# DANIEL MARTIN

◆

"JOHN FOWLES IS FANTASTIC . . . HE
IS JUST ABOUT THE BEST THING THAT
HAS HAPPENED TO THE ENGLISH OR
AMERICAN NOVEL IN OVER TWO
DECADES . . . he brings back to us all the
virtues of the novel at its peak—the excitement,
the color, the drama, the human passions, the
sense of place and scene, and above all the social
concern . . . he has developed a novel not
only big physically but emotionally compelling,
intellectually stimulating and rewarding,
atmospherically both varied and vivid, humanly
absorbing. . . . Characters, people, that is, who
live with you so fully as to create that magic
world of great fiction which is truer than life
because it is life described and illuminated and
extended and enlarged beyond our own normal
experience—and which therefore increases
our own life."

—*Maxwell Geismar*, NEWSDAY

"BEAUTIFULLY WRITTEN . . . A
MASTERLY FICTIONAL CREATION . . .
HIS BEST PIECE OF WORK TO DATE!"
—THE NEW YORK TIMES BOOK REVIEW

*(Please turn the page)*

# DANIEL MARTIN

John Fowles

## A TOTEM BOOK
### TORONTO

First published, 1977, by Collins Publishers,
Toronto, Canada


This edition published 1978
by TOTEM BOOKS
a division of
Collins Publishers
100 Lesmill Road, Don Mills, Ontario

ISBN 0 00 222020 2

Printed in Canada by
Universal Printers Ltd. Winnipeg

The crisis consists precisely in the fact that the old is dying and the new cannot be born; in this interregnum a great variety of morbid symptoms appears.

—ANTONIO GRAMSCI,
*Prison Notebooks*

# Acknowledgments

The passages from Gramsci come from *Selections from the Prison Notebooks of Antonio Gramsci,* edited by Quintin Hoare and Geoffrey Nowell-Smith, Lawrence and Wishart, London, 1971. Those from Georg Lukács are from *The Historical Novel,* translated by Hannah and Stanley Mitchell, and *The Meaning of Contemporary Realism,* translated by John and Necke Mander, Merlin Press, London, 1962 and 1963. The three extracts from the Stratis Thalassinos (Stratis the Mariner) poems by George Seferis are as translated by Edmund Keeley and Philip Sherrard in *George Seferis: Collected Poems 1924–1955.* Copyright © 1967 by Princeton University Press. Reprinted by permission of Princeton University Press. I am grateful to all the above for permission to quote.

JOHN FOWLES

# DANIEL MARTIN

# The Harvest

But what's wrong with that man?
All afternoon (yesterday the day before yesterday and
    today) he's been sitting there staring at a flame
he bumped into me at evening as he went downstairs
he said to me:
"The body lies the water clouds the soul
hesitates
and the wind forgets always forgets
but the flame doesn't change."
He also said to me:
"You know I love a woman who's gone away perhaps to the
    nether world; that's not why I seem so deserted
I try to keep myself going with a flame
because it doesn't change."
Then he told me the story of his life.

—GEORGE SEFERIS, "Mr. Stratis
Thalassinos Describes a Man"

Whole sight; or all the rest is desolation.

The last of a hanger ran under the eastern ridge of the
combe, where it had always been too steep and stony for the
plough. It was now little more than a long spinney, mainly of
beech. The field sloped from the wall of trees, westward, a
gentle bosom, down to the open gate onto Fishacre Lane.
The dark coats lay there in against the hedge, covering the
cider-jar and the dinner-bundle, beside the two scythes that
had been used to clear the still-dewed hedge swathe much
earlier that morning. Now the wheat was half cut. Lewis sat
perched behind the faded carmine reaper, craning into the
sea of blond stems for stones, his hand on the mower-lever,
always ready to lift the blades. Captain hardly needed the
reins; so many years of plodding, just so, down the new
stubble next to the still-standing ears. Only at the corners did
Lewis cry, softly, coaxing the old horse round. Sally, the
younger horse, who had helped on the steeper ground, stood

tethered beneath a thorn not far from the gate, cropping the hedge, her tail intermittently swishing.

Bindweed ran up the stems of the corn; seeding thistles, red poppies; and lower, the little cornfield violets called heart's-ease; with blue speedwell eyes and scarlet pimpernel, shepherd's glass, herb of the second sight. The field's name was the Old Batch—*batch* from *bake*, some ancient farm's own annual bread was always grown here. The sky's proleptic name was California; the imperial static blue of August.

There are four figures in the field, besides Lewis on the reaper-binder. Mr. Luscombe: red-faced and crooked-grinning, one eye with a cast behind his steel-rimmed spectacles, a collarless shirt with a thin gray stripe, darned, the cuffs worn, cord trousers with peaks at the back for the braces, but held up also by a thick leather belt. Bill, his younger son, nineteen, capped and massive, six inches taller than anyone else on the field, arms like hams, a slow giant, clumsy at all but his work . . . but see him scythe, dwarf the distort handle and the blade, the swaling drive and unstopping rhythm, pure and princely force of craft. Old Sam in breeches, braces, boots and gaiters, his face forgotten, though not his limp; a collarless shirt also, a straw hat with the crown detached on one side ("lets in th'ole air a bit, doan'ee see") and a tuft of wilted heart's-ease tucked in the black band. And finally a boy in his midteens, his clothes unsuited, a mere harvest helper: cotton trousers, an apple-green Aertex shirt, old gym-shoes.

They work in two teams, on opposite sides of the field, one clockwise, the other anti-clockwise, stooking. Clutching a sheaf in the right hand, just above the binder twine, never by the twine itself, then moving on to the next sheaf, picking that up in the same way in the left hand, then walking with the two sheaves to the nearest unfinished stook, a stook being four pairs of sheaves and a single "to close the door" at each end; then standing before the other sheaves propped against each other, lifting the two in each hand, then setting them, shocking down the butts into the stubble and simultaneously clashing the eared heads together. The simplest job in the world, it might seem to Queenie, back from her morning's cleaning at the Vicarage, who stands there in the lane beside her bicycle a moment, watching in through the open gateway for the idle pleasure of it. The boy waves from the top end of the field and she waves back. When he looks again, a minute later, she is still there, the beige summer hat with the band of white silk and the artificial rose in front, the drab brown dress, the heavy old bicycle with its fret of skirt-protective wires over the back wheel.

The boy sets the first two sheaves, the founders, of a new stook. They stand, then start to topple. He catches them before they fall, lifts them to set them firm again. But old Mr. Luscombe shocks his pair down six feet away, safe as houses. His founders never fall. He smiles lopsidedly with his bad teeth, a wink, the cast in his eye, the sun in his glasses. Bronze-red hands and old brown boots. The boy makes a grimace, then brings his sheaves and sets them against the farmer's pair. The insides of his forearms are sore already, his fingers not being strong enough to carry the sheaves far by grasp. If the stook is some way off, he hoicks them up against his side, under his arms, against the thistles. But he likes the pain—a harvest pain, a part of the ritual; like the stiff muscles the next morning, like sleep that night, so drowning, deep and swift to come.

The crackle of the stubble, the shock of the stood sheaves. The rattle of the reaper, the chatter of the mower blades, the windmill arms above them. Lewis's voice at the corners: hoy then, hoy'ee, Cap'n, back, back, back, whoy, whoy. Then the click of the tongue: jik-jik, the onward rattle and chain and chatter. Thistledown floats southward across the field, in a light air from the north, mounting, a thermal, new stars for the empyrean.

And the day will endure like this, under the perfect azure sky, stooking and stooking the wheat. Again and again old Luscombe will shred an ear from its haulm and roll the grains between his heavy palms to husk them; cup his hand and blow the husks away; stare; then take a grain and bite it in half, the germ with its taste of earth and dust, and then spit it out; and carefully put the remaining grains in his trouser pocket, for the poultry, that evening. Three or four times the reaper's noise will stop abruptly. The stookers will stand and see Lewis climb down from his fenestrated iron saddle and know what it is again: the knotter is choked. A spew of unbound wheat behind the machine; the toolbox open. Lewis is brown and shy, much smaller than his younger brother—the family mechanic, and taciturn. The nearest pair of stookers will come and gather armfuls of the unbound wheat; take three strong stems and rope them, then lead them under the armful and rick the ends where they meet, one twist only, but tight, tucking the ears under the bind to hold it firm; leave Lewis to his labors over the knotter and walk back to where they left their uncompleted rows. In silence, apart, treading the crackling stubble.

At one Mr. Luscombe will pull out his old fob, then cry to the field and start rolling a cigarette. They will straggle to the hedge by the gate, sweating, Lewis last, having taken Captain from the shafts and tethered him in the shade beside Sally; stand around the coats. The cider-jar will be unbunged. The boy is offered the first drink, from a tin mug. Bill lifts the whole gallon jar, tips it into his mouth. Old Sam grins. And the boy feels the sour green swill down his gullet, down both gullets; last year's brew, delicious as orchard shade in the sun and wheat-dust. Lewis sups cold tea from a wire-handled can.

Long and distant, over the uncut serried rods of wheat: the five men walk along the lane hedge to the shade of an ash. Old Sam stops to urinate against the bank. They sit beneath the ash, or sprawl; out of the dish-cloth, white with blue ends, a pile of great cartwheels of bread, the crusts burnt black; deep yellow butter, ham cut thick as a plate, plate of pink meat and white fat, both sides of the bread nearly an inch thick; the yellow butter pearled and marbled with whey, a week's ration a slice.

Thic for thee, thic for thee, says doling Mr. Luscombe, and where's my plum vidies to?

Ma says to eat up they, says Bill.

Beauty of Bath, crisp and amber-fleshed, with their little edge of piquant acid. Still Primavera's, thinks the boy; and much better poems than bruised and woolly Pelham Widow. But who cares, teeth deep in white cartwheel, bread and sweet ham, all life to follow.

They talk a little, having eaten; the cider again, and nibbling apples. Lewis smokes Woodbines and stares at the reaper in the sun. The boy lies on his back, the stubble pricking, slightly drunk, bathed in the green pond of Devon voices, his Devon and England, quick and tortuous ancestral voices, debating next year's function for this field; then other fields. A language so local, so phonetically condensed and permissive of slur that it is inseparable in his mind, and will always remain so, from its peculiar landscapes; its combes and bartons, leats and linhays. He is shy and ashamed of his own educated dialect of the tongue.

Then there comes across the voices, from far off, five or six miles, the faint wail of a siren.

Torquay I reckon, says Bill.

The boy sits up, scanning the sky to the south. They are silent. The wail dies, changing pitch. A cock pheasant bells disyllabically up in the beeches above the field. Bill sharply raises his finger; and before it is fully up, a remote crump. Then another. Then the faint bass roll of a wing-cannon. Three seconds' silence; then the cannon again. And once more the pheasant bells.

Caught-ey on the hop agen, says Mr. Luscombe.

One o' they hit-and-runners, agrees Bill.

They stand out from the shade of the ash, watching south. But the sky is empty, blue, in peace. They shade their eyes, searching for a speck, a trail, a plume of smoke; nothing. But now an engine, at first very faint, then without warning louder, closer, abruptly welling. The five turn cautiously back beneath the ash. The long combe is flooded with the frantic approach, violent machinery at full stretch, screaming in an agony of vicious fear. The boy, who is already literary, knows he is about to die.

Then for a few world-cleaving seconds it is over them, over the upper half of the field, only two hundred feet or so high, camouflaged dark green and black; blue-bellied, Balkan-crossed; slim, enormous, a two-engined Heinkel, real, the war real, terror and fascination, pigeons breaking from the beeches in a panic, Sally rearing, Captain the same and tearing loose from his tether, a wild whinnying. He canters away, then subsides into a heavy lumbering trot across the field. But the giant botfly is gone, trailing its savage roar. Mr. Luscombe runs, almost as heavily as his horse, bawling. Whoy there, Captain. Easy, boy, easy. Then Bill running as well, overtaking his father. The old horse stops at the edge of the uncut wheat, trembling. Another whinny.

The boy turns to Lewis: I saw the pilot!

Was 'er one o' they or one o' us's, asks Old Sam.

The boy shouts at him. German! It was German!

Lewis holds up a finger. Somewhere to the north they hear the Heinkel swing west.

Dartmouth, says Lewis quietly. He'll go out along the river.

As if something about that great sear of machinery, the quickness and inhumanity of it, the power, has impressed him; sweating away with rotten old horses, saved from the army by the farm . . . old Celtic softness for metal Romans. In midfield his father pats Captain and leads him gently back toward the reaper. Bill looks down toward the three by the hedge; then mimes a shotgun, following the Heinkel's flight, and points up the hill to where he would have had it fall. Even Lewis has a wry grin.

But then, though their ears stay cocked as they walk up into the field, no sound, no more war, no stuttering hammer of wing cannon, no crumps from the direction of Totnes or Dartmouth, no Hurricanes in pursuit. Only, as Lewis flicks the reins to start Captain on again and the stookers stoop to gather their first sheaves, a stertorous sound from the high azure. The boy looks up. Very high, four black specks, rolling, teasing, caramboling into one another as they fly westward. Two ravens and their young; the sky's eternal sleeping voice, mocking man.

Mysteries: how the pheasant heard the bombs before the men. Who sent the ravens and that passage?

Our daily bread: sheaves and stooks, the afternoon wearing on, the light ash-shadow creeping over the stubble. Inexorably the reaper dwindles the wheat. The first rabbit runs, a cry from Lewis. It zigzags among the unstooked sheaves, leaps one like a hare, then takes cover inside a stook. Bill, who is nearest, picks up a stone and creeps close. But the rabbit is away, racing white scut, and the hurled stone flies harmlessly over its head.

Soon after three the field begins to fill with people, as if they had been secretly watching all the time and knew exactly when to appear. Two or three old men, a fat young woman with a pram, a tall gipsy with a lurcher at his heels: the saturnine "Babe" with his lantern jaw, man of darkness, constable's horror, distiller, or so rumored, of applejack in Thorncombe Woods. Then the Fishacre hamlet children dribbling back from school, seven or eight of them, five small boys and two little girls and an older one. The open gate is like a mouth; it sucks in all who pass. Queenie and old Mrs. Hellyer, though they must have walked up especially; and others, adults and children. Then little Mrs. Luscombe of the dark eyebrows, humping the tea-baskets. Beside her, a gentle-faced woman in a gray-and-white dress, severe and even for then old-fashioned, with an incongruous Eton crop . . . the stooking boy's aunt. And still more.

Now the wheat is six or seven swathes in breadth and some fifty yards long. Lewis cries at a corner to the nearest male bystanders.

Crawlin' with the buggers!

They all gather round the last piece: stookers, children, old men, Babe and his lurcher: a black-and-liver dog with a cowed, much-beaten look, always crouched, neurotic, hyper-alert and Argus-eyed, never a yard from his master's heels. The young woman walks up on swollen ankles, carrying her baby son in her arms, the pram left by the gate. Some have sticks, others pile stones. A ring of excited faces, scrutinizing each tremor in the rectangle of corn: commands, the older men knowing, sternly cautious. Doan'ee fuss, lad, keep back. In the rectangle's heart a stirring of ears, a ripple of shaken stems, like a troutwave in a stream. A hen pheasant explodes with a rattling whir, brown-speckled jack-in-the-box, down the hill and over Fishacre Lane. Laughter. A small girl screams. A tiny rabbit, not eight inches long, runs out from the upper border, stops bemused, then runs again. The boy who helped stook stands ten yards away, grinning as a wild band of children sprawl and tumble after the tiny animal, which doubles, stops, spurts, and finally runs back into the wheat.

Doan'ee 'ee dreadle the corn, bellows Mr. Luscombe at the eagerest boy. Young devil. Now Lewis whistles shrilly on the other side of the path, pointing. This time it is a big rabbit, racing for the lane hedge, the lurcher's side. The rabbit is through the human ring, jinking through the stones and sticks and stooks. The gipsy gives a low whistle, long-dying. The dog streaks away, using all its greyhound blood, its lethal dexterity. The rabbit escapes once by a last-second change of course. The lurcher flashes past, a little spurt of red dust from among the stubble as it twists back. It has everyone's eyes; even Lewis has reined in. This time the dog makes no mistake. It has the rabbit by the neck, shakes it violently. Another whistle from the gipsy, and it runs swiftly to its master, bent low, the still-kicking animal locked in its long jaws. The gipsy takes the rabbit by its hind legs, lifts it away and up and chops down with his free hand, just once, on the neck. Everyone there knows how Babe came by the lurcher; it is a village joke, like his nickname. The Devil came to Thorncombe Woods one night to thank him for selling so much rotgut to all they Yanks back over the Camp; and brought him the lurcher as a present. But as they watch man and dog, they know he isn't there because he needs the rab-bits; he has every moonlit night and field for miles round for rabbits. But his is an ancient presence, and quasi-divine, of a time when men were hunters, not planters; he honors fields at cutting time.

Lewis starts the reaper off again. Now a rabbit springs every few yards, small and large; some terrified, others determined. Old men pounce, flail with their sticks, stumble, fall on their faces; and the children too. Guffaws, screams, curses, cries of triumph; the silent lurcher racing, twisting, snapping, merciless. The last swathe. Then a scream of pain, like a tiny child's, from the hidden blades. Without stopping, Lewis points back. A rabbit drags away, its hind legs sliced off. The boy who stooked runs and lifts it: the red stumps. Little green balls of excrement fall from the anal fur. Convulsive jerking, another scream. He chops, then chops again; a third time; then casually turns and throws the corpse toward a pile of others. Doe-eyes glazing, whiskers, soft ears, snowy scuts. He moves closer and stares down at the pile, a good twenty now. And his heart turns, some strange premonitory turn, a day when in an empty field he shall weep for this.

He looks up and sees his aunt and Mrs. Luscombe, the only two people in the field who have not joined in the massacre. They stand by a tablecloth spread on the stubble beneath the ash-tree, talking and watching. Beside them there curls up a twist of blue smoke; an old black kettle perched on stones. The final rabbit, the one most certain, hemmed with hunters, runs straight between myopic Old Sam's legs and outpaces all the boys who chase it. The lurcher tries to streak through them, loses balance and sight, at last permits himself a frustrated yelp, looks desperately around, so many shouting, pointing, urging bipeds; then sees the bobbing scut and sets off again. But the rabbit reaches the hedge a good few yards clear. The gipsy whistles. The dog lopes back, its tail down.

Then the prize-giving. Old Mr. Luscombe stands by the assembled kill; a little embarrassed, unused to playing Solomon. One here, one there, a small one to a child, a fat brace to Babe, another to Old Sam. Then six to the boy who stooked.

Take 'en down to the ash-tree, Danny.

And "Danny," whose preferred name is Dan, walks down the field, three pairs of hind legs in each hand, Nimrod, to the spread tea.

Little Mrs. Luscombe, with her eyebrows like commas, stands hands on hips by her twig fire, grinning at him.

You caught all they then, Danny?

I got two. One didn't count actually. It was caught in the blades.

Poor thing, says his aunt.

Mrs. Luscombe is politely but firmly scornful.

You didden have a stone wall round your garden, m' dear, you woulden weep tears for *they*.

And his aunt smiles at him, maternally, as Mrs. Luscombe takes the rabbits, weighs them, approves, palping their haunches; picks a good couple.

There's your supper, Danny.

Oh I say. Really? Thanks awfully, Mrs. Luscombe.

Are you absolutely sure? asks his aunt. Then: I don't know what we'd do without you.

Where's Father? asks the boy.

It seems the Rural Dean has called. About the porch.

He nods: nursing his solitude, his terrible Oedipal secret; already at the crossroads every son must pass.

He says, We'll just finish the stooking.

And he walks back to where they have gone back to work, but there are many more hands now, as in a Breughel. The children vying to lug the farthest sheaves closer for the men; even Babe sets to for that last twenty minutes.

Then back under the ash-tree, as ritual as Holy Communion, the old pink-and-white check cloth, the bread, the quart bowl of cream, the pots of raspberry and black-currant jam, the chipped white mugs, the two teapots, a browny-black with yellow bands, the same brown as the cake with all its hoarded sultanas and currants. Best the illicit scalded cream, its deep yellow crust folded into the voluptuous white. No cream since time began could equal it; the harvest hunger, sun, the circle of watching children, the smell of sweat. Byre and meadow and breath of Red Devons. Ambrosia, death, sweet raspberry jam.

Did 'ee see 'un, ma? Did 'ee see 'un, Miz Martin? Us-all coulda touched 'un, coulden us, Danny?

Later.

He is alone among the highest beeches, over the stooked and now empty field, the marly combe; where he comes each spring to find the first moschatel, strange little transient four-faces, smelling of musk. Another mystery, his current flower and emblem, for reasons he cannot say. The sun in the extreme west, as he likes it best. Its slanting rays reveal the lands in a pasture-field on the other side of the valley, the parallel waves where an ox-plough once went many centuries before; and where he must pay a visit soon, childish, but another of his secret flowers, the honeycomb-scented orchid

*Spiranthes spiralis,* blooms on the old meadow there about now. He clings to his knowledges; signs of birds, locations of plants, fragments of Latin and folklore, since he lacks so much else. The leaves of the beeches are translucent in the westering sun. A wood-pigeon coos, a nuthatch whistles somewhere close above.

He sits with his back to a beech-trunk, staring down through foliage at the field. Without past or future, purged of tenses; collecting this day, pregnant with being. Unharvested, yet one with this land; and that was why he had been so afraid. It wasn't death, the agony in the mower's blades, the scream and red stumps . . . but dying, dying before the other wheat was ripe.

Inscrutable innocent, already in exile.

Down, half masked by leaves. Point of view of the hidden bird.

I feel in his pocket and bring out a clasp-knife; plunge the blade in the red earth to clean it of the filth from the two rabbits liver, intestines, stench. He stands and turns and begins to carve his initials on the beech-tree. Deep incisions in the bark, peeling the gray skin away to the sappy green of the living stem. Adieu, my boyhood and my dream.

*D.H.M.*

And underneath: *21 Aug 42.*

# Games

"You do."

"No."

"But you must do."

He smiles in the darkness.

"Jenny, in writing there aren't any musts."

"Then can."

He says parentally, "You ought to be asleep."

But he stands unmoving, staring out of the window into the night; out of the dark room, over the palms and poinsettias and castor-oil plants in the garden, beyond the garden. Downtown, the endless plain of trivial jeweled light. He closes his eyes a long moment, shutting it out.

"All the ghosts here. They get you in the end."

"Now you're being phony romantic."

"You mean I haven't yet been seen sitting dead drunk in a corner of the commissary."

"Oh Daniel. Come on."

He says nothing. A silence. A flicker of lighter flame. On the glass of the window he catches her momentary face, the long hair, the amber shadows of the couch. A whiteness where the indigo kimono, unsashed, lies open. A nice angle; nicest because no lens, no stock, could ever record it. Mirrors. The dark room. Leaving the red point and sign of rebellion in the glass, one with the distant blue, diamond and garnet lake of sky-signs.

She murmurs, "Give a little."

It is terrible, like a nausea at times like this, but an unkilled adolescent in him still prizes the thousand-times-seen view; remains excited, smug, achieved; mocks all he has known, learned, rationally valued.

He turns and crosses the room to a fake Biedermeier table by the door.

"Do you want anything?"

"Only you. And neat. Just for once."

He adds water to his whisky, tastes it, adds some more; turns.

"I really ought to tuck you in."

"For Christ's sake come and sit down." Her head twists, staring at him over the back of the couch. She says, "You're making me act."

"Sorry."

"I have enough of that during the day. If you remember." He goes and sits beside her; then leans forward and sips his whisky. "When did it begin?"

He divides conversation into two categories: when you speak, and when you listen to yourself speak. Of late, his has been too much the second. Narcissism: when one grows too old to believe in one's uniqueness, one falls in love with one's complexity—as if layers of lies could replace the green illusion; or the sophistries of failure, the stench of success.

"This afternoon. When you ran over. I went out and wandered round the lot. All those empty stages. Just a feeling of . . . wasted time. Effort. Something."

"And having to wait for me."

"It wasn't your fault."

"But it was that?" He shakes his head. "The star and her stud."

"That's just the old dialect. The myth."

"But they still believe in it."

"One must pay the natives something, Jenny."

She sits with an arm crooked on the back of the couch, observing his face in profile.

"That's what I hate about the Prick. He thinks he's so cool, so this year, baby. Every time he sees you he gives me one of those looks. Those little old way-back looks. One day I'm going to ask him why he wears condoms in his eyes."

"That should add zing to your scenes."

She stands and wanders across to the window, stubs out her cigarette—yes, she is acting—in a pottery dish by the telephone; then stares out, as he had, at the infamous city's artificial night.

"It's the one thing I'll never understand about this creepy town. How they've so totally managed to ban naturalness from it." She turns and comes back, stands with folded arms, looking down at him. "I mean, why are they all so frightened of it? Why can't they just accept we have our own private little English . . . oh Dan." She sits, and makes him put his arm around her; takes the hand and kisses its back, then

[ 12 ]

leads it to a bare breast and holds it there. "All right. So you walked round the lot. That doesn't explain why . . . come on."

He stares across the room.

"I suppose it was about reality. Failures to capture it. Those stages, the flats still standing there. Movies no one even remembers any more. How all the king's plays and all the king's scripts . . . and nothing in your present can ever put you together again."

"Tell me when to touch the tears from my eyes."

There is a little rush of air down his nostrils; he gives the bare breast a gentle squeeze, then removes his arm.

"Proves my point."

"Well someone's fishing."

"Not the smallest hook."

"You don't even . . . *and* you know it."

"Only by local standards."

"Balls."

"Darling, when you're—"

"Oh Gawd, here we go again."

He is silent a moment. "When I was your age I could only look forward. At mine you . . ."

"Then you need your eyesight tested."

"Not really. If you want to know what the shored fragments are worth, ask the ruin."

" 'Why then I'll fit you. Hieronymo's mad again.' " She sits away and grins at him in the night, raises a reproving finger. "You'd forgotten that was the next line. Right? You shouldn't get literary with actresses. We may be cows, but we can always cap you."

"Stage point. Not a real one."

She looks down. "You're such a lousy casting."

"Inverted vanity. Looking back at my immortal oeuvre."

"Oy veh. So we aren't Shakespeare."

He murmurs, "I think I'd better go."

But she makes him sit back, once more put an arm round her, and lies with her face against his shoulder.

"I'm being flip."

"With reason."

She kisses his skin through his shirt. "I know you're in ruins somewhere. It's just I hate having to feel I'm making them worse."

He pulls her a little closer. "You're one of the very few fragments that make sense."

"If only I . . ."

"We've settled all that."

She takes one of his hands. "Tell me about this afternoon. What really happened."

"It was on the old *Camelot* set. It suddenly hit me. How well I matched it. The betrayal of myths. As if I was totally in exile from what I ought to have been." He added, "Done."

"And what's that?"

"Good question."

"Try."

"Something to do with the artifice of the medium."

"And?"

"That if I could ever hope to describe it, it would have to be beyond staging or filming. They'd just . . . betray the real thing again."

"What's 'it'?"

"God knows, Jenny. The real history of what I am? This is all disgustingly solipsistic."

"As you once convinced me all art was."

He waits, staring across the room.

"I've spent most of my adult life learning how to use the least possible words, how to get scenes crisp. How you pack your meaning in between the lines. How you create other people. Always other people." He pauses again. "As if I'd been taken over by someone else. Years ago."

"What kind of someone else?"

"Some kind of fink."

"Rubbish. But go on."

He strokes the side of her hair. "It's such a soft option. You write, Interior, medium shot, girl and man on a couch, night. Then you walk out. Let someone else be Jenny and Dan. Someone else tell them what to do. Photograph them. You never really stake yourself. Let it be no one else. Just you." He stops stroking, pats her hair. "That's all, Jenny. I don't really want to start a new career. Just a way of saying I'm sick of screenplays."

"And Hollywood. And me."

"Not you."

"But you wish you could go home."

"Not literally. Metaphorically."

"Then where we began. Memoirs."

"I've invented quite enough paper people without adding myself to the list. Anyway, libel. I couldn't make reality honest."

"Then write a novel." He sniffs. "Why not?"

"I wouldn't know where to begin."

"Here."

"Idiot."

She sits away on her knees, contemplating him.

"Seriously."

He smiles. "With the ravings of the male menopause and a naked film-star in Harold-Robbins Land?"

She closes her kimono. "That's a filthy thing to say. About both of us."

"Sated with sex and trying to remember his Aristotle, he outlined his theory of—"

"I'm not a film-star. I'm your Jenny."

"Who's being much too indulgent."

"You've got the money, you could make the time."

"Too many dead fish on my conscience."

"What does that mean?"

"That I've gutted too many of the damn things to create a living one."

"Then you know the traps. I don't see what you've got to lose."

"My last."

"Your last what?"

"The thing cobblers are meant to stick to."

She is silent, scrutinizing.

"Is all this to do with the new script?"

He shakes his head. "It bores me into the ground, but I can do scenario in my sleep. Like a computer." He stands and goes to the window again. She twists round on the couch and watches his back. After a moment, he goes on, but in a quieter voice. "If you run away, Jenny, you can't find your way back. That's all I meant. Trying to . . . it's only a pipe dream. Trying to crawl back inside the womb. Turn the clock back." He turns and smiles across at her. "Late-night maundering."

"You're so defeatist. All you have to do is put down exactly what we've just said."

"That's the last chapter. What I've become."

She looks down, a little pause; a "beat," in the jargon.

"Bill was on about you the other day. Why you've never directed."

"And?"

"I told him what you told me."

"And what did he say?"

"Something rather perceptive. How being a perfectionist and being scared are often the same thing."

"That was sweet of him."

"And right of him?"

He smiles through the darkness at her accusing face. "Calling me yellow will get you nowhere."

She waits a moment, then stands and walks to him, and kisses him quickly on the mouth; pushes him back so that he has to sit in an armchair by the picture window; kneels on the carpet and rests her forearms on his knees. A faint light from the city sky outside.

"Positive thinking."

"Yes, Jenny."

"My Highland great-grandmother had the second sight."

"As you told me."

"This *is* the first chapter."

"And the next?"

"Something will happen. Like a window opening. No, a door. Like a door in a wall." She kneels back, arms folded over her breasts, biting her lips, playing sibyl.

"And through it?"

"Your story. Your real history of you."

He has a tired grin. "When?"

"Before you have your way and we . . . go our separate ones." His grin dies. "You *can* reconstitute this conversation? It's very important. You must remember it."

"I only want out because I'm in love with you. You realize that?"

"Answer my question."

"I shouldn't think so."

"Then I'll try and write some of it down for you. Tomorrow. Between takes. Just the gist."

"And my question?"

"Or a version of it, anyway."

They stare at each other. In the end he says quietly, "God, how I loathe your generation."

And she smiles up at him, like a praised child, so overcome that in the end she has to bow her head. He reaches forward and ruffles her hair, then makes to stand. But she stops him.

"Wait a minute. I haven't finished with you yet."

"This is mad. You must get your sleep."

She turns to the telephone table behind her; kneels there, switches on the lamp; pulls the Los Angeles directory out on the carpet, stares at its cover a moment, then gives him a speculating look back. He sits perched forward, ready to go.

"Jenny."

She stares down again. "Something solitary. Devious." Then she opens the directory, crouches to read its small print. "Oh God, there aren't any English names."

"Tell me what you're doing."

But she says nothing. Suddenly she turns toward the back, riffs pages quickly; halts, cranes, finds something; flashes a grin at him.

"Eureka. Wolfe."

"Wolf?"

"As in lone. But with an *e*." She runs her finger down a list of names. "That's it. *S*. You can't get more wriggly than that. Altadena Drive, wherever that is."

"Behind Pasadena. And if you——"

"Shut up. Stanley J. That's no good." She closes the directory, examines him like a coper before a doubtful horse, then points. "Simon." She folds her arms. "Since you're so simple, too. You may drop the *J*."

He looks down at the carpet. "How long is it since you were spanked?"

"But you can't use your own name in a novel. Anyway, it's so square. Who'd ever go for a character called Daniel Martin?"

He says, since they are used to back-references, conversational jumps in either direction, but gently, "I really do, sometimes."

She folds her hands on her lap, playing demure innocence now. "She's only trying to make sure she gets the dedication."

He stands. "If she isn't in bed in one minute, she's going to get what she really deserves. A massive flea in the ear for coming on set with bags under her eyes."

Stridently, making them both start, the telephone on the table behind her rings. Jenny grins, still on her knees, delighted.

"Shall I speak to Mr. Wolfe, or will you?"

He turns to go. "I should leave it. Probably some nut."

But she says his name, not teasing; a tiny trace of fear at his suggestion. He stops, stands half-turned, looking at her indigo back as she twists and lifts the ivory receiver. He waits, then hears her say in her cool public voice, "Yes, he's here. I'll get him." And she holds out the receiver, biting her lips again.

"Long-distance. From home. They transferred the call."

"Who is it?"

"The operator didn't say."

He draws a breath and walks back to where she now stands; almost snatches the receiver from her hand. She turns away to the window. He confirms his name, and is asked to hold the line. He eyes the girl's profiled face. She raises her hands and shakes her hair loose, knowing he is watching; as if she has just woken from sleep. She cannot press the smile out of her lips.

"I shouldn't get excited. A hundred to one it's just some moronic Fleet Street tattle-monger short of a paragraph."

"Or my Highland great-grandmother."

And she contemplates the midnight infinities of Los Angeles, insufferably English and amused. He reaches out, catches her arm, pulls her brutally toward him; and tries to kiss her with anger, but she is laughing too much.

In his ear, distances.

Then a voice; and unbelievably, as in a fiction, the door in the wall opens.

# The Woman in the Reeds

The wind blows the indolent arms of the willows sideways and ruffles the water of the long reach. The distant wooded hills to the west and the intervening meadowlands are stained with summery cloud-shadow. On the far side of the Cherwell a young man, an undergraduate, poles a punt upstream. In the bow seat, facing him, a girl wearing sun-glasses reclines. She trails the fingers of her right hand through the water. He is twenty-three years old, and reading English; she is two years younger, and reading French. He wears army-surplus denim trousers and a navy-blue polo-necked sweater; she is in a dirndl peasant skirt, a dark green busily embroidered white and red; a white blouse and red Paisley headscarf. By her bare feet lie a rush basket, sandals and a strew of books.

The young man would pass, even today; all except his short hair would pass. But even then her full and folksy mid-calf skirt, the puffs in the short sleeves of the blouse, are dated; the colors too bravura, too eager to escape the accusation of bluestocking . . . and faintly irritating, because such a plea is unnecessary. She is, to use a student cliché of the time, very nubile; has both a sexuality and a distinction, a kind of warm elegance and consciousness of it that is almost an indifference. Her younger sister, for instance, dresses much better; wouldn't be seen dead in a tatty old peasant skirt. But the girl in the punt takes greater risks, perhaps because she is engaged (though not to today's gondolier), perhaps because she knows her standing, her reputation, is safely beyond the odd gaucheness, showiness, affectation. Only that previous winter, in fishnet tights and a long auburn wig and a student's gown, she had brought the house down in an ETC revue sketch. *If Rita read Greats* . . . the Rita's other name being Hayworth. And it hadn't been all the clever cracks about Aspasia and *hetairai* or the climactic song (composed by the young man poling): *Symposia were cosier when I wore my negligée;* but the decided and visible oomph of the mimesis.

[ 19 ]

She has fine pronounced eyebrows, very clear, direct brown eyes complementing a hair that is almost black in certain lights; a classical nose, a wide and always faintly smiling mouth, even in repose; even now, as she watches her own fingers in the water; as if she is always remembering something amusing told her an hour before. She and her sister have a nickname all through the men's colleges. They are known as the Heavenly Twins, although they are not twins, but a year, both in age and study, and in many other things, apart. In their respective second and first years they sometimes dressed alike, and so a false parallel was drawn. Now their mark is made, and they have decided to be themselves.

They descended on Oxford with one other slight difference. They had lived abroad a lot, for their father had been an ambassador. He had died the year the war started; and their mother had remarried a year later—to yet another diplomat, though this time he was an American. The two girls had spent the war in the United States, and an aura of that culture still clung about them . . . a frankness, a trace of the accent (then, it later disappeared), a certain freedom other English girl students of their age, brought up amid rationing cards and the wail of sirens, lacked. They also had, though they were not ostentatious in that way, wealth. Their English parents had not been poor; and their American stepfather, though he too had children from a previous marriage, was reputedly far from poor. They were privileged in so many ways; and to have good brains and good looks on top of everything else seemed almost unfair. Neither had close female friends at the university.

The girl looks up to the young man at work.

"My offer's still open."

"I enjoy it. Honestly. I need the exercise. Revising like a maniac these last three days." He pushes on the pole, recovers it, stabs it forward till he feels the soundless thump on the river-bottom, waits till the onward motion of the punt brings it vertical, thrusts down, makes a little adjustment to the direction by using the trailing pole as a rudder. He grimaces down at the girl.

"I'm going to plough. I feel it in my bones."

"Sez you. I bet you get a first."

"I'm leaving that for Anthony."

"He's worried about ancient history. He thinks he may only get an alpha minus." She lowers her glasses professorially, guys gloom. "I'm vulnerable on Thucydides."

He grins. She turns and watches the river ahead. Another punt comes downstream, with four other students in it, sophomores, a girl and three men. They look across at the pair in the upstream punt. One of the young men turns and says something to the girl; and all four look again, idly, casually, as would-be sophisticated passers glance again at local celebrities, Zuleikas and princes of the senior year. The cynosures make no comment; they are used to this.

A few hundred yards later the young man lets the pole trail longer than usual and wipes his forehead with the back of his hand.

"I say, Jane, I'm getting hellish shagged. And starving. I don't think the Victoria's on."

The girl sits up, solicitous.

"Well let's tie up here. I don't mind."

"There's a cut just ahead. We could go up there a bit. Be out of the wind."

"Fine."

In a minute they come in sight of the cut, an old drainage dike at right angles east from the river and running between two willow-hedged leys. The public footpath is on the other bank. At the mouth of the cut is an old peeling notice-board: *Private. Landing forbidden. By order.* But, as they discover when they head in to the mouth, another punt lies moored there. Two undergraduates sprawl at opposite ends of it, reading, an open bottle of champagne between them. The gold-foiled neck of another bottle pokes up, suspended by string, from the cooling green water beside the stern-seat. The taller student of the two, with a mop of blond hair and a faintly flushed face, glances up at the intrusion. He has strange vacuous eyes, a glaucous gray-green.

"Good God. Jane darling. Daniel. Don't one's friends *ever* leave one in peace?"

Daniel slows his punt, grins down at the blond head, the textbook in hand.

"You bloody sham, Andrew. You're reading."

"Well not quite really, dear boy. Rotten old governor. Bet me a hundred I won't get through."

Jane is amused. "How sickmaking. You poor thing."

"Rather fascinating stuff, actually, some of it. Isn't it, Mark?" The other student, an older man, grunts in dissent. "I say, do have a mouthful of fizz."

Jane smiles again. "Unlike you, we truly have come to work."

"How revoltingly plebby of you both."

They grin. Daniel waves and poles on. After a few yards Jane bites her lips.

"Now it'll be all round Oxford we're having an affair."

"Bet you it won't. He'll be too scared it'll be all round the Bullingdon we saw him swotting."

"Poor Andrew."

"Rich Andrew."

"I always wonder what really goes on in that tiny head."

"He's not such a fool as he sounds."

"Just a flawless imitation?"

He laughs, as he steers the punt through the encroaching paddles of water lilies, the flowering sheets of water drop-wort. The wind shakes a little shower of white petals from a thorn-tree on the bank. The girl lifts a skein of dropwort and holds it up, so that a chain of drips slide beside the punt. Then she lets it fall.

"Won't this do?"

"There's a sort of pond a bit further up. Or there was last year. Nell and I used to come here." She gives him a studied look over the tops of her dark glasses. He shrugs and smiles. "Just for a quiet alfresco snog."

"How revoltingly pastoral of you both."

He smirks. A sedge-warbler chatters ahead in the reeds, he swings the punt round a first projecting screen. Beyond, a much denser curtain of reeds and bulrushes stretches across the water.

"Damn. It's got overgrown. I'll just have one bash."

He sinks the pole and thrusts with all his weight at where there seems most water between the barring stems. The girl gives a little scream as they crash into the first green barrier, bows her head protectively in her hands. The flat prow pushes some three yards in, then hits a soft obstruction, rises slightly, stops.

"Bugger."

Jane turns and looks forward over the side. And then—as he tries to extract his pole from the mud—her head flashes round, her mouth open, incredulous, horror-struck.

"Daniel!"

She buries her face in her hands.

"Jane?"

"Go back, go back."

"What's up?"

She twists away to the far side of the punt, her hand over her nose and mouth.

"Oh I can smell it. Please go back."

But he leaves the pole, steps forward over the slatted seat-back, looks beside her; and sees.

Just beneath the surface of the water, pushed down by the punt's nose, a naked human buttock, grayish-white. There is an opening in the reeds where the back and head must lie. The bottoms of the legs are in the water, invisible beneath the punt.

"Christ."

"I think I'm going to be sick."

He turns hastily, forces her head forward, down to her knees; then scrambles back to the rear of the punt, frantically jerks the pole out of the mud, nearly overbalances, recovers, begins levering back. The punt hesitates, then slides back free of the reeds. He sees the hideous, obscure shape bob slowly to the surface.

"Jane, are you all right?"

She stays with her head down, but gives a faint nod. He maneuvers the punt awkwardly around, then thrusts it violently away back toward the river, around the first stand of reeds, then alongside the bank, jamming it secure with the pole. He kneels beside the girl.

"Are you all right?"

She nods, then slowly looks up at him, and in a strange gesture takes off her dark glasses, and stares at him.

"Oh Dan."

"How bloody horrible."

"It . . ."

"I know."

For a moment they stare at each other's death-riven incomprehension; their shattered morning world. He presses her hands, then looks back toward the mouth of the cut. "I'd better tell Andrew."

"Yes, okay. I'm all right now."

He stares at her anxiously a moment more, then stands and jumps ashore. He runs through the long grass toward the river. The girl sits with her head bowed on her drawn-up knees, as if to shut out sight.

"Andrew! Andrew!"

Their two faces through the willow-leaves; he stands on the bank above them.

"We've just found a body in the water."

[ 23 ]

"A what!"

"A body. A dead body. I think it's a woman. In the reeds."

"Good God."

The student called Mark, who is several years older than the other two, tanned, a moustache, clear gray eyes, known only to Daniel as some obscure crony of Andrew Randall, who has obscure cronies everywhere, stands and steps ashore.

"You're sure?"

"Absolutely. We ran right into it. Over it."

Andrew comes beside them. "Where's Jane?"

"Just back there. She's okay. Just shocked."

Mark says, "We'd better go and see."

"Hang on, dear boy." Andrew scrambles back into the punt, rummages in a coat, comes out with a silver and leather flask. The three stride quickly back along the bank. Jane looks up. Andrew goes down beside her, uncapping the flask.

"Try a drop of this, Jane."

"It's all right now."

"Orders. Just a sippington."

She takes the flask, swallows, chokes momentarily. Mark glances at Daniel.

"You'd better show me where it is."

"It's a bloody awful sight."

The gray eyes are dry. "I landed at Anzio, old man. And have you ever seen a long-drowned sheep?"

"For Christ's sake, we were right on top of the—"

"Yes. Well let's make sure."

Daniel hesitates, then follows him down the bank to where the reeds stretch across the water.

"About there." He points. "In the middle."

Mark kicks off his shoes and climbs down into the reeds, parts them, then takes a cautious step forward. His leg sinks. He feels for footing farther out. Daniel looks round. Jane is standing now in the long grass, watching from forty yards away. Andrew walks toward him, holding out the flask. Daniel shakes his head. The reeds close behind Mark, half-masking him, as he sinks above his knees. Daniel stares at a tuft of purple hyssop on the bank. Two shimmering blue demoiselle dragonflies with ink-stained wings flutter over the flowers, then drift away. Somewhere farther up the cut a moorhen croaks. Mark's back, his khaki pullover, disappear in the dense green stems that have closed behind his passage; the susurrus, the squelches and splashes.

Beside him Andrew murmurs, "Bet you a fiver she's a tart. Our gallant American allies again." Then he says, "Mark?"

"Roger. I've found it."

But Mark says nothing more. He seems to spend an inexplicable time hidden there in the reeds, silent; occasionally a reed-head bends sideways. In the end he comes heavily back, then clambers up on the grass, wet to the loins, his feet cased in black mud, a stench of stagnancy; and something sweeter in the air, hideous. He grimaces at the two others, glances back toward where Jane is, speaks in a low voice.

"She's been dead some time. Stocking round her neck. Her hair's full of maggots." He reaches down and tears off a handful of grass and brushes the worst of the mud away. "We'd better steam on up to the Victoria. Get the constabulary."

"I say, what a bore. I was just getting into silage. To say nothing of the champers."

Daniel looks down, unamused. He senses in them both a contempt for him . . . the bohemian, the effete middle-class aesthete. It is as if he is being cheated of his own discovery. But he did not land at Anzio; or indeed see any action at all during his two years' wasted time in the army. They walk back toward Jane. Mark takes command.

"You two'd better wait here till the coppers turn up. I should take our mooring. And for God's sake keep everyone away. They won't want anyone else trampling around. Come on, Andrew."

Andrew smiles at Daniel. "You owe me a fiver, old chap."

"I didn't take the bet."

And Daniel gets a momentary amused stare, the age-old quiz of the aristocrat. The flask is held out.

"Sure you won't have a nip? Look a bit pale round the gills."

Daniel curtly shakes his head. Andrew blows a light kiss to Jane, then sets out after his friend.

Daniel mutters, "My God, I believe they're actually enjoying it."

"Who's the other man?"

"Christ knows. Some war hero."

Jane takes a deep breath, gives Daniel a faint smile.

"Well. We're in the news again."

"I'm terribly sorry."

"I suggested it."

[ 25 ]

Mark shouts back and points to the bank where he stands. Daniel waves. "You walk down, Jane. I'll bring the punt."

When he reaches the mouth of the cut, she is standing there between the willows. At her feet stands the unopened bottle of champagne. She pulls a face.

"Sir Andrew Ague-prick's parting gift."

He glances back and sees the other punt already a hundred yards away, heading for the far bank to gain protection from the breeze. He tethers his own, then climbs up beside Jane, lighting a cigarette. They sit down facing the main river, their backs to the horror a hundred yards behind. Another punt comes down opposite them, five or six people, a girl poling inexpertly, a scream, laughter as she nearly loses the pole.

"Did he say how old she was?"

"No."

She reaches and takes the cigarette from his fingers, takes a puff, then passes it back.

He says, "When I was a kid, helping with the harvest during the war, a rabbit got caught in the mower blades of the reaper." But he doesn't go on.

She stares out over the river. "I know what you mean. Like things in dreams."

"It's all I can remember about that day now. The whole summer."

She leans back against the willow-stem beside her, turned a little toward him, her head tilted back. She has left her dark glasses in the punt. After a moment she closes her eyes. He glances at her face, those eyelashes, that mouth, the grave girl under the sometimes outrageous one. She murmurs, "On the banks of the gentle stream."

"I know."

And silence falls between them. Two more punts pass on their way back toward Oxford. The clouds are thickening, a steep, opaque rain-mountain coming from the west, over the Cumnor Hills. The sunlight disappears. He looks up at the sky.

"Are you cold?"

She shakes her head, without opening her eyes. Overhead a huge American bomber, a Flying Fortress, roars slowly down westward below the clouds on its way to land at Brize Norton. Perhaps Andrew is right, it carries the murderer: he chews gum, in a baseball hat, watching a panel of instruments, up there. The thing is two miles away, a mere speck, when she speaks.

"Maybe it's right. That we should have found it."

He turns, to see her eyes open, watching him.

"How do you mean?"

"Just . . . the way we've all lived these last three years. And reality."

"It's been the most marvelous three years of my life."

"And mine."

"Meeting Nell . . . and you. Anthony." He stares at his feet. "All that."

"But has it been real?"

"I thought we had a truce on metaphysics."

She is silent a moment.

"I was revising Rabelais last night. *Fais ce que voudras.*"

"Since when was that a sin?"

"Perhaps what we want isn't what is. Or ever could be."

"But we've done what we want. At least part of it."

"Inside something which is . . . literary? Like the Abbaie de Thélème. Not anything real at all."

He cocks a thumb back. "If you're saying *that's* reality . . . honest to God, some Carfax tart who got picked up by—"

"Like your rabbit in the reaper?"

"But that's not us."

"Are you sure?"

"Of course I'm sure." He grins drily up. "Anthony would be deeply shocked if he heard you talking like this."

"Perhaps that's a fault in Anthony."

"I shall tell him every word you said."

She smiles gently, then bends forward, buries her head against her clasped knees, speaks into the peasant skirt.

"I'm just scared that these will have turned out to be the happiest years of our lives. For all four of us. Because we've been in love, we've grown up, we've had such fun. No responsibilities. Play-acting. Games."

"We've still had the fun."

Now she props her chin on her hands, and surveys him. Then without warning she stands and walks back to the champagne bottle and picks it up by the golden neck. She brings it beside him, then once again without warning swings her arm and tosses the bottle out into the river. It splashes, sinks, bobs back to the surface a moment, then sinks again, and for good.

He stares up at her. "Why did you do that?"

Looking at the river, at the place where the bottle sank, she says, "Are you and Nell going to marry, Dan?"

He searches her oblique face.

"Why on earth do you ask that?"

She kneels beside him, avoiding his eyes. "I just wondered."

"Has Nell said we aren't?"

She shakes her head. "You both seem so secretive about it."

"Do you realize you're the first girl I've been out alone with, apart from Nell, for at least eighteen months?" He pushes her arm lightly. "Oh Jane, come on, love, for Christ's sake . . . you may be transatlantic orphans, but you don't have to play the heavy sister. I mean why else should I be so desperately looking for a job here next year?"

"Guilty. Sorry."

"Nell feels marriage and final years don't go together. So do I. And getting formally engaged is—" He breaks off, covers his eyes. "Oh Christ. A brick. The man has dropped a brick."

"So *vieux jeu?*"

"Oh God."

"No. Be honest."

"You know what I meant."

"We're freaks?"

"Of course not. Just that . . . well, you're not Nell. And Anthony's not me."

She bows her head in acceptance. "I see."

He eyes her, then sits up. "Jane, is this why we're out together?"

"In a sort of way."

"You absurd old thing."

"Mother hen."

"Anthony knows?"

"He suggested it."

He gives a sniff of amusement toward the hills.

"I get it. When he comes back tomorrow, he's going to sneak off alone with Nell. It's a bloody conspiracy."

"Converting the heathens."

"I suppose he can't help it. I must say I thought better of you." She smiles. He adds, "I wonder where they'll find their corpse."

"Idiot."

He leaves a pause. "On the matter of secrets . . . *are* you going to let him convert you?"

"I haven't made up my mind yet, Dan."

"You ought to have met my father. That would have put you off the whole shoot for life."

"Should one judge faith by people?"

"I still hope Anthony doesn't succeed."

"Why's that?"

He stares across the river at the clouded west. "You don't know what it's like. Not even Anthony. Living in the shadow of a church. It forces you to hide so much, you can't imagine if you haven't been through it. The unreality of it. Like what you were saying about Oxford. Only far worse. Not even the fun." He contemplates the dark hills. "I could become a thousand things, but I'll never be a Christian again as long as I live."

"Spoken like a true Oedipus complex."

Their eyes met, and they smile, then both look down, with that acute self-consciousness of young adults, ever sensing new situations, new knowledges, new awarenesses; drowned in self-interest, blind to all but each new moment's tendrils. He looks at his watch.

"They should have got through by now. I'll go and look."

He walks back into the field a few yards out from the willows, scanning eastward for dark figures. After a moment she comes beside him, searching also. She speaks without looking at him.

"I think Nell's very lucky, Dan. That was something else I wanted to say."

"No luckier than Anthony."

She whispers, "All these lucky living people." And then, before he can decide what a certain wistful dryness in her voice can have meant, she speaks more normally and points. "There!"

At the far end of the field, farther to the south than they had expected, five figures appear from the willows: two in uniform, three in civilian clothes. The two uniformed men carry waders slung over their shoulders. Another man carries a rolled-up stretcher. Another has a black box slung over his shoulder. Daniel waves, and one of the uniformed men gravely raises an arm in acknowledgment.

Watching them walk through the sea of buttercups, he says, "Why did you throw that champagne in the river?"

He glances at her beside him. She looks down into the grass at their feet.

"It just felt right."

He puts an arm round her shoulders and kisses the side of her head. She remains staring at the grass.

"Why did you do that?"

He smiles. "For the same reason."

# An Unbiased View

This isn't what I promised to write, just before you ran away. But it's still pure fiction. Of course.

About Mr. Wolfe. Not you.

It was at Claridges. A first-floor suite full of Louis-something furniture. Not too bad, perhaps the three of them canceled one another out and for once there was at least a pretense they were looking for actress rather than lay potential. I knew Dan was slightly drunk and I wasn't impressed. Or I was disappointed. After the script. He hardly said a word, not even when we were introduced. A kind of bored leer (he must have been drunk, he normally never puts on like that with total strangers). Bill and the man Gold did the chat. I sensed Dan was trying to dissociate himself. So why was he there? I think I thought he was rather pathetic, really. Like some character out of Hemingway. Or the man in *Under the Volcano.* You can see I'm tough and wise and sensitive and virile and literary and lost and totally above all this because I'm drunk.

Terribly dated.

At one point I mentioned I'd been in one of his plays. We'd done it for two weeks in Birmingham as a run-in for the main season, a pretense of honesty before the crap started. I said how much I'd liked it. Actually I hadn't, it's one of his weakest (I now know, having read and re-read them all), but I wanted to say something. I knew Dan couldn't be for much in the decision, that he must be there mainly out of courtesy. Perhaps I was already sorry for him.

He said, Good.

It was the only time I found him interesting. He said "good" like: you stupid, pretentious bitch. As if I were some Chelsea nithead.

I said, trying to remind him I was a cut above mere drama school, And my tutor at Sussex was an admirer of yours. (Well, he had once mentioned Dan's name.)

He slid his eyes at the other two.

He said, I think the girl really wants the part.

They grinned, and I had to smile. That left him not smiling, and carefully avoiding my eyes, the mean bastard.

He once said to me later, You know why I spend so much time paring dialogue? Because I loathe actors. Those were always two things about him. He wasn't a playwright, a dramatist turned scriptwriter. All he did, I write dialogue. Once he put it: I'm a dialogue installer and repairman. Another time: At least most screen-actors never learn to act. That was my sin, that day.

They'd run the two previous parts—already picked me, it seems. It wasn't much more than a formality. He claimed he was very drunk at Claridges, not slightly drunk, and couldn't remember anything. So he'd better not alter this.

A bit more than medium height, graying a little at the fringes. The hair cut more American than British. Trend-conscious American executive. Bill's wild locks and Mexican moustache made Dan look very passé. He always had that faint air, very much that male type physically, of the Duke of Windsor when he was still young. Rather a sullen-shy face, but the body not gone to fat. A good mouth, his best feature. His eyes too fixed and pale, I never really went for them, despite their occasional sexiness. A sort of challenge, they always stared slightly. When he was bored, he used it consciously, as if he was somewhere else, and wished you were. It was a rudeness I rather got to like, probably because I learnt how to control it. If it was aimed at me, I knew how to kid him out of it. And useful, if it was aimed at someone who bored me as well. As they often did, obviously. Agreeing on what's a bore is a main reason the thing happens.

I've just re-read that last paragraph and it's too based on that first meeting. I make him too stony, too static. He moved lightly, he was never physically clumsy. Sometimes I wished he was, it was as if he'd studied not being clumsy, how to be deft. Contradicting what he felt about acting. So usually he'd come on a shade too urbane (this is in public). The much-traveled man of the world and all that. On the other hand (as he knows) I hate men who can't handle hotels, restaurants, waiters—success life, if you have to lead it. I suppose doing it well inevitably means role-playing.

A good escort, as publicity would say.

I still can't define his essence. Something in transit, hardly ever altogether with you. I used to think it was the age thing, but it was much more than that, not just those moments when he slipped on his father, his uncle face, like the time he first talked marriage, up in the Mojave. When I explained why not, he went young again. Absurd. He got the faces in exactly the wrong order. If he'd asked me young, it might have been so different. I was falling in love with him (or the idea of him) then, on the brink of losing my cool, I knew it would come up and I knew the answer would come from way beyond a prepared decision, if he chose the right moment. Out of instinct, the time and the place and the mood. He'd never have muffed it so badly in a script.

Not just in transit. Self-contained. Very planned and compact, like his handwriting. Like a good leather suitcase in an airport lounge, neatly locked, waiting to be taken somewhere else, with a destination label you can't quite read. Or when you could go closer and did read, it was just the name and the airport the other end, and you hadn't heard of either. To begin with I found this very attractive. Not quite being able to read him, which also meant knowing it couldn't last, he was passing. Realizing he was (and not just in the literal sense) deeply divorced. Homeless, permanently mid-Atlantic, in spite of the way he clung to his Englishness in accent and idiom, the kind of parenthesis he always let you see round his Americanisms, and his queer old patriotism—what I thought of sometimes as his Visit-Britain self, chatting with picturesque old gaffers in an oak-beamed country pub and quaffing his tankard of ale. I used to get mean about that, a nasty little Seventies bird: if he loved it so much, why was he here?

That was a place we didn't meet. I've never been a country girl (thank Christ, says she). It shocked him that I didn't despise Los Angeles on sight. Or want to go back to the boring old Mojave desert.

And Tsankawi. Oh God. But I can't deal with that now.

I remember the day, early on, it was night actually, he first came out about his country retreat at home. All the time he was describing it, the landscape, Devon, the wild life, his childhood—as if all that was why it meant so much to him, I sensed something else. What he really needed was not the place, but an excuse to talk about it. He hardly ever lives there, it's really just a hobby, something he's acquired on the way to what he actually is. Which of course he knows—or rather, since he's as scared of not seeming to see his own paradoxes as a good chess-player of exposing his queen, he thinks he knows. He said it once, when we were talking about *Citizen Kane* (he may alter this if I've got it wrong): how the great master-stroke was the Rosebud symbolism, how the worst corruption of the corrupt practitioners of a corrupt art was the notion that you could *buy* back innocence. Like a Mafia contribution to the local priest—as if that would save you if there really were a Heaven and it truly judged. I didn't tell him I couldn't see why being objective about his pseudo-farm let him out, either.

But I didn't dislike him for it. He never realized he wasn't ugly when he was fallible.

And his father being a vicar (I hadn't then realized *The Empty Church* was autobiographical). I laughed, I just couldn't believe it. I didn't really believe it till the day we were out driving down to Marineland and got into a freeway crawl, and he started singing hymns. Guying them, all their Christian nonsense. But he'd remembered so many. That was another moment I loved him. He was fun to be with sometimes.

So the self-contained thing was really just a symptom of his inability to relate to anything but a *place* where he didn't have to relate, except verbally, and after a few Dettols. I never got far beyond even that secret. To his real ones, like Caroline. I hated the way he used to talk (before I had it out with him) about her, by implication so dismissively, contemptuously, as if she were some useless secretary he was stuck with at home, instead of his own daughter. All right, so her mother's screwed her up and given her values he despises. But it was transparent that in fact he was simply hurt, resentful . . . and not only about the past, having lost her, but also about having got hooked on me, the incest bit (but what did he think he sometimes was for me?), and hating it and loving it.

Then all the murk behind his broken marriage. I gave up trying to penetrate that. And his other women, his quite *grotesque* evasiveness about that, if I got nosy. As if I might be offended, as if that kind of past ever made a man less attractive. I shouldn't call him a smart leather suitcase. He's really an old split parcel, done up with fifty thousand clumsy knots. He outrages all my Scottishness.

All this was summed up on that weird last evening (the

second-sight thing was nonsense, but it was strange, Dan, I *did* feel something was going to happen to us). When you, I mean he, talked of chasms. And I told him he meant barricades. I hope he'll think very hard about that, if he ever reads this.

I'm running and running him down, but all this actually made us more equal. I never realized so clearly before that "old" minds are also young minds in old bodies. (Unkind, I mean nice no-longer-young bodies.) There were increasingly times when I felt older. I *was* older. When that extraordinary call came, he was like a child, a small boy who is frightened and excited and trying to hide both by being "mature." Somebody truly, actually, for God's sake really wanted him. He felt set free, I could feel it. I was very angry, which I hid. Not that he decided to go, but had the nerve to drag me in as a pretext. I don't know why I should sometimes have been worried about using *him*. At least I've been open about it.

I look back now and I see that its all happening, something like it, was inevitable. After Tim and I broke up and I ran wild, it was always in the air. It had to be someone like Dan, in the end. This was an element I brought in from the first (though it wasn't calculated, I'm really saying he's also taught me to be more honest). It had had to happen, it had a kind of dialectical inevitability, *therefore* it must one day change to something else. That "therefore" was always around. Made it a stage, in both senses.

It was Harold, in the Birmingham days, who gave me the clue. He said: All good actresses are whores. Because on top of the normal need to experience, we have a professional *duty* to experience. I was conscious of that long before Dan. I was very conscious of it when I split with Timothy. Even at the worst of it, our fighting and screaming, a secret little Jenny-doll sat in my brain licking cream. That first screen part was full of the cream she'd been licking, if I'm frank.

Dan came to the airport to meet me at Los Angeles. With the studio publicity woman and her photographer and roses in cellophane. He claimed it was because Bill couldn't make it, he was just standing in. Which spoilt it. A little. But he wasn't drunk, he was dry and rather paternal, a different person from Claridges. And when we were at last in the limo away into the land of the fries and the burgers he described his own first arrival years before, unmet. The feeling totally alien and lost. He saw me look at one of the monopod hoardings, with some absurd giantess of a drum-majorette slowly spiraling on top. He said, You have to decide one thing here—which is real, you or Los Angeles. Right?

I said, Right.

I turned that into a mantra. It was the nicest, the best thing he ever gave me. "Los Angeles" means anywhere.

I was in flakes and they made me go straight to bed when we got to the hotel. I was to have a free day before the publicity grind and fittings and the rest. There was a list of flats, apartments, to look at. I'd decided that somehow living in an apartment would mean like being in digs in rep. A tin of coffee, a box of detergent, a kettle to boil. I might need that. The publicity woman had planned to take me looking, but Dan offered to combine it with a drive round the sights. I think he saw something in my face, she wasn't my cup of tea at all. Frightened me with all that career-woman processed-cheesecake charm.

He picked me up at ten the next morning. I hadn't been able to sleep well, I kept on getting up and staring out of the window. So this is America, this is the place, that's Sunset Boulevard down there. Nine tenths of me was still in London, dear little Belsize Park. I was scared, I was glad Dan was going to be there to shepherd me in the morning. He was in the Polo Lounge, drinking coffee and reading the day before's London *Times*. Very reassuring. And I even felt excited for a while, just a tourist. But it grew too much, we saw too many places too far apart and I began to get in a panic again, going all instinctive instead of practical. He was patient and neutral. Like an estate agent, bored but hiding it, with a rich client. And then I began to think he was secretly watching me, trying to make up his mind whether I really was right for the part and I felt annoyed that he wasn't sure. He said later he liked what he called my being choosy. He'd just been curious, "anthropological." I didn't think of him in a bed way at all. No. I did once, in a ghastly bedroom we were both standing in. And dismissed him at once. He tried to put me off the place I finally said yes to. But I fell for the view. I'd realized by then that I'd never find room-shapes and furniture I could happily live with. So I hired the view. We had a late lunch back at the hotel. He offered to drive me round some more, but by then I wanted to be rid of him. I went and slept.

That same day's evening Bill had flown back from New York and he and his wife and Dan took me out to dinner. It was for me to meet Steve as well, but he hadn't turned up, though he'd been supposed to make the same flight as Bill.

Who brought profuse apologies. Steve was busy laying, of course (as he told me as soon as we did meet, the next afternoon). It was like the birds-of-paradise with the note from him (*Thrilled to be working with you—Steve*) I found waiting with all the rest of the florist's shop. From the hotel, and Bill, and the man Gold, and the studio—none from Dan, though—in my suite when I arrived. Each card written in the same hand. When I thanked Steve for flowers and message, he just opened his hands, a typically lousy piece of acting. He didn't know what the hell I was talking about.

But I'd already heard enough about him by then. At dinner that first evening Bill and Dan had finally drunk enough to be bitchy and more honest. I learnt for the first time that Steve was neither of them's first choice—the man Gold had pulled box-office.

Steve has some hang-ups, said Bill.

He's a prick, said Dan.

I can handle it, said Bill. It is there.

And then Dan smiled at me, the faintest wink, partly at that clumsy use of "it," but something nicer. Both tender and wry, some kind of simple English current between us in the posh-lousy eating-place. An alliance. And it said he'd decided to like me, we'd find a way to cope with the Prick. Which we didn't, but never mind.

Then next days: meeting the Prick, fighting wardrobe, the awful run-throughs, re-writes, arguments. Trying to get it to the P. that I didn't want to make it quite yet in the sack, thanks very much all the same. One god-awful statutory evening alone with him and his hang-ups—well, what Dan would call anthropologically quite interesting, they all seemed so calculated, part of his image, and ludicrously dolled up with Nam and all the okay political attitudes. I got very prim and English with all his sloppy clichés. He'd have done fine as a beach bum or a gigolo. It was trying to be a thinking actor. *And* irresistible penis. I let him kiss me at the end. Killed the groping before it got anywhere, and any repetition of it.

All this was against the (for me) whole freak background of California. Of course I knew my real career (thou dark enigma) didn't depend on this one film very much, if at all—Dan didn't have to teach me that. But I had some sort of culture shock. I couldn't tell the P. what I really thought of him, as I would have back home. He had to be made to want to help me a little, with all the sex scenes ahead. And then the awful synthetic gloss (I hadn't met Abe and Mildred then, remember) over the other people in this world, the constant gescheffting, gossiping, organizing, like hundreds of little plastic cogs in a clock that won't keep real time anyway. Nothing ever seemed to stop, one always had to be doing something, planning something, saying something that was "meaningful." It was like a foreign language I couldn't speak (not American English, the movie-biz use of it) yet had to listen to because I could understand it. All those boring evenings with people I never wanted to see again. Worse even than boring publicity. Feeling I was being dragged down into the gloss and the plastic and the piddling self-importance, all of which made me long for England and people who do their own thing naturally and not because it's a trendy little phrase. Long for hours that drift and conversation that hops about and has silences, with nobody really believing one another or expecting to be believed, because it's all a game. All you pointed out to me later about old and recent users of a language. The awful give-away of trying to be "meaningful."

Sorry. All *Dan* pointed out to me.

Which made me look forward—more to that than to Dan—to an evening with him. His suggestion, very tentative, an English exiles' evening, just the two of us. I had lost touch with him a little after that first day. He was around during the read-throughs and I'd got to admire him professionally. The P. was always coming up with "better" (shorter) lines, or no lines at all because he could get it across by some piece of fantastically subtle sub-sub-Brando (Jesus) *shtik* which he could never quite demonstrate, let alone explain. Bill and Dan must have agreed how to handle it. Bill would sound sympathetic and interested, Dan would finally shoot him down. I think they were right, it was the only way. But it was so long-winded. And the P. started taking against Dan and the whole script and tried to enlist my support. I used to sit there silent in all the gas and think how much simpler the whole bloody process was at home.

So our evening. We drove back over the hills to the San Fernando Valley and some dotty Russian place, where the food came in dribs and drabs, with endless pauses, and not what we'd thought we'd ordered anyway, but delicious. I pumped him discreetly, his past. Learnt he was divorced, one daughter only three years younger than me and trespassers keep out. I did. But his career, his plays, why he'd stopped writing them, movies, America . . . he talked a lot and I responded and he listened when I began unloading all my own naïve feelings about California. I knew we had a wavelength, something I'd doubted before. He came in for a nightcap when we got back to my apartment. Ten minutes later he pecked my cheek and left. I wanted him to. Which doesn't mean that it wasn't a lovely evening and a great relief.

Shooting began, locations, and I hardly saw him then. Just very occasionally he would appear, he'd already started on the Kitchener script. But then he was there one day during the sequences at Malibu and we had a talk between takes. I was getting pissed off, they seemed to need so long to set things up and Bill never seemed satisfied until we'd done three takes more than necessary. I used to get driven straight home after shooting and then stay in, go to bed at eleven, ten sometimes. A model young actress. But compared to dressing up and going out and being a sex-object and wildly bored . . . I started turning down everything. I had a courtesy meal with Bill and his wife, but I think that was all for a whole week. It was strange, I rather enjoyed it. Cooking the bits I'd scribble Martha to buy when she came in to clean. Or sometimes I'd stop off in the studio car and pop into a health-food place or a deli. Kitchen around a bit, watch the inane TV. Read. Write home like a schoolgirl. It was Dan's fault. I was trying too hard to prove California was unreal, not me.

Some of which (not that last bit) I found myself telling Dan between takes at Malibu. We were paddling, like elderly trippers at Southend. The stills man took a photo of us I've kept. Both staring at the sea at our feet. I suppose I was trying to tell him my simple Anglo-Scottishness was stronger than this alien culture. And honestly no, I didn't feel lonely at all. Yes, of course I'd ring if . . . and suddenly knowing I *was* lonely. That was where the digs illusion broke down, the other girl I'd have had to chatter with. It was a kind of bottling up, that was why I was writing so many letters. It was just someone to talk to, no more than that. I'd stopped the jack-and-jill, I was getting on perfectly well as a temporary nun.

I said, I've discovered a sensational health-food store.

He gave me a side-look. Is that an invitation, Jenny?

It hadn't really been. Then suddenly was.

Tonight? If I promise to leave by ten?

I knew I had to come to a decision, as soon as I'd said yes. It had all been very guarded, casual, space for withdrawal on both sides. But I knew "check" would be attempted. I thought about it a lot, that is, about a whole aspect of Dan I haven't mentioned before—the fact that he has a name. On the other hand, knowing that by the highest standards he never quite got there, that his plays are really rather square, that among my generation in the theater there are a dozen other writers we are more interested in, more "with" . . . which he knows, though it's always been a taboo subject between us. He assumes I despise him theatrically, at best a sort of toleration. And perhaps I always assumed too much that he didn't really care. Then something else: the fact that, in (silly) terms of having your name in the papers, I've always before gone down rather than up for my men. I'd known for some time that that wasn't healthy. As if it wasn't enough to give my delightful body-and-soul to them, but there had to be the press cuttings as well.

It was partly vanity. Handing out the privilege of sleeping with Jenny McNeil in return for her privilege of despising them for not having made it—which is exactly how Timothy once put it. And outraged me, I was so sure my living with him proved I was a democrat, that I saw through all the ballyhoo, I might be an embryo star but my feet were on the ground. It was also a fear, almost a little girl's fear that I should one day wake up and all this would burst like a bubble, so better not risk too much. But the other thing was paramount. I always felt safer when there was something in lovers I could despise. I couldn't even call it political, a justifiable Women's Lib attitude. It went much deeper, to a nasty little self-centered terror of being challenged and disturbed. Reduced to equality.

I'd thought often about all this since I came to California. It may shock Dan, but it did play quite a part. He wasn't *very* famous, or someone I admired *deeply* as a writer. Just quite famous and quite respected—which meant I could still despise him a little *and* still feel he was a long step up from nonentity. He was perhaps going down and I was perhaps coming up, but for now the balance of success and experience and professional respect and everything else was heavily on his side. Except physically, I'd be doing him no favors.

This all sounds so vilely calculated. I kept changing my mind about him (or *it*) through the rest of that day at work. And there were *honestly* all kinds of simpler things. Wanting to know him better, thinking how it would put the Prick's nose out, feeling excited, both emotionally and sexually. I suppose I saw Dan as a sort of challenge. I remember having had a shower and staring at myself naked in the mirror, before he came. Feeling strange. Just not knowing. I've always known before.

Then wanting, much later that evening, after eleven, him to make a move. He'd been pumping me, much better than my attempt at it during our Russian evening. I suppose the Cats are right, you do need regular confession. Like menstruation. He'd coaxed out of me what I really felt about the film, about Bill, about the Prick (we agreed on that name for Steve that evening). Everything. My never being quite sure what Bill wanted or what dotty new improvisations the P. would suddenly introduce into a scene, and why Bill let him get away with it so often. Dan was nice: the rushes I'm not allowed to see, I was doing fine. Even the ever-pessimistic Gold was impressed. But what I liked best was knowing Dan himself had passed me.

Then the talk finally wearing thin, as if I was hinting that he should go, but it was only because I didn't know how to say that he didn't have to.

A fantastic silence. It seemed to last forever. He was lying on the couch, feet up, staring at the ceiling. I was sitting on the rug beside the log-place, hearth is too nice and old a word for it, back to the wall, staring at my toes. I was wearing a shirt, no bra, a long skirt. No make-up. He'd come in a blazer, foulard, studious informal like a smart Angeleno. Only he'd taken the blazer off. A blue flowered shirt.

He said, if this was a script, I'd have the man get up and go. Or the girl get up and come. We're wasting footage.

He turned his head on the couch and looked across at me. I didn't like that corny way he'd put it. He wasn't smiling and I didn't smile back. After a moment I stared down at my feet again. He got up, picked his blazer off a chair and just exited. Without a word. Not even a good night or a thank you for the meal. The door closed and I was left sitting there. Perverse: he'd have to do better than that and I still didn't want him to go.

But he went. I heard the outside door open and then it was slammed shut. Silence. I ran to . . . I don't know, at least say something. And he was there, leaning by the front door, *inside*, staring down at the ground. The old trick.

I turned back into the room and he came after me, switching off the lights. I remember he put his arms round my back and kissed the back of my head.

I said, Dan, I'm not on the pill at the moment. That's all.

No problem. If that really is all.

I put my hands down on his and said, I didn't want you to go.

He began to unbutton my shirt, undressed me, without kissing me again after that first touch. Then himself, and I was still half-perverse, I just stood there waiting, looking out at the lights all the way to the ocean, hearing the freeway traffic down below: all those funny, streaky, wobbling thoughts when you know it's this, a new thing, a new man, where is this room, who am I, who cares, why.

He came and put his arms round my shoulders and led me to the couch. We lay down side by side and he ran his hand down my body, watching me. Almost as if he thought I might flinch. As if I'd never had sex before.

He said, I've been wanting to ring you all week.

I said, I wish you had.

We kissed then. I was simple, passive, no games, I let him do what he wanted, responded just enough to show him I wanted him to do what he wanted—there was still something uncertain, I wasn't sure I wanted him for this, though I didn't mind. Anyway, it never is natural the first time, one's taking notes, comparing, remembering, waiting. In the end we went on the floor and I thought of tomorrow. Seeing him again, after this. Then his body. How lucky men are to have it so simple.

He didn't say anything. Neither of us said anything for some time. We just lay there, the way you come out of a film sometimes and you don't want to talk about it. I thought how little I knew about him. Wondered how much he did this sort of thing. There was very little unit gossip about him. Wondered what he really thought about me. His age, his past, my age, my past. He broke the silence. First he reached out and traced the line of my mouth.

Jenny, in the argot of this barbarous province what I've just done is lay a broad. The only way to kill that argot is to break the rules of the ritual that accompanies it. By the rules I should thank you for a nice fuck, dress and drive home. But I'm going to take you to bed and sleep, just sleep, beside you. Kiss you in the morning. Make your coffee when your call comes. You understand, if tomorrow you feel it's all a mistake, fine. I just want to be sure that for now we behave like European humans. Not movieland apes.

He was leaning on his elbow, watching me in the darkness.

I said, It already is tomorrow. I'm still here.

He kissed my hand.

Okay, then just one more speech. I've been in love often enough in my life to know the symptoms. As opposed to the lay-the-broad ones. But love is a sickness of my generation. Not yours. I don't expect you at any point to catch it from me.

Is that a request or a prediction?

Both.

And that was it. We went to bed. We didn't sleep. There's something about one's own bed, most belonging there. And the way he held me. And thinking about what he'd said, and how it hadn't needed saying, it was almost insulting because it really meant I might just be a broad who went in for one-night stands and then that I was too young and shallow and 1970ish to understand love. It was square, anyway. But it also said he was less cool, or more vulnerable, than I believed. And something wicked: Daddy-o wants me. All his years, his women. Till suddenly I wanted, and truly to say yes, and turned to tell him.

(To be continued. It's 1:30, I'm mad.)

# The Door

"Daniel? It's Nell."

"Who?"

"Your one-time wife."

His arm drops from Jenny's shoulders.

"Caro?"

"She's fine." A hesitation. "I'm sorry for this god-awful hour. We can't work out the time-change."

"I'm still up. It doesn't matter."

"I'm ringing about Anthony, Dan."

"Oh God. Is it all over?"

"No, it's . . . as a matter of fact I'm with Jane. In Oxford. She wants to speak to you." He says nothing. "Are you there?"

"Just temporarily speechless."

"She'll explain. Here she is."

He glances at Jenny, then puts his free hand to his head like a pistol. She stares at him a moment, not laughing now, then looks down and turns away toward the center of the room.

"Dan?"

"Jane."

A strange mixture in his voice: both warmth and offense, and above all incredulity. There is a tiny pause on the line.

"I feel awful disturbing you like this. So out of the blue." A longer pause. She says, "Can you hear me?"

"It's just that yours was the last voice in the world . . ."

"I'm sorry. It was so kind of you to send that message via Caro."

"I'm only sorry it's had to be so long."

He expects a response to that; but she is silent again. He is trapped in two pasts, an immediate, still in that room, and a very remote; between two things he fears, emotion and unreason.

"How is he?"

[ 44 ]

"He's in hospital now. Here in Oxford."

"It's such foul luck for you all."

"We've learnt to accept it."

Again there is a silence, and he seeks frantically for a reason why this should be sprung on him.

"Is there some treatment over here you want me to . . ."

"I'm afraid it's beyond that. No one can do anything now." Another hiatus. "Dan, I've been trying to gather courage all week to ring you. I don't quite know how to say this, after all that's happened." Again she holds back, then plunges. "He wants to see you before he dies."

"To see me!"

"I'm afraid so. Rather desperately." She adds, "He's very ill. But quite clear-headed."

He feels like a man whose foot finds an abyss instead of a pavement.

"But Jane, with all the sympathy in the world, I mean, all that's so . . ." Now he is the one who seeks refuge in silence. He makes his voice less demanding of escape. "You two were right, for God's sake. I've long forgiven you both completely. Do tell him that." When she doesn't answer he says, "This is what it's about?"

"Yes . . . partly."

"You know. With all my heart. Total absolution. As far as I'm concerned."

"He particularly asked me to say it's . . . unfinished business."

"But my dear, I . . . I mean . . . Well can't you just tell him? He can take it as read."

"It's not a whim, Dan. I wouldn't be troubling you otherwise."

And she waits; as she always would, once a question was posed, a demand stated. Her pressures were always more those of silence than speech.

"Can I give him a ring?"

And then complete silence. He says "Hallo?"; then again. Then he heard the first voice, Nell's, sheathed and neutral.

"It's me again."

"What's happened?"

"Nothing . . . she can't talk for a moment."

"Nell, what the hell am I supposed to do? I've just offered to ring the hospital."

"He wants the living presence, I'm afraid."

"But why, for God's sake?"

"I don't really know. Only that he apparently talks of nothing else."

"I asked Caro to say if I could do anything, before I left."

"I know. I suppose it's something to do with dying." He feels her searching for a reasonableness. "We've tried to explain it's very difficult for you. But he's become obsessed by it. I saw him only yesterday evening. It's not just Jane."

"I don't understand why I couldn't have been given some warning."

"Jane's been lying to him. He's under the impression that she's been trying to get in touch with you. But she didn't want to involve you. I've only just come in on all this myself. I'm the one who's finally forced her to do something about it. We've been arguing most of the night. You'd better blame me."

"How long have they given him?"

"Not very long. It's not only the dying. How long he can talk coherently." She added, "I understood from Caro that you'd finished with the current film."

"More or less. It's not that."

"Oh yes. There was a photo of her in the *Express* the other day. Congratulations."

"Oh for Christ's sake."

She says evenly, "If you think it's been easy for Jane and me to watch—"

"I'm not wholly devoid of imagination, Nell. Now for fuck's sake pack it in."

His voice has something rare in it: a rawness. A silence. Then as if satisfied, the old weapon once again proven good, she retreats into simplicity.

"I'm sorry. We're not blackmailing. Just begging."

"It's all such ancient history now."

"Not for Anthony." She added, "But it's totally up to you."

He wavers, calculates, stares out at downtown Los Angeles six or seven miles away; feels strangely frightened, as if the reflection in the glass is his own accusing ghost; like an empiricist threatened with supernatural pattern, though he thinks not of doors, but of traps, returns out of freedom, the digging-up of corpses; of more than one death.

"Is Jane still there? Can I speak to her?"

"Wait . . . yes, all right. Here she is."

"Dan, I'm sorry. We're both in a rather overwrought state."

"All right, Jane. I understand. Now listen. Cast your mind

back a thousand years. Do you remember a day when you threw a full champagne bottle into a river? And you said, when I asked you why, I can't remember the exact words, but something like, It *felt* right. Do you remember that?"

"Just."

"Then forget all these years of silence between us. All the anger. The betrayal. And give me one more equally inspired total judgment. Would it feel wrong if I didn't come? Do *you* want me to come?"

"I haven't the right to say, Dan."

"Not unless I ask. Which I just have." He adds, "I'm between films. I was coming home soon."

And he waits, he sees, already, as he sometimes does at the very early stages of a new script, permutations, forks, openings to exploit.

"Anthony would be eternally grateful. If that doesn't sound too silly."

"And you?"

At last she says, "Please. If you possibly can."

"And there's very little time?"

"No."

The decision is on him, almost before he knows it is there, and he feels—the image is from seeing, not experience—like a surfer, suddenly caught on the crest, and hurled forward. It is both a moment of will, as if, like the surfer, he was waiting for this; and simultaneously one of abandonment . . . no sooner willed than transferring will to the wave.

"Okay. This call's costing you the earth, so listen. Tell Anthony I'm on my way. Give him my every sympathy. And just put on Nell for one moment more, will you?"

"I sometimes think I ought to have thrown myself instead of the bottle."

"I shall demand an explanation of that when we meet."

There is silence, the last. Then she says, "I don't know what to say, Dan. Forgive me."

Then it is Nell again.

"I'll try and get a flight tomorrow. Just warn Caro I'm coming back, will you?"

"I'll telephone her this evening."

"Thanks."

And he puts down the receiver, meanly, before she can find a tone of voice for whatever repentance or gratitude she too feels. Then he stares into the lit plains of the California night, seeing Oxford, a gray winter morning, five thousand miles away. From somewhere below there rises the neurotic switching wail of a patrol-car siren. Without turning, he says, "Two fingers, Jenny. Straight, please."

He stares at the glass when she silently brings it, then up into her eyes with a wry smile.

"And fuck your great-grandmother."

She holds his eyes, probing. "What's happened?"

"My erstwhile brother-in-law wants to see me."

"But I thought . . . the one with cancer?"

He swallows half the whisky. He stares down at the glass. He looks up at her, then down again. "We were very close once, Jenny. I've never really talked to you about all that."

"You told me they'd excommunicated you."

He turns away from her eyes, looks out again over the endless city. "He was my best friend at Oxford. We were a . . . sort of quartet. The two sisters. He and I." He gives her a diffident grimace, searching her reaction. "Ghosts."

"But . . ." she lets expostulation trail away. "You're going?"

"It seems there's not much time left." She stares at him, and her eyes show two kinds of hurt honesty, both a childlike and an adult. If he tells her a lie then, it is also partly to himself. "It's Caro, Jenny. We've torn her apart for so long. I can't refuse the olive-branch now it's offered."

"Why does he want to see you so much?"

"God knows."

"But you must have some idea."

He lets out a breath.

"He's a professional philosopher as well as a Catholic. They do rather live in a world of their own." He reaches and takes her hand, but again looks out into the night. "His wife's someone special. Very . . . meticulous over personal relationships. Very scrupulous. She wouldn't have broken so many years of silence without . . ." but he doesn't finish.

She withdraws her hand and turns away. He watches her light a cigarette by the couch.

"Why did it feel right to throw a full champagne bottle into a river?"

"It was just her way once of suggesting we'd all been living in a false paradise at Oxford." He goes on a shade too quickly. "All very involved. I'll tell you one day."

"You don't have to defend it. I just wondered."

But she avoids his eyes.

He says, "Perhaps it's for the best."

"Thanks very much."

"A breather."

"I didn't realize it was a race." She picks up an ashtray and empties it unnecessarily into a wastepaper basket. "You won't come back?"

"They only want you for three weeks more. With any luck."

She leaves a silence. "Well. That'll teach me to make jokes about second sight."

"Yes. It was a little uncanny, that."

She glances at him, accusing.

"Ask me to marry you again."

"I try not to repeat silly mistakes."

"Your whole life's a mistake. You've just told me so."

"All the more reason for not dragging you into it."

"I shouldn't have said yes."

"Then what?"

She bends and plumps a cushion. "I think about it. Quite a lot. Much more seriously than you do, I suspect. For all your talk."

"Then you should know why it wouldn't work."

"I know the signs are bad. All you say." She obstinately arranges cushions, then picks one up to examine some loose braiding. "I just wonder if the fact that you won't trail round after me and I won't give up everything to darn your socks isn't really rather a good thing. The best I'm likely to get. Given the squaw bit doesn't attract me at all. That it wrecked my only other . . . serious relationship. Would always wreck it with anyone normal my own age." She says, "I'm trying to be honest."

"Then it definitely wouldn't work, Jenny. The one component such marriages need is a core of dishonesty. I don't think we two could ever manage that. In the long run."

She puts the cushion down. "You don't seem to realize I need you. In so many ways."

"Need someone."

She turns from the couch and sits in an armchair, hunched forward, head bowed. "I feel frightened already."

"That proves I'm bad for you. And always would be."

"I've got to decide about the new part."

"You know what I think. He's a good man. He'll get the script up. You should do it."

"And take myself off your hands." She says, "I'd know you were waiting. You'd be there."

"I shall be. For as long as you want. You know that." He searches for a placebo. "And you can move into the Cabin. Abe and Mildred would love that."

"I might. And don't change the subject." She draws on the cigarette, blows out smoke, then looks up at him. He still stands by the telephone. "I notice you're not admitting that I'm also the best *you're* likely to get."

"You're shopping for bargains."

"You hide. That's even worse."

"What do I hide?"

"Your past."

"Not cool. The past."

"That's a stupid, slick, evasive, answer."

She spaces the adjectives, like little whiplashes. He turns away.

"So is a great deal of my past."

"Stage point. Not a real one." He says nothing. "And so's most of everyone's past. I don't know why you imagine yours is so peculiarly awful."

"I didn't say awful. Unpurged." He goes and sits on the couch, at right angles to her chair. "It's not a matter of statistics, Jenny. Or even individual history. Purely of personal awareness." She will not help. He says, "I misled you, it wasn't really a feeling of emptiness I had this afternoon. Much more the opposite. Like having eaten too much. Undigested deadweight. A millstone."

She contemplates the end of her cigarette.

"What did your ex-wife say that annoyed you?"

"That thing in the *Express.* Couldn't resist a dig."

She stares at the carpet. "Is it the same for you?"

"Is what?"

"Still hating. I heard you say, It's all so far away."

"Will this seem far away, twenty years from now?"

"Whatever happened, I shouldn't want to hurt you any more."

She will not look at him; and he watches her face for a moment, the tenacious thwarted child in it, the jealous young adult; and feels a strong need to take her in his arms, to thaw this ice—but suppresses it, notes and commends himself for suppressing it. He regards the last of the more than two fingers of the Laphroaig.

"We had all our values wrong. We expected too much. Trusted too much. There's a great chasm in twentieth-century history. A frontier. Whether you were born before nineteen thirty-nine or not. The world, time . . . it slipped. Jumped forward three decades in one. We antediluvians have been left permanently out of gear, Jenny. Your generation knows all about the externals. The visual things. What the Thirties and Forties looked and sounded like. But you don't know what they felt like. All the ridiculous decors of the heart they left us encumbered with."

She does not answer for a long moment.

"Hadn't you better ring the airport?"

"Jenny."

"It's not a chasm, Dan. It's a deliberate barricade you erect."

"To protect both of us."

She stubs out the cigarette.

"I'm going to bed."

She stands and crosses the room to the bedroom door; but stops there and looks back at him.

"You'll please notice that I meticulously, scrupulously, do not slam the door." And once through she sets it, with an ostentatious precision, half-ajar. Then she glances up again at him.

"Okay? Old-timer?"

She vanishes. He sits in silence for a few seconds, then finishes the whisky. Then he goes to where his jacket lies and takes out a pocket diary, through which he leafs as he walks back toward the telephone. He dials a number and, waiting for an answer, stares back across to the bedroom door—which like that other door, like reality itself, that ultimate ambiguous fiction of the enacted past, seems poised eternally in two minds; inviting, forbidding, accusing, forgiving; and always waiting . . . for someone at last to get the feeling right.

# Aftermath

The police car dropped them at the top of the North Oxford
road where Dan had his digs. The sky had clouded over completely, and there was already a spatter of rain. They walked
quickly between the lines of solid Victorian houses, staid and
donnish, too trite to be real. The wind had loosened some
leaves. Autumn came drear and viciously premature. They
said hardly a word until they were in his room.

It was the best bed-sitter in the house, first-floor back, overlooking the garden; but equally chosen for its landlady, a
Woodstock Road Marxist who, having somehow got herself
on the approved list, allowed her student lodgers freedoms
unusual for the time. One put up with erratic meals and
Communist Party pamphlets for the rare privilege of being
able to do what one liked both with and in the privacy of
one's room. Dan's exhibited what passed for advanced taste
in 1950. He had some private money besides his government
grant and the Art Nouveau craze was still twenty years from
ubiquity. Small portables in the style could be picked up for
a shilling or two in any junkshop.

What could one deduce today from photographs of that
room? Theatrical interests: a pinned-up collection of pre-
1914 music-hall and musical comedy star postcards (which
he still has somewhere and occasionally adds to), a toy theater rather too prominently on a small table by the window
over the garden, above the mantelpiece an original Gordon
Craig set-design sketch (then his proudest possession, foolishly given much later to the woman cited in his wife's divorce action), a framed playbill with his own name on (as
joint librettist of the revue the previous winter), a batch of
masks from a production of Anouilh's *Antigone* (hardly *fin
de siècle* and already announcing a suspect eclecticism). Academic interests: a case of English literature texts and a cartoon on the wall showing Professor Tolkien being trampled
underfoot by a Russian Stakhanovite bearing a lettered ban-

ner, on closer examination an undergraduate porting the runic proclamation: *Down with Anglo-Saxon.* (Of priceless value since *The Lord of the Rings,* but unfortunately burned only three weeks from where we are, to be precise on the last day of the owner's Final Schools, along with the abominable *Beowulf* and a number of other ancient printed instruments of torture—all in revenge for the third-class degree frequently admonished and duly received.)

Family background and personal life: difficult, yet the very paucity of evidence tells a tale. No family photographs, I seem to remember, though there was one, a blurred snapshot of an old stone doorway with the illegible (but he knew it by heart) date 1647 above that half came into that category; and there were very probably on display some stills of the various other OUDS and ETC productions Daniel had had a hand in; and there was certainly one, misty-edged and studio-posed, of Nell on the table used for a desk—and at present cluttered with all the evidence of panic cram. The most striking effect was of a highly evolved (if not painfully out-of-hand) narcissism, since the room had at least fifteen mirrors on its walls. True, they had been collected for their Art Nouveau frames, or at least allegedly; but no other room in Oxford can have provided such easy access to the physical contemplation of self. This little foible had been cruelly lampooned (if it wasn't that at Oxford any lampooning is less cruel than none) in an undergraduate magazine the previous term. There had been a list of "characters" in the manner of La Bruyère. Daniel was dubbed Mr. Specula Speculans, "who died of shock on accidentally looking into a mirror without its glass and thereby discovering a true figure of his talents in place of the exquisite lineaments of his face."

It must be remembered that this callow attempt at a personal decor existed against—or because of—a background of austerity, rationing, and universal conformity. Britain was still deep in a dream of siege. Of its time, it was daring. People who went to parties in it were honored, and told less fortunate friends about it afterward. An added piquancy was the well-known landlady downstairs, who raged against the viper she had taken to her bosom and the bourgeois decadence of his fancy pots and pieces and his general attitude to life—or so Dan liked to pretend to his guests. The truth was that the elderly comrade, despite her eccentricities, was no fool and knew her young men, and their potentialities for the cause, a good deal better than they knew themselves. Not one whom Dan had shared that house with, and who had like him achieved some public notice in later life, had become a Communist; but rather more remarkably none had become a Conservative, either.

Jane knew the room too well to notice it at all that afternoon. She went to the window and stared down at the garden. After a moment, she pulled off the red headscarf and shook her dark hair loose; but still stood there holding the scarf, brooding.

"Do you want a drink, Jane?"

She turned and smiled faintly. "Tea?"

"I'll go and fill the kettle."

When he came back from the bathroom with it, he found her standing in the corner where he kept his exiguous kitchen.

"Only dried milk."

"It doesn't matter."

"I could pinch some fresh off old Nadya Constantinovna."

"No really."

"She's out."

"Honestly."

And she came with two cups and a teapot, spoons, and knelt by the fireplace. He put the kettle on the little electric coil he used for heating water, then went to the corner and fetched the dried milk, tea, sugar. Then he sat down on the rug opposite her and watched her measure out the black leaves into the pot.

"Is Nell coming round?"

He shook his head. "Essay night." She nodded. He sensed that she did not want to talk. Yet the feeling of emptiness in the silent house, in the day, in the time of day, made the vacuum embarrassing to him.

"Shall I put the fire on?"

"If you like."

The gas-fire phutted at his match, began to flame blue and gold; sparks of incandescent pink. The kettle started to add its slow voice. They echoed a kind a deep purr in Dan, for all his slight unease and Jane's silence. Already his dialogue-inventive mind, the monster that then still seemed a joyous gift, was secretly rehearsing various amusing ways of telling what had happened: that pompous half-education of the policemen's voices, Andrew's impossibly blasé behavior, that "I landed at Anzio, old man" . . . and then something else, not only the event, the gray buttocks like uncooked tripe, the reported maggots seething in the hair (which Dan would claim for his own eyes too)—but having been with Jane, the idol of her year, the almost celebrated already.

All of young Oxford knew she must one day be more famous, truly famous, with those gifts (much more serious than just taking off Rita Hayworth, her Vittoria in *The White Devil* had proved that beyond doubt) and looks. She sat, one arm back, leaning sideways a little, staring into the gas-fire. Deep down it wasn't her vivacities, her powers of mimicry, her mobility, all she could be on stage; but what her face showed just then, a sort of pensive inwardness. She was very much two people, one had long ago realized that, much more complicated than Nell; which was what matched her, against all superficial probability, with Anthony, who was in so many ways the antithesis of them all—the Greats scholar from Winchester, already halfway to becoming a don, applied, logical (in all except his religious beliefs, at that time almost as much a dandyism as collecting Art Nouveau mirror-frames); rapidly analytical and aphoristic. Young Oxford men who were mature, like Mark, in terms of war and death, were two a penny; everyone knew the story of the proctors' bulldog who had clapped hands on a student caught drinking in a pub—only to find that his victim was the young colonel whose batman he had been during the war. But Anthony had a different maturity, an apparently much surer knowledge of who he was and what he intended to be. He was widely envied Jane, but their relationship seemed incongruous only to people who knew neither of them well. Behind the masks their complementarity was striking.

As he might, though less concisely, have put it at the time; in simple fact he was in love with her. That was why he was embarrassed. For some months, at least two terms, he had known this; and that he was trapped. His future marriage to her sister was broken long before that day. Webster's immortal line: strange geometric hinges. His sense of guilt ought to have been attached to Nell; but in fact it was much more oriented toward Anthony, and not at all, or very little, because on that particular occasion Anthony had granted himself a week-end's break (some monastery in Gloucestershire that went in for the instant retreat) from his final grind.

Dan still felt a baffled privilege, to have got on so well with Anthony—baffled because he still couldn't really understand what the brilliant Wykehamist saw in him. He knew much better what he had himself taken from the relationship—the contact with a much more fastidious and incisive intellect, with a psyche far more certain of both external and internal values, far less easily corrupted by new ideas and the ephemeral. In a way, Anthony *was* Oxford; Dan was merely a visitor. He had learned far more from him than from his tutors, if the truth were known. But there was that one great flaw: he could never quite shake off a deep, though carefully hidden, conviction that it was a friendship between unequals.

In fairness to Dan, and to historical accuracy, it must be said that in terms of undergraduate prestige—so closely connected with undergraduate notoriety—his feeling of inferiority would have seemed odd to his contemporaries. He was a far better known, and perhaps even envied, student of his time than Anthony; of that group who escape academy and achieve more than a mere college reputation and who, later, in retrospect, give their whole university generation its characteristic stamp. But like Jane, he was also two people, though far less prepared, or able, to admit it than she. Perhaps it was mainly in his secret feelings toward Anthony that he did admit it; and in those toward Jane. He was even a little jealous of her gender, her young womanhood, which he felt allowed her both a more natural and a more mature attitude; she could both mock and be affectionate in ways he could not. They would, in fact, usually take the same side in any argument against Anthony, conspiring in guying him gently if he became too outrageously the young don. But it was a stage alliance, would-be worldly-wise thespians sniping at intellectualism; and hid the truth of where the real affinities lay.

So Dan watched this apparent proof, the prize he had not won—and, to complicate matters, which had even seemed partly stolen from him, since he had known Jane before Anthony, had even first introduced them, had really only held back before that introduction because he was in awe of her. Now he took what consolation he could from this substitute intimacy, in the softly hissing silence. The sky seemed to grow darker, strangely dark for midsummer. It began to rain outside, more heavily. The kettle boiled and Jane leaned across and lifted it; filled the pot. She was still filling it when she asked her astounding question.

"Do you and Nell go to bed together, Dan?"

Her intent, downlooking face.

"Dar*ling* . . ." he gave a little puff of shocked amusement; of pure shock, really. She did not smile, but set the kettle on the hearth before the fire. He had one virtue, I suppose. He read other people's moods fast; caught their intonations, usages, changed millimeters of mouth- and eye-shape; but only the moods, not the intentions.

He murmured, "Hasn't Nell . . . ?"

"Sisters don't always talk about things like that." She put a spoonful of milk in each of the two cups. "You mean you do?"

"Doesn't everybody?"

Again, they didn't, and far from it, in those days; and the comparatively few that did kept up a convention of secrecy about it. But Dan had never been a young man to keep his hard-earned and very far from innate sophistication under a bushel. One has to have some substitute for honesty.

"Anthony and I don't."

He couldn't understand why she should want to tell him. Knowing Anthony's views, he had not supposed that they did; both he and Nell had decided quite definitely that they didn't.

"The Catholic thing?"

She passed him his cup; little flecks of undissolved white powder floated on top.

"Yes."

"It means a lot to him."

"Yes."

"Under the squibs and epigrams."

She smiled faintly, but for the second time that day she seemed to be reproaching Anthony. A shifting of deep grounds, a sudden mystery, a hinge's first faint creak. She sipped her tea.

"I'm not a virgin, Dan. There was someone else. In my first year. Before I met Anthony."

Which pierced something hitherto virgin between them.

"He knows?"

She made a grimace. "This is rather why I'm telling you. It's a sort of rehearsal."

"Oh Gawd."

"It's so stupid. If I'd only told him at the beginning. Then it seemed too late. I'm sort of trapped now. It's not what I did. But that I haven't told him before."

He offered her a cigarette, lit a spill and held it out, then lit his own.

"And he's never thought to ask?"

"For someone so intelligent, he's rather bizarrely trusting. He assumes things about people he'd never assume about a theory of logic or a syllogism." She drew on the cigarette. "At least that's what I used to think."

"And now?"

"I wonder if he isn't rather frightened. Which frightens me every time I try to screw courage up to tell him."

"You'll have to tell him some time."

"I can't just before Finals. He'd be bound to see it as . . ."

"As what?"

She had such fine eyes, soul; sometimes she looked young, she did at that moment, staring into the fire, younger than Nell.

"The Jesuit in him. So badly timed, I must be trying to say something else. He'd look for it."

"Are you sure he doesn't think about you as one more step in the dark?"

She smiled. "I suppose I am a stand-in for the whole she-bang. Now you mention it."

"Is he putting a lot of pressure on—about the Catholic thing?"

"You know what he's like." She shrugged. "He doesn't lay down the law. It's all Gabriel Marcel and personal choice. Falling over himself not to decide for me." She leaned back on an elbow, moving her legs from the warmth of the fire; but still stared into it. "I've suddenly realized what Rabelais was on about this week. How he's really more modern than all the St. Germain-des-Prés crowd. Far more of an existentialist. That's what I was trying to say on the river. When you think how utterly obsessed by self-denial England's become. Outside the little world we've made for ourselves here. I feel there's something about Anthony and his religious side that's rather the same. Always thinking about the past and worrying about the future. Never actually managing to enjoy the present. And Rabelais is just one gorgeous long raspberry in the face of all that. There are passages, you . . . you suddenly feel he's the only sane human being who ever lived." She stared at her cigarette. "I tried to explain all this to Anthony the other evening."

"And he didn't quite follow."

"On the contrary. Everything. Except the fact that I'd just been to bed with the man. In spirit."

Dan grinned down. "But you didn't quite put it that way."

"It's how it felt. Adultery as well as heresy. Especially when he read the ethical riot act over my poor little female mind."

"Come on. He's not like that."

"Of course not. He was quite funny. Because he was so sure I couldn't be serious." She began tracing patterns in the worn Turkish carpet beneath the rug. "His problem is he can only be himself. You and I can be other people."

"Now you're denying him imagination. That's not fair."

"Not imagination. But acting on it. He could never write plays. Novels. Anything where you have to be someone else. Not in a thousand years." There was a silence; suddenly she shifted ground. "I can't make out if Nell likes him or not."

Again he was shocked. "Of course she does. You know she does."

"She doesn't realize he disapproves of her?"

Dan gave her a quick look then; but her eyes remained on the carpet.

"That's news to me too, Janey."

Liar: it was long sensed, and feared. And now the afternoon really started to show strange facets, cracks, reversals of time; was hinged indeed. It seemed there was almost a malice in her, a determination to force scales from his eyes; and at the same time a nakedness, as she let him see all these buried feelings.

"He does try to hide it. Even from me."

"But what's he got against her, for God's sake?"

"I suppose he suspects you go to bed. Fears something in me that he fears in her. He does rather take the sexpot image at face value."

"But that's at least half a mask. He knows that."

"I know."

"And I'm just as bad."

"No, you pass. You're a child of nature. His proof he's not a prig." She slid him a glance. "Is all this shocking you?"

"I think he's being terribly inauthentic."

"He's also authentically fond of you both."

"Thanks a million."

"And he tries to understand."

"But he can't have it both ways. He can't pretend to our faces that he likes Nell—and then pity me or something for having fallen into the clutches of the Scarlet Woman of Babylon."

"Fear for you."

He stared at her, but her own eyes were lost in the fire. Again he felt left a step behind.

"Is this what you were trying to say on the river? About Nell and me getting married?"

"How do you mean?"

"In your and Anthony's considered opinion, we shouldn't?"

"It's not something I have a considered opinion about."

He was silent, then gave a sour little sniff. "I thought at least we'd gained your qualified approval." He went on: "So why did you say Nell was lucky?"

"Because I think she is." She said slowly, "And I haven't got a considered opinion because I'm not able to judge properly."

Once more he tried to force her to look at him.

"Why not?"

"Because."

"Come on."

Her voice dropped. "Because I'm jealous of her."

"Because the bed thing's not a problem?"

"That would be just envy. I said jealousy."

It took a moment or two to sink in. But the intentness of her eyes on the carpet . . . he looked down at his own stretched-out legs, he was sitting with his back to the wall beside the fire; and felt like someone led blindfold to a precipice. She murmured in the silence, *"Fais ce que voudras."*

"This is getting rather complicated."

"Perhaps it's a long-overdue simplification."

"But you and Anthony, I thought . . ."

She turned away on the other elbow. He stared at her back.

"All this summer, whenever the four of us have been together, you won't look at me. Unless you absolutely have to. And I've had to force myself to look normally at you."

Her head bowed, face hidden, she waited.

"I didn't realize."

"That you've been avoiding my eyes?"

"Your side of it."

"No idea at all?"

"Just . . . once or twice. That evening at the Trout."

"Why did you think I held your hand like that?"

They had strolled out to Rosamund's Bower when the pub closed. Nell and Anthony had gone on ahead. He had been very conscious of her hand lightly in his in the darkness . . . but it had not said this.

"I thought it was just sisterly."

"I hated Nell that whole evening. I had no nice sisterly feelings at all."

There was silence. The back of her head, the line of her body. The rain had lessened, but it stayed overcast. He forced out his confession, as if reluctantly. What he really began to feel was a delicious excitement.

"It's mad. But I think I'm in love with both of you."

"That's exactly how I feel."

"God. What a mess."

"It's my fault. I wasn't going to bring it up."

"That thing in the reeds."

"I suppose so."

"It goes back quite a long way with me. You were such a success . . . I didn't know how to get near you."

Another silence.

She said, "It's like catching 'flu. You have it before you can do anything about it."

"Except there are simple ways of treating 'flu."

She left a pause.

"One usually goes to bed, doesn't one?"

A long moment. He whispers, "Jane?" She lies curled away, perched on an elbow. "You can't really mean that."

She shook her head. "It's so difficult to explain. I feel in some way Anthony's made me miss something. What you and Nell have. What my body dreams."

"Rabelais?"

"I suppose to be wild and wanton."

"Wild and wanton" was a stock undergraduate phrase of the time, and always used mockingly.

"But what you just said . . ."

"I do love him, Dan. In a strange sort of way it's because I love him." She added, "Want to love him."

He felt more and more out of his depth, yet unable not to go on.

"Want to know if you can love him?"

There was a silence, and when she broke it her voice was so low he hardly heard the words.

"Just once. An *acte gratuit?*"

He stared at his shoes. "And tomorrow?"

"If we knew exactly what we were doing. That we could keep it . . . outside time. As an exorcism."

He swallowed secretly. "An exorcism of what?"

"What must happen. What will happen."

"Knowing we love each other?"

"Knowing we once wanted each other. And that at least once we'd had the courage to admit it."

He could feel his sexual excitement on the rise; and an ungovernable desire not to resist it, despite what he then said.

"I don't know how we could ever face them."

"We seem to have managed to hide things so far. Even from each other."

He said, "It's not that I . . ." but once again his sentence floated away.

He felt paralyzed, stunned by the enormity, ravished by the strangeness. The silence grew, and she did not move. From across the gardens at the back there drifted through the rain the sound of an oboe, a rise and descent of progressive scales, skilled and rapid. Then a break.

She sat up and faced him. He felt she was looking at him for the first time. Those gentle but penetrating brown eyes, searching his; something oddly virginal about her at that moment, of a schoolgirl, a seventeen-year-old frightened at what her elder self had done; but with a faint smile that did not deny, yet somehow counterbalanced the innocence. Perhaps it was provoked by something still wavering in his own expression, for the smile also held a tiny hint of a challenge; or of a tease, as if she were proposing no more than a dare.

The student oboist began to play Delius, and she reached her free hand across the rug, almost formally, like a medieval bride.

# Passage

Daniel nearly missed his flight, owing to a traffic snarl-up.
For once the sky was almost smogless, a lovely midwinter
Californian morning. The gray-haired Polish cab-driver kept
cursing freeways in general and the San Diego in particular,
but he was in far more of a rage about it than his fare: an I
in the hands of fate, Isherwood's camera, not unhappily
reduced to watching himself, as if he were indeed a fiction, a
paper person in someone else's script . . . the seed of a hypothesis, like the "Simon Wolfe" planted in his mind the
night before. Perhaps that ancient gibe about him, Mr.
Specula Speculans, had not been quite fair: a love of mirrors
may appear to be only too literally *prima facie* evidence of
narcissism, but it can also be symbolic of an attempt to see
oneself as others see one—to escape the first person, and become one's own third.

In his already rather low valuation of the novel (a dismissal Daniel knew perfectly well was on the one hand a
cheap conditioning of his *métier* and on the other a product
of the lazy assumption that he was long past finding in himself, poor asthmatic cripple, the athleticism of imagination
and long wind the form must need) he reserved an especially,
and symptomatically, dark corner for first-person narration;
and the closer the narrative I approximated to what one
could deduce of the authorial I, the more murky this corner
grew. The truth was that the objectivity of the camera corre-
sponded to some deep psychological need in him; much more
to that than to the fundamental principle of aesthetic (and
even quasi-moral) good taste that he sometimes pretended lay
behind his instinct here.

What did dimly occur to him as he sat half-listening and
half-abetting his driver's determination to show that he was
now truly American—America is a perfect society, perfect
societies have no snarls and flaws, so what the goddam hell is
going on—was that perhaps this flinching from the I inherent

in any honest recapitulation of his life was no more than a fear of judgment; and that (Jenny's reported remark concerning perfectionism had also lodged much closer home than she may have realized) doing what he obscurely wanted was intimately bound up with doing what he obscurely hated. He even tried it out: "I missed my flight (or I nearly missed my flight), owing to a traffic hold-up on the San Diego freeway"—and did not like the sound and feel of it one bit.

At last they began to crawl forward, to within sight of the accident, the flashing lights, that were causing the stopped lines of impotent quadrirotal man. In his characteristic English fashion, Dan carefully filed away this added reason for why he was condemned to be what he was: how clear it was, if he ever did attempt the impossible, that anything would be better than to present it in the first person . . . even the absurdity of a mythical Simon Wolfe.

I was also very tired that morning. Jenny hadn't released me for another hour. There had been tears, not quite for the first time since we had met, but for the first time over our private relationship.

The idea for her picture had come during a stint on another script in Hollywood three years previously. The studio had found me one of those British girl secretaries who work their way round the States—though not very attractive physically, she had possessed a sense of humor and a long tongue. I enjoyed her dry coffee-break accounts of her various work-experiences and abortive romances before she came to me, I'd long wanted to contrive something on the Anglo-American cultural comedy . . . so Jenny was now a trained English nanny in a millionaire household in one of the chic canyons, fighting a losing battle against both her employers and her off-duty boy-friend—Steve Anderson's part. She could play the character close enough to her real self. Steve was and is the most frightful young bore, but his part also offered scope for his real-life fixations and dedicated self-involvement. I'm afraid director and script-writer had deliberately cultivated a certain amount of off-camera antipathy between their two stars. I didn't tell her, but I had in fact begun to respect Steve in the can, if not in the flesh. On screen, in the rushes, her controlled insularity and his would-be "Method" sloppiness mixed rather well . . . as we had hoped. We had also lied about his not being our first choice.

It was a white lie, since we had very much wanted a girl to

whom the Californian dream-nightmare was as fresh in reality as it had to be in the story. I knew how insidious the place is, how fast it warps the stranger to its own peculiar ways, so her virginity there was important. That also meant the film was going to be a tougher proposition than she realized. I played pig at Claridges partly for this reason: to warn her that whatever her local successes she was now stepping out of home movies, in both senses, into a very different and potentially much more lonely world. Then we were scared she might be overawed by Steve's ill-deserved reputation (and get to hear how much more he was taking). I watched her like a hawk during those first days, for purely professional reasons . . . which became more personal ones, of course, though I liked her all the better for apparently deciding that she didn't need my help. She showed a brisk blend of tact and independence, ancestral Scottish qualities I value far more than the second sight.

Like so many pretty, and far from stupid, girls in the business she was in a slight dilemma—incipiently crucified by her own good looks. It is not perhaps the kind of crucifixion the ordinary girl can have much sympathy for; nevertheless, it exists . . . and Jenny had the camera image that conforms too closely to current notions of what is sexually desirable in young women to escape. A certain leggy fragility, an elegant insouciance, a well-boned, fine-mouthed, candid-eyed eager frankness about the face . . . a nice ongoing kid, the lens said, searching as well as enticing to go to bed with; a twentieth-century princess, provoking very nearly the same dream as the real princesses who had once languished in their walled castles and haunted another age besotted with the concept of the unattainable.

She had done a little modeling work at home, and knew well enough how to get herself up to kill, and to "project," vanities she didn't always resist. Even tired, with her completely natural face, she couldn't always lose that air of vacuous distinction and effortless beauty that highly photographable women, the Shrimptons and Twiggies of this world, acquire. She was conscious of it, of course; and had a special clown's grimace for when she knew I had caught that look. I remember another evening, we'd been to a party and she had looked ravishing even with some expert competition, and I said so when we got home. She went straight into the bathroom and washed her face off. When she came out she said, "I forbid you to like me for that."

This problem of being her own young woman, not just the chauvinistic male world's dream of the type, distorted her in another way: her frostiness with men who took her at the obvious surface valuation was sometimes painfully gauche—and indeed misled me in the beginning. It was right for the part, that aloofness; but in private I found it rather silly, all this gazelle-like shying-away from the slightest wrong approach, even though she grew to hide it better. Another self, both warmer and less assured, I caught only glimpses of in the early days. None of us could really get near her, and it was hard to tell what was genuine and what was being tried out in pursuit of a working persona in a very alien environment.

It was Bill who warned me that she might be withdrawing too much. By then the thought of giving her a shoulder to rest on was not just a matter of production need or simple human charity, yet there did remain an element of calculation . . . which remained in substance, even if it changed in nature. She did need me, or someone like me, in Los Angeles; but it remained very open whether she needed me anywhere else. This doesn't mean that we had not achieved a very real affection. I could have fallen heavily for her, and become intolerably possessive; but I had sinned in that area often enough before to know that to take one's partner's independence as a challenge is the straight road to disaster. Wanting her was bound up with the notion of changing her, and I liked her too well as she was. Just as "I believe in God" is generally a synonym for "I believe in not thinking," only too frequently "I love you" is a euphemism for "I want to own you." I sincerely wanted to leave Jenny in the public gallery of her own freedom; and at the same time I was still also in love with both her body and her independence.

The tears were partly spoilt-child tears, glycerine drops; and also more genuine ones. I gave way to the blackmail. We'd forget the whole evening, it had never happened. She'd fly back as soon as she was released. It was just a temporary separation. Training, she said; and I let it pass.

Then I had driven back to Bel-Air, which is not where any Englishman in Los Angeles can normally afford to live—and where I lived purely by kindness and an old friendship. An early script I did for Columbia failed to meet with studio approval and they brought in Abe Nathan to help me rewrite it. He had more or less given up the trade by then, but he was still on call for crises. I was piqued, and prepared not to like him one bit. But not all studio decisions are crass. The story needed the "doctor," and I needed the lesson; I fell for the professionalism, and even more for Abe himself—as I did for his wife Mildred when I came to know her as well. He might wear the full livery the old Hollywood forced on its educated slaves—be cynical, lugubrious, obscene, suspect the worst of everything and everybody—but he failed abysmally to hide the fact that this persona was very largely a matter of Batesian mimicry (the evolution in a harmless species of the appearance of a dangerous one); and that underneath the waspishness lay a shrewd, humane and fundamentally tolerant mind. I had let him read every one of my scripts ever since. Even though the recipes of his own heyday no longer worked, he retained a very sure nose for the weak spots in the new ones—and in much else besides.

Mildred and he live in the wilder, less posh section of Bel-Air—"where the quail still speak Spanish." Theirs is not the opulent mansion the place is more famous for . . . not even a swimming-pool, though that is an invert ostentation; but a pleasantly ramshackle garden, incongruously studded with classical statues, the weather-proofed plaster props from some forgotten Roman epic, with the "cabin" up the hill. Abe built it to write in himself, but he had long let me appropriate it when I was in town. It lacks one or two hotel amenities, but is buried in greenery and birds' voices. I can be alone there, or with them down at the house. I don't like Los Angeles, increasingly detest those famous hundred suburbs in search of a city. But Abe, Mildred and the Cabin would make hell itself tolerable.

I had packed when I got back there, then snatched four hours' sleep, to be woken by Jenny's voice again on the telephone. Her own wake-up call had just come in. She was her normal self again; apologized for being "silly." Need was reaffirmed. I would broach the matter of her taking over the Cabin. I would call from home as soon as I could.

I went down to the house. Abe was already about and he gave me coffee, while I told him my news. Of course Jenny could take over the Cabin if she liked; whichever, he and Mildred would see she didn't get too lonely. I wanted this for more than the obvious kind reasons, since Mildred and he represent a formidable combination of Jewish commonsense and New England frankness. Few secrets survive for long near them. Jenny needed to get to know them both out of my presence, to be their temporary *shiksa* daughter instead of my cute little British bird. I was hopeful that as soon as she revealed my view of our relationship, they would take my side. They approved of Jenny as a person, but not of cradle-snatching. They also knew my past much better than she did . . . and my faults.

There *was* an element of doing a far, far better thing, killing two lapses with one exit—but we really were viable only in a culture where nobody ever grows old (especially if they are rich and successful) and trading in well-screwed for younger flesh is an accepted way of life. I had known a number of father-daughter marriages there. The girls weren't all the high-class platinum hookers of the old days; most were rather demure and reserved creatures, and some even had a sort of dignity, or perhaps it was just a smooth complacency at having side-stepped the tedium of being young and broke. It was the men who seemed to me more made the fools; and besides, Jenny had too much sense, too close an attachment to the freedoms of her generation, ever to deny herself the full potentialities of her future . . . and however hard I might have tried to subvert her from them. She had, or sometimes pretended with me that she had, a jejune notion that she'd seen it all; that I was, as she brutally (too brutally to be convincing) estimated, the best she was likely to get. But that was a nonsense passing time must explode. I had no right to encourage such an illusion; and I had categorically no wish to pick up the emotional tab when it was shattered.

I suppose the experience with Nell formed me there, no doubt on a predisposed Freudian pattern. Living with a woman has always seemed to me an artificial situation, pseudo-dramatic in nature; that is, an area where invention and concealment are as important as reality and honesty. I have always needed secrets. I write that clinically, not vainly. I live in front of too many wrong decisions, I cannot rid my life of them, the least I can do is to hide them from my lady guests . . . that is the practical theory, at any rate. Perhaps I had grown to like Abe and Mildred so much simply because they were clear proof that the theory is inadequate; that better relationships can exist. They are two people who have principally defined my own Englishness by their lack of it. I once outraged them both by arguing that most English anti-Semitism, like most English anti-Americanism, sprang out of sheer envy. They did not like simple evil explained as complex loss, or failure to evolve. You poor sons of bitches, snarled Abe, deprived of the gas-ovens . . . but that wasn't the point.

We took off. After a minute, by craning back, I could even make out Burbank and the roofs of the Warner lot stages, under one of which Jenny must have been facing the first take of the day. I did feel a guilt then, tenderness, a protectiveness. She would never be an outstanding actress, as the middle-aged woman I had spoken to the previous night might once conceivably have been, and I knew she hadn't fully accepted that as yet: the closed options, the compromises to come.

East, at altitude, over the deserted mountains of north Arizona and the toy gash of the Grand Canyon: there had been talk between Jenny and myself of driving back overland when her work was done. But that was a foregone experience I didn't regret, since there was another chasm beside that of age. The life we led in Los Angeles had allowed us to overlook it, turn it into another toy gash of no more than a trivial passing significance; but in another context, on the ground, I knew it would always have presented a much more formidable obstacle. It was my fault, in the sense that I had effectively reduced it to the status of one more secret about my past . . . though in this case, not only with Jenny.

Anthony and I originally moved from cursory acquaintance—being of the same year at the same college and with a shared staircase to our rooms—to friendship precisely because of this "secret." I was already engaged in burying or suppressing it, but it was still close enough in my past to be partially uncovered.

The summer term of 1948, our first university year: by chance I went into his sitting-room one day. Our shared servant was retiring and I was collecting for a leaving present for him. On Anthony's desk I saw a flower in a jam-jar—a stem of the Man Orchid, *Aceras*. A few moments later we discovered a common interest, though with me it was largely a memento, an echo of former days. With him it was far more serious; as with so much in his life, such an interest could be only methodical, deeply pursued, or non-existent. Scientifically I had learnt enough botany as a schoolboy to find my way round the old copy of Bentham and Hooker we had at home; and I had in my teens fallen prey a little to the orchid mystique. I disclaimed anything more with Anthony, and thereby disclaimed the whole buried continent that nature had been for me in my adolescence. I was ashamed of it already, and nothing in his obviously much greater expertise encouraged me to reveal the truth . . . then or later.

I had always thought Anthony priggishly above the rest of us, a typical Greats scholar. He dressed rather formally, and there was a kind of studied quickness, a purpose, when he walked across the quad that I'd always found affected. He seemed to have few friends. On the other hand (one must put it in such childish terms) he didn't wear glasses or hunch— nor did he belong to that equally disagreeable faction, the hearty. He was slightly taller than me, with very regular features and vaguely challenging eyes—though I think that was simply because he had the curiously un-English habit of looking you in the face when he talked to you. I now found, as we talked about orchids, that they could also be amused and friendly eyes. He wanted to know more; where I had botanized, how serious I was. I was flattered, I suppose—this apparently fastidious and already reputedly brilliant young professor in embryo had time for me. He once said, years later, when I'd been ribbing him about a newspaper report of some flagrantly fake stigmatization in Italy, "I'm surprised you don't believe in miracles, Dan. How else did we meet?"

He took me out to Watlington one day very soon afterward; and that led to other days, and other knowledges of each other. But we first surmounted the barriers between us across orchids. Barriers there were; we were very different young men, even in college and university terms. I was already writing for magazines, had one foot in the university theatrical door; wore a frivolous (and very false) persona, did an absolute minimum of academic work. I knew a lot of people, I would have said I had a lot of friends, but they were almost all like myself, at Oxford to mix, to prink and prance, to enjoy themselves, bound far less by real affection and interest than by a common love of the exhibitionistic. My own personality had undergone a very thorough revolution since adolescence, and even since my arrival at Oxford after war service. I had rejected so much. I was writing myself, making myself the chief character in a play, so that I was not only the written personage, the character and its actor, but also the person who sits in the back of the stalls admiring what he has written. All my other "friends" were also more or less onstage; the difference with Anthony was that he sat beside me in the stalls.

With the orchids, I took his view: one must keep such interests to oneself and fellow-enthusiasts, and not bore other people with them. He wasn't a nature-lover at all, I didn't realize that at the time. He just happened to be a crack field botanist—which goes also, I suspect, for his subsequent professional work as a philosopher. But I've never had the patience (or the mental equipment) to read his books. When he became a don, philosophy became like botany, he wouldn't talk about it any more to the lay world. Another even more important realization came much later: that he was a kind of father-substitute, though we were almost exactly the same age. The idea would have outraged me at the time, and killed the friendship, as I believed I had consciously "killed" the spirit of my father and his antiquated world. I do not know if Anthony realized this. He was certainly sufficiently astute to have done so, though he had no time for Freud. I am trying to say that he was good for me in the sense that he resurrected, if only very tenuously and intermittently, a self—or an unresolved dilemma—I had foolishly tried to dismiss; and nefarious in the sense that our relationship was set in a minefield.

In our orchid-hunting I never really rose above the role of shikari—I found the game, he shot it. The thrill for me was finding the rare ones—my first (and last, alas) Monkeys near Goring, a solitary Fly under a sunshot whitebeam at the edge of a Chiltern beechwood. His heaven was a wet meadow full of dull old Dactylorchids: counting and measuring and noting down the degree of hybridization. I wanted to find the flowers, he wanted to establish some new subspecies. I lived (and hid) poetic moments; he lived Druce and Godfery. My solitary boyhood had forced me to take refuge in nature as a poem, a myth, a catalysis, the only theater I was allowed to know; it was nine parts emotion and sublimation, but it acquired an aura, a mystery, a magic in the anthropological sense. I have spent years of my adult life ignoring it, but the long traumas of adolescence stamp deep. It still takes very little, a weed in flower at the foot of a concrete wall, the flight of a bird across a city window, to re-immerse me; and when I am released from deprivation, I can't stop that old self emerging. I feared driving across America with Jenny simply because I knew we should pass so many places where on my own I should have stopped; not as a serious naturalist would have stopped, though I might have pretended that, but as a bitter and repressed child once hid in the green Devon countryside.

All that side of me remained completely overborne in Anthony's antiseptic presence; nor did I see his singlemindedness then as a defect—it simply proved the hidden softness and greenness in myself. Lying about it all began with him . . . and with Nell and Jane, too.

I knew Jane only very slightly during that first year; she was already talked about, had already made a hit in the OUDS, whereas I knew myself still very immature. Nell hadn't appeared then. One day at the Kemp, wanting to show off to Anthony, I introduced him to her. She was groaning about Descartes, some essay she had to write; Anthony began to explain. I had to go to a tutorial and I left them, secretly amused that two such unlikely people should have found anything in common. It didn't happen overnight. I think he took her out a couple of times before term ended. They spent the long vacation apart, but apparently they wrote letters; and by the end of the calendar year, they were paired off. And Nell had arrived, my consolation prize. She was prettier than Jane, and the later sex-pot persona was still hidden behind the fresh-woman's reserve. I thought we were perfectly matched, the four of us. I enjoyed, when access was granted, Nell's naked body very much, and throughout my second year that obscured my real feelings.

During our two remaining summers as students the two girls often came on our orchid expeditions; and always mocked us in their different ways. I mustn't make Anthony sound humorless, but he had everything neatly compartmented in his life. All obsession was bad taste. He seldom laughed at himself, but he would always laugh at the girls' teasing. "I think I'll just sketch this labellum" became a kind of in-joke among us. I was never quite sure what it meant, but it always made us twist with secret laughter. We used it most against other people. In a way it made Anthony the odd man out; and hid the truth. That is, I was the real outsider. For the girls, nature was an occasion for drifting walks and idle picnics, listening to the nightingales on Otmoor while Anthony and I botanized; for him, a crossword puzzle, a relief in concrete objects from abstract ideas. And for me all I would never regain.

When much later, after the divorce and the vitriol, I felt that I had finally set this side of myself in perspective, the solution seemed simple. But putting down new roots, after all that had happened, in an early landscape was much more difficult than I had imagined. I got bored at the farm in Devon,

I grew lonely, I found the magic I remembered had somehow disappeared and that the nature of actuality verged on the repetitive and monotonous. I had of course failed to see how much the past magic had depended on past deprivation; and the present deprivation was of all that I had constructed to counter it. I began my peripatetic existence, working more and more away from Thorncombe. Only frequent exile made the place possible.

I was also trapped by a far more spurious myth and magic, since all this coincided with growing success in the film world, which presented me with a renewed opportunity—akin in essence if not in detail to my reaction to Oxford—to wear a mask and invent a character . . . once more to write myself. I let myself be dazzled by the gilt chimeras of the career: that happiness was always having work, being in demand, belonging nowhere, the jet life, the long transatlantic phone call about nothing. I became one third American and one third Jewish; the one third English I camped up or suppressed, according to circumstances. Jenny is right: I used it as a weapon when I was bored, and disowned it when I was amused; demoted it to a Cinderella role. It was vilely exploited by the other two of me.

I even thought of getting rid of Thorncombe, I used it so little. It distressed me when I returned after long infidelities, and seemed to show those mute reproachful eyes that forsaken gardens and buildings acquire. I would see the way some tree or shrub I had planted had grown, and long for that close daily knowledge of the little world around one that only peasants understand. Then I would once more fall in love with the place. It came less to matter that I knew that within a fortnight I should feel restless again. Thorncombe felt right; and I was wrong.

Perhaps all this is getting near the heart of Englishness: being happier at being unhappy than doing something constructive about it. We boast of our genius for compromise, which is really a refusal to choose; and that in turn contains a large part of cowardice, apathy, selfish laziness—but it is also, I grow increasingly certain of this as I grow older, a function of our peculiar imagination, of our racial and individual gift for metaphor; for allowing hypotheses about ourselves, and our pasts and futures, almost as much reality as the true events and destinies. Other races look at themselves in the mirror, and either live with the reflection or do something practical to improve it. We paint an ideal, or a dream, self on the glass and then wallow in the discrepancy. Nothing distinguishes us more clearly from the Americans, nothing characterizes better the very different ways we use our shared language—the way they use it as a tool, even when they are being poetic, and the way we treat it as a poem, even when we are using it as a tool; and it is the same with the enormous semantic subtleties of middle-class English intonation and the poverty of nuance in even the most intellectually sophisticated American equivalent.

These two dialects seem to me two reactions to the same thing: the craving for freedom. The American myth is of free will in its simple, primary sense. One can choose oneself and will oneself; and this absurdly optimistic assumption so dominates the republic that it has bred all its gross social injustices. Failure to succeed proves a moral, not a genetic, fault. "All men are born equal" becomes "No decent society can help those who fail to stay equal." The myth becomes so pervasive that it even ends up as the credo of those, the underprivileged, who most need to disbelieve it. I have seen it in even the most intelligent liberals there, people like Abe and Mildred, impeccably sympathetic in their attitude to things like Medicare, Black anger, environmental control and all the rest; yet still they hanker after the old and other American dream of freedom to cash in on other people's inequality. From the beginning Americans came to America to escape two things: political tyranny and fixed odds in the struggle for life, and they have never realized that the two aims are profoundly hostile to each other—that the genetic injustice of life is just as great as the old European economic injustice. Their system dealt with the latter by assuming an equal dispensation of energy, talent and good luck to all men; and now they are smashed hard on the reef of the far deeper injustice.

All this was of course also the English assumption in the sixteenth and seventeenth centuries. But we have long abandoned it. Injustice and inequality are in the nature of things, like Virgil's tears, and we have removed freedom from all living reality. It is a thing in the mind, a Utopia we secretly retreat to from our daily ordinary world; just as I have always lived far more in the mind at Thorncombe than in reality. That is what permits in England our extraordinary tolerance of national decay, of muddling through; our socializing conservatism and our conservative socialism. Our society, and its actual state, is nothing; merely the dead real

world, not the living imaginary one; and that is why we have
evolved a language that always means more than it says, both
emotionally and imaginatively. With the Americans it is the
reverse: they mean and feel far less than they have the habit
of saying. In both cases, it is to the same end: to find a place
to be free. The outward cynics may live in the States; but the
fundamental ones, the true quietists, live in Britain.

I am trying to exculpate myself, not explain cultures. My
attitude to nature, my past, Thorncombe, must be partly a
product of my own history and genetic make-up; it is also because I am English.

But to make the flight from California and Jenny, that
bout of self-pity the previous night, seem some kind of positive (or American) response to all this would be very false. I
had no serious desire to examine my past or re-create it in
any shape or form; and of course I cheat here. One does not
think coherently without a much stronger pretext than mere
time to spare. Anything that makes the dozing man on the
707 that day, stuck in what is after all only a continuity shot,
high over the monotonous rectangled wheatlands of the Midwest, appear in the least certain of what he was doing would
be absurd.

Perhaps the only symptom of imminent life-change was a
negative one. I had no project in mind after the wretched
Kitchener script. I couldn't get out of that, I was contractu-
ally committed; but both man and period, in the month I had
been messing with them, bored me to death. With my daughter Caro now working and Nell long remarried, I couldn't
even pretend that I had needed the money, so I had had to
look for some other motive; and I had decided that it was essentially a need to validate self-contempt, to create one last
straw that broke the conditioned camel's back.

I remember, when Anthony and Jane and Nell and I spent
our summer in Rome, standing before some comically awful
painting of a saint flagellating himself. Even Jane, a convert
by then, found it ridiculous, Catholicism gone dotty—which
allowed Anthony to put us right on the principle, if not this
present manifestation of it: how self-mortification was universal because it was absurd and necessary. He based a great
deal on the absurd-and-necessary at that time—and in that
side of his life—and I didn't take it very seriously, having already made something of an art of not causing myself anything but pleasure. But here I was, over twenty years later,

flogging myself over the back with Kitchener, a man I liked less the more I knew about him, and a project of formidable technical difficulties; and not even allowed to write, given the production cost of sinking old cruisers, the one scene I would have enjoyed . . . the old buffer disappearing forever beneath the waves off the Orkneys.

And what should follow that, I did not know. I was not really flying to New York, and home; but into an empty space.

# The Umbrella

> What can a flame remember? If it remembers a
> little less than is necessary, it goes out; if it re-
> members a little more than is necessary, it goes
> out. If only it could teach us, while it burns, to re-
> member correctly.
>
> —GEORGE SEFERIS, "Man"

My mother died just before my fourth birthday, and I really
cannot remember her at all; only the dimmest ghost of a bed
surmounted by a tired brown face—the brownness being due
to the illness that killed her, Addison's disease. My father was
a hopeless incompetent on the domestic side and the unmar-
ried of his two sisters had moved in long before the death.
Being a parson's child helped. There was no doubt, when I
was little, that the brown face had "gone to Heaven." In that
at least I was lucky to be born where I was; four generations
into the Church of England, with a substitute mother who
would have done very well as the nicest kind of practical An-
glican nun. Aunt Millie was ineffably devoted to making
good, and one of the few things I regret bitterly (as opposed
to merely regretting) was that I never gave her enough credit
for it. She had to bear the brunt of so much that I dared not
reproach my father with. When I was young, I took her for
granted; when I grew up, I despised her for her dowdiness
and her simplicity; at her funeral ten years ago I had tears in
my eyes, and perhaps that will gain me a slight remission on
Judgment Day.

He always seemed old to me, more like a grandfather than
a father. Having married very late, he was only a year short
of fifty when I was born, and his hair was almost white by
the time I begin to recall him clearly. If I have to use one
phrase to describe his attitude to me, it must be something
like a detached and quizzical puzzlement. From the photographs it seems clear my mother was no beauty; she was

thirty herself when they married, and some kind of secret I have never quite pierced lay over her. It certainly wasn't anything sinful, but more to do with a suggestion of folly on my father's part. He never reminisced about her; Aunt Millie did, but in the sort of kind terms (her gentleness, her respect for my father, her gift for music) that suggested some defect had to be excused. One defect was certainly of birth. She had been one of his parishioners in Shropshire, where he had a living before I came into the world, and her parents had been grocers—quietly successful ones, "provision merchants" was Aunt Millie's description. Like her son, she was an only child. She seems to have become a village spinster when they died; educated and provided for, but I suppose with the classification of "trade." She played the organ in his church. I can't imagine what happened, whether in some innocent village way she trapped my father, or whether it was a case of two profound sexual timidities, a scholarly and a genteel, taking refuge in each other's arms.

Much later, in the Fifties, a letter came out of the blue from a woman who had read a newspaper interview with me, and who claimed she was some kind of second cousin. It was more about herself, she had a dress-shop in Birmingham, but she remembered my mother from before the marriage, that she sewed beautifully and had a medlar-tree in her garden. She didn't know why she remembered the medlars, which she spelled meddlers. I answered her letter politely, in the kind of way that discourages further communication. When I bought Thorncombe, I got a medlar and planted it; but it died two years later.

My father: it wasn't until I went to boarding-school that I realized how outstandingly dull he was as a preacher, a handicap which was partly imposed by his general humorlessness and partly by his lifelong habit of sailing high over village heads. He was not at all a religious or a saintly man, even by the modest standards of the Church of England. He was something of a theologian, but rather in the way an army officer might have an interest in regimental history. He had a considerable collection of sermons and doctrinal pamphlets from the seventeenth century; but the eloquence and fluent imagery of that period never once went with him into the pulpit. I used to cringe with embarrassment, sitting in the Vicarage pew and seeing how restless he would make the congregation as he droned—he had a special pulpit voice some of the cheekier village boys had the knack of imitating, especially when they met me out of range of adult ears—interminably on toward Sunday lunch; or luncheon, as it was always called. I have admired the pruned and clipped ever since. He conditioned me there, as in so many things, by antithesis.

I sent him, during my first term at Oxford, just before he died, an Arber reprint of Hugh Latimer's 1549 *Sermon on the Ploughers,* one of the greatest pieces of hammering prose-poetry in the history of the English language, let alone the English church. He thanked me for it, but made no comment. It was meant to be a gentle revenge, but I think he took it as a sign that what he saw as certain doubts in me might after all survive the "reefs of higher education"—a phrase I once heard him use in a sermon on a characteristically irrelevant favorite bee in his pulpit bonnet: recruitment to the ministry.

He never, beyond some very cursory reference, introduced current world events into his sermons. They were always remorselessly dry and rarefied. One of his more educated wartime churchwardens had the temerity to suggest that a few more topical allusions would not come amiss; but Father remained convinced that the village had quite enough of all that in the newspapers and on the wireless, and continued adamantly in his old course. On another wartime occasion a Negro chaplain from the American camp nearby came and preached to a packed church—drawn not by piety but by curiosity to see how this mysterious chimpanzee would perform. He had a fine voice and presence, and a touch of the revivalist in manner; and he stunned us, he was so warm and good. But not my father, who in a rare descent to cattiness condemned him in private afterward as "overenthusiastic." He was using the word in its technical church sense, of course; the following week he went fifteen minutes over time on the Arian heresy, just to put us all in our place.

I can see now that his real fear was of any nakedness of feeling. He had a bizarre use of the word "demonstrate," which he twisted, or spread, to include any exhibition of anger, conviction, tearfulness . . . any strong emotion, however innocent or justified. Other visiting preachers who showed a touch too much fervor, protesting parties in some village argument, even myself unfairly blamed for some misdemeanor . . . *if only the good man would rely less on the demonstrative; all this demonstration doesn't help the lady's cause; do not demonstrate so, Daniel.* It was not that he would have expected me to sit silent, if I had a reasonable excuse; simply that I had dared to advance natural temperament as self-justification. The word covered countless other things, in my case: sullenness, excitement, even mere boredom. He had some extraordinary Platonic notion of the perfect human soul, in which all the manifestations he counted as "demonstration" were missing, or totally controlled. I dread to think what he would have made of the more recent political sense of the verb and noun.

Yet—or perhaps, the English being what they are, because of this—he was counted a good parish man. He was endlessly patient with the most garrulous old spinsters, sympathetic to the (slightly) more enlightened. Like many Devon villages, we had no real squire—there were various larger country houses in neighboring combes where we were on visiting terms, but in the village itself he was the *de facto* social and symbolic tribal chief; on every committee, consulted over everything. I think he filled that role well enough. He certainly believed in it, which was one good reason he was not truly religious. His real faith was in order; and his mildly privileged place in it. There were peasants; these were farmers and shopkeepers and, during the war, a heterogeneous collection of elderly evacuees in rented cottages; and there were people like us. I was never allowed a shadow of a doubt (perhaps because the truth about my mother's background might have created one) as to where we belonged. Proof hung forever on the dining-room wall; an oil-painting of my great-grandfather, a bishop no less. To be fair, and even if his marriage had not proved it, father was not a snob. We might be out of a better drawer than the rest of the village, but we must never show it. No distinction was ever to be made between those it was our duty to be with pastorally and those it was pleasant to be with socially.

In essence he was a subtle—rather than classic—example of why the military and the ecclesiastical, cross and sword, so often seem just two faces of the same coin. He wasn't a stern man at all, in spite of his lack of humor, which sprang much more from a diffuse absentmindedness, almost an unworldliness, than any intrinsic disapproval of laughter. There was nothing in his personal nature that overtly tyrannized the household, indeed, he was always at his most patient where some fathers might have ranted and thumped the table; and I am sure it was not simply because I was an only child, and technically motherless. I was hardly an angel before I went to boarding-school at fourteen, yet he never once used physical punishment on me. He disapproved of it, even in the village school, though he finally sent me to where the juniors were caned once a fortnight with monotonous regularity. The real tyranny came from the totally accepted belief in the system, the existing social frame. Just as a soldier cannot question orders, the hierarchy of command and all the assumptions that underlie it, nor could we. One might at a pinch discreetly object to the outward manner of some other vicar from a neighboring village, or of some high-up from clerical headquarters at Exeter, even of the bishop himself; but not to their right to be exactly who they were. During the war, of course, that was in the nature of things; all social evolution was petrified, which was the main reason Labour won that first election afterward. Though quite unconsciously, and despite his being an arch-demonstrator, father must have approved of Hitler for keeping progress so firmly at bay.

I tried to put it all in the play I based on him; one other parallel I made there still holds, I think, and that is the way the English turn all outward freedom (as contrasted with that of the imagination) into a game with set rules: one where every freedom is allowed except the freedom to break those rules. I suspect the Anglo-Saxons were a much more taboo-dominated crowd than the Celts they drove out of England. If the Romans brought civilization, the German tribes brought ritual codes, which have survived in our hideous national inventiveness over games proper, the art of wasting time according to someone else's book. I particularly loathed team games at school—as I have ever since—though I thought at the time it was merely because they were an obvious emblem of the whole sadistically stereotyping system. But I see now it was one more negative way in which Father and his world-outlook conditioned me.

We lived very simply, though much more out of parsonical good taste than necessity. The living (or both livings, since we also had a neighboring parish-hamlet in our cure) was well endowed, and my father had several hundred a year private income on top of that; and there was the money my mother had left in trust to me; even Millie had a small income of her own. That came to seem like another hypocrisy, when I realized in later boyhood that our supposed poverty was really mere thrift. No doubt a good deal went on charity and the upkeep of the two churches, but the former certainly didn't begin at home in terms of birthday presents, pocket-money and the like. I have been careless with money ever since—one more item on the bill.

My father had one real passion, which endeared him to the village and belatedly endeared him to me as well. That was a mania for gardening. Though he would potter about on our occasional picnics and botanize with me, he did not really approve of wild plants and nature. He drew some analogy between horticulture and God watching over a world; in nature things happened behind your back, could not be supervised and controlled. At any rate, his own garden and his greenhouse he adored. That and the seventeenth-century texts he liked to browse over were his only real indulgences—very nearly his sin, in the case of gardening. If he couldn't get cuttings of rare shrubs honestly, he was not above stealing them, with a mixture of blatant casualness and ill-concealed guilt that was delicious. He always carried an umbrella, on even the most unlikely days, to hide his ill-gotten Irishman's heels and seedlings in. It was one of the few things Aunt Millie and I were allowed to tease him over; and assumed monstrous proportions when one day one of his victims happened to be in our garden and spotted a successful scion of some precious rarity from his own. Father was shamed into an outright lie about its real provenance, and he wasn't allowed to forget it.

All my most affectionate memories are of him standing in his greenhouse, wearing the ancient and faintly episcopal purple baize butler's apron he used for gardening. Sometimes, in hot weather, he would take off his dog-collar and be taken by some unsuspecting stranger for the full-time gardener we did not actually permit ourselves. As an adolescent I got bored with all this side of his life, I wanted to read books and roam the countryside during my holidays, but when I was younger I used to help him pot and all the rest. He bred carnations and primulas especially; used to exhibit, before the war, and judged shows to the end. If we were short of humor and several other kinds of light in that house, there were always flowers, a feeling that the large garden was a part of the family.

It seems absurd now. A small boy rushing in to breakfast: The *Osmanthus* is out! The *Clematis armandii*! The *Trichodendron*! They weren't Latin and Greek to me. They were like our dogs and cats, loved and very familiar. There was a walled kitchen-garden as well, but Father had no interest in vegetables. Thrift was abandoned enough to allow a man to come in twice a week to look after them. His prides there were the fruit-trees, the apples and pears some previous incumbent had gone in for and my father added to; old gridded espaliers and gnarled cordons, their fruiting-spurs as brittle as charcoal. I suppose people still grow them, Jargonelle and Glou Morceau, Musk Bergamot and Good Christian; the russets and pippins and wardens and codlings and nameless ones—Aunt Millie's Tree, the Yellow Devil (because it used to rot in the apple-loft), the Green Spice. I knew them as other little boys knew county cricketers and football teams.

And I owe him other poetries, quite literal, though like so many true gifts from parents to children, they took many years to mature. When I was a child he liked, or at any rate regarded it as his duty, to come and read to me at bedtime, if his work allowed. Sometimes, as I grew older (though not nearly old enough) he would read a simpler passage from one of his seventeenth-century texts—I think more for the sound of the English than for the religious content, although he may have hoped for some Coué-like benefit. Occasionally he would try to explain the doctrinal situation behind one of these passages in terms a small boy might understand, as a less abstruse father might have tried to convey the real history of cowboys and Red Indians. I certainly grew up with a vision of some very confused theological gun-slinging, and a distinct sense that the Church had once been a much more exciting place to inhabit.

I can see now he always wished I was older; it was as if he foresaw that when the nine-year-old he read to became the nineteen he secretly dreamed him to be, such conversation would be impossible: I should have escaped him. But I mustn't make him too austere and unworldly. He very rarely returned from his occasional sorties to Exeter, where he always found time for an hour or two in the antiquarian bookshops, without something for me: it was usually a story by one of the boys' writers of his own childhood, a Henty or a Talbot Baines Reed, and I would much rather have had the latest Biggles or a Beano Annual, but I still enjoyed them.

Once he handed me, after one of these expeditions, a book of fables. The price he bought it for is still on the fly-leaf: one shilling and sixpence. He had obviously glanced at it, decided the English was suitably simple and edifying, and the pictures pretty and harmless. I thought the queer little uncolored prints terribly dull; at first glance, a really measly present. But in fact it was a Bewick, the 1820 anthology of his work patched together round Gay's *Fables*. Though I didn't realize it then, it was my first contact with a great English original. At the time (I was ten) I thought the book a ludicrous and shameful error on my father's part, because turning through the pages for the pictures I came on one I knew he couldn't have noticed in the shop: the famous cut of a doctor of divinity spurning the solicitation of a one-legged beggar, while behind him a dog pisses down his gown—a little moral tale whose concise brilliance I was to remember all through my childhood . . . and beyond. Then there were other scandalous scenes of ladies with bare breasts. I was shocked particularly—and fascinated—by the one that was headed *Indolence and Sloth:* the sleeping young man with the jordan under his bed and the two women, one naked and the other clothed, beside it, seeming to discuss something as they watched him. I was tempted to show this gross lapse of caution to Aunt Millie, but didn't, in case my father promptly descended on the book and confiscated it.

Just how great and quintessentially English an artist Bewick is I still have to learn each time I look at him; but at least the small boy came to realize something intense and private in the artist that called to his own nature. He began a little, through the years, to see with Bewick's eyes, as he was later to see with John Clare's and Palmer's . . . and Thoreau's. That dog-eared copy of the *Select Fables* is now the last book I would ever sell.

A somewhat similar thing was to happen two or three years later, when I was in the throes of first puberty. One wet day, in despair, I pulled down a dull-looking book from an upper shelf in my father's study. It was the first volume of Herrick's *Hesperides;* by benign chance the page fell open at one of his coarsest epigrams and I saw a word in print, fart, I had hitherto imagined was something one only giggled over, out of reach of adult ears, at school. Up in my room I read on. Much of it I couldn't understand, but the mingled brutality and eroticism of what I could was a revelation. I was to purloin those two volumes countless times again during the following years. They had a profound influence—the secrecy with which I had to steal them, rearranging the books so that no empty space showed, then hiding them in my room . . . but, with a healthier secrecy, their lyrical genius and Herrick's underlying pagan humanity also seeped into me. His former "lothed" living at Dean Prior was within cycling distance of us, and I must have been one of the youngest votaries who has ever stood before his epitaph there, though I think it was less out of gratitude than sheer disbelief. How could someone of my father's calling ever have been allowed to write such wicked verse?

Later, at Oxford, I had one day to produce an essay on Herrick for my tutor. I wasn't so foolish as to make it quite autobiographical, but it did make an engaging minor poet out to be a pinnacle of human sanity and supreme exponent of love of life—he was my Rabelais, of course. "Very interesting, Mr. Martin," said my tutor when I had finished reading. "And now perhaps next week you would be kind enough to write me an essay on Herrick." The snub was deserved; but I was dealing with someone who had only read the man . . . not lived him.

My father did do some censoring. Another bedtime book he read from was the Jacobean collection, *The Shirburn Ballads.* It was not until he died and I was going through his library before the great bulk of it was sent for sale that I discovered the *Shirburn* is not just an anthology of hymntunes; the religious ballads were the only ones he ever read to me, to my recollection. I had already been set at literal Latin and Greek at my prep school, and my father read English verse with the emphatic stress of his own classical schooldays. He particularly liked the broadsheets in the rhythm of the amphimacer, which indulged this love of a heavy beat—we would even get them at Sunday School occasionally. He would stand there, waving his free hand like a would-be conductor, making me go red as the kids around tried to stifle their giggles . . . how could he make such a fool of me with his stupid poem-reading? But now, at least in their bedtime renderings, they are among my good memories of him.

> All that heart can conceive,
>   ear can hear, eye can see,
> All, and more, I possess,
>   sweet JESU CHRIST, by thee.
> Heaven and earth, all therein,
>   Life, limb, thou gavest me.
> Have I not cause to sing
>   Jesu, come thou to me.
>
> Though the world tempt me sore,
>   though the flesh trouble me,
> Though the Devil would devour,
>   my refuge is in thee. . . .

It was not to be. But I think if it ever had, it might have come more from that private voice; its endless long-short-long, the due pause it gave every caesura, those little rocking boats of primitive faith. He used to send me to sleep with them sometimes; but to the best of sleeps.

Our 1930s were not like the world's; not shadowed at all to this small boy, but endlessly leafy, sunlit, ancient-walled, secure, spaced by bells; all smell of mown grass and islanded from towns. The only real shadow lay beyond the iron gate that led through into the churchyard. My unknown mother's grave; but even that seemed mainly protective, quietly watching. Each autumn we planted her two favorite primroses round the border: Quaker's Delight and the wild oxlip, the true plant from East Anglia, not the primrose-cowslip cross. My father had a clerical friend there who used to send seed especially. By late April the grave was always a quilt of lilac clusters and tall pale-yellow heads; after Sunday matins, people would stroll down the path to admire it.

The war came, and puberty for me, and a much darker chapter; so dark that for years I let the earlier days stay buried. I began having serious doubts after a year at public school. It was only partly that I lacked the courage (nothing conforms like a dormitory of small boys) of my mercilessly teased and mocked C. of E. background. The boredom I had felt in secret for years, the endless, endless, endless round of hymns, prayers, collects, psalms, the same faces, the same voices, the same corpus of beliefs and routines that didn't seem to tie in at all with reality, all that was now translated to a world where to express one's boredom with chapel was the done thing, not the forbidden. Small boys' arguments for atheism may not have much logic or cogency; but they came much faster and (though I knew how to cover up, even then) more attractively to me than to the others. So too did the pleasures of sexuality; I fell into that, from the profoundly sexless and emotion-banning ambience of the Vicarage, like Adam himself. I had agonizing feelings of shame and guilt, of course, and masturbation and blasphemy became inextricably interwoven. Every indulgence in the one threatened the traditional punishment of the other . . . heavens opening, thunderbolts raining, divine anathema. But nothing happened in fact.

I remember talking about all this with Anthony years afterward at Oxford, and his smiling and saying that to derive disbelief from a failure to punish was almost as bad as deriving belief from a certainty of grace. I was never in danger of the worse sin. I discovered the unholy pleasures of gossip and malice; they seemed honest after fifteen years of imposed charity in the discussion of other people's faults. And I became very eager indeed to prove I was no tame victim of my background; swore and blasphemed, swopped filth with the best, after lights out. I discovered new aspects of myself; an inventiveness, even though it most often manifested itself as a skill in lying; a tongue, an extrovert mask. I also wanted to succeed, with a ferocity that might not have been predicted of my earlier years, and I worked hard—though that was partly out of guilt for so many betrayals in other matters. We also had the standard English classics at home and I was better read than most of my contemporaries. I continued to read more all through my school career. My discoveries there (the shock of Samuel Butler, and the joy) also increasingly sapped my respect for my father and his faith.

The real severance came after an event that must wait to be told. But by the age of seventeen I was a fully-fledged atheist, so convinced that I went dutifully—if gracelessly— through all the old observances when I was home for the holidays. I went on going to church and even taking communion from my father's hands right up to his death in 1948, without an iota of belief and a mounting quota of sins. I thought it was adult to deceive the old man so, though it was mainly condescension . . . and kindness a little. He had faced up to the fact, before I left school, that I was not going to keep up the family tradition; and at least outwardly, taken it with a resigned equanimity. But I think he secretly hoped I would one day change my mind, and I lacked the heart to destroy that last illusion.

I even managed, dimly, to begin the reconciliation with my rural background. School, other minds and other places, to say nothing of the growing aestheticism of my view of life, at least allowed me to see that it had its charms, even though it still—and for many years to come—had to be presented to one's friends as so much unspeakable drag. The lovely rich peace of the countryside, the calm of the Vicarage, its fine garden . . . even our two churches. I had the ghastly Late Victorian architecture of the chapel at school to put them by now; and began to see them as connoisseurs of Devon churches have always seen them: for as good a pair—even without their celebrated roodscreens and splendid fifteenth-century painted rows of Apostles and Elders—as any in the county. The one beside the Vicarage had a massive fluted and streamlined tower soaring (the simile comes from later times) like a space rocket within its cone-capsule. It was nobly airy and light inside, thanks to its huge Tudor windows; then the churchyard beyond, the two elms and the yew, and Dartmoor in the distance. It also held my favorite religious pin-up, who had somehow managed to gatecrash the more orthodox assembly on the roodscreen, the pagan figure of the Cumaean Sibyl. My father always pointed her out to visitors, to show his broadmindedness—and show off his ability to quote from the Fourth Eclogue.

Our second church was smaller, its tower sitting like a barn-owl in the green dusk of its long-deserted combe. All its old box-pews were still in existence, and it had a womblike peace, a domesticity, a femaleness, and we all secretly preferred it to the grander building nearer home. Curiously, it always attracted good congregations, in spite of its inaccessibility; people would come from far and wide in the area, even during the war. One church was magnificent stone prose, but the other a folk-poem. I shall never rate consecrated ground; yet I know in which churchyard I would rather lie . . . and it is not, alas, beside my parents.

And finally there was Aunt Millie.

She was a thin, small woman, in retrospect always with something faintly (and quite misleadingly) of the Radclyffe Hall era of lesbianism about her—perhaps it was just that she always had her straight gray hair cut in a kind of Eton crop, invariably wore "sensible" clothes and broguelike shoes, had no apparent feminine vanities at all. Nothing, in reality, could have been less butch than her placid composure. Her one small vice was smoking, and that and the severe hair and the glasses could give her face a semblance of intellectuality, as if she were hiding another personality. In fact I realized during my adolescence that she was very nearly simple-minded, quite at sea with any print outside *Good Housekeeping* and the parish magazine—and the local newspaper, of which she read every line, and every week. If I could with some reason curse my father for our way of life—he was at least intelligent enough for some sort of choice to be imaginable—it was impossible with Millie. Her one skill was thinking the best of everyone and everything within her domain of knowledge.

If my father had been the commandant of a concentration

camp, she would have come to see the necessity of genocide—but not out of evil . . . out of a total lack of belief in her own ability to judge. Her real religion was not in church, but in her view of other people's motives, of the import of village scandals and tragedies. She had a phrase she would use to conclude discussion of all but irremediable disaster: *Perhaps it's for the best.* Even my father would look gently over his spectacles at her before some such applications of this optimism. Once, when we were alone, and she had said it of something that even Dr. Pangloss could have seen was for the worst, I laughed at her. And she said quietly, "Hoping is no sin, Daniel."

I harried her abominably, like any spoiled son his mother. She *could* share my budding literary enthusiasms if only she'd try, she *could* move with the times a little more, cider-cup was *not* the end of the world at a tennis-party . . . poor woman, it wasn't fair at all.

She was much nearer sainthood than anyone else in my life—the kind of sanctity Flaubert defined for all time in *Un Cœur Simple.* I didn't read that masterpiece until she was dead; and recognized her, and my own past arrogance, at once. She was still alive, living with my other aunt, her married sister in Cumberland, when the divorce with Nell took place. She wrote me a long rambling letter that tried to understand what had happened, tried very hard not to blame me, but significantly did not try to pretend that perhaps it was for the best, though she did end, the dear old fool, by pressing me to go out to "one of the colonies" and "start a new life." I had passed several light-years beyond her comprehension by then . . . but not her forgiveness. That outreached all time and space.

I disowned all this world for so long simply because I saw it as freakishly abnormal. But I see it now as no more than an extreme example of the general case. My contemporaries were all brought up in some degree of the nineteenth century, since the twentieth did not begin till 1945. That is why we are on the rack, forced into one of the longest and most abrupt cultural stretches in the history of mankind. Already what I was before the Second World War seems far more than four decades away; much more like the same number of centuries.

And then what we once were is now severed in a very special way from the present—reduced to an object, an artifice, an antique, a flashback . . . something discontinuous, and disconnected from present being. My generation wanted to shed unnecessary guilt, irrational respect, emotional dependence; but the process has become altogether too much like sterilization. It may be a remedy for one problem, but it has created another. We are saved from breeding relationships we cannot feed; but we are also prevented from breeding those we need. All pasts shall be coeval, a backworld uniformly not present, relegated to the status of so many family snapshots. The mode of recollection usurps the reality of the recalled.

Under the tyranny of the eye, that glutton for frontiers, this is the prime alienation of the cinema; always inherent in the theater, yet obscured there because of different performances and productions of the same text. But the final cut allows no choice, no more than the one angle; no creative response, no walking around, no time for one's own thought. In the very act of creating its own past, the past of the scenario and the past of the shooting, it destroys the past of the mind of each spectator.

Images are inherently fascistic because they overstamp the truth, however dim and blurred, of the real past experience; as if, faced with ruins, we must turn architects, not archaeologists. The word is the most imprecise of signs. Only a science-obsessed age could fail to comprehend that this is its great virtue, not its defect. What I was trying to tell Jenny in Hollywood was that I would murder my past if I tried to evoke it on camera; and it is precisely because I can't really evoke it in words, can only hope to awaken some analogous experience in other memories and sensitivities, that it must be written.

I draggle kicking down the back lane to Fishacre, sent out by Aunt Millie to tell Father the carpenter from Totnes has come, he's forgotten and gone visiting old Major Arbuthnot who has gout and wax in his ears, about the rehanging of the tenor bell. Burning May, the hedges dense with cow-parsley, whose coarse bottom leaves are stained brick-red with the lane dust, whose spoked heads are taller than mine and dense with insects; flies, drones, rust-red grenadiers. Late afternoon. I've broken off a hollow parsley stalk, made a blowpipe out of it, poisoned Amazonian grass-haulms skittering in the sun, they won't fly straight, stupid, it's so hot, and I wanted to play in the garden before prep., lost in my "house" in the copper beech. A woodlark sings over the huge hedge, in the distance somewhere, bell-fluting trisyllable, core of green, core of spring-summer, already one of those sounds that creep into the unconscious and haunt one all one's life, though all the little boy in the lane thinks is the name and clever-clever knowing it—the name, not the bird. Now a plane drones slowly over, high in the azure, very different from the future-hidden Heinkel, and I stop and watch it. A Tiger Moth. Another name. I also know the real (though do not know that in that unconscious "real" my redeemer cometh) tiger moth: the fluttery, zigzag-striped, chocolate-and-cream, black and red-orange Jersey Tiger. We catch some every year in the garden. The airplane is more interesting. I'm good at names. I shoot it down with a grass-stalk.

My father appears, wheeling his bicycle up the hill, with a little girl beside him. I run down toward them, making like a messenger. The little girl is pudge-faced, her name is Margaret, they call her Squinty Four-eyes in Sunday School. She is cross-eyed and wears spectacles. I give my father the message and he says, "Oh dear. Oh yes." Then, "Thank you, Daniel." He hands me his umbrella to carry. Margaret stares at me. I say, "Good afternoon." She looks up at my father, then squints at me and says "Lo." She is walking up to see her auntie in the village. We trail back up the lane, my father in the middle, me to his left carrying the umbrella, Margaret a little behind, making strange purposeful thrusting strides every so often to keep up. I am eleven, she is ten. I like one girl in Sunday School, but it is not Margaret. I do not like girls, but I like sitting near this other girl and trying to sing louder than she does. Her name is Nancy. Her summer-blue eyes do not squint. They stare at you (she is eleven also) and make you hold your breath. She beats us all at it.

The woodlark sounds again. I tell my father. He stops. "Yes, so it is." He asks Margaret if she can hear the pretty bird. This time she squints at me before looking up at him. ("Us 'urd a birdy, Mum, 'n Mr. Martin 'e tell us 'er name!" Little upward tonal leaps at *Mum* and *name*.) Now she just nods gravely. Dopy little cottage oick. I am angry with her because she'll get the ride now, not me. And sure enough, when the lane levels, it is her fat little legs that are lifted over the extra saddle on the crossbar. She wobbles off between my father's arms. He goes slowly, but I have to trot. And the stupid umbrella. I am furious. We have a car, an ancient Standard Flying-12, but on some days my stupid father will use his rotten old bicycle like this. His pale-beige summer visiting coat, his dark-gray trousers in bicycle clips, the straw panama with the black band which can't blow off, there's an eyelet in the brim behind attached by a safety pin to a sort of black bootlace that ends in a watch-chain bar pushed through his buttonhole. (Though at least I am spared the shame of the children of the vicar of Little Hembury five miles away. Their father has been seen cycling in knee-length shorts and a solar topee; and reported to the bishop for it, what's more.)

We cross the main road, then on down the lane to the village. I sulk, I refuse to keep up, they disappear. I dread the thought of meeting anyone. They will laugh at me, carrying the ridiculous gamp. Village boys, worst of all; and worstest of all, since I am a day-pupil in a preparatory school outside the next village, I am condemned to uniform—stupid gray shorts with a pink-and-white canvas belt done up with a snakeshead clasp, stupid long gray stockings also banded pink and white at the top (dear God, how I hate pink, and shall do all my life); stupid black shoes I have to clean myself every day. Stupid, stupid, *stupid*. I seethe. I let the wretched umbrella flop and trail behind me, ferrule scraping on the patched macadam. I come around a bend, I see my father at the gate of the council-house where Margaret's auntie the midwife lives. He looks back toward me, talking. Margaret stands half hidden behind her fat aunt. I wish I was anyone's child but a vicar's. My father raises his straw hat to the midwife, then turns away and stands in the lane waiting for me. I impersonate heat exhaustion and atrocious exploitation.

"Come on, old fellow."

I say nothing. He examines me. I am demonstrating.

He says, "Ladies first, Daniel. That's a rule of life."

"I'm hot."

"Do you want to ride now?"

I shake my head and avoid his eyes. I am breaking another rule, squandering all credit, by doing that (not saying, no thank you) and he knows I know it.

"Then you must walk home on your own. I have the man waiting." I say nothing. "Shall I take the umbrella?"

"I'll carry it."

I will give him nothing; not even what I hate.

"Very well."

He reaches out and ruffles the top of my head. I pull my head away. People may be watching from the council-houses.

I look to see if they are. Then he does something unprecedented. He makes a joke.

"I have lost a son. But I have found a gargoyle."

I watch him ride sedately off. Then I go the back way home, carrying misery and a large black umbrella through a perfect afternoon.

My *Rosebud*.

# Gratuitous Act

The now of then is coming down toward New York over a white landscape; snow, the beginning of the world where winter is real. Dan sets his watch to Eastern Standard time.

I doubt if that bed-sitter scene in the Oxford of 1950 sounds credible now; the sin and seriousness of it. It remains the most awful, in Dr. Johnson's sense, and the most strange coupling of my incelibate life. It must also, I suspect, have been one of the most awful in the more ordinary sense. I cannot remember the details of the act itself at all, beyond the realization that Jane was not as adept as her sister. With Nell there were already flirtations with perversity—or what passed as perversity in those days—and we had become by dint of practice quite skilled in sex-manual terms. With Jane there was a physical naïvety, a surprising innocence; she was passive, once the boats were burned. We got under the bedclothes, and I possessed her, and I don't think it lasted very long. I remember those minutes far more for their profound and delicious wickedness, their betrayal, their impossibility-actuality, their inextricable association with the woman in the reeds; above all, for their saying, once the strange geometric hinges had opened, that certain returns to innocence were now forever banned. We seemed to take a step (that whole first postwar period, sated with the sound of marching, was obsessed with private step-taking) not into darkness so much as uniqueness; no one could ever have done this before, no other age could have had our emancipation, our eagerness to experiment. Perhaps it was really our first step into the twentieth century.

I think of Jenny, her simplicity and careless grace, the way she slips out of clothes into nakedness, into sexuality, as easily as a seal into water. The fuss of those days, the multiple guilts and ignorances . . . Rabelais has won with a vengeance now; and everything is much tamer. No uniforms and uniformity to exorcise; no *id* to release; no tense long years between puberty and the full exploration of what puberty brings. No doubt we gained in one way; so much had to be sublimated for so long that at least we acquired the rudiments of a genuine culture. Jane and I were five years younger than our children, at the equivalent age, in terms of sexual precocity and its physical and linguistic expression; but five years older in most other things. That is one more chasm.

Our surrender to existentialism and each other was also, of course, fraught with evil. It defiled the printed text of life; broke codes with a vengeance; and it gave Dan a fatal taste for adultery, for seducing, for playing Jane's part that day. It might seem good, as great yet immoral art can be good; good in sacrificing all to self; but we didn't realize the non-exchangeability of life and art. In reality that day Dan did not understand what was happening; that as he had been led in, so must he be led out.

They lay clasped afterward, in a state of delayed shock, far more Candide and Cunégonde than would-be young intellectuals. Then they lay on their backs, side by side and hand-in-hand, and stared at the ceiling.

Dan said, "What are we going to do?"

She pressed his hand. "Nothing."

"We can't . . ." but he did not finish the sentence.

After a silence she said, "I do love Anthony. And Nell loves you."

"But we love each other."

Again she pressed his hand. "We could have loved each other."

Their fingers were interlaced, and he squeezed.

"We can't pretend this hasn't happened."

"We must."

"But it would be such a lie. Such a . . ."

"In parenthesis."

He was silent. He wanted to look at her, but could not; could only stare at the ceiling above.

She said, "Our secret. They mustn't ever know."

"It's like living with dynamite."

"That's why it had to be exploded. I've been terrified Nell will see."

For the first time, then, he felt used. But he had forgotten what she had said on the river: about the real and bathetic future that faced them.

"It's not fair."

Again there was a silence. Then she said, "When we came

back here, I arrived at a sort of decision. That I'd let you make love to me if you wanted. But if that happened, I would marry Anthony . . . as a Catholic."

He did look at her then.

"But that's mad." He sought for words. "In those terms, you've just committed a mortal sin."

"For which I must now to penance." She had a small smile, but she held his eyes, and he knew it was not being said lightly. She added, "And you."

"All our lives?"

"May I have a cigarette?"

He turned and reached for them and lit two, then passed her one. She sat up, out of the bedclothes, and he put his arm round her. She leaned her head against his cheek.

"I also decided I should never feel guilt about this. Ever."

"But you've just said we must do penance."

"I'm sorry, I know it's not logical. I'm not ashamed of having wanted you. But I would be if I couldn't stop. If wanting you became more important than hurting Nell and Anthony."

"You didn't even enjoy it very much."

"I did. It was just how I imagined."

He said, "Okay for a rehearsal."

She pressed her head back against his and ran a hand down his thigh beneath the bedclothes, then pinched the skin gently. He lifted a hand and cupped the small breasts together, then moved it up to turn her face and body. But they had hardly begun to kiss—and Dan to feel, though he was never to know, that everything was still in the balance—when there was the sound of the front door being slammed below. Dan had locked that of his own room—but they were instantly terrified, staring at the wooden panels as if a figure might burst through them, like a shape in a movie cartoon. It flashed through his mind that it might be Nell, after all; and she would wait until Lenin's widow returned home and ask her to let her in . . .

Never so frightened, before or since; but the footsteps were too fast and heavy. They did stop outside the door, and knock, then try the handle: then accepted defeat and went on upstairs. The two in the bed heard the steps cross the ceiling, from the room above. It was Barney Dillon, the student who lived upstairs.

Jane turned and put her arms around Dan and gave him one quick, wild kiss; pushed away, stared him in the eyes for a long moment. Then she was out of bed, dressing; and he the same. They straightened the bedclothes, all in a fevered silence. From upstairs there was the sound of a radio, the faint beat of music; more footsteps. They felt, or at any rate Dan felt, both relieved and still frightened. It could have been Nell; and it could still be Nell. He also felt already defeated, deceived, almost as if Jane had conspired to bring this interruption. She was brushing her hair, intent on her face in one of his mirrors. Then she was holding out her hands and taking his.

"I must go. In case he comes down."

"But—"

"Dan."

"I'm never going to be able to hide it."

"You must."

"There's so much we haven't said."

"And couldn't ever. It doesn't matter."

She kissed him again; and again was the one who broke it off. She stood for a moment with her head buried against his neck. Then she said, "Please see if the coast's clear."

He cautiously unlocked the door. They tiptoed downstairs, Jane with her shoes in her hand. She slipped them on at the front door, while he looked out down the street.

"It's okay."

But she hesitated, then looked down from his face. "I'll go and see Nell later." Nell's and her own college were very close. She added, "Unless you want to."

He shook his head. By which he really meant, I don't know how you can . . . though he saw the necessity. She raised her eyes and met his.

"If I can help it now, it's because I couldn't before. Do you understand that?"

He said nothing, he was still trying to understand. But in the end he nodded. Her eyes were strange, they had almost a despair, a searching for something he could not give. She leaned forward, kissed him impulsively on the mouth. The next moment she was slipping quickly out of the door. He closed it, and remained staring a moment at the latch; trying to imagine what he had barred from his future, what punishment this crime would exact; his own dissociated hand on the final lock.

He tiptoed back upstairs and went along to the bathroom. When he went back to his own room, he shut the door loudly, so that it could be heard upstairs, if Barney was listening. Everything there seemed inalienably changed, strange to him; most of all, his own face in his mirrors; yet suddenly he felt a strange amusement, he even smiled at himself. After all, it was fantastic, incredible, really rather marvelous; terribly avant-garde and adult; and left nothing, for it was so like Jane to be so intense and dramatic about the future, definitely decided. It had happened, that was the essential; and all kinds of buried feelings of inferiority toward Anthony lay mysteriously but profoundly alleviated. Once more Dan had begun to write himself.

And so well that he found, after ten minutes or so, as if for a first test, the poise, the chutzpah, to go up and see Barney Dillon.

# Returns

I had an hour to wait at Kennedy for my flight to London. I ought to have spent some of it ringing David Malevich, who I knew was in New York, about the Kitchener script. But I felt too tired, too remote from the present. So I gave myself the prospect of one more transatlantic call about nothing, and sat in the departure lounge bar. The surfer surrendered to the wave, indifferent to what happened for as long as the journey lasted; something in me wished it would last forever. Again, Jenny, in that simile I had not yet read—and which indeed she hadn't yet written—was halfway right. I did feel like a suitcase with illegible labels, safe for as long as I was locked. I managed one practical thing between the whisky sours. Not trusting her mother, I sent a cable to Caro saying I was on my way.

Caroline at least had become a less menacing fault, in both the geological and the self-blaming sense, in my life. For so many years she hadn't seemed my daughter—merely something I had once given Nell and was ungraciously allowed to see again from time to time. Repressed suspicion haunted our brief encounters. Nell had conditioned her to see me as the rat; and on my side I saw far too much of the mother in the child. She even took after her mother physically, though not mentally—not that that was unmixed consolation. If she lacked Nell's sharp tongue, she also seemed to lack every other kind of intellectual acuity. The country world she had followed Nell into when she re-married, the riding, the wretched boarding-school for upper-class fools she had been sent to (Nell's choice, my expense) . . . none of that helped. Through her teens I tried, too hard, to inject some culture, some rudimentary awareness that not all human decency resided in the rural-Tory view of life. But she seemed impervious, or just embarrassed. Then two years before Nell and I had had to face the problem of a career for her. There was no chance of her getting into the most indulgent university.

She didn't want to go abroad. In the end we settled for a secretarial course run for similar poor little rich girls in Kensington.

I began to see a great deal more of her then; and at long last discovered someone I could like, under the veneer of debby silliness. There was an embryonic independence, in which, vainly, I saw my own genes at work; an affectionateness, and a marked new attitude toward me. I learned more about Nell and Andrew and her hitherto shrouded life at Compton. She was no cat, and it was largely reading between the lines. But it was clear that living in London, even though it was in a hostel run like a prison-camp, had woken her up to the fact that she'd been partly brain-washed at home; and especially over me. We had a long-delayed little father-daughter affair, in short. I was allowed to tease her out of some of her follies and she teased me out of some of mine. She had boy-friends, there was nothing unhealthy about it. One day she spontaneously brought up the absurdity of our meetings when she was younger—the stiffness, the boredom—and we kept laughing, remembering yet one more ghastly week-end or afternoon. It was marvelous: like seeing a capsized boat right itself, and knowing that no serious damage had been done—that in a way there was almost an advantage in the long being capsized.

That previous summer she had finished her course and after a holiday, got herself a job. She had had a choice of several and took the one I advised, with . . . let's call it the *Sunday Timeserver*. The others were all in the City and I preferred her to do something with more human interest than share-prices and learning business jargon. She had no writing ability at all, but life—however humble—on a big newspaper seemed less likely to bore her. There was by then a more permanent young man. I knew they were going to bed together and that marriage was likely one day; so it was just a matter of keeping her occupied and getting her some experience of life outside Gloucestershire and Kensington. She fancied a flat of her own, but I suggested she take over mine while I was in California. It was the flat in Notting Hill Nell and I had graduated to at the end of our marriage; old-fashioned, but large, and on a ninety-nine year lease. It seemed silly not to use it. So Caro moved in, and a month or two later I moved out. She didn't write very often, but when she did she kept up a pretense of "awfulness" at not having found anywhere else to live: a pretense that hurt. It defined much that remained not quite natural in our relationship. It was the same with money, over which she was careful (a virtue she must have picked up from her stepfather). She had refused to let me continue her allowance when she started work, on all sorts of excellent grounds (the "fortune" I had already had to "fork out" on her education, and so on), yet I felt frustrated. Jenny was quite right: I did complain far more about these minor flaws than allow the major assets in our new knowledge of each other.

The thought of soon seeing her again was a genuine pleasure, though it was accompanied by an equally genuine guilt, since I had stayed a good deal longer than I originally intended in America. I knew Caro must know why. Jenny had been mentioned once or twice in my letters, but not the full extent of the relationship. News of that must have reached her by now, and I anticipated a trace of jealousy. She hadn't written at all for the last three weeks. On the other hand she was her own mistress now, and in a much more open world, and I counted on the ill wind at Oxford that blew me home to help us together again.

The flight was called. I boarded and promptly spread myself over three seats. But I could see it was going to be mercifully uncrowded—we were due in London at 2 A.M., not when the wise normally arrive. I tried to decide which I wanted most: the meal, or sleep. I decided it was sleep, and I sat waiting for the take-off.

All my adult life I have believed that nothing controls our destinies beyond our genes and external events. The manifold ways so many Californians try to escape from rational causation—the dotty religions, the chasing after Gurdjieff, Ouspensky, any crank, the fifty thousand therapy centers and deep-meditation ranches, the astrology, the mania for ESP and drug mysticism . . . all that had never provoked anything in me but contempt or a laugh. I had already been badly shaken that previous evening; and now the god of coincidence decided to kick me while I was down.

A last passenger came into the cabin. I glanced toward the aisle as he passed, and he down toward me. He had run to fat a little, was balding fast, but still that same vaguely louche, vaguely quizzical smile—though for the tiniest beat the face wished, too late, that it hadn't looked down and seen me. Only the surprise was genuine, and on both sides.

He said, "Good God." Then he shuttered his hand quickly

across his face, and said what I had said a few hours previously. "Ghosts."

And I finally knew that day in Oxford did not want to die.

At the time one was proud to introduce him, despite the lop-sided smile, always probing, like a leech, for exposed skin. Dillon the wit, the gossip, a pillar of *Isis:* in those days publicity was myrrh and frankincense, and Barney could dispense it. He was another of the mature ones, though in a very different way from Anthony; already in Fleet Street, already on the as yet unforeseen television screen, charming to the unknown and needle-sharp with the innuendo in the back of the known. Even then he had the knack of world-weary authority in his film and theater reviews, of elaborate malice in his gossip column, of pathological egocentricity convincingly passed off as solid honesty in his more serious pieces. He was an amusing mimic, too.

Dan found him stretched on his bed. Barney also was in his last year. He winked up at Dan from his book, playing the spiv.

"Sell you a pass for a fiver?"

Daniel grinned; held his line.

"I'll sell you a scoop for nothing."

"I buy it in cubes, mate. Not granulated."

"Seriously, Barney. Something fantastic . . . but *fan*-tast-ic."

Dillon stared at him; then smiled cautiously.

"So give."

A week later, this appeared in his gossip column.

> We have it straight from the hearse's mouth that one of our budding Ben Jonsons is peeved beyond words—a merciful release, some may think (not us, we like the lad). Seems he was absent-mindedly propelling the wrong Heavenly Twin recently down a retired backwater when . . . okay, so you read the papers too. Why the peeve? The said backwater has a certain reputation, my friends, and has told more than one Nell in its thyme. The unfortunate pair claim they were there for a quiet read. Haven't met such charming innocence since the girl who went to *In Which We Serve* to improve her tennis. These strolling players, when will they learn?

It was not the tone that offended Dan when he read it, but the brevity.

And now I was standing, a quarter of a century later, and taking his hand.

"Barney. Long time."

"Incredible. I was talking about you only yesterday."

He shook his head, full of some bewilderment he couldn't communicate, but wanted me to know he felt. He had a briefcase, a mac over one arm; a rather ostentatiously up-to-the-moment suit, studiously informal, an open-necked shirt.

He said, "With Caroline." He must have seen I was nonplussed. "On the blower. Hasn't she told you?"

"Told me what?"

"She's my secretary now. As of three weeks ago."

"But I thought you'd left . . ."

A stewardess came up and smiled at him. She evidently knew who he was.

"We're winding up the elastic. If you'd take your seat, Mr. Dillon."

"Oh Christ. I'll fucking well report you." He transferred his grin at her to me. "She knows I'm the all-time air coward. Super to see you, Dan. Just let me dump my stuff. I'll explain."

I watched him go down the plane and find an empty row of seats. The same stewardess hovered around him, and there was more badinage. If he hadn't slept with her, he apparently wanted to suggest it. I noticed an English couple across the gangway; they also knew who he was, must have seen him on television.

There had been a period after Oxford when we had kept in fairly frequent touch . . . occasional dinners, parties, first nights. I was writing plays, and he was reviewing. He was very friendly about the first two plays, and did an almost gushing profile of me for a theater magazine soon afterward. Then for a time he moved to other fields, and we drifted apart. But he was back in the theater column when my fifth play, the one about the break-up of my marriage, came on in London. He very comprehensively panned it. To give him his due, he delivered warning privately that I was about to be slaughtered; and made some sort of apology for having to do his duty . . . and it was poorly reviewed elsewhere. I didn't resent the technical side of his attack, I knew I had made a mess of things there; but I did resent his use of private information, the references to "unassimilated personal experience" and the rest. It didn't matter, at the time, that he was quite right; I felt, if not an old friendship, then at least an old acquaintance had been betrayed, and I decided to cross him off my list of people I wanted to know. In the nature of our two lapping worlds, we had met occasionally from time to time since. He had also done some film reviewing, and I couldn't complain of unfair treatment when our paths had crossed in that way.

It was less anything personal that I had always disliked in Barney, in fact, than that he was a critic. No creator can like critics. There is too much difference between the two activities. One is begetting, the other surgery. However justified the criticism, it is always inflicted by someone who hasn't, a eunuch, on someone who has, a generator; by someone who takes no real risks on someone who stakes most of his being, economic as well as immortal.

I certainly could not call Barney a failure in worldly terms; yet something of that also hung about him—indeed has continued to hang around all my Oxford generation. As with Ken Tynan, so many others, I certainly can't except myself, destiny then pointed to far higher places than the ones actually achieved. Perhaps we were too self-conscious, too aware of one another and what was expected of us, too scared of seeming pretentious; and then, in the 1950s, we were fatally undercut and isolated by the whole working-class, anti-university shift in the English theater and the novel. Tynan's famous rave for *Look Back in Anger* was also a kind of epitaph over *our* hopes and ambitions—over the framework of middle-class tradition and culture that we had all been willy-nilly confined in. All this reduced us to watching and bitching; to satire; to climbing on whatever cultural or professional bandwagon came to hand, accepting the fool's gold of instant success. That is why so many became journalists, critics, media men, producers and directors; grew so scared of their pasts and their social class, and never recovered.

Barney himself had over the last decade become more and more of a television personality, latterly on a chat show of his own. I had even seen it once or twice. He was a little too concerned for his own image; tried to trade one-liners with a professional comic; interrupted too much with a well-known politician. As with all camera-conscious performers of that merciless medium, he finally made one wonder what he was trying to hide, why he couldn't be himself. This particular show had brought him a good deal of local fame—money as well, obviously—but watching it, I had not been able to help remembering the old Barney and his cynicism. He had had higher standards once; and the one thing he had never been in the Oxford days, was unnecessarily nice to the famous. Probably he would have said that he had matured . . . but gadflies don't mature, they simply die. One of his shows I had turned off halfway through. Whatever anger I had once felt about the review had given way to a boredom with the hollow shell he, as minor emblem of all our generation, had seemed to have become.

And now the hollow shell came and sat beside me, and fastened his seat-belt. We were on camera. The couple opposite kept sneaking looks across.

"I've ordered Scotch. Yes?"

"Fine. Tell me about Caro. I thought you'd left the paper."

"We pissed and made up." He shrugged. "Just a new column. Keep my hand in." He slid me a sour grin. "I'm so bloody famous now. I can remember the days when I was lucky to get the corner of a table. Now it's an office and secretary."

"Is she any good?"

"Splendid. Taken to it like a duck to water."

"I'm glad."

"Holds the fort and all that. Bosses me about. Even learning to spell." I smiled. "She's sensational. Really."

He seemed very eager to be nice. But my mind was already reaching ahead to Caro. Though I couldn't recall ever having talked of Barney to her, perhaps Nell had, and I wondered for a moment if she had known, or half-guessed, that he was not someone I liked the thought of her having to work for; whether there wasn't a little element of revenge for my infidelity with Jenny. We began to taxi. I asked what had brought him over to the States.

"Piece on the elections. Usual crap." He screwed up his mouth. "This fucking country. It kills me. They just never seem to grow up. You must find that?"

"Sometimes."

"Of course, on the Coast . . ." he shrugged, then probed. "I thought you were doing a script out there."

"I'm coming back to see Anthony Mallory, Barney. Caro's . . . ?"

"Yes, she told me. Bloody awful." He paused. "I thought—" He broke off, then smiled. "Sorry, not my business."

He obviously thought what Caro must have told him: that Anthony and I hadn't communicated for years. I explained the situation, and we talked about Anthony, and cancer, for a little while.

"Oh well, be a nice surprise for Caro. You have a very admiring daughter. You know that?" He squeezed his nose. "Actually, Dan, before I forget, she asked me to give you a ring. Send you her love and tell you about the new job. I've been so goddam busy and then today I decided to cut out early and had to cram fifty-nine—"

"That's okay. I'll tell her."

We waited for take-off, at the runway end. The engines roared up in test, and he was silent a moment. He gave a little sniff of self-amusement.

"Jesus, I hate this form of locomotion."

"Intimations of mortality?"

"Is it all worthwhile, I ask myself."

"Come on. We've survived."

"Oh sure. In five thousand pages of fish-and-chip wrapping."

"Balls."

He stared bleakly down the cabin, then pulled his mouth to one side and shrugged. "When I look back."

"From the top of your profession?"

"Big deal. As they say." We began to run. "Actually I've been here about a TV show as well. They have a crazy idea I might be the new David Frost. I told them, I don't even want to be the old David Frost." I duly grinned. "Seriously. I'm running away at the moment. Supposed to be having lunch with one of the putative sponsors tomorrow. Sit with him through the pilot." We took off. He stared past me out of the window. "It's going to kill me, if it goes through. Kills me at home, that fucking series."

"I thought you were very good. When I've watched."

"Who switched it on the second time?"

I smiled again. At least it was nice to be back where undertones were not missed.

"You try over here. There's not much competition."

I stared out at Manhattan rising in the distance; the termite towers. He loosened his seat-belt.

"Caroline tells me you're on an epic."

"Hardly. Historical. Kitchener." I said, "And doomed before it starts."

"Yes?"

"We're off the record, Barney."

"Of course, dear boy. Just curious."

The stewardess came with our whiskies. Barney gave her a smile and a "Bless you." We talked movie business for a few minutes. I felt he was acting all the time. He sat listening, staring down at his glass, swilling the ice-cubes round, unnaturally deferential; as if he would rather be chatting up the stewardess. Then he began to talk again about television, its ephemerality, the "stupefying quantity of horseshit" his own programs involved. It was a trauma, or ordeal, I had long been through myself—the tyranny of the mass audience, the need to suppress instinct, education, subtlety and a dozen other things in favor of the bedrock truth of the human condition: that the majority is ignorant and wants, or at least pays money, to be treated as a moron. Audiences are *shmucks,* as a celebrated old Hollywood director once put it succinctly to me, and *shmucks* hate brains. Then Barney went on about the horrors of now being recognized everywhere he went; but no one walks into that blind. All art, from the finest poetry to the sleaziest strip-show, has the same clause written in—you will henceforth put yourself on public show and suffer all that that entails. Still, I felt some sympathy for him; and a certain wry amusement, at finding myself in Jenny's role now. Perhaps he sensed it. We had a couple more whiskies, and he raised his glass.

"Well, here's to Caroline, anyway." He drank, then said, "She seems to have survived the divorce pretty well."

"By some miracle. It's been nice getting to know her this last couple of years."

"You probably didn't miss much. Speaking from bitter personal experience."

"I've forgotten . . ."

"Three boys. The oldest won't speak to me, the middle one can't, and the youngest does. He's the one I hate."

He'd said that before, no doubt, in El Vino's.

"And beyond the epigram?"

"Margaret's problem, really. I've opted out. I felt pretty much the same about my own old man. They don't bother to hide it. I suppose that's progress."

I tried to remember Margaret; a small woman with a smile that tried too hard, and who said nothing unless spoken to; never seemed quite to want to be where she was. She hadn't been at Oxford, and I knew very little about her.

Barney stared down the cabin. "Roll on the Republic. Let some other poor bastard bring the little horrors up."

"I'm sorry."

"My fault. Never enough time. Or the patience." He took a breath, and another mouthful of whisky, then changed the subject. "You're coming back here as soon as . . . ?"

"No, I'll finish the script at home."

He gave me one of his old smiles: knowing and searching.

"Is it really home for you now?"

"England? Good lord, yes. I've got a small farm down in Devon."

"Caroline told me. Sounds nice."

We drifted then to the state of Britain. Of course I had recognized symptoms I shared: doubts and disillusions, grasped-for apples turned to wax, dreams become ashes. But I would never have come out with that to him. You can practice self-deprecation and get away with it with those you love; but not with those you despise. I decided he was anxious that I shouldn't say too much about the past to Caro. He too wanted a favorable report: he had problems, he didn't take himself too seriously.

They started bringing round the meal and I used that, my not having slept and not feeling hungry, to break off the conversation. He was very anxious we should have lunch one day soon if I was in London. I made the right noises. Then I lay down. Sleep came deep and dreamless, like all slumbers of the damned.

# Tarquinia

They had one golden period. Anthony heard of an empty flat in Rome and the four of them spent six weeks in it during the high summer of the year that followed their last as students. The three graduates had gone down only in the academic sense. Anthony was now teaching at Worcester and Dan was stage-managing at the Playhouse; on a pittance, and really living on the eight hundred a year he had inherited. Anthony and Jane had married in December. She was four months pregnant by the time they went to Rome. Their wedding had been formal and formidable, with a full panoply of relatives; Dan was best man. Jane had been officially received into the Church a month previously. In the new year they moved into a cottage at Wytham. Dan and Nell had had a much simpler registry office ceremony as soon as Nell had taken her Finals, and Rome was their token honeymoon. A year before Dan would not have believed it possible that he could go through with such an arrangement. But much had changed in the interval.

He would have liked not to see Jane for weeks after their *acte gratuit*. But that very next afternoon he was working in his room when she appeared with Anthony. It happened so fast, as of course she had intended, that he had no time to dread the meeting. Their names as the discoverers of the corpse (whose murderer was never found) were already in the morning newspapers. Anthony seemed wrily amused, wanted to hear Dan's side of it. He had to be treated normally . . . as Nell already that day had had to be treated normally. She knew he was cramming and had arrived just after breakfast on her bicycle, on her way to her first lecture. She had been easy to deceive. She showed no suspicion, merely a shocked excitement, so ghastly, so extraordinary, "their idyllic little cut . . ."

He found he could look at Jane without embarrassment. He even felt a belated pity for Anthony, and discovered how

easy it was to pull wool over trusting eyes; and began to condone himself. It had been a comedy, a ten minutes' madness.
He felt himself running away, already devaluing the reality,
even comparing Jane physically to Nell, telling himself he
really preferred Nell, he wasn't jealous. But then Anthony
left the room a moment to go to the bathroom, and they
were left alone. It was a warm day, she was sitting propped
on the window-sill over the garden, and Dan was lying on the
bed. They said nothing and avoided each other's eyes, and
the truth behind the comedy was there. Then suddenly she
swung her legs to the ground and came across to the bed. He
stared up into her eyes.

She said slowly, " 'If it were done . . .' "

"Okay."

"Nell?"

"All right. She came round this morning."

And he stared until she had to turn away. She put both
hands on the mantelpiece and stared down at the unlit gas-
fire.

"Are you angry with me?"

"Do you remember how that *Macbeth* speech ends?"

"No."

" 'Then we'd jump the life to come.' "

She opened her mouth to say something, then closed it.
There was a long moment.

"I had quite a talk with Nell last night. About you."

"Comparing notes?"

She swallowed the sarcasm, then spoke simply.

"You are angry."

He put his hands behind his head and stared up at the ceiling.

"You seem to wish it had never happened now."

"Only if it leaves you bitter."

"So what did you and Nell decide? I'm good enough for
her?"

They heard Anthony outside, his voice; and guessed that
he must have bumped into the man who had the front room.
They had been at Winchester together. Jane said nothing for
a moment.

"Dan, if I stop it now, I can still be happy with Anthony.
If it went on . . . and Nell does want to marry you. Perhaps
more than you realize." She gave him a little glance down
from where she stood facing the mantelpiece. "We'll always
be closer in one way to each other than to them."

"In sheer dottiness."

She smiled, then spoke more gravely. "In what we gave up for them."

The door opened, and Anthony came briskly in. Jane turned to face him.

"Darling, the poor boy wants to work. So do I."

He hated her then. She had sounded just like Nell. The circumstances might justify her acting a bright normality, but that reminder of how well she could act tainted what had just gone before. There she had cast herself as wisdom, self-sacrifice, already trying out for her future role as a Catholic convert. Yet the strangest thing was that he felt that somewhere she did love him, understood him far more deeply than her sister, still wanted him physically more than Anthony. What had happened was like an attempt to break out of a myth of herself . . . into that of Rabelais; but that once proven false, too expensive morally, she found herself now double-chained in the old one.

But all this was long past by the time they went to Rome. Perhaps she contrived it—at any rate they were not to see each other alone again before Final Schools began. Then they had the long vacation apart, the two girls having taken Anthony to the States to stay with their mother and stepfather. Dan was invited and could have gone, but he had already found reasons not to: he didn't want to miss the job at the Playhouse, he had neglected Aunt Millie, he knew he was going to get a bad degree, he had an idea for a play . . . all of which hid the real reason why he remained proof to all Nell's sulks and blandishments. He felt an inherent poison in the situation by then; an almost Jacobean claustrophobia, incest, and he knew only separation could purge it. He did have one very brief chance to discuss it with Jane; and she agreed, it would perhaps be better if he didn't come. After a week or so he began to miss them. He felt himself orphaned all over again, emotionally as he was literally. Aunt Millie and Cumberland—where she now lived with her married sister, Dan's other aunt—reminded him only of what his own family could not give him. The long letters that began to arrive from Nell were some compensation, though she teased him about "dates" and "beaux" on Cape Cod, where they were holidaying. Secretly he took offense, but that did not survive ten minutes when she came back; ten seconds . . . her arms had gone around him on the platform at Oxford, then her mischievous whispered voice in his ear: *Where's the nearest bed?*

From then on, what seemed like a small miracle had taken place. Jane and he tacitly avoided being left together. Sometimes he searched her eyes, when they were—unobserved. She would smile gently, and look down. Nothing was to be said, the matter was eternally closed. It had something to do with her conversion, which subtly altered the relationship among all four of them. It was not that they talked about it—the same principle applied as with the orchid-hunting, its discussion was strictly for initiates. But over that winter something died in Jane; more and more he saw her surrender in his room as something slightly hysterical; an overcerebral girl trying for a part she did not want, or trying to reproduce in real life one she had occasionally played, the revue sex-clown.

He suspected at first that her withdrawnness was also acted, over-identification with her new role. The commitment to Catholicism seemed continuingly absurd; he could not see why it was necessary at all. He had never understood that part of Anthony instinctively, even if he could have explained it intellectually. Perhaps there was some element of sexual jealousy, but he felt he genuinely resented this enslavement to what he saw as sophistry, an abstruse confidence trick . . . to the flaw in the other man, not his virtue.

On that side the most surprised, oddly enough, had been Nell. It gradually became clear that her own nature had needed Jane's more flamboyant old self as a complement. It was almost as if she had been led by her sister into a cul-de-sac, and was now left to find her own way out. For a time, that winter, she played the spoiled child to their more adult selves. She kept complaining to Dan. *She had that frightful Madonna face on again all evening, why have we all got so dull, honestly I don't know her any more* . . . but something in Nell was eventually mollified, especially when the marriage took place and the newly-weds moved out to Wytham. Dan was always busy at the theater in the evening and Nell went out there often to be with Jane. They went furniture-hunting, things like that; became as close, though much more privately, as when Nell had first arrived and they earned their university nickname. The Catholic "thing" was accepted, and became unimportant.

Then there was Anthony's prestige; the handsomely achieved First, his rapid passage into senior philosophical circles, the assurance of a fellowship as soon as he showed he could teach and fit in. It didn't alter him at all, if anything he played down his enhanced authority *en famille*, but it, and a happiness he couldn't quite hide, did affect them also. It proved Jane's wisdom, or at least made her decision easier to understand. For Dan it brought twinges of career, as well as the other, jealousies. He did not envy academic glory, but he wanted success. A play he had secretly submitted to a London agency in December had been turned down by every management who read it. He carried that failure with him for months afterward.

Then Nell had changed. Their relationship had never had—or so it seemed to Dan—the innate rightness and conviction of Jane and Anthony's. They understood each other, they pleased each other in bed, they liked to be seen around together. But there was always in Nell a hint of shallowness, of fickleness, an impatience. She liked amusing parties, amusing people, flirting; what Jane had once called ogle-sprinkling. She had always used her good looks far more than her sister, to compensate for something she lacked. But Jane's new sobriety began to affect her. She started working hard, and became serious in other unexpected ways: took to playing housewife in the Beaumont Street flat Dan had moved to. Marriage became inevitable. She grew, by comparison with her former self, whatever is the female equivalent of uxorious. Dan quite liked it; and when Jane was announced pregnant, whatever dim hankerings, or dissatisfactions, he still harbored disappeared. He finally accepted that Nell was his lot.

But by then, the spring, Dan had written his fourth or fifth play, I forget now. This time he had had the sense to dramatize a world he knew as opposed to ones spun out of an inexperienced imagination; and the sense to seek advice. By good luck one of England's more famous and more thinking actors turned up at the Playhouse. Dan braved him with his play; was made to rewrite several scenes, and drop one or two. But then the kind man instituted himself fairy godfather for the script in London. By May Dan knew he had taken the first essential step toward being a professional dramatist. He had signed his first contract. *The Empty Church* did wonders for his morale, if not his bank-balance; and demolished whatever remaining doubts Nell may have retained about him. He even thought he detected a faint wistfulness in Jane at the news, and he was man enough to crow inwardly at the thought of that. But in sum it was a good year for all of them, full of promise, at a time when what you are doing for yourself seems much more important than what you do to, or have done to you by, other people.

None of us had ever been to Italy before—it was all new and amusing. We even loved the heat; adored the ramshackle but airy old tile-floored flat; the endless siestas and sightseeings and picnics out in the Campagna. We couldn't rush about, the heat and Jane's pregnancy prevented that. Nell and I went off on our own occasionally, but we functioned well as a foursome, seemingly better than ever before. Between Jane and myself—and of course in Rome we were from time to time obliged to be alone—there was a total silence about the past. I thought we had become enormously mature, to be able to pretend so convincingly that it had never happened, to discuss a painting together or go around the corner shopping like two old friends. She was in awe a little of her own baby, while Anthony had an acute crisis of first-child neurosis about her and its safety; but even that susceptibility to couvade seemed endearing and fallible. If we all laughed at his fussing there, he made us laugh in turn about the sillier Catholic side of Rome. They both wore their religion very lightly. Nell and I used to tease them about Sunday Mass: they would debate (putting it on for us) churches like a pair of gourmets over a Michelin guide. We used to celebrate our own mass while they were out, making love in the sun on the terrace. We decided they were incipiently square, but nice to know.

The real bible that summer, for all four of us, was *Sea and Sardinia*. Imperial Rome, we agreed, was vulgar beyond belief. All good lay with Lawrence and the Etruscans. We pursued them wherever their sites lay in range. We were playing pagan, of course; and eternal Oxford aesthetes.

The climax and epitome of those blue-and-ocher weeks took place at Tarquinia. The tombs were still locked away from the public at that time, but Anthony pulled the name of one of his new Senior Common Room friends on the curator and we were allowed a tour. It was early evening when we finished. It had been a memorable experience: in my case some kind of avatar of so many things I had derived from the Devon countryside as a boy. I felt it spoke more deeply to me, even though Anthony knew far more about the Etruscans in scholarly terms. I think it was also the first time I had a clear sense of the futility of the notion of progress in art: nothing could be better or lovelier than this, till the end of time. It was sad, but in a noble, haunting, fertile way.

We went back into the little town and sat about drinking wine . . . holding forth, as one does at that age, about our feelings, how terribly moving it all was, how—then suddenly decided that we would give ourselves the night there. We tried two or three hotels, but they were full of holidaying Italians.

However, a waiter in one of them told us of an isolated *pensione* down by the sea three miles away, and the two girls and I overruled Anthony's doubts. The place had only one free room left, but it contained two double beds, and we dismissed the ancient taxi that had brought us. We had a long meal and more wine under a vine-trellis outside. It was very airless and afterward, a little drunk, we idled along the beach beside the silent, listless sea. Then Nell and Jane decided they wanted to swim. So we undressed, pairing off by sex, not marriage. I saw the two girls wade in, then both turn and call to us. They stood hand-in-hand, like a pair of sea-nymphs, in the starlight. For a moment I wasn't sure which was which, though Jane was an inch or two taller than Nell. I was thinking, He's never seen Nell's breasts and pubic hair before.

She said, "Oh they're hopeless. They're shy."

They turned and went on wading in. The beach ran out very shallowly, for a long way. Anthony and I followed. The girls ahead of us stood with the water round their waists, then plunged forward, one of them with a small scream. Then they were swimming. A few seconds later Anthony and I plunged as well and swam out to join them. They had stopped where they could just stand, having discovered the sea was phosphorescent. Glaucous trails glimmered behind each movement. We made a circle, talking about the phenomenon, swirling our arms through the mild water. Then Jane reached out her hands to Anthony and myself and we made a ring as Nell in turn took our free hands. It was ridiculous, childish, as if we were about to do a round-dance or play Ring-a-ring-a-roses. I think it was Nell who made us begin to circle gently. The depth we were in made any but very slow movement impossible. Four heads without bodies; touches beneath the water. I felt Jane's bare foot, but I knew it was by accident. I could see Anthony smiling at me opposite.

Perhaps those beautiful tomb-walls somewhere inland behind the beach; perhaps the fact that the holiday was near its end; no, something deeper than that, a mysterious unison, and strangely uncarnal, in spite of our naked bodies. I have had very few religious moments in my life. The profound difference between Anthony and myself—and our types of mankind—is that I did for a few moments there feel unaccountably happy; yet I could see that for him, the supposedly religious man, this was no more than a faintly embarrassing midnight jape. Or I can put it like this: he saw me as the brother-in-law he liked, I saw him as the brother I loved. It was a moment that had both an infinity and an evanescence—an intense closeness, yet no more durable than the tiny shimmering organisms in the water around us.

I tried repeatedly in later years to put those few moments into my work—and always had to cut them out. It took me time to discover that even atheists need a sense of blasphemy. And loss. Like the vanished Etruscans, we should never be together like that again. Perhaps I knew that then, also.

# Petard

One of the hostesses woke me, we were coming into London. I went and had a wash; set my watch forward once again. Barney was standing by my seat when I returned.

"Dan, Margaret's meeting me. Can we give you a lift into town?"

I should have liked to refuse, but it seemed churlish. At that time of night I wouldn't have to ask them in for a drink. We got off the plane and through passport control together; and waited for our luggage together. He went to fetch a trolley from the far end of the hall. I felt unreal, in a bad dream, still not properly awake. He was grinning when he came back.

"Either you have a marvelous daughter or I have a telepathic secretary."

I looked back through the customs counters. I couldn't distinguish Caro's among the scatter of distant faces, but Barney said, "She's with Margaret. I think you have your own transport." A hand waved, and I waved back. I'd told her in the cable not to wait up for me, let alone fag out to Heathrow. The luggage began its slow-motion spill. None of it fell well for me; and I don't mean the luggage.

Barney's wife was still an unimpressive little woman, tired and faded under the set smile and the make-up. She had not aged well; but then she had always seemed to me anomalous, suburban to Barney's urban. I vaguely remembered their house, in never-swinging Muswell Hill. Caro looked oddly apprehensive, no doubt at not having told me herself about the new job. She flashed one look at Barney, then I was hugging her. I held her severely away by the shoulders.

"I thought I gave orders."

"My own boss now."

I embraced her again; and heard Barney's voice. "Not to worry, Caroline. I've given you a marvelous reference."

"Thank you, Mr. Dillon."

I took the little edge in her answer to be mocking: knowing he was sneaking home ahead of plan.

"Dan, you remember Margaret?"

"Of course."

We shook hands, there was a brief four-way conversation about Barney's coming home early, small worlds . . . nothings. We moved outside, I led the way with Margaret. I heard Caro ask Barney how some interview had gone, but didn't catch his answer. When they came up beside us, he was asking her not to ring him the next day unless it was "desperate."

"And for God's sake don't tell anyone I'm back."

"Right."

Renewed insistence from Barney that we have lunch one day soon: we saw them into their car, then I wheeled the trolley on down to where Caro had parked her Mini. I stood watching her while she unlocked it: she was wearing a long coat I hadn't seen before. And a face. She held the door open while I maneuvered the suitcases into the back.

"I know why you've come. Mummy told me yesterday."

"Is she in Oxford?"

"The Runt's got mumps rather badly. She's gone back to Compton for a couple of days." The Runt was her ten-year-old half-brother, Andrew's son and heir: they went in for a sort of Mitfordian family slang. I straightened and looked at her.

"Surprised?" She nodded, and looked down.

"I feel very sorry for him, Caro. In spite of family history."

"I know, Daddy."

Her Daddy's often had faint inverted commas around them; but these were stamped hard. She went round to the driving-door and unlocked that. I bent myself in beside her.

"I was very close to him once."

She looked through the windscreen. The Dillons' car, ahead of us, moved off.

"It just seems rather sad that something like this has to happen to bring you together again."

"Darling, if you came to tell me that your generation of the family thinks mine have behaved like cretins . . ."

"I came because I love you. Right?"

I leaned and kissed her cheek, and she switched on the engine.

"I rang Aunt Jane this evening. When I got your cable."

"How did she sound?"

We moved off. She made a bad gear-change and grimaced.

"In control. As always. We talked about me mostly."

"I'll try and catch up with some sleep. Then I'll go."

"Yes, I said I thought you would." She hesitated. "She's very grateful."

"I was looking for an excuse. I've missed you out there."

She said nothing for a moment, though she had a small smile.

"Is she nice?"

It had to come, and I was glad she had brought it so quickly into the open.

"Yes. And I still missed you."

"They say she's very bright."

I left a pause. "Did it shock you?"

"Don't be silly. I used to rather fancy you myself."

"Now I'm the one who's shocked."

"I used to tell my best friends at school about you. How devastating you were."

"Like the H-bomb?" She grinned. "Yes?"

"When I was little and you took me on that grand ancestral tour in Devon. That was the first time I'd really thought about you and Mummy. I couldn't think why she'd ever left such a nice man." She added, "Of course, that was before I really knew you."

"If you weren't being so sweet . . ."

The grin lingered, but I sensed something troubled underneath, something that couldn't be said, that had to be hidden under this teasing. She jockeyed to get past a late truck. We headed for the tunnel to the M4.

"And how's Richard?"

"That's all over, as a matter of fact."

I gave her a quick look. She was a shade too set on her driving; but then she twitched her mouth and shrugged. I had once watched her show-jumping at a gymkhana, in her horsy phase. Whatever she lacked elsewhere, she took her fences straight and brave.

"Since when?"

"About a month ago. Since I last wrote."

"Someone else?"

"Just . . ." and again she shrugged.

"Poor old Richard. I rather liked him."

"No you didn't. You thought he was an Old Etonian nit."

Contradicting me like that was not new. She had taken to

it during the time I had set to work on her debutantisms; telling me she might be a fool, but she knew my true opinions from those I sometimes humored her with.

She said, "And you were right."

"Do you want to talk about it?"

We came out of the tunnel. I had that dislocation of long journeys, where nothing, even familiar landscape, has reality; where most of you is still where you came from. The awful winter dankness of England.

"It all happened down at Compton, really. We went for the weekend. I suppose seeing him being given the future son-in-law treatment was the last straw."

"Hardly his fault?"

"He's so fantastically square. Under the surface. Honestly he was horrid, he was lapping it all up. Sucking up like mad to Andrew. Pretending he was interested in milk-yield and shooting and God knows what else. I suddenly realized what a phony he is. Not only about all that."

"Then you're right to chuck him out."

The unfortunate Richard had been very much a male equivalent of Caro; not university material at all. His family owned a famous London publishing house, and he'd been learning the trade on the fine old English principle that since natural aptitude is clearly inherited, no practical demonstration of it need ever be required. He had picked up some vaguely left-wing views among the properly resentful underlings he would one day mismanage—or perhaps he just needed to try out on me opinions that must have been unspeakable at home.

"He was *so* beastly, you've no idea. He had the nerve to say Fleet Street was corrupting me. He told me one day I was getting sharp. 'Rather vulgar, dear girl.' I threw a gin-bottle at him, I absolutely saw red. The bloody nerve of the man." She said, "And don't grin."

"There is some of the flat left?"

"This was at his place."

"Good. Never throw your own gin."

She bit her lips. We climbed up on to the M4.

"You knew from the start. You could have told me."

"With my track record in picking ideal partners . . ."

"You must have learnt something."

"Too late."

She digested that. "Are you going to marry her?"

"Her name's Jenny. And no, I'm not."

"I didn't mean . . ."

"I know you didn't."

Cross-purposes; they were always inherent between us. Something in her had changed. Perhaps it was no more than the normal effect of six months in a new world. I had an idea that she had had a bruising in Fleet Street; and bruising back had become her defense. The "rather vulgar" I wouldn't wear; but there did indeed seem a new sharpness, some sort of shift from innocence to aggression. The crack about fancying me would not have been possible six months previously; not the implicit reprimand about older-generation stupidity.

"And the job?"

"Love it. Even the mad hours."

"And your new boss?"

"It's fun working for him. Lots of variety. I seem to spend half my life on the telephone."

"Why didn't you write and tell me?"

"I was a tiny bit afraid you'd be . . . I know he gave you a terrible review once."

"He's given me good ones as well. And no excuse."

"My dreadful English."

I sensed something embarrassed in her, and tried to relieve it.

"Never mind. Now I'm back."

But evidently her mind was still running on my being offended by Barney.

"Actually it's half how I got the job. I had to do some typing for him, and he asked about the name." She added, "I couldn't very well turn it down. It's quite a promotion."

"Of course. I'm delighted for you."

After a moment she said, "Mummy told me you'd never really liked him."

"That's all from before the Flood."

"Did you talk on the plane?"

"We had a chat. Old times. All that. About you."

"He rather envies you actually."

"I was given that line a bit."

"He means it. Envy's the wrong word. He says he admires almost everything you've done."

"And nothing he's done himself."

"He's terribly insecure. Underneath." I said nothing. "They're all the same, you can't imagine what a bunch of self-pitiers they all are. We all get it. The secretaries. And the rivalries, you know, they're so petty, if A gets half a column

[ 121 ]

more than B, or C has a private lunch with his nibs or D gets a new byline mug-shot. If they didn't go to El Vino's and backbite each other every day they'd go mad. Actually Bernard's better than most of them. He can at least laugh about it."

He had always used his proper first name in print; but I deduced that he would have preferred me to use it to his face now.

Caro said, "It's absurdly like the village at home, really. All spying and gossip and everyone knowing everything about everyone else."

I had to smile to myself: this new-found authority and objectivity I had been careful in the past not to try to woo Caro with the glamorous—or what is publicly considered glamorous—side of my own life. Whatever narcissism I had had at Oxford, I had managed to ban from my life that particularly odious variety so peculiar to the movie world. My study at the flat has books on its walls, and still a mirror or two; but not those ultimate lying mirrors, the framed awards and gilt statuettes, the posters and cast stills; and I had similarly kept her away from famous names. I began to suspect it hadn't really been necessary.

We talked then about family things, about Uncle Anthony, what Jane would do, their children. She became more the daughter I had left behind in the summer. We arrived home and I carried my suitcases up the stairs behind her. I felt fatally awake by then, the wretched time-lag was taking its usual toll. Jenny would be in her apartment five thousand sunlit miles away, having a shower perhaps after the day's shooting, the evening still ahead; or she might have acted fast and already spoken with Mildred. I saw her gathering up her bits and pieces for the move to the Cabin; had a great desire to call California; and killed it. The weaning had to commence.

There were fresh flowers in the living-room, an unopened bottle of whisky, Malvern water and a glass by the fireplace. Caro played the dutiful daughter, switched on the electric fire, made sure I noticed all these signs of the welcome-home. I kissed her.

"Now bed for you. You're ten times nicer than I deserve."

"When do you want breakfast?"

"When do you have to be in?"

"It doesn't matter. With Bernard officially away. As long as I'm there by midday."

"I probably shan't sleep much. You wake me when you get up."

"I've made the bed and everything."

"Bless you. And for fetching me. Now hop it."

She went, and I poured myself a whisky, then stared around the room. There was a new cushion on one of the settees. But nothing else—bar a pile of mail, which I wasn't going to face till the morning, it seemed exactly as I had left it months before, and that disappointed me. I had hoped Caro would give herself a little more freedom, though I knew that for her "home" must always mean Compton . . . Versailles to a cottage, no comparison.

I had stayed there only once, long before Nell became its chatelaine. Andrew had thrown a famous ball for his twenty-first birthday and all fashionable student Oxford had descended—cars, coaches . . . one group from the Bullingdon side of his life had even turned up in a coach-and-four, someone blowing a posthorn. Compton Nine-Acres (it had nearer nine thousand in fact, in those days) wasn't perhaps a great house as country-houses go, but it was impressive enough: the gardens, the parkland, the seemingly endless rooms, all that spaciousness and graciousness. It was a very long way from any world I was familiar with. I suppose that even then that celebratory week-end was an anachronism, a tacit farewell to the old days, Andrew's father's terminal fling against the post-war socialist present. It must have been one of the last full-blown traditional occasions of its kind—there wasn't only the ball, there was a tenants' and village party on the lawn the preceding afternoon. Tennis, cricket, croquet, riding; endless champagne and superb food for those days of rationing. Some scarlet-uniformed local band, their silver instruments under the shade of a huge beech; a pair of trousers being hauled up a flagpole; and Andrew drunk throughout. Even Anthony enjoyed it, though he hardly knew Andrew at college; we were there largely because of the girls, of course, not that Andrew then showed any particular interest in them. At Oxford his sex-life was a little of a mystery. One would see him about with girls, and he was reputed to frequent a Mayfair brothel; but one associated him much more with hunting, beagling and drinking. We half suspected he was slightly queer; and I remember Nell being certain he would be "hopeless" in bed.

I knew from Caro that the house and its old *façons de vivre* had gone the way of all things—that death duties had severely diminished the estate, the park had largely gone under the plough, that Nell had to make do (and complained endlessly) with the help of an Italian couple and a daily woman from the village. But just as I had envied Andrew that departed world in my one glimpse of it, so I still envied Caro its remnants. It was all very well condemning such worlds, politically—nothing easier. But it was like some of Ezra Pound's poetry. You could blow the philosophy to bits; the lines and images still haunted you.

I sat there sipping my drink, once more tempted to blame Nell for everything and thinking of the immediate future. Presumably she would very soon be back in Oxford at Jane's side; and whatever other reconciliations might take place, I doubted whether there could ever be a sincere one between us two. If I had been technically and legally guilty, I still saw her as the first cause. No doubt all divorces repeat the Adam and Eve situation. Genesis is as silent as the grave concerning what happened when they were expelled from Eden, except for their producing a corpse and a murderer by way of children. Our Cain-and-Abel had been a total unforgivingness.

For nearly three years after the action I virtually did not speak with Nell. Occasionally she brought Caro to London, usually I went down to Oxford for the day. We would exchange a few frigid commonplaces over the child's head at the hand-over place, and when I brought her back. I was prepared, after a while and for purely civilized reasons, to be warmer, but Nell wasn't. Then one day she wrote to say she wanted to meet me in London without Caro. She had something to discuss. I presumed it was to do with the alimony. I could afford more then, though I wasn't going to give it without a battle. Nell was very far from poor, and she knew I knew that. We met for lunch. But she hadn't come for a finer pound of flesh. She was going to marry Andrew.

My first reaction was an incredulous repetition of his name. I had read of his father's death at about the time of our divorce and I realized he had come into the title; but I still saw the condescending young drunkard of our joint past, the impossible drawl, the posing, the blend of Regency rake and Tony Lumpkin . . . to say nothing of the summary he had been of all we at least pretended to despise. His one virtue had been a kind of outrageousness, that was why one had tolerated him. I wasn't forgiven that instinctive response to the news and by way of punishment she would tell me very little of how they had met, except that it had been some six months before, by chance, in Oxford. Now he "happened" to be very much in love with her—"fantastic though that may seem." I noticed that she did not say she was very much in love with him. Her line was much more that she had to think of Caroline, who apparently "adored" him. They had been to stay at Compton.

I had to accept the fact, improbable though it was; but I couldn't understand why it had to be announced to me in this face-to-face way. Nell made a little speech about Caro being my daughter and my "presumably" having some "faint" interest in her future; and there were new financial arrangements to discuss. I wasn't taken in by this sudden descent from crowing to consultation, and I suspect Nell half-hoped I would be violently angry or try to stop her—or it may have been that Anthony and Jane, though they had by then banned me from all contact with them, were still prey to scruples and had argued that she must do this. I am quite sure she was not angling for some sort of reconciliation; it was far more as if I must be made to see what I had reduced her to . . . which was absurd. He was rich, he had a beautiful house, he was a baronet; and I could even believe he was in love with her, since he must have had free range over any number of eligible young county dollies from his own world. Perhaps she didn't really know herself why she had come. She was very nervous, and taking the first major independent decision of her life, and I might have been kinder.

So she duly became Lady Randall. We had met more than briefly only three or four times since then. On all but one occasion Caro had been present, and we had been on our best behavior. The other time Andrew had been there—that was the most recent meeting, to discuss Caro's future now she had to leave school. It had been rather comic, since after a stiff beginning (we two men hadn't seen each other since Oxford) Andrew and I had decided that we were, beyond the barriers erected by our very different ways of life and political convictions, both reasonably amusing and interesting fellows. He had matured and quietened down considerably. My old rural self liked the shrewd squire in him, his still not quite dead love of the outrageous clearly took to the show-business gossip I offered on my side. We talked about the old days at Oxford. Nell grew increasingly silent as the evening drew on and Andrew and I got agreeably drunk. I knew he would have been happy to have me down to Compton; and that such sanity would take place over Nell's dead body. I was very glad she was now his wife when we finally left Wheeler's and said goodbye.

All water under the bridge; and sitting there in the flat, with more whisky, my thoughts returned to Jenny. I wanted to hear her voice; or her voice as reminder of a simpler, less sentenced present. Perhaps Nell was right, there had always been an aura of despair about the flat, of makeshift and wrong choice. I was staring at the telephone, very near to giving way. Then suddenly the real present was in the doorway again: Caro, in a long dressing-gown. I knew at once that something was wrong. She had been supposedly gone to bed for at least twenty minutes, and now she wore the air of a both disobedient and reproving child.

"I can't sleep."

"Have a whisky then."

She shook her head, but came into the room. She went to one of the windows, the curtains weren't drawn, and stared out.

I said, "Caro?"

For three or four seconds she said nothing.

"I'm having an affair with Bernard, Daddy." She stared down at the street below. "I'm very sorry. I didn't know how to tell you earlier."

I felt shock, but no flash of disbelief; if anything, a fool for not having worked it out for myself. They had both thrown dust in my eyes, but there had been enough clues.

She murmured, "Please say something."

"How did it happen, for God's sake?"

She shrugged, still turned away: how does it ever happen? I wanted to ask what on earth she saw in him. He had looked to me every year of his age, I had even congratulated myself on not looking so pouched and raddled, physically gone to seed. . . .

"I didn't know he was coming home with you. The last time we talked he said another two days. When I saw . . . his wife, I wanted to run away. But she saw me first."

"She doesn't know?"

She shook her head. "I suppose she suspects. Their marriage has been empty for years."

"Are you in love with him?"

"I feel sorry for him. I don't know."

"This is why you didn't write?"

She nodded, and I thought for a moment that she was going to cry. I went and fetched another glass, poured a little whisky in, went to where she was.

"Come and sit down."

She let me lead her to the settee and sat down beside me.

"Does your mother know?"

"No, I . . . I'd rather you didn't tell her. Just yet."

We both looked at the glasses in our hands.

"Why are you telling me?"

"Because I've spent most of my life not telling you the truth. Because . . ." but she shrugged again.

"You seem rather miserable about it."

"Only about having to inflict it on you."

"And?"

"Meeting his wife like that." She added in a lower voice, "His coming back without telling me."

"Do you imagine you're his first infidelity?"

"I'm not a total innocent."

"Then you know the score. Margaret, he doesn't leave." I added, "God knows why." She said nothing. "Is this why you dropped Richard?"

She shook her head. "That's been coming for months now."

"But it is why you're his secretary?"

"I'm quite good at my job. Incredible though it may seem." She glanced at me. "Why's that funny?"

"Because your mother once threw the same unjustified sarcasm at me. In another context."

"I'm sorry."

"My dear, your ability to take shorthand isn't what worries me."

"But that it's someone you despise."

She was staring down at the carpet. I said evenly, "I don't despise him personally, Caro. Or not more than anyone else in that world."

"Which you advised me to enter."

"Guilty. But in the hopes you'd see through it."

"As Bernard does. Far more than you seem to realize."

"But goes on living in it?"

"He's not as lucky as some people. Apart from anything else he has a wife and three children to support."

"All right. Fair enough." She remained obstinately looking down; the gymkhana again, but now she was like a rider who has forgotten which fence comes next. "Tell me why you like him."

"Because he's sad. And gentle. On his own. And grateful."

"So he ought to be."

She left a pause. "Also I can talk to him."

"Is that an accusation?" She shook her head, but not very convincingly. "Come on. Out with it."

"Talk seriously."

"What about?"

"All sorts of things I can't talk about with you. Or Mummy."

"Such as?"

"You don't seem able to understand that anyone could love you both. For all your faults." She went on before I could answer. "I know she can be a bitch, I know you can be at least half the selfish bastard she thinks you are. It's not just you two. The whole family. We seem to have banned and buried so much."

"You know what happened."

"It's not the past. It's what I feel about you both. *Now*."

"And he listens?" She nodded. "How serious is he?" She said nothing, and I had to coax her. "If that doesn't sound too old-fashioned."

"He feels guilty about . . . his wife."

I doubted that; or suspected that such a guilt, or decency, was too attractive and convenient a ploy to be as disinterested as she made it sound.

"And if one day he decided he wasn't anymore?"

"I haven't lost my head. It's not like that."

There was a silence. I drank from my own glass; she still had not touched hers.

"Is this what he was supposed to telephone me about?"

"We did discuss it. He knew what you'd feel."

"Did you?"

"Not at the beginning."

"And I haven't much ground to stand on, have I?"

"That's nothing to do with it. At all."

"Are you sure?"

"Daddy, I'm not ashamed that you're still rather an attractive man. I know you can't be Andrew."

"What does that mean?"

"I know you despise all that world as well. But he's a much better father than you'll ever be." She added, "Perhaps just because he's always there. And he can handle Mummy."

I left a silence.

"You seem to think I despise everything, Caro."

"You expect everyone to think and feel like you." She added, "I'm not blaming you, you're probably right about Fleet Street, but . . ." again she shook her head.

I didn't know whether she was accusing my career or my nature; it was not a new accusation, though it had never been brought quite so near to the bone before. My only consolation was that it must hide a certain doubt in Caro herself.

"Will you at least promise me that when you're married you'll have more than one child?"

She searched my eyes. "Why do you say that?"

"Because single children are always intensely self-absorbed. But also they can't imagine that anyone else might ever actually need them. It isn't quite as simple as their never having time for anyone else."

"I just meant your work." She managed a rueful little smile. "Anyway, it's too late now to trade you in."

"At least we're agreed on something."

She passed me her glass. "I don't want this." I poured its contents into my own and she stood up and went to the fireplace, her back to me.

"Are you angry because he didn't tell you himself?"

"I can see it was difficult. I just wish he hadn't tried so hard to sell himself as a pathetic failure. I don't know who he's trying to kid."

"I should have thought you would. You always——" but she bit the sentence off.

"Go on. Truth time."

"You don't exactly oversell your own professional life."

"That's mainly because I've seen too many movieland children drilled into uncritical admiration."

"I've only very recently realized how much you've conned me. Quite a lot of people at work think I'm rather lucky to be your daughter."

"That's a press-clippings view of life."

She was silent a moment. "When Bernard moans, he's much more convincing. People are always attacking him. Nobody attacks you."

"Sweetie, all this is proving my point. Middle-aged men may seem mature and knowledgeable and all the rest of it. But when they have to have girl-friends of your and Jenny's age, they're not. Deep down they're still frustrated adolescents. Running scared. They're in a panic."

"What are you in a panic about?"

She said it with a strange mixture of shyness and aggression. But it touched me, it defined so precisely the gap between us. I thought of Jenny's dry impatience before the same line. Even allowing for the three years or so of difference in age, Jenny was a much shrewder and less dependent girl; but I half sensed what could drive fathers and daughters to incest . . . that need to purge the spoken of the unspoken, to institute a simplicity in place of an obscuring complexity.

"That's something we'll talk about another day. Or night." I could see from her face that she felt she was being fobbed off. "Caro, Jenny's had a lot of experience. She's acquired a kind of . . . armor? I don't want you hurt. Used. That's all."

We seemed to have reached an impasse. Caro was sublimely ignorant of Freud—and of classical tragedy, for that matter. I could imagine, given the narrow limits of her cultural world and the British mania for television, that Barney had more mundane attractions for her. He was a household name in his way; and just as for the masses he wore a liberal intellectual's face on camera, I could guess that the Pagliacci face he showed Caro in private would be convincing enough. It would have been child's play to seem both glamorous and vulnerable to such an innocent—who probably felt in addition out of her depth, in need of a protector. If my own bill of health was cleaner it was only because Jenny had an innate scepticism and the resolution to inflict it when the sobs grew too loud.

"Will you tell him you've spoken to me?"

"I'll have to, won't I?"

Then more silence. Mine was spent in strangling impossible questions: what's he like in bed, have you brought him here, how widely known is it . . . she was pretty enough to have made it a physical thing, but there must have been a dozen other girls in that building with her looks—and with a comfortable superiority in what constitutes attraction, at least for men like Barney, out of bed. I felt angrier and angrier, almost like picking up the telephone and having it out with him there and then. In the end I got up and went to the whisky again. I wanted to put my arm round her, but it seemed wrong; cheating.

"Why *have* you told me this, Caro?" She looked down into the fireplace and said nothing. "You could have gone on in secret."

"And not bothered you?"

"That's a foul hit."

"Sorry."

"Then tell me." Still she was silent. "Do you want me to do something about it?"

"Just understand me, I suppose."

"And give you my blessing?"

She turned away.

"Why did Jenny McNeil fall in love with you?"

I felt the force of the petard then.

"Love's hardly the word."

"Then whatever word you do use."

"So you can use it back?" It was too harsh, and I went on quickly. "She was simply a bit thrown by the life out there. Feeling lonely. And hardly short of experience with younger men." I said, "Who aren't all like Richard, you know."

"I realize that."

"I'm not angry, Caro. As long as you're happy."

"I was. Until today."

"I'll get over it. You must show me a little grace."

She nodded, then turned and sat on the arm of a chair.

"I'd better tell you something else."

"What?"

"I spent this afternoon looking for flats. I think I've found one I can afford."

I did want to be angry with her then, I'd very much have liked to be an American Jewish or a working-class father, anything other than feeling caught in that dreadful English middle-class trap of never showing or saying what you really feel. I certainly saw that I was to be taken at full tilt . . . or not at all.

"I'm going down to Thorncombe as soon as possible."

"I think I'd rather."

"Where is it?"

"Near Parliament Hill. Kentish Town, really."

"That's pretty grubby, isn't it?"

"It's quite a nice house."

"You must let me—"

"I've saved a lot. Living here."

We had a little argument about that, but she was adamant; and I realized that "Kentish Town" was partly symbolic—not only her father was being rejected. I also remembered that it was on the way to Muswell Hill. The place fell vacant in a couple of weeks, it seemed. It was furnished, but she wanted to "borrow" a table and one or two other things. Perhaps she wanted to give me at least one small chance to feel still needed. Then there was a silence, too little and too much to say. She stood and took her last fence; came and stood in front of me, leaned forward clumsily and kissed me on the cheek. She let me hold her for a few moments. Then she turned and left the room.

Cut.

# Forward Backward

Six hours later, ten o'clock on a chilling London winter morning, a dank mist over everything outside: I had finally got some sleep, though not nearly enough by the time Caro was tapping on my door. Lying there, I felt the next stage of the long-journey disorientation: I had never left London, California was a dream. I must have had depressive real dreams, anxiety ones, though I couldn't remember them, perhaps because the real anxieties flooded back with the gray daylight—Caro's news, the coming ordeal later that day at Oxford, I must try to ring Jenny, then David Malevich, all that mail waiting, my accountant, my dentist . . . a great deal too much reality.

Caro helped. I was given the full treatment for breakfast, no Continental nonsense; a dry look askance from the electric stove. She was trying, she said, to make up for "last night," and reconciliation was easy. She told me more about the flat, across the table while I ate, and I tried to accept it as a natural thing: wanting to strike out on her own, live like other girls. We didn't mention Barney at all. I started questioning her about Jane and Anthony. Over the last two years I had got her to talk, if not quite openly, at least unemotionally about Compton and its inmates, but the same wasn't true of her Oxford relatives. I knew a little of what had happened to the three children, Caro's cousins; but I had no very clear picture at all of what Jane and Anthony themselves had become. Though she hinted at a certain puzzlement with Anthony, he could be so dry, you didn't always understand whether he was being serious or funny, I had detected a strong affection in her for both of them. They'd always treated her exactly as if she were their own daughter, she felt that. She thought Aunt Jane had "gone off" the Catholic thing, but it was "sort of something" one didn't talk about. She was terribly efficient, lots of committees and things, much more practical than Mummy; an awfully good cook, I'd love their house. Uncle Anthony was still dotty about orchids, there was one he'd found at Compton two or three years before, but she couldn't remember its name.

I took the impression, amid all her chatter, that Jane had changed much more than Anthony. What memories I had of her on the domestic side were of a distinctly slapdash approach to food, nor could I associate her with worthy committees and left-wing causes—I gathered that latter detail from something Caro dropped in about Andrew: how he sometimes called Jane her "Red aunt" . . . though no doubt the faintest shade of pink would seem red to him. My final picture was of a brisk, well-organized and self-possessed woman who contrasted rather favorably in Caro's eyes with the temperament and occasional bossiness of her own mother.

She took herself off just after eleven, giving me messages for them in Oxford. I promised to ring her that night, we'd have a whole evening together as soon as I could get back. We kissed. Then I stood at the window and watched her slight figure cross the misted street below and walk up toward the Underground station. She turned and waved, and I waved back.

Then I went and looked in her room—the one she'd had as a baby, though it had been two or three times redecorated since then. It was rather sad, in some way like Jenny's apartment in Los Angeles; depersonalized and temporary, a shade too tidy, as if she were still living in a hostel. No litter of clothes, of cosmetics, none of the junk one might have seen in the room of a student of her age. No books. A painting of an old carthorse, worn and frameless, that we had bought off a stall in the Portobello Road one Saturday morning just before I left for California. There were some snaps of the family down at Compton stuck in the side of her dressing-table mirror; and I saw one of the Cabin at Abe's that I had sent her. I suppose I was looking for some positive evidence that Barney came to the flat . . . or letters, I don't know. But I opened no drawers. I was really looking for Caro.

Perhaps her room at Compton was the same; her other room I knew, down at Thorncombe, was certainly so. That whole enterprise I had also had to count, at least with respect to her, as a failure; another, if more complicated, hoist from my own petard.

She had come to me one Easter in the early 1960s, for a whole week. She was just eleven, and we'd never spent such a long time alone together. I felt trepidation about it, and so must have she. We had a very sticky first day together in London; and then somehow we got on to grandparents. It seemed suddenly to dawn on her that there were two on my side that she had never met. I told her a little about my life at her age, and I saw a spark of interest, a curiosity that was new in our relationship. There and then I abandoned the program I had vaguely in mind for our week in London: the museums, the kids' films and theaters. I proposed on the spot a trip down to Devon, her "grand ancestral tour." She was faintly shocked at first, with the old gravity of little girls, but then took to the idea with such excitement that I kicked myself for not having thought of it earlier. I had been there only once, on a rather similar trip with Aunt Millie some six years before, since my father had died. I suppose it had been nagging at my unconscious for several years. But now it abruptly assumed the same attraction for me as it evidently did for Caro. It was still for jokes, really; I had the place in perspective, or so I considered. Every year I sent the present incumbent five pounds to have my parents' graves tended; and I was fool enough to think I could push the place into oblivion at such a price.

So we went to the church and stood by the graves of her grandparents. She looked both embarrassed and sad . . . and I made her giggle a little, the sermons, where I had to sit so many Sundays, the Apostles and Elders on the rood screen, the Cumaean Sibyl, the fusty absurdity of it all. Though something, at the graves, had made me feel sad, too. For the first time in years I remembered the wild oxlips and the Quaker's Bonnet primroses that had once always carpeted my mother at the time of spring.

We called at the Vicarage. That looked much the same outside; but the old kitchen-garden had gone, and all its fruit-trees. Now a new village hall and half an acre of tarmac stood in its place; and for the moment that seemed a worse desecration than if they had bulldozed the church itself. Around the house some of the old garden remained, though it was obviously now in far less skilled hands. But the *Osmanthus* still flourished, the myrtle, the *Trichodendron* had branches full of hanging red buds . . . and I was even able to show off to Caro and the current vicar's wife over the names.

I had booked us into a hotel at Torquay, but I drove Caro there—for my sake, not hers—by way of Thorncombe. That was how I learned it was for sale. It was already empty and I made the fatal mistake of letting her talk me into a poke around. Rather to my surprise, in view of the grand country-house she lived in herself, she loved it; I was touched . . . for reasons she knew nothing about, though as we wandered in the yard and peered through windows I told her a part of the people who had once lived there. She wished I lived in a place like this, she could have a pony, I could go to church again—we had already made an enormous leap in those days away, and she was timidly learning how to tease me—I laughed, and teased her gently back. Perhaps I'd buy it just for her. She knew I wasn't even remotely serious, and so did I, although I had incidentally learned she did not like my living in London. On the way out I noticed the date of the auction on the board by the lane.

Nor had I forgotten it, or the secret depths of the day, when I had seen her into bed that same evening. I sat down in the lounge over a book, but not reading. As with all significant places on that emotion-charged map of childhood and adolescence we carry round with us in later life, my first sight of Thorncombe after so many years had been disappointing. It had lost all its green secrecy, its hiddenness, its charm; it seemed dwarfed, trite; perhaps because I was with Caro, and she was enthusing innocently but trivially over something a little sacred. There were other factors, of course: I too was tired of London, for over a year I had been traveling. I began to feel the need of somewhere to retreat, to rest up . . . I was tempted. But then I saw all the disadvantages, the futility of pretending that I was not now rootless by choice as well as career; the idiocy of returning where one was still remembered, as I had discovered over a cup of tea at the Vicarage, by a very different self. By the time I went to bed, with Caro asleep on the other side of the room, I had dismissed the whole idea.

The next day we drove farther west, but we kept a small joke going about the place. I would have to buy it if she really wanted it; and she pretended she did. I knew it was nothing as a practical wish, but very far from without meaning as regards ourselves. I caught her looking at me once or twice, strangely, and blushing when she was caught; and I knew what that was about as well. We returned to London, she went off home, and I missed her a great deal more than ever in the past. I kept seeing her standing beside me in the churchyard, not knowing what to make of those two yellow-lichened stones; and saw myself in her.

A week before the auction I caught a train to Newton Abbot, hired a taxi, went to the agents, then straight out to Thorncombe. It was a gray afternoon, and it began to drizzle while I was there. The tired ghosts, the empty rooms. I went to bed that night in the Newton hotel more or less certain that I was on a wild-goose chase. But the next day dawned brighter, I gave it one last chance. I wandered round the orchard, went up the hill through the beechwoods behind, and some of the old magic crept back. I did not want the thirty acres of pasture that went with the place, but the agent had told me they could easily be sold off later, or let for keep. The buildings needed a lot of money spent on them. A hideous row of breeze-block pighouses had to be got rid of, an equally unsightly Dutch barn. But I began to see how the old farmhouse with its still splendid doorway and the two ancient stone barns behind could be converted.

It wasn't entirely romantic nostalgia that finally made me put my money down; but quite as much a kind of anger that so much had been allowed to go to rack and ruin. I had detected an apologetic note even in the agent's voice. Too much land had been sold off to attract serious farmers; too much else was ruined for it to attract private buyers. Meanwhile it stood rather like an old farm dog—not a chance simile, I could remember just such a dog from the summer when my whole being had lain in that house and how sure its place had been there—an old wall-eyed Welsh collie called True, and as safe from the shotgun as an aged human being. Then I told myself it was simply a cutting job, a potentially good scene that needed the blue pencil and a rewrite. And Caro: this money says I love you.

Of course she had come to stay, even spent holidays there, brought friends, and her own pony down in a loose-box from Compton; but by that time puberty and her smart boarding-school had fatally adulterated the innocence of eleven. In some strange way it had seemed even to distance us. I sensed that for her it was at best an amusing little place, at worst rather dull and—her stepfather's vocabulary—"plebby"; and then I so obviously wasn't very serious about it myself. Caro never belonged there, had never, beyond that brief first passion, which had really been with discovering herself my daughter, been in love with it. We had used it a little more during that last year or so, but I still felt she came under duress. It was not home. She had not been once on her own, in my absence.

I had, when she finished her secretarial course, seriously thought of taking her with me to California. But there was the remembrance of the fiasco over Thorncombe, the need for her to find her own feet and work for a living (or at least go through the motions) in London; a not wanting to plunge her into such a totally alien environment and culture, where I should inevitably have to leave her on her own a lot; the then attachment to Richard and—last but not least—the problem of Nell, who I knew would fight the idea tooth and nail. My final decision had also been selfish: the lupine hater of encumbrance in me, if it did not foresee Jenny, did script other situations where Caro might be a nuisance. I think that if she had only hinted that she would have liked to come . . . but she didn't.

And now I went into the living-room and stood staring at the mist outside, trying to decide whether to risk Oxford by car or to take a train. There had been fog warnings on the radio, according to Caro. The meeting began to loom large. It was not that I couldn't imagine what might happen, be said and felt. As at so many potentially fraught junctures in my life I could invent too many variations, almost as if I lived the event to its full before its limited reality took place. All writing, private and mental, or public and literal, is an attempt to escape from the conditioned past and future. But the hyperactive imagination is as damaging a preparation for reality as it is useful in writing. I knew I wouldn't say the things I was already rehearsing; and couldn't stop rehearsing.

In the end I made a practical American in me lose patience with the introverted Englishman and rang the RAC weather center. They did not recommend journeys by car; so I found out the train times. Then, without giving myself further time for thought, I dialed the Oxford number Caro had given me. The voice of a girl with a foreign accent answered. Mrs. Mallory was out. But as soon as I said my name she was less formal. Mrs. Mallory was at the hospital, but she had said I might call. She was expecting me, a room was prepared. I tried to explain that a hotel would do . . . but no no, she expect you here. The young lady, or her English, sounded peremptory about that, so I told her what train I was catching; and that I should be with them soon after six.

# Breaking Silence

I arrived at Paddington early and had a first-class compartment to myself, but it filled before we started. Something about those five other masked faces, buried in their evening newspapers and magazines, at last landed me back in England: that chosen isolation, that hatred of the other, as if we were all embarrassed at having to share our means of travel, even though it was first-class, with someone else. When we drew out of the station the elderly woman opposite me glanced up at the ventilation window. It was slightly open. A minute later she glanced again. I said, "Shall I shut it?"

"Oh well if . . ."

I stood and shut it; and received a frozen grimace, meant to represent gratitude, from the lady and two or three covertly disapproving examinations from my male fellow-passengers. I had committed the cardinal sin not of shutting the window, but of opening my mouth. No other caste in the world who are so certain that public decency and good breeding is silence; or who by carrying it to such lengths create such an impression of tribal homogeneity . . . I was wearing clothes bought in California, a polo-necked pullover and sports jacket, not a suit and tie, and perhaps they read something alien in me—a danger, someone to be taught the English way. I didn't really disapprove of it; I noted it, like an anthropologist, and understood it, as an Englishman. Being forced to share a confined space with people to whom you have not been introduced was an activity dense with risk: one might be held to ransom and forced to give some item of information about oneself. Perhaps it was just a matter of accent: a terror of revealing, in even the smallest phrase, one's class, or some dissonance between voice and clothes, opinion and vowel-sound.

It disturbed me far more than usual, that absolutely normal English silence. It seemed not relaxed at all, but almost explosive, a silence like a scream; perhaps because it seemed so characteristic of my own past—and of the family I was re-entering. I had analyzed this fear of exposure, this onanistic fondling of privacy, long before; once used it successfully in a play; but its persistence baffled me. It went marching on through the youth and sexual revolutions, through the permissive society, swinging London and all the rest. Hide, hide, hide, hide. Of course it was nothing, in that train: simply six middle-class people wanting to be left alone. But its private transference to a personal world, its murderous use as a killer of tolerance and trust, as agapicide, had principally ruined my marriage. We had used our silences like sabers, in the end.

Dan and Nell decided, perhaps in reaction to the other menage's philoprogenitiveness, not to have children for at least a year. There were—or so they argued—economic reasons. He had to see how his dramatic first-born would be received, had to prove he could follow it. They both wanted to move to London. Nell needn't have worked, but of the two sisters she was at that time much closer to the then unformulated ideas of Women's Liberation. Of course it was partly pretending: we both had private income, indeed together just about enough not to have needed to work at all. If we had money troubles, then as later, it was because we were born squanderers—Dan in reaction to his upbringing, Nell in conformity with hers. Neither of us ever showed anything but a very intermittent skill at economizing.

The Empty Church, the play that attempted to exorcise my father's ghost from my life, came on. It received fair to good reviews, benefiting a little from the charity traditionally extended to new names. It had rather a slow start at the box-office, but then picked up. Dan had his first real publicity. I suppose he ought to have seen a red light then: Nell was far more emotional, manic-depressive about it, than he was. She took the praise at face value and the criticism (most of it justified, if one's going to copy Ibsen one has no business with melodramatic tricks) as a personal affront . . . almost as if what was under attack was her choice in marrying the playwright. She was stupidly rude one evening at a party—they had just moved to London—to the New Statesman drama critic. He hadn't even given the play a bad review, merely spelled out some reservations. That spawned their first serious row, when they got home. It didn't last long, she cried and they made love. Dan even had to stop her writing a letter of apology the next day. At the time he put it down to overiden-tification. In reality it was a first declaration of career jeal-ousy.

What had finally brought them to London was not only the modest success of the play, but the quite unexpected arrival of a film-script offer. Dan had supposed it was a reward for the talent for realistic dialogue revealed in the theater; a bet-ter agent might have warned him he was simply being snatched up on the cheap. The story, based on a rotten novel about a war-time romance, was not worth reading, let alone filming. But he was very green, he thought he saw new angles, he knew he could improve the dialogue, and the money, though next to nothing by future standards, tempted. He was also having problems with his next play. I can't pre-tend that he hesitated, and Nell was for it. The well-known and profoundly ungifted British producer who had bought the book flattered him in the manner of his kind and they both happily swallowed that as well. At one point they seemed to be seeing a new film every evening—and tearing its script to bits afterward or trying to pick up lessons from it. Dan read the movie-making classics and had the usual love-affair with the professional jargon—all that bastard attempt to direct on paper which every decent scenarist in the history of the business has always run a mile from.

Nell found herself a job soon afterward. One of her college friends had already got some minor editorial position with the same publishers who were to re-enter my life later in the form of Caro's rejected beau. They were short of a reader and Nell was successfully recommended. The pay was crimi-nally poor, barely covered the money she spent on clothes, and nothing serious was sent her way. But she was allowed to work largely at home and she and Dan were still dewy-eyed enough to think that that compensated for the exploitation and the drudgery. They took turns at the same typewriter. All this was in a tiny mews flat they had found near the Bromp-ton Road, before SW3 had achieved its current *chic* and crip-pling prices.

It was a happy enough winter. Jane had Rosamund, with-out problems, and Dan and Nell became the baby's god-parents. They still saw quite a lot of Anthony and Jane, either at Wytham or when they came down to London. Dan had by then realized that no amount of dialogue improve-ment could hide the basic silliness of the story, but the first draft he sent in met with more approval than it deserved.

It was a typical British film production: a bad idea in the first place, done on the cheap from top to bottom, and based on the legitimate assumption that the great British cinema-going public had no taste and the illegitimate one that only water divided the United Kingdom from the United States. In the novel the hero had been English, but "American interest" had killed that from the start—not that it would have made any difference to the two hours of rubbish that eventually hit the odeons.

It took some years for Dan to realize that the total failure in England to develop a decent commercial movie industry, let alone something better than a constipated trickle of serious film-makers, is at least partly due to our unerring flair for backing bad directors . . . or to the corollary notion that some semi-illiterate cameraman or ingratiating phony must know more about reproducing life than anyone else. He should have learned from that first director, who had merely managed to fawn his way into the grand conspiracy of mediocrity that has dominated the home industry for the last twenty-five years.

But all this is in retrospect. Dan did a second draft, was drawn into the first fringes of the celluloid world—like a foolish shrimp into a sea anemone. Already feelers were out about another script, and he was beginning to see his way through with the new play. Writing that became a great relief after the script, so much so that he insidiously argued himself into believing there was a creative as well as an economic argument for following both professions. Even Nell had a promotion of sorts—to proof-reading. She had an unusual feminine ability to be meticulously accurate in punctuation and spelling, a something else she did not pass on to Caro. The appallingness of *her* written English was one of the few things they were able to agree on in later years.

But by this time, the spring of 1952, faint rifts in the lute were already appearing. Dan had to be on hand while they shot the indoor scenes—there were very few locations, it was all being done with stock footage and back-projection—at Pinewood. Already Nell had begun to complain about the "excitement" of Dan's life and the "dullness" of hers. He was scrupulous about taking her along to parties and showings and the rest, she even came down once or twice to the studio, but their side-by-side working existence was over. He had taken, even before shooting began, to doing some of the rewrites at the office in Wardour Street. He was given a miserable little cubbyhole there, but he now found it easier to write away from Nell. Perhaps it was partly embarrassment at having, at home, her read what he wrote; but even with the play . . . she was always hovering over it, wanting to see each scene the moment it came off the typewriter. That began to irritate Dan—unfairly, she was trying to cling to the joint existence. As he worked away from home more, so did she; correcting proofs at the publishers, making friends with her fellow-editors. In spite of this, they both started feeling the mews flat was too small. Her first silences germinated there. Increasingly he was late home.

At this stage the blame is almost all Dan's. The work Nell did was pettifogging and monotonous, especially for a graduate with a better degree than he had managed to get himself. He was doing exactly what he wanted (not the same as he really needed) and she was marking galleys and time. He had also fallen a victim of the glamours and vulgarities of his new world—however disparagingly he might talk of it with people like Jane and Anthony.

The commercial cinema is like a hallucinogenic drug; it distorts the vision of all who work in it. What is at stake behind the public scenes is always personal power and prestige, which reduce the industry to a poker-table where every player must, if he is to survive, become some kind of professional cheat, or hustler. Success is always with the two-faced; and one can no more enter the game innocently (though Dan did his best) than a house with *BORDELLO* in neon lights across its front. That its madams, pimps, whores and bullies masquerade publicly as "distinguished" directors and stars, famous producers and agents, simply shows how much there is to hide.

It cannot be an art, in this form. No art could so invariably prefer the crook to the honest man, the Tartuffe to the plain-speaker, the mediocrity to the genius, accountancy to all aesthetic and moral principle; could instal a debased argument from populism, pandering to the lowest common denominator, at its heart. One day history will ask why so few truly adult films were ever made in the two countries with the most opportunities; what fatal reaction it was in the forced marriage between the Jewish and the Anglo-Saxon race-minds that generated so much corrupt shimmer, and so little real substance; and why such a hugely disproportionate amount of the lasting proof that the cinema can be an art, and a very great one, has come from countries outside the English-speaking world.

Dan very soon proved his own failure to ask such questions. He committed his second infidelity to Nell during this first picture. The female lead had been given to a girl whose face and legs were already a familiar stand-by on the cheaper sections of Fleet Street. She later went to work in America and got a celebrated nickname: the "British Open." She became a course all self-respecting West Coast studs had to have played over at least once. Studio gossip out at Pinewood claimed that she was already being laid—even between takes, according to one of the grips—by the *passé* American star who had been brought over to ensure the foreign distribution. Dan first found her synthetic and stupid. But only a producer as gormless and a director as sycophantic as the ones the film had would ever have cast her as the emotion-torn upper-class WAAF officer she was supposed to be playing. Then she grew faintly pathetic, a victim of circumstance, a casting martyr. It wasn't only the stale old sadness of peddled flesh. She did seem to have some occasional notion of how bad she was. That generally made her performance even worse but she was a trouper, in her fashion. She was also the first woman that Dan had met whose reputation was based purely on her sexuality. He began to realize after a week or two that for some reason she preferred his company to that of most other people around the stage. She was getting a fair amount of publicity build-up and Dan had to spend some time doing last-minute rewrites, but when they were both idle they took to chatting together.

He used to tease her a little; innocuously, and she was too dumb to be dry back, but she liked having her pin-up image gently mocked. It gave her the illusion that she could see through it.

This type of non-actress always craves the nearest tame intellectual's reassurance: I know that now and that it isn't really the wistful modesty the more skilled practitioners can make it seem but just an indispensable adjunct of big tits, like the dress cleft to the sternum or the shirt one size too small. Their motives are no more humane than when Circe asked Ulysses up for a drink . . . or those of Delilah turned barber. Not that Dan's motives were humane, of course; he was simply, if unconsciously, looking for a personification of all he felt seducing him elsewhere.

She had met Nell, she knew Dan was married; she must

also have known that she disturbed him physically. It came to the point when he knew he could have her for the asking. The day before a free day on her schedule, she asked him to "drop by" if he was in town and anywhere near her Curzon Street flat. He had said he must be at the studio. Too bad, she murmured; and her heavily ironic eyes said the rest.

I don't know what it was: whether mere lust or some perverse need to prove to myself that "success" was the highest moral good instead of ordinary human decency; whether it was Nell's increasingly frequent sulks and moods; whether it was the fatal memory of that afternoon with Jane, which by then had become a proof that wild selfishness can be got away with . . . and echo tenderly, poetically, secretly—while Nell could still remain nice, when she chose, to come home to. At the time I blamed the last most: Jane.

The shooting was almost finished before it happened. Dan had stopped going to Pinewood and was working on the final revisions of *The Red Barn*. Nell had gone to her office to proof-read. Just before midday the telephone rang. That voice. Circe claimed she had a script she wanted Ulysses to read, if he was free for lunch . . . Dan suddenly found both ropes and mast were imaginary. He took a taxi, went to Curzon Street, and screwed her. To be exact, he had not gone with that definitely in mind; but his usually inventive imagination had failed for once. The door had been opened by an already naked girl. He could only have turned and walked away. Many years later he met her by chance, indeed even sat opposite her at a Hollywood dinner party. She was more famous, or infamous, by then, and perhaps she was being discreet; but he had the impression that she had completely forgotten that they had ever been to bed together.

It had been done in silence, at some length; she had proved better at sex than at acting; and it had happened only that once. Deep down it confirmed his experience with Jane, though this time the dialogue about whether there was to be a future was cut down to two or three lines. He wasn't going to break up his marriage, she didn't expect him to; so let's get on with it. There really was, rather to Dan's surprise, a script she had been offered. He took it away with him and probably she expected him to bring it back and claim reading fees. Instead he talked about it with her over the telephone and returned it by post. She didn't seriously object when he killed further conversation, at least carnal, dead. She behaved as she was, beneath the dramatic pretensions: a sporting amateur, and satisfied as soon as flesh had trumped brains.

I mustn't dismiss this too lightly; the cynicism came later. Dan left the flat feeling stunned with self-shock; and I remember he had a miserable afternoon. He wandered across Hyde Park and ended up, heaven knows why, in the Geological Museum; perhaps because it was devoted to the non-human. Then he sat for an hour or more in a pub, even though he knew Nell would probably be home before him and he would have to invent some alibi. In fact she stayed on late to finish a set of proofs and he was given ample time to collect his wits and his damaged mask. It was very clear to him that he had done something wicked and that he must not let it happen again. But of course he had graduated; with Jane there had been a deeply suppressed but mutually recognized feeling, a justifying sense of uniqueness, of enormous difficulty, that this was (at least in hindsight) a springboard to higher, nobler things; to the life she now led, in fact.

But now he had done it with a slut, not only in a brothel decor but in a brothel way; only the money had been missing. He underwent the usual sequence of guilt and self-justification—he had been trapped by Nell, he needed freedom . . . by which he principally meant, though he hardly admitted it to himself, the freedom to exploit his growing success. So Nell became a foolishly high premium he had paid to insure against failure in life, both sexual and professional. He had long known he was not unattractive to women, but the adventure in Curzon Street went to his head after the first shock of it. He decided he must be very attractive—and I use "must" in both its descriptive and prescriptive sense. He adopted the disgusting habit of trying out this charm much more consciously than before. Always well out of Nell's sight, of course. He told himself it was only a game, a little revenge.

And also a little recompense, since outwardly he did try quite hard for a while to be more concerned for Nell. In July he handed in the finished version of *The Red Barn* to his new agent, waited to have his first reaction (warm and excited), then drove off with her for a holiday in France. They idled down to Provence, eked out four weeks there, then idled back. It was a success from the start: the weather, the food, the countryside, the sex, the suddenly discussible feeling that they had drifted apart during those previous months. Dan telephoned back to London from Avignon; both theater producers who had by then read the play wanted it . . . he and

Nell had the most expensive dinner of their then lives that evening, and came to other decisions over it. Nell would stop working and go in for motherhood, they would find a bigger flat or a small house as soon as they got back. That was delayed beyond the three weeks—Nell's holiday allowance—originally planned. She sent her letter of resignation from a drowsy little port, charmingly free of the vulgar mob, called St. Tropez.

I think Dan might at some point during that happy month have confessed to the Curzon Street coupling, but he had some buried terror as to how confession might then run on; or he clung to his secrets. In truth he remained intensely selfish. But the sun gave Nell a new body, contraceptives were abandoned, the heat made them both continuously randy, and if he still surreptitiously eyed other female bodies, it was without envy. They ran out of money (both permitted and illegal) and had to make do on the way back with flea-pits and cheaper and cheaper picnic meals; but even that had been fun. For months afterward the experience remained their true honeymoon; and not only because Nell proved to have conceived first time around. What the holiday also proved, alas, was that they could be happy (as at Oxford) only in the unreal, not the real. But neither of them saw that then.

*The Red Barn* was, I think if not genuinely new, at least fresh. It was probably lucky that I had only the sketchiest notion at the time of what Brecht was getting at. I came on the idea by pure chance, happening one day to pick up a contemporary account of the William Corder trial. All Maria Marten had meant to me before was the type exemplar of ham rural fustian. But I saw at once that there was an entertaining historical play to be disinterred. It had taken me some time to realize that William was the central character, not Maria; and I did take enormous pains over the dialogue. But the play's success was a team job: it had the best series of sets of its year, five fat and a number of good small parts. The cattle were with it from the start.

The anatomy of first major success is like the young human body, a miracle only the owner can fully savor . . . and even then, only at the time. Dan, at any rate, went through that following winter in a state of smug euphoria, well above the flak from minor setbacks. The only serious professional disappointment was the failure to get a New York production going; but in the New Year the play went on in Sweden and

West Germany, with negotiations for rights in progress with several other countries. The private clouds on the horizon did not seem very important at the time.

Though the ninety-nine-year lease I bought of the Notting Hill flat was probably the best business deal I ever did, unaided, in my life, Dan and Nell began having doubts as soon as they moved in. It was partly that miserable drive to keep up with the Joneses that is endemic in the show-business world. They started to feel they had quite unnecessarily undersold themselves. The sort of people they now began to mix with all lived in so much nicer surroundings—and so much more stylishly above their income, in many cases. They had seen small houses—in St. John's Wood, in Islington, in Fulham, and then promptly compared them unfavorably with the cottage at Wytham. A cottage there was on the market and they secretly hankered after that at the same time as they found a dozen reasons for its impossibility. For the first time in his life Dan now had an accountant: the cost of the lease in London meant they could not sanely afford the price of the cottage. Everything in the new home had finally to come from Heal's and they ran up huge bills. That did not prevent Nell from frequently blaming him later for not buying what they could not afford.

She had a tetchy pregnancy and took increasingly against the flat. One day it would be too large, the next it was "mad" not having realized a garden for the baby ought to have been the priority. Increasingly she resented being left alone, increasingly she harked back to our "dear little" mews. Cooking had never amused her, and in the last months of her pregnancy we took to going out almost every evening. I came to learn it was a way of avoiding rows. I mustn't exaggerate, she shared some of Dan's euphoria over the play, there was the baby . . . most of the time it was merely a feeling that the flat was probably a mistake, but not one of primary importance. Caro was born on April 10, and for a time other problems were forgotten. Dan had completed the first draft of his next play; and in the same week that he became a father he signed for his second filmscript.

I suppose the most terrible marriages are where the child is the wedge (or is used as the wedge) that splits the stone. Caro proved difficult, she seemed to run the gamut of all the ills that babies can make themselves heirs to, and she exhausted Nell both nervously and physically. I think I bore my share, I worked at home during the first draft. But somehow

Caro became tacitly like the flat itself: a good idea at the time, but only too often an apparent mistake in the actual experience. Then there was a certain amount of sisterly rivalry—Jane, pregnant again herself, had turned into a model mother, and Nell felt obliged to run in that race. I tried to persuade her to give up one of the two spare bedrooms we had to an *au pair* girl—anyone to keep her company, even some out-of-work actress. But Nell would neither cope nor admit that she could not cope; later she claimed that it was solely fear of what would happen when she took herself off to Wytham.

She did that more and more as the summer wore on and I had to spend more time away from the flat. I would see her and the baby solicitously onto the train at Paddington; and then return too happily to the flat and my work. I usually went down to fetch her at the next week-end, but my periods of freedom assumed the aspect of holidays. She had traveled that Oxford line so much more frequently. Perhaps the real trouble started there: in the bond among the three of them and the children in Oxford, from which Dan was now partially excluded—though it was not apparent to him then.

From this time on, I feel less guilty. Nell began to stew when she was in London and mull over the injustices of her new role. They rapidly grew far worse than the old ones at the publisher's—as with the mews, that tended to become a beautiful broken future instead of the disliked stopgap it had actually seemed to her at the time; and would suddenly seem again, with that illogicality I find the least endearing thing in the female sex, if I proposed the simple solution of asking her old employers for work she could do at home.

The hopeless downward progression of this kind of situation, especially when the two involved have more than their ration of intransigent selfishness, has become so familiar nowadays that I won't spell out all the stages. Such changes in a person's character, and in the character of a relationship, don't announce themselves dramatically; they steal slowly over months, masking themselves behind reconciliations, periods of happiness, new resolves. Like some forms of lethal disease, they invite every myth of comforting explanation before they exact the truth.

I suppose nothing was more symptomatic of the hidden cancer than Nell's reversed attitude to my film work. She began to resent it without distinction—with some reason in the case of the first film when it appeared. The critics slated it, though two—one of whom was Barney Dillon—saved my embarrassment a little by excepting the script from their general thumbs-down. But the new script promised better, and I was enjoying the experience of working with Tony. He was not a great director by any stretch of the adjective, but not a fool, either, and a marked improvement on his predecessor.

The plot was based on an original idea of his, a psychological thriller, which we called *The Intruder* at the time, though it was released as *Face in the Window*. He knew what he wanted and made me work to get it; and at the same time was open to ideas. I learned a lot from him also on the business of demarcation lines. Nell took against my enthusiasm when I came back from sessions with him, and I began to hide it . . . if it still wasn't spoken, it was implicit in her attitude that I had sold out, I was on the grab for quick success and cheap limelight. Anthony and Jane's names were invoked one evening, when something *had* been spoken. They couldn't understand why I should want to get involved in such a corrupt *demi-monde*, why play-writing was not enough . . . or so she said. They certainly didn't say so to my face, though I sensed a growing distance between us, a breakdown of vocabulary and shared values. The cinema also internationalizes; and I began to see them as obscurely provincial. Two forms of profound obstinacy were gearing up for battle; and I resented the fifth column Nell now formed in my own camp.

One evening, it must have been in July or August, I came home to find Nell and Caro had decamped to Wytham without warning. We had had a long row the previous night and she had still been asleep when I left for the office after breakfast. I went down and fetched her back at the week-end. Perhaps Anthony still knew nothing then, but I could see a questioning and reproachful light in Jane's eyes. Nell had certainly talked to her. That made me very angry, though I managed to conceal it.

I was by then doing the second draft. Because there was some mess-up over the availability dates of one of the chief actors, there was a hurry to get the new film off the ground. I was given a room at the production office and a part-time secretary. Andrea was two years older than me and half-Polish—not really a humble secretary at all, but already well on her way to being one of the best production secretaries on this side of the Atlantic: a kind of regimental sergeant-major, though her breed must use tact and a cool head where the other struts and bellows. I liked her at once for her professionalism: impossible not to admire the speed and accuracy with which she typed out my drafts and would talk about them, sometimes suggest a useful cut, point out a weakness. She didn't attract me physically, she had rather a heavy body and there was something about her of that accusing resignation of the career girl. I didn't know then that she had been married, since she seldom talked about herself. The only thing Slavonic about her, or at least not English, were her eyes. They were very fine, very direct, almost jade-green, much lighter than hazel. It all happened very slowly; began merely as a feeling of relief, the contrast between never knowing how an evening with Nell would end and coming to rely on that useful, intelligent camaraderie in the office to give some point and sanity to daily life. She came sometimes when I went to show new scenes to Tony, who used to fire off his own suggestions faster than I could write them down, and I could see he felt the same about her as I did myself: that she was a pro to her fingertips and a good shrewd head to have at one's side.

We had no relationship outside work. Usually she went out and bought me sandwiches, occasionally I took her out to lunch in one of the cheaper places nearby. But finally I came to hear a little about her broken marriage. It had been to one of the Poles who had escaped to Britain and become a fighter ace. Peace had turned him into a sadistic drunkard and dabbler in expatriate politics. Now she lived with her Polish mother somewhere behind Marble Arch. Just how much of a monster he had been, and remained, to her in private I did not hear in detail until later, but that was already hinted at. She was a dry woman and had her share of the gallows humor that hangs over movie-making like the smell of malt over a brewery; but she gave the impression that this was defensive, cryptic coloration. Something in her had been badly hurt by her marriage. I lost her when the production schedules and all the rest had to be got out, and I missed her. I was very careful not to talk much about her to Nell. They met once or twice and Nell didn't like her, or professed not to; but she was beginning to dislike everyone on that side of my life by then and she evidently saw no cause for sexual jealousy.

There was some final rewriting to be done when we started shooting, again down at Pinewood. Tony notoriously hated working with idle faces watching behind him, and I didn't go to the sets very much. Andrea and I were often alone in the production office. I started going down there when it was no longer really necessary. Word gets round the film industry much faster than in any other artistic world; and the word was that this script was good, that Tony was pleased with it, that I was learning fast. I was reliable . . . I basked in that. I wanted to learn the other techniques of my new business, too. Secretly I even had dreams of directing myself one day.

I had about this time—with plenty of unhelpful advice from Nell—to face up to what I wanted to be. Another script was already in the offing. It was not really a dilemma. I knew (or thought I knew) that the cinema could never be as serious for me as the theater. But it was fun, and it brought in the money. If I wanted to say something really personal and "important," it could only be on the stage. The new play I had in mind (which eventually became The Production) would establish that: that I had the compromises, the false pressures and premises of the film world in perspective. But I felt I wasn't ready for it for a while; and perhaps I was also a little scared of insulting the goose that laid the golden script-fees. I was certainly too close to the present production to invent safely unrecognizable characters.

Above all there was the need to prove to Nell that she was wrong. When I took the third script, however, there was a marital lull. She seemed to accept that I was not going to give up this alternative career; and that if she couldn't approve of it, she could at least approve the money it was bringing in. My new agent had seen to it that I was no longer in the bargain basement. I indulged Nell. I knew we were spending too much, but if it brought more peace at home I felt it was justifiable.

Then something predictive: one noon down at the studio Andrea seemed a little depressed, Dan asked her why, and she said it was her birthday, something about birthdays when you were a child . . . how you never quite grew up enough to treat them as ordinary days. Dan went straight to the canteen and bought a half-bottle of champagne. She laughed, they drank it. Then at lunch Dan announced the birthday to the others, there was more champagne . . . it was nothing. By chance afterward he and she went back to the production office alone together. The empty half-bottle sitting on her desk: she turned and kissed him. It wasn't the kiss, which was quick and affectionate, against his cheek not his mouth. But something in a fractional hesitation of the embrace, a waiting, an equally brief look in her eyes before she turned away to make some phone-call. Dan knew she was saying the camaraderie was on her side a pretense. That was all. Someone came in, and the next day it was exactly as before.

Then a few nights later: Nell and Dan had just gone to bed and he made one of those gestures all husbands and wives evolve and recognize as a suggestion. It was very sharply rebuffed. He said sorry; as lightly as possible. But Nell lay stiff as a rake. After fifteen seconds of that she got angrily out of bed and lit a cigarette; another sort of preamble he had come to recognize only too well.

"What is it this time?"

"You know damn well what it is."

"That's why I asked the question."

She hated what she called his "B-movie sarcasms." She said nothing, but ripped one of the curtains aside and stared out at the night.

"I don't know what you want out of life."

"I want a divorce."

He had come home late and they had had to rush out to dinner with friends—to be precise, with the girl who had got her the former job at the publishers and her husband. Dan knew she hadn't enjoyed the evening, that she had been brewing over something, and had put it down to the other girl, the tittle-tattle about publishing: the illogical envy of a career she did not really want again. But this was something new.

"Why?"

He waited, but she said nothing. He was suddenly very scared, he had some notion that Jane had been mad and . . . he asked why again.

"You know why."

"That I deprived you of a job you loathed when you actually did it?"

"Oh for God's sake." There was more silence. Then she said, "You're a bloody good liar, I'll give you that."

"I don't begin to know what this is all about."

"It's about the affair you're having with that Polish cow."

He let out a breath—outwardly of amused contempt for the accusation, inwardly of relief.

"Okay. Let's have it. Or was the letter anonymous?"

"You admit it?"

"I admit absolutely nothing. Except that I wish you were a Polish cow. Instead of a paranoiac little English bitch."

"Yes, you'd love that."

Dan got out of bed to go to her, but she turned on him before he could reach her. He could see her face in the streetlights from below. It managed to look both frightened and venomous—or obsessed. And it stopped him: the feeling that she had undergone some secret change of personality, that he no longer knew or understood her at all.

He said, "It's not true, Nell."

"Her ex-husband telephoned this afternoon. And told me a few facts about her. You're apparently beating a well-trodden path. I suppose you know that."

"But the man's a bloody lunatic. She's already had to get a court order to stop him pestering her mother. The whole office knows that."

They stood six feet apart, facing each other.

"He sounded very sane to me."

"Well we'll see what the law thinks. I'll sue the sod for slander."

"He says it's all over Pinewood. Everyone knows."

But there was a slight climb-down in her voice.

"Nell, the man's deranged, for Christ's sake. Apparently he started doing this with her mother last year. He's a Catholic, he won't give her a divorce, he . . . honest to God, how can you belive such rubbish?"

"Because it could so easily be true." Dan turned away and found the cigarettes. He must have been angry, because he felt like agreeing with her—and telling her why. But she jumped on. "He saw you going into her flat last week."

"I gave her a lift home. She asked me up to meet her mother. Just a drink. That was all. Half an hour."

"Which you forgot to mention."

"I seem to remember you were too full of the horrors of motherhood for any normal conversation that evening."

She digested that. "Do you usually give her lifts home?"

"She's running a production office, for God's sake. She's usually the last to leave. No."

"You seem to know an awful lot about her."

"As I have a perfect right to. She's also good at her job. And a nice human being." He took a breath. "Liking her is not infidelity, Nell."

She had gone back to staring out the window. Dan sat on the end of the bed.

"I suppose you tell her all about the paranoiac little English bitch you made the mistake of marrying."

"That's so cheap I'm not going to answer it."

There was a silence; it was rather like a medieval joust. After each tilt she had to think up some new trick of attack.

"You're cutting me absolutely out of your life. I know nothing about you anymore. Sidney rang this afternoon." Sidney was Dan's new agent. "About the American offer. I don't even know what the American offer is."

"It's another possible script. Nothing's settled yet. And I haven't cut you out of my life. You've done that yourself."

"You're becoming something I don't understand."

"Because you don't want to grow up. You want nothing to change."

She gave a bitter sniff. "Of course. I simply adore this ghastly white elephant of a flat and being cooped up in it every day while you go off and—"

"Then let's move. Let's get a house. An *au pair*. A nanny. Whatever you want."

"As long as I leave you in peace."

"I see. I drop everything so that you can have someone to row with all day long."

She spoke in a quieter voice. "I don't know why Anthony and Jane can live such an affectionate and civilized life together and we—"

"Oh *fuck* Anthony and Jane." But when he went on, it was more evenly. "If anyone's having an affair, it's you. With them."

"Thank you."

"Well it's true. If you wanted to marry a don and live among the dreaming spires, then why the hell . . ."

"Because you were different then."

"Thank you."

"You started it."

And so on, and so on. It ended in her tears, and a new batch of resolutions. But they had no consistency. She rang up her friend, and started reading again; but then got bored with that. First, she would stick it out at the flat; then we had a brief phase of house-hunting, only to discover that prices were beginning to rise; and neither of us ever felt certain we really liked what we looked at. Once again her heart became set on somewhere in the country—that became the priority. She blamed London, in some moods, for everything that had gone wrong.

Perhaps the greatest irony was that the incident brought Andrea and myself an important step closer to what finally took place. I felt I had to warn her about what the wretched Vladislav was doing and somehow I couldn't bring myself to do so in the office. I had to wait several days, but then Nell and Caro and I went down to Wytham for the week-end and Nell decided to stay on till the Wednesday—or rather, in pursuit of one of the new resolutions, did not want to stay on, but I talked her into it. So I took Andrea out to dinner one evening—I didn't mislead her, I told her I had something rather difficult to say. I think she must have guessed, though she was shocked when she knew, very apologetic, wanted to meet Nell to explain . . . but Nell had made me promise not to do what I was doing. She had rather rapidly promoted the "Polish cow" to "poor woman."

At last, at the Chinese restaurant we went to, I was given the full story of Andrea's marriage. She'd been in the WAAF during the war and her knowledge of Polish had made her posting and work obvious. She had fallen for Vladislav, married him in no time; his fundamental instabilities had seemed natural enough, part of the stress of scrambles, missions, swastikas stenciled beneath the cockpit. But peace, the deal with Stalin, had turned him anti-British; as did his failure to make it as a commercial airline pilot. He was already drinking heavily by then. Andrea had been dragged through the Polish thing and the Catholic thing and the expatriate thing; and had also discovered that she could never have children . . . all of which had left her with a kind of sad contempt for everything Polish (except her mother) and a continuing guilt over the rogue male she had married. Becoming what she was now had saved her life; or at any rate, her own sanity. Even then I sensed a much deeper despair than the cynical shell she sometimes wore at the office suggested. She felt trapped in some hopeless way. In effect she was both Nell and Dan: Nell, in leading a life that did not satisfy her full self; and Dan, in feeling she had been tricked into a wrong marriage. She told me she had had a number of affairs since the marriage died, but it had always seemed as if "some other woman" was involved. One such liaison (it shocked me to learn—not its having happened, but my not having realized it) had been with Tony, a year before. He was married, with a family, it had all been conducted in great secrecy. They're all rats in our business, she said, even the nicest.

I mustn't make Andrea sound too coolly objective about herself; or too stolid and sexless physically. She was what the French call a *belle laide;* someone whose charm grew very slowly on you. The body misled, especially beside the twenty-year-old birds producers hire to make their coffee and soothe their eyes and egos. But the face was really rather striking and the eyes were remarkable, incomparably the finest I have ever known well. This produced a little advantage for her, since they were always the thing one wanted most to look at. She was not a woman it was easy to keep at a distance, there was something of the conscious *femme fatale* about her. Perhaps it was a compensation for the purely physical attractions prettier women can use. She certainly knew she possessed more magnetism than most men realized when they first met her. Then she was older than I was—and not only in the literal sense—perhaps something vaguely maternal about her body . . . I don't know.

In return, that evening, I talked a little about my own marriage. It was not moaning, I even justified Nell's attitude—and a good deal more to Andrea than I secretly did to myself. I suppose outwardly the evening must have seemed to confirm that any other relationship than that of colleagues and good friends was impossible. I kissed her on the cheek and pressed her hand when I took her home; then got in the taxi and went off. I could imagine going to bed with her by then, but not in the manner of my two previous adulteries. Neither her temperament nor our working relationship would have allowed a brief liaison.

When she killed herself in 1962, it depressed me for weeks. I hadn't seen her then for several years and it took me some time to understand why it seemed a much greater loss, and guilt, than outward circumstances warranted. It wasn't even a feeling that if our eventual two years together had ended in marriage instead of force of circumstance, or mutual refusal to disrupt our ways of life, then she would never have ended her existence. I knew her too well by then and the depressive streak in her nature. It was far more a feeling that she had had the last word about all our private lives, all our profession, all our age. God really had been a frustrated and paranoiac alien; and we had all been members of that seedy Polish veterans' club he had wasted his life drunkenly managing off the Bayswater Road. I never came face to face with Vladislav, but I have seen him ever since she died; implacably behind each scene of the great illusion.

People in the carriage began to stir and shift. I saw streetlamps mistily reflected in black water. We drew, in our scrupulously maintained English silence, into the most English of all cities. Mother Oxford, Venus-Minerva, triple-haunted, hundred-tongued; Shakespeare's Verona and every student's Elsinore since molding-time began. Not a city, but an incest.

# Rencontre

I recognized Jane at once, as I stood in the throng waiting to get through the ticket barrier. I waved and she raised a hand briefly in return; as if we hadn't seen each other merely for a few days, instead of sixteen years. A woman of forty-five in a long leather coat, fur-trimmed at neck and hem; bare-headed, no bag, hands in pockets; the face seemed much, much older, but she had retained something of that old discreteness, some aura of difference from everyone around her. Even if she had been a total and chance-glimpsed stranger, I should have looked at her twice. An elderly passenger ahead of me spoke to her as he passed. I saw her smile. They exchanged words for a few moments. It was that leather coat—it had a faint flamboyance, a staginess. She didn't seem to have gone gray, her hair must have been tinted, though it was less dark than I remembered, a shade more auburn; quite long, fastened loosely with a silver comb at the back. She retained a slightly Spanish air, always part of her *Gestalt* in my memory. In every other way she looked a stylish don's wife, very much in her own city.

She was still talking to the other passenger when I reached the ticket inspector. But she excused herself then, and he went on. She didn't move, she had only the smallest smile as I came to her. At the last moment she lowered her eyes. There was a bizarre moment when neither of us seemed to know what to do. She still had her hands in her pockets. Then she took them both out and reached them to me.

"I've forgotten my lines."

I pressed the extended hands, then rather awkwardly leaned forward and kissed her cheek.

"No lines needed."

She did look me in the eyes then; a hint of an old irony—or perhaps a question, I couldn't tell.

"You haven't changed."

"Nor have you. You look stunning."

"Wrong participle."

In close-up she looked her age. There were lines of tiredness as well as of natural years. She wore no make-up. I sensed too a hidden fear. She was very uncertain of who I was. We both smiled, the way strangers do at their own stiffness.

"The car's outside."

"Fine."

She turned and led the way out into the night.

"I'm . . . we're so grateful, Dan, I . . ."

"I was due back. Honestly."

She glanced down at the wet pavement, then bowed her head in reluctant acceptance. We walked over to where she had parked her car. She faced me across its roof.

"Can you stand seeing him this evening?"

"Of course."

"I thought you might like a drink first. We could stop off at the Randolph."

"Marvelous. And I'm taking you to dinner afterwards."

"I've got something in. The *au pair* . . ."

"I insist."

Again there was a tiny clash of wills; and again she resolved it with a shrug of concession.

On the short journey to the Randolph she told me, clinically, almost indifferently, what the medical situation was with Anthony. What was initially a primary cancer of the stomach had become general; palliative surgery had failed. He was already surviving beyond the original prognosis. We exchanged news about her children, other relations, Caro. I said nothing about Barney. During these banalities I was far more aware of a secret happiness than a sadness; all those forgotten—I had not seen Oxford for sixteen years, either—and yet not forgotten streets and buildings, the woman driving beside me; but something much deeper than that, the strange reversals of time, of personal histories . . . moments that you are glad, for once, to have survived to. Perhaps the presence of death always does that. Lost values regain meaning, to be still alive becomes the fundamental luck each ordinary, compromising day manages to bury.

We found a table at the Randolph. She took her Russian-looking coat off: a trouser-suit, a plain cream shirt, a brown-black bull's-eye agate in pinchbeck at its neck. She seemed taller and thinner than I remembered; perhaps it was just the clothes. I ordered her a Campari and a large Scotch for myself. The waiter had hardly turned his back before I brought the small talk to an end.

"I've imagined today a good many times over the years, Jane. But never quite like this." She stared at the table in front of us. "It was all my fault. I just want to get that out of the way."

She murmured, "All our faults." Then, "That's one of the few articles of faith Anthony and I still agree on."

"You're not a Catholic anymore?"

The smile was more natural. "It has been a long time, hasn't it?"

"I spent last night pumping Caro."

Still she smiled, though she looked down again.

"I lapsed years ago, I'm afraid."

"And Anthony not?"

"He's taken the last rites. What they call the Sacrament of the Sick nowadays. I think." She must have realized how odd that vagueness sounded. "The crows visit him, anyway." Then she said, "It's become one of those areas of non-communication over the years. What they say every decent marriage needs."

The waiter came with our drinks. I noted that double recourse to "they"; and had a few moments to discard the illusion that envied marriages must be flawless.

"And the children?"

"Have taken after their godless mother."

"I didn't realize."

She sipped her Campari. I had waited to see if she would make a toast out of it. But I wasn't to be given such an obvious, if trite, clue to her real feelings. She began to puzzle me, perhaps because I had come with so many preconceptions . . . or misread Caro's view of her. On the one hand I had expected more of a brisk maturity, on the other I had imagined a greater warmth. That permanent faint smile I had always associated with her seemed to have disappeared; and so had all her ancient vitality—that mute electricity, disturbance, poetry with which she had always charged even the most trivial meeting; in a hurried wave across a crowded street, a smile between other heads at a party. What I began to feel was a deep reserve, and I didn't know what it hid.

"I suppose if faith can take blows like this, it must be real."

"He's always been rather good at deriving certainty from incompatible events." She added, "Or truths."

"The ultimate absurdity?"

"Something like that." She made an effort to be more communicative. "He hasn't been morbid about it—rather brave, actually. Very philosophical indeed. For a philosopher. But it's much closer to him now than anything else. The real dialogue is all with that." She made a little grimace. "The eternal verities or something."

"That's understandable?"

"I suppose so. *Chacun á sa mort.*"

"Did he say that—or you?"

She gave a token grin. "He'll die an Oxford man. All ironies intact."

I examined that grin.

"My guess is he's not the only one who's being brave."

She shrugged. "Nell thinks I'm being very hard about the whole business." Again I watched her face in profile, her searching for words a foreigner might understand. "She's become rather odiously conventional and Daily-Telegraphish over these last years."

"So I've gathered from Caro."

"A pillar of the county. I think we underrated Andrew."

"He was never as silly as he made out."

"I remember you used to say that."

"She's been happy with him?"

A very cursory smile: as if such things didn't matter. "I think as much as it's in her nature to be."

"I'm glad."

But my eyes remained avoided. We both watched a group of students sitting across the room. They made our small dandyisms of the late 1940s look very puny indeed. I was increasingly set back by her; she was so unforthcoming, disconnected, as if she wanted me to deduce, without saying it, that I was not here by her choice. I could have done with a little more of the conventionality she had just accused Nell of. I made another attempt to bridge everything that lay between us.

"What does he want of me, Jane?"

"Just to rewrite the past a little?"

"What does that mean?"

She hesitated.

"We haven't talked about you, Dan. Or the past. For many years now. I know he's very anxious indeed to see you, but he hasn't really . . . vouchsafed why." She went on in a quicker voice. "The trouble with being highly civilized people is that one has techniques for burying highly uncivilized truths. All I really know is that he grew very distressed when I tried to suggest we had no right to force this on you." She added, "That at least was . . . authentic."

"Then I'm on his side. I think you had."

"All this doesn't mean I'm not very grateful you've come." For a moment I had her eyes, almost her old eyes; a candor, a self-mockery. "I'm not in a mood to see much hope or reason in anything at the moment. You mustn't take any notice."

Which of course made sure that I did: it was increasingly strange, as if our former relative status was now reversed so completely that some indication must be shown in every sentence and gesture. I was far too important and famous now, she seemed to be saying, to have serious time for a backwater being like herself.

"It would be a miracle if you felt anything else."

"Perhaps." Her smile was very artificial, and she leaped, absurdly, to yet another apology. "Before I forget, Nell asked me to say she was sorry about what she said over the telephone. About your friend, she . . ."

"I rose to the bait."

"I've only seen one of her films. I thought she was very good."

"She may go places. If she keeps away from people like me."

"Presumably she has views on that?"

I glanced across at the students opposite.

"She belongs over there, Jane. I'm the wrong table."

"She wants to marry you?"

I shook my head. "I'm just shepherding her through her first experience of Hollywood. Trying to delay the inevitable."

"What's that?"

"Her believing in it."

She smiled down, but once again there was a shade too much conventional politeness of response, a suggestion that her mind was somewhere else. I saw her glance surreptitiously at her watch.

"Should we be going?"

"He'll have had his so-called supper by now."

"And ours? Where does one eat these days?"

We had a further short argument over that, Nell had brought a brace of pheasant from Compton on her last visit

. . . but I made her give in, and on the way out I booked us a table at the Italian restaurant she recommended while she rang home to warn the *au pair* girl. Shouldn't I stay at the Randolph? But it was her turn to be adamant. We set off for the hospital.

For once a camera would have done better; the queries in eyes, the avoided looks, the hidden reservations on both sides, the self-consciousness. I still retained an image of feminine wax stamped by Anthony and his views of life; but it seemed that some sad middle-aged variant of an original self, an independence now turned to an indifference, had taken the place of that. Nor did she conform to what I had expected from Caro; for some reason I was not being shown that face.

I knew I had to rediscover her, along with a system of communication: one that could be quite exceptionally devious, and hide a profound narcissism . . . and could also be sharply censorious. No town is farther, when it wants to be, from the tame conversational norms of the rest of middle-class England, with all its conditioned evasions and half-finished sentences, its permanent poised flight to the inarticulate. I had lived for so long in exile, in a world whose only "test" was one's degree of craftsmanship in a given context, and aeons from this tiny society that lived essentially, for all its outward academic orientations, by ideal and abstract—and frequently absurd—notions of personal truth and behavior.

I had also, behind the apparent deference, felt obscurely condescended to; the way intellectuals will condescend to peasants, make all kinds of urbane adjustment for their ignorance. It made me feel that I must come with a smell of the vulgar outside world I inhabited; that at least one reason why she was not more explicit about what she really felt was that I was too tarnished and blunted by the second-rate minds of a second-rate world to understand. That could co-exist with the fear that I was now the worldly-wise one, from well beyond this ivory castle with all its linguistic and ethical punctilios. Our little argument over eating out or in symbolized it. I demanded some recognition of what I had become; and she granted it, though it was silly. She had objected to the Italian restaurant as soon as she mentioned it—it was "so absurdly expensive"; as if to say that money ought to be a problem in our lives, we should never have progressed from studenthood.

So I felt baffled as we drove through the misty streets, and disappointed; and increasingly nervous—knowing how far away the woman beside me was, and guessing her husband might be even farther. Once again I had a sharp and sudden longing for the girl who was physically far away in Los Angeles and whom I had just demoted from reality to a good deed; not for her body, but for her franknesses and simplicities, her presentness. Film excludes all but now; permits no glances away to past and future; is therefore the safest dream. That was why I had given so much of my time and ingenuity to it.

# Crimes and Punishments

The effect of public on private history is mysterious; or perhaps I should say—since our century can hardly be accused of not trying to solve the enigma—mysterious to me. All my life I have veered between a belief in at least a degree of free will and in a determinism. The only clear conclusion I have come to is that what have appeared to be my own freely taken decisions provide very little evidence of more wisdom than the blind dictates of destiny. One of the monsters in my father's seventeenth-century theological bestiary was quietism; it always sounded attractive to me when he denounced it . . . the notion that both virtue and vice were the enemies of grace. I certainly haven't found the grace, but neither have I found any good reason for supposing that to surrender to one's nature pays any worse dividends than resisting it. The problem, of course, the ultimate catch, is knowing what one's true nature is.

I can't remember that the national misery of that first decade after the war, the general resentment that having won the bloody thing, we now had to pay for it, particularly worried anyone in the milieux that I inhabited. It seems to me today that the one abiding drive of all my generation—and I do not mean just my class—was intense selfishness. We watched the imperial and commercial underpinnings of our culture collapse without regret (that came later), mainly because the disappearance of a national mission gave our selfishness more *Lebensraum*. If most of us were liberals in public, we were all parties of one in private—foreshadowing the many desertions to the right that took place in the Sixties. The current situation, with everything determined in terms of the entrenched rich versus the would-be rich, was already latent.

Most of us still saw the confrontation in the context of Marxist theory. The true face of British organized labor and its party had yet to be seen. None of us quite guessed how crypto-bourgeois and conservative it would become or how the country's political life would perish away into a sluggish battle less between "Tories" and "Socialists" than between the comforts of apathy (historical destiny) and occasional fits of free will, or mutual blackmailing between capital and the power to strike; or how the remaining national virtues (civic decency, hatred of violence and all the rest) would one day come to seem as much a result of sheer indolence as of positive choice. Even the absurd nostalgia for the imperial and military past that has appeared like a toadstool on rotting wood in recent years (and which I was by no means sure the sceptical line I was taking over Kitchener in my script would counter, though it had been an initial reason I took the thing) springs far less from political conviction than from a puzzled sense that the selfish present is somehow selling us all short.

Like so many individual members of its armed forces in that first decade of "peace," the whole country felt itself demobilized—from centuries of boring old duty to others, false prestige, spurious uniformity of character and behavior. The 1951 Festival of Britain was not at all the herald of a new age, but the death-knell of the old one. We then broke up into tribes and classes, finally into private selves.

I am not against this, in principle. I have never felt "British" since my schooldays . . . only English, and even that tenuously most of the time. But I think it is clear now that we made a bad mess of the transition from nation of brain-washed patriots to population of inturned selves. We failed to see what was really happening; and just as we also failed to evolve new political parties to meet the needs—and dangers—of an increasingly self-centered society, so also we lacked the honesty to throw away the old masks. Obsession with self was everywhere, yet we treated it like some personal secret that had to be hidden from everyone else . . . so on with the Puritan motley—endless public concern about the economy, about Britain's new role (as if it were some distinguished actor), the Suez farce, the more recent rantings against pornography and the permissive society, the triumph of Carnaby over Downing Street, of television bread-and-circuses over true democratic feeling. All that my generation and the one it sired have ever cared a damn about is personal destiny; all the other destinies have become blinds. This may be good, I no longer know; but the enormous superstructure of hypocrisy and the clouds of double-talk emitted in the (still incomplete) process must make us stink in the nostrils of history.

I am not pretending that Dan was honest and prescient; ready from the beginning to murder an unborn child rather than leave his smallest desire unsatisfied—though I wish now he had trailed a touch more sulfur and rather fewer compromises and lies. If he did stand a little more substantially for the future than most of his contemporaries, it was merely because he had more offered to his selfishness—and more opportunities to indulge it. I think Nell stood no chance.

The age of self offered him old sins he could convert into supposed new freedoms. It set her in a cage. That was her real jealousy; and his real adultery.

Dan was already, like the entire country faced with the Hottentots who begin at Calais, closing up. The intense private world, part pure imagination, part imaginatively altered reality, that he had lived in since childhood now came into its own. If it had sometimes seemed a perversity, a wickedness, in the past, it was now, with success, forgiven and sanctified—and boldly took over the course of his life. It was less and less inclined to brook interference, distraction, claim-jumping. Nell became a threat, a potential interloper, who might one day sneak in and assay the "gold" in those hidden gray brain-folds—and find it lacking. I suspect our growing incompatibility was at least as much a matter of history as of personal psychologies.

If I had been born into an earlier world, where society punished the heretic, I should very probably never have betrayed Nell—or at any rate I should have concealed the betrayal much better. But I was what the Victorians banned from their arts: a dramatist. I think they condemned and castrated the theater for so long because they knew the stage is a long step nearer an indecent reality than the novel. It tells secrets publicly, it gabs to strangers, its lines are spoken not by anonymous print, in a solitude like that of defecation or masturbation, merely in the single mind, but by men and women in front of an audience. The novel, print, is very English; the theater (despite Shakespeare) is not. I was always conscious of this paradox, of my all-hiding private self and my lying public one; my unwritten *Sonnets* and my all too written *Plays*.

In 1954 I did my first "big" script—the fourth chronologically. The locations were to be shot in Spain. I went out to

Hollywood for the first time, since it was also my first encounter with a "big" producer—a sacred monster . . . and like all his kind, much more the noun than the adjective by the standards of any sane view of man. Nell and Caro came to America with me, but they stayed with her mother and stepfather on the East Coast. During my three weeks alone on the West I slept with a girl who picked me up in the bar of my hotel. She wanted an entrée to the world I had just got my own precarious foothold in, but she was much more a wry tramp, of the kind Preston Sturges made Veronica Lake portray so well, than an ambitious whore. I grew to like her both in and out of bed, not least because she had an easy day-to-day acceptance of life that contrasted very pleasantly with Nell's increasing need to live in anything but the present. I found even her naïveties and ignorance (she was only a month or two in from the Midwest herself) endearing—especially as my own superiority in knowledge was tenuous in the extreme . . . no more than a product of what I was picking up each day as I went along.

It was also my first encounter with someone who had deromanticized sex, who seemed to regard it, like so many Americans, as a mixture of anatomy and gastronomy—to be discussed before, during and afterward, like a meal. I wasn't used to such frankness, and it fascinated me at first, though that side of things began to lose its charms before I returned to Nell—and has gone on losing charm ever since. Limbs are nouns and action verbs, and there is nothing more profoundly destroying of all but skin pleasure than the need to assess and analyze what is really a perfectly sufficient language in itself; and like music, to be enjoyed best in silence. I am not blaming Elaine for conforming to her culture—indeed I owed her a lot for helping me to understand it, and my own.

In short, it was an affair with America itself. Despite Elaine, I didn't quite realize during that first visit how far California is from the rest of the United States. I liked it a lot, though less for intrinsic reasons than for its total non-Englishness and the endless facilities it offered me for suppressing that side of my nature. I felt very little guilt over her; or just enough guilt to keep our three weeks of dates and sex-games as clandestine as possible. I telephoned Nell almost every day—less out of solicitude than to be sure she wouldn't suddenly fly out and surprise me. I suppose I had become quite amoral by then; or sheiklike. Nell didn't repel me physically, which made her physically easy to deceive—and like most women, she set great store by that lying test. I also quite enjoyed the week I spent with her in Connecticut before we returned home, not least because the visit to Hollywood had given me a cachet in her parents' eyes I had previously lacked.

Our working holiday in Spain during the location filming, later that year, was not a success. We rented a small villa just outside Valencia, near the beach, and there was a Spanish maid to look after Caro. But Nell grew bored with the long set-ups. I could hardly blame her, they began to bore me myself, but this was the first time I had seen such stuff, involving many hundreds of extras, and I felt I had a professional duty to pay attention. I was also kept busy by my sacred monster, whose anxiety and incipient megalomania began to soar as shooting approached and remained at a sustained high pitch throughout the ensuing weeks. I had been warned that this always happened by the young American director who was also being given his first big chance, and we managed to weather the floods of four-letter abuse and the constant threat of being sacked. Scenes that had been "great" a day before would turn overnight—usually the one before shooting— "lousy." All through the writing the wretched old man had showered me with his own ideas, delivering them with all the delicacy of a calving glacier . . . and these dreadful whims and notions of his had a habit of floating back weeks and even months afterwards, as barren as icebergs, but always threatening to sink any intelligent course the director and I advocated. All this added more fuel to Nell's distrust and contempt for the whole activity.

She developed an equally strong streak of intellectual snobbishness over the petty rivalries, the shallow chat, the general monomania and absorption in "shop" that characterizes movie people on location the world over. It is, or was then, a world without university graduates and any terms of reference outside the one art and industry; and as irrationally hierarchical as Ancient Egypt. Her contempt for me grew in strict proportion with my refusal to dismiss it *en bloc*. In turn I felt my script, that precious seed from which sprang all this energy and spending of money, was insulted. Nell took to passing her days on the beach with Caro and the maid. I had a reason for not objecting to that; a continuing fear that someone among the production people who had come over from Hollywood might have had wind of my little affair there. I didn't want any of them to get too close to Nell.

Some months later, we were now in the spring of 1955, I was back in London and on my second script for Tony. Andrea was again the production secretary, the long immanent feeling between us one day boiled over . . . I don't know how Nell finally guessed what had happened, but to prove her guess she hired a private detective. I came home one evening to find a carbon of his report laid out for me to read. She and Caro had disappeared. After the initial shock it came as a relief. In the end I rang Oxford. They must have been expecting the call, for Anthony answered, refused to fetch Nell, refused to discuss anything over the telephone—and insisted on coming down to London to see me.

A couple of days later he appeared at the flat and I took him out to lunch. I expected to have one of his ethical riot acts read over my head, but he was surprisingly matter-of-fact. Jane and he had realized for some time that things weren't going well, it was a matter for my own conscience, he didn't propose to judge the rights and wrongs of it all. I suspected that he was secretly frightened of me, perhaps of what I might say about Nell and her habit of retreating to Wytham at the drop of a disagreement. He was outwardly understanding, almost deferential toward my professional life and world—in a way no true-blue Oxford don, as he was by then, would ever truly feel at heart.

Nell was "very hurt" and would talk of nothing but a divorce. Yet he thought, if I wanted to make some attempt to mend the marriage, that Jane and he could argue her into at least waiting a while before she took action. He pressed for that course—and (perfectly fairly) used Caro as an argument; but too quickly agreed that as much damage could be done by constantly rowing as by separated parents. I then told him—I bound him to secrecy, which he observed—that there had been other women. I gave no names or details, but I could see the disclosure shocked both of him: the middle-class Englishman as well as the Catholic philosopher. I detected something Jesuitical in his outward reaction; in former days he would have had that out, tried to discover what drove me to such behavior; now he evidently thought it more politic to play the man of the world.

He had to be back in Oxford that evening and we parted about three, having grown increasingly guarded and remote with one another. My lack of contrition (except over Caro) and my general acceptance that I was the man I was (which was not the man he had thought) must have distressed and angered him. But he showed no sign of it on that occasion. Very probably I do him an injustice, he was sincerely trying to appear neutral, but the paradoxical effect of all this diplomacy was that I wished we had been more brutal with each other. I decided he had been playing priest. He had condemned me in secret beyond appeal; the courtesy was for the already damned, not the possibly innocent. I think the real trouble was simply that I still respected his judgment and that he supposed I now despised it. I am trying to explain what happened later.

I then alternated between moods of not caring a tinker's curse and less frequent ones of regretting the world I had cut myself off from. I didn't miss Nell at all except in minor domestic ways. But then Andrea moved in, and even that need was canceled. I did miss Caro, though disgracefully little, if I am honest; I think the major loss seemed to be of Anthony and Jane. It told me something of why I had married Nell in the first place; but it did not help—what is it in Langland about love being lighter than a linden-leaf, more piercing than the needle's point?—my sense of rejection.

I had parted with Anthony on the understanding that mine was the next move. The weeks passed, I did nothing. I can't pretend it was Andrea's fault; she was unpossessive, she made no demands on the future. But that virtue in her did not make returning to Nell any more attractive. In the end it was Nell who moved, by means of a solicitor's letter. I did not defend the action. Nell was ice-cold in court—she came alone, without Anthony or Jane—and I think did not look at me once throughout the proceedings. If I looked at her, it was almost out of curiosity. She seemed already of the past, like a character from a forgotten play. I had intended to have a word with her afterward, to ask after Caro, to establish some kind of truce now that the divide was final; but my first attempt toward that was cut dead. It never even came to words. I hadn't pressed for access while the legal machine was rumbling on, but now I had it officially. Caro had had her third birthday, and I wanted to see her. I wrote and asked Anthony what to do about it. It was eventually arranged that I should go down to Wytham. Nell would not be there.

So I drove down one day—to find that Anthony had also funked a meeting. The door was opened by Jane. There were her own two children and Caro, whom she successfully used throughout my hours there as a foil to anything but a very cool and armored politeness. She claimed that Anthony had a noon tutorial and a busy afternoon, and Wytham was too far to get back for lunch. I felt defeated long before I left. Every endeavor I made to get us off the trivial and immediate was rebuffed. Did she think I was totally to blame? It was for me to judge. But she must have some opinion? What good would there be in her telling it? Not the tiniest reference was made to that summer day in our past. I was tempted to bring it up; but I knew it would receive nothing but a snub. I had not used it properly, I was unspeakable. So I nursed the grotesque unfairness of her blaming me for a sin she had first taught me to commit. It was almost as if my worst infidelity had been to her, not Nell. I knew she was putting on an act, she couldn't be as calm and collected as she was pretending; yet something in her was not embarrassed, and that irritated me most. She was like some heroine from Jane Austen, a Fanny Price, deeply certain that she lived by some central moral tradition and deeply oblivious of the fact that the failure of anyone else to live by it might represent more than a contemptible lack of taste.

I discovered a little about Anthony and herself—how they were looking for a house in the city—and about Nell. She, it seemed, had got a part-time job cataloguing in the Taylorian and might take a flat in the house, if they could find one large enough. I wondered if Anthony really wanted that, given his past secret feelings about Nell, but I couldn't ask. A few facts were being given, not the realities behind them. She went off shopping after lunch with her own two children and left me for an hour with Caro. It seemed a very long hour, alone with a child I had grown a stranger to, in a house from which I was banned in everything except physical fact. The telephone rang, but I didn't answer it. Jane said it would probably have been Anthony, when she returned. I tried to make her sorry for me over Caro, the difficulty I had had in keeping her amused; which was answered by something about children living in the present, and trying to preserve that; then that she was "afraid" they all felt the less I saw of Caro at this stage, the better. We had to gear ourselves to her need of me, not mine for her. Jane said, She'll look for you one day, I expect. That was the nearest I came to a kind word.

If she baffled me conversationally, she confused me in an even more frustrating way psychologically. Of the four of us we two had changed most, but in diametrically opposite directions. All her old flashes of teasing, of frankness, of intuitive warmth, seemed to have been extinguished. I was finding Andrea quite exceptionally pleasant to live with: we had no rows, but enough friendly arguments to stop existence becoming saccharine. She cooked well, she made love well, she had a perfect tact about my work—went out to do her own in the morning and came back every evening to help me with mine if I wanted or to tell me the latest gossip, if I wanted that. She was also, in a Continental rather than an English way, a genuine culture addict. I saw more new exhibitions and went to more concerts in a month with her than in a year previously with Nell. Yet for all this I left Wytham once again knowing that I wished I had married Jane. I can't explain it. I hated her that day. Outwardly and consciously I left feeling deeply humiliated and telling myself that Anthony had turned her into a cold and lifeless female prig. I made up my mind I would never visit Caro in such circumstances again (and didn't, from then on I met her in Oxford itself or Nell brought her to London).

I was bitterly sarcastic to Andrea about my reception, when I got back to town; too bitter, as she soon pointed out. I suppose I felt failed and fallen. Like Lucifer: *I will exalt my throne above the stars of God* . . . and set it among the stars of Hollywood. It continued to feel like that on occasion for several years more; a hollow ambition masking a just exile.

But my major sin was still to come, though I had had the thing in mind well before that visit to Wytham actually took place. I have no excuse whatever for what I did—now, that is. At the time I saw reasons: the need to analyze it all, exorcise it, the belief that my treatment of this not very original situation was new in its depth and frankness, had a general application. A negative justification might have been that the film-script business, with its ready-found themes, was already making me lazy in invention. I did start the play with everyone fairly well disguised, and of course it remained so in terms of backgrounds and minor details. I made Anthony a public-school master in the West of England, myself an up-and-coming painter, Jane and Nell schoolfriends, not sisters. Anthony became a young Establishment Tartuffe, Jane his yes-saying wife; Nell, against my will, I had for dramatic reasons finally rather to flatter—showing her "honestly" torn between art and convention, whether or not to forgive the infidelity that sparked the action.

A number of her rows with the painter were almost verbatim from our own; and a final scene, with the Anthony-figure justifying his interference to the now wifeless painter by a display of impervious self-righteousness was—as he must have recognized at once—a blatant parody of that first meeting we had had when Nell left me. It was technically one of the better scenes in an otherwise bad play, which aggravated its injury. Andrea failed me for once, letting sympathy cloud her usually clear view of what went and what didn't. But I doubt if she could have stopped me: I was hell-bent on letting them know what I really felt—and that I had much more power to take public revenge than they might imagine.

The play got very guarded reviews. There was a general complaint that the schoolmaster and his wife were caricatures, that the whole thing was too static in action, too onesided in plot. One or two criticisms, including Barney's shakedown, were sharply hostile. But the review I most feared and craved, like some tyro urban guerrilla with his first bomb, had already come. By a malign chance (not one I was responsible for or could avert) Oxford had been on the out-of-town run. I have kept the letter, which is dated January 9, 1957.

Daniel,
Two evening ago Jane and I saw *The Victors* here in Oxford. I think the title is bad. It seemed to us a defeat of every human decency. It is not just a question of the vicious travesty of our true relationship that you have seen fit to put on the stage; or the fact that you know many people will immediately recognize, or think they recognize, the real names behind your totally (and I must presume deliberately) inadequate attempt to conceal them; not even of the incomprehensible way you have discharged most of your bile on Jane and myself—and over matters you must know have no foundation whatever in our actual behaviour. What shocks me far more than all this is your apparent desire to demonstrate that you are not responsible for your actions and that your inability to be faithful to Nell was accordingly her and our fault, not yours. This argues such a hopeless corruption of any normal sense of morality—and I am certainly not writing as a Catholic or a philosopher, but simply as someone who once believed himself your close friend—that very possibly this letter will mean nothing to you. I have serious doubts now as to whether you have any personal honesty or powers of self-judgment left.

No doubt all art has to be based on life; and no doubt much of it has to be based on life in the form of the artist's own experience. I can also see that some such experience might justify public revenge. What I cannot see is how any responsible artist can use his art to transfer his own clear guilt, and in a closely circumstantial manner, to the innocent. Even if Jane and I were not Catholics, with Catholic views on the subject of marriage, the notion that we should have intrigued to make Nell leave you is ludicrous. In fact what advice we gave, right up to the divorce, was precisely the opposite of what you pretend we maliciously worked to achieve. The buried motive you imply at one point (that the pedagogic buffoon supposed to be myself is in love with the painter's wife) is still more odious proof of your outrageous need to pervert reality. You are also gravely mistaken if you think that I am envious of your successful career. Whatever inclinations I might have had there could in any case not have survived this revelation of its effects on your character.

We have searched our consciences, gone through our more recent behaviour to you, and we still do not understand why we have deserved this. We no longer feel anger, but pity. I don't know if it was something always inherent in your present way of life, but our conclusion is that somewhere you have taken a very wrong road. We cannot believe that a part of you does not know this and that you will, if you ever recover your senses, bitterly regret that you ever wrote such a childishly vindictive essay in distortion.

We cannot answer you in kind or in public, we cannot sue you for libel, we can only suffer in silence. You knew that too, from the beginning. And what are we to tell Caroline, and our own children, when they are old enough to read and understand your play? "Genius forgives all" is a dubious proposition at the best of times. And I do not think you come into that category.

We want no answer to this—no excuses, justifications, what you will. I have informed Nell that neither Jane nor myself will in any circumstances act again as intermediaries or provide a meeting-place for you and your daughter. From now on you will please deal with Nell's solicitor about such arrangements. We cannot put any other interpretation on the play than that you intended to drive us to this. We are only too clearly dead for you; and from now on you must be dead for us.

It was handwritten and signed with his full name. I passed it straight to Andrea—we were having breakfast—and watched her face as she read. It stayed impassive when she looked up.

"Surprised?"

"Not really."

"Will you answer?"

"Ears of stone. No point." She glanced back at the letter. "Of course they followed the party line over a reconciliation. But I bet you they got it through to Nell what they really thought about me." She still looked at the letter, as if it convinced her rather better than I did. "He'll have loved composing every word of that little commination."

"What's a commination?"

"Ash Wednesday. God's curse on all sinners."

I told her then, because I so desperately needed to have at least one person on my side, about Jane. That gained me a partial absolution; in time, because we discussed it a lot, an almost total one, so far as Andrea was concerned. I think that in some way she equated Jane's "duplicity" with her own husband's use of the same religion to justify his terrifying egomania.

For many years now I have accepted that Anthony was right. I deserved nothing else, and especially as he knew nothing of what had happened between Jane and myself. Only two years previously I had had to have it out with Caro, why I had written the wretched thing; it had proved useful, both as a test to myself that I had acquired objectivity and in opening up a previously forbidden area between us.

*The Victors* killed one other thing besides a friendship. I did write two more plays, but my heart was in neither of them. It is not only human kind that cannot bear too much reality.

# Catastasis

It is absurd to speak of a feeling of estrangement so soon after meeting someone from whom one has been estranged for years; yet that was what Dan felt with Jane. His sense of discomfort was not lessened when they arrived at the hospital. She switched off the engine, then reached under the dashboard for a book. She held it on her lap a moment.

"I'll take you up, Dan. But Anthony wants to see you alone." She didn't look, but she must have realized that he was taken aback. Once more his imagination had let him down: he had seen Anthony in bed, Jane on one side, himself on the other—at least that inducement to reunion, celebration of old times.

"Why don't we meet at the restaurant? I can get a cab or something."

"No really . . ." she raised the book, she had come prepared to wait. Then she turned and opened her door, to cut any further discussion short. He wondered why she had left the announcement so late. Plainly something about it embarrassed her, like his very presence. She began talking a little too circumstantially, as they walked toward the entrance from the car-park, about how good the hospital was. Dan felt more and more like a soldier being pitched into battle without proper orders.

They got into a lift and rose to the third floor; down a corridor to a crossroads of them. A sister sat at a desk, writing. As Jane went forward, she looked up, smiled in recognition, but Dan couldn't hear what was being said. Jane was to go in first and warn Anthony that he was there. He watched her disappear down one of the side-corridors. Two men in dressing-gowns passed, arguing about a chess-game. He wanted to smoke, but there was a sign forbidding it behind the sister's desk. She had returned to her writing. Once more Dan began rehearsing sentences he knew he probably wouldn't say; and stared at a notice-board, without registering a single thing its pieces of paper meant. There was some absurd echo of childhood, waiting outside the headmaster's study. He wished he hadn't come. It was a scene he would have avoided in a script. At last he heard Jane say his name.

He followed her down the side-corridor. She stopped some yards short of an open door at the end.

"In there."

"Right."

"Not too much commiseration. It doesn't help."

"I'll try."

She hesitated.

"Well, I'll leave you to it."

Still she hesitated, as if she knew she should say more. But then with a nervously formal smile, as if she had done her part, delivered her parcel, she turned back to the open space where the corridors met.

Anthony was not in bed, but sitting in a wheel chair by the window; a closed glass door beside it led out to a small balcony. A thin man in a blue silk dressing-gown, a dark green tartan rug around his bottom half. The face gave Dan a shock, he hardly recognized it. Anthony had always looked a little older than he really was, Dan's own age, but now he seemed like a man of sixty. He had lost no hair, but it had grayed with a premature completeness. His cheeks were sallow and wasted. He looked very tired, there was a ghost of a more famous Anthony—Eden—about him, and only the eyes and the smile resurrected the person Dan had once known so well. He went without speaking to where the dying man sat and took his outstretched hand. It was retained. There was a moment's silence, a shared emotion, an immediate and mutual recognition of what had been so lacking with the woman outside.

"I feel like an intolerable spoilt child."

"Nonsense."

"All this way."

"I was coming back. No problems."

Anthony searched his eyes. "It's fantastic to see you again, Dan. For once that wretched word is exact."

"I could use sadder ones."

The sick man gave a little shrug of amusement.

"One begins by apologizing to everyone." He put on a voice. " 'I say, I'm most frightfully sorry, but I understand I'm done for.' Absurd." He smiled. "We become very vain, Dan. We take the sympathy for granted." He gestured. "Now do have a sherry. And forgive me for not being able to join you."

Dan did not want any, hadn't drunk sherry for years, but knew himself awkward standing there. On a table beside the door there was a tray with a bottle of Amontillado and glasses. The room was small, but there were flowers, books; over the bed, a cheap reproduction of Mantegna's *Saint Sebastian*. It seemed hardly likely that the hospital would have put it there. The intention would be sardonic, not inspirational. He uncorked the bottle and poured his sherry.

"Jane's looked after you all right?"

"I'm going to take her out to dinner. If I may."

"She'll love that."

Dan turned; and tried once more.

"Anthony, I've had strict instructions not to—"

"Then obey them." They both smiled at that old incisiveness. "I'm not in any great pain now. I'm only here to spare Jane various tedious chores. I can be rather tactless, cytogenesis."

"Okay. But I . . ."

"Your being here speaks better than any words. Even from someone of your skill with them." He retained his former rapidity of speech; paused a little more now between sentences, that seemed to be all. Dan raised the glass.

"Then to the good past."

"Amen to that. Now come and sit down."

There was a metal and plastic chair, which left Dan sitting a shade higher. Anthony watched him, almost hungrily, smiling, his hands in his dressing-gown pockets. It was disconcerting: just in that first minute there was more affection, rapport, than in the previous hour with Jane outside. One at least of Dan's fears was quenched. But he got to know that smile in what followed. It was fixed, more and more a mask; his own was the same, if for different reasons. Anthony's eyes had kept their directness, their always strange need to observe yours. They seemed both sceptical and feverish, as if a last black flame burned in the mind behind them.

"So how's the real world?"

"As unreal as ever."

"No regrets?"

"Thousands."

"But not professional. You've done extraordinarily well."

"In the movie world that's *prima facie* evidence of eternal damnation."

The smile was momentarily genuine.

"Well. We've enjoyed them. The ones we've seen."

"One or two I don't blush for. But I've made far more money than self-esteem."

"And you've got a lovely hide-out now? Where you were born? Caro's told us about it."

"Just a farmhouse. I hardly use it."

"Good orchid country?"

It was so fired; like some forgotten joke.

"Greenwings in one meadow. One quite nice colony of *spiralis*. When the sheep don't get them. Early purples. That's about the lot."

"You know *aestivalis* has re-appeared on one of the New Forest sites?"

"I didn't."

"By some miracle." It was all teasing, fencing. "You remember that wild-goose chase?"

They had gone down to Hampshire in pursuit of the elusive Summer Lady's Tress, one of the rarest British orchids. A long and azure weekend, interminable scrambling through bogs and over grass-tussocks; and not a sight of the plant.

"Of course."

"But you've lost interest in all that now?"

"I still botanize a bit when I'm down there."

"I've missed you at Watlington. No one else ever quite—"

He smiled, as if to admit he was being foolish. Dan knew he meant to put him at his ease; but he wouldn't leave him with his eyes; trying to decide who he had become, which way to move into the real conversation. Dan looked down at the sherry.

"I've missed you in far more places than that, Anthony."

At last Anthony looked down as well, then murmured, "Yes."

There was a silence.

"I've just told Jane—I've long accepted I have only myself to blame for what happened."

Anthony was silent a moment more; then smiling again. "Let's at least thank heaven I didn't take up the law." Dan queried him. "I'm told nine parts of the judge's skill is in the sentencing. I doubt my abilities there."

"You shouldn't. I deserved it."

He was surveyed; almost savored. "That's another false inference from first appearances."

Dan shook his head. "That at least I've got sorted out."

Anthony watched him, then looked down and fiddled with the dark green rug.

"Dan, alas, I haven't much time . . . I have to be doped for the night in a little while."

"I'll come in again tomorrow. As often as—"

The condemned man nodded, but it was almost with an impatience.

"I haven't forced this huge journey on you for quite nothing."

"My dear man, you've forced nothing on me. Except regret that this ever happened."

Again Anthony hesitated. Dan had a growing sense that he too was not at all as he had been imagined, perhaps because something in him had aged, or simply atrophied, that stayed almost boyish, unblunted, in the don; who now fiddled again with the rug, truing a line in its pattern to the line of his legs beneath. His hands were unhealthily white.

"I'd like first, Dan, to assure you that easing my conscience has only a very secondary part—and no part at all in my asking you to come here—in what I wish to say. When I was first told, I was very frightened. Bitter? Having spent most of one's life on linguistic analysis and ethical theory doesn't help one damn little bit when it comes to it." He looked up at Dan with a humorless smile. "Nor does faith and theology. All you can feel at first is a crashing sense of injustice. Divine or natural makes no odds. You can't think about the past. Only about the future you'll never see. But that state of mind becomes so painful, and pointless, that you have—or at least *I* had—to rationalize myself out of it. My own solution was to attempt an honest evaluation of my own life—my work, my marriage with Jane, everything. I've tried to strike a true balance. That has meant re-examining matters I've spent a great deal of time—and only too successfully—forgetting. And from there to considering whether anything can still be done about them. You're with me?"

"Of course. But you really mustn't—"

"No please. Just let me finish." He folded his arms. "Another notion you have to rid yourself of is that of punishment. I have sinned, therefore I die. They know all about that here. They're very convincing on the carcinoma—or at least my species of it—as an example of pure hazard. But rather less so on the necessity for such a principle in the natural scheme. One's reduced to the homely saw. It's an ill wind . . . that sort of thing. In this situation, very obviously the good it blows depends on the victim. Not without its humor, as a matter of fact—I detect in myself a desire to do good in direct proportion to my increasing inability to do anything but think about doing good." They smiled, cautiously, still uncertain of each other. "I'm not indulging in self-abasement before the . . . eternal throne. I daresay I've collected enough green stamps to satisfy Saint Peter. But that idea of a divine customs-and-excise man was never very plausible, was it?"

"I've always had too much to declare to be able to afford to believe it."

Anthony's smile deepened momentarily. "In my case I'm afraid I should be tempted to argue the toss over certain articles. I think I could make out a case for some of my past mistakes having brought good in the end." He hesitated fractionally. "One of them was bullying Jane into the Church. Has she . . . ?"

"Just the fact. Not the reasons."

"She's bearing up much better now as a convinced pagan than she would have as a lukewarm Catholic. Even I can see that." He sniffed. "I now head a family of apostates."

"I'm sorry."

"No need. Let's hope Heaven takes credit cards in lieu of cash these days. We're all in a bad way if it doesn't."

"And your own beliefs?"

Dan realized, as soon as he had spoken, that it was a question better not asked: it sidetracked. Anthony hesitated, then there came the more natural smile.

"I heard a lovely joke the other day. About the young priest in a very advanced seminary who went to his superior and said: I have the most terrible sin to confess. Whereupon he flung himself on his knees and covered his face in his hands." Anthony covered his own. " 'Reverend father, I don't know how to tell you this, but I can't bear the cross of my guilt and shame any longer.' 'Yes, my son.' " Anthony looked up, with a naturally haggard and clownishly woebegone face. " 'I've tried and tried, but I still have absolute faith in Christ!' "

Dan grinned. "And you're in the same terrible condition?"

He pulled his nose. "Hardly. Enough to call myself a Catholic still. But I do promise you, Dan, you're not here to ensure I have on a clean pair of spiritual underpants when the . . . accident happens. Nothing like that." He was trying to get down to an unbeliever's level, and too hard, with that third attempt at a dismissive image; but Dan smiled dutifully. "It's much more a matter of engineering. Of correcting a design failure." He added, "A little revenge on Madame Sosostris. And her wicked pack of cards."

"I understand."

He contemplated Dan a moment: knowing, as Dan was soon to learn, that he didn't.

"You're not so kindly here to be forgiven for that play. I can't recall exactly what I wrote to you at the time, but I very much doubt if I should want to withdraw the substance of it. Even today."

"No argument."

"But only because even if you had known what drove me to write my letter, writing your play would have remained wrong. That doesn't quite let me out, however." Dan searched the drawn face. It looked down and then up at him again. There was a faint dry quiz in the eyes. "Before we married, Jane told me that you and she had been to bed together. That was always the joker in the pack."

Dan bent his head. "Oh God."

The voice was light.

"I know Oxford philosophy has—in many ways deservedly—become every clever writer's favorite Aunt Sally. We do rather tend to waste time over modern equivalents of how many angels can stand on a needle's point. I should quite understand if you regarded all this as very ancient history. Hardly worth crossing the street to discuss, let alone your real journey."

"I had no idea."

"As we intended." Dan's mind struggled to get back to the ancient history; and the light this strange new fact threw over it. His instinctive first reaction was a blend of outrage and absurdity: how much they must have had to hide, and how condescending their silence had been. Anthony went on. "Let me add at once you are forgiven for that now, with all my heart. I wish I could say you were forgiven at the time. But you weren't."

"I was just . . ."

"I know. And that she was mainly to blame. And I was to blame. If anyone was innocent it was you."

"That's letting me off too lightly."

"It doesn't matter now, Dan. Sexual mores are very transient. My students have taught me that." Once again he smoothed the rug over his knees. "If Jane had been less hon-

est . . . or was dealing with someone who prized his own sophistries less highly. Who had such a capacity for straining at
intellectual gnats and swallowing emotional camels."

"If you blame yourself, I think you're still being guilty of
that."

That brought him short a little. There was an acknowledgment of it in his gentler voice.

"Mind has dominated our marriage, Dan. And all its toys.
Not flesh. Or heart." He put his hands back in his dressing-
gown pockets. "That's what enabled us to keep our secret.
What obliged you to marry Nell. Must take some of the
blame for your writing of that play. For this silence between
us all these years." He said nothing for a moment. "By appearing to condone you, I made sure that I never could. At
that time."

"I don't see how you could do anything but hate me."

"I think I felt envy most. In retrospect."

"Envy?"

"Inasmuch as you represented another life-principle."

"Betrayal?"

"Let's say human fallibility."

"That's a virtue?"

"A corrective. To the would-be in spirit."

"Now I don't understand."

"My main contribution to our marriage has been intellectual arrogance. Jane's has been the patience to tolerate it."

"That hardly squares with her leaving the Church."

"She gave me a complete freedom of choice in the beginning. I need never have seen her again. There are more ways
of being arrogant than demanding conformity of religious belief. Mine was to suppress all the instinctual side of her
nature. To persuade her that even the most ridiculous decisions can be justified by mind."

"Now you're making her your fool."

He had another humorless smile, as if he had Dan cornered.

"My victim."

"But . . . your marriage hasn't been a failure."

"How should you know? After all these years?"

"Because I can't believe she'd have lived a lie. She's not
that sort of person. Her dropping the faith proves it."

"I rather think that was a poor substitute for dropping her
husband." Dan was suddenly back at the Randolph, listening
to various unread messages in Jane's tone of voice, those

tinges of cynicism, indifference—which he had put down as much to Oxford, playing English, as to anything biographical. "The very fact that what I am saying is partly conjecture, that is, that I don't know if Jane would fully echo these views, does rather prove my point."

"Isn't there a simple remedy for that?"

"If it weren't so well known that truth is bad for the dying." He added, "And as I have had to learn, some diseases are beyond simple remedies."

Though he spoke without bitterness, the accusation was implicit.

"You're being very hard on her." Anthony said nothing. "Surely one knows these things? By instinct. Intuition."

"Perhaps I've spent too long with that verb 'to know' to trust it very much. I'm merely saying that if my blind obsession with things of the mind has in some profound way—a way even Jane herself may not be fully aware of—curtailed, censored, what you will, her true nature, then . . ." but he uncharacteristically caught back whatever he was going to say. Dan was presenting some problem he had not foreseen. He went on in a much less incisive voice. "I don't want to die without having done something about it."

"But what you call censoring is the price of any lasting relationship. And people like Jane don't just lie down and let themselves be mutilated out of recognition."

That amused him. "You ought to go and dine at one or two high tables here."

"Career deformation. That's not the same."

"Simply less severe than marriage deformation? Which is the greater sin? Adultery or adulterating?"

Dan opened his hands. "My dear chap, it's in the rules of the game. Because I wouldn't observe them, wouldn't let Nell adulterate me . . . that's why we broke up. You know that as well as I do."

"All right. And if you had kept the marriage intact by letting her pattern your behavior? Would you have been happier?"

"How on earth can I tell?"

"By telling me whether you've constantly regretted the divorce."

Dan looked down at his sherry glass. "If I haven't, it's only because I'm congenitally unfaithful to women."

"Whereas I have been congenitally, as you put it, faithful

to one woman. Is there so much difference? At least you've rationed out your exploitations."

Dan remembered an old gibe about Oxford: that the most characteristic don in its history was Lewis Carroll. He couldn't quite hide his feeling that they were getting very near pure nonsense.

"Anthony, look, I've had barely an hour to get to know Jane again. I can see she's changed. But she doesn't strike me as a deformed person at all. And I know from Caro. She adores Jane. I can imagine what it's like for you, how the temptation to be harsh with oneself and . . ." he was getting a shade too near exasperation, and he controlled it. "You know what I'm trying to say."

"Terminal paranoia?"

"Of course not. But one can be overscrupulous?"

There was a little silence. Dan felt an unreason in that wasted face, an obstinacy, almost an irritation at being deflected from this long-nursed doubt.

"Would you have married Jane, if I'd broken things off at the beginning?"

"That's an impossible question. And you must know it."

"But you were in love with her?"

"I desired her. As I've desired dozens of other women since." Anthony's eyes observed intently, too intently for comfort, and Dan lowered his own and shrugged. "I'm not a Casanova, Anthony, but I have slept around a good deal. I really do have an irredeemable liking for the impermanent." Still Anthony said nothing, and he was reduced to raising his glass. "May I have another?"

"Please."

Dan stood up and went back to the table with the sherry. "And anyway, there was always Nell."

"Is there someone now?"

"Yes." He glanced wrily back. "And young enough to be my daughter."

"I'm considered very square these days. I haven't seduced a single student." Dan smiled, and he went on. "You feel no responsibility towards her?"

"Of course. And especially in warning her what I am."

"Then you're showing greater honesty than I ever have."

The door opened and a young nurse stood there. She said nothing, simply gave Anthony a mock-severe warning look. He said, "Not yet." She nodded indulgently and disappeared.

"You're sure . . . ?"

"No, no. Just nannying."

Dan went with his glass and looked out through the glass door; nearer to Anthony, but turned half away. A car passed, then two students on bicycles, in the mist-filled street below; the roofs of Oxford, a city that seemed several centuries behind the one he had just left in California. He thought again for a moment of Jenny, of how much more he would have liked to be having dinner with her than with the woman outside; with the unspeakable past. He felt psychologically stifled; the claustrophobia of academic life, of the something beneath all its sophistications, its brains, that remained eternally adolescent, as chlorotic as a plant denied sufficient light—and privileged, unhardened by the realities of the world outside. That also stood for the whole of England.

"You said something about correcting a design failure."

"I suppose I meant no more than what good might come from pointing it out." But he went on quickly, "No, that's rather less than frank. It's mere hypothesis, Dan. A kind of . . . hope against hope that you might one day find time to help disinter the person Jane might have been from beneath the person she now is." He stared up at Dan and for the first time, strangely, there was a tinge of formality in his eyes. "If you could consider becoming her friend again."

"Anthony, I wouldn't be here if . . . I tried to get a message to you both. Through Caro. Months ago."

Once again he had the impression that he had unnecessarily forestalled a direction Anthony was not going to take.

"Yes, it . . . did arrive." He smiled. "You're wondering why it wasn't acted upon. Or why only now."

"A little bit, yes."

"Death's rather like a certain kind of lecturer. You don't really hear what is being said until you're in the first row." He said, "It's helped me to win my battle, Dan. Jane is losing hers." He hesitated. "She didn't want you to come today. I don't know if you've realized that."

Dan looked down again out of the room: the dead street.

"She blames me still over Nell?"

"I don't think that has anything to do with it. And blame is not the word." His voice was less incisive now. "She's reacted to the past in a very different way from myself. I suspect you've become in some way an emblem of all that our marriage has lacked. The broken keel on which she now considers it was built." There was a moment's pause, then he went on. "You must excuse me, Dan. I'm not exposing the

problem very coherently. I decided I wanted very much to
see you about a month ago. It was partly Jane's reaction
when I broached the matter that made me realize how much
she and I had hidden from each other over the years. None
of this has been discussed openly between us. Her reluctance
has purportedly been at the inconvenience it would cause
you. The vanity of supposing you would even remember who
we were." He added, "In which she may be partly right."

Dan was leaning now against the wall by the glass door;
for once Anthony was avoiding his eyes, speaking to the gray
hospital floor.

"But mainly wrong."

Anthony smiled up. "But at least she's partly right in thinking that my motives are essentially selfish. I'm really asking
you to do something that I failed to do myself, Dan. And I
know. Impossibly. After all these years—not, alas, knowing
you anymore. Simply guessing. Praying. Now that you have
been given the missing card."

And for a few moments, but once again moments of that
hinged, geometric nature that destroys time and conscious notion of sequence, the two men sought something, a mystery
and an understanding of it, in each other's eyes. A code of
intercourse was being broken, another proposed; and Dan, if
he could not grasp its full significance consciously, knew that
whatever the state of Anthony's specific faith, he retained a
far deeper one in a universal absolute. His seeming obliviousness to time, interval, to all the outward rest, was in fact a
mere function of that: what I ask is timeless . . . a preposterous, but true, demand of personal moral being. You may
wonder at me, laugh at me, despise me for professing both a
faith and a discipline the world increasingly despises: but that
is neither who I am at this moment nor why we are here.
Perhaps it was the proximity of death; yet it seemed to Dan
as if he had always been mistaken in one assumption: that
this man was a philosopher merely by intellect and a cast of
mind. Underneath, and movingly, lay something very primitive and simple, of the innocence of childhood; and also of
true adulthood, of that other philosopher who had once preferred hemlock to a lie.

"Anthony, of course. If trying will help . . ."

"But I ask the impossible?"

"I didn't mean that." He looked down at his sherry. "Just
that—well, it's rather up to Jane, isn't it? She must have
many far closer friends now."

"What she needs is someone who both knows her and doesn't. Who can remember what she once was. She's become very withdrawn, Dan. I think not only with me." He considered his next sentence in his mind, then spoke. "Perhaps the most profound breach in our marriage has been over the question of whether we have some control over our lives or not. One reason I can't talk with her about all these matters is that our marriage has become the standing proof that my case has no validity. I preach in an empty church, which proves my sermons are worthless. We're reduced now to a tender convention. Dying husband, dutiful wife."

Dan went and sat on the end of the bed, and stared at the foot of the wall beneath the window.

"I didn't know about all this, Anthony."

"How could you? We've largely hidden it. Even from our own children. Certainly to the world at large."

"Have you tried recently to . . . ?"

"I forced her to lie for years over her true religious beliefs. Which began the closing-in process. I won't now do it over something much more important. She also has a formidable pride. I'm not prepared to blackmail that, either."

"Then judgment without trial?"

"On the contrary. Trial without judgment."

"Does she know you were going to tell me this?"

"She must . . . yes, in a sense, she must know. But I'd prefer you to keep it to yourself now, Dan. In fact, I insist." Dan said nothing, feeling more and more out of his depth; caught in a game he had almost forgotten how to play; aware of that woman sitting out there, knowing and not knowing. Anthony went on. "This must sound very peculiar. But I insist for, how shall I put it, tactical reasons? On the supposition that you are prepared to forgive us both."

"You know there's no question about that."

There was another little silence.

"I'm also profoundly grateful to have been allowed to share my life with her. At another level. I speak in terms of what you both sacrificed. The act may have been immoral, but what followed . . . my gratitude is partly the selfishness of a beneficiary of your decision. But it does exist."

Dan smiled. "One satisfied partner is above average for the course."

"But below average in a serious match. Even in golf, I believe."

Something very peculiar had happened to his sense of time.

For Dan they had become strangers, with very different histories and even cultures now. For Anthony, it was still as if they were then closest of friends; and over the years he had acquired no replacements.

Again Dan smiled at him; then glanced at the Mantegna reproduction over the bed.

"I begin to understand why you have that hanging there."

Anthony's mouth showed a quirk.

"Very bad taste. Even my witty Jesuit friends are not amused." But he would not be distracted; braced himself back and looked across the room. "Dan, you once said something to me that I've always remembered. You'd spotted some nice orchid I'd walked right past—*insectifera?*—I can't recall now, but we were telling the girls about it that evening. Your nose for them. And you said that I knew only how to look *at* orchids—not *for* them. Do you remember that?" Dan shook his head at the questioning eyes. "Well. When I think of the vain thousands of words I've wasted, both orally and in print, on abstract propositions and philosophical angel-counting. Instead of . . ." he shrugged.

Dan remembered Barney: this pandemic of self-deprecation.

"I won't wear that. Quite apart from anything else you've taught hundreds of young men to think."

"Only as I think myself. I thank heaven for the stupid ones. At least they escaped contamination."

"Balls."

"Precisely. In another sense. The academic glass-bead game."

He had his hands in his dressing-gown pockets, and again he braced himself back a little against the chair, as if he felt discomfort—perhaps pain, despite his disclaimer. He smiled drily sideways at Dan.

"I'm sorry. This must seem singularly like self-pity. It's just that everyone makes too many allowances for the dying. As if the soft center is what one needs."

"You also know perfectly well that looking-at is a much more important activity than looking for."

"Perhaps with orchids. Not with self. I have looked *at* myself. All my adult life. But as I am. Not as I might have been, or ought to have been. That's what permitted me to turn you into the living exemplar of all that Jane and I had supposedly risen above."

His self-distaste was in his voice; and his face.

"All right. By impossibly high Christian standards, you lacked charity. That doesn't mean the basic judgment was at fault."

"But the standards of judgment were." His eyes were on Dan's. "And your accepting the sentence so meekly proves it."

"Why?"

"My dear fellow, a judge who tried a case—that of your play—so clearly involving his own interests would be a disgrace to justice. Especially when a previous private decision of his—one you were unaware of—had very much helped cause the crime in question. That you now have the kindness to tell me the sentence was right proves your comparative innocence."

"But who provoked that original private decision? And why do you think it only happened once? That we backed out almost as soon as we'd walked in?"

"Because you incorrectly assumed I was the injured party."

Dan shook his head. "Something much simpler. I wasn't good enough for Jane. And she wasn't bad enough for me."

"I think I might very well have convinced you otherwise. And even if it were true, you still might have benefited each other far more deeply than . . ." but he stopped at the second term of the comparison.

Dan swilled the last of the sherry in the bottom of the glass. Anthony was not to be deprived of his arrows; and the present archer left a silence. The martyr gave another curt rictus of self-mockery.

"All this deathbed melodrama. I did also very much just want to see you again. Hear about your life."

"The Oscar in the loo?"

"Not all ashes, surely?"

"Not if you live it from day to day. As I mostly have."

"There are worse philosophies."

"Until you do your accounts."

"One moaner is quite enough in this room."

Dan smiled down from his reproof. "I suppose I've become like Jane. A determinist. More or less opted out."

"Opting out is not compatible with determinism."

"Unless one's a born taker of the easier road."

"That's defeatism. Not determinism."

"One can choose one's bit of flotsam. But it's all going in the same direction?"

Anthony raised a finger.

"I detect Saint Samuel à-Beckett and his fancy French nonsense. Arrant romantic pessimism."

"Now you're being hard on Beckett."

"No harder than Pascal would have been. Or Voltaire, for that matter. *Mutatis mutandis.*"

"I suppose not."

"I had one of my most serenely self-satisfied Oxford colleagues trying to sell ecological disaster to me the other day. It seems I'm quite extraordinarily lucky to be able to walk out of such a flop. I told him he was at perfect liberty to join me."

Dan laughed. "But that he won't doesn't necessarily disprove his case?"

"You must allow me the suspicion that the play isn't really half so bad as the doomsters pretend. After all, the one evil thing in creation is also the one thing that can think." He gave Dan one of his quizzes. "I'm still defeated by the conundrum of God. But I have the Devil clear."

"And what's he?"

"Not seeing whole." He stared at the floor. "One of my students a year or two ago informed me that the twentieth century was like realizing we're all actors in a bad comedy at precisely the same moment as we realize that no one wrote it, no one is watching it, and that the only other theater in town is the graveyard."

"What did you say to that?"

"That he should drop philosophy and take up your profession."

"Unkind."

"Not at all. You're locked up in the untenable dream, we're condemned to the tenable proposition. The word as game. The word as tool. Just as long as the one doesn't pretend to be the other."

"You never play with your tools?"

"Oh I couldn't deny that we have self-abuse in common."

And they smiled, I think for the first time completely without reserve, perhaps because they had both recalled an old kind of dialogue, a fondness for such puns, word-play; because they knew this first meeting was drawing to an end . . . and if they hadn't, on either side, found what was expected, there was something—an unchangingness, behind all the outward shifts of circumstance. Time lay quiescent, if not defeated. Anthony straightened again.

"Dan, I can't tell you how essential this has been for me. What a gift you've brought."

"For me as well."

"I do have the strangest kind of optimism about the human condition. I can't explain it. It's . . . well, I think a little more than mere faith. There is something sillier than the theory of perfectibility."

"Imperfectibility?"

Anthony nodded. "Just that we shall come through. In spite of all our faults. If only we learn that it must begin in ourselves. In the true history of our own lives. Instead of putting the blame on everything else under the sun." He gave Dan a faintly mischievous look. "I sometimes think I shall bequeath a last mystical catch-phrase to the world. Turn in." A moment, then he pulled at his rug and said, "And I better had. Going trite is even worse than going maudlin."

"You're allowed an aria." He didn't know what that meant. "Old Hollywood jargon. There's a famous Goldwynism. 'Cut that goddamn speech, arias went out with Shakespeare.' "

Anthony's head lifted, he approved. "I must remember that." He sought Dan's eyes. "You do understand what I've been trying to say, Dan?"

"Of course."

"I know Jane better than anyone else in the world. In spite of everything. She does need help. A Good Samaritan."

"I'll try my best." Dan reached out and touched his hand, then stood up. "And I'll come in tomorrow. Give you the full horrors of my world. Reject Spengler then, if you can."

"I should enjoy that."

"And don't worry about the past. The major design faults were in things. Life. Not us."

"As long as you'll agree that the only remedies do lie in us. As we are. Not were."

"Done."

The sick man extended a hand and Dan took it. Then, with a gesture that at last revealed a buried emotion, Anthony joined his other hand to those already joined. But his eyes, looking up into Dan's, still intent, still smiling, stayed dry.

"All we haven't said."

"Spoken. No need."

"Then have a nice dinner."

"And you sleep well."

"Modern pharmacy solves that."

He let go of the hand. Dan turned at the door.

"Shall I ring for someone?"

"No, no. They'll come."

He raised his hand: and still that smile. It had the faint air of a benediction—or the air of a faint benediction; something as two-edged as the piece of artistic genius and morbid religiosity that hung over the bed.

He had already decided what I had become, and he did not want me to see. So I spent that last moment looking at him, not for him.

# Jane

"All right?"

"Fine."

"I'll just go and say good night."

I waited where I had found Jane absorbed in her book, and felt myself left standing in more senses than one: the immediate clearest sentiment was of embarrassment at now having to face an evening with a woman who wished I hadn't reappeared in her life, and whom I had more or less promised to lie to.

The revelation about Anthony's complaisance in pre-history seemed on reflection less unexpected, less extraordinary, than this casting of me as the savior of someone who very evidently did not want to be saved. I began to feel that I had been obscurely gulled, had allowed the pathos of his situation—for all his rejection of that element in it—to silence me. I ought to have argued more. He had had the advantage of surprise, and none of my own rehearsals had foreseen such a drastic change of basic premise . . . or anything but a very casual resumption of relations with Jane in the future.

Perhaps the illness and the drugs had unbalanced him; perhaps it was all some kind of tortuous revenge on his wife; perhaps he'd been pursuing the same line with other people. But she would surely have warned me beforehand, if that had been the case; and her behavior hardly denied his diagnosis. I think the greatest shock lay in this possibility that an event I had always believed had disturbed my own life far more deeply than hers, but which I had in fact long relegated to the category of spilt milk, had finally—if Anthony was to be believed—affected her more deeply. But it was all so retrospective, so past; like going into a theater and finding a production one had seen there half a lifetime before still on stage. Of course there was a sense in which he and Jane had continued to inhabit the theater, the past must in that way have continued more present for them; but not for the first, or last, time that evening I had a feeling that I had landed among children—or certainly among people whose values had remained bizarrely petrified. Yet I also knew a more subjective side of me had been moved by Anthony and resurrected from behind the hardening years—a kind of greenness, but with the good as well as the bad aspects of that metaphor, what we had lost as well as what we had gained.

Jane was not long away, and then we were in the lift going down, side by side, facing the doors. There was a moment's awkward silence.

"How did you find him?"

"Rather hair-raisingly brave about it all."

"As long as it wasn't a complete waste of time."

"Of course not."

There was no other word for what she had said but graceless. Her tone had effectively denied the token negative. I do indeed hold a resentful hand: now guess how strong it is. She looked in her bag for her car-key.

"He's asked me to let you have all his orchid books."

"That's very sweet of him."

"They're probably hopelessly out of date."

"I doubt it. And I'd still love to have them."

"I'll look them out."

The lift doors slid open. By the time we were in her car again, it was very clear that she wasn't going to ask me what had been said. At least I was to be spared lying about that. Either she knew or she didn't care. Anthony had at least convinced me that he wanted to dissolve the years of silence. She was very glad that they were still there; and proceeded to underline their existence by a determined, if outwardly bland, normality.

We got ourselves to the Italian restaurant, but again someone knew her. We stopped, she introduced me to the couple; my name, that was all, as if she would have been ashamed to go into the reason for my presence. There was a little exchange about Anthony. Then we went to our table across the room. She explained who they were: an English don and his wife, from Merton. I had the impression she would much rather have been sitting and talking with them—a tit for my secret tat about Jenny. When the menu had been gone through and the food ordered, she asked me about my work. We chatted, she sat in her cream shirt with the agate brooch, elbows on the table, hands lightly clasped, the head calmly poised, considering everything in the room but my face.

Slowly, almost reluctantly, I found myself accepting Anthony's view: there was something obstinately elsewhere in her . . . more than that, snubbingly elsewhere. Despite her show of politeness, I soon began to smell the same contempt for my movie world as her husband had suggested she felt for his religious and philosophical ones. None of her questions seemed innocent.

"And you've given up the theater completely?"

"Nothing new to say. Or perhaps just unable to adapt myself to the fashionable new ways of saying it."

"Isn't the cinema the same? The same problems?"

Our first courses came. I have spent a good deal of my life observing people's minute but betraying gestures, and I noted the quickness with which she picked up the spoon for her melon. I decided that at least one assumption she might be making about me needed destruction.

"In my branch of it it's a little like being an industrial executive. Maintaining the standard of a staple product? Which is entertainment. Vehicles for current stars. The odd dose of truth one tries to smuggle in is incidental. Just part of the packaging. Status comes from box-office record. At most, craft."

She delved into her melon. "And you've settled for that?"

I extracted the backbones from my grilled sardines.

"I have all sorts of excuses, Jane. But Anthony's just seen through them. He called me a defeatist. Then a romantic pessimist."

She was faintly amused. "And Beckett was duly cursed."

I smiled and tried to catch her eyes, but they were studiously intent on the melon. "You don't agree?"

"Oh yes. But not for Anthony's reasons."

"Then why?"

She shrugged. "Just that literary melancholia so often precedes fascism. Rousseau, then Napoleon. Chateaubriand and the Restoration. The Twenties."

"Rabelais remains a god?"

Another brief smile: nervous and dismissive.

"I'd forgotten about that."

"But he came to pass?"

"A misunderstanding of him."

I had meant the permissive society; but I wasn't sure what she meant.

"He certainly entered my life again last night. Do you remember Barney Dillon?"

She paused a moment over her melon. "She's told you?"

I gave her a surprised look. "You knew?"

"I was up in town for a day last week. We had lunch together." She went on scooping out the flesh. "She's always rather tended to tell me things she's afraid to tell her mother." I realized she meant to apologize for pre-empting the confession, but I detected a buried reproof.

"You've told Nell?"

"She asked me not to. How did you react?"

"As calmly as I could manage."

"I shouldn't worry. She's very sensible."

"You can't approve of it?"

She hesitated.

"You should see some of the young men Rosamund shacks up with. I've learnt that disapproving doesn't help."

"He's such a damned phony. I can't tell you." I told her about the flight from New York, the meeting at Heathrow: Barney's devious silence.

"I haven't met him for years."

"You must have seen him on the box."

"Occasionally. He seems rather good at that. As they go." She finished the melon. "That was delicious."

I knew, unless she had changed profoundly, she couldn't really think thus of him, or no more sincerely than she had said "delicious" of the melon. She was merely using an old Oxford trick to snub me: always contradict people who show their emotions in order to goad them into showing more. Perhaps she guessed from my silence that I wasn't buying it, because she went on.

"If they really need help, they come."

"If only I could understand what she sees in him."

"She's not a fool. In spite of Nell's attempts to turn her into one."

I lit a cigarette between courses, a bad habit Jenny had got me out of during our liaison.

"At least I begin to see why she likes you so much."

"The feeling is mutual."

A cool common sense, perhaps; but it appeared to be implying that I couldn't accuse Barney of my own nature and crimes. I changed the subject to her own children. Rosamund had left Cambridge and was now a research assistant in the BBC, and coming down to Oxford every week-end. Her younger sister Anne was having a year in Italy as a part of her language course; Anthony had insisted she go through

[ 199 ]

with it. And the benjamin, Paul, whom I'd never seen, was a fifteen-year-old boy at Dartington. I knew from Caro that he was a tricky child—"he never says a word" was the description of hers that had stuck. I did not get a clean picture of him from his mother—he had emotional and academic problems, but she seemed to regard it as a passing phase . . . or perhaps as one more little opportunity to show me I was a stranger, not a family friend. Then there was talk about Comptom, about Oxford and how it had changed. I even dragged a little out of her about her own life, her committees and good causes; but not a word about Anthony, except in passing, or their marriage. The punctilious lack of curiosity in her as to what we had said became more and more chilling.

Increasingly I knew I was being tolerated for Anthony's sake, purely out of courtesy. The more we talked, the clearer it became that we had nothing in common, not even a former "sin" and an inability to forgive it. The "bequest" was revealed as ridiculous, based as it patently was on, if not a misconception, a severe underestimate of how Jane valued me. It now began to be something to be stored and told to Jenny when next we met. Not keeping *her* in my life came rapidly to seem an impossibility. This and the previous scene had to be told, and she was now the only one who understood my language. The dialect here was hopelessly archaic.

Or so I was thinking by the time the coffee came; and a silence, one of those silences more revealing than any words. I made one last attempt.

"Are you going to go on living in Oxford, Jane?"

"I'm not sure. All my friends are here now. Andrew's suggested Compton, but I . . . Nell and I are both against it. He doesn't quite realize our capacity for getting on each other's nerves." She had been smoking, and now she stubbed out the cigarette; and seemed to speak to the ashtray. "I'm also thinking of joining the Communist Party."

She didn't look at me, but she must have been aware of the fatuously surprised face I showed for a moment. For another moment or two I took it as some metaphorical crack about Nell and Andrew. But then she suddenly looked me in the eyes, with a tight little smile, as if she knew I knew you can't deliver such information as casually and inconsequentially without having saved it up and timed it.

"Are you serious?"

"I'm flirting with the Maoists and the International Marxists as well. They're much more fashionable, of course."

Then she said, "Anthony isn't to know, by the way. I've not decided yet. It's as much . . . I suppose intuitive as intellectual."

"Because it feels right?"

"Just slightly less wrong than the other alternatives."

"It certainly makes a change from the usual order of conversion."

"It know it's rather unreal here. At Oxford. They're much more sophisticated than elsewhere in the country."

"Russia?"

She had a thin smile. "People in glass houses?"

"But . . . I mean, fine, with backward peasant societies. But we're hardly that now."

"Just a backward capitalist one?"

"Still conditioned to certain freedoms?"

She took another cigarette, and leaned forward for me to light it.

"I haven't any Joan-of-Arc illusions. I hate violence. And dogma. I know they seem to be the prerequisites of change. I couldn't even follow the Catholic party line. I'm not pretending I have a good record in that way at all."

"But?"

She traced the rim of her coffee-saucer with a finger-tip.

"I suppose I have a perhaps very naïve dream of an intelligent Marxist society. A system that could one day translate theory into something viable locally . . . what Mao's done for China." She looked up across the room. "It's partly the futility of university life. The smugness of it. The impracticality." She gave herself a dismissive smile. "I don't really know. It's probably just a foolish illusion that the Left needs people who feel as well as think."

I watched her, she was looking down again, and remembered how good an amateur actress she had been in the old days. She had been acting ever since I arrived, was still acting, but the role had changed. I suspected the attitude to me hadn't; it might seem like a rapprochement, an attempt at explaining what lay behind her mask. But it was really putting up another fence—a private version of an iron curtain.

"Is this a common thing here nowadays?"

"I'm not being trendy, if that's what you mean."

"But how much the reverse?"

"I can think of four—no, five avowed SCR Marxists. One of whom I can't stand."

"And Anthony doesn't realize at all?"

"He knows I have strong left-wing sympathies. He shares some of them. I don't think he'd be very surprised."

"Then why don't you tell him?"

"I think it might hurt him."

"Nell knows?"

Her lips pressed together.

"We've had a couple of shouting-matches about it. One only three days ago. She's managed to pick up all Andrew's sillier views of life. None of his humor and tolerance. He treats all this as a joke. Nell takes it as a personal affront, I'm afraid."

"You have my sympathies there."

But they evoked no response, or only a very tangential one.

"The house, you'll see, it's quite large, I shan't really need it all. I'd like to see it used in some way when this is over." She gave another dry look across the room. "Perhaps I'll just be Lenin's widow all over again. Everyone's joke landlady. Pamphlets for breakfast, propaganda for supper."

"Well. It's what Oxford's famous for."

"Except I think this lost cause is only counted so among the timeserving intelligentsia. The monstrous regiment of academics turned media men." She paused. "I'm afraid I've come to regard TV and Fleet Street liberalism as the nastiest right-wing conspiracy yet."

"Audience corrupts. Even more than power."

"I don't see why the cleverest have to be the most corrupt. And devote so much of their cleverness to perpetuating social and genetic advantage."

"You ought to go abroad more often, Jane. They're just mannikins. Bantams on a midden."

"But I don't live abroad. Your midden happens to be my country."

"And mine. But *touché*."

My smile was barely returned. Underneath those exchanges we had begun to annoy each other, perhaps both sensing that we took each other too lightly, though in different ways. The waiter came with more coffee, which she refused. I didn't really want any myself, but I took some all the same, to keep her sitting there. He went away, there was a silence. I avoided her eyes when I spoke.

"Am I included in this general anathema?"

"Why should you think that?"

"Because I've just met someone who *was* glad to see me."

She was silent a moment, then she said, "Perhaps women

change more than men." But she shook her head. "I'm sorry. I am truly and immensely grateful for your coming."

"Even though I'm a semi-expatriate and capitalist lackey."

She looked down, and her voice dropped. "You're putting very unfair words into my mouth."

"But you wish silence had never been broken."

She took a breath. I knew she was tempted to snub me again; yet that behind the poised woman and her weapons lay someone very far from balance. She stared down at her empty coffee-cup, as if the answer lay in its black grounds.

"I don't know what Anthony has said to you, but I can guess they concern things I regard as very private. That have far more to do with the present than the past. That's simply all, you must believe me." She hesitated, and then there was suddenly an undertone of something much more natural. "I can't at the moment take the past, Dan. In any shape or form."

She had used my name, at last, for the first time; and for the first time I clearly saw a strain. She was mortal after all. I left a pause.

"Anthony kept going on about the two of you having ruined my marriage. By implication, my life. I pointed out that you have no right to give yourselves that kind of guilt. I haven't not enjoyed my life, Jane, for all its faults and failings—and I was always fully capable of ruining my own marriage. And I did. That's one thing. The other is that he hoped you and I would become friends again now. My own instant conclusion is that there's an appalling lack of corrupt and conscienceless men in your life. I think you need at least one. I've also got Anthony to report to tomorrow. And Caro. I'd like it to be that some hope, however small, was established."

She had stared down through that and for a long moment she continued to do so, but there was a trace of a rueful smile, some sort of admission of defeat.

"Nell did warn me."

"Of what?"

"What she called your vicious habit of calling everyone's bluff but your own."

"You used to have quite a low handicap at that game yourself."

"I seem to have grown out of practice."

"I can't understand why you should wish to continue what was always an inhumanity."

"It's nothing to do with you personally. But with a use to which I feel you're being put. Quite unjustifiably."

"Isn't one definition of fascism the belief that you have a right to judge for other people?"

I detected what I had sensed with her husband, an insecurity, almost a gauche anxiety when faced with someone from another world . . . all very well to despise and dismiss it, as I felt sure she did—very probably on artistic as well as political grounds—and all very well to despise her own enclosed academic world, her city: but it was where she lived, and she was not used to people, to situations, to men who had dropped, or could drop, the local sign-system, the conventions she knew best.

Her eyes down, she murmurs, "I'm no longer the person you knew, Dan. I'm sorry for not hiding it better. It's not your fault at all."

Dan hesitates, then reaches across the white cloth and touches her hand lightly. She says nothing. He beckons for the waiter.

Outside we found that the mist, not quite echoing what had just happened between us, had thickened. It was very nearly dense fog, and there was hardly any other traffic about. I knew we were crawling up the Banbury Road, but I lost all sense of distance. Jane edged along in second, peering intently at the nearside curb. We talked a little, spasmodically, about her new political convictions. I didn't argue, merely prompted gently. She became self-deprecating, even apologetic; as if it were a matter of aesthetics, the flower-arrangement of British political life needed a red branch somewhere in it; as if the universal postwar rejection of Communism in Britain were a kind of unfair social ostracism; then—perhaps with more reason—as if it were a matter of chemistry, equal valences. If Russia needed its Solzhenitsyns, then Britain needed them too, in reverse. There was also an element of middle-aged women's liberation, a need to shock both herself and those around her, a reaction against premature widowhood and all its threatened emptinesses. And I had finally a strong whiff of Oxford eccentricity. I wondered if she had any idea what a decision like hers would have meant in America, where the iron really bit.

We turned off the Banbury Road into a side-street. At last Jane swung the car out and turned in over a curb-ramp into a garden. She parked short of a garage beside the house. I rescued my overnight bag from the rear seat, and waited while she locked the doors. There were lights on in a semi-basement, and I could see a kitchen as we walked over the gravel. There were also lights above, on the ground floor, shafting the mist. Victorian brick and white woodwork, steps up, a tiled porch.

Jane stands looking for keys in her handbag. But a blurred shadow appears through the colored glass panes of the front door and it opens before she can get them out. A thin young French girl in a black pullover and jeans. She wears gold-rimmed glasses, pigtails tied with two red ribbons and face out of *Phèdre*.

# Beyond the Door

I couldn't follow the rapid exchange in French, but the girl was clearly in some sort of Gallic agony at having failed to get hold of us earlier. She would hardly let us into the hall. It was striking, with Pompeian red walls and a grotesquely massive set of carved Victorian banisters, painted white, beside the staircase. I glimpsed some nice paintings; a spectacularly florid cast-iron hatstand, also painted white. An old Jane lurked in that subtly theatrical red-and-white space, though I didn't note that at the time. The girl demanded all our attention. Eventually Jane put an arm round her shoulders to quiet her. I asked what had happened.

"The hospital have been trying to get in touch." She made a little grimace of apology at such fuss. "Dan, this is Gisèle."

The girl gave me a nervous, silent bob.

"I'd better see what it's all about. Do go and have a nightcap. I won't be a moment."

She gestured to the girl to look after me. There was a table with a telephone on it beside the stairs.

"Did they say. . . ?"

"Sometimes he can't sleep. He likes me to read to him." Her eyes flicked, for my benefit, toward the face behind her. "We're a tiny bit alarm-prone." She smiled. "There's some Armagnac. Do help yourself."

I went into the room after the French girl. It stretched the depth of the house, two original rooms knocked into one, with a vaguely proscenium-shaped arch left between them. Many books, more engravings and paintings, some pleasant old furniture, a grand piano at the far, garden end—which reminded me that Jane had once played passably. A lit alcove of ancient pottery; bits of Tanagra mounted on plastic cubes, a small Greek kylix. A line of invitation cards on a mantelpiece, an old Oxford form of snobbery; a modern terracotta head of a boy among them, I presumed the son. A crowded room. Not that I took much of all this in: the French girl

[ 206 ]

had turned and closed the door. She seemed very anxious that I should know she was still upset.

"Did they tell you what it was?"

She stared at me, then shook her head. "*Je m'excuse, monsieur. Je suis . . .*" then she shook her head again. I offered her a cigarette. "*Non, non . . .* I am okay."

I had in fact already half-guessed what it was; or at least what I hoped it might be: a change of heart in Anthony—a hearing, on reflection, after we had left, of what I had been trying to say; a sudden need to break his self-imposed silence with his wife.

Jane's voice came from outside, too low to be distinct. I stood by the fireplace, the girl still stood by the door, like some kind of watchdog. She waved a hand, managed a bit more English.

"If you like to drink something . . ."

"Fine. Don't worry. I'll help myself."

The drinks were on a console table in the rear half of the room. I poured a Scotch. The girl stayed by the door, abandoning all pretense that she was not listening to what went on outside. I moved down beside the piano and looked out over the fog-hidden garden at the rear of the house. Perhaps it was the brooding isolation there, the blanketed silence, but I had a feeling of dislocation. A swiveling Jacobsen egg-chair stood by the window, with a book lying on its seat: *Selections from the Prison Notebooks of Antonio Gramsci.* I could see little markers, Jane was evidently reading it, and I picked the volume up. Many passages had been marked in pencil, some heavily, with double vertical lines beside them. "*For each individual is the synthesis not only of existing relations, but of the history of these relations.*" "*Structure ceases to be an external force which crushes man, assimilates him to itself and makes him passive, and is transformed into a means of freedom, an instrument to create a new ethical political form and a source of new initiatives.*" Those last eleven words had been further underlined in the text. I leafed idly through the pages, trying to find some written comment; but there were none . . . or just one passage. It had an additional exclamation mark beside it. "*The philosophy of praxis is consciousness full of contradictions, in which the philosopher himself, understood both individually and as an entire social group, not merely grasps the contradictions, but posits himself as an element of the contradiction and elevates this element to a principle of knowledge and therefore of action.*"

I replaced the book, feeling the girl might think I was prying; but she seemed oblivious of me, and stood hidden, still by the door, behind the side of the arch joining the two rooms. I began to look at other books on the shelves that lined the walls, serried and silent regiments of philosophy and would-be human wisdom. Then there was the little ping from outside of the receiver being replaced. I saw the girl move away from the door. But we heard the sound of another number being dialed, and a few moments later, Jane's low voice again. The conversation didn't last very long. Again the receiver went down. Total silence followed. The French girl looked through the arch to where I stood, as if it was all my fault; then away. I let the silence run a few moments more, then put down my glass and with what tried to be a pacifying smile, went out into the hall.

Jane was standing only a foot or two from the front door, quite motionless, her back to me, her hands in the pockets of her outdoor coat, staring into the night. She must have heard me come out, but she didn't turn.

"Jane?"

Still she didn't move. I went a step or two closer.

"Has something happened?"

Her head did shift a fraction around toward me then. I saw the faintest smile, for all the world as if I had just said something silly.

"Apparently soon after we left. He managed to get out on his balcony." She faced the night again. "And over the rail."

"You don't . . ."

"I'm afraid so."

"Dead?"

"They think it would have been instantaneous." She gave a minute shrug. "By the time they found him . . ."

I went a step closer, trying to understand how her shock did not match mine; I think more, almost, in shock at that than at this thunderbolt.

"Jane?"

"Who was that man on Scott's last expedition?"

"Captain Oates."

She gave the ghost of a nod. I heard the girl in the doorway behind me, and went and took Jane's arm.

"For God's sake come and sit down."

"I'm all right, Dan. I've just rung my doctor and told her not to worry." She touched my hand, but only to release her

[ 208 ]

arm, then turned and smiled back at the French girl—who spoke first.

"*Je ne savais pas comment . . .*"

"*Oui, oui. Il n'en voulait plus. C'est tout.*"

The girl, with a far better sense of occasion than Jane, covered her face in her hands. Jane went and took her shoulders, then kissed her lightly on the head and murmured something. The girl looked up, I don't know whether in amazement at this Anglo-Saxon sangfroid or in horror at Racine reduced to . . . Jane turned to me.

"I think I need some tea."

"You need something stronger than that."

"No, I'd rather . . ." she smiled at Gisèle. "Go on."

The girl went hesitantly away, another dubious look at me, still as if I were in some way to blame. She disappeared down past the staircase to the basement, and I followed Jane into the living-room.

"I can't believe it."

"I know."

"Did they say. . . ?"

"The nurse who saw him to sleep said how relaxed he seemed. He was talking about you."

She stooped and took a cigarette from a box, then the light I held out for her.

"Had he ever. . . ?"

She drew deeply on the cigarette, breathed the smoke out.

"No. Not once."

"And no note?"

"They can't find anything."

She turned away to the mantelpiece, and stared down at the hearth. It was made with a coal fire, but hadn't been lit.

"It couldn't have been a mistake? If he was drugged?"

She shook her head. "I don't think so. They . . ."

"But why this of all nights?"

She said nothing, stayed without moving, then walked toward the bayed front windows of the room. I was left staring at her back. After a moment she ran both her hands back over the sides of her hair, then pressed the back of her neck a moment, beneath the silver comb, as if she were sitting up in bed, waking out of some nightmare.

"It's not your fault, Dan. In any way at all."

"I wish you'd sit down."

"Really. I'm all right. I was prepared. It had to happen soon."

Yet something about her seemed totally unprepared; as if she had just missed a train and was lost in prospect of the person she would now fail to meet. She stood with her back turned, holding an elbow in one hand, the cigarette near her mouth with the other. I went beside her.

"Come on. Let's have your coat."

A moment's hesitation, then she unbuttoned it and let me take it from her shoulders. There was something almost sullen in her averted face, far more like a woman who had just been mortally and irremediably offended than one who had received a profound shock. I put the coat over the back of a sofa and went down the room to where the drinks were. I could still see and hear him so vividly, and the most incomprehensible thing seemed that we hadn't known, sitting there in that restaurant—that one could be eternally deprived of another human being so close in space, immediate in time. That old phrase of his, "correcting a design failure," returned with a ghastly and macabre irony. Absolving that ancient sin, or making sure I knew exactly what absolution entailed, had for some incomprehensible reason assumed more validity in his mind than the fresh "sin" of suicide. He had been at death's door, his self-awarded euthanasia had merely forestalled Atropos by a few weeks, but the timing . . . it was like being the victim of a bad practical joke. I went back with a tumbler of brandy. Jane glanced at it, but shook her head.

"You have it. I really don't want any."

"Just a mouthful."

She gave in, she took a sip, but put the glass down at once on the window-ledge in front of her.

"I'm so sorry you've been dragged into this. It's unforgivable."

I said gently, "You must try to pity him a little."

She turned away to find an ashtray. Then she stubbed out the half-smoked cigarette with an unnatural care and persistence.

"I pity us both, Dan."

For a moment then there was something more honest in her voice; a tinge of despair, of real feeling. But as if she regretted even that small concession to normal reaction, she immediately looked at her watch.

"I must let Rosamund know. And Nell."

"I'll ring Nell. In a minute."

She hesitated. "Perhaps. If you wouldn't mind."

"Of course not."

She took a deep breath. "It's the thought of all the fuss. The arranging."

"I should let Nell take care of that.".

"There'll have to be an inquest, I'm afraid."

"Never mind."

"They wondered if you'd come to the hospital with me to-morrow morning."

"I wouldn't dream of letting you go alone."

"I feel so embarrassed, I—"

"Don't be ridiculous."

She looked down, she was going to say something more, but Gisèle appeared with the tea-tray; and Jane seemed glad of the excuse to move and clear a space on the marble coffee-table in front of the fireplace. The girl made a gesture of willingness to go away, but Jane made her stay. I gave up; refused tea, went and collected my glass of whisky; then suggested I ring Nell.

Out in the hall I prayed for it to be Andrew who answered; and after a long pause, the prayer was granted. It was a relief to hear ordinary reactions of shock and then solicitude: another male voice and mind. I put him off attempting to set out at once, though he said they were fairly free of fog at Compton. They would be in Oxford by lunchtime. No, she'd rather not talk to Nell tonight; yes, I'd tell her they were "shattered and heartbroken." I'd hold the fort till they came. And yes, I looked forward to meeting him again too.

I went back into the living-room and Jane took her cup of tea and my place at the telephone. The call went on for twenty minutes or more, during which I tried to make conversation with the French kid: where she came from, how long she'd been in Oxford . . . Aix-en-Provence, a month, apparently Jane's younger daughter had stayed with her family in France. I couldn't imagine what she was thinking, these English with their phlegm, their stone-cold blood, their infantile questions about Cézanne and the ruin of the Côte d'Azur. But Jane seemed to have found a brisker, more normal self when she came back. Rosamund had cried, it seemed, then decided it was perhaps for the best . . . she too would be here for lunch. Then there were banalities: what food Gisèle should buy the next morning, where everyone would sleep, when and how to let Paul, and Anne in Florence, know, and . . .

About half past twelve Gisèle went down to the kitchen with the tea-things and Jane took me up to my room—the absent Paul's. I saw poster-diagrams: one of English building styles, another of medieval armor, with all the bits and pieces labeled and explained. A lot of books, rather an ominous lack of the usual decor one expects in a boy's bedroom. History was evidently his thing, and I smelled a little don in the making. Jane looked cursorily round to see I had everything I might need. Again she was playing hostess; treating me like some academic stranger, far too distinguished—or transient—to be bothered with the trivial upsets of her private life.

"Will you be all right, Jane?"

"Yes. Really. Please don't worry." She looked down at the bed between us. "I do hope the mattress isn't too hard."

"My dear, it's not the hardness of mattresses that worries me."

She met my eyes for a moment, and I wasn't smiling. She looked down again at the bed.

"One survives as one can."

"At least Anthony was frank with me."

She turned away to a window. The curtains were already drawn, but she pulled them a little closer, then fiddled with their edges. She had taken off her suit coat, and there was something in the way she stood, the flagrantly unnecessary fussing with the curtains, that was childishly mulish; willing, that is, to be argued out of it.

"He did tell me that all wasn't well between you." I waited for her to answer, but she said nothing. "Whatever else he meant by this terrible thing, it can't have been that you and I have nothing to say about it." I tried a more practical approach. "Anyway, we surely have to decide what's to be said tomorrow. Publicly."

At last she turned from the window, though she wouldn't look at me.

"You must be so tired."

"I'm still on California time. And please sit down."

There was a Windsor chair by a table-desk in the corner of the room behind her. She looked round at it, as if she were the stranger there, then moved, turned the chair a little; and sat in it, sideways to me, her arms folded.

I sat on the end of the bed, turned away from her.

"May I tell you what he said to me?"

"If you think it will help."

I leaned forward, elbows on knees, and chose my words very carefully: his self-accusing mood, his feeling that he had denatured her real personality during their marriage; my objections; his asking me how I should know the reality of the situation after all these years, and my obviously not being able to answer that. I stopped, there was a silence.

"Did he give a reason for telling you all this?"

"He said you'd told him about us. Before the two of you got married."

There was a telltale hesitation, though her voice was quiet.

"Yes. That's true. I did."

"I wish I'd known." She said nothing. "He rather suggested everything that went wrong had stemmed from that."

"From my telling him? Or our not telling you?"

"I think he meant both. The general hide-and-seek that went on."

"We did discuss telling you. There seemed reasons not to at the time."

"What were they?" Silence. I drew a breath. "Jane, everyone is going to wonder about the timing of this. We can't not talk about it now."

There was a further pause, but then she spoke.

"Your relationship with Nell?"

"Nothing else?"

"I suppose self-preservation on my part. I felt I'd betrayed you a little. And Anthony. He was so much happier pretending to forgive you in secret. Not having to face up to the fact that he could never forgive you in reality." She hesitated a moment, then went on. "One always finds good reasons for doing what one wants."

"He kept on talking about correcting a design failure. I think the underlying idea was of some mythical true marriage between you and me that he'd . . . prevented." Again she refused my invitation to comment. "Almost as if you were some locked cupboard to which I had the only key. My feeling was very strongly that he was not only living in the past, but he'd blacked out on all subsequent reality. I did try to suggest that. But I don't think he really heard."

I waited for her to agree or disagree. The door was ajar, and I heard the French girl as she went on her way to the floor above. A door up there shut quietly, and we heard faint footfalls on the ceiling over our heads; as once before, in very different circumstances.

At last Jane said, "Part of him never grew up, I'm afraid."

"I didn't realize the lines were so broken. Broken at all, in fact."

"Ours grew into one of those marriages where the partners survive by hoarding secrets from each other. Forbidden areas."

"It seems such a change from the beginning."

"I think our supposed total frankness in those days was always rather . . ." but she did not finish the sentence.

"There doesn't seem much supposed about the total frankness that drove you to tell him about us."

"Except that from then on our marriage was based on a secret I'd kept from him."

"But not for very long." She said nothing. "When did you tell him?"

"When we were in the States. That summer."

"He took it badly?"

She shook her head, in a kind of ancient despair; let out a breath. "He was as innocent as a new-born child, all his life, about the workings of his own unconscious. It set a pattern. Of course we didn't see it at the time. One never does. But slowly, over the years, telling each other what we truly felt about anything became like . . . I suppose, like throwing away trump cards. Not the done thing at all."

"But you guessed why he wanted me to come?"

"I suspected you'd be in some way asked to pick up the bill for his penance."

"That's putting it very harshly."

"You haven't had to spend most of your life listening to Catholic double-talk."

I smiled, still with my back to her. "Which your new faith is free of?"

"At least theirs is mostly about social salvation. Not private."

I remembered what he had said about all improvement in the world starting from the individual. It must have been at least in part a retrospective admonition to himself; and perhaps also a reaction to a hopelessness in the woman I was with. But I didn't want us to wander off into some general discussion.

"Obviously there's a straightforward reason for what he did. I suppose people will swallow that."

"They'll have to, won't they?"

She was saying every sentence, and especially that last one, as if it were potentially final, the matter closed. I found some cigarettes and offered them, expecting her to refuse, and to seize the chance to take herself off; but she accepted one. I stood and lit it for her; then sat on the bed again, facing her this time; and now, staring at the foot of the curtains, she spoke without being prompted.

"We managed. We weren't unhappy in the day-to-day. There was quite a lot we did agree on. The children."

"He said something else. That he was eternally grateful to you."

She had a sere smile. "That's called kissing the cross. In the trade."

"I won't take that."

She said nothing for a moment.

"I made him suffer, Dan. Terribly."

"You never discussed separating?"

"Several times. Before the illness."

There was the sound of a crawling car outside, and I felt certain it must be a visitor for the house. It even stopped, but then we heard it go slowly on.

"And what prevented you?"

"Oh, the usual thing. A sort of shared guilt. You know, one's made so many mistakes that splitting up just seems . . . one more? And the children." She half glanced toward the head of the bed. "Paul especially. He's rather had to bear the brunt of it. The girls understand. Rosamund knows all about it, she's been a . . . great help. Very intelligent about everything."

"Why *did* you tell him about us?"

She shook her head, she no longer knew. "The Church? I had all their rubbish about sin and absolution floating about in my head. Anthony on truth. I hadn't realized then that Anthony on truth was always really Anthony on masochism." But she said that less bitterly, almost wrily. "It was probably the wrong choice. But I don't think it matters. It wouldn't have been any different if I'd fully matched his immaculate conception of me. It's had much more to do with temperaments . . . emotions. Perversities, perhaps." She grimaced. "We're not very unusual. Almost the standard North Oxford marriage."

"He talked about hating me for years."

"You mustn't take Catholic eggheads' judgments on themselves too seriously. It's their speciality, moral mountains out of molehills. His never very secure masculine nose was left permanently a little out of joint. That's all. And it did give him a lovely chance to play Jesus Christ and the woman taken in adultery." She stood up and fetched an ash-tray from a chest of drawers by the door, then set it on the bed beside me before she sat again. "What you said at dinner. Having only yourself to blame for the break-up with Nell. It was the same for us."

"I'm not letting Nell off scot-free."

"Of course not. It takes two." She stared at her hands, at the curl of cigarette smoke that rose from them. "It's all very well for him to lie on his deathbed and say he's eternally grateful to me. It was something that didn't get said very often in this house." She shook her head again. "It's so dishonest. If you're not presently grateful, what is the point?" Now I was the one who waited. "We came to know the danger areas too well. I had a period of shouting at him. But we grew too civilized for that. Too lazy. One can spend two hours in *Hedda Gabler*. Not ten years." After a moment she said, "You get so sick of brooding all your life away over your own problems."

"Yes, I know what you mean."

Very quietly, discreetly, from upstairs came the sound of radio music. I saw the French girl writing, frantically home; or in some diary. And out of nowhere the past was with us, former selves, almost uncannily, in a silence that was not like the other silences of that night, but an ancient remembered kind of silence, very characteristic of her more serious side. An old empathy down through the body of the years, and tinged with sadness, futility, like some old garment one had once loved, but could never wear seriously again: I wasn't even sure that she was not manipulating me, hiding a shift of defensive position under the guise of true confession. My inquisitiveness had to be defused, she had conceded that; and was doing it by presenting a very banal version of events. I had never had any belief in the "noble" theory of tragedy: that only the falls of the great can achieve such status. But just as childhood memories get grossly magnified in absent adult memory—all return is a form of bathos—I knew I had been guilty of cherishing a kind of noble legend of our joint past. Yet there lingered, perhaps because Anthony had just done something so far from banal, a feeling of half-truth in all that she said.

"Nell knows the situation?"

"By inference." She leaned back. "Not for lack of interrogation. Though mercifully she's dropped all that since the illness. I think she's tried to pump Roz, but . . ."

"I've been through that. With Caro."

"She got far worse since she became mistress of Compton. Little worlds where you must control everything, or you feel threatened."

"I can imagine."

"I really don't know her anymore. That side of her." She added, "She's been very good these last few months. It's just this ghastly need to dragoon us all into her scheme of things."

"Insecurity. She would never admit it."

"It's not all her fault. I've lost the art of being what people want me to be. It's become rather a nasty little habit. Destroying people's expectations. As you must have noticed."

I smiled, partly at the fact that she wasn't smiling herself.

"Now you mention it."

"I tell myself I'm simply in search of lost honesty."

"Is that the right adverb?"

"Then honestly in search of lost simplicity."

"Not a quality I ever associated with you."

"We all went to such a bad school."

"Yes."

There was another silence. I handed her the ash-tray so that she could stub out her cigarette. She spoke in a brisker voice.

"You're so lucky to have lived in a world that knows it's artificial. Ever since Freddie Ayer the mania you must have here is soccer. Heaven help you at a philosophical dinner-party if you can't discuss Liverpool's last match or the metaphysics of four-three-four and the floating winger."

"You should hear a would-be intellectual film-producer discussing Lévi-Strauss."

"At least he's trying?"

"A lot more than you can imagine."

We smiled down from each other's eyes. The music upstairs had stopped, and the house, the city, lay in peace. I saw Anthony lying on his back, staring sightlessly, the ultimate cold of death; yet somehow still listening. Once more she folded her arms.

"I think there's something I'd better tell you, Dan. Which nobody else knows." She was staring down at her curtains again. "What you said just now about Anthony's wanting us to be friends . . . it, well actually it gave me an enormous sense of relief." Her eyes rose to meet mine. "There's someone else. These last two years. We've tried to keep it very secret. But I was frightened Anthony might have guessed something."

"I think he'd have told me. And I'm delighted."

She gave a shrug, killing too much delight. "It's all been rather complicated. He's another philosophy teacher here. Not literally here at the moment. He's spending a sabbatical at Harvard, for a book on William James."

"I'm sure you needn't feel guilty."

"It's just the . . . it's so ludicrous, the kind of incestuous pattern things seem to fall into. We've all been close friends for years now. I know his ex-wife quite well. She's remarried. She lives only just round the corner." She pulled a dry face. "One of those Iris Murdoch situations."

"Shall you marry?"

"I think that's the general idea."

"It sounds a very good one."

"He's several years younger than I am. I . . . you know. One's time of life. All that." She paused a moment. "He was Anthony's student originally. They've gone rather different ways philosophically, but there's always been that Oedipal undertone. The Jocasta thing."

"And you share the same politics?"

"He's quite active in the local Labour Party." She added, "He doesn't take my flight further left very seriously. You know what dons are like—any deviation from their own views becomes a tutorial situation. Silly students getting uppish again."

I smiled. "But obviously you like him?"

"Yes, very much. He makes me laugh, he writes very funny letters. Comparing the horrors of Harvard to our own brand. To Anthony as well. Very often I hear everything twice over." Then she said inconsequentially, "Sometimes I think I never want to hear the word ethics again as long as I live."

"I don't think the total lack of them I'm familiar with makes things any simpler."

"Just this feeling that the real informing spirit of Oxford remains the posh prep school. Preternaturally clever little boys playing at being adults."

"But nothing stands in the way now? Even ethically?"

"Only my instinct that he'd be much better off with someone younger. Not me."

"That's his decision. And speaking from contemporary experience, there are problems that way too."

There was a tiny grain of mischief in her voice.

"Nell will be pleased to hear that."

"Then I forbid you to tell her."

She smiled.

"If you'd keep this other skeleton in the cupboard quiet."

"Of course."

"He offered to give up this year at Harvard. But I made him go."

"Why on earth don't you go out and join him? When the conventions have been observed?"

"I'll have to see how Paul takes it."

"Problems?"

"He's fully capable of facing them rationally. It's the emotional side, he tends to suppress everything there. I suppose in imitation of his parents. It would have been easier if I'd had another girl. He's rather modeled himself on his father."

"And rejected you?"

"In the way fifteen-year-olds do."

"He'll get over that."

"As long as I don't seem to be rejecting him."

"He gets on with your friend?"

"Yes. Rather well." She smoothed her trousers. "It's simply the potential shock of having to accept him as a stepfather. On top of everything else. We've had awful problems with his schooling. He's a weird child—hopeless at any subject that bores him. Won't even try. Totally intractable. Anything to do with history, quite the reverse. A horrid little monomaniac."

"You mustn't sacrifice your own happiness to him."

Her brown eyes appraised mine; and for a moment there was an old light in them. She looked drily down.

"I think you're going to like Rosamund."

"Her view?"

She nodded. "I am aware of it. It's a matter of . . . finding the right time?" She glanced at her wristwatch. "And talking of time."

It was half past one, but for a moment neither of us moved. I stared at the floor.

"You're not angry with me for forcing this on you, Jane?"

"I'm angry for having to force it on you."

"I suspect all that's being forced on me is something that was long overdue." She said nothing. "What went on in those years. I have the strangest idea that if we'd all stayed close, it wouldn't have turned out like this. I don't know . . . in some peculiar way we complemented one another. Even Nell." Still she was silent, but it was a silence that had lost its hostility. "It's all been such a comedown since. As you predicted."

"All woe?"

"No. Of course not. But far too many artificial substitutes."

There was another silence then, but she broke it finally by standing and pushing the chair back true to its table; then stopped a moment there and spoke to the wooden top. "The situation is really very drab and ordinary, Dan. In spite of what's happened tonight." She picked up the ash-tray, took it back to the chest of drawers, spoke there again with her back to me. "You've caught me at such a bad time. I think I've managed to retain some sort of sense of humor." She turned with a smile. "I'm just not managing to show it at the moment."

"I haven't forgotten you as Lydia Languish."

"Fifty million years ago." She moved to the door, awkwardly, and aware of it. "I said we'd be at the hospital about ten."

"You'd better wake me."

She nodded, hesitated over saying something, or perhaps over doing something—a kiss on the cheek, a token embrace; decided not to.

"Sleep well."

"And you."

The door closed on her. After a moment Dan went and stared in the little mirror over the chest of drawers. He looked as tired as he felt. But five minutes later, in bed, in darkness, he knew sleep was in no hurry to come. Yet he felt relaxed, as he would sometimes after a good day's work—relaxed, though one's mind is still alive and reviewing; as if he had refound some old charge of curiosity about existence, of irony, enigma, secret purpose. He should perhaps have felt sorrow for Anthony, and some guilt, but even that seemed to have a richness. He felt saturated, diverse; if not justified by self, at least justified in temporary destiny, hazard. He had never, at least since leaving Nell, been fond of adding complexity to an already quite sufficiently complex life, and in some way the fact that he knew, as he lay there, that he no longer wished he had never come to Oxford proved this reentry into the past had answered some previously unseen lack.

Like all self-conscious writers Dan had always associated success in work with the breaking of established codes; or to be more precise, with keeping a balance between the expected, obeying his craft, and the unexpected, obeying the main social function of all art. Another of his grudges against his own particular *métier* was that it put so much more value on the craft than the code-breaking side; that even the smallest departure from the cinematic established and sanctified had to be so fiercely fought for. He had never been a literary experimenter, an avantgardist; but he would not have been a writer if ordinary expectation, life as it is, had satisfied his deeper psychological bent. And now—this seemed very near the heart of it to him—he felt that life itself had backed his view: had broken codes he might have flinched at breaking if he had been inventing the situation, had performed a kind of magic not with causality, but the timing, precipitation and conjunction of the results of causality. It was like an unsettling of fixed statistical probability, a release from mire, a liberation, a yes from the heart of reality to the supposed artifice of art.

He knew it when his mind, drifting at last toward sleep, drifted also to the Kitchener script. Perhaps its recalcitrance was really a challenge; and now the challenge assumed the face of a relief. He would meet it, he would solve, given this lead, the problems somehow. Perhaps his relief had a more selfish and personal strand, at the thought of his also hazard-granted escape from the kind of existence that had apparently soured and finally dominated this Oxford house. He thought of Jenny; of how distant she was, and mercifully, from all that was symbolic and archetypal in a boy's bedroom. In England, Oxford; the involute and its academy; middle class and middle age. He went to sleep.

Mr. Specula Speculans snores there now; so it must seem. But even the humblest dialogue-fixers and life-inventors must have such moods, however unapt, however callously oblivious of other human suffering, to survive. They live not life, but other lives; drive not down the freeways of determined fact, but drift and scholar-gipsy through the landscapes of the hypothetical, through all the pasts and futures of each present. Only one of each can be what happened and what will happen, but to such men they are the least important. I create, I am: all the rest is dream, though concrete and executed. Perhaps what Dan always wanted of his looking-glasses was not his own face, but the way through them. This kind of mind is self-satisfied only in the sense that one must suppose God is self-satisfied—in an eternity of presents; in his potentiality, not his fulfillment. A perfect world would have no room for writers: vampires who sleep with a slaked smile while philosophers fall from windows, men and women are tortured, children starve, the world dies of its own greed and stupidity. It is even worse than that. If Dan did smile in his sleep that night it was because his unconscious seemed to believe that a perfect world would have room for no one else.

# Webs

I was awakened just before nine by Gisèle's voice outside the door. My "daughter from London" was on the telephone. When I came down to the hall, Jane, in a housecoat, passed me the receiver with her hand over the mouthpiece.

"I've told her what's happened."

"Bless you."

I announced myself to Caro, and watched Jane disappear downstairs.

"Oh Daddy. How *terrible* for you."

"Less for me than . . ."

"Is she. . . ?"

"She's being very brave."

"I couldn't believe it when she first told me."

"I know." I gave her my own brief, and very censored, account of what had happened: our meeting, he'd given no clue, he must have decided on it for some time.

"It seems so strange. Almost as if he was just waiting."

"I think he was in a way, Caro." I hesitated, abruptly realizing for the first time the practical problems of explaining— or rather, not explaining—what had really happened. "Seeing me must have seemed his last piece of unfinished business. You mustn't think of it as an act of despair. I suspect it was much more one of relief. Peace, if you like."

She mulled over that for a moment.

"Aunt Jane says you've been marvelous."

"Hardly."

"That wasn't how it sounded."

"We've talked. You were right."

"I'm glad." She paused, "At last." Then, "At least that."

"You needn't rub it in."

"I wasn't."

"And you—how are things?"

She hesitated. "I went to see the flat again yesterday evening. Now it makes me feel I'm walking out on you."

"Which proves you aren't. Go on. You take it."

"I did say I would, actually. I've got first refusal till tomorrow. But—"

"No buts. They want some money?"

"Just the first month's rent."

There was a pause.

"I rang originally because . . . actually a telegram's just come for you."

"Have you opened it?"

"I thought I'd better."

The further pause gave the game away. "From Jenny?"

"Do you want me to read it out?"

"Please."

She must have had it in front of her. "It says, 'Tibou China'—is that right?—'misses you but has me now stop please call your tonight Jenny.' " Caro added, "If that makes sense."

"Yes, that's fine."

"Who's Tibou China?"

"One word. *Tibouchina.* It's a shrub that grows outside the Cabin. Jenny's moved in. That's all."

"I thought it must be a Pekinese or something."

"A Brazilian. I'll take you to Kew one day and show it to you."

She murmured, "All these plants and women in your life."

"Only one for real. Her name begins with C."

"I bet."

"Will you be in this evening?"

"If you want me to."

"Not if . . ."

"You have priority."

"I'll catch a train this afternoon. Let's go out to dinner somewhere."

Another hesitation. "Would you come and see the flat?"

"Of course. Let's do that."

"Don't be horrid to Mummy. She can't help it."

"I'll try."

"And what you promised. Not telling her yet. Please."

Now I hesitated. "But you have told Jane?"

"I had to have someone."

"I'm not getting at you, Caro. Just she'll be hurt if . . ."

"I can't handle you both together."

It wasn't the time to argue. "Okay. Don't worry."

"And all I didn't say to Aunt Jane."

[ 224 ]

"She understands."

A moment, then there was a kiss down the line; then disconnection.

Fifteen minutes later I was shaved and dressed and down in the kitchen. It was still misty outside, but clearing, already a hint of blue sky on its way. The weather, it seemed, rejected mourning. Another large room, a dead forest of varnished pine, all the equipment at the garden end, a round table at the front: Jane sitting at it, the girl busy making coffee. There were some opened letters, the *Times* and the *Guardian;* but not the *Morning Star,* so far as I could see.

"Caro feels she was inarticulate."

"Not at all. She was sweet. Do you want bacon and eggs, Dan?"

"Just coffee."

Apparently she had already rung her daughter in Florence; and spoken to the school, then to Paul himself, in Devon. Anne was flying home as soon as she could. Paul, who hadn't been told the manner of his father's death, had seemed to take it reasonably well. And now she was preparing a list of other people to ring. Her hair was loose, she looked less tense, almost as if she had slept well. Perhaps it was the girl, having to act a little in front of her. The kitchen was agreeably domestic after the theatrical hall and living-room upstairs—cottagy, rural in comparison.

"I like the house. I didn't have time to say that last night."

"You should see Gisèle's home in Aix."

She had retreated again into the mundane; into being English, talking about anything except what must have been uppermost in her mind; denying, it occurred to me, all the psychological laws of art . . . or at any rate, my art ("Her ravaged face shows the horror of the previous night"). Gisèle's family lived in a lovely eighteenth-century *hôtel,* her father taught at the university in Aix. She was musical, it seemed; of near professional standard at the violin. But reality soon returned, in dark-gray trousers—all I glimpsed as I followed Jane's sudden look up to the front garden outside.

"Oh God. Here are the crows."

"His priest?" She closed her eyes and nodded. "Shall I see him?"

"Would you mind? I simply . . ."

"Of course. I'll say you're not dressed yet."

I stood up. The front doorbell rang.

"If you could just ask if he gets a Christian burial. Or a stake through his heart at the nearest crossroads."

I smiled and turned to go upstairs, but she stood and came after me, lowering her voice, as if Gisèle must be spared such obscenity. "Dan, one detail from last night. They said he had a crucifix in his hand when they found him. You'd better feed that to his holiness."

I stared at her a moment, trying to discover why I hadn't been told this before. But the bell rang again. I touched her arm and went to answer it.

He was a young man, with a trace of a Scottish accent and much more than a trace of knowing what the invisible mistress of the house thought of him. He expressed his formal condolences, he quite understood; of course, of course, Mrs. Mallory would not feel up to seeing anyone—I would have got rid of him on the doorstep, if it hadn't seemed not quite the place for the question I had to ask . . . or perhaps it was just that no one born into a vicarage and its divine simplicities can ever see a priest without seeing an adult child as well.

We sat in the living-room and I explained about Anthony and the crucifix: how there may have been a loss of faith in his own courage, but not in his church. The priest lowered his head and murmured, "The poor man."

"This won't prevent his being buried according to the. . . ?"

"Oh no. We're . . . long past that stage." He gave me a nervous smile. "I don't even have to obtain a dispensation. I can assure you there will be no difficulty at all. In this case." He made a little explanation of the new doctrine on culpability. But then he said, "I take it you think a verdict of suicide will be returned?"

"It was hardly a balcony one could have fallen from by mistake."

"Yes, of course. I see. Most distressing."

I told him that I had spent that last hour with Anthony; went on a bit, how he had seemed reconciled to his fate, what a surprise it had been, but (using what was apparently my interlocutor's favorite adverbial phrase) of course in the circumstances . . . it was a touch absurd, justifying Anthony to this rather humorless young Scotsman. He seemed so ill-at-ease, so anxious not to offend, so unconsciously blinkered by his calling; a very long way, in sect as in character, from

John Knox, and finally almost more in need of comforting than the widow downstairs.

He went at last, in another cloud of condolence. If Mrs. Mallory would care to ring him about the Funeral Mass, if he could help in any way . . . ritual, in a world already stifled with it.

I found Jane peeling potatoes when I returned downstairs. I told her what Father Buchanan had said, and she shrugged, as if she were disappointed at his tameness, although I was thanked for coping with him. She went away to dress and I glanced through the newspapers in the living-room, not really reading anything, for very soon I heard her voice outside on the telephone. It was light, brisk, forthright. *Oh John, I thought I'd better ring to tell you that Anthony's died . . . Susan, I'm afraid Anthony took his life last night . . .* and so on. It seemed to me she was overdoing the detachment. These bald announcements were evidently provoking the usual offers of help and sympathy—which gave her a chance to rebuff them: firmly, if politely. I began to wonder if our rapprochement of the night would hold, whether she regretted it now. In the little shelved alcove of classical antiquities near where I sat I saw two small Etruscan bronzes. Tarquinia, that moment there . . . it seemed as remote symbolically as it was historically.

A few minutes later we left for the hospital. Beneath her outdoor coat she was wearing a dark red shirt and a tweed skirt; no mourning for Electra, as for the sky. The mist had made way for a cloudless blue.

It was very discreet and English. Anthony's doctor was there—he had already dealt with the identification formalities—and some hospital bigwig and the staff sister concerned; agreement that no negligence was involved, no sign had been given . . . I was politely questioned as to Anthony's apparent state of mind, and professed myself as shocked and mystified as everyone else. Then there was talk about the inquest, a suitable undertaker's firm. A cardboard box with his belongings, a radio, the Mantegna reproduction, were handed over.

Jane showed no sign of strain until we were outside and in her car again.

"I think if there was an airport here I'd ask you to drive me to it and put me on a plane for the far side of the world."

She spoke quietly, drily, out of the windscreen at the hospital courtyard. But it was the kind of statement I had looked for in vain on our way to the hospital: an admission that the distances of the previous evening could not be restored. A uniformed man beside an ambulance chatted up a West Indian nurse in the sunlight. She kept grinning, splendid white teeth.

"It'll all be over very soon."

"Yes." She switched on, and we moved off. "I suppose they took our word for it."

"I'm sure."

"I don't see why you have to be at the inquest."

"It must be part of the rules. And anyway. Now I have a friend in Oxford."

"Some friend."

"I'm so glad we talked last night."

"As long as I didn't shatter too many illusions."

"You didn't shatter anything. Or only frosted glass."

She smiled. "You give me a nostalgia for America."

"Why's that?"

"I remember when I first came back here after the war. How closed everything seemed. As if everyone spoke in cipher." She took a breath. "And I was the only one *en clair*."

"I know the feeling." I slipped her a look. "And talking of America."

"I sent him a cable. First thing."

"He'll come back?"

"I asked him not to. Just yet." She added, "He's got his research work. The fare. It would be silly."

She stopped at a little row of shops, to pick up something she had forgotten to ask Gisèle to buy. I saw a small coffeebar opposite, suggested we have a cup—I had a reason to have her to myself for a few minutes and so, it finally emerged, did she. I put mine point-blank, as soon as we had sat and ordered.

"Will you come and stay at Thorncombe, Jane? It's very near Dartington."

She gave me a slightly embarrassed smile, then glanced down. "As a matter of fact I drove past it last spring with Paul. Caro had shown him where it was on a map." She murmured, "Unforgivable curiosity. It did look very sweet."

"Then you have no excuse. Seriously, whether I'm there or not. The old couple I've taken on are always happy to do the honors."

"Ben and Phoebe?"

"Caro's told you?"

"They sound like Philemon and Baucis."

"If Ben didn't drink himself blind every Saturday night.
But that and his wife's ways with green vegetables are the
only real hazards."

"It would be nice."

"You must bring Paul over."

"He'd love that. Though I couldn't promise it would be
very apparent."

"I've had abundant training. When she was Paul's age. Before she tumbled to Nell."

"I know she loves it now."

"She hardly ever goes there."

Our coffees were brought. Jane stirred hers, then looked
me in the eyes.

"I have a tiny special relationship with Caro, Dan."

"I know you do. And I'm very grateful."

"I feel it would have been tactful if I'd pretended I hadn't
known about Barney Dillon."

"That's silly."

"I felt you were offended."

"Only that you aren't more against it."

She looked away, searching for the right words. "I think
she has to escape from Nell. From Compton, all of that. And
she can't do it through you . . . without hurting her mother."

"I do realize that."

"I'm trying to say children like her don't have many roads
from what they are to what they'd rather be. I know what
you must feel about him, but that's really not the point. I
think it's a kind of lesson she has to learn. I'm sorry, I should
have said all this at dinner last night." She hesitated, then
went on in a lighter voice. "And her real love-affair of these
last two years has been with you. That's not a guess."

"Which makes me feel even more to blame."

"It's a small break for freedom."

"Out of the frying-pan."

"But she has so little room to maneuver. She's surrounded
by adults she has to get in perspective. And whom she's terrified of offending. And you really mustn't discount Andrew.
That bond. The reverse of the traditional situation has happened there. The more she's reacted against Nell, the more
he's become the mediator. Her ally."

"I've guessed that. I am grateful."

"As long as you realize it's created another conflict. She
put it very naïvely but touchingly to me the last time we
met. She said, If only you all believed in the same things."

"Poor kid."

"You don't mind me saying this?"

"Of course not. I wish I knew if she was fed up over what's happened in California."

"We didn't really talk about that. But I don't see why she should be."

I stared down at the table. "I've been very naughty, Jane. Over Jenny. She's rather too close to what I'd have liked Caro to have been. She's literate, she reads, she thinks. . . ." I shrugged.

"And also found you more interesting than men her own age?"

"I know I haven't a foot to stand on. I suppose it's just Caro's particular choice of guru."

"Can you blame her for taking him at the general valuation? He's quite well seen nowadays. In all senses." She tilted her head at my skeptical look. "Yes, of course. A servant of the system. But that may be a part of the lesson she needs."

"And telling Nell?"

"I suggested this morning that she left that to you."

"Well it wasn't. I was once more ordered to keep my mouth shut."

She smiled. "Then you must let her do it in her own good time."

"I can see she picked a lousy father. But a perfect aunt."

She looked out of the window. "I nearly broke down two years ago, just after Roz started at the BBC. I ran away to London and did what decent mothers are never meant to do—threw myself sobbing into my daughter's arms and told all. She was marvelous. So much more mature than I was at her age." She played with the handle of her cup, then gave me the moral. "I suspect one loses a lot if one hides too much behind one's years."

"She knows about . . . you haven't told me his name?"

"Peter. Yes. She greeted that breath-taking confession by telling me that if I hadn't been such an old square I'd have found a lover years ago."

I grinned, and saw in her eyes a spark of an old animation, a love of sending things up; but then she looked down, though she was still smiling. Through all of this I had been increasingly aware of a defect of imagination on my part. I knew what she had said of Andrew must apply to her as well. That however badly she had treated me, it had been repaid handsomely in her attitude to my daughter; that her "tiny special relationship" was something much more important than that. I recalled a little incident from the beginning of Caro's life. Rather inconsistently, since we had held their own first child at the font, Nell and I had refused to have Caro baptized; and though Anthony and Jane hadn't argued over that, there had been some complaint about our depriving the baby of its natural godparents. It had all been got over lightly enough, but I could still remember Jane saying she intended to be her godmother whether we liked it or not. I began belatedly to realize that she had been it to a degree few fully titled godmothers felt necessary in practice.

I deduced too that I was perhaps less strange to Jane than she had first led me to believe . . . often seen through Caro, at least. But just as I knew Caro's understanding of Jane, at least as transmitted to me, was very partial, I wondered how accurate my own portrait had been. It seemed clear I was being told, if gently, that I hadn't thought hard enough about Caro's problems. I felt tempted to justify myself. But I also knew Jane was on much sounder grounds there than with her views on politics and our past. My judgment of her shifted during that closer conversation over the coffees: we were back with that old touchstone of "feeling right." She had felt very wrong to me through most of the evening before. But now I recognized something in her that had not, at least in this matter, changed. She might hide and hide, speak in cipher, betray her true self, but she was still capable of a tenacity of right-feeling—that strangest of all intransigences, both humanity's trap and its ultimate freedom. It was not unlike as it was with Jenny when she was to put down her feelings about America; that is, I left the coffee-bar secretly chastened, or revised, concerning my too easy first sentence upon Oxford and its modes and mores. In a way too it was a practical demonstration of Anthony's last contradiction of me. No true change except in ourselves, as we are. A rarefied idealism, perhaps; but I no longer felt so sure it was provincial.

Jane told me more about Rosamund on the way back . . . and the girl herself, whom I hadn't seen, except in the very occasional photograph, for so many years, came out as soon as we drove up to the house and parked behind her own small blue Renault. She was tall, taller than her mother, long-haired and long-limbed, a shade too lanky and strong-mouthed to be very attractive physically, but there was a frankness about her that I liked. She resembled her father, much more his face than Jane's. The two women clung to each other a long moment, then Rosamund turned and took my hand. I made her lean forward and kissed her on the cheek. She said, "I'm so glad you were here"; with a good straight look, it meant the words.

I very soon learned that she was the practical member of the household; a brisk production-assistant efficiency was initiated. Paul must be put on the train, and she'd meet him herself at Reading. Phone-calls had started coming in, and Jane was set to answering some of those that needed it. I was given a drink down in the kitchen, while the two girls busied themselves with the lunch. The smell of food, we were to have the brace of pheasant I had rejected the night before. Rosamund talked about herself, not Anthony; her life in London working at the BBC. Then a gray Jaguar drew up outside, above us. I glimpsed the bottom halves of Nell and Andrew. Jane opened the door upstairs to them, and they didn't appear for a few minutes.

When they did, Nell pressed my hand after our token kiss-on-the-cheek with more warmth than for a long time past. Then I had Andrew's grip, and that ancient sizing and amused stare. He was wearing a dark-gray suit and our old college tie, and only his weather-bronzed face seemed rural. He had sidewhiskers now, and was balding; a central strand of wheaten hair, a little reticulation of beetroot veins under pouched eyes, those curious, faintly glaucous eyes . . . an example of that cross between the Saxon peasant and the Viking that has become over the centuries one of the well-bred English faces; Viking in the raids on convention, Saxon in the fundamental placidity and contentment. It was clear that, as in history, the Saxon had tamed the Viking. He had brought a magnum of Taittinger, and began to chaff Rosamund.

"Still bedding down with that frightfully clever what's-his-name fella?"

"Andrew, do you mind?"

Nell cried across the room. "Darling, he's trying to be discreet and refined."

I caught Jane's eyes assaying my reaction. Then the telephone was ringing upstairs again.

Andrew interested me: how good such people were to have in such situations—their style, panache, natural command. Though the only one of us who was formally dressed, he was by far the least funereal. He got the champagne cooled and opened, managed to suggest without offense that it was all rather a caper, lovely to be here together with all the cross-talk and the sun coming through the window. I'd never seen him like this, with Nell's side of the family, and the last lingering unlikelihood in the marriage soon disappeared. Of course he had never been a quarter of the languid fool he used to pretend to be as an undergraduate, living in a manner that was already totally outdated except among his rich clique (heavy with memories of fathers who had been up in the Evelyn Waugh period); and he must have seen through the county, as a bride-market, far more thoroughly than any of us ever realized. I guessed that he had somehow made a choice of which traditions and rituals were worth keeping and which could be dismissed: live like a squire, work like a farmer, think like a free man . . . and make out you are only the first. It functioned. There must have been some sense in which he had married below himself; but one saw why. He needed this more open, tolerant world quite as much as his title and his outward role in life.

He and I, and Nell came with us, strolled out into the garden while lunch was laid at the table where we'd been sitting. They were more serious then. Nell, as always, was probing, inquisitive, suspicious. Why, why, why, what had Anthony said to me, what did I think, what had I guessed . . . all of which I sidestepped. I might have been a little franker with Andrew alone; with Nell I felt determined in silence. Fortunately Andrew's presence meant she couldn't delve too deeply into the past. Then we discussed Jane, and things grew a shade more honest. Yes, we had talked. I'd gathered the marriage had had its problems . . . the Catholic thing. And yes, she'd told me about the Communist Party "nonsense."

"It's purely emotional," said Nell. "Just being bloody-minded. She'll drop it now he's dead. She needed a safety-valve, that was all. I tried to tell her. But of course she won't listen to me about anything these days." She went on before I needed to answer. "At least half of it's this ridiculous Women's Lib nonsense she's picked up from Roz."

I smiled. "Obviously not from you."

"My dear man, fêtes to the left of me, fêtes to the right. I do good like nobody's business. When I'm not playing six maids, a nanny, and his lordship's valet. I mean, I'd have a case, I do need liberating. Andrew, stop smirking."

She was still quite pretty for her age, still had her quickness; but something in her—once much more occasional than constant—that had always been both insecure and insensitive had got worse. If her sister had forgotten how to play conventional roles, Nell had remembered only too well.

Andrew said, "Ought to marry again."

Nell made a duck's mouth at me. "Ye olde country saw."

"Not an argument against it, dear girl."

"But darling, *she* is. She's fallen in love with stewing."

I murmured, "Then Andrew could be right."

"For heaven's sake. I wouldn't be against it. Honestly, Dan . . . strictly between ourselves, any normal woman would have walked out on Anthony years ago." I felt like reminding her that she had once used this supposedly model marriage to belittle our own, but she was going on. "You know, there was a time when she was coming and staying with us a lot and I knew perfectly well what was going on, but . . . oh well, it's all history now. It's the way she's always been." She looked round, accusing the backs of the houses. "It's this dreadful inbred city. She's never grown out of it. Don't you think?"

"I've just had three months in California, Nell. It seems rather civilized after the dream-world over there."

"Are you back for long?"

"As long as I can make it."

"Andrew and I . . . we thought you might like to come down to Compton with Caro for a week-end or something." She widened her eyes, a familiar old signal that she was being terribly sincere, and murmured, "If you could stand the squareness. But please."

"I'd love to. That would be fun."

Andrew said, "Jolly good." Then, "Do you shoot, Dan?"

"Only dice. And that neither well nor often."

"Splendid. We'll get out the old backgammon board."

"Oh Andrew, for God's sake." She raised her eyebrows at me. "At the last totting-up I owed him eight hundred thousand pounds."

"A little over my limit."

Andrew flicked an eyelid, over her head. "Play for pennies, actually."

Nell asked how Caro had seemed. She knew of course that she was working for Barney, and we discussed the pros and cons of that: it was clear that, being the slave of a system herself, she saw the new job favorably. No doubt the association added an agreeable little vicarious feather to her local social hat. I told them about the new flat, and sensed a small struggle in Nell between being secretly pleased that I was forsaken and alarmed that Caro was striking out on her own. She thought she was "rather silly" to have dropped Richard. But when I said I thought she needed something better than a charming young clot, I saw something in Andrew's, if not Nell's, eyes that agreed. Inevitably she asked if there was "someone else"—Caro was being so cagy. I played innocent; I'd try to find out. We were called in for lunch.

It was much more enjoyable than I had anticipated, mainly thanks to Andrew; and bizarre, since I felt that they were surreptitiously using me for a celebration. There was some kind of suppressed relief at its all being over with Anthony and it had to be expressed through a surrogate; and by carefully not mentioning him, or what he had done. I was a little the prodigal son, informally re-accepted into their world; and it was much more a love-feast than a wake. On my side there was my knowing that I had missed their company more than I had ever admitted: the banter, the trivial news about other relations, children, the cross-currents—the lost familiarity of it all, in both the literal and the normal sense of the word. I had become too used to one-to-one relationships, even with Caro; to artistic or commercial or sexual codes of behavior; everything but this loose, warm web of clan. It was, after all, a modest secular equivalent of that nightbathe at Tarquinia so many years before.

Rosamund drove me to the station about three, on her way down to Reading to meet her brother. As soon as we moved off—I'd been reminded during the lunch that I was technically her godfather—I spoke.

"You seem to have a stunning relationship with your mother, Roz."

"You've been talking?"

"Yes."

"She's had rather a rough time these last years."

"So I understand."

"Does she seem changed to you?"

"Only at first."

I asked her what she thought of her mother's extraordinary prospective leap to the left—if it was not straight backward. Rather surprisingly she seemed to share Nell's view of it, though with a better understanding and much more sympathy.

"I think it's been mainly struggling for survival. It's so stupid she never had a career. That's not preaching Lib, just what she is, really. I even have to pretend I enjoy my own job less than I really do. I mean she's glad for me, but it's also what she ought to have done. And she knows it." After a moment, she went on. "I used to blame my father. But there's something in her I don't really understand. We do talk a lot, but there's always that final block. She sort of slides off into commonplaces. Starts justifying what she is. I think she gets frightened if she looks back too much."

"She's not alone in that."

"I suppose one can't win. One day I shall curse myself for not having had children younger."

"At least you'll have done what seemed wise at the time."

"Didn't you?"

"Do I have to answer that?"

She smiled, then slowed down and stopped to let a string of uniformed schoolgirls pass over a crossing. Her question came abruptly.

"Do you know why he did it?"

I left a little silence. "I think it was an act of charity. At least in intention."

"It's only these last two or three years I've realized how totally unsuited they were to each other."

"I doubt whether totally unsuited people last that long, Roz."

"All right. But if it hadn't been for us . . ."

She moved off again. She meant, us children.

"They did set themselves fiercely high standards. They're never very easy to live up to."

"I've never understood why they had to be so savagely applied to you." She said, "I hear about worse stabs in the back every day of my life." A moment, then her tone changed. "Are forgotten goddaughters allowed to ask very personal questions?"

I flinched inwardly. "Of course."

"*Was* there any truth in that play you wrote?"

"It's just how it seemed at the time. One against three."

"I really meant something between my father and Nell."

We were rapidly getting into dangerous waters. "No truth at all. Malice, I'm afraid."

She was silent for a few seconds.

"It's so strange. All these years. You've been so completely taboo. I half expected horns and a cloven hoof."

"I did wear them once."

She grinned, but I suspected she knew she hadn't been honestly answered, and I jumped in before she could dig further.

"Are you glad she's going to remarry?"

That got a sharp look. "You *have* been talking."

"Most of last night."

She turned down toward the station. "He's . . . very charming. Very alive. I'm all for it. Even my father would have been, in a funny kind of way. The last time I saw him—on Sunday—he kept going on about it."

"Her remarrying?"

"Not specifically. Her needing a new life." She added, "I almost wish now I'd told him." She turned to me again. "Did you ever understand your parents?"

"I only knew one."

"I forgot."

"And I'm just, very dimly, beginning to understand him."

"I suppose understanding them would make things terribly dull."

"I rather suspect that goes for life in general."

She smiled, she accepted that; happy career girl.

Three hours later Dan was passing on her love to Caro, along with the other news. To begin with Caro was rather flagrantly solicitous, as if she were partly to blame for what had happened. But though she was curious as to how he had "found" Jane, she was not as inquisitive as he expected over the suicide itself. She wanted to know how her mother had been, as well. The conversation in the garden was duly reported—and the invitation to Compton. All this was as she drove Dan north through Maida Vale to see her flat. So many of his conversations that day seemed destined to be shifting, both literally and metaphorically. Too full of his own news, Dan was slow to realize that his daughter was hiding something. But Compton led them to what had hitherto been avoided.

"Daddy, you don't have to nag at me. I know I should tell her."

"The longer you leave it . . ."

"It's just . . ."

"Just what?"

"I can't face doing it over the 'phone. She never lets me get a word in edgeways, anyway. She hardly hears what I say. It's always the latest Compton disasters."

"Mothers get envious of daughters. Feel they've been deserted. That's quite common."

She said nothing for a moment.

"Were they always like that? Mummy and Aunt Jane?"

"Like what?"

"So different."

"You must put some of the blame on me. What happened between us."

"That's Aunt Jane's line."

"We do both know what she went through."

"You don't know what I go through. She really liked Richard. He was so revoltingly safe. She'd have had me married off to him on the spot." She braked with an unnecessary sharpness to let another car draw out of a side-road. "I know what she'll do. She'll blame it on herself. For ever letting me out of her sight. And poor Andrew. He'll get it."

"Then it's not your problem. And I think he gives as good as he gets."

"I don't know how he stands her sometimes."

"Caro."

"It's only because I feel guilty about her."

"You must sick it up."

"And because my ears have been burning all day."

"That's ridiculous."

"The problem daughter."

"We all agreed they're much more interesting than the straight ones."

He had said it lightly, to make her smile. But whatever had been building up, or waiting, now broke surface. She did not smile, but drove a little way in silence. Dan glanced at her.

"What is it?"

"Nothing." But a second or two later she spoke again. "I told Bernard today that I'd told you."

"And?"

"He asked me to say he was sorry about . . . you know."

"It was difficult for him. I can see that."

"Actually he'd like you to have lunch with him one day." That took Dan so completely by surprise that he hesitated fatally. "There is his side of it."

"Which I know."

She hesitated; then crashed through her fence.

"You're so good at forcing people to give wrong impressions of themselves."

"From bitter personal experience?"

"You do lead people on."

"To lying about themselves?"

"That's the whole point. He wasn't lying."

"I was asking in general."

"I never know what you really feel."

"I thought I'd made it plain in the present case."

"When I told Aunt Jane, all she said was, Are you happy?"

"Darling, you're not being consistent."

It was said almost fiercely, and Dan left a pause.

"Do *you* want me to meet him?"

"It doesn't matter. It was just an idea."

After a few moments he saw her eyes blink, as she watched the road ahead. He let her drive a hundred yards, then looked again.

"Pull in. There's a space ahead."

She obeyed, parked, switched off the engine, then sat with her head bowed, like a disobedient child. He took her hand and pressed it, and felt a pressure back.

"This is so silly, Caro."

"I know."

"If your mother and I get overprotective about you, it's very largely because we made such a mess of loving each other."

"It's just I'm so tired of . . ."

"Of what?"

"If I love one of you back, it always seems to be betraying the other."

"That's our stupidity. Not something wrong in you." He pressed her hand again. "Is this why you didn't tell me you'd already told Aunt Jane?" She nodded. "Then let's get one thing straight. I'm not jealous of your relationship with her. Or with Andrew. I've nothing but gratitude for the way both of them have helped. And even your mother and I are getting less stupid. She really was falling over herself to be nice to me today."

"Oh God."

"It's all right. I did the squirming for you."

She managed the shadow of a smile, then reached with her free hand toward a box of tissues under the dashboard.

"If the thing with Bernard makes you happy, then I won't argue about it."

"He was annoyed that I told you."

"He has no right to be."

"I don't mean with me. Not really annoyed. Just . . . I suppose embarrassed."

"That you were honest?"

"I don't use words very accurately. It's not that he didn't understand. That wretched meeting you on the flight."

"As long as he didn't suggest that someone trendier would have kept their mouths shut."

She shook her head. "It was my doing something he felt he ought to have done himself. That's really why he wants to see you."

Dan still held her hand. "And you want me to?"

"I know it must seem pointless." She hesitated. "Daddy, he's not trendy at all under the surface."

"Then tell him all right. If he really wants to."

She pressed his hand, and took a breath.

"What did you and Aunt Jane decide about me?"

"That deciding about you wasn't on."

"Beyond salvation?"

"Our interference."

"I bet it was all Freud and Marx and God knows what else."

"I'll tell you when it's over."

"I'd rather know now."

"That's not fair. You'd be able to prove us wrong."

She did, again, smile briefly at that; a fall, but back in the saddle now.

"It's realizing that someone does seem to need you. I wouldn't go to bed with him to begin with. I thought it was just . . . the usual thing."

"Go on."

"I mean need you for . . . non-family reasons."

"I understand."

"I did think about it. What you'd all feel."

"You mustn't worry about that. It's the oldest madness in the species. Parents thinking the product of their own genes will somehow be everything they failed to be themselves."

"It all sort of hit me today." She sighed. "Mummy's really going to blame you, you know that."

"I shan't let her, Caro. This whole business of your working in London was agreed between us."

"I wouldn't blame you for wishing I was different."

"My dear child, I wish almost everything was different, starting with myself. But we have to make the best of what we are. And you and I could have done worse these last two years—you'd at least grant that?"

"You know."

"You mustn't think everything can be said in language.

That because we keep up a kind of teasing relationship that that's all I really feel. Phrases like 'I love you' always secretly mean a sort of uncertainty. That's the only reason I don't say them. And also because I know you know this."

"I do deep down."

"Then hold to that." He leaned and kissed the side of her head. "Now shall I drive?"

"No, I'm okay." She pressed his hand a last time and reached for the ignition; stopped, turned and put her arms around Dan's neck for a moment; then went back to starting the engine.

He was shown around the flat. It, and its district, did not appeal to him much; but it seemed reasonably clean, the price not too outrageous, and there were no two ways about Caro having set her heart on it. So Dan gave his *imprimatur*, and Caro her check for the first month's rent, and they went on up to Hampstead Village and had dinner. All through it Dan underwent a small tug-of-war between affection and . . . not quite boredom, but a malaise. Inevitably the past was with them, and his memories of Anthony; but so much remained that still had to be censored. There was a point where he felt almost like telling her, as Jane had told her own daughter, at least part of the truth. So much prevarication, so much standing on dignity, on the assumption that younger generations can never understand older ones; almost as if children were brought into the world only in order that their parents might have secrets from them—and surely the kind of secrets whose unfolding might have been of much more real value than the stale old outward teachings of experience that were sheltered behind. Judging it more creditable to pass on general theory than practical reality began to Dan, that evening, to seem more and more like a smug papal infallibility, an attitude that reason and honesty mocked at every turn. He had felt it with Rosamund, earlier that day; she had asked a sensible and honest question. *I once went to bed with your mother, and your father knew it and could never forget it.* So simple, so many doubts and enigmas cleared at a stroke; having thought which, Dan went carefully on maintaining his daughter's myth of the past.

Back at home, when they had kissed each other good night, he couldn't sleep; and he had to wait until the time-difference allowed Jenny to be back at the Cabin. Caro had seen the telegram; that at least need not be hidden. So he booked a call, then read into the small hours until it was put through.

The line was poor, and they seemed every mile of the real distance apart. Mildred and Abe had been sweet, "all you ever said about them." She'd thought she'd "quite enjoy" his being gone, but she didn't, she needed someone to nag. He let that part of it, and her little bits of other news, come first. Then he told her his own.

"Oh *Dan*. How *ghastly* for you. Just this last night?"

"Yes."

"But *why?*"

Once again Dan was plunged into the prevarication business; and this time with someone who knew him better than the other two young women of his day. He temporized rather than prevaricated; theorized as he had theorized to Caro, to her mother and stepfather.

"But to make you go all that way and then . . . Dan, you're not telling me everything."

"No. Not really. Not quite all."

"Then what?"

"I'll tell you all about it. But not now. It's just . . . some sad old birds come home to roost."

"You once told me any story could be told in five lines."

"This isn't a story, Jenny. One day. I promise."

"I know your promises."

"But not how much I'm missing you."

"Sweet talk."

"I wish it was."

"This is hardly the way to drop me in the ashcan."

"I'm aware of that, too."

"If only I could see your face."

"Just tired."

"Is it terribly late?"

"Two thirty."

"Oh God. You poor thing."

She asked about Caro. He said she was fine, and silently charged the truth there also to a later settling. Then there was questioning about Jane, Nell, what it had been like meeting them again.

"Anthropologically interesting?"

"In a way. All sweetness and light. On that side."

There was a break, then she said, "Hey, by the way I'm trying to do what I promised."

"Which promise?"

"About us. Trying to write it down."

He had forgotten. "Seriously?"

"I probably shan't send it to you."

"You shouldn't take me at such absurd face values."

"I'm rather enjoying it. I'm not sure I shan't write a novel myself." She said, "I don't know why people make such a fuss about it. You just write down what you remember. What you felt. And it's all there."

"All?"

"Enough. I doubt if your horrid yellow pads and pencils have ever been put to better use."

"Someone's asking to be put across my knees."

"Yes please. Anytime."

They rang off a minute later; a less flippant minute. Her last words were, "I'm not ready yet. I need you still." It was not a plea; simply from a part of her, the Scottish part perhaps, that didn't tease or rebel, but took a sober, almost clinical, view of what she could do, and couldn't.

Dan went to the window and stared out at the London night. A movement in the street below, four stories down, opposite, caught his eye. There was a row of shops, and it was apparently the night their rubbish was collected. Dustbins, cardboard boxes, black plastic sacks stood on the pavements outside their doors. A nocturnal tramp was bent over one of the piles; rummaging quietly, almost fastidiously, like someone picking over lots at an auction sale. Beside him stood an ancient hoodless perambulator. Dan went back to his desk, took a pair of binoculars from a drawer, switched out the light, then returned to the window and focused down on the man. He wore a black homburg hat that had lost its band, an overcoat tied with string, a pair of gumboots. His face was invisible beneath the hat, turned away as he scavenged; but he was obviously an old man. He came up from a cardboard box with three or four wire coat-hangers, examined each in his mittened hands, for defects, then placed them in the pram beside him. There was something obscurely comic about him, contented and professional, grateful the city was asleep, the street deserted—as if he was merely following a regular routine with these shops at this time of the week; and something Victorian, anachronistic, almost timeless. He was both very real and, under the street-lights, on the empty stage of the night, theatrical. Beckett again, and waiting for Godot.

Watching him, Dan felt a strange sympathy, almost a need

to go down and talk to him, to play the modern Mayhew for a few minutes; find out how he lived, he felt, he philosophized—perhaps even ask him up for a cup of coffee. He knew it was not true charity or curiosity; but to regain reality in a day that had somehow cast Dan himself as unreal: too full of polite lies, unnatural smiles and urbanities, conventional middle-class behaviors. All through it he had felt like someone locked up inside an adamantly middle-class novel; a smooth, too plausible Establishment fixer out of C. P. Snow, not a lone wolf at all. What called down there was the reality of solitude; and for a moment Dan envied it as a rococo mechanical canary might envy a real bird singing in the woods outside the room where it silently and impotently stands waiting to be wound up again.

In spite of having just heard Jenny's voice, of knowing Caro was asleep a few yards away, of all that day's reconciliations, of having been so variously enmeshed and enwebbed in female minds and female sensitivities, Dan had an unaccountable sense of having hidden from something, or of failing to see something; of an incompleteness less defined by the banal enough polarity before his eyes of true poverty and privileged comfort than glimpsed through and beyond it . . . what Beckett had glimpsed, behind his ambiguous symbolisms and "arrant romantic pessimism": the loneliness of each, the bedrock of the human condition. I am what I am. What is, is. Dan imagined that he was looking at his lost real self down there, in that shadowy figure; a thing living on the edge of existence in a night street of his psyche; beyond conversation and invitation, eternally separate.

But then, as he watched, he was returned to theater again. Another figure suddenly appeared, walking across the street from the pavement directly beneath where Dan stood. A policeman, he went up to where the old tramp worked. The man turned to face him. The helmeted constable went close, looked down into the pram, and the two stood talking. Dan watched, in suspense, waiting for the latterday Bumble to appear. The tramp seemed to be speaking a lot, answering some interrogation. He lifted aside a bundle in the pram for the policeman to see something underneath, and they seemed to discuss it. The tramp even lifted it a little, so Dan could see: an old wall-clock, rejected time.

Then Dan saw the policeman's hand go to an upper pocket—and really did feel like playing the *deus ex machina*, opening the window and shouting down in protest at the absurdity of booking a harmless old man. But the policeman did not produce a notebook. Merely a packet of cigarettes, which he held out to the old fellow; who took one with a grateful nod, stored it carefully in his overcoat pocket, and touched his black homburg. Then the policeman walked on.

Which leaves our hero caged behind his window above, obliged to smile to himself, like an inefficient god who sees a lapse in his creation repaired by what he had forgotten to institute.

# A Second Contribution

It's silly to remember him by such an un-English flower, whose name I can't even spell. I could ask Abe, but it doesn't matter. I count how many have opened each day. Actually they're a bit, don't smile, to me like wild roses at home. In shape, if you forget that lovely color. I'd give my soul to find a velvet or a corduroy of just that bluey violet. I'd wear it once a year, in memory of you. They make me want to smoke again. No I don't. I have to be cruel now, and I've been looking forward to it.

Him. Mr. Wolfe.

I liked Dan least here—not literally here in the Cabin, of course. But in the house with Abe and Mildred. Those absurd pool games. The way he and Abe used to play Minnesota Fats and Paul Newman, hustling each other like mad for dimes and quarters, endlessly arguing about how much "English" to use in their shots. I was cast by Abe as a feed, a Scottish fellow-sufferer. You never knew the only decent thing that ever came out of that damn country was a crooked way of hitting a pool-ball?

Mildred's head around the door: Chow, people. Abe's lugubrious Edward G. Robinson face: Eat, eat! You crazy? He just took me for all I've got. Mildred would look at me and roll her eyes upward. When will they grow up. The boys. Abe: The trouble with broads is they have no imagination. And Dan stands there, purring at me, cue in hand: Isn't this great, aren't they lovely people?

I was always a generation behind, ten thousand generations behind little sour-sweet Abe. Dan's first more than casual description of him, on the way to my first evening here in Bel-Air—I can still remember bits. Potentially great screenwriter, reformed alcoholic, knows everyone, made quite a pile, etc., etc. The punch-line was: And if you don't love him by the end of the evening, you can walk home by yourself.

Strange, I never heard him go out on the limb like that for

anyone else. And stranger still that he didn't know, even then, that in these matters I am my own young woman. Something trumped something there.

That same first evening, at dinner. Dan had told Abe he'd got the wrong director for some old movie I'd never heard of, and Mildred backed Dan. It was Nick Ray, not Abe's John Somebody-else. Mildred told him he was getting senile. Dan bet a thousand dollars it was Nick Ray. Abe wouldn't take the money, but only because "I don't want to give you an excuse to take this charming young doll to burger joints for the next six weeks." He turned to me and put his pudgy little paw on my wrist. "Jenny, the time has come when I have to explain a couple of things. My wife's such a dumbhead no one else ever married her. As for your lousy limey boyfriend he eats my food, he sucks my brains, he cheats at pool and he makes googoo eyes at my wife behind my back. He didn't tell you that, hn?" I played along, I said I didn't know how he stood Dan as a lodger. "You think there's another place in town that would take him?" He wagged his finger at me. "You know he tried to kid his last girl his name was Sir Beverly Hills Hotel?" Then: "Where do you think he buys his towels?"

Then he looked at Dan and his wife: "As I was saying, the reason Nick Ray took that picture . . ."

It happened all the time, at the beginning. Mildred and Dan even seemed to force him into corners so that I could watch him being a performing bear. All right, he was jolly, a nice little Jewish wisecracker. But it used to go on too long. After all, Mr. Wolfe, who was it taught me to look for all that imagery in the local argot? The constant references to sodomy and copulation, to screwing and laying and pecking order (fuck-you order, yes?). And how one can't treat everyone in sight as a prostitute and then expect to put out an unprostituted art. Or who was it told me Abe was so right that day he held forth on why they violined so much in the old days? Because the real private language and behavior was so crude and coarse, men so cocksure and orange-horse about all women being their panty-dropping playground that they couldn't act love on screen without seeming silly to themselves. So the men had to camp it up as etiquette-crazy beaux, and the women had to seem to be fooled by it, always swooning toe-to-toe on their marks, to compensate. It took freaks like Cagney and Bogart to break that up.

And the Jewish need to handle what you possess. The

ghetto hang-up; turning the audience into Cossacks, then telling yourself you had to please them at all costs. He was on about it last night—how when he started the whole industry was run by Jews and yet a Jewish-looking actor couldn't get a job "as understudy to a crowd extra." The Cossacks wouldn't have liked that. But the Jewishness kept creeping through. The poor *shmucks*, says Abe, they thought the goys were just Jews with pink skins and straight noses.

I've got sidetracked, but not really.

It wasn't Abe, but Dan trying to keep up with him and swap meannesses. Not realizing it was square when Abe did it, but endearing, and anyway he couldn't help himself. With Dan, just square. And horrid, when he used the same sort of language he pretended to have analyzed and to despise. It was so much better when they discussed things, America, politics, whatever, seriously. And I could feel the real affection and respect they had for each other.

Mildred I liked all the way down the line from the beginning. Dan never realized—at least I suspect he doesn't—how much she has put into that marriage. I guessed it before, and begin to know for sure now.

Dan has faults of perception. That's what I learned at Mildred and Abe's. Not quite seeing what made them work was one of them. A lovely man around a dinner-table or over a pool-game must take it out on someone in private. Mildred told me in so many words: He always needed people, I guess I always needed him. His latest thing (by the way) is an innocent (Mildred is always there) pretending he's crazy about me. But because Mildred is always there, there's something not innocent about it that I can't describe. Needling something in their past, not their present. I'm not sure if I'd have liked him as a young man.

Not quite knowing what makes *me* work is another blind spot, this is where I meant to begin. After the first shock, I didn't mind Dan deciding he had to go, I didn't even really mind his seizing on it as an excuse for a cool-off period. But I did mind his assumption that I'd see it his way, silly little temperamental female thing, as soon as he was gone. If he was bored with me or if I had shown I was bored with him, if one of us had to get hurt rather than go on shamming something we didn't feel . . . no, it was the gall: that he must know what was best for both of us. Going all Sidney Carton and far-far-nobler-thing, as if I'd only a month between me and eternal spinsterhood. I've now decided what it is that drives him to behave like this. I had a first suspicion that he simply wanted out because I threatened to become a problem in England. His daughter and all the rest of it. But I think it's more complicated—and a lot worse—than that.

He has a mistress. Her name is Loss.

All this is bound up with what I've learned about America.

I have to imagine a secret Dan who actually *likes* loss—both all he's lost in the past and all he has still to lose. In some way to him loss is a beautiful, fertile thing. I don't mean he wallows in it or moans about it (that would reveal too much), but he's discovered that he's much happier as a self-appointed loser than as a winner. It was there during the phone-call when his ex and her sister spoke to him. A kind of excitement as he sniffed a lovely old loss-area. Now what's happened is that I too have become a potential loss-area. That's why he's so tender, so outwardly understanding: he's really saying, quite literally, get lost. The more I think of it, the more creepy it becomes. Like some strangler caressing a girl's neck and quietly weeping because he's going to kill her in a few minutes.

I half believe the man is such a fool he thinks this is rather romantic. When all it really is is Romantic with a big R, straight out of my unfavorite period in literature.

One's misled, but only because he isn't standing over a stormy sea or racing round the Blethering Heights in a wild Byronic hair-do. But that's truly what he is: a professional melancholiac, and enjoying every minute of it. He didn't ask me to marry him up in the Mojave, he asked me to refuse to marry him. I feel livid now that I didn't say yes. Just to have called his bluff.

It enrages me to think that I even once saw him as Mr. Knightley to my Emma. I must have been mad.

What I've decided I like about America (you were like dark glasses, I've seen so much more since you left) is that they simply don't understand this awful English attachment to defeat and loss and self-negation. I hated the Prick two days ago. He came in feeling depressed about something, and my God, didn't he let us all know it. Almost his best performance yet. But at least he wanted to do something about it, wasn't hiding it. The stiff upper lip is absurd, I henceforth disown it completely. I will *not* be a vase and ashes on someone's mantelpiece.

You come to the United States not knowing what to expect. Then all your worst prejudices are confirmed. It's a nation of automata piling down the freeways in search of a life that isn't worth having anyway. What a joke that word is: *free*way. Then their obsession with doing things by the book—if the book says this or that makes you happy, you must be happy. You suddenly realize how astoundingly free (or at least suspicious of other people's recipes) society is at home. That's why I fell in love with Dan. He seemed free in an unfree culture, and I was scared. Partly because I know California is the future and England is already a thing in a museum, a dying animal in a zoo. No pride left (or what pride there is, in the wrong things) and so all intent on dying nice and quietly. Wrinkle City time. I was hating America (or this part of it) and feeling hopeless about home. Nowhere to go except *him*.

Then slowly tiny things dawn on you and you see you've got America a bit wrong: that perhaps all the stupidity and the tastelessness and the inequality and the violence and the conformity are just the price of keeping a national energy alive. They exploit themselves so foully in many minor ways, ones we'd never tolerate at home. That day you took me round Farmers' Market, just to show me how they've bred their fruit and vegetables to fit Madison Avenue notions of what they ought to look like. Huge red A-for-apple apples tasting like sugary sponge. Gigantic insipid tomatoes, huge flavorless lettuces. The heresy that size and looks are everything, all other values nothing. Which you see in the way the brainwashed ones talk, entertain, behave. Idiotic cheap models of how successful people should dress, speak, furnish their houses.

The woman who told me she had to drive thirty miles in wherever-it-was for what she called "butcher's meat," as if it was some fantastic delicacy like genuine Beluga or French truffles. That lovely decal. *Supermarkets save time. But for what?*

I know Mildred cooks like an angel, and there are good restaurants. But you keep thinking, thank God for Europe and tiny little unambitious tradesmen . . . who are really craftsmen, and respected as such. I know some people here know. Abe, I went at him about this the other day and he made a natch joke about it: If Americans ever figure out how they sell themselves so much they don't need and don't want, they'll all try to emigrate back to Europe.

And yet there's a sort of forwardness, an independence, a lack of servility. A hope. At least the will, if not the means.

The way they use English, instead of letting it use them. Things we have no notion of. So I begin to see it as a choice of how you pay the bill. At home we do it by being apathetic and hierarchical, by clinging to the past. Here they do it by looking forward to a dream world, where everyone succeeds, everyone's rich and happy. Horrors like the supermarkets and the freeways and the smog and the sprawl are just incidents on the road there. The wagon-trail myth. Today's problems aren't problems, but proofs of tomorrow's new frontier. You drive on, at all costs. With us, you make do with what you are. They're eternally stuck in the first few pages, when we reached the last chapter ages ago.

I remember, do you, Dan arguing with me that the uniqueness of the Anglo-Saxon race-mind was its mania for equality. Claiming it can be seen right back, even in feudal times. Magna Carta, Parliament, the common law and all the rest. But with us it reached its zenith in the seventeenth century. Cromwell and the Commonwealth. We had our chance then, and funked it. Or rather, those who wouldn't funk it took the chance over with them to America. Of course the American soul has become hopelessly mixed. But there's still something about it of the other English road. Dan said once, This is where Cromwell never died. I laughed, I could see the old boy standing beside Sunset in his iron top and leather boots. Sorry, folks. Dan didn't think it was funny.

But what I don't see (to the point at last) is how he can believe this and yet secretly remain so English of the English who queued up to cheer Charles II back ashore. If only he could pick up a little of the American faith in themselves. In the present, however bad. If I had a magic wand, I'd wave it over his head and leave him just as he is, but American. It's a shame, really. He was born into the wrong culture. He makes me feel so free, by comparison. I don't think this is just the age thing. Mildred said something shrewd about him. She'd said, Dan's the most English Englishman I ever met. And I said, But he isn't typical at all, really. She shook her head: Honey, he's just learned to hide it. That's all.

We've talked a lot about him, by the way. I sense she wants to tell me things she knows and I don't. Other women, perhaps. And she wants me to tell her things I know. We fence, but affectionately. She has great tact. The official state of play is just a temporary separation. I don't want anyone else's opinion on us, however well-meant.

I'm more than half writing to myself, you know that. Telling you all this nonsense you first told me. But vain thing, you'll know what that means as well. I don't really mean it about dark glasses.

I miss you so much. Every hour of every day. And night.

*Next morning.* I will send this, after all. I've just asked the two quails, and they said it makes no sense—but if I loved you, I should.


This was yet to come, of course. But one little Jenny-coined epithet needs a gloss. It derives from a story Dan told her, perhaps the saddest and most revealing of all native American jokes.

A Brooklyn boy gets a job as a stable-lad in a plush Long Island mansion. Each morning he saddles a horse and leads it around to the front of the mansion and waits for the daughter of the house to come down the steps and go for her ride. He falls in love with her—so badly that he begins to mope, to eat nothing. One day the stable-master takes the boy on one side. The boy tells him what it's all about; how the girl never speaks to him, never looks at him, seems unaware he exists.

"Listen," says the older man, "you gotta do sump'n with dames they have to notice."

"Like what?"

"Like paint her horse orange. She has to notice that. You get talking. Then you're in."

That night the boy paints the horse bright orange from nose to tail. The next morning he saddles it up, then leads it around to the steps in front of the house. The girl comes down, stops, stares at the horse, then at the boy holding it.

"Someone's painted that horse orange!"

"Yeah. Me. Let's fuck."

# Interlude

It is, of course, the women in Dan's life; not the men. Perhaps there was always some cunning streak of homosexuality in him, even though he had never, since his first years at boarding-school, felt any physical attraction toward the gay world. But in his relationships with his own sex there had always seemed an incompleteness: even with Anthony, with Abe, with a handful of other men he had known well over the years. He had very rarely sought male company for pleasure, perhaps because it threatened his always precarious sense of uniqueness. He saw himself too easily in other masculine faces, mannerisms, machismos, ambitions, failings; his own sex always seemed to lack the variety and unpredictability of women—they could be told, whereas all interesting women had to tell themselves, slowly and subtly if they were really to please him; and not consciously so, but in their nature.

One can't dissociate the kind of man he is from the vulgarest kind of vanity, the Casanova aspect of the beast; from the notched tally, the quite literal cocksureness; but his real attitude there was at least partly, he would say centrally, botanical—botanical in his twist of the word, not the normal and proper sense, such as Anthony had demonstrated. It was not categorizing and counting, but searching. He liked looking for women who would interest him, for new specimens; or more accurately, he expected the events, hazards and situations of his professional life to provide encounters. He was even rather passive about this, rarely making the first move, but letting the new face and psyche display itself to him before he showed his own cards. He had never slept with a prostitute—or at least with a clear professional; and the two women he had coupled with only once have both been mentioned. That side of a relationship had never seemed an end in itself; and he had always despised, or more latterly, pitied, the men for whom he knew it was.

He was arguably not even looking for women in all this, but collecting mirrors still; surfaces before which he could make himself naked—or at any rate more naked than he could before other men—and see himself reflected. A psycho-analyst might say he was searching for the lost two-in-one identity of his first months of life; some solution for his double separation trauma, the universal one of infancy and the private experience of literally losing his mother. He had in the past applied Freudian theory, insofar as the subject can be his own analyst, to his own history. But the trouble there was that he had always led a reasonably happy sex-life. Whatever Freudian horrors and truths he might arrive at by the book seemed denied by reality: he was neither dissatisfied nor guilt-ridden as he was. He enjoyed both his compara-tively casual and his longer-lasting affairs; he occasionally felt sad when they were over, but never for very long. Very sim-ply, he enjoyed the process of knowing each. Indeed, as he grew older, this pleasure became less and less dependent on sexual involvement; almost more fun, that one had to deci-pher a Caro or as just now, a Jane, without the benefit of the closer context.

All of which Jenny is to get slightly wrong: his mistress was not loss so much as that he expected the loss of all his mistresses, and in more or less direct proportion to his discov-ery of them. There were always, inevitably, elements of cal-lousness, selfishness, self-secrecy. One cannot without some infliction of pain tell another human being: I've examined you, experienced you, learned from you, and it's been amus-ing and interesting, but now I'd like to move on.

A novel is written in the two past tenses: the present per-fect of the writer's mind, the concluded past of fictional con-vention. But in terms of the cramped and myopic fictional present . . . if Jenny accuses Dan (has still, of course, in the chronology of this reconstruction, hardly put pencil to paper, let alone had Dan read the result) of a love of loss, she is being disingenuous, since she knows he likes her too much to hurt her; that if she insists, they continue. Above all she knows he knows that behind her reproaches lies a very old-fashioned little nucleus of personal vanity; a myth of per-manence. She will not be one of a chain, she will last. Because Dan—like Britain herself—has a sharp sense of the relativity of all supposed absolutes, she supposes him defeated . . . for which she mustn't be blamed, since he wears that mask at times. Yet it is much more a mask of excuse, a sacrificial pawn, than an emblem of some deep truth, or true presentiment in him.

My other two sisters: a fable.

I met them in London at the party following a private showing in the late 1950s, a year after I had split, true to pattern but amicably, with Andrea. The film had nothing to do with me, I was simply there as a casual friend of the director, and I had come meaning to stay no longer than courtesy required for the usual drinks and hyperbole afterward.

However, some of the cattle were there as well, including two girls who had had small parts in one sequence. They couldn't act, but they photographed well, and I had caught a glimpse of something piquant. It so happened that I had come to the showing with a script problem of my own. I was halfway into that early attempt at a cross-racial love-story that was finally released (with a compromise ending I foolishly let myself be talked into) as *Dark Encounter*. It was to be shot here, to get the Eady money. I had down a very long scene between these two main characters that needed breaking—an interlude, some little bit of sideplay that broke tension and might also snag the white hero's otherwise too smooth progression toward his black girl; something to remind him that pig-skin also has its charms.

After the two girls had done their short scene, during the showing, my mind had wandered off the screen, or through it, to my own embryo picture. I saw a way of using them, then several ways; a potentiality of development. Minor characters in scripts are rather like knights in chess: limited in movement, but handy in their capacity for quick turns, for fixing situations. I hadn't noticed what the final credits revealed as two sisters before lights went out, but I was interested to see them there afterward—and promptly got myself into conversation with the more available.

Her name was Miriam, though she wasn't Jewish; but as *echt* Cockney as the Mile End Road, a fact that had been coached out of her voice in the two or three lines she had spoken during the film. She had an oddly delicate face, a slim little body, rather striking clothes; and an equally pretty blend of naïvety and suspicion. All this was before the London working class came into their own, and the type was very fresh, at least to me. I was much more familiar with vacuous young starlets from the Home Counties (or who at least aped that background) asking to be tossed to the nearest fat old ·

shark in Wardour Street—and whose only notion of a Cockney accent was to replace an impeccable middle-class *a* by an impeccable middle-class *i*. Miriam was making some attempt at gentility, but her real voice kept breaking through.

Whatever else, she wasn't stale flesh. She wanted to know who I was, at first wouldn't believe me ("You're all such bloody liars in this business"); then more than made up for it ("Oh fantastic—d'you reelly write that?"). It was all career-furthering, of course, and in someone less engaging I should have fled a mile from it. But she amused me. I got her to talk about herself and discovered she was very far from new to show business—or at least one branch of it. Both her father and mother had worked the halls; and so had she and her sister. She pretended to be shocked that I had never heard of the Fairy Sisters. It had been dancing and a bit of crooning, "only we couldn't reelly do neether, you know, it was criminal we even got paid"—a sniff and a gauche grimace—"sometimes." I gathered it had been mostly summer seaside work, concert parties. Their agent had got wind of the two bit parts in the present film, and they had been taken on. I presumed at the usual fee, since I noticed her younger sister across the room seemed permanently attached to the producer's side: a man I knew was a well-known old goat. From time to time she threw covert little glances across at where Miriam stood with me. I had from both an impression of innocence, behind the knowingness.

I decided I could use Miriam, and perhaps her sister as well; and even that it would be a pity also not to try to use this chips-and-vinegar voice rather more than I had at first envisaged. A better director might get a better performance. I was attracted, too; she had a kind of homemade style—a rather prescient one, as it turned out, in terms of clothes and class. I said there might be a bit of work in the script I was doing, I couldn't promise anything, but maybe we could have lunch together . . .

She fluttered her eyelashes.

"Oh yeah. *And. . . ?*"

"I'd be much more devious if I wanted that."

"Much more what?"

"Straightforward."

She sniffed. "I'll bet." Then she said, "You wouldn't catch me comin' on me own."

"As many bodyguards as you like."

She didn't in fact take much persuading. We compromised,

as regarded chaperones; her sister would be present. Her name was Marjory, but Miriam called her the Drag. Punctuality was not her strong suit, it seemed.

Either of them's strong suit, as I was soon to learn. They appeared late, and without apology, for the lunch. They looked out of place, and they both knew it—were biting their lips and sniffing at each other as soon as they had sat down. I knew this hadn't happened very often to them before. Under the not totally false pretense of needing to know their backgrounds better if I was going to write them in, I pumped them. They began to thaw. They had, for the world they were now in, a delicious lack of self-consciousness. It was all a game, fun, codding and being codded. I soon felt a little like an uncle giving two school-kids a treat. They enjoyed everything so: the food, the wine, the other people around us, the money being spent. They were also curious about me. I talked about Hollywood and dropped a few famous names, because I knew they wanted to hear them; and then went on to be more honest about the movie business than they can have been used to. I wasn't promising anything definite. The younger sister, Marjory the Drag, who was perhaps the prettier of the two, was also the less loquacious; a hint of something drier, or more sullen, about her . . . at any rate, remaining more on her guard, rather as if she were the elder sister. She was nineteen, Miriam a year older.

There must have been some pre-arranged signal. But a shade too abruptly the Drag was gathering her things.

"Sorry. I got a date."

I asked who it was with, when she'd left. Miriam shrugged.

"I dunno. Some bloke."

I suggested the name of the producer.

"That's just nights."

"I've roughed out a scene. Would you like to come and read it?"

"Yeah, okay. You promise you won't laugh."

There was no suspicion now; only a becoming modesty, and I had trouble not smiling.

On the way back to the flat in a taxi, she suddenly broke into what I was saying.

"Honest, you don't 'ave to spiel. I been around."

"I'm not kidding you about the picture."

"I know." She gave one of her sniffs. "I 'ad you checked out."

"Good."

"Couldn't work out at the showin' whether you was a crook or just bloody daft."

"And now?"

"Obvious, innit? Now you know 'ow dumb we reelly are."

But that went with a pressed mouth and a grin that wasn't dumb at all, and cut any amount of normal dialogue.

And that was that. We did go through a brief pretense of reading the scene—she wasn't very good, but by then neither of our minds were on the script. When it came to it, she was out of her clothes and into bed before I was; and the same blend of opposites in her behavior out of bed carried there as well. She contrived to be both gently prudish and very far from sexual ignorance; shy and inquisitive; cool and affectionate; both aware she was nice to go to bed with and a little bit puzzled as to why I should take the bother.

There was only one false note. We were still lying there, and she said, "D'you want me to 'op it now?"

"Do you want to go?"

"Not if you don't want me to."

So I set about discovering her. She and the Drag still officially lived at home, in what I grew to think of, by the way they exaggeratedly pronounced it, as Orrible Acne. They wished they didn't, there were always rows, less those of Cockney puritanism ("I mean, they couldn't, all accounts me dad's been the randiest old bastard of 'em all") than of professional fear. The parents did some kind of old-style patter-and-song routine, got up as a pearly King and Queen, an act the two girls had once been a part of. It was a sort of jealousy, she thought; an envy " 'cos we're tryin' to make lives of our own." And it was stupid, she'd been let into the bloody facts of life when she was fifteen, and they knew all about it, and who it was, and did nothing about it. It had been a member of an acrobatic team on the same bill. "I was soppy daft about 'im, you know, didn't give the poor bleeder a chance reelly. Me mum wanted to take 'im to court, only I said I'd say that. You know, if 'e'd . . . but fair's fair, innit?" There'd been a lot of blokes since, but they hadn't lasted; she was growing out of Horrible Hackney and its young men. And her sister?

"Oh Gawd. Honestly . . . 'e's such a bloody old pervert. 'E fancies me as well. Know what I mean?"

"I can guess."

"I told 'im, get lost. Wish she would."

After a moment she said, in a tone of briskly indifferent

curiosity that was very characteristic, "Am I okay? You like me?"

I proved I liked her. Then we slept a little, and it was half past six. I was ahead of schedule on the script. We agreed that she'd stay the night, then we went to see a film and had a late supper. When we got back she telephoned her parents in Hackney; it was the briefest of calls. She wouldn't be back; she was fine. With a friend. I know what I'm doing, Mum. Then, well that's 'er business, innit? She put the receiver down and pulled a lugubrious face at me.

She moved in the next day, at my invitation. I already knew she was going to be very simple to live with; and in that sense I used her, I wouldn't let her interfere with my work, I suppose I rather treated her as a pet animal—someone I was prepared to feed and dress and make love to, and teach a little, but not someone I could ever give my heart or full attention to. She was one of those girls who are both shrewd and ignorant over many things, and with the usual defense mechanism: suspicious of all superior knowledge. Reading was beyond her, though she tried intermittently. But I soon discovered she had a mind of her own over other things: clothes, food, the films we saw, the odd exhibition. Some of the knowledge flowed my way, especially over the films. One of the supreme idiocies of commercial film-makers is their ignorance of how the mind of the ordinary audience works. All the sneak previews and reaction analysis reports in the world are not worth half an hour with the real thing; and still today, if I think I am going over audience heads, I sometimes try to see as Miriam saw. She was a sucker for sentiment and spectacle. But I introduced her to some classics and what serious contemporary cinema was around. After a first sniff and reluctance, she fell agreeable fast for quality, and I think not just to please me.

I jump ahead a little: "she" should really be "they." Miriam did some elementary shopping and housework, but there were still long hours to fill while I worked; she very soon took to going out on her own during the day. To see her parents, her sister, or so she said; sometimes she just went to "the flicks." She failed only once to return. But she rang, she was with "me Mum," the old man was being a pig, he was pissed, she wanted to stay the night. She came back late the next day.

I was glad to see her; the gabble, her ghastly evening retold.

A few days later, she did return to the flat when expected, but not alone. This time her sister was with her. She had, I suspect under strong pressure from Miriam, walked out on the idea of sleeping her way to stardom. The girl did look unhappy and vaguely shocked, and rather touchingly aware that I was not running a home for waifs and strays. It would only be for that night, she couldn't face all the argybargy at home. There were two spare rooms, I couldn't very well refuse; and even if Miriam was content with her submissive role, I felt some other return besides my leisure hours and the odd hand-out "for pocket-money" was called for. We stayed in, they cooked, with more enjoyment than skill, a meal. I heard their low voices in the kitchen, and it was somehow rather pleasing, their ordinariness and sisterliness; a certain shyness between them during the meal, a tendency to giggle, as during our first lunch together; and then alone with Miriam in bed later, I had all her worry I should feel I was being taken advantage of, "lumbered" with her problems. She told me more about their home, their parents.

It was mainly about her father—he was one of those ugly variants of the sad clown, all jollity and bonhomie on the boards or in a pub, but a moody, flashfisted tyrant in his home; even worse, there had been "things" when she and Marjory were younger . . . "Honest, Dan, I couldn't tell you . . . course, 'e was always 'alf pissed." Then said shyly, "I don' mean whatchermercallit. You know. Jus' . . . you know."

"But all that's over now?"

"Sure. Only when we was little. Just you don't never forget." She paused, then went whispering on in the darkness. "What's so terrible, 'slike it was the only way 'e knew 'ow to be our proper dad. Ever since 'e don' want to know us. Like it's all me Mum's fault we even exist. 'E's such a mean old bastard, you can't imagine. You want me to shut up?"

"No. Tell me."

"Frinstance month ago I was down 'ome and I went to fetch 'im outa the boozer for his Sunday dinner. You know, 'e was all over me, drinks all round, showin' me off like I was every dad's dream. Then we got outside an' . . . oh Christ— you know. No bloody warning, 'e starts callin' me 'n Marjory every fucking name under the bleedin' sun. I could kill 'im sometimes. Honest. And the way he treats me Mum. You just can't imagine."

But I could, only too well, behind her few remaining reticences; and began to realize the strange, almost noble, sense of working-class responsibility that kept the two girls at least morally at their mother's side. They showed me a snapshot of her one day, a woman in her early forties, her hair done tightly back, a faintly gipsy face, but worn, resigned before its time, though she was smiling. They'd begged her to walk out, but they were up against another kind of martyrdom there. There was the act; the fear of what the "old bugger" would do if he was abandoned. I read an East End Mycenae, the workings of inexorable fate; very trite, perhaps, but very real. As I lay that evening listening to Miriam as she rambled on, I knew I had done something more than pick up a charming mongrel; but landed myself with someone I must not hurt. The next morning I said Marjory could stay until she could face all that: the venom of Laius.

Her shyness turned out to be rather illusory, or more a matter of previous insecurity than anything very innate. Miriam tended to boss her about and they developed a dry little slanging relationship—or must always have had it, and now hid it no longer. Some sort of equivalent of my attitude to Miriam began to be passed on: judgments or information I had given to the elder sister were now—sometimes a good deal more bullyingly and peremptorily—visited on the younger. Playing umpire was not difficult. Their spats amused me, and were never serious. Once or twice they joined to argue against me. More and more I was treated as a kind of oracle-cum-encyclopedia-cum-butt: why didn't I believe in God or an after-life, why did I vote Labour, what was expressionism about, why did I despise fish-and-chips . . . and then one day they found to their amazement that I'd never been to the dogs. So I was dragged out to Haringay, and lost some money—or they lost it for me—and felt uncomfortably like an off-duty ponce; but enjoyed it. Their shrieks and moans when their sure-fire winners once again failed to make it, and their chatter all the way home; and Miriam's clinging young body, when we went to bed.

I remember that night in particular. Her sister had been with us for five or six days by then and it was clear to me that she wasn't going to leave unless she was told. Miriam kept telling me she was like her old self again; it was rather as if I had performed some miracle cure. They were also both broke. They weren't grasping, never asked for money; and never refused it. I apparently had plenty, they were simply grateful, but not conscience-stricken about what was spent on them or I gave to Miriam. But this night, it must have been bothering her secretly, she was lying in silence; then she kissed the side of my neck and whispered.

"D'you fancy my sister?"

I thought back then to a tiny incident at the greyhound stadium earlier that evening. One of the dogs, the one Marjory had put her money on, stumbled as it came out of the trap and picked up hopelessly late to stand a chance. She had turned her face against my shoulder in despair and disgust. I'd laughed, and put my arm around her for a moment. Miriam had seen that.

"Don't be silly. I like you much better."

"Why's it silly?"

"Being jealous."

"You're not saying my question."

I kissed the top of her head. "I like you both. But only you in bed."

There was a mulling silence. "You don' understand. Dan. I wouldn't mind if you did."

I patted her bottom. "Come on. That's dirty talk."

Another beat. "She fancies you."

"How do you know?"

" 'Cos we talked about it."

"Then you shouldn't have."

"It's only 'cos we like you. 'Cos we're grateful." She said, "If you'd like it too."

I should have said firmly then that I didn't; but such darkness, closeness is very different from daylight. Part of me did not dislike the idea. But I think above all I was curious.

I said, "If you really liked me, it would have to make you feel jealous."

"Honest. I wouldn't mind." She kissed my neck again. "If I knew you . . . you know." Then she said, "I don't mean anything nasty. Like ol' Doodah. Us both together. Nuffin' like that."

I was tempted to joke her out of it, to pretend that I was disappointed it could not be "both together." But I knew she was trying, in her tongue-tied way, to say something generous—and however implausible, obscene, what you will, her proposition might sound. She was saying that she knew she and I had no future, the distances were too great; that she and her sister were glad to have landed up with me; that . . .

"Does she feel in the way?"

I felt her nod. "Yeah, a bit."

"I won't push her out, Miriam. If that's it."

"Just thought I'd mention it."

"You're sweet. And extraordinary." I lifted her head and kissed her mouth; then turned us on our sides, her back to me, and held her. I thought the matter was closed, we would settle to sleep. But after a few moments she whispered again.

"Any day now I'm not goin' to be no good."

"We're due for a rest."

That baffled her a moment. But she nodded again, and then there was silence.

I had no idea, the next day, whether she had passed on to Marjory the result of that whispered conversation; I could see no evidence of it. I could also not help seeing the offered substitute in a new light, or at least a franker one. Having had them side by side now for several days, I had begun to sort out their particular charms. The younger had the less independent mind, but also a greater consciousness of men; another blend, this time of impudence and slyness, also a sort of greenness, an underlying innocence, perhaps because of that year less. She was less inhibited, yet a shade more schoolgirlish.

Two nights later, I had gone to bed and was reading. The girls were in the kitchen, they made themselves cocoa every night. I heard their voices, then they went into Caro's old bedroom, where Marjory slept. A few minutes later, someone stood in the doorway of my room. It was Marjory. She was in a short nightdress. It was the first time I had seen her in anything but daytime clothes.

"She wants to sleep on 'er own tonight."

I was embarrassed enough to pretend that I thought she was just a messenger.

"Oh. Okay."

She did not move.

"She said I was to come. And go away, if you said."

"Then she's disobeying orders."

She said nothing, looked at the ground, then up at me again; she had a nice mouth, and it had an oddly trepid glum smile, which hung suspended in the air, Cheshire-catlike, while she waited. Now I looked down, at my book, and kept my eyes on it.

"I think you'd better go away."

"Don't you like me?"

"Of course I like you."

"What then?"

"I don't want to take advantage of you. Or Miriam."

She let a moment pass. The nightdress was very short; puffed sleeves that didn't suit her—or any woman, in my experience. The legs proved she needed something slimmer and simpler.

"What you readin'?"

I had to smile at that, it was so obvious; and she promptly looked hurt.

"I only asked."

"I told her quite distinctly that I didn't want this to happen."

"She said you was jus' bein' decent."

"One has to try to be that sometimes."

She tossed her hair. She was leaning against the side of the door, her hands behind her back.

"You do 'ave to try then?"

"Don't be cheeky." She looked down. "I'm happy the way it is."

"I'm not. And me feet are bloody freezin'."

I weakened.

"Go and fetch the cigarettes."

"Then can I stay?"

"Just to talk. For one cigarette."

She disappeared, then returned and stood at the end of the bed, lighting two cigarettes. The nightdress was not opaque. She came round on the unoccupied side of the bed and passed me mine.

"Can I sit by you, Dan? Me feet reelly are cold."

I drew a breath. "Until I say out. Then out."

She climbed demurely in on the far side of the bed. There was a great waft of perfume. She slid a glance at the book I was reading.

"Is that po'try?" She craned to look closer. "I wish you'd read me a bit. Like you do Miriam."

I realized my bedroom had fewer secrets than I had supposed. It was Bullen's anthology of seventeenth-century love verse, *Speculum Amanti;* and I had one recent night read some to Miriam.

"I can't. It might give you ideas."

She had her sister's sniff. "Bet it's not as filthy as that old jumper." I had forsaken pajamas with Miriam; and had pulled on an old sweater by way of a bed-jacket. My elbow was nudged. "Be a sport. Just one little bit."

"I thought we were going to have a serious talk."

"In a min."

I began reading. But by the end of the first stanza she was nestling closer. She wanted to read the print. Then she was reaching across me for the ash-tray, and ended closer still; a few lines later my right arm was lifted and placed around her shoulders, and a bare leg touched the length of mine beneath the blankets. She did stay good and little-girlish till the end of that short poem and through most of the longer one that followed; but then, having put out her cigarette, her body turned and a leg came up and across. By the third poem a hand had crept beneath the bedclothes, and the nightdress ridden so high that the continued wearing of it became absurd. I closed the book. Her face was turned against my shoulder, her eyes closed.

She murmured, "Don't stop. I like it. 'Snice."

Which might have come better from me; I spent a brief five seconds examining the moral implications of what was about to happen—then turned out the light and began to examine the physical ones. She was no more innocent than her sister, of course; and at least in the dark, a good deal less prudish.

I regretted my weakness the next morning. Marjory had left the bed, I could hear them both in the kitchen and I knew they had to be faced, which I did with an unassumed dry diffidence. They sat silently at the kitchen table, biting their lips. Then Miriam slid a little look up at me.

"'Oo gets top marks then?"

"Equal first."

They exchanged looks, then began to giggle; recovered, and that was it. Somehow guilt and embarrassment, all the possible consequences, could not survive with them. I had the sense to let them dictate matters, to observe whatever taboos they felt were still necessary. No other reference was ever made to "marks"; I never had them "both together," either. Out of bed I was to show no favoritism—indeed, they rather avoided all physical contact with me or insisted that I was shared, that I held each hand in a cinema, whatever it was. Watching television they would usually sit together away from me, like sisters of a much younger age; but they'd been brought up in a tough school, regularly left alone at nights when they were still very small. Despite their nagging, they still liked to feel each other very close.

I remember them talking one day of sharing toys, dolls, their closeness then; and understood a little better how they could share so without jealousy the grown-up toy they had found in me.

That was principally it, of course. We somehow hit on a blend of reciprocal curiosity, affection and physical pleasure that was totally free of love. Even the physical pleasure was mostly mine, I suspect; at separate times they both confessed they liked best the lying in the dark and talking. They would often have talked all night, if I hadn't stopped them. They had been starved all their lives of confession—had never met a professional word-man before, someone who could coax, listen, correct them without hurting them. Marjory especially had a lovely fresh sense of recall: school outings, theaters they had played, music-hall characters, tricks of the trade, relatives. She was a better mimic than Miriam.

One evening they did their former act for me in the living-room; some quite deft footwork in the dancing, but the one song they tried made them break up . . . and mercifully. Neither had been in tune; and the sad ghost of a dead art, a dying form of entertainment hung over it all. On top of that, I now felt a clear responsibility for them. The first draft of the script had gone off, and the scene into which I had put them—I had decided to use both—had been passed in principle, but I still couldn't promise them the parts till the production team came over and casting began. I had warned them, and they hadn't seemed to care; but I cared. Their agent was pestering them to "fill in" with some of the old work, but they weren't interested. They used to talk about modeling, cabaret, all sorts of silly ideas; and I became less and less sure I shouldn't be backing their agent. Deep in both of them there was a driftingness, a fecklessness; or perhaps I should say a courage of the kind Brecht immortalized. As long as they had the price of a cinema ticket and a bag of chips, and somewhere to kip, they would survive. It used to irritate me at times, but I also knew it was a middle-class irritation, a conditioned one.

We lived like that for seven or eight weeks. Then I had to go to New Mexico, where the director-to-be of my script was finishing a Western, to discuss some rewrites. I told them they could stay on in the flat while I was away, and they said they would. But it was not very much of a surprise when I came back one late afternoon just before I was due to leave to find them gone. It had been in the air. Laid out on my desk was an Old Etonian tie—they must have seen it in some posh tailor's and decided I'd like the pattern—and a pair of dreadful

Siamese cuff-links. I hadn't taught them everything and I was a little hurt that they hadn't noticed I never wore cuff-links. Nicer was a bunch of chrysanthemums—and nicer still a scrawled note: *We'll never love no one 'arf as much.* I had edged them out of double negatives; and they'd learned to spell "half" like that from my script. That note, I still have.

I telephoned Hackney, but they weren't there; and were still not there every time I tried in the two days before I had to leave for the States. Nor could their agent help. A fortnight later, when I came back, I tried him again. I had in the meantime sold the idea of at least testing Miriam and Marjory to the producer and director. But to my horror the agent told me they'd just left for Germany to join a dancing troupe, some night-club in Munich. He assured me it was "straight up," he strictly didn't export for the white slave trade, and that he'd let them know the film possibility was much firmer now. He even gave me their address, and I wrote to it. But I never had an answer; and when casting started they still couldn't be traced. They had left the troupe in Munich only three days after they joined it. Their mother thought they were in Italy, but "they never wrote." Something tired and resigned in her voice gave me a final guilt: I had helped wean them and now she was bereft. I changed their two scenes in the script. I've never seen or heard of them since.

They were the two most civilized feminine creatures I have ever known; and I can hear them sniff-and-giggle if they ever read this. They had in retrospect a stunning honesty, and a tact, and an intelligence. Our relationship could never have lasted much longer than it did. But I remember it now as a glimpse of an ideal world, perhaps even of a future: not in some odious male chauvinist sense, the access to two bodies, the indulging in the old harem fantasy, but because it was so free of all the encumbrance, the suppuration, the vile selfishness of romantic love. For two months we made it: without spite, without tears, without possessiveness; with nothing, really, but human profit. And it was mainly their doing, not mine.

Jenny picked up some silly psychology game at work one day, and made me play it. If one had to pick three partners for an eternal desert island, which sex would they be?

"Three women."

"I knew you'd say that."

"Then you needn't have asked."

"Balanced men say one man and two women."

"Certainly better for mixed doubles."

"What you don't know is that three women means you hate women. You want to see them destroy one another."

"I once knew two who never would. That leaves me only one to find."

"It jolly well wouldn't be me."

"Then that leaves us two to find."

But she wasn't mollified. "Who were they?"

"Angels in disguise."

"You're making them up."

"One day I shall make you up."

"What makes you think you're not doing that already?"

"Against the rules."

"What rules?"

"Of the present tense."

"Pig." I smiled, but she didn't. "I keep having to revise what I hate about you most. I've now decided it's the loathsome way you use other people's games to play your own."

And I recalled then something one of the sisters, I can't remember which, had once said to me.

"What I like about living with you's the way you make it all like a game. Like it doesn't matter. 'Slong as we're all happy."

An apparent compliment, at least inside the walls of Jane's once admired abbey; but I had remembered it because it had hurt, faintly, even then. The frustration I felt when they disappeared may have been partly that of thwarted generosity, of not fulfilling the offer I had used to seduce them. Time may have made it partly a source of pleasure, as Jenny was to claim. Yet there has always been a sense in which those two have haunted me, as the dead haunt, making missed opportunities eternal—and making even this exorcism by the written word a vain and empty thing. It is not that I wish it had never happened, or that I do not accept that it had had to end. I simply wish they knew they never really left.

I gave them a little money, a temporary haven, a few facts about life. In return I received, though I did not see it at the time, a lasting lesson on the limitations of my class, my education and my kind. I have called them "Miriam" and "Marjory" here, but I suspect better names could have been found among those of nine far more famous sisters: Clio and Thalia, perhaps.

"You mean—Christ, Dan, what you been doin' all your life? Your age . . . and you never been to the bloody dogs!" She grimaces across me at Marjory, mouths like a gossiping old backyard mum. "It's 'is books. 'E loves 'is books." Marjory mouths silently back. Miriam sprawls forward across the kitchen table on an elbow. I am no longer there. "Shall we take 'im then? Just for jokes? Course, we'd 'ave to make 'im promise not to talk posh. Case they chuck 'im outa the stadium." Marjory puffs, stifling a giggle. Miriam tilts her head, surveys me with a blithe mock ignorance. "D'you reckon you could be'ave like an ornary 'ooman bloke, Dan? Just for one evenin'?"

Miriam has very clear gray-blue eyes. They taunt, they live, and I envy with all my heart every man who has had them since.

# Hollow Men

It began inauspiciously. Barney was already primed when we met at the restaurant and if I'd had any sense I should have turned straight around and walked out before we spoke a word. He wore an appropriately wry and circumstantial grin as I approached, but his eyes said something else. We met for a chess-game and however many sacrifices he might make on the surface, his strategy was not to lose it: at least to fight for a drawn match. I was warned at once. He would use any too obvious anger I showed. We were to play with English pieces.

Anthony's death at least took care of the preliminaries. This was three days after the little heart-to-heart with Caro, and the suicide had been reported briefly in the national papers. There had been a short obituary in the *Times*; and of course Barney would have heard all about it from Caro herself. He was a good enough newspaperman to have guessed that a story lay behind the public facts, but he was preternaturally uninquiring there—I suspected on Caro's advice. It must have been damned awful for me, he could imagine what a shock . . . we ordered, and he asked for another double gin and tonic.

Once again I tried to see him through Caro's eyes—that is, tried to ignore a couple of discreet raised hands to other entering customers, chat with the head waiter, the reek of the expense-account life around us. It seemed a highly unnecessary place to meet; an uncharacteristic tautology. I did not have to be reminded that he was a successful "personality" now.

He did finally broach the matter, though with his eyes on his glass, not in my direction. We were on a wall-bench, side by side.

"I hope Caro's told you how bad I feel about not telling you on the plane, Dan. I frankly didn't know how to play it."

"I'm not blaming you for that."

He gave his old twisted smile. "But you are blaming."

"Wouldn't you?"

"I suppose." There was an awkward pause. "I've never exactly been top of your list of favorite people. I realize that." I refused the offer to deny the valuation. He took another mouthful of gin. "Look, Dan, the reason I felt we ought to meet . . ."

The waiter brought my smoked salmon—Barney had said he was trying to lose weight—and he had to break off a moment. The place seemed full of people like us: klatsches of men, very few women, talking business, doing deals. Next to us on my side there was evidently a publisher and one of his authors: I heard talk of some disappointing American sale. It was "their" fault, not the author's . . . he was above transatlantic heads. I knew from the publisher's orotund voice that he wouldn't have known a transatlantic head if it had been sitting on the plate in front of him, but the pen seemed happy to imbibe the sepia.

"It's categorically not having a bit on the side. She's the nicest thing that's happened to me in years." I squeezed lemon over the pink flesh, and trusted he would note the parallel. "I mean that. Very seriously."

"I think I'd be happier if she was just a bit on the side."

He was silenced a moment. The publisher had high hopes of Germany. I began eating. "That's hardly fair to Caro, is it?"

"I don't want her hurt, that's all. She's a good deal less sophisticated than she sometimes makes out."

"I wouldn't like her so much if I wasn't aware of that."

"Then you know what I mean."

"I've told her. She wants to forget the whole thing, she only has to say. She knows what I am, Dan." I began to resent this insidious lapping of my name against the stone in my face, and he may have sensed it. He said, "Perhaps better than you do. Behind all the shit."

"My dear man, I'm not concerned with what you are. Simply with what might happen to her."

"You seem pretty certain I must have a bad effect."

The wine came, and he tasted it impatiently. It was poured, set in the ice-bucket. I decided to move my bishop.

"As you know, I've recently acquired a girl-friend who's not much older than Caro. You're not going to catch the pot calling the kettle black, Barney. But I know damn well that whatever they fall for, it's not our youth and blue eyes. There must be something unhealthy in it. At least on their side."

"Hardly be for lack of choice, can it?"

"That's not the point."

Neither of us wanted to be overheard, and all this part of the conversation was conducted in a tacitly conspiratorial way.

"You forget I'm an old hand at the unhealthy relationship. I've had a bloody lifetime at it."

"Your marriage?"

He drew a breath.

"I believe that's what some people call it."

I ate my salmon. "Presumably something kept it alive."

"The usual happy blend of sadism and masochism."

"Come on."

He left a pause. "You're lucky, Dan. You've missed all that."

"All what?"

"When you get beyond the hatred to the inertia. When you've metaphorically buggered each other so often that it's become a way of life." I said nothing, and he tried again: a little more honesty. "It's the kids. You know. At least she's never taken it out on them. We made a deal. Her price for letting me go my own unsweet way. I'm not really complaining."

"I've forgotten how old the youngest is."

"Twelve. I'm hardly free yet, if that's what you mean." He eyed me surreptitiously. "I've told Caro all about it. It may be a mockery, but if that's the way Margaret wants her pound of flesh, it's not something I feel I can welsh on."

It was absurd: now he was defending his decency as a bastard.

"I haven't the least desire to see you make an honest woman out of Caro."

"I didn't imagine you did, dear boy. I'm just trying to explain the situation."

"Your wife knows?"

"That side of my life is my own business. Part of the treaty." He stared across the room, then leaned back; began sacrificing again. "I got so pissed off with intellectual women at Oxford. I used to envy you. Your lot. Never quite making it with you. I sort of fell for Margaret by reaction. As if I really did believe the clever ones bored me. Instead of just wanting them. My old man was a railwayman, I don't know if you remember."

"Vaguely."

I remembered well, in fact. He had brought it up rather gratuitously in one of the interviews I'd watched.

"All that Methodist bullshit. Marks you for life, once you've been through it. The myth of the nice little woman." He gave a subdued sniff. "I didn't get the other side of the message. It takes a nice little man as well."

I finished eating and leaned back; and joined him in staring across the crowded room.

"You can hardly have picked on Caro for her brains."

"I've had the clever ones since then. Clever and nothing else." He paused. "I don't want to sound offensive, Christ knows we all moan about our kids. But I don't think Caro's brainless by a long chalk. Okay, she's disappointed you academically. But she's got quite a gift for handling people. Getting their number. And I don't just mean on the blower."

"I'm glad to hear it."

I can't have sounded it, and he left another small silence.

"I don't know if she told you, but she was out of her depth in the office at the beginning. I wanted to help her find her feet a little." I waited. "I've never gone in for the Fleet Street *droit-du-seigneur* game. That's not how it happened. I would like you to believe that. I was . . . taken by surprise as well. I know what it must seem on the face of it." He glanced to see how it seemed on my face. "I fully understand you must feel you need this like a hole in the head. But between Caro and myself—she gives me a lot, Dan. I hope I manage to give her something in return. Something that as a matter of fact I thought was dead in me."

Once again he was silenced, as our Dover soles were brought and served.

"As long as it's not a desire to take a permanent lien on her life."

"You said yourself, we're a little bit in the same boat. At least give me credit for sharing some of your feelings."

There was a sharper edge in his voice.

"Okay, Barney."

"That's not at issue. If I could just get it across that I think she's a smashing girl, that she's made me very happy, that I don't want to hurt her. That I didn't pick on her. It came totally out of the blue. A two-way thing."

Against my will, I began to feel he was trying to say the truth, at least as regards the unexpectedness. Perhaps there had always been something profoundly anomalous in him, atavistic, beneath the hard-boiled persona. . . . I knew there must be something more in his marriage, however slightingly he spoke of it, than what could be described by words like "deal" and "treaty." There also a parallel existed between us: his Methodist upbringing, my Church of England one. The shared rebellion, the enduring guilt at levels deeper than logic and reason can ever purge: it was an uncomfortable feeling, like finding oneself in the same cell, and for the same crime, as a man one repudiated on every other ground. I picked up my knife and fork.

"Shall we leave it at this?"

"Has Caro suggested anything different to you?"

"No." I began to dissect the sole.

"It was decent of you to come. I realize you didn't want to."

"I loathe having to play the Victorian papa. In this context, it's doubly absurd."

"One's dear old homegrown Eumenides."

"If you want to put it that way."

He was still smoking, drinking wine now, indifferent to his food, but watching me at mine. "She's terrified of hurting you—you know that?"

"I'm prepared to be hurt as long as she's happy. I've no right to any other attitude. I've tried to tell her that."

I had a feeling he'd have liked to go on, and we should have entered a discussion of Caro's feelings about Nell and myself. But perhaps he guessed that I would not have allowed it.

"How's the sole?"

"Excellent."

"They try. More than you can say for most these days."

He began eating, and we passed on to American food; then other things, leaving Caro in parenthesis, the match duly drawn. I felt depressed, secretly angry at not having been angrier, at having been so determined not to lay myself open to attack, and brought under scrutiny as a parent. I saw myself, too, in Jenny's father's place. She was a late and youngest child and her parents—her father was a doctor in Cheshire— were both in their early sixties. We had never really discussed all that, either. They knew about us, she assured me they were broadminded, they wanted her to lead her own life . . .

Someone stopped by our table on his way out—another face from television, though its owner was better known as a columnist. I had read a piece by him only that morning, written with the mordant wit that was his trademark—and his downfall. Over the years he had clowned too much to have his moments of *saeva indignatio* taken very seriously. I was introduced, there was a little barbed backchat between him and Barney—a different and somehow much more real Barney, on guard, on duty, wearing his fencing-mask. Apparently the man was to appear shortly on Barney's program, the thrust and parry was mainly about that. Barney asked me what I thought of him, when he went off. I said something about finding him a shade wasted: a potential Junius who had sold out to his own lesser gift.

"I want to have a go at him on that."

"Without forewarning him?"

"He knows he's good enough to have it asked—why he isn't better." It was said drily. Then Barney shrugged. "Anyway, who could be a Junius in a culture that's forgotten how to read?"

"But he hasn't done too badly out of it?"

"Oh sure." Once again he was dry. "The best we have."

I smiled; and wondered whether that famous putting-down Barney had just appropriated, of a bad prime minister by a jealous rival, was not the single most English remark of the postwar years; behind all our discourse, and well beyond the political. What had gone wrong was less people than climate; less men than milieu—and the particular one we were in, that day, seemed most to blame. At all those tables, other men like us—and there really did seem, though it must have been fortuitous, an absence of younger or older faces—other middle-aged men hustling each other or preparing to hustle the world outside, in some ultimate treachery of the clerks.

Dan knew he had no right to stand aside, since the commercial cinema must certainly be counted as one of the audience-manipulating media; but he felt a nausea. So many other students he had known at Oxford had been sucked down into this world, with all its illusions of instant power; were in politics now, in television, on Fleet Street; had become cogs in the communication machine, stifled all ancient conviction for the sake of career, some press-lord's salary. Barney had gone on to mention one of the other undergraduates who had shared their lodgings, who had then been a good deal further to the left than the rest of them; and who had spent the last fifteen years in the Beaverbrook empire . . . had stayed a socialist in private, according to Barney. Dan remembered him well, he had been rather an Orwellian figure, an austere and sardonic young odd man out, despising both of them. They had used to call him Krupskaya's darling, he had pleased their landlady. Barney said it was a matter of compartments.

"The one union you'd better be fully paid up with if you want to stay on Fleet Street is the Amalgamated Society of Schizophrenics."

"He never felt like that."

"Oh, he thinks he still gets a message through."

"On that paper?"

"Simple. Kid yourself the kind of tiny nuance your pro friends pick up rings a bell throughout the length and breadth of the suburbs." He slid me a look. "And sheer professionalism. You mustn't underrate that. I know one paper last year where part of the course for their tyro subs was analyzing the brilliance of friend Goebbels' work in the Thirties."

"I think I've heard enough."

"Maybe you have the quaint old belief that people buy newspapers to be informed."

"Just amused?"

"Not even that. Excused. From boring things like thinking for yourself."

"Is this why you switched?"

"To telly? God knows. Lolly. A probably misguided notion I can do the three-card trick as well as the next man. And let's face it, it is where it is. To kill two clichés with one lie." He went on less cynically, as if he suddenly saw he was countermanding the image he had presented when we were discussing Caro. "There's honestly not much option nowadays, Dan. Heaven help the poor sod who can't stake himself a claim on the tiny screen. He'll never make it to the top."

Dan really wanted to go, as they sat talking over the coffee; yet also enjoyed, secretly, this ancient English game of hiding in the trees and judging the world outside. He was reminded, too, of Jane's contempt for the "time-serving intelligentsia." Her repressed violence had seemed naïve, faintly comic; but now, helped by his personal animus, he felt himself nearer to her view than he had admitted. He had no belief in her cure for the disease, but he began to second the diagnosis. When the history of the period came to be written, the communications industry would have to go in the dock. Somewhere in Britain a conduit between national reality and national awareness of it had been fatally blocked. One might argue that it was inevitable, too predicated by factors beyond human control, for any one section of society to take the blame; and certainly the public who allowed the block to take place, and to endure, had also to be charged. But Dan had a vision of a clogging spew of pundits and pontificators, editors and interviewers, critics and columnists, puppet personalities and attitude-hucksters, a combined media Mafia squatting on an enormous dungheap of empty words and tired images, and conjoined, despite their private rivalries and jealousies, by one common determination: to retain their own status and importance in the system they had erected.

His was the most familiar of all twentieth-century dilemmas, of course: that of the man, the animal, required to pay in terms of personal freedom for the contempt he felt at the abuse of social freedom—and unable to do it. It was like being caught between two absurd propositions: between "Better dead than Red" and "Any freedom is better than no freedom"; between the sickness of fear and the sickness of compromise. One feels a pervasive cancer at the heart of one's world; but still prefers it to the surgical intervention that must extirpate the attacked central organ, freedom, as well as the cancer.

Barney had migrated to brandy by then. The restaurant was already emptying, yet for some reason Dan sat on, listening mainly, prompting a little, and avoiding argument. Barney had returned to his own dilemma: how no one really listened any more, nothing registered, an audience of fifteen million was an audience of no one, the speed of forgetfulness was approaching the speed of light—the letters he got, the cranks who misunderstood the simplest things that were said. He even dragged Caro back in, how he felt she was the first person "in years" who actually did listen to and understand him: the cost of being a cynosure of the cretins and the Aunt Sally of the fastidious.

Dan knew what was being stated: that when everyone wanted instant fame and significance, the lasting kinds were unattainable. Perhaps theirs really had been the unlucky generation. They had just caught the last of the old Oxford, which had trained them to admire and covet the enduring accolade of history, *aere perennius* as the supreme good . . . and just as the essential corollary, all the stabilizing moral and religious values in society, were vanishing into thin air. Reality had driven them, perhaps because they were pitched willy-nilly into a world with a ubiquitous and insatiable greed for the ephemeral, to take any publicity, any celebrity, any transient success as a placebo. Barney's world had even fixed the rules of the game to make such shoddy prizes easier to gain and to bestow, and tried to cover the fixing, so that to criticize the glamorization of the worthless, the flagrant prostitution of true human values, the substitution of degree of exposure for degree of actual achievement, now invited an immediate accusation of elitism and pretension, of being out of touch. It infested all the morbid areas in their culture, the useless complications and profit-obsessed excesses of capitalism, the plastic constructs: tellyland, popland, movieland, Fleet Street, the academic circus, the third-rate mortalized by the fourth-rate . . . Dan thought grimly of a bit of jargon he had read somewhere in California. The cosmeticization of natural process. But Barney had said it. The real function was not to amuse; but to excuse from thinking.

And now he was maintaining that the only honest year of his professional life was the one he had spent on a provincial newspaper before coming to London. It was clear that he judged himself fallen between the wise mediocrity and a genuine reputation. Time. Fear of death, the wasted journey, which was part of the old Puritan fallacy: life is either a destination, an arrived success, or not worth the cost. The soap-bubble bursts, and looking back, there seems nothing.

Dan knew that once again his sympathy was being wheedled in an oblique way; that he was also being maneuvered, and more successfully than he allowed Barney to realize, into confessing his own self-disillusionment—that they were in the same boat in more senses than the one he had admitted; but rather to his own surprise, when they finally stood on the busy Covent Garden pavement outside the restaurant and shook hands, his was not quite a merely token grip. He would never like Barney, he would never forgive him over Caro, but he suddenly felt too old to hate him. He had hardly turned away into a taxi when a memory of Thorncombe came to him: of a rabbit dying of myxomatosis that he had chanced on one evening in one of the fields—how he had stared at it, then walked on. He knew he should have dashed its brains out on the nearest gate-rail . . . but when one has the disease oneself?

He spent the rest of the day and evening alone at the flat. Caro was going straight from the office to a first night with Barney. Dan worked for a time on the Kitchener script, but his heart wasn't in it; the depression that had begun at the lunch lasted. He would have liked to have ring Jenny, but the difference in time prevented that, and he knew he didn't really want to discuss Barney with her. They had spoken again, and she knew what was happening there. He thought of ringing Jane in Oxford, but knew, or suspected, he would get little sympathy in that quarter, either. He couldn't work, he couldn't read, he couldn't face the television. In the end he wandered aimlessly around the flat, trying to decide whether he should sell it. Perhaps Nell had been right, and there had always been something hostile in it, distancing and alienating, vaguely forsaken; then Caro's imminent departure—the last good reason to keep the place, and even that, now, had gone. No one loves me, no one cares.

He waited till midnight, but she did not show. Soon after that, he wrote the day off as a loss (quite wrongly, since to feel biologically determined, fundamentally futile, was at least to look at the face his culture spent so much effort on avoiding); and went to bed.

# Solid Daughter

Caro appeared in a dressing-gown. I had already finished my own breakfast. She looked at me with a half-guilty, half-shy smile, and for once refused a fence; moved to get herself some coffee. I asked her about the play, having just read an unenthusiastic review of it in the *Times*. It had been that sad, sour, Norwegian answer to Shakespeare's *Tempest: When We Dead Awaken*.

"I enjoyed it. It was fun." She saw my sceptical grin. "The evening. Not the play."

"Did Bernard?"

"He thought the production was rather gimmicky."

"That's what the *Times* says."

"Yes? We had a drink with him, actually. During the interval."

This time I suppressed my smile at being made to feel provincial—and a fool for not seeing that the past determination to protect her from the false glamours of my own world would make her leap at any other . . . and quite naturally. She came and sat down opposite me, nursing her coffee-mug; then did take her fence.

"I hear we didn't actually come to blows."

"All very civilized."

"He was grateful." She looked down. "Was the food all right?"

"Yes. I was impressed."

"I had to bully them to get a table. It's always so crowded."

But then she was shy again, uncertain how to go on.

"He didn't change my feeling, Caro. We left it that . . . but he's probably told you. As long as you're happy."

"He said he talked too much."

"Not really. And it was interesting."

She sniffed. "I can see I'm not going to do any better with you than I did with him."

"Nothing you don't know already."

"I bet."

"Cross my heart."

"I bet you spent all yesterday evening tearing your hair."

"I did a little. But not about you. About the flat." She queried me. "Whether you'll ever need it now. Whether I shouldn't sell it and find something smaller."

"Just because I—"

"It's not that. I think I'm going to take a year off, Caro. As soon as the present script is finished. And live down at Thorncombe."

"Thorncombe!" She tilted her head. "What's going on?"

"Nothing. Just wondering how you feel about keeping it on. I could also sublet until you wanted it."

But she was suspicious now.

"Are you sure this isn't because I'm ratting on you?"

"Don't be silly."

She gave me a look under her eyebrows.

"You'll go mad with boredom."

"Probably."

"What happened at Oxford?"

"I've been toying with the idea for some time. And yes, a little. Even Bernard; a little."

"Why him?"

"Wanting a sabbatical? We agreed that's what we envied about academics."

"That's absurd. He'd die without his work."

"I feel like making a run for it while I've still got a chance of surviving. And now you're such a liberated and urban young woman."

She eyed me. "You're a meanie. You've been holding out on something."

"I won't go unless I have your permission."

She stared at me, then stood and got more coffee; then decided to make herself some toast. She spoke as she cut the bread.

"I don't know how Jenny McNeil stands you."

"Nor does Jenny McNeil. Sometimes."

She put her slice of bread in the toaster.

"One parent moaning about living in Outer Siberia is quite enough."

"I promise not to."

She grimaced across the counter that divided the kitchen. "You don't seem to realize how peculiar you are, your lot.

Going around pretending what ghastly failures you are. Honestly, that play last night. I thought it was stupid. All that stuff about not having really lived. It's so depressing." She went on before I could answer. "Did your father keep implying to you that his life was all one huge mistake?"

"No."

"There you are then."

"But the first rule of his was that you never say what you really feel. Would you prefer that?"

"Not if it was the only alternative." She stared down at the toaster. "That's why I like Aunt Jane so much. She's the only adult in my life who actually seems to have done something about it."

"About what?"

Her toast popped up, and she came back with it to the table.

"What you've just said." She buttered, and I pushed the marmalade across. "She said something about you the other day. When we had lunch. When I was going on about the way you've always made me feel I ought to be ashamed of what you do."

"What did she say?"

"How you'd always been two people."

"We're all at least that."

"She said you seemed to have cut yourself from your past more than anyone else. Even when you were all still at university."

"I had a Victorian childhood, Caro. I had to get rid of it."

"Then she said you'd done the same to Oxford. When you left."

"There's nothing very unusual about that. So do most graduates."

"Then Mummy."

"That also happens."

"She wasn't getting at you."

"I'm sure she wasn't."

She was taking an unconscionable time over spreading her marmalade, searching for words.

"She was trying to suggest why I might be a problem for you. Something you can't leave behind. Like everything else."

"My dear girl, I'm not going to Thorncombe to leave you behind. I shall raise blue murder if you're not down there at least once a month."

She began to eat, her elbows on the table. "Do you think she was right?"

"I'm not sure I like all this psychoanalysis at breakfast."

She gave me a very direct look.

"Please."

"I could have involved you more in my working life. But I've never wanted you to like me for that."

"You say my grandfather banned emotion, but you . . ." then she shook her head.

"I what?"

"I just wish you'd talk to me more. About you. Instead of its always being me." She waved her toast. "You suddenly spring this thing about the flat and Thorncombe at me, and I feel I'm back at square one. This mysterious person who flits in and out of my life. And who doesn't seem to understand I miss him now when he's not there." She suddenly put her toast down and stared at it on her plate; set her hands on her lap. "I'm really trying to tell you why I asked you to see Bernard. Why I told you. Aunt Jane didn't realize what she said was rather a shock to me. I mean, I had felt . . . you know. What we said in the car."

"Go on."

She picked up the toast again, breathed out. "Just that I have a lot of past to get rid of as well."

"And I could help more?"

"I do feel much closer to you now than to Andrew. But it's absurd, I can still talk to him more easily." She gave a little nod to herself. "And I think it's because I know him, and I don't know you—I feel I don't know you. That somewhere you don't want me to know you."

I stared at the table-cloth between us. It was such a strange time and place for this attack . . . no, the wrong word; for this quite legitimate challenge. I had that sense of metaphysical cuckolding that must come at some point to all fathers: flesh of my flesh, but something beyond my genes, and her mother's. And I remembered Barney's compliment about her: getting people's number.

"Is this to do with my going to California?"

"I did miss you."

"Did you want to come?"

"I . . . thought about it."

"You should have said."

"I felt you didn't want me."

"I funked your mother. I thought about it, too."

[ 283 ]

"I assumed it was something to do with Jenny McNeil."

"Absolutely not. That happened there."

And we were left, after this little tumble of confessions, in a silence, writing other scenarios. I stood, and touched her shoulder on my way to the coffee-pot on the stove; and spoke again from there.

"Caro, I suspect you have a notion that life gets simpler as you grow older because you can control it better. But for a lot of us it doesn't. It just exhibits a repeated pattern, and all one can predict is the recurrence of the pattern. As if one was fed into a computer at birth. And that's that. This is what begins to haunt people at my age. Bernard's. Whether we can ever escape what we are." She said nothing, and I sat down again. "You're asking me to pretend that I have no doubts about my life. If I did that, then I think we really would be back to square one. Also I'm a writer. We're traditionally very poor hands at one-to-one relationships in the flesh. Much better at inventing them for mythical other people. One reason I want to take this coming year off is to try to analyze all this." I looked down. "Perhaps on paper. I'm thinking of trying a novel."

"Seriously?"

"Secretly. So please don't pass it on. That's an order."

She smiled; a small girl's inquisitive smile.

"What would it be about?"

"Tropes and metaphors."

"What are tropes when they're at home?"

"All the things I can't tell straight."

"Why is it such a secret?"

"Because I don't know if I can do it."

She gave a mock reproving look. "So much for rectangular things."

I grinned, she had harked back to a sarcasm I had once inflicted on her, in her more debutante days. She had asked me (with an air of accusation) why I knew "so much" about "everything." I had said something about the difference between truly knowing a lot and knowing a little about a lot; and how, anyway, most of my knowledge came from those "queer rectangular things with cardboard covers" that were stacked on the shelves of the room around us; implying that such knowledge was there for anyone who—unlike Caro—picked up the knack of reading. Ever since, books had become "rectangular things" in our private vocabulary.

"And why are writers bad at relationships?"

"Because we can always imagine better ones. With much less effort. And the imaginary ones grow much more satisfying than the real ones."

"Is that why you try to leave the real ones behind?"

"I don't know, Caro. Perhaps. The real trap when we dead awaken is not so much that we find we never really lived. But that we can't write anymore. You create out of what you lack. Not what you have."

She watched me a moment, as if this elementary truth about art was new to her; then glanced at the kitchen clock.

"Oh God. I must go." She stood and transferred her breakfast things to the counter, but then gave me a smile down. "Can you remember what it was like? Trying to understand what everything's about?"

"Of course."

"I'm a pest."

"No."

"You're not angry with me?"

"Never."

She hesitated, searching my eyes, then went away to dress. But she came into the living-room a few minutes later, and across to the table where I worked. Then she stooped, with a wordlessness and quickness I liked, and kissed my cheek; and went back to the door, but turned there.

"As a punishment for being such a míz, you're going to have to eat my veal blanquette tonight."

"Do you want me to buy anything?"

She thought.

"Indigestion powder?" A grin. "You're safe, actually. It's one of Aunt Jane's recipes."

Then she was gone, and Dan was left to reflect undisturbed on the recipe-provider's judgment on him. It was fair, but it rankled that she should have had to explain him so to his own daughter. No doubt it had been put tactfully, as Caro had suggested; and with even less doubt it would not have been put at all if she had realized Caro was to pass it on; but beneath the diplomacy he recognized that old compulsive attraction to systems of absolutes that had once driven Jane into the Catholic Church and now apparently threatened to push her halfway to Moscow . . . all that had caused the original schisms between them. Clearly she had been hiding it when they met—or rather, hiding it increasingly as the meeting became on the surface more open and truthful. Somewhere Dan was still the responsibility-shirking grasshopper, she the dutiful ant.

But very soon after Caro had left he was already, partly proving his own argument to her about writers, thinking less of Jane in the flesh than of her uses, when reduced to certain moral attitudes, artistically; as an emblem of his own guilty conscience, perhaps precisely because of the feminine and characteristically English cast of her nature. The secret lay somewhere in what he had always liked least about her and Anthony: the streak of priggishness, of censorious insularity, of parochial ethics. Behind all that lay an essence of what he had to come to terms with, and let himself be judged by. He began to see the ghost of a central character, a theme, of a thing in the mind that might once more make reality the metaphor and itself the reality . . . a more difficult truth about the invention of myths than he had had the courage to tell Caro. Spending a page or two on it is not quite outraging verisimilitude, since that morning Dan did, for an hour, pushing Kitchener to one side—and very possibly some of the uncomfortable home truths just told—start assembling a few notes on why he should leave the sanctuary of a medium he knew for the mysteries and complexities of one he didn't.

# The Sacred Combe

I remember as a boy putting the familiar old poser to my father: If God created the world, why did he allow evil in it? I received the familiar old answer: so that man may be free to choose between good and evil and then, with Christ's help, show moral perfectibility. This pat solution to the conundrum did not really satisfy me. Perhaps an already budding scenarist sensed that an appallingly over-length script had been written for the job; and an embryo cynic certainly wondered why the system could not have been planned to provide at least an equal power of choice, and of will, in the victims of it.

At the time I asked the question I was like every other middle-class child, educated to see life in terms of success in examinations and games; but the other two great principles of the then English middle-class view of life, that only cads cheat, that sportsmanship is next to godliness, were foolishly instilled in us—as over-riding controls—even more rigorously than the laws and techniques of the lessons we studied and the games we played. It was handing us a balloon in one hand and a sharp pin in the other. Sooner or later the two were bound to make contact—and of course have made resounding contact all through English (and American) history, as time and again the distended belly of social injustice has been lanced by the fair-play fanatic on the central committee of the national psyche.

Abbot's bellies and arrows out of secret leaves . . . during a brief spell between contracts in the early 1960s, I tried to write a script—purely to please myself—on Robin Hood. But I committed the cardinal error of making my (largely invented) version grimly realistic and unromantic. It failed signally to get off the ground; no one I showed it to liked it. Just as I failed at the time to see its true bearing to my own past, I had failed to see why we have turned this archetypal national myth, perhaps the only one, outside the Christ story, that literally every English person carries in his mind all through his life, into a matter for afternoon TV serials and the sides of breakfast-cereal packets; for the Walt Disneys and Errol Flynns of this world. It is a myth based on hiding, and therefore we have hidden its true importance ever since it first balladed and folk-rumored its way into being—though even that genesis, from a people, not a single mind, gives the real game away. It is too profoundly about being English not to need endless camouflage, belittlement, relegation, good-humored contempt . . . for eternal children, not contemporary adults.

It is also a good deal more relevant to the general artistic experience than the fashionable parallels drawn by some English and American novelists with the Creator of my first paragraph. If there is a God, he or she (or it) must be supremely and chillingly unconcerned about a number of things to which individual thinking and feeling specks of matter rightly give priority—pain, equality, justice, and the rest. The only sustainable divine parallel is with a completely aleatory artist, who composes his work on purely random principles, and who therefore does not compose it at all . . . and even then this hypothetical God is evidently playing with such infinitely more complicated dice that the analogy is worthless.

The one principle the ordinary writer tries to abolish from his work, at least in the finished text, is precisely that of randomness. He calculates, plans, strives where the great question-mark is indifferent and leaves all to hazard; and his final, revised product is in intention as rigid and pre-conceived as a piece of machinery or an architect-designed building. Nor is he creating *ex nihilo*, but out of pre-existent memory-stores and experience; so he is re-arranging or inferring, even when he writes about what has never happened or even what will or can never happen.

Much more significant is the desire to create imaginary worlds other than the world that is the case—a further matter in which the God of the theologians seems personally not interested. This desire, or need, has always been strongly linked, at least in my own experience, with the notion of retreat, in both the religious and the military sense; of the secret place that is also a redoubt. And for me it is here that the Robin Hood—or greenwood—myth changes from merely symbolizing folk-aspiration in social terms to enshrining a dominant mental characteristic, an essential behavior, an archetypal *movement* (akin to certain major vowel-shifts in the language itself) of the English imagination.

I can illustrate it in a very different way, once more with my father's help. He had another minor theological interest (as with Dissent, based on disapproval, not sympathy) in the Oxford Movement of the 1830s; and I remember Keble and Newman and the other flirters with Rome received particularly black marks for that very singular, and very English, part of their heterodoxy, the theory of reserve: the necessity of hiding inner religious mysteries and feelings from the vulgar. To my father this showed the inherent Jesuitry of Rome; but coming from a man with such a hatred of "demonstration" and "enthusiasm," who indeed in most daily matters was a perfect embodiment of the theory he so disliked, it was not convincing. Misled by externals, he had simply failed to see how quintessentially English the Oxford Movement was.

I experienced this retreat (or reserve) much more strongly when I wrote plays, but it had continued with my occasional original scripts; and though it became a very tenuous concept with other people's themes, such as the one I was currently engaged on, even there it existed for as long as the treatment remained partial, fluid, still malleable. I might complain, but I also knew it was in many ways the most enjoyable time, and precisely because of this necessary aspect of retreat, of secrecy . . . as one might feel to be the first man ever to set foot on a desert island, a new planet. No one else had yet been there, however stale the place might turn out to be when it was finally thrown open to the world.

Many years ago I chanced on an English translation of one of the most fascinating of all self-revealings in European literature: that strange Frenchman Restif de la Bretonne's masterpiece, his romanced autobiography, *Monsieur Nicolas*. There is a passage in the early part of the book, where he is describing his peasant boyhood in a remote Burgundian village in the 1740s, that entranced me when I first read it, and which has ever since given me a label for, and a key to, this inward retreat.

He tells how one day, his father finding himself without his usual shepherd, he was allowed to take out the family flock; and how, wandering with it, he came on a secret valley in the hills behind the village. He had never heard anyone speak of it before; it was miraculously lush, green, secret, and full of birds and animals . . . a hare, a roebuck, a pair of wild boar mating. A hoopoe, the first he had ever seen, flew down and began feeding in a tree of wild honey-pears. He felt these creatures were in some way tamer and more magical here than outside, so that he had a sense of trespassing. But it immediately became "his" valley in his mind; he returned there, built a little monument of stones, cooked picnic meals over a fire; and even consecrated the place—in another entrancing passage—with a gathering of other young shepherds and shepherdesses, feeling "the state of man before kings and laws and prohibitions." Using a dialect word of the region he baptized the place simply *la bonna vaux:* the valley of abundance, the sacred combe.

Restif's is, in fact, a quite uncannily close premonition of a vision the English associate more readily with the Samuel Palmer of the Shoreham years: of a place outside the normal world, intensely private and enclosed, intensely green and fertile, numinous, haunted and haunting, dominated by a sense of magic that is also a sense of a mysterious yet profound parity in all existence. Of course it recurs again and again in literature and art, in one form or another, from the sublimities of the Garden of Eden and the Forest of Arden to the 1930s hokum of James Hilton's Shangri-La. But perhaps because my discovery of Restif's life, mind and sensibilities (his eroticism, his acute sense of presentness and pastness and his instinctively cinematic eye also appealed deeply) was, despite the language barrier, one of those experiences that go well beyond the literary and objective into something like the finding of a lost parent, a lost elder brother, perhaps because *Monsieur Nicolas* has mysteriously failed to gain its true place among the other great autobiographies of European literature, and so outside France remains in itself something of a secret, my own favorite Quarlesian emblem for this phenomenon remains *la bonne vaux.*

It is this, the sacred combe and all it stands for, that explains why I was losing patience with my profession; and also, far more profoundly than the earlier reason I gave, why the cinema has never had patience at all for the English.

The film cannot be the medium of a culture all of whose surface appearances mislead, and which has made such a psychological art of escaping present, or camera, reality. For us English the camera, a public eye, invites performance, lying. We make abundant use of these appearances in our comedy, in our humor; socially and politically; but for our private reality we go elsewhere, and above all to words. Since we are so careful only to reveal our true selves in private, the "private" form of the read text must serve us better than the publicity of the seen spectacle. Furthermore the printed text allows an escape for its perpetrator. It is only the spoor, the trace of an animal that has passed and is now somewhere else in the forest; and even then, given the nature of language, a trace left far more in the reader's mind (another forest) than outside it, as in the true externally apprehended arts like painting and music.

With film-making our real "block" is our secret knowledge that any true picture of the English must express what the camera cannot capture—the continual evasion of the inner self, the continual actual reality of saying one thing and thinking another. Or one might reverse the proposition: no novel about the English that can be successfully filmed is a true picture of them. The eternal bar is that the elusive and eluding nature of the English psyche is profoundly unsympathetic to visual representation; and our baffled inability to make good films about ourselves, or to produce artists of the stature of a Bergman, a Buñuel, a Satyajit Ray, springs very largely from that.

I had in any case nurtured a deeper and less local quarrel with the cinema and its child, television. All art is a surrogate for the individual imaginations of its audience; but these two are beyond that role now, and into that of usurpation. They sap and leach the native power away; insidiously impose their own conformities, their angles, their limits of vision; deny the existence of what they cannot capture. As with all frequently repeated experience, the effect is paradigmatic, affecting by analogy much beyond the immediately seen—indeed, all spheres of life where a free and independent imagination matters. The much-proclaimed ephemerality of television is no consolation; one might as well argue that since no one cigarette can in itself cause cancer, smoking holds no danger.

In short, and in spite of their vaunted virtues as disseminators of popular art and instant democracy, I had long begun to smell something rotten in the state of both these dominant media; a little, perhaps, as an otherwise dutiful German official might once have begun to wonder about the Nazi Party, I had begun to see something ominously stereotyping, if not positively totalitarian, in the machine and its servants. Somewhere the cinema, like television, was atrophying a vital psychic function: the ability to imagine for oneself. But, just as there were no doubt many Germans who did not like the Nazis, yet felt treachery to their country a worse crime, I had for years blinded myself to these feelings, and to a great extent because I was not their victim. It was illogical, to say the least: because Dan was proof to the drug, he could allow himself to go on manufacturing it. But he had found other reasons too.

As every Marxist critic has pointed out, this withdrawal from outer fact into inner fantasy is anti-social and inherently selfish. Every artist lives in an equivalent of my old Oxford room, with its countless mirrors; and just as something in the cinema, its community art aspects, the comparative quickness of the creation period, had at the beginning seemed healthy—away from masturbation into copulation, in the terms the industry so cherishes—the same something had in the end increasingly starved me of this solitary pleasure in retreat, in reentering *la bonne vaux* . . . and perhaps made me seek compensation in other forms of retreat, of the kind Jane had suggested to Caro.

I knew it was far more this that was driving me toward the idea of a novel than any intrinsic love of the form. As a reader, drama and poetry had always meant much more to me. I simply sensed a far greater capacity for retreat in fiction. In Robin Hood terms I saw in it a forest, after the thin copses of the filmscript . . . and a risk. So much of the work I now did in the cinema was guaranteed from the start. Only too often the money had been there, the studio will was there; and the process was almost automatic, even in its occasional snags and disappointments.

I had had a sequence in the Robin Hood script that I see now was more prescient than I realized at the time. As a relief from the action and barbarity of some surrounding episodes, I imagined a summertime when the living grew fat under the greenwood tree (the quintessence of *la bonne vaux* is its transience), and the morale of the band disintegrated; when what began as something lyrical and idyllic turned slowly sour, when the outlaws *in* nature became the outlawed *by* nature, self-indulgent and lazy, as privileged in their way as the privileged men outside they had first taken to the woods to escape. This had perhaps lain obscurely behind my feelings about Barney and his world—and my own, by extension: of a privilege gone sour, habitual, conditioned. We had allowed an elision from hating our own twentieth-century Sheriffs of Nottingham, our society, the way the world was going, into being content merely to retire to the sidelines.

In the script I had solved this inertia by violence, the rape of a village girl by two of the band; then Robin's rage and self-rage, the first expressed in a summary move to hang the two men, the second by a forgiving them, the acceptance of his own ultimate responsibility, as the leader and will of the enterprise.

And now, in London that morning, under the influence of the last twenty-four hours, and of that at least partial confession to Caro of what I had in mind—a confession I hadn't really intended, had half come out with to placate her, half to make it a little more difficult to renege—I began to see the kind of trap I was in. A potentially further retreat, with no guarantee that I could return from it as I had made my Robin Hood (convenient man of action, puppet, hireling . . . a high-scrupled brigand—at least I read Byron with more understanding afterward) return.

One note I wrote that morning ran: *A character who must be seen in flight, like a bird that has forgotten how to stop migrating.* Then: *What makes him stop?*

The irony is that all artists, at least in the process of creation, are much more "divine" than any first cause one might arrive at, theologically or scientifically, on the evidence. They are not of course genetically, environmentally or technically free; imprisoned inside whatever gifts they have, whatever past and present experience; nonetheless, even that limited freedom is far greater, because of the immense forest constituted by the imagined, because of the permission Western society grants them to roam in it, than any other form of human being, except perhaps the mystic and the madman, can attain. That is the one reality, and it is largely unconnected with the reception the public accords the eventual product of the retreat.

But the distinction between the craftsman and the true artist is precisely between knowing what one can do and not knowing—which is why one occupation is safe, and the other always incipiently dangerous. I had only to glance back over my work to know which category I belonged to in the overwhelming bulk of it: it reeked of safety, mainly because it had been written out of what I (and my studio masters) knew the world wanted to hear, and less and less out of my whole knowledge of reality, both personal and public. My most damaging substitute retreat had been from the awareness of that. That was the horror of landing that drove the bird endlessly on: the risk of the real ground.

The wilderness, whose worst temptation is not to return.

If I had a preferred line in the modern novel, it was the one that began with Henry James and descended through Virginia Woolf to Nabokov; all, in their different guises, of the confraternity, the secret society, who have known, and known exile from, *la bonne vaux*. We all like to think such personal preference reflects a general criterion, but of course it also, always, stems partly from personal failing—betrays what we lack, what we long for from and in our lack. I made one other note that morning.

*If a life is largely made of retreats from reality, its relation must be of retreats from the imagined.*

# Rituals

A number of far more mundane things seemed in any case
determined not to make Dan's literal retreat to his own South
Devon combe easy. There was the inquest and the funeral to
follow; a feeling he should not walk out on Caro during her
last days at the flat—they had, that evening of the breakfast
psychoanalysis, talked a good deal more, and far more affectionately. On the flat itself they both havered; and finally
elected to postpone a decision for a while. Dan hoped her
side of the havering represented a tacit recognition that the
affair with Barney must end one day.

Finally there was David Malevich, who had put the
Kitchener hangrope around the writer's neck; and now
proceeded to tighten it. Dan had telephoned New York the
day after he got back from Oxford, only to find, from the
producer's secretary, that she had been about to ring him.
Her boss was out of town, but flying to London in a few
days' time, and urgently wanted a meeting. That "urgently"
jabbed Dan's conscience. Between domestic and family
things, he tried to get back to his last. The premonition he
had had that night in Oxford turned out to be not quite illusory. There was at least a trickle of badly needed new ideas;
and if he still half-wished he had never taken the film on,
some of its technical problems began to seem more interesting than tiresome. Being in England again helped; the
wretched old protagonist had always seemed doubly unreal in
California.

Malevich was a long way from the stock satirical notion—
some crass bespectacled toad surrounded by telephones, tits
and cigar-smoke—of the American producer. He did not
even look the part, being tall, slim and dauntingly fit and
young-looking, despite his near-baldness, for his fifty-five
years. He had once reputedly allowed a dispute with an actor
he wanted—over an extra twenty thousand dollars—to be
settled by a tennis match; and beaten his much younger op-

ponent three sets to love. One version of the story has it that at the end of the game he went up to the net and offered the money back on condition it was spent on tennis lessons. But I doubt that. He was hot on budget-paring. He neither smoked nor drank, and dressed as soberly as a New England businessman. He would have passed very well as a successful corporation lawyer or a Wall Street banker, both professions he was suited for not merely physically and in his clothes.

This was the third script Dan had done for him and he knew Malevich listened intelligently and kept his personal whims well under control when they disagreed; and also would not tolerate his directors improvising on final drafts—which had gained him the sobriquet "Genghiz Khan" with at least one of them. Dan was unkind about him to Jane, since it was he who had once held forth about Lévi-Strauss's ideas . . . and not really tryingly at all. He was literate for his trade, even though he tended to use its jargon when talking business. Beneath the showbiz acumen and the skill at packaging, there lay a romantic idealist, almost a dreamer. He had come to the cinema after a successful spell as a Broadway impresario; and had managed to remain his own man in a world where almost any independence is taken as a vicious personal affront.

He had had one or two disasters, and a high failure rate (including one of Dan's two previous efforts) in terms of projects he had never managed to push beyond script stages; but over the years his guesses as to what new trends—or returns to old ones—would bring audiences in had proved a good deal more perspicacious than most of those of the big studios. He once took a script he had touted round all the majors without success and did a co-production deal behind the Iron Curtain; it was not a world-buster, but it grossed considerably more than the costly white elephant one of his Hollywood refusers had wasted a fat part of their annual budget on. A year or two later Malevich had somehow got hold of a copy of their internal cost-and-return breakdown (not the sort of figures that ever see the public light of day) and promptly had it bound up with a copy of his own balance-sheet, then sent it to the studio head concerned along with a brochure about retirement homes in some remote corner of Florida. He retained an engaging venom for anyone who had ever turned him down without good reason.

Dan, not having done cast-of-thousands work since his attempt at the genre in the days with Nell, had laughed when first presented with the Kitchener idea. But the producer had argued in his usual dry, obstinate way, his theory being that despite Vietnam there was a considerable latent nostalgia in the States for imperialism, and especially when someone else could be seen to be doing the imperializing; then there was the war stuff, the other famous historical figures who could be pulled in by the hair of their armpits, the political intrigue, the exotic locations. He had read Kitchener up; and what Dan knew about the old man at that stage could have been written on the top of a matchbox. He made the error of ceding a little ground: he might just be interested if the folly of imperialism could be shown, and there was the nice irony of that famous finger recruiting for the world war imperialism had finally caused. Malevich treated this obvious idea as a stroke of genius—precisely why he had come to Dan, he wanted a sound script before he started assembling the rest of the package. Dan didn't fall for that, and still played coy.

But then there was a letter assuring him there was no shortage of development finance; percentage, if he wanted it that way; the golden was added to the vanity carrot. It took another lunch. But by then Dan had done a first research himself and decided that Kitchener was an odd enough character (there were a number of interesting pre-echoes of T. E. Lawrence, as Malevich had already pointed out) to give him a foothold. He knew that the weird and Dombey-like mixture of acute shyness and determined megalomania could be turned into an agreeably complex part for any actor worth his salt (just as this same mixture helped him guess why Malevich, a Yugoslavian Jew in his origins, had developed this unlikely interest in the man who invented the concentration camp). Even the lack of any visible sex-life in Kitchener, either straight or bent, had potentiality.

The old man himself had never really been Dan's problem, in fact; it was simply the mass of material that had to be included, all the places and events, all the Gordons, Bothas, Curzons, Churchills and the rest who had to be marched on. Something had to give, either proper dramatic development or historical facts, and the juggling Dan was reduced to had been what irritated him most. He had settled (rather as a drowning man clings to a lifebelt) for one small formal trick. He wanted to catch Kitchener somewhere in mid-career and at some central focus geographically; and then sally from that point in flashback and flash-forward to the rest of his life. Many years before, when he was living with Andrea, he had

[ 297 ]

been to Egypt. She had had a touch of pleurisy one winter, was off work, both depressed and depressing; almost as soon as she was fit to travel Dan took her off for a cruise down the Nile. They had stayed on a few days at Aswan, and fallen for one of the islands in the river there: Kitchener's Island. Dan had no very clear memory of it, beyond its exotic trees and liquid green peace against the surrounding desert, the feluccas drifting by, but that seemed a good calm launching-pad for all the sorties into the blood-and-thunder—the other countries, other times.

I knew David well enough, when he duly turned up in London and we were sitting opposite each other at the Connaught, not to pretend that everything was going fine. He listened to my problems; agreed with one or two things I thought could be dropped, balked at another, the 1894 row with the Khedive, which I knew would cost me time and David money—at least he'd like to see it on paper. Having won that point, he went on to praise the idea of using Kitchener's Island as a kind of hub for the spokes of the rest. I described the place as best I could; its advantages for the story.

"I like it, Dan. We won't beat it."

"A similar island won't be too hard to find. It's getting that desert background."

He eyed me, nodding his head. "Maybe we should think again?"

"I'd hate to do that. There must be somewhere."

He sipped his apple-juice, then suddenly gave me a little smile. I should have remembered he was also a first-class card-player.

"Alternatively you could ask what the hell a busy man like me's doing here."

"I thought you'd told me." He had said he was going on to Rome about another project.

"I'm flying to Cairo first. Tomorrow."

"You don't mean . . ."

"Want to come along?"

"Shoot in Egypt?"

He grinned. "The Israelis do it. All the time."

"Well exactly—isn't there a slight political problem?"

"Jews with guns and Jews with dollars are two different things." He made a gesture of giving away. "You have your island. The way their Washington embassy are talking . . . anything."

"And you don't mind . . . ?"

He shrugged. "So I'm barred a couple of bridge-games."

"That's marvelous, David."

"I hear the light's something."

"As good as California. Better. No smog."

"They even have some kind of set-up down at Aswan. Studios, technicians. If we need them. Extras a dime a hundred. Per week. Camels for free." He began to eat again, but couldn't resist prodding his fork at me. "You still don't know a good producer when you see one."

"And the Cairo scenes? Suakin?"

"Could you make it tomorrow?"

I explained about Anthony.

"That's too bad." He thought a moment. "This is what I'd like, Dan. Soon as you can, you get yourself out there—it'll make a nice trip? I'm flying straight back from Rome to New York, but I'll have my office give you who to meet and what to see. They'll fix everything there. They want us in that badly." One of his eyelids twitched. "Daughters, wives . . . you name it."

"I think you're confusing Arabs with Eskimos."

"Not the gentlemen I've been talking to."

"I'm delighted."

"So let's enjoy it." He decided he didn't want any more of his steak, and leaned back. "When's Jenny McNeil through?"

"Three or four weeks. If they don't run over."

"Take her. I hear she's earned it." He saw me hesitate. "No?"

"I'm behind as it is, David. I'm not sure I shouldn't scrub it. I have been there. Enough for what I need."

"And you know what I do to writers who don't deliver on time."

"My point."

We were smiling. He looked down, then up at me, more serious. "I want this to be really something, Dan. Screw the date. If you need a couple of weeks more . . ." he opened his hands. "What's two weeks?"

"Let me sit on it."

"Just tell the London office. They'll fix the visas, all that junk."

"Fine."

He folded his arms. "Now let's talk directors. Guess who I had lunch with last week."

But in the taxi home Dan decided firmly that he must not go. It wasn't necessary; just a perquisite of the profession; the eventual director's and location manager's job, not his. He was also more behind than David had realized, nowhere near even half-finished, and with less than half the contract time to run. In addition it seemed one more running away from all those lives he had just re-entered: a resort to that most pernicious and enduring "privilege" of the film world, the supposed freedom to be above all normal considerations of duty, routine, economy, self-discipline. He didn't even tell Caro, when he saw her the next morning and she asked how the meeting had gone.

A day later he was in Oxford again, to attend the inquest. He went straight to the court where it was held, as his train cut the timing rather thin. Jane and Rosamund were there, and Andrew, who had driven over that morning; Nell had stayed behind to look after his son and heir, still ill with the mumps. There were two or three ranks of other people, one or two obvious reporters, what Dan presumed were a sprinkling of university friends and colleagues, though perhaps mainly just the unemployed curious. The medical and post-mortem details were gone into, the nurse who had last attended Anthony gave her evidence, the ward sister on duty that night; then Jane was put gently through it. Yes, she had been surprised, it had been against all his religious beliefs. He had never discussed doing such a thing. She could not recall ever having discussed the matter in general with him. There were no family or financial problems that might have caused him distress. He had been kept fully informed of the prognosis, he was well aware that he had little time left . . . and so on. She was very composed, level-voiced, and especially when the elderly coroner asked her if she knew of any special reason why he had chosen to "terminate his life" on that particular evening.

"Of none at all." She went on, "He had seen an old friend—my sister's former husband—whom he had particularly asked to visit him. I know he was very much looking forward to this and so far as I could tell, both from my husband and Mr. Martin afterwards, he greatly enjoyed it."

"You were not present yourself at this meeting?"

"My husband asked if in the circumstances he could be

selfish and have Mr. Martin to himself. They were very close friends here as students, at the same college, and they hadn't seen each other for many years."

He did not press the point, but Dan saw him write something down; and had an abrupt and nasty intuition that he was not going to get off so lightly. It was soon put to the test, when he took Jane's place.

"May I ask why you had not seen the deceased for so many years?"

"There was considerable bitterness at the time I was divorced by Mrs. Mallory's sister. I was very largely to blame for that. I'm prepared to explain why, if you think it's relevant."

"I am concerned only with that evening. May I take it your meeting was essentially one of reconciliation?"

"Yes."

"And the mood was as one would expect?"

"Very much so."

"Did you discuss other matters?"

"What had become of us over the years. That kind of thing."

"Was suicide mentioned, however obliquely?"

"Not at all. He even made fun of me at one point for having rather pessimistic views on the state of the world."

"Was any other anxiety or unhappiness—other than the obvious one caused by his medical condition—mentioned?"

"He was a little sceptical of the value of his academic work. But a certain amount of self-denigration there had always been a trait in his character. Ever since I first knew him."

The coroner permitted himself an austere smile.

"And in your opinion of no significance to this inquiry?"

"I am sure not."

"As you left, did you have any hint given you of what he intended to do?"

"None whatever. I said I would visit him again the next day. He showed every sign of looking forward to that."

"In retrospect, is it your impression that he had formed his resolve before you met him? Or for some reason, after?" He stopped me answering. "In other words, do you think it was premeditated or done on the spur of the moment?"

"So far as our meeting indicated, the latter. But I think it was more in his nature—and his profession perhaps—to act in a premeditated way."

"You are suggesting, hypothesizing, that his mind was made up before this meeting of family reconciliation—and that in effect, once the meeting was happily concluded, nothing remained to hinder a previous decision?"

"I find that more plausible."

"To the extent that he had been to blame for the rift between you, he felt atonement had been made? I believe you came from America at his request?"

"The answer is yes. To both your questions."

"But he did not put it to you that some last debt on his conscience—perhaps more considerable than anyone realized—had been honored?"

"He was sorry it had taken so long. So was I."

"But it was not said explicitly—now I can go in peace?"

"Definitely not."

"Or implicitly in any manner?"

"If I had had the least suspicion, I should have warned Mrs. Mallory before we left the hospital."

He hesitated. "I am not clear why this meeting was not arranged sooner."

"I presume it was because I was in America." I jumped in before he could pursue this line. "I did mention when we met that I wished we hadn't left it so late . . . in the course of his illness. I can't recall his exact words, but I think this very kind but quite unnecessary desire not to trouble me with his personal tragedy was not overcome until recently."

"By which time it had evidently gained considerable importance in his mind?"

"Yes."

"Did he seem to take an undue portion of the blame for this unhappy relationship between you?"

"I was not only legally but morally the guilty party in the divorce action. The real cause of war was a play I based on the circumstances of the divorce, but which travestied the true parts played in it by all concerned."

The coroner smiled.

"Your frankness does you credit. But it doesn't answer my question."

"I'm sorry. I thought he was being overscrupulous in taking any blame at all for what had happened."

"May I inquire where he considered himself at fault?"

"In not having forgiven me my sins?"

"A deficiency in the quality of mercy?"

"He felt he had strained it."

"And though unjustly, condemned himself? How severely?"

"I mustn't give a false impression. All this was discussed quite lightly. Not without humor. Rather as two people smile at past mistakes."

"But may he not, especially in view of his religious convictions, have viewed the matter more seriously than his outward manner suggested?"

"I find it hard to believe that his suicide represented some form of penance or self-awarded punishment. His behavior throughout our conversation was perfectly rational. He even told a couple of amusing stories. I found him emotionally and psychologically very little changed from the man I remembered."

"You are saying in effect that although this guilt he felt for not having healed the rift earlier may have been a minor factor, it cannot have been the prime cause?"

"In my judgment. And I know Mrs. Mallory shares my view. We have of course discussed the possibility."

He looked at his notes again. Dan had an idea that he knew he was not getting the whole truth and was half-inclined to dig further. But in the end the coroner nodded. Dan could stand down. Very soon after that, it was all over.

He went back and had lunch with them all, and met Jane's other two children, Anne and Paul. Anne turned out to be rather like her elder sister; but he got nowhere with Paul, his only consolation being that Andrew's attempts to jolly the boy along did not succeed much better. There was something oddly withdrawn and sullen about him, determined not to join in; as if he was part Orestes determined to avenge his father's death and part didn't want to belong to this family at all. He too was rather tall for his age, Anthony's child again, but totally without his directness. He seemed prepared to look at anything but other people's faces. Jane tried to cover for him, but Dan could sense her inner trouble.

He had no chance of speaking with her alone, but Andrew had come determined to organize the family week-end at Compton, and suggested the next but one, in a week's time, since it was then a Friday. Anne was returning to Florence, Roz wasn't sure she could come, but Dan said it would suit him and, he hoped, Caro. Then it emerged that Jane wanted to take Paul on back down to Dartington for the Monday following—and Dan joined in the organizing. Caro and he would drive up to Oxford and take them on to Compton; and then he'd go down with the two of them to Devon. Jane and her son could spend the Sunday night at the farm, then she could catch the train home when she wanted. He could see she was inclined to refuse, she turned for tacit support to Paul—he shrugged, "I don't mind," as if he did—but Dan had a better ally in Rosamund. He had begun to take to her even more during that lunch: there was something positive about her, where Jane stayed veiled, oblique. Andrew had started ribbing her about Germaine Greer and Dan liked her forthrightness. She lacked Jenny's looks, but she had similar qualities elsewhere. She drove him to the station again and this time he made her promise to have dinner one day soon in London.

The day after the inquest saw the arrival of Jenny's "first contribution." It gave Dan a shock: less at the side of it that was critical of him, but at its distancing; a certain sharp, too sharp objectivity, the "you-and-me" made "them." That she could write so candidly was less of a shock, since he had once, without her knowledge, read one of her letters home before she had sent it off. That had been about Los Angeles and the film, written to amuse, to an actress friend, but even there he had felt a tiny alienation, a revelation of someone he did not know.

Love is so strange, so conducted, since time began, under the illusion that it brings the lovers closer together; which it does, of course, in all sorts of physical and psychological ways. But it is also based on some profoundly blind assumptions, the prime fantasy being that the nature of the loved one during the first passionate phase is the everlasting true nature. But that phase is an infinitely delicate balance of reciprocal illusion, a meshing of wheels so finely cogged that the slightest atom of dust—the intrusion of hitherto unrecognized desires, tastes, twists of character, any new information thrust into the idyll—can wreck the movement. I knew this, I had learned to watch for it as one learns to watch for signs of familiar disease in certain plants; I had even seen it happen over other smaller incidents earlier in my relationship with Jenny. When she discovered my father had been a vicar, time stopped for ten minutes; but that made me faintly comic, and she forgave me. Assimilated, these threatened obstacles join. I am simply saying that her writing stopped a morning for me; as some reviews do. By the time we spoke again, by chance that evening, since she rang me during her Californian lunch-break, I was recovered, though not quite prepared to admit it.

"Has it come?"

"Yes."

"Are we on speaking terms?"

"Just about."

"Dan."

"Yes, Jenny."

"Well say something."

"I can hardly say I didn't know you had it in you."

"You *are* offended."

"Just slightly stunned you can be so honest."

"It's not you. Just an idea for a character."

"Liar."

"I cried twice today. Thinking about you. Wishing I hadn't sent it."

"You write very well."

"I wish you'd burn it. Pretend it never happened."

"No chance."

There was a silence.

"It's because I miss you so much. It's talking to paper instead of you. That's all."

"But more frankly."

"You don't ask why I miss you so much."

"Tell me."

"I've decided to take that part. I've said yes."

"Good. I told you you should."

"Now I feel I've burnt my boats. Done your dirty work for you."

"Don't be silly."

She said nothing for a moment. "You know who I learnt more frankness off."

"Then the teacher feels taught. Professional jealousy." There was another pause, I could almost hear her breathe out in frustration. "And scared stiff that if he doesn't sound hurt you won't send him any more." Still she said nothing. "You can't leave it just there."

"It was trying to tell you how it felt. In the beginning."

"I'm interested in how it feels."

"It feels you may soon be the first man to be strangled via satellite."

We went on like that for another five minutes, though I let her know by the end that she was being more teased than resented, just as her determination—"if I have written anything more"—never to let me see it was maintained in the same spirit. By the end of the call I had become the one to be forgiven . . . or not forgiven. I was reminded that while I was going through a jolly evening in "my book-lined study" she would be spending her afternoon naked in bed with the Prick. She was not as squeamish as some actresses about that kind of scene, and the one I'd written (of course long before she got the part) was post-coital, more comic than passionate. I knew she hadn't been looking forward to it, but she had rung off before I realized that her call had been as much about this, to get a little courage, as about what she had written. I woke myself up early the next morning to ring her in the Cabin when she got home. The scene had gone not too badly, not too many takes, and we made up: I had been pretending, I wasn't really hurt, and I wanted to read more.

I have never much liked funerals, perhaps because one of my father's peculiarities was expecting Aunt Millie and myself to be present when he officiated at those of anyone who had the smallest standing in the village, and I had sat through so many of the accursed things. Anthony's gave me no reason to change my mind. The Catholic version of the ritual provided one slight variation, and there was a nice little donnish speech in praise of the defunct from one of his faculty colleagues. The event attracted a rather sparser assembly than I had expected. But Jane told me later that she had encouraged people to cry off. There were still more than enough to crowd her living-room for the middle-class attempt at a wake-party that followed the committal.

I hardly spoke to her that day, but I watched her. She seemed more under strain than at the inquest, perhaps because she had to play the kind of role she claimed was now beyond her; so many polite questions, smiles at condolences, educated chatter. She had worn a black coat throughout the service and the burial, but had rebelled enough to wear a peasanty yet chic brown-and-white dress underneath, with a choker of jet beads; and somehow this, together with a sort of vivacity she put on with her less intimate guests when we returned, made her seem brittle and remote. The dress was only a minimal flouting of convention, but it was there.

I had glanced at her in the cemetery when ashes to ashes, dust to dust, the coffin was lowered. She had been noticeably dry-eyed, holding Paul's hand. The two girls, and Caro between Nell and myself, even Nell, were obviously moved; but Jane had, for a few seconds before she bowed her head, an almost indifferent face, a shadow of that same buried resentfulness of our first evening in Oxford. I suppose everyone unconsciously glances toward the widow on such occasions, and I was not the only one. There, too, something was being announced. I wondered about the man at Harvard, whether he knew how to deal with the difficult woman she had now become. I knew he was not there, having managed a word with Roz before we assembled at the graveside. I tried to probe her mother's mask at the wake, when she came up to refill our glasses. I was standing with Caro and some aged aunt of Anthony's.

"Are you all right, Jane?"

"Yes, fine. This is the bit I can stand." She glanced round behind her, where there was a scattering of Anthony's Catholic cronies, some in uniform, then grimaced. "I suppose you don't know a good rite of desanctification?"

"Laughing at it will help."

"You think?"

But then she moved on, as if she did not care how conventional she seemed.

Before our week-end at Compton, I took Roz out to dinner. It meant slightly hurting Caro, who became inquisitive as soon as I said there were things Anthony had said I'd rather pass on alone; but I mollified her by making her waste an hour one evening with me poking round a jewelry antique shop for something she thought Roz might like, by way of penance on my side for having deprived her of so many years of birthday presents. We finally picked out a silver and moss-agate necklace, and Caro also (if you can't beat them, buy them) came away with something smaller than chanced to catch her eye.

Roz seemed to like her present, and certainly not to have expected it; and promptly took off the beads she was wearing and put on the gift. The evening went well. I heard a little of her own life, at work and in private; then I led us to the past. I gave her a much more circumstantial account than I had orginally meant to, though I hid even the faintest suggestion that her mother and I had ever known anything but friendship. I took the blame, tried to explain my misguided motives over the play, and made very sure that she knew I saw her parents' reaction had been the only possible one. A little of this she had gone over with Jane, it seemed; and she told me how Jane had once said of me to her that I ought never to have married Nell and that I wasn't altogether to blame. For a moment I had a curious sense of Jane herself having once been on the confessional brink with the girl opposite me.

"Did she tell you why?"

She smiled. "I'm only a niece. But even I find her a bit much at times."

"She's changed. Much more than your mother, I suspect."

"That's just her problem. Jane's. Not changing. In spite of all her talk about it."

"You don't take it seriously?"

"I'll believe it when I see it. You know, it's her Catholicism. Somewhere that's still there underneath. It's all very well her going through the Funeral Mass like someone with a bad smell under her nose. Talking about the crows and all the rest. Deep down that's where she still is. In some strange psychological way. All the sin-and-guilt bit."

"But transferred to a different creed?"

"We argue about it."

"And she doesn't agree?"

"She usually does one of her retreats. I haven't had her life, I can't know. Etcetera."

It wasn't difficult, after my own soul-baring, or semblance of it, to keep Roz talking about her parents. I didn't really discover anything I hadn't already been told by Anthony and Jane themselves . . . or guessed at. It was more a case of a new angle on known facts; a dramatic irony. Roz had a revealing habit of calling her mother by her Christian name, yet always referring to Anthony as "my father," which seemed to reflect the reality of that household during the latter years . . . not anything so simple as a male being ganged up on by his females, but a zone of unspoken distance between male and female intelligences. She repeated a very similar phrase to one I had heard from Jane: there was so much that never got said. And it wasn't that she hadn't loved him, simply that she never knew how to approach him except along certain prescribed lines, sometimes it was "terrible, almost as if we were his adopted children and he had to show an interest." I asked if their following Jane out of the Church had disappointed him.

"Obviously. But it never came across like that at the time. I was sixteen, Jane knew what I felt . . . we went off one day, just he and I, on one of his orchid jaunts and I spilt the beans—and he was marvelous. Talked about doubt, and faith—you know, as if it was a philosophy problem. Asked me to try a little longer. But when I said at the end of next term that I still felt the same, he didn't argue at all. He was absolutely reasonable, never tried to win me back. I think with Anne he just gave up—accepted the same thing was happening. I see now it isolated him unbearably. It's absurd, he even protected us from ever remembering the problem existed. Catholics who didn't know the scene, they'd come to dinner or whatever, and innocently bring up something, just Catholic chitchat. And he'd kill it stone dead." She paused, then said, "I did mention it the last time I saw him. My losing faith."

"Whether it had hurt him?"

"That I was sorry it *had* hurt him."

"What did he say?"

"That he preferred me as I was to what he had tried to force me to be." A tiny tremor crossed her face, and she looked down.

"Let's change the subject."

"No." She shook her head, and smiled up. "I'm . . . it's just . . . being too late now."

"He was very honest and very shy of emotion, Roz. That's a lethal combination, when you're faced with ordinary mortals."

"Yes, I know."

"And your potential new stepfather's more outgoing?"

"Oh Peter's fine. He's supposed to be very brilliant, but he enjoys life. He can be rather a clown, actually."

She told me a little about him. He came from the North, from Tyneside, a shipyard worker's son "only you'd never guess"; a major scholarship to Oxford, Anthony's student, never looked back. There were two children by his first marriage, he had been the guilty party, he fancied himself as a rogue male in those days. The girl had been one of his graduate ex-students and there had been something of a scandal.

"Why didn't he marry her?"

"I honestly don't quite know. Jane says he wanted to, but something went wrong. His ex-wife's a frightful little bore, she still lives just round the corner from us."

"Yes, I heard."

She gave me an amused quiz. "You seem to have heard an awful lot that night."

"The Gestapo would have been proud of me."

"I'm just rather surprised you got anywhere."

I looked down from her eyes.

"I was given a kind of commission by your father, Roz. Of course he didn't know about Peter, which rather lets me out,

[ 309 ]

but he did ask me to keep the breach closed. And I very much want to do that. Not just because he asked me to. With all of you. If it would help."

"I think it already has. We also had a talk. After I drove you to the station that day."

"As long as she didn't feel I forced her to say too much."

She smiled. "She felt she'd forced you to listen too much."

"At least we have a good go-between."

She touched her agate necklace. "Now she's been so shamelessly bribed."

We talked about Paul then, and other things. Roz had to work the following Saturday, and had had to give up the idea of coming with us to Compton. But she promised to come down in the spring to Thorncombe with her current boy-friend. It was not quite mere avuncular charity. Following my re-entry into the family orbit, I had begun to have dim memories of the spirit of the place as it had once been long before I bought it; indeed, why I had bought it . . . if one can buy ghosts. But they must wait.

# Compton

Caro had wheedled herself the Friday afternoon off, and we were on our way soon after lunch—in my Volvo, not her Mini. She had hesitated fractionally when told her week-end was pre-empted—by her need to square her conscience with her mother as much as by me—but that was all. We had actually gone to the funeral on the understanding that the deed should be done at some point there. However, the fence-taker quailed when it came to it, and I could hardly blame her. It was neither the time nor place, and the sight of so many Oxford faces had produced a febrile, socializing mood in Nell when we returned to the house. Once again, on our way back to London, I had found myself in the unaccustomed role of defending mother against daughter—not altogether convincingly. I had been the loser too long not to enjoy this proof that I was now the more conversable.

She was a little too determined to be gay on the second journey to Oxford—there was a touch, although she would have hated me for saying it, of her mother's febrility about her. It transparently hid a nervousness: Nell to be faced with Barney, myself to be faced with Compton. She began once more warning me, almost as if we were visiting total strangers, about how *Country Life* it all was, I must be "good" . . .

In the days that had passed we had tacitly dropped all mention of Barney. She was usually home, when she stayed out, soon after midnight; but at least once, I happened to be awake, I heard her letting herself in well after three. It showed the next morning, though I said nothing. She looked permanently tired, in fact; but not, however hard I searched, unhappy. She was moving into the new flat that following week and at least I consoled myself that there she would not be turfed at such ungodly hours out of whoever's flat or bed they were presently borrowing. I couldn't quite understand why she had to return home as it was; however, that was also forbidden ground. But in other matters we had both set out to understand each other better. I told her about Jenny, about Abe and Mildred; and more of why I had left her mother for Andrea. Then one evening when she was in, she saw on my desk the messy pages, covered in corrections, from the Kitchener scene I had been working on all day; said nothing; but suddenly during supper, an hour later, asked if she could try to type it out.

"Not worth it. It's so far from final."

"I just thought . . ."

I waited a moment, then got up and went and found the scene; came back and put it beside her, and kissed her head. She had played secretary for half an hour, and I used what she finally appeared with as the basis for an impromptu tutorial about script-writing and its problems. The scene still read weakly, and I explained why. It was really a lesson for me. She was suddenly the younger child I had never known: full of questions . . . perhaps for the first time understanding what such work was about. It was not what really had to be said, but it helped.

We arrived in Oxford. I had a more private experience of the affection I knew existed between aunt and niece. Jane herself was in a much more relaxed mood than at the funeral; a definite, if guarded, air of release from nightmare, of composure regained. We had an early tea with them, and then she took me upstairs while Caro, ungraciously helped by Paul, washed up. There was a small carton of books and botanical papers to do with orchids: what Anthony had asked I should take.

"I haven't included all his drawings and notes and things, other than the ones in the margins. Paul's not interested, but I thought he might like to have them one day."

"Of course. And if he'd ever like these back."

"I'm sorry he's being so boorish. He needs to be back at school."

"Taking it hard?"

"It's difficult to get through at the moment. I think he needs either to be completely alone with me or away from me. These last few days, so many people have been dropping in. He's so unreasonable. For a basically rather bright child." But as if she felt she was unfairly unloading her troubles, she smiled. "Anyway. Roz, you have won."

"And been won by."

"I was got out of bed at midnight to hear about your evening." She added, "And the present that wasn't necessary. But was loved."

"Caro chose it."

"Roz was thrilled."

She looked down at the books between us, aware that I was searching her eyes for more than these trivialities.

"Survived?"

"By some miracle."

"And what news from America?"

"He's written."

The telephone began to ring outside, and she went to answer it. By the time she finished, Caro and Paul had appeared from their chores, and we were four again.

We talked in the car, of course, but somehow everything was dominated by the brooding young adolescent in the back seat beside his mother. The weather was heavy and gray; windless, no rain, and quite mild, but with an oppressive and seemingly immovable canopy of cloud. If it had needed a presiding human spirit, Paul would have done for the part. Caro fell over herself to involve him in whatever we were talking about, and he would give some answer; but he never volunteered anything. If something was said that had the rest of us smiling, he would look at Jane—I saw this once or twice in the driving-mirror—but not in the way children sometimes look at their parents for guidance in their own reaction; much more to blame it, as if he knew she was putting on an act . . . even though it was no more than that of ordinary civility. He sat, too, strangely thrust back, like someone who doesn't trust the driver. It occurred to me, when we were climbing into the Cotswolds, that he really wanted to be in the front seat, and I suggested he change places with Caro.

"No, I'm all right."

" 'Thank you,' " murmured Jane.

He left a really killing little pause, exquisitely timed to show he was being coerced.

"Thank you."

His behavior was so grotesque that I began to feel sorry for him. Plainly the death had disturbed him much more deeply than he was prepared to show; and I could recall my own childhood well enough to remember those moods when every tenderness, like every well-meaning briskness, only drives you back farther into your shell. But I couldn't remember my sulks lasting more than a day. I decided we should leave him in his misery, and when once more Caro got rebuffed, I touched her arm and managed to signal that she stop trying.

We arrived at Compton just before dusk. The lodge-gates—the lodge itself was lived in now by one of Andrew's tractor-drivers, it seemed—were open, and we swept up one of those endless drives that demand a barouche, or at least a Rolls, if one is to arrive in appropriate style. Then we were in front of the gray Palladian house; gravel, some impressive urns and balusters, half the façade in bleak darkness—they nicknamed that the Frozen Wing, since it was too expensive to heat except on special occasions; but the graceful tall windows on the ground floor of the other half shone a welcome yellow in the twilight. A door opened: Andrew looming in a bulky white polo-necked sweater, Nell slight beside him, a dumpy schoolgirl of Paul's age in jodhpurs—Caro's half-sister Penelope, or Penny: two Irish setters—they came down the steps, dogs and people, and there was a great shaking of hands, embracing, cross-talk; then Andrew helping me with the luggage. When we came into the splendidly proportioned hall, I saw a little boy in a dressing-gown sitting at the top of the first curved flight of stairs.

"That's the Runt," said Andrew. "Still in quarantine."

Jane and Caro stood at the foot of the stairs, talking with him, and I was brought forward by his father.

"This is Caro's daddy, Andrew. Say howdy-do."

The boy shuffled to his feet, and bobbed his head. "Howdy-do. Sir."

Nell murmured, "He's been rehearsing that all afternoon."

Whatever else Andrew had had to sell to make the estate viable, it had evidently not been paintings or furniture, and the interior of the house came as something of a shock to me. It had impressed me long ago when I was there for his twenty-first, but I had expected to be less awed this time. I think what surprised was not so much the decor in itself as the fact that anyone could still live in such surroundings in contemporary England. It lacked the frigid museum feel of stately homes thrown open to the public, it was clearly lived in, and with an easy informality, but there lingered something artificial, unreal in its space and elegance, its predominantly eighteenth-century chairs and sofas and pots and paintings. We had gone into the drawing-room and sat around a fire in a loose circle, but that still left three-quarters of the room unoccupied. It was a little like a film set, one half expected a side open for the camera. We had drinks. Nell sat with curled-back legs on the carpet in front of the fire, while Andrew sprawled and chatted to me about Volvos, he was thinking of trying one. Penny, who evidently took after Andrew and was a bad case of puppy fat, sat on a huge settee between her aunt and Caro, while Paul huddled, silent as always, in an armchair.

I was reassessing Caroline, reminding myself that it was a miracle she had ever escaped at all from this, and wrily reflecting that I had never really asked her what she didn't like about Compton, the place; there must have been something, the shutawayness of it, the provinciality, the patent unreality in terms of the way most of the country lived—and something more interior still, some flaw in its psyche. And I speculated a little about Jane as well, how she reconciled all this with her new-found political instincts . . . with Gramsci and the philosophy of praxis. In that matter I had begun to suspect that Nell and Roz were nearer the truth than I had at first supposed. The subject had not been mentioned since it was first thrown in my face, and increasingly it came to seem a histrionic, if not positively hysterical, gesture of defiance . . . or certainly of "consciousness full of contradictions"; of self-liberation, if one took a kinder view, but still essentially a gesture. For all that, I was glad she was there.

Nell began to tell us the week-end program. There was only one formal engagement, a Miles and Elizabeth Fenwick were asked to dinner for the Saturday evening.

Caro said, "Oh you didn't ask that ghastly daughter!"

"Darling, I do have some tact. He wants to meet you, Dan, actually."

"Me?"

"It's all rather involved. His prospective son-in-law, it's a sister, not the ghastly daughter Caro loves so much, he's trying to enter the film business. I think putting money up rather than anything else, and he's got in with some character called Jimmy Knight—have you ever heard of him?"

"No. Is there a production company?"

"He'll tell you. Really all Miles wants is to have someone convince him it's not utter madness."

"I'd be lying if I told him anything else."

"They're going to marry anyway. It's all rather pointless."

"Then I'd better lie."

"No, do say what you think. I'm making him sound an idiot. Actually he's an M.P."

"Indisputable proof to the contrary," murmured Jane.

Andrew and I laughed and Nell raised a finger at her sister. "One more crack like that and you'll be sitting next to him." She turned to me. "If you could just chat him up for a few minutes. Please."

"Of course."

"Otherwise there's riding, walking, guided tours, Ping-Pong—"

"Table tennis." It was Paul. We all looked at him. He brushed back his long hair, then stared at his knees. "That's its proper name."

"I beg your pardon. Table tennis."

Caro said, "You're making it sound like some dreadful seaside hotel."

"Just a dreadful country one, darling."

Andrew broke in. "Play snooker, Dan?"

"I play pool in America a bit. Same principle."

Andrew winked at me. "That's settled us, then."

Nell stretched out an accusing arm. "But not for you-know-what."

"Of course not, dear girl. Perish the thought."

I had her grave eyes. "You watch him. He was down in the village only last week, cheating the old-age pensioners out of their beer money."

"Rubbish. I was doing my squire thing. They expect me to win." His eyes flicked lazily toward Jane. "Wouldn't tug their poor old exploited forelocks if I didn't."

She smiled. "No rise."

"Foiled again."

Nell grimaced at me. She was still sitting propped on one arm in front of the fire.

"I went down to the cowshed the other day and the two cowmen are there and our shepherd and the tractor-drivers and God knows who else, all in a huddle round Andrew, and I think how sweet, how marvelous it is, the way he gets them so involved in running things . . . not a bit of it. The football pools. Merely where they're going to put their wretched little crosses this week."

"Jolly serious business. New opium of the masses."

She waved a hand at her husband.

"I wouldn't mind if it was just a fiendish plan to keep their minds off asking for more money. But he's worse than any of them." She looked at Caro. "Do you know what he did just before Christmas? He offered Vicar a free share if he'd pray for eight draws at midweek Evensong."

Caro grinned. "What did he say?"

"Good on him. That he'd do better praying for Andrew's soul."

Penny said, "It was only joking, Mummy."

"Don't you be so sure."

I caught Jane's eyes for a moment, a hinted smile down; she knew and I knew that Nell was trying to be kind, to put us at our ease, suggesting she had problems that both of us underestimated; and was also proving the very opposite.

A few minutes later I was being hustled. The snooker table was only half-size, and distinctly dilapidated, down in a long cellar beneath the house, with a central heating boiler intermittently roaring away somewhere close by. There was a table tennis table as well and for some reason a fruit-machine. Andrew looked up as he set the frame; a wink.

"Fiver. Just for mustard?"

"If you insist."

"Always get it back. Just threaten to tell her ladyship."

I smiled, and chalked my cue. "Do you still gamble for serious?"

"Absolutely not. Lost ten times more money at Oxford than in all the years since. Matter of principle." He leaned to cue off for first break. "Just a hard-working farmer these days, Dan. Behind the airs and graces."

"Caro's told me."

As we played we got through a little conversation about Caro, and I guessed he had picked the game as a convenient way to say casually, between strokes, what might have been more awkward face-to-face: his liking for Caro, concern for her; which gave me my chance to thank him for having been such an excellent stepfather. He won that first frame rather easily, and though I won the next, I suspect it was only because he let me. By that time Paul and Penny had come down and begun to play table tennis together. I think they must have been sent down, rather than of their own wills. Paul was evidently rather good at the game, and the overweight schoolgirl opposite him as plainly not. With monotonous regularity he smashed every third or fourth of her amateurish returns. It was very near sadism in the circumstances. He gave her not a chance; and though her constant running to retrieve the small white ball from some corner may have been helping her weight problem, it was almost demoniacally selfish on his part. He refused point-blank to accommodate his game to hers. Andrew must have felt the same after we'd watched half a dozen or so of the rallies. We were leaning against the snooker table. Suddenly he decided to join in.

"Come on, Penny. I'll thrash him for you."

She gave up her paddle to her father, who showed a brisk game of higher class. He was clowning a bit, but I could see Paul took it very seriously. Then Caro came down; they were "getting sloshed" upstairs and it was time to join them. I went with her, and on the way she asked demurely if we'd had a nice game of snooker.

"I always rather liked him, Caro. Much more than your mother and Jane did, oddly enough—when we were all undergraduates."

She pulled a face. "It's all universal love upstairs, as well. I feel I don't know anyone anymore."

"I expect we'll manage a good row before we go." I gave her a look. "Just as long as you aren't the cause of it."

"I've made a bedtime appointment." She grimaced again. "I don't know what I dread most. Her hating Bernard. Or her wanting to ask him down." But she went on quickly. "I'm sorry she asked the Fenwicks. Actually he's quite amusing. A bit of an old rake. It's his third marriage."

It turned out Caro had even met the tyro Sam Goldwyn whose venture I was to advise on. He had been at Eton with Richard; "just like him, really, only stupider." She then rather contemptuously revealed, as if she knew I would be ashamed that she'd even met such people, that he was a lord. Which at least relieved my conscience about not saying the truth.

We had, despite the formal surroundings, an agreeable enough supper. Nell's Italian housekeeper, who evidently knew how to cook, brought the dishes in, but left us to serve ourselves; and the presence of the three children kept the talk on a safely anodyne level. I talked farming and rural things with Andrew. Jane chatted to Nell about all the people she'd heard from, Caro listened with one ear to them, with another to her half-sister, who was clearly in the full throes of the pony mania she had once suffered from herself. Even Paul was forced to join in a little.

But as always happens when people are being studiously on their best behavior, there was once again a faint, though not unpleasing, air of unreality over the occasion. Perhaps it was partly the house, the deep silence outside, that curious air the traditional English upper classes, in their traditional backgrounds, manage to give of being in a play by someone else—of being so used to such surroundings that they no more own them than actors own a theater set. Rather absurdly give, since no class is in fact more tenacious of its property. Yet in all outward ways the only true member of the upper classes there, Andrew, was the most natural. Exhibiting another trait of the species, he managed to suggest that he supposed we all lived more or less like this.

From time to time I caught Caro giving me looks, trying to guess what I was thinking; and more surprisingly, though more discreetly, Jane as well . . . as if she were speculating about whose side I was really on; who I really was, after all these years. I even suspected she hid an inward amusement, to see the grasshopper brought to bay like this, made to do his duty. Yet however convincingly she played the familiar guest in her sister's house, there remained something intensely guarded about her, not natural in itself, and not natural in regard to her own old nature. It wasn't quite the usual Oxford guardedness, of a fundamentally sceptical mind dissembling behind obedience to the conventions of circumstance; but something deeper, more fraught, perhaps really the reverse, what Roz had suggested, a faith dissembling behind scepticism. It was enhanced by Nell, never one to let silences grow. Jane said less as the meal wore on, and that did recall one still-centered aspect of her old self. She continued to intrigue me; and to repel as well. . . . I glimpsed that other less attractive aspect, of a superior moral judgment, of eternally denying her real self to lesser mortals. It underlay her new dogma, and her old, was far more perennial than them, was perhaps what she unconsciously sought in them . . . a justification for something not very far removed from the Oxford Movement's theory of reserve, in fact. Their value as dogmas was less intrinsic than that their abstruseness, their mysteries, their esoteric jargon, kept the ordinary herd conveniently at bay.

But she remained different; she reminded me slightly of one or two women writers I had known—of a withholding, not exactly male, but springing from an independence of feeling that was also not female; that came perhaps in their case from the experience of the retreat into the imagination, but which in isolating them from the commonality of their sex, isolated them too from the other. I felt confirmed in seeking some clue in Jane that might be central to what I wanted to write myself; but less and less sanguine of success. She had evidently ended by baffling Anthony. She was not the sort of woman ever to be understood empirically, logically—indeed that was part of the problem, that she could discuss herself lucidly and frankly, and yet still live in a darkness . . . not merely inscrutable, but almost calculatedly two-faced; although that suggests hypocrisy, and this was perhaps simply a matter of self-preservation, of knowing that the feelings of the "dark" self would destroy too much if allowed to show. This interpretation was backed by something more concrete I noticed about her: how everything she said, at least that evening, seemed to be in inverted commas, in some subtle way distinguished from some hypothetical sentence she might have more truthfully said. I knew she must be making an effort, like all the rest of us, so in a sense this was unkind. But I was left with a strange impression, denying the parallel with a woman writer, of someone with a profound mistrust of words; who waited for something better.

I found Nell alone when I came down to breakfast. Apparently Penny was already out in the stables. Andrew was amusing his son for an hour, Jane and Caro were not yet up, and Paul was off somewhere on his solitary own. The sky had cleared overnight, there was sunlight outside, and a gracious vista. That was hardly the adjective for Nell's eyes when she had poured me coffee.

"It's lucky I've sworn to be all smiles this weekend. Even if it kills me."

"Caro?"

"When you'd gone to bed."

I tried to look contrite.

"I have been going at her to tell you, Nell."

"Don't worry. You've been cleared."

"I was presented with a *fait accompli*. That night I came back."

"It's not your fault." She lit a cigarette. "Or both our faults."

"I think she also has some of our virtues."

She breathed smoke down her nostrils; there was an old glint of aggression in her eyes, a challenge.

"We are getting soft in our old age."

"More honest."

"And as a matter of academic interest . . . ?"

"I think she'll survive. As we have."

"In our fashion."

I glanced drily round the elegant dining-room, but she re-

fused the invitation to take herself more lightly, and stared
down at the polished rosewood of the table between us.

"I know you think I've tried to turn her into a daft deb."

"That's selling yourself short. And over Barney I'm at least
equally to blame."

"Except that she doesn't apparently think so."

"Why do you say that?"

"She seems to adore the job. London. I had to bear the full
brunt of that last night. As if all I'd ever been was some kind
of prison governess."

"She knows she's been naughty. I've had the same treatment. Been reminded of all my sins."

"Which are they?"

"Still treating her as a child. Not being frank with her."

She left a silence, then spoke with a candor that took me
by surprise.

"What infuriates me is that she told Jane first."

"I gather Jane's long been the person she goes to to discuss
what she feels about us both."

"I am her mother."

"I'm not trying to excuse her over this, Nell."

"Is it so unreasonable?"

"Of course not." I felt tempted to remind her that she had
hardly told her own mother "all" before we married; but held
my tongue.

"I just don't understand what goes on with her generation."

"You've told Andrew?"

She mimicked his voice. "Living it up a bit, isn't she?" I
smiled, but she did not smile back. "I feel conspired against."

"Not by me."

"I have done my best."

"I know." Her eyes remained doubting. "Look, Nell, for
God's sake. I can't stand the man . . . she told you I had
lunch with him the other day? At his request?"

"She mentioned it."

"At least he convinced me it's not just a cold-blooded
seduction. He's become a jaundiced TV idol who knows his
world is sick and that he's trapped in it . . . you know. But I
think we have to believe he has something she needs. Unlikely as it may seem."

"She says there's no question of marrying."

"I got that from him as well."

I told her more of what he had said to me about his own
marriage. Through the window behind Nell I saw Paul walk-

ing across the gravel, head down. She stubbed out her cigarette, and then I received her wide-eyed "I can face anything" look.

"Do you blame me?"

"For what?"

"Letting you have so little say in her education."

"That's got nothing to do with what's just happened."

"But it was a mistake?"

"I plead the Fifth Amendment."

She retreated into dryness. "I was simply trying to work out if I have one Bolshie in the house, or two." She added, "Your daughter's always been rather silent about that."

"I try to believe in simplicity, Nell. Rather as lapsed Catholics try to regain faith. It's more a longing than a reality."

"Do you think I don't miss it too sometimes?"

"There are always prices."

"I know what Jane thinks of me. The way we live."

"My impression is she's not too sure of what she thinks of anything."

She got up and turned away to a window; there was an elaborate Victorian wire plant-holder there, and she fiddled a moment with one of the houseplants it contained.

"I know she's been useful as a sort of family ombudsman. It's just the way she plays Minerva to us ordinary mortals." She began rather petulantly snipping away the browning flowers from some succulent. It was a childishly revealing fragment of behavior; chopping off awkward heads, trying to suggest she was a harassed housewife; but finally, and absurdly, suggesting the mind of the lady who once thought brioches and bread were the same thing. "I sometimes think she takes us at the silliest face value. As if we didn't have constant anxieties about keeping this place up. All of that."

"It's an old illusion of people who live outside palaces."

"Palaces!" She gave the embittered sniff of inside knowledge. "You ought to see the estimate we've just had for repairing the roof." I smiled, but she turned from her flowers and caught my expression. "All right. But what is the answer, Dan? To let the rain in?"

I was saved the trouble of finding a reply, for Jane appeared with Caro. I didn't know till afterward that Caro had placed a ban on all public discussion of the matter; which lost Nell the good point I gave her for changing the subject when they came in.

I wasn't alone with Jane till after lunch, and then only briefly. We were all to go for a walk, and she and I were waiting outside and ready before the others. She leaned in the
weak winter sunshine against the stone balustrade in front of
the house, in a pair of borrowed gumboots; she had never
been much of a country-woman, and she somehow contrived
to make it clear that in that she had not changed. She smiled
as I came up to her.

"I hope you don't feel overorganized."

"It makes a change."

"*Vie de campagne.*"

Andrew had taken me before lunch on a long tour of the
house and the farm buildings in what had once been the
stable block. We had discussed Caro's news. His reaction was,
of course, shrewder than Nell had suggested. In his own way
he took my view: one could only keep one's fingers crossed.
He had no particular feelings against Barney; "can't stand
any of those TV johnnies, if I'm honest"; and exonerated me
from any taint of conspiracy. He said something about the
dangers of mollycoddling young animals; then that horses
need a fall or two. Although he didn't openly criticize Nell, I
had gained the impression (as in retrospect what she had said
to me at breakfast confirmed) that a point he had long argued now stood proven. Our talking did not diminish my respect for him. He had that formidable easygoingness of the
landed farmer; half out of knowledge of his social position,
perhaps, but also half out of his familiarity with natural
process. It was a virtue of privilege that became a privilege of
virtue of a kind.

"You know Caro's crossed her bridge?"

"Only too well." She looked down at the gravel. "I've been
severely reprimanded for coming between mother and daughter."

"She's an idiot."

Jane smiled, said nothing. I leaned beside her on the balustrade, facing the house, and broke the silence.

"You forget places like this exist."

"If you're lucky."

"You do very well. The hair shirt doesn't show."

She smiled again. "It's not the house. What houses like this
do to people."

"Possess them?"

"Embalm them, I think." She stared up at the bland front.
"Caro uses a word to me about Nell sometimes. Rather more

[ 323 ]

_ouble-meaning than she realizes. Mummyish." Then, "I'm being catty."

"I can't quite work out why I mind it all so much less in Andrew."

"He was born mummified. At least it's natural in him."

"Steady, comrade."

She kept a faint smile. "It's not politics, Dan. A little matter of free will. Every time I come here I go through a sibling nightmare."

I glanced at her. "Not in a thousand years."

She shrugged. "Oh . . . not in this form. But there are other kinds of . . . not escaping what one is."

"Your friend in America?"

"No." She shook her head, though the negative had already been firm. "I suppose just my years."

"Shall I go and fetch you a walking-stick?"

Her lips pressed together.

"I see Roz has found an ally."

"Of course. Tease the poor old thing on every possible occasion."

"Like a knot it would be much simpler to cut."

"Now you're being an idiot as well."

She acknowledged the reproof, but then, as if to administer one of her own and to justify her idiocy, slipped me a gently ambiguous side-look.

"How wise you were to stay out of all this, Dan."

"That's an odd adjective."

"Fortunate."

"Not to have had gangrene—merely amputation?"

"I suppose I meant that in a way."

She was staring at the gravel, as if my metaphor had frozen something in her, disinterred what she had not meant. Caro and her half-sister appeared, and we stood and strolled to meet them. I said nothing more, but her fortuitous reference to mummification had reminded me of that offer to go to Egypt—or to be precise, that I could, if I cared to change my mind, pick up a telephone and in five minutes arrange to go there. Her remark about wisdom, though said without overt malice, held the now familiar warning. I had mummifying privileges as well; remained relegated, in her eyes, to some lower, blinder world. It seemed to me that here was where her real lack of freedom lay: in the incapacity to compromise. It was redeemed only, and only partly, by her incapacity to forgive herself least of all.

It was also related to Nell's unanswered question: whether it really helped to let the rain in. Somewhere Jane clung to a deep intuitive belief, as she had once in Catholic doctrine, that all, at least in her own life, was determined, predestined; which had led her into the oldest fallacy of all, that any external change was better than no change . . . a credo no more tenable than her one-time whim for the Rabelaisian dreamland where everything goes. All she had substituted for that and its Catholic successor—and perhaps that change of horses had most to do with their common unattainability, so convenient a proof of despair in personal freedom—was some egalitarian Utopia in which Compton would overnight become an old persons' home, a holiday camp for trade union officials, heaven knew what . . . functions I wouldn't have disapproved if they had been practicable, but that was not the issue. The only true and real field in which one could test personal freedom was present possibility. Of course we could all lead better, nobler, more socialist lives; but not by positing them only in some future perfect state. One could so clearly only move and act from today, *this* present and flawed world.

Which was the lawn, crossing a haha, the parkland beyond, blue and gray distances over the green, the two setters bounding and racing about, the casual train of us: Jane walked ahead between Caro and Penny, then Paul and Nell—the latter perhaps determined to prove that two could play at sympathetic aunt, but the boy did seem a shade more amenable now—with Andrew and myself bringing up the rear. Figures in a landscape, his landscape; the first of his line had "grabbed" it—his word, we had talked about it during the tour—after the Restoration. The baronetcy itself had come for staying true to the monarchy during the Commonwealth. Of course, in the manner of his kind, Andrew played all this down, as if his three centuries of ancestors, this same prospect, earth, trees his grandsires planted, meant nothing to him . . . that ultimate vulgar modesty of the very rooted and assured. I wondered how deep a hold it all had on him, beneath the bland, dismissive surface, the man who talked—with very clearly signaled inverted commas—of "the peasantry" and "playing squire" and "her ladyship."

By chance, later that afternoon, I was given some clue. We had walked a mile or so to a hill, where some forebear of

Andrew's had built a folly—a rather gloomy stone tower with pointed Gothic windows, but with a nice view over the gentle Gloucestershire valley south and the village. Nell had wanted to go back then, to get the dinner organized, but Andrew had a sick ewe, we could see the flock in a field below us, and the party split. I went on alone with him, while the others returned to the house.

His shepherd had put the ewe in a little pen of hurdles beside a green-and-white caravan—which had been rather a conspicuous eyesore when we looked down from the folly, Nell had even complained about it, but it was needed for the March lambing. A rough shelter of corrugated iron had been rigged in one corner of the pen, and the animal stood weakly off a litter of straw inside it when Andrew arrived. He asked me to stay outside, and I watched him catch and then expertly turn the invalid on her back and examine her. One or two of the rest of the flock watched from a hundred yards away, then went on with their grazing. After a minute he came back.

"Any luck?"

He shook his head as he retied the binder twine round the hurdle he had opened to get in. "Looks like a goner. I think it's pneumonia, but I'd better get the horse-doctor in. Damn things invent a new disease every winter." He saw me looking at the caravan, as we turned away. "Sorry about that. But you can't turn off good shepherds for bad taste."

"They're hard to come by now?"

"Like gold. And they know it." He went behind the caravan and came out with a crook, and we began to walk toward the rest of the flock. "Ought to jack 'em in, really. Sheep. Bit of an economic luxury these days."

"Then why not?"

"Like so much else. If the dear old commissars are going to take over . . ."

"I can't believe that's a serious reason."

"No? I wouldn't like to bet on the Runt being able to take over when I'm gone. The way things are going."

"That must sadden you."

"Sometimes." He shrugged. "Has its pleasures, Dan. We're the foxes now."

"But surely not quite yet run to ground?"

He grinned. "While it lasts." We stopped to survey the flock, but he went on talking. "Years ago, when I started, just after the governor died, I hired a bad egg. Good ploughman, but Union up to here." He leveled a hand to his chin. "He started to preach the gospel, I had a spy down at the pub, I knew all about it. Could have chucked him his cards, but I didn't. Decided I'd sit it out. Then one day he said he was leaving, an uncle had left his wife a bit of money and he was going in for pigs. Come his last pay-day we had quite a set-to. I pulled his leg a bit, about getting to know the other side of the picture. Not a fool, he knew his stuff. History, statistics, all that. And that was the final thing he said to me. 'Enjoy it while it lasts.'" Andrew left a pause. "Always remembered that."

"Did he gain any disciples?"

"Some of the younger ones. Didn't last. One thing about the land, the guv'nor doesn't work, they all know it. That's why I'll still do a day or two's ploughing, whatever." He winked at me. "Very simple fellow, your average peasant."

I said, "You're not fooling me, Andrew."

"Just my dear sister-in-law."

"Not even her, I suspect."

"Clever girl. Lot of bottom in her yet. Do hope she gets over it."

I wasn't quite sure if he meant Anthony's death or her contempt for his way of life; and wasn't to find out, because he had spotted a ewe with a limping hind-leg and had a small chase before he could crook her over . . . and then we moved on to the problem of foot-rot.

We did return slightly to the subject on our way back to the house, because he told me about his old "chum" Mark, from that long-ago day of the woman in the reeds. I had asked after him. He had apparently sold his Hampshire farm in the late 1950s, and now farmed in New Zealand; had tried, was still trying, to persuade Andrew to follow his example. But Andrew felt he had left it too late, and anyway "her ladyship wouldn't stand for it."

All of this was as we were coming up through what was left of the park to the house, and I began to see he would be separated from it only by a new Cromwell and Commonwealth; that the tenacity, and the courage that went with it, existed—and at the same time a blindness, a need to turn everything into a game, a playing of hare-and-hounds, a gamble. His now harmless love of betting, his little "matter of principle," was a good deal deeper than a quirk of independence, a mere atavism. He knew the odds were hopelessly against him, that history, the overwhelming new awareness of personal rights that had followed universal education and the universal publicity of the new media (let alone their political embodiment), must win now. There was no real argument between Jane and himself, since the matter was effectively decided. In a few decades at most, her side must have their way. He would double and double, but never escape; the tail of a species, of a failure to adapt; and as we came up the steps to the gravel in front of the house I did finally see a justice in Jane's remark about being born mummified, since his failure to adapt was a result of the huge superstructure of land, house, tradition, family he had to carry; but the analogy was better made with the last of the brontosaurs, whose armor dragged them down.

Monsters . . . and curiously, a quite literal one delayed us a minute from going indoors. I had been aware as we approached the house of a low jet somewhere in the distance behind us, but as we went up the steps its distant roar became anomalous and I looked back. I could see the plane four or five miles away, on a downward path.

Andrew said, "Concorde. They're testing the damn thing at Fairford."

"My God. It's the first time I've heard it."

"Wish I could say the same."

The roar was strange, sky-filling despite the distance of the aircraft, seemingly too all-invasive to emanate from that tiny sliver of machinery in the dimming winter sky. I heard a voice from the house: Caro and Jane, and the two children, stood by the front door, watching with us. Andrew took a breath.

"Had a great protest meeting soon after it started. Down at Lechlade. Absolute shambles. Local Bolshies screaming at each other—the Fairford union men were all out in force. Our lot no better. All our would-be politicos trying to sit on the fence in case they lost votes. Just about summed it all up, really."

"Three blind mice?"

"Sixty million of the, dear boy. If you ask me."

And with that comprehensive judgment on his nation, he turned his back on the future.

Only two nights before, in the flat, I had pulled down that old copy of the Shirburn Ballads inherited from my father.

*Why dost thow put thy confidence*
*in strange and stately Towres?*
*Why takest thow such pleasure*
*in building sumptuous bowers,*
*Reioycinge in thy pastures,*
*and Parke of fallow deere?*
*Repent therfore, oh England—*
*the iudgement day is nye.*

The anonymous Jeremiah of the broadsheet ballad might
well have got a certain masochistic enjoyment from our evening, as it turned out, I had been told more of our guests before they arrived. Fenwick was a highly successful barrister
as well as a politician; he had a safe Tory seat "just over the
border"; but wasn't at all, I was assured, "countrified." He
had acted "brilliantly"—at least successfully—for Andrew
in some planning dispute that had gone to public inquiry.
Rather a gay old dog out of his chambers, his present, third,
and much younger, wife was American: I'd like her.

I didn't very much, though she was more interesting than
her English equivalent. She showed a fashionable Manhattan
background and a solid Wasp frame of values in an aura of
Anglo-American high society; good looks, she must have been
in her mid-thirties; and though the accent had almost disappeared, she retained a characteristic transatlantic female insistence—putting even Nell in the shade—on getting her fair
share of any conversation. That is, over her fair share. She
was shallowly cultivated in the arts, and perhaps aware of it.
All her value-judgments were like a snip-snap of scissors; as
if, if she did not diminish all she saw, she might seem *passée*.
She had faintly porcine features, a delicate white pig. Every
so often the M.P. gave her veiled, somehow speculative looks,
like a man with a new pet. She was a common enough type,
of course; I knew Californian equivalents on the fringes of the
higher echelons of the movie world. Such people had always
seemed to me peculiarly un-American, far more in love with
the foibles and manias of caste than with the Republic. The
present lady did nothing to change my view; she had simply
emigrated to where she had the British caste system to play
with as well.

Her much older husband interested me a good deal more.
He still had a handsome mane of grizzled hair and enormous
bushy eyebrows over penetrating gray eyes; and he was very
obviously not short of *savoir vivre*. He gave a pleasant im-

pression of quizzing everyone he spoke to, being amused by them—and assessing them pretty shrewdly at the same time. Before dinner I saw him sit by Jane, and overheard something about Anthony; and watched him thaw out any hostility she may have felt toward him on other grounds—some story, and she threw back her head, genuinely amused.

I was sent off into a corner with him myself soon after that, and delivered a short alphabet of production company hazards. Fenwick was concerned not only as the father of the potential bride but as an old friend of the lordling's mother. The young man was very evidently hell-bent on entering the visual *demi-monde,* and the names of one or two well-known fashion photographers he went about with were held out as proof of his artistic bent—held out with a dry inquiry, as I imagine in court of Queen's Counsel might have pretended to support a dubious precedent in order to demolish it later. I suggested that stashed young aristocrats had been every conman's delight since time began; and received instant agreement. It was very soon clear that I was teaching, in spite of the deference shown to my opinions, a grandmother to suck eggs; Fenwick knew all about the folly of production without distribution guarantees, and the rest. The only slight mystery to me was that with all his knowledge of the world he had not guessed that this latterday Marmaduke was very probably laying every starlet and model he could put his hands on— and that the daughter would be eventually happier in a nunnery. But that was hardly in my brief. I already sensed a blind spot in Fenwick's intelligence; or perhaps it was just a profound cynicism.

The dinner went agreeably. Fenwick was a good raconteur, even against himself; and he had a tiny touch of that rare quality, demon—a gift for being a shade sharper, more contradictory, more outrageous than normal convention permits. It was based on a supreme self-confidence, on the certainties of a man who had lived and mixed a lot, but it was lightly, self-mockingly, worn. I heard him reproaching poor Caro a little for having forsaken the country for "the worst den of iniquity in the Great Wen" ("The great *what?*"); but with the gentle astringency of an old hand at amusing young women. All reference to politics was fastidiously avoided; the Fenwicks must have been warned to keep off the subject . . . or perhaps already knew. Jane had met them before at Compton, it seemed.

I received my due ration of that inevitable lionizing every professional in the film business comes to dread—the endless naïve questions about the technicalities, the pricked ears and fatuous smiles when yet another star's name is dropped, like a swine before pearls—but even that was more intelligently done than usual. The conversation moved on to my present job, the Kitchener script. I talked a little about him, though in that company I played down the folly-of-imperialism line and concentrated more on the psychological enigma. Fenwick had listened to this in silence, but now he smiled across at me.

"I met him once. Shook hands. I was seven years old."

"Good Lord—where was this?"

"At Taplow—the Desboroughs'? Just before the war, in 1914. He had the most extraordinary eyes. Very pale blue, and a terrifying squint. They toned it down in the famous poster. Enormously tall. Like meeting a skyscraper."

"Did he say anything to you?"

Fenwick cast me as his seven-year-old self; gave me a severe look under the shaggy eyebrows. " 'Always look people in the eyes, my boy.' I must have been staring at his boots. You know Osbert Sitwell's description of him?"

"The godlike thing?"

"I can vouch for that. Tremendous physical presence. Like a magnet, one couldn't look at anyone else."

"You still have an admiration for him?"

"As a magnificent beast. As a general . . . I remember once hearing an *obiter dictum* from Winston on the subject." He put on a creditable Churchillian voice. " 'The hero of Omdurman would rather have kissed his Satanic Majesty's arse than contemplated the smallest strategic decision.' " We laughed, and Fenwick pinched his nose, then countermanded too much humor with a raised finger. "Mind you, I can also remember the shock of his death in 1916. Of course no one knew the mess of it he'd been making behind the scenes. I was at prep school. We were solemnly hauled out of class, all the staff, even the maidservants, I can recall one of them bursting into tears . . . the headmaster . . . the dreadful news, as if nothing now stood between us and the Prussian hordes." I made a quick mental note of that, it might be a way of doing a scene. Fenwick leaned back, a hand reached out to the base of his glass of Burgundy. He move it an inch; a judicial adjustment, but in something more than the glass's position. He smiled up at me. "I wonder if we're capable of judging men like Kitchener anymore. His faults weren't really the essence of it, you know. Like dear old Montgomery. I suspect it's because he wasn't credible as a person, even as a general, that he did become so credible as a national symbol. A badge. The whole nation wore him for those first two years of the war." He raised the bushy eyebrows, and warned me. "And you may find someone who can act him. But you'll never find that presence . . . that emblematic quality."

"We are very aware of the problem. We're toying with the idea of Max von Sydow—the Swedish actor? We'd have to dub his voice, of course."

We wandered off to acting and casting; Churchill, where Fenwick felt interpretations based on him had failed; and then to other things.

Finally Nell was on her feet. The gentlemen were to be left, it seemed, though she tried to lessen the ridiculousness of this old ritual by pointing down the table at Andrew.

"Twenty minutes. Or I shall come and pull you out by the scruffs of your necks."

"Yes, marm."

Paul went with the women, and I was left with Andrew, Fenwick, and a decanter of port; and at last, politics. The subject had been banned for Jane's sake, not mine. Andrew had moved from his end of the table and taken a chair beside Fenwick, making him the tacit focus. But I had his lazily probing look; and the sense of a question that might have been asked earlier.

"You still a socialist, Dan?"

"I think I need prior notice of that."

Fenwick said, "I should think so too."

But Andrew persisted.

"By vote." I smiled across at Fenwick. "Hardly out of faith in all its elected members."

"My dear fellow, we all have that problem. Or rather, the country has it."

"The credibility gap?"

His sceptical gray eyes examined me.

"I think electoral blindness is a more accurate phrase."

"In what way?"

Again Fenwick had two fingers splayed across the base of his balloon-glass of brandy—he had refused the port—revolving it a little. He looked up at me. "People like you? Highly intelligent chaps with their heads in the sand?" It was said half-jocularly, and not at all as a challenge—even faintly as if he were disinclined to broach the subject.

"I'd like to know what I'm blind to."

"Mobocracy?"

"Strong word."

"All the signs are there. Contempt for us poor boobies who have to represent you, for democratic process, for law—for anything that gets in the way of having one's cake and eating it." He folded his arms, leaned back a little. "In my view it's not even a party matter anymore. The only difference is that my lot—some of us—say that the situation is suicidally dangerous. And your side pretend it isn't—have to, to keep their masters quiet. But they know."

"The unions?"

"They too have their masters."

"Under the bed?"

That amused him. "Very much in it, I should have thought."

"But any remedy must seem like witch-hunting?"

He glanced with a hint of regret at Andrew beside him, as if he wished he hadn't plunged us into the topic; then gave me a rather more serious look, as if my presumption was involved as well—but he would give me the benefit of the doubt for the time being.

"I'm speaking very much off the record, among friends, after an excellent dinner." He paused a moment. "I see it like this. I don't believe in delaying inevitable confrontations. You two are too young, but I watched the ostrich game being played all through the Thirties—by my own party, among others. My generation paid the bill for all that. Hoping for the best." He eyed me with a sort of sardonic benevolence. "If you don't believe in parliamentary democracy and social order and a modicum of free enterprise, very well, you may sit back and enjoy the spectacle of the country sliding into chaos and an eventual bloodbath. But if you do have some belief in those things, however circumscribed by a no doubt admirable concern for the less privileged—then I'm bound to suggest you're supporting the wrong party." He raised a quick hand. "Some good men, of course. Both on the Front Bench and behind. But they have less and less say. Once the cards are down, I give them as much chance as the moderates when Robespierre and his disciples set up shop."

"There's surely still some way to go before . . ."

"I think that theory will serve as an excellent epitaph on the tomb of the British. Here lies a nation who believed itself exempt from time."

"Are you saying the process can't be reversed? It's too late?"

"My dear man, the history of this century is one of increasing madness. If one stands for reason in public affairs, one can stay sane only by assuming that the game is fixed. I see very little hope indeed for reversing the process, as you put it. And most certainly not when people like yourself— and you are indisputably in the educated majority these days—are apparently content to stand by and watch the worst happen."

I took the decanter that Andrew pushed to me. "You don't see a curtailment of free enterprise as the inevitable price of a fairer society?"

"Ah. Then perhaps you can tell me what is fair about a society in which there will be no freedom at all?"

"But that's like saying a nuclear holocaust is inevitable. It's possible, it may even be probable—but present reality is surely choices?"

I realized I was getting the same sort of look as his wife earlier during the dinner.

"Very well. Let that be conceded. Nineteen eighty-four may never come. But my guess is that in twenty years' time, it may well be less, this will no longer be a free society. Your party will have been blown aside like thistledown. Mine won't even exist. If Parliament survives in some form, it will be only as a rubber stamp. All the power will be in other hands. You may if you wish regard me as a nervous old passenger who has the presumption to warn the captain and crew that their seamanship does not satisfy him. But I see no purpose in doing that after the *Titanic* has struck. And if you think our present ship of state is being properly navigated and conducted . . . well."

He gave a little shrug. His voice, though still light, had grown obscurely sarcastic, as if this Tony Lumpkin and the film-world fellow had to be taught the realities of life.

Andrew said, "I wonder if the dear old proles really have that sort of energy."

"With respect, Andrew, that is supremely irrelevant. Their future masters *have* got the energy. It's the apathy among those who ought to know better that I find so distressing. In both parties, alas," He gave me a dry smile. "I'm certainly not attaching all blame to you."

"Nor to some much-needed social progress, I hope."

Now I was being impertinent. "I accept virtually all that has been done by both parties since the war to better the lot of the underprivileged. The sick, the needy . . . of course." He tapped the table. "What I won't accept is the leveling down—the treating of all talent, energy, self-sacrifice, hard work, as a crime. I will not accept that a universal norm of impoverished mediocrity is conducive to social health. Why should you be paid the same fees as a writer ten times your inferior? Why should Andrew here be denied a fair reward for all the improvements he has made on his estate? What you socialists seem incapable of realizing is that dragging everyone down to the same level is not only a chimera—a genetic impossibility, quite apart from anything else—but counter-productive. It doesn't help the bottom half of society. Absolute justice will always be a myth, because life is fundamentally unfair. But it is unfair for a purpose." I tried to speak, but the hand was raised again. "Forgive me. But put all politics on one side. No form of life can survive on the basis of enforced equality. That is a biological fact. The whole of evolution depends on the freedom of the individual to develop in his own way. All history, human and natural, demonstrates that—again and again."

"China?"

He looked at me as if he were a judge examining, over the glasses he did not actually wear, some outrageous proposition from an inept young counsel.

"China remains to be seen, my friend. What I say is certainly true of the West. Of Europe and America."

"But I don't see, if at least half Britain thinks more equality is desirable, how it can be stopped from having its way— except by force, of course."

Now I had made a *faux pas,* and the demon showed a little flash of malicious delight, hidden under a pretended ruefulness, at the error.

"I must disclaim the least desire to be a colonel *à la grecque.*"

"I didn't mean to suggest that."

But I had, and he knew it. He declined more brandy. "This country's last chance of waking out of its coma is very rapidly disappearing. That is all."

"Is this a general feeling at Westminster?"

He gave a puff at such simplemindedness.

"There's only one general feeling at Westminster. That independence must be stamped out at all costs. The new Holy Trinity is constituted by the three Chief Whips. That's why this whole issue, which in a sane country would dominate election debate, is very carefully pushed into the background. The policy-makers in all three parties are in complete agreement on that. Heaven forbid that we should ask the electorate to stop and think about anything central in their lives. Beyond money, of course."

There was a silence, then he gave me a more natural smile, as if I shouldn't take him too much at face value. "I can assure you my views are regarded as electoral poison by most of my colleagues." He glanced at Andrew. "Including our mutual friend, I'm afraid."

Andrew murmured, "Rather an ambitious fellow, that."

"So I understand. Well. Good luck to him."

"And you really think it will end in a bloodbath?"

"I think the notion that we shall all obediently queue up for a place in the Marxist paradise is based on a fallacy about the British. Of course we're very good at enjoying deprivation when faced with a Hitler—an external threat. My own guess is that we shall lose our sangfroid when it is imposed from inside. It will suddenly dawn on countless people, and by no means just on middle-class liberals like yourself, that they've been flagrantly led up the garden path. I have no doubt they will be extremely frustrated and very angry. And at the same time they will by then be faced with a very considerable apparatus of state repression of dissidence. I rather doubt if the ethos of the cricket-field will see us through that."

The door opened from the drawing-room, and Caro was standing there with a smile on her face. She held up a hunting-crop.

"I am commanded to show this."

Fenwick threw up his hands in mock dismay. "My dear, you make the most charming whipper-in. Especially as your father was just about to defeat me on all counts."

I left the room with a feeling of absurdity—of an almost calculated nonsense. The port, the brandy, the eighteenth-century room in the candlelight around us—generations of squires must have held forth like that, worlds going to pot

. . . with less reason, yet surely with more conviction than Fenwick. He had been so patently playing games, outlining his case with no more apparent personal involvement than if it had been some brief he had taken on in the course of his other profession and was explaining to two juniors. I found it vaguely humiliating. There was some echo of the old rotten-borough days, that he should be allowed, however peripherally, to decide our communal fate; and not because of his political and black-millenary beliefs, but because of his seeming indifference to their real import. It was very much as if they amused him far more than they alarmed him.

In some profound way, behind all his reasons and his experience, he was no more than an egotist—he had what I had always detected, and loathed, in Conservative philosophy, at least on the ground, embodied in its individual adherents; the belief that the fortunate must at all costs be allowed to retain their good fortune. It remained, despite the talk of meritocracy, of the pseudo-biological plea Fenwick himself had advanced, despite all the leftward shifts in his party since 1945; always this fanatical rear-guard determination, like that of a dog being dragged toward a kennel, not to give a selfish inch out of the status quo. Perhaps, like all politicians, he had been not very seriously trying to pick up a vote; or did it out of devilment, to kill a boredom. But I should have liked him better—and perhaps listened harder—if I had detected the faintest tinge of real despair or bitterness in his voice. At least Andrew had turned this surviving a huge historical and social change into a matter of personal challenge . . . still a game perhaps, but where the stakes were very real.

In Fenwick I sensed a far worse apathy than the one he had accused me of—if I was indifferent to the outcome of the "war," he no longer cared that he had lost it; and I could only assume that that was because he knew he would not personally have to pay its indemnities. He had had his rich and enjoyable private and professional life, and nothing could take that away now. The cynicism I had suspected as regarded his daughter—that he was sacrificing paternal common sense to a title—merely reflected this. He was closed off, and self-content; and it seemed to me that his kind of intelligent Tory, with so handsomely more than enough intellectual equipment and experience to see that there was more to conservatism than a rabid selfishness, and yet who demonstrated it more profoundly than the most blinkered and stupid ordinary member of his party, was doubly repulsive. At heart he simply believed in what he was; and the system was secondary.

I didn't of course analyze my dislike of him in such detail at the time. But I didn't forget that evening, not least because, although I remained enough of a liberal to despise his pessimism, I knew there must seem, to someone like Jane, a psychological similarity between us; a shared malice of defeat . . . for all that I hid mine better. At least I came out of the room and the argument with a need to declare a dissociation. I knew it as soon as we were back with the women. I had collected my coffee and took it across to where Jane was sitting—just far enough away to be out of earshot of the others if we spoke in low voices.

"Have you settled the future of the world?"

"Civilized life in this country has twenty years left at most. You'll be delighted to hear."

"Encouraging news."

"From the horse's mouth."

"I wish I'd been there."

"I'll give you the full details tomorrow." I gave her a look. "Then you can tell me where I join as well. And speed the day."

She was smiling. "I'm glad it wasn't all in vain."

"I wouldn't mind if he was just a plain old-fashioned reactionary. But he's Pontius Pilate into the bargain."

"Anthony rather liked him. He had a thing about barristers. Professional jealousy, I suppose. The way they're prepared to argue for anything. At a price."

"Is that a gentle hint that people in glass houses . . . ?"

She gave me a quick look, half-amused, half-concerned.

"No."

"I'm not doing a glamour job on Kitchener."

She stared across at the others, who were looking at a painting by the coffee-table; her voice dropped a little.

"Please don't turn me into a prig, Dan. I feel quite enough of a social leper as it is."

"You shouldn't have such powers of intuition."

"A belief in which is a prime symptom of male chauvinism. Or so Roz tells me."

"I've had that from Jenny McNeil. I remain unconverted."

"Shame on you." But then, as if to kill this polite fencing, she glanced round to the far end of the room, where Paul and Penny were leaning over a table playing some game. "Paul has a favor to ask."

"What's that?"

"His term project's on ancient field-systems. There's some famous complex of the things in Dorset."

"Go that way tomorrow? Fine."

"If it isn't . . . he has worked it all out on the map. If you could bear leaving a little earlier than we planned."

"Let's. It's prettier by that route, in any case."

"He's so absurd. Apparently we passed right by some other place he wanted to look at on our way here yesterday."

"Shall I go and talk to him?"

"That would be kind."

Penny and he were doing a huge jigsaw. Paul was embarrassed still, but there was an effort to sound grateful that the trip was on. He went away to find a map—and a sheet of paper on which he had worked out an itinerary, with mileages carefully noted. He showed me some paperback on the subject, with an air-photograph of the site. It was "very important," he told me, with an odd mixture of aggressive defiance, professorial authority and doubt whether I would be in the least interested. I saw some ox-plough ridges in the illustration, and told him one of the Thorncombe pastures still showed them; and for the first time I existed in his eyes. How wide were they, were they straight or curved . . . and when I told him there was an early nineteenth-century deep-map of the farm knocking about somewhere, when it was much larger, and with all the old hedgelines marked, I had clearly begun to make a conquest; or at least found the key to the "little monomaniac" Jane had spoken of. I was saved from too long a lecture by Nell and Jane herself, who came to pack the two children off to bed. There was a discussion about the changed plans. Then the two kids trooped off to say their goodbyes and disappear.

The Fenwicks left soon after eleven, and we talked about them. Andrew seemed to think he had been "putting it on" for my benefit; and revealed that there was little love lost between Fenwick and their own much younger local M.P. Nell thought he considered himself a failure, fatally split between his two careers, too close to too many who had become judges or got cabinet posts not to be secretly soured. We didn't discuss his end-of-the-world prognosis for Britian.

Then Caro stood and said she must go to bed, she felt so

tired, although I suspect "so tactful" would have been more accurate. The four of us sat on around the fire into the small hours, discussing her, and Barney, then Paul's problems and "moods." It was all done very equably and reasonably, and even much more frankly, as regarded Caro and between Nell and myself, than ever in the past. The always inherent animosities seemed genuinely allayed, we managed to talk about her as another human being, not a potential tug-of-war rope; and we even agreed on a joint policy of not countenancing any closer contact with Barney ourselves. Jane's shrewdness and Andrew's common sense helped, of course.

There came a silence. Nell was sitting on a stool, her back against a settee in which Andrew lay sprawled and already very nearly asleep. Jane had kicked off her shoes and was curled up in an armchair on the other side of the fireplace. Now she received a look from her sister.

"Well. That just leaves one last family problem."

"No thanks."

"Jane, as we're all being so terribly sensible and understanding, I don't see why you shouldn't make a contribution." Jane contemplated her, then smiled and shook her head. "I know we're very square and quite delicious to provoke and . . . come on."

"Come on where?"

"Own up."

"To having a mind of my own?"

"That you aren't sure."

"All I'm sure of at the moment is that I don't want to talk about it."

"We worry about you. All the time." She nudged Andrew's leg. "Don't we, Andrew?"

His eyes opened, but he spoke to the ceiling.

"Constant topic of conversation."

"I'm flattered. But unmoved."

"I promise not to argue." Jane drew a breath, and half flicked a glance toward where I was sitting. She was wearing an evening shirt and a long skirt, both rather severe, very muted patterns and colors compared to those the other women had worn. "And you've told Dan. So don't pretend it's all a great secret."

"It's because I'm not pretending that I don't want to talk about it, Nell."

"You've decided?"

"Not yet."

Nell stared at her a moment, as if she were not her fool, then invoked my help.

"Dan, don't you think she's mad?"

"I think if she must, she must."

"You sound just like Andrew." She gave Jane another resentful look. "It's so ridiculous. You've got more brains than all the rest of us put together."

"Perhaps I have. On this."

"You don't even dress like a lady Marxist." Jane smiled. "Let alone speak like one."

"I find that rather cumbersome to travel with."

"Because you see through it."

"Some of it."

"Then why?"

"Because a clumsily expressed truth remains a truth?"

"You might at least think of your poor children before you become the laughing-stock of Oxford."

"I think a great deal about children. And the world they'll have to live in."

"The dear old salt-mines?"

Jane smiled again, and held her tongue. I watched her stare into the embers of the fire; and felt a certain sympathy for Nell's exasperation with this withdrawal into the gnomic and sibylline. I received some of the accusation in her eyes.

"You can't agree with her."

"I understand the feeling. If not quite Jane's answer to it."

"Well so do we. No one expects society to go backwards."

Still Jane smiled faintly and stared into the fire; not to be tempted. Andrew gave a little snort in his sleep.

Nell said to her, "All right. But just as long as you know I think you're the most horrid slippery eel that ever was."

The petulance of her voice, the spoiled-child resentment that didn't quite manage to hide an affection, took me back very sharply to our earlier days together—to when Nell had often played this role in our arguments . . . the youngest of four, the indulged in part, the conscious clown. Yet paradoxically, behind this superficial semblance, their real relationship had changed. Emotionally and psychologically Jane was somehow now the younger sister; the greener, the less certain. And almost as if to hide it, she suddenly put her feet to the ground, moved across and knelt beside Nell, bent and kissed her cheek briefly, then stood again.

"It was a lovely evening. I'm going to bed."

Nell gave her a dark look up.

"That won't get you anywhere."

But she stood herself with a kind of chiding forgiveness, and pressed Jane's hand a moment before she turned to Andrew and shook him till he woke from his slumbers. A brief look passed between Jane and myself: a diffident little grimace on her side, as if she was embarrassed to have me the spectator of such behavior; and especially hated whatever sympathy she detected in me toward it.

# Tsankawi

When I went to New Mexico, just after Miriam and Marjory walked out on me, I had plenty of free time. My director was busy with the Western he was shooting, and our script discussions had to be in the evening. The unit was based on Santa Fe—for once they were giving the butte landscapes a miss and shooting mainly in those last southern outriders of the Rockies that stretch down over the desert into the state. It was my first visit, and like many people before me—most famously D. H. Lawrence, of course—I fell for the area almost on sight.

Along with San Francisco and New Orleans, Santa Fe is one of the most humane of all American cities; by some miracle it has so far managed to ban the skyscraper, and the literal low profile there extends to other things. I think it was Lewis Mumford who pointed out that most American downtown architecture is an attempt to create distance between people—to crush ordinary humanity and all its proper scales out of sight. Perhaps because it has opted out of the high-rise rat-race, and has attracted a huge art-and-crafts colony, Santa Fe is noticeably relaxed; provincial, perhaps, but proud of it. The Spanish Colonial adobe buildings with their pretty patios, the sweet-pungent incense of the *piñón* logs that pervades every New Mexican dusk, the marvelous light and air of the high desert, the cottonwoods, the old colonnaded shops around the sleepy central plaza, the cathedral bells chiming through the night . . . it's not at all the America of the European myth, and I liked it very much that first time, and have not changed my mind since.

But Santa Fe could have been a far less attractive town than it is without seriously damaging my regard for the surrounding landscapes. There are more spectacular ones in the United States, but none has quite the pure balance, the classical perfection and nobility, almost the Greekness, of the ranges that border the Rio Grande between Santa Fe and

Taos fifty miles to the north. Some skylines will not be forgotten; one from my childhood, of the southern edge of Dartmoor, is like that. It has always haunted my dreams; and the secret template of its contours still inhabits outwardly quite different vistas. The Rio Grande valley here is also one of the great Pueblo Indian centers; and though I wasn't much taken by their modern villages down in the valley reservations, I fell in love with the abandoned "medieval" mesa sites on the outliers of the Jemez mountains that face Santa Fe across the rift.

Their atmosphere is paradoxically very European—to be precise, Etruscan and Minoan . . . that is, they are haunted by loss and mystery, by a sense of some magical relationship, glimpsed both in the art and what little is known of their inhabitants' way of life, between man and nature. This must have been what so attracted Lawrence. Then they are magnificently placed, each village acropolis pedestaled on its cliffs of pink volcanic tufa over the endless green pine-forests and vast plains. Their horizons are ringed with mountains, whose basal conifers dissolve into the amber-gray of the higher aspen-woods, then the snow and the dustless azure of the sky. The views are infinite, of a kind most city-dwellers have forgotten exist; of another gentler and nobler, as yet unvitiated, planet. The nearest European equivalent I know is Phaestos in Crete.

I took Jenny there, very briefly. She had a two-day break and talked me into it, since I had already been rather dewy-eyed to her about my attachment. So we caught a jet out of Los Angeles to Albuquerque one evening and drove up to Santa Fe by night. It was all a little naughty, since only super-stars are allowed to put themselves, and shooting schedules, at risk like that; and fun. She had her first Mexican food, and liked the casual old *posada* I had booked us into; the bitter night air, the aroma of *piñón* smoke, the endless Indian-trader shops with their folk-pottery and rugs and jewelry, the playing truant.

I took her the next day to see Puye and the Frijoles Canyon in the Bandelier National Monument, under the hidden shadow of Los Alamos. At Puye she scrambled enthusiastically up and down the serried rows of cliff-dwellings, tried to coax the chipmunks, asked endless questions, wandered over the acropolis; was shown a towhee and a flicker and various other mesa birds; kept kissing me, like a schoolgirl, I was so kind to bring her to such a fantastic place, and so clever to know about it. All this went on again at Bandelier, which is a rather different site, secret—*la bonne vaux* turned museum—in a canyon bottom; asleep and wooded and inturned, and as remote from our stock picture of "Red Indians" as can be imagined . . . a timid planter culture not very far removed from the Garden of Eden. Their still-present plants, the yuccas and the cylindrical prickly pears, the medicine herbs and the dyeing weeds, seem to have a kind of numen, an equal status, all that the young Restif once felt on the other side of the world. It's almost a smile, said Jenny; look, we've lasted longer here than you moldy old human beings.

We drove east back down to Santa Fe in the splendid evening air, all roses and ochers and greens, with the tree-covered folds in the mountains behind the town lying like a gigantic crumpled velvet rug; a limpid and cloudless winter sky above, a light no camera has ever captured, or ever will, since its essence is in its depths, not its colors or vertical planes. We wandered round the old town again before dinner. I bought her a silver and turquoise bracelet in one of the tourist shops that stayed open late; we sipped margaritas, we had a meal, we made love; and it had been a flawless day.

All of which Jenny was to describe from her own point of view, since those two snatched days were the basis of her last "contribution," whose real arrival was to come later; whose writing I now recast (but as she granted I might, at the beginning); and whose drift was why, despite her third and still-to-be-inserted contribution, she would not "give me up." In Los Angeles, she was to write, we were always "in brackets"; and for a few hours, in New Mexico, our one escape, outside them.

What I have to describe, why I cannot use her version, is cruel, and she can't be blamed for it in any way. She wanted to do more shopping the next morning, we would drive out and see one more ancient Indian site, and then straight from there down to the highway to Albuquerque for our evening plane back to California. The site was a place called Tsankawi, archaeologically less famous than Puye and the one at Bandelier; but it was the one I had always liked best, my trump card, the quintessence of the whole region. I had returned to it several times on my first visit, and twice again since then.

I have never quite understood why some places exert this deep personal attraction, why at them one's past seems in some mysterious way to meet one's future, one was somehow always to be there as well as being there in reality. It is a feeling I had very strongly when I bought Thorncombe—that my real need for the place came from the depths of my unconscious, and only secondarily from the various conscious reasons I found. There were, with Thorncombe, quite conscious reasons of an emotional and nostalgic kind, so the analogy isn't quite true; but the more apparent absurdity of comparing a Devon farm and a place like Tsankawi is not quite so silly as it must seem. In some way, the mesa transcended all place and frontier; it had the haunting and mysterious personal familiarity I mentioned just now, but a simpler human familiarity as well, belonging not just to some obscure and forgotten Indian tribe, but to all similar moments of supreme harmony in human culture; to certain buildings, paintings, musics, passages of great poetry. It validated, that was it; it was enough to explain all the rest, the blindness of evolution, its appalling wastage, indifference, cruelty, futility. There was a sense in which it was a secret place, a literal retreat, an analogue of what had always obsessed my mind; but it also stood in triumphant opposition, and this was what finally, for me, distinguished Tsankawi from the other sites: in them there was a sadness, the vanished past, the cultural loss; but Tsankawi defeated time, all deaths. Its deserted silence was like a sustained high note, unconquerable.

On my last visit, some three years before, I had persuaded Abe and Mildred to come along; perhaps to see if the place could withstand the sort of reality they—or at least Abe—represented. I didn't forewarn them in any way that they were treading on slightly holy ground, and we climbed the half-mile or so from the road to the top of the mesa against a flood of lugubrious wisecracks from Abe, who is not a foot-oriented American. Was I sure the local St. Bernards carried a good brand of tequila, why did all Englishmen—it was rather cold—think they were Captain Scott, he loved Indians in movies, but could he please cancel the reservation . . . and then, when we were standing before a particularly dense honeycomb of cave-dwellings, he said, This must have been the garment district. He did finally, at the top, concede it was a great view; but still couldn't resist asking which lot it was I wanted them to buy. Mildred, astute soul that she is, saw I was less and less amused, and took me off: Abe was an agoraphobe, space and solitude like this secretly terrified him.

Then she told me about a wood near a house where she had spent childhood holidays in Florida, its belonging forever to its vanished Seminoles, how you never entered it without feeling you trespassed. She said, Like you broke some law. She felt the same here. A beautiful, beautiful place.

She meant it kindly, to set up a little Anglo-American conspiracy against Abe's "crassness"; but rather overdid it as we wandered back to the car, demanding to know why he was such a misery, why he couldn't leave the ghetto behind, how he had the nerve to call *her* a Puritan . . . and so on. It wasn't fair, historically or presently, he actually took a rather un-Jewish pride and interest in his rambling Bel-Air garden. When we got into the car he made a sudden move to get out again.

"Hold it. I think I left my scalp back on the trail."

All of which should have warned me that I could not expect other people to share my feelings; it was not only an English obsession, but a very personal one, and I compounded it by a childish failure to see that one can't expect even the most sensitive first visitors to have the reactions one has oneself acquired only by repeated knowledge. Because for me the place was a little bit beyond words, I foolishly demanded an immediate awed silence in everyone else.

Jenny and I arrived at Tsankawi just after noon. It was another peerless day, almost summer-warm out of the light wind. We parked beside a woolly forest of rabbit-brush, and at once there seemed a good augury: a loose flock of bluebirds, gorgeous in the sun, like passerine kingfishers, flying from pine to pine away from us. Again, I had not warned Jenny that she was about to undergo a test. We walked hand-in-hand up the first slope to where a huge rock platform, a kind of natural apron stage, jutted out from the first low cliff. It immediately pleased the actress in Jenny, she walked away to the end, struck a Sarah Siddons pose, grinned back at me. She was in blue that day, pale chinos and shirt, a pink headscarf, the freckles more conspicuous than usual; her most innocent self. We went on up a slope to the second brick-colored tier of cliffs, pitted and pocked with cave-dwellings; following the old Indian trail, where countless generations of bare and moccasined feet had worn a furrow, a foot or more deep in places, across the gentle bulges of the soft tufa . . . beautiful abstract sgraffito curves made by some patient giant; and all around, below us, the sea of pines, the broken valley plains, the distant snow-capped mountains.

We wandered along the foot of the upper cliffs and I showed her the petroglyphs beside each cave entrance, the Jungian mandalas and the trail sentinels, oddly majestic though kindergarten-simple men with one raised and forbidding arm, scratched in the rock; then farther on, a plumed serpent incised around the blackened wall of a shallow ceremonial cave. Then we collected some *piñón* cones and shook out the seeds and cracked the cases—the soft kernel is edible—and got our fingers coated in the aromatic resin; sat and smoked for a while in the lee of a great rock, her back against my shoulder, staring out over the landscape at our feet. It was very warm there out of the wind, and Jenny took off her coat; then a little later unbuttoned her shirt, and let it fall apart, aired her breasts in the sun. We sat in silence for a minute, my hand on her bare waist, almost asleep in the warmth.

"I wish I could take all my clothes off. And be had."

"Right here?"

"There's no one around."

"You had your ration last night."

She gave a nudge back against my shoulder. "All those caves."

"You must ask me to tell you about a spider called the brown recluse. To say nothing of scorpions, tarantulas, black widows, vampires, rattlesnakes, outraged Indian ghosts . . ."

"Fink."

"I shall treasure the idea.

"You're just lazy. No imagination."

I chucked her waist. "Too much."

She turned her head a moment against my shoulder. "Tomorrow. Horrid pretending again. Sitting here will be a thousand years away already. It won't seem real."

"One can come back to places."

"Not for the first time. It's never the same."

"And sex would alter that?"

She said nothing for a moment.

"Only knowing one would always be together would alter that."

Then she twisted her head up, kissed me quickly on the chin and sat away. She began buttoning up her shirt, stood to tuck it in, grinned down. "Now let's be happy sexless tourists again." And she reached out a hand to pull me up.

We drifted a farther few hundred yards along the foot of the cliffs, then found a place where we could scramble up to the top of the mesa. The central pueblo there has eroded away to little more than a circular wall of earth. It was probably founded in the twelfth century, but no one knows why—since there is no evidence that these were warlike cultures or at that time threatened by any—it was built so inconveniently high above the valley bottoms where the crops were grown. Its position puzzles anyone—especially an American anyone—who seeks a pragmatic explanation for everything; yet it seemed very clear to me that the departed Indians wanted, perhaps for some religious reason, to be poised between heaven and earth, in a perfect balance.

We sat on the highest mound of rubble, facing toward the Sangre de Cristo mountains thirty miles to the east: Taos Mountain and the Rockies north; and over the desert south the Watermelon near Albuquerque. One could see as far as the earth's curvature allowed. Much closer at hand, two miles away over another mesa, two ravens spiraled and called, their voices indistinguishable from those that I sometimes hear in Devon still; a bird; a voice, that always shifts me, thirty years in the tiniest fraction of a second, to boyhood. And Jenny beside me, her hands clasped around a raised knee, small tongues of wind in the licks and curls of hair that escaped from the headscarf.

"What are they?"

"Ravens."

"I thought ravens were just British."

"Holarctic. All over the Northern Hemisphere. Where they have space to survive."

She stared at them a moment, then gave me a sly look. "They're not saying 'Nevermore.' "

"He got it wrong. Evermore was the real message."

" 'Ghastly grim and ancient raven . . . Quoth the raven, Evermore.' " She bit her lips. "It's not as good."

"And blame everything but your own species."

She swiveled round to face me, rested her elbows on her knees, chin cupped in hands, staring at me, amused.

"I've trodden on someone's corn."

"The foot malady or the false sentiment?"

"Come on. What's wrong with Edgar Allen and me?"

"The only real nevermore in this world is sticking out of the forest behind you."

Tsankawi is on the fringe of the Los Alamos atomic-bomb laboratory area. We could just see the top of a huge silver hangar several miles away; occasional watch-towers over the wire fence that runs for hidden miles in the trees. Jenny glanced round, then back.

"I still think it's a lovely old ham poem."

"That's because you're a lovely young ham actress."

She eyed me. "I don't like that."

"A bird blind to ornithomancy."

"What does that mean?"

"Divination by flight and call. The Romans went in for it."

"Did they throw all disbelievers to the lions? Like you?"

She was still staring at me, no longer teasing.

"You did recognize that junco this morning. I have hopes yet."

"Why isn't it enough that I just love it here? That I don't want to know all the names and the frightfully scientific words."

"Because you shouldn't justify contempt from ignorance. In anything."

"But that's just what you're doing. Despising me because you don't know how I feel. That being here with you means more to me than just being here with the birds and the bees. And the ravens." She said, "I'm a people person. That doesn't mean I'm blind to everything else."

"Don't let's argue."

"I'm not arguing. Just complaining."

"Okay."

"You get so uptight when I have my own ways of seeing things." I didn't answer, and she added, "And use words like uptight." I smiled at her, and she held my eyes a moment, then turned and lay on an elbow. "Anyway, what's the point. My next man will probably be just as bored with the nature bit as everyone else."

"I thought we'd agreed not to play that game."

She said nothing. There was a heap of loose earth from a chipmunk burrow just in front of her. She picked out a shard, began idly brushing it clean. Then she held it for me to see.

"Isn't that extraordinary—there's a hole in one corner. Someone must have worn it as an ornament."

It was some two inches square, with a pattern of black lines and heavier zigzags on a pale gray background; and I could see the hole, carefully drilled by some squaw hundreds of years ago. Jenny held it against her blue shirt.

"Isn't it pretty?" She sat up on one arm, began sifting through the earth. "I wonder if there are any more." Two more shards came to light, but smaller, less conspicuously marked. Again she tried her perforated shard against her shirt. "If you had four or five like this, in a pendant, they'd be heavenly." Suddenly she put a hand up and tapped her forehead. "Dan, I've got a marvelous idea. That little jeweler's studio on Fairfax. They could mount them on silver wire. All my people at home I can't think what to buy for."

It was a subject that had already come up that morning in Santa Fe, as I had stood watching her sort through countless trays of rings and bracelets and beads, her taste in agonized conflict with her hatred—half ancestral and half from the fierce determination not to be a mere spendthrift film-star—of being fleeced. With one exception, a necklace for her mother, what she had wanted to buy out of liking she had refused to buy out of price.

"There speaks a true Scot."

"Boo. They'd be much more personal."

And she was on her feet, looking round, then saw more spoil a few yards away. I watched her kneel by it, begin scrabbling in the loose earth again, and almost at once she was showing me another large shard.

"Look, it's so pretty. Even nicer."

She was like a small girl, obsessed by finding the wretched shards. I sat there, as she wandered farther away, every so often kneeling. I saw her pull off her pink headscarf at one place, and then when she stood again, she held it by the corners, an improvised bag.

I am still not quite sure what combination of factors it was that made me feel offended. The double attempt on her part to raise the banned topic of our future and a corollary feeling that it had been less raised seriously than as a disguised taunt; the little show of independence on the matter of nature; the feeling that she did not sense this place's uniqueness, for her it was merely a variation on the others; a feeling of transience, unrecapturabilities, abysses, the worm in the rose; that it was against all probability that I would ever be here with her again—a feeling that was more often a pleasure, since impermanence adds a zest to experience no fixed marriage can ever achieve—but which now, in this vast Olympian landscape, seemed sour and bitter.

The two ravens' calls became more frequent and I saw them attacking a red-tailed hawk—the noise even distracted Jenny and she turned from forty yards away to point the cause out to me—that had encroached on their territory.

Though the Americans term the bird a hawk, it is in fact a mere racial variant of the English buzzard, indeed indistinguishable at a distance, just as the mobbing behavior was indistinguishable from similar scenes in any South Devon sky; which took me back to Thorncombe, my past there and my present, and the impossibility of weaving Jenny into any lasting future.

*I am a people person;* and I was so little one, in any deep way, that this must always—even if there were not so many other obstacles—stand between us. This minor coincidence, of seeing two species and a common behaviorism of the English countryside reproduced in a very foreign and remote one, somehow seemed to prove it; all my lasting relationships were with this world of quasi-arcane knowledge and experience . . . not merely of course in a natural-history sense, but because I was fundamentally an observer and storer of correspondences—like some iceberg, with nine tenths of what really pleased and moved me sunk well below the understanding of the people I moved among, and however intimately. I mustn't suggest I thought of all this with some sort of guilt or regret; it was much more with a wistful vanity, a perhaps rather smug knowledge that I was much more profoundly English than Jenny realized; because it was less the outward manifestations that gave the game away than this peculiarly structured imagination, so dependent on undisclosed memories, undisclosed real feelings.

We are above all the race that live in flashback, in the past and future; and by a long blindness I had got myself into the one artistic profession where this essence of Englishness, this psychological and emotional equivalent of the flashback (or flash-forward, flash-aside) lay completely across the natural grain of the medium—which was a constant flowing through nowness, was chained to the present image. Of course I had used flashbacks in scripts, and indeed was about to use them massively in the one on Kitchener, but I had never really liked them. It was part of the gospel I had imbibed (from Abe, among others) that they were intrusive, clumsy, a kind of bodge good carpenters strive, except in one or two rare cases like *Citizen Kane,* to avoid.

The tiny first seed of what this book is trying to be dropped into my mind that day: a longing for a medium that would tally better with the real structure of my racial being and mind . . . something dense, interweaving, treating time as horizontal, like a skyline; not cramped, linear and progressive. It was a longing accented by something I knew of the men who had once lived at Tsankawi; of their inability to think of time except in the present, of the past and future except in terms of the present-not-here, thereby creating a kind of equivalency of memories and feelings, a totality of consciousness that fragmented modern man has completely lost.

It was an idea, a flash-forward, that pronounced itself unattainable almost as soon as it arose and I can't recall now whether I even thought at that moment in terms of the novel. If my mind ran on anything practical, it was in terms of a return to the theater . . . partly Jenny, she retained a strong love of the legitimate stage, and nagged at my pessimism about it. But I felt a discontent at how vastly out of reach of my actual craft this actual moment, Tsankawi, Jenny, the ravens and the hawk, all the steeped resonances, were; so infinitely beyond camera and dialogue and dramatic art, as unreachable as all the landscapes beyond the limits of my eye. In that most pure and open of places, I felt like a man in prison.

I had to attach these feelings to some present object of discontent; and I decided, quite unfairly, that it was Jenny's shard-hunting. Never mind that the things lay in thousands all over the top of the mesa, it was in some way sacrilegious, almost as vulgar as Abe's inability to react to a strange environment except with wisecracks. She was using the place, and she should have sensed she had no more right to its artefacts than she would have had to those in a church or a museum . . . or someone else's house.

I am not now defending this obviously very strained analogy. I even told myself at the time that my irritation was absurd; and even if it had some faint justification (a notice down by the road did ask people not to remove any manmade object from the site) the proper response was to suggest gently to Jenny that some places had earned their unrifled peace. She would have understood, especially if she knew it meant something to me. But naturally—or unnaturally—being English I had no sooner given her a black mark than I determined to say nothing about it . . . that is, I used the incident to award myself a good one: not for pretending to condone her, of course, but for having once more concealed my own hiding-place in the trees.

And it was not really about Tsankawi at all. From Jenny I was secretly demanding an even more impossible reaction: to the fact that I was a lot more in love with her than with anyone else for many years. Never mind that I was quite sure that it would never work out, that it wasn't fair to her, that we were doing the right thing, that I had very carefully set a sort of subjunctive mood between us that could only view a lasting relationship, and any discussion about it, as in bad taste if not treated as a hypothetical game; I still wanted her to read what was hidden. She was quite right. When I asked her to marry me in the Mojave, it was done in a way to invite refusal; almost out of curiosity, to see how she would answer. I even approved the half-mocking, half-affectionate way she said no. But I suppose I was also looking, as all men do, for a sacrifice of her real self, or at least of all the parts of it that conflicted with the more concealed elements of my own.

The continuing temptation to cozen her, to explore the possibility of a marriage, to lie and suggest she could be a wife, have children, live with me *and* lead an acting career, was strong enough for me to deserve some credit for having resisted it. One of the perennial lunacies of the film world lies in the contract squabbling that goes on over just this matter of credit in the titles—who precedes who, how large the lettering, how long the footage; and my case that day was analogous. Jenny was not giving my renunciation enough billing; and looking back, I suspect the real offense in the shard-collecting was that she did not show enough respect to the lost civilization of me. I was the potsherds, and all they apparently meant to her was ornament, cheap gifts to sisters and friends.

She came back some twenty minutes later, with her pink scarf bulging, and squatted by me to show what she had found. She'd decided they would look even prettier framed in silver. I teased her about this abrupt departure from ca'canniness. Deception was easy, and she was absorbed in composing her pendants, laying out little rows of three and five, changing them, mulling over her hoard. But then we lost our solitude. A young couple appeared from below, and Jenny rather guiltily covered her finds with her scarf. They passed close by us, a wave and a hi. The young man had their child on his back, carried papoose-style; his rather severe-faced young wife ahead, in a long hippie skirt. They had a nice feeling of closeness, unpretentiousness, simplicity; of research students, perhaps, or from some intelligent commune. But they intruded, and not only on the place. I saw it in Jenny's eyes as well, as she watched them walk away. She did something rather strange then. She uncovered the shards and stared down at them.

"Dan, do you think I'm naughty? Should I leave them here?"

It was something to do with that young family, their being native Americans, their faint air of a brave poverty; not with me.

"I don't think they'll be missed."

"I so want something to remember these two days by."

She looked up into my eyes then, with a serious, almost childlike, candor she sometimes had in private. I smiled, since she did not.

"Then pack them up. If we're going to catch that plane . . ."

It was so sad, these sudden bad vibes between us, and not being able to say anything, or rather saying anything but what we ought to have been saying, knowing I'd lost Dan, but not why. Guessing why, trying to guess why. Then being frightened. Actually I felt angry, I wish I'd spoken. It's the most terrible feeling of all, suddenly realizing you don't know someone. I suspect men like it, or don't mind it, or don't notice it. But it destroys women, you've no idea. I thought it was that couple with their baby, but I didn't know. And *you* didn't know what those two days meant to me, because I was thinking all the time, that is what being married to him would be like, on our own, and I knew I'd never want to travel with anyone else, and the nature thing, honestly I was beginning to learn, at least not to want to fight you over it, at least to *begin* to understand what it was to you . . . you don't realize how close to you I'd felt all that second day—the first as well. That's why I wanted sex, but not just sex. That's why I laughed at your ravens. You understand so many outer things about women, but I sometimes think none of the inner ones at all. Or perhaps it's even worse, you know them and pretend you don't. You know I don't really know what I think, who I am, where I'm going. That girls like me do really, deep down, need protection societies.

When you withdraw like that, and just ban me.

I wanted to ask you to marry me. I can remember the exact moment, it was when we got back in the car, and you were looking at the map to find the road. No I didn't, I wanted to cry. I mean, we should have settled it there, one way or the other. We were both cowards. You've corrupted me terribly in some way, perhaps the way the English have always conned the Scots. Suggesting your way is somehow subtler, more sophisticated, works better in the end, and our silly Gaelic honesty is just provincial.

There. I've written nothing for five minutes, I've been crying, just out of spite. Hatred of you. Hatred that you aren't younger. That you're so far away. That I shan't be able to tell you this when we speak next over the phone.

You *knew*. You should have said *something*.

# Westward

We were on our way by half past ten, dispatched in a soup of good feeling and new resolution. The past was forgotten, we were civilized people now; they must all come and spend a night at Thorncombe, with Caro and myself doing the honors; and I was even, in a moment aside with Nell, commissioned ("it's because she won't talk about it with anyone") to try to knock some sense into Jane's recalcitrant head. A shade too much, this philadelphian mood, and partly due to the presence of the various children; and I might have been dry about it with Jane as soon as we left. But I had Paul beside me to do the map-reading, or to pretend to do it, and we were obliged to continue playing parts.

We set off into one of those clear-skied but misty, intensely still winter days—not too misty to make driving difficult, but dissolving every view into grayness a mile or two away; the sunlight was endlessly gauzed, the overhead sky only dimly blue. I enjoyed its Englishness: when half of what can be seen is always veiled, can only be imagined . . .

The whole day was to have Englishness, roots, at its center or at least softly looming at all its edges. Paul, after an initial shyness—he seemed to wake up every morning with that problem to conquer—proved vulnerable on his current hobby-horse; though at times he became a little incoherent, suddenly finding himself at brinks where his information abruptly ended, he had acquired an impressive knowledge—for a fifteen-year-old, and as far as my own very near total ignorance could tell—of medieval agriculture. He did tend to produce facts in a Would-you-believe-it kind of way, like the old Ripley strip-cartoon; but facts he possessed . . . about "closed" and "champaign" (hedged and unhedged) England, manorial systems, the ox-team, plough design and ploughing techniques, rigs and lands and lynchets. He had a folder with him, where it was all drawn. I kept having to snatch glances down as I drove; obviously a very neat, painstaking child, not a bad draftsman, and with a much maturer handwriting than his outward behavior would have led one to expect. I asked him why he had grown so interested in the subject; a mistake, I ought to have known it is not a question, however tactfully it is put, adults can ask without suggesting a concealed condescension. He hesitated a moment.

"Just I find kings and queens and all that stuff a drag."

"So did I. But we never had a choice."

I told him about the horrors of my own boarding-school then; and Jane joined in from behind . . . how lucky he was to be his age, we hinted, and at an enlightened place like Dartington. He showed a certain macabre interest in the canings and all the rest I had had to undergo in my own adolescence; and then with a certain puritanical perversity commented that a bit more discipline wouldn't hurt some of his friends at Dartington. I had a feeling that this was an oblique reproach of his parents for having sent him there; that he wasn't so "difficult" as they thought. But it may have been a disguised olive-branch to his mother. He reminded me a lot of Anthony: a certain deep stubbornness, which he hadn't yet learned to handle, and which certainly didn't seem redeemed, in however embryonic a form, by his father's sense of ironic humor—but which would probably make him a genuine scholar one day, and possibly a formidably arrogant one. I hadn't forgotten how he had smashed poor Penny's returns at the Ping-Pong table. He was rather pathetically in need of winning something.

Jane didn't say very much, just enough to coax him if he had forgotten something, or not explained well enough . . . a shade too much maternal anxiety there, and Paul sensed it; but this time made me his ally, not the scapegoat.

We turned off the A30 at Shaftesbury and went south to find Grimstone Down—without difficulty, Paul had done his home-work—and sat in the Volvo and ate the sandwiches Nell had insisted on giving us. Paul was so eager to start looking that he left us before we finished. We watched him a moment, book in hand, already searching for his Celtic fields.

"Thank you for being so patient, Dan."

"He really has got it up."

"I wish he could discover some other key. Between being a sulk and being a bore."

I was in the front, half-twisted toward Jane in the back, but I looked through the windscreen to where her son was standing, trying to orient himself.

"As long as he finds a girl with a sense of humor."

"Some hope."

"I don't know. He's not bad-looking."

"It's not that. His hatred of being laughed it." She added, "Roz thinks I fuss about him too much."

"Well . . . speaking from sad experience."

"I thought you never knew your mother."

"My substitute one. Her fussing prevented me from realizing how much I owed her. Until it was too late."

"That's still better than never at all."

I glanced back, amused. "I always used to envy you two. So cool and casual about being Foreign Office orphans."

"We had to be, to survive. All those nannies, screens of servants. Even when we were *en poste* with them. My father was just someone in evening dress who kissed us good night." She began gathering up the debris from our lunch. "I was sorting through some old photos the other day. There was one of him in all his ambassadorial finery. Quite impossible to shed a tear over . . . even of anger. Like a tailor's dummy." She said lightly, "I think I'd rather fuss."

"But it's not the only alternative?"

"I do try not to."

"I'm hardly one . . . with Caro on my conscience."

She left a little pause. "We had a talk on the way back, Dan. After we left you yesterday afternoon." I had her brown eyes for a moment, then she looked down. "I'm going to pay a more discreet role in future."

"With Caro's consent, I hope?"

"Yes, she . . . agreed."

"I've tried to follow your advice with her these last ten days."

"I felt very bad about that afterwards."

"Don't be silly. You've been right from the very beginning about her. That day at Wytham."

"I've forgotten."

"You said she might need me one day. But not then." I smiled back. "For which I hated you at the time."

"It sounds insufferable. I had forgotten."

"You were right."

"I had no right to say something like that."

For a moment, what had lain behind that day at Wytham was in the air, but unbreachable.

"It helped me get through those years. In retrospect."

"They hurt?"

"Not nearly as much as they should have. Just once intolerably. The first time I brought her down here."

"Yes, I do remember that. I heard Nell's side of it. It upset Caro as well."

"It was very strange. We suddenly realized who we were. It went both ways. Also as you predicted."

"The infallible Pythia of Wytham."

"Long forgiven. And repaid through Caro."

"I was so unbearably sure of myself then."

"We all were. In one way or another."

A hundred yards away, down the road, we saw Paul look back, with a vague reproach, toward us. I heard Jane shift.

"I think we're due for another lecture. If you could stand it."

We found Paul set back to discover that things at ground level were a lot more confusing than in an air-shot; but I suggested we walk on and eventually we came to a bend in the lane that we could see on his photograph, and we knew where we were. The deserted upland, brown earth covered in flints, Jane being dutifully interested, Paul holding forth again, a flock of lapwings wheeling over our heads, the soft green Dorset countryside to the south in the pale sunlight, my being treated as human by Paul—suddenly he sought interest and agreement from me rather than his mother, as if any man was better than *her*. I rewrote history. I had married Jane, he was our son, we had such outings all the time . . . at least I wondered how different we two adults might have been by then, if we had spent our lives together. I might have been a better writer, or at least a less transient playwright; and perhaps she would have gone on to the career that once beckoned—the stage. But I rather doubted whether I should have made her a better woman.

There was some clue in that reference to her well-to-do and largely foreign childhood, not that I hadn't heard the pros and cons of it discussed often enough in the old days. Jane, and perhaps Nell as well, had always been destined to search for the reality behind the tailor's dummy; and were probably thereby equally destined to unsatisfactory marriages of one kind or another. It must have been an unconscious factor in Jane's choice of Anthony. Their mother had always been something of an elegant cipher, far too used to status and money and the petrified hierarchies of the old embassy life ever to abandon their underlying principles. She had not been a fool, in fact rather a dry and amusing woman for her kind, but she was supremely egotistical at heart, a fact that her generosity as a grandmother in terms of presents and money had not concealed from either of her daughters. Nell was much more like her—something I had noted again during that weekend; but some streak of the same intense respect for self inhabited Jane as well. It didn't really matter that she must now despise her mother's kind of life, whose second-marriage American phase had not differed essentially, give or take a culture, from its first; she still inherited a certain determination to see everything in her own way.

But at least it was a function of looking-for; her son, like his father, was very evidently absorbed by looking-at . . . he had that same obsessive singularity of purpose, seeing nothing now, or seeming to see nothing, but his field-systems. Any distraction, our stopping a moment to look at the lapwings, another few moments when Jane and I tried to work out from the map what a hill across the valley with an earthwork on top of it was called, irritated him. One of Anthony's stances in our student days had been an only partly pretended contempt for poetry, indeed for fine writing of any kind. I remember one of his epigrams: *The metaphor is the curse of Western civilization.* It had been no good pointing out that all language, even the most logical and philosophical, is metaphorical in origin, it was the rhetorical use of metaphor that was evil . . . he even tried to condemn Shakespeare once for having written *Hamlet* instead of clinically forestalling Freud by three hundred years. He wasn't serious, of course, merely dazzling us with arguments for the impossible. But he had a much more genuine hatred, almost a fear, of what could not be collected, classed, precisely defined, noted down; I mentioned earlier his obsession with the *Dactylorchis* group of British wild orchids, which hybridize with bewildering frequency—I think the fluid frontiers between their species seriously upset him, and they were rather less a botanical challenge than a nagging flaw in his would-be highly ordered nature of things. Paul, consciously or unconsciously, was in his footsteps. Perhaps that was what Jane had really meant by "another key."

This very ancient earth, first turned before the Saxons came, its flints broken and rebroken and broken again by the ploughshare, by countless anonymous generations even more obscure than my Pueblo Indians in the Jemez, seemed to say this silently for me . . . it was a cold, austere, rather sad place. It would have done, as Jane pointed out, perfectly for a Tess turnip-hoeing or stone-picking. It was also rich with time, the mother of metaphors. Science was like the camera there: a prison.

We had finally, an hour later, almost to drag Paul away. He was quite evidently content to spend all day, and night, tracing the old ridges and whatnot over the fields. But I promised that I'd drive him over into Dorset again one day, perhaps in the summer, and give him more time to measure and explore. It would have been quicker to return to the A30, but I suggested we go by the southern route, via Dorchester, which Jane didn't know; and soon we were going past Hardy's statue, mournful and traffic-disapproving as ever, and climbing up into the coastal hills past Maiden Castle and across what is for me one of the frontiers of that mysterious entity, the West of England . . . the first glimpse of silvery Lyme Bay reaching down to Start Point and, on days clearer than this, of Dartmoor on the western horizon; the first smell of home, Paul's dull old champaign England at last left behind, the green and closed, dense with retreat, ahead.

We stopped and had a cup of tea in the last "foreign" town, Bridport; then were into Devon, the first deep red fields of marl, facing a pearly sunset, all lemons and greens, the sun sinking fire into vapor, the squat dusk silhouette of Exeter Cathedral on its hill. It was dark by the time we were going through Newton Abbot, the nearest town of my childhood, every street and corner known, and better known still every bend and hedge and barn on the road up out of it and away. Then Paul was in the headlights, undoing the gate from the lane for me; and up by the house the front door opened, they must have been listening for the sound of the car: old Ben and Phoebe waiting, as if they were the real hosts . . .

For nearly a year after I had bought the farm and the builders done their job, it was empty when I was away from it. The already derelict garden grew increasingly unkempt. During one absence the roof leaked over one of the bedrooms and brought half a ceiling down with it, a wretched mess. I had had one of the barns behind the house converted into living accommodation, I didn't quite know what for, perhaps as a studio, perhaps as a den for Caro and her schoolfriends . . . and somehow the place never got used. There was the strong feeling of a white elephant, of a silly auction bid come home to roost. Then I had a script, three months' work, and I decided to do it at Thorncombe; and face a few property-owning responsibilities at the same time.

Many of the older people in the village remembered me, though I rarely shopped or went there at all. I could hear the church bells occasionally, and that was enough. But one evening, soon after I was installed for my three months, I went to the village pub to buy some cigarettes. An old man there knew me. He had briefly helped look after the vicarage vegetables in the Thirties—and I suddenly, if dimly, remembered his face. He had disappeared in the war, someone else had done the digging. In fact Ben was the son of the bow-legged old man with the heart's-ease in his hat from my wartime harvest-field. Now he was in his sixties.

I bought him a pint of cider, and asked him, after the usual chat, if he still did a bit of gardening. He played Devon-canny, he wasn't up to heavy work anymore, he didn't know, he had a back, he'd have to ask the missus, maybe he'd cycle over one day. I did raise the question of money, but "bless you, it weren't that." It was, of course. It always is, in Devon—and when I pressed, he shook his head in disapproval at my folly. "T'aint like th' ol' days, rates's gone up something terrible"; which neatly skewered both my father's past parsimony and the present real deciding factor. But I think also he was deathly curious to see what this odd cup of foreign tea, "ol' Parson Mart'n's son," had done with the place.

He turned up the next afternoon, as promised, and clicked his tongue over the state of the garden, though he thought the house and barn were a proper neat job; accepted another glass of cider in the kitchen. I made the second gesture he had been waiting for, a marked contribution to the local inflationary spiral, and clinched it by insisting that he count bicycling time into wage-time. Old Ben knows a sucker when he sees one, both in a rosebush and on the tree of life. Thus I acquired a part-time gardener . . . and a rather sad village history. He and his wife Phoebe had no children, his two brothers and a sister had all left the village; and he had a drink problem. I learned later from Phoebe that he was also a rough character in his cups, she had twice left him in the past. My father must have known all this, and been playing practical Christian; or perhaps, as I did, he simply grew to like the man. He was a slow worker, but very thorough; in spite of his demon, palpably honest; and devoted to his wife.

I didn't meet her till a month later. His bicycle had a

puncture one day and I gave him and it a lift into the village in the car. She was gossiping with another old girl at the front gate of their tiny cottage as we pulled up, and insisted I come in for a cup of tea . . . a typically Devon-faced little woman, younger than him, still faintly girlish, squirrelishly inquisitive, in spite of the gray hair. I took to her at once, even to her innocent curiosity—"Ben says 'tis all so pretty what you done, Mr. Martin." I said it might be pretty, but it wasn't very clean, I wished (because I'd already tried to find one) all the village girls didn't go off to Newton Abbot for work nowadays. Nothing was said to that, except the usual comment on the decline of village mores, but the seed must have germinated, because a few days later Ben turned up with a proposition. They had a neighbor who drove into Newton every day for his job; and who would bring him and Phoebe over in the morning and pick them up when he came back. She had done maid's work once, she'd clean the old place up proper. She got bored at home. It really was a tiny half-cottage, like a doll's house.

I came to know the simplicities and subtleties of their two souls very rapidly; though she was outwardly philosophical about it, Phoebe's inability to have children had deeply scarred her somewhere. There was a kind of underlying metaphysical bitterness in her that balanced her general disposition to mother anything in sight. She was the boss, too, despite Ben's occasional violence—I very soon heard about all that as well, how he had broken her arm once, how they'd had to lie to the doctor, how he'd kill himself, dreadful old rotgut he would drink . . . and they were a mine of village gossip as well, and slowly linked me closer to the place. I'm sure everything about me equally got carried back there. I told them enough about my past since leaving the village and my present to satisfy their curiosity, and they met Caro. Phoebe took to cooking me a hot lunch when she came. Her kitchen notions were very simple, and she boiled every green vegetable to a mash, but I came to look forward to it. Rather rapidly she began to take charge of the domestic side of things; and the house was much, much cleaner. She was long-lapsed chapel, but her devil remained dirt. When I had to go away, we agreed she would continue coming once a week to give the place a dust, while Ben kept on as usual with the garden. I left the keys with them without fear.

This went on for two years more. Then one day when I was there again they came in great distress: their cottage had been condemned. They didn't own it, of course, and paid an absurdly low weekly rent for it, a few shillings; but the owner wasn't contesting the order . . . had even initiated it, according to Phoebe, to be rid of them. It wasn't even sure they could be rehoused in the village, a bureaucratic cruelty that infuriated me so much that I went into Newton Abbot the next day prepared to have someone's blood; but met my match in a clerk obviously used to handling people like me. It was not quite as bad as Ben and Phoebe thought; they couldn't have a council house because they were for families, but old people's homes were planned for the village, and they would have priority there. She even showed me a list, with their names newly penciled in.

So I took them on. They could have the converted barn rent-free, and we'd come to an agreement over the work they did. I made them go away and think about it for a day or two; and had the pleasure, when they diffidently said that if I was sure, then yes, of knowing that for once in their ill-starred lives something had turned out well. Phoebe once said to me, about their lack of children, "If us only knew what 'twas we done wrong, why the Lord had to punish us so." My father at least would have been pleased with the blow struck against the God of Methodism.

It wasn't quite a decision I'd never regretted. Their personal and functional failings I grew to live with: that is, Phoebe's cooking and Ben's drinking. He did now confine it, at least when I was about, to Saturday nights; and I got used to the clatter of upset pails, the bangs and dangs and bumps and buggers, as he negotiated the last stretch home. One such Saturday I'd gone to bed and heard through the open window his drunken singing, strangely solitary and forlorn, down the hill opposite the farm; he was almost poetical then. He always walked to the village for these weekly sprees, being rarely in a state on his return to manage even that primary mode of transport without difficulty; on at least one occasion (so Phoebe told me) he spent the night sprawled in some hedge in a drunken stupor, and didn't get home till dawn. Luckily it was summer. But he tamed the garden, began to grow lovely vegetables, and all the simple cottage flowers. Plants were the children he'd never had, and he doted on them.

Phoebe also came gradually to accept that garlic and origan and suchlike exotic fancies did not drop one dead at the first mouthful, and learned, except in occasional reversions, to cook vegetables and meat something short of total extinction. And she kept the house beautifully.

What bothered me much more was their continual presence and gratitude. I suppose it counted as a very soft billet for them, and they were frightened of losing it, of growing too old to cope; and I, as usual, was a little frightened of the responsibility they represented. But the most difficult thing to bear was their simple frame of values. It is all very well, in theory, from a city life, to laugh at village parochialism, the yokel assumption that the rest of the world thinks and behaves like us here; but that is also to laugh at a philosophy that has carried generations of land people through bitter and savagely exploited times. Any Freudian could nail Phoebe's obsession with polishing and the spick-and-span; but what was also entailed was a faith in certain elementary decencies of existence—in method, habit, routine, as a prerequisite of continuity. This is a wisdom that only people who have spent their lives in and surrounded by plant-growing and animal-tending can ever profoundly gain. They can't put it in words, but they feel it. I saw it in Ben. His praise for his own plants and flowers was always grudging, there was always something not quite right; yet sometimes I would spot him on his own staring at them or touching them. This wasn't some elementary form of false modesty; simply his bone knowledge that if everything grew perfectly, the world—and he—had nothing to live for. He had really grasped a very profound truth: that failure is the salt of life.

It was the more carnal condiment in my own that was the great problem: not simply to make them accept that I was sleeping with someone I wasn't married to, but that I had no intention of marrying; and also that it was a matter, or series of matters, to be kept secret from my most frequent visitor, Caro. I did eventually take the bull by the horns and explain to Phoebe that there were other masculine sins besides Ben's. If she was shocked—it would have been more at my frankness than at the actual fact—she hid it. It wasn't their business, they owed me so much, live and let live . . . I was showered with all the old adages of village tolerance, rather along the lines of Aunt Millie's eternal "Perhaps it's for the best."

But if that gave me license to live and love as I wanted, it didn't quite surmount all hurdles. I sensed a lingering, though completely hidden, disapproval. Perhaps Ben and Phoebe were shrewd enough to work out that they were better off with a succession of mistresses, in both senses of the word, than with a permanent wife with a domestic mind of her own. But I knew their profound belief was that I ought to settle down instead of "carrying on"; and I took a little to judging friends, and not only the ones I shared my bed with, by Phoebe's reaction . . . how much she would chat with them, how discreet or voluble she would be, how much put on her old maidservant self or show her real one. It was all rather absurd, perhaps; but people got a bad mark if they didn't get on with Phoebe and learn to walk the delicate tightrope between giving her a hand in the kitchen and taking possession of it. I was allowed to laugh at her faults—and more latterly, Caro—but other women had to learn to be diplomats.

I had once or twice rebelled under this gentle tyranny and contemplated easing them out of my life. But then there were all the times I was absent, and to think of them there was reassuring; the returns, the hearing their hoarded quanta of news, gossip, the pleasures of an intense small world after a diffuse great one, their Devon voices . . . and the ghosts of all the others in that house.

# Phillida

*O what a plague is love!*
*how shall I beare it?*
*She will unconstant prove,*
*I greatly feare it.*
*She so molests my minde*
*that my wit fayleth.*
*She wavers with the wind,*
*as the ship saileth.*
*Please her the best I may,*
*she looks another way.*
*Alacke and weladay!*
    Phillida flouts me.

In the vicarage days Thorncombe had been owned by a family called Reed. They were of that now nearly extinct class, the educated yeomanry. There weren't many like them in the parish; plenty of uneducated yeoman farmers with thick accents and thicker grammar, but the Reeds were different. Though they all had the accent of the South Hams, they articulated clearly, without most of the dialect words. There were six in the family—headed by a widowed grandfather, the senior churchwarden, "Old Mr. Reed," a great favorite of my father's, constantly cited as an example of a "natural gentleman." The patronizing cliché is foul, but he really was a splendid old fellow, with an innate dignity and courtesy . . . almost a grandeur. With him, you could believe about the backbone of England. Elsewhere you played polite to those who lacked a standard accent; in his patriarchal presence you wanted to be it naturally. He was never "Old Reed"; he had earned his Mr. I remember him best for his lesson-reading. He knew many of the great passages of the Bible by heart, and he would recite them in a slow, deep voice straight from memory, not looking down at the lectern, with a simple conviction I never heard in my father . . . or in many far more accomplished actors in later life, for that matter. He is excepted for eternity from all I have ever hated in the Church of England. He was like a folk-song, a folk-poem; Drake and Raleigh's voice. My father might preach and practice faith, but Old Mr. Reed was it.

He was too old to work Thorncombe by the time the war came, and that was done by his son, who was nondescript by comparison: a rather taciturn, softspoken man in his early fifties. He had a wife and three daughters, the youngest of whom was the Nancy I had once liked to watch covertly in Sunday School and who was so good at staring out. The elder two, the twins Mary and Louise, helped their parents run the farm as soon as the war started. They were regarded as odd by the village, always dressed more like men than women, except at church; eternally in breeches, jumpers and shirts, a pair of wiry, brown-faced agricultural Amazons, though they were slightly built. Their skill and toughness and general air of self-confidence intimidated me before I really knew them—I thought they were very unattractive, as girls.

The Reeds had a fine herd of Guernseys and made the best cream in the district; still brewed their own cider; poultry; the mother was a crack bee-keeper as well, my father wouldn't touch any other honey. Although the farm was at a far corner of the parish, and of course they didn't come into the category we could meet on equal social terms, we had quite a lot to do with them. There was church business—Mrs. Reed was also a leading light in the Mothers' Union—which meant that messages had often to be taken out there. Then during the war, food . . . my father shook his head at such scandalous defiance of the Holy Laws of Rationing, but there was a surreptitious trade in cream, butter, eggs, chickens, "fat rabbit" (illegally killed pork), all over the village. We did well from several quarters. There was an air of the tithe in kind about it, as Aunt Millie claimed. But our main supply line ran from Thorncombe.

I was in love with the place long before that. It was isolated, orcharded in a little valley of its own, backed up against a steep wooded hillside and facing south-west. A simple whitewashed house, with just one touch of distinction, a plain but massive stone porch with the date 1647 carved on it. I was attached to that porch and its simplicity even as a small boy; it, too, had faith. And the house inside as well, always with that characteristic Devon smell, rich and sweet, of old cowdung and hay and beeswax; and it was comfortable, immensely lived-in. There was some good china, solid old furniture, a lack of the cheap-bargain trash, the linoleum and oilcloth so prevalent in the average farmhouse of the area. At Thorncombe life wasn't centered around the kitchen, though it was used for ordinary meals. Perhaps it was the preponderance of women in the household. It always made me strange to myself, in those days. There was the class thing, the way Mrs. Reed always made a fuss of me, gave me tea, lemonade, a glass of cider when I was considered old enough; the vicar's son, the honored guest; and Daniel suddenly conscious that he didn't sound natural—or rather, that this was one place where it permanently worried him that he didn't. Then it had some mysterious warmth, some inner life, some grace that we lacked at the Vicarage, although ours was a bigger, more spacious home, with an infinitely finer garden. That must have been partly the girls, an unconscious dream of sisters, of a true mother, not poor Aunt Millie; partly the analogous aura of sexuality; and living close to animals, the earth, to the tangible, not the spiritual. I always looked forward to going out to Thorncombe. My father made me share my unskilled labor among as many different farmers as asked for it during the wartime harvests, which riled me secretly. I was for the Reeds first, and everyone else afterward.

And Nancy.

The agonies of Nancy.

I virtually forgot her for two years when I went to boarding-school. I knew she had gone on to the local grammar-school in Newton Abbot, was a day-girl there. I saw her on holiday, in church. She seemed rather gauche and fat and to have grown much shyer, to have mislaid her old tomboy self—it was difficult to get a glance now from her eyes, let alone a stare. I was no better. I had heard too much sex talk in the dormitory and taken most of it literally. Mine was not a particularly queer school, but queer undercurrents were rife and they disturbed me. I had to lie—and supposed I was the only one who had to—about my own sexual experience. Of course I had kissed girls, of course I had touched their tits, of course . . . the full distance one was excused, that was for later, but my real total inexperience was shameful. I found one or two other boys attractive, and I hated it; being blasphemous was one thing, but secretly perverted was another. I blamed home—not without some justice; the other boys all seemed to have sisters and sisters had girl-friends and dances and wizard parties . . . while all I got was the odd tennis afternoon with dull and stand-offish creatures who seemed far more interested in hockey and ponies and each other than in walks in the shrubbery. Not that even that was on, given the phalanx of adult chaperones who generally supervised such occasions. I was terribly scared of being laughed at, too, if I did make some timid advance . . . or if a fuss was made, and Father or Aunt Millie heard. School at least drove girls out of mind. We met none, saw none who were remotely attainable. There was work, and the feel of a shared repression and impossibility. But on holiday at home I was condemned to my own resources and Portnoy's complaint.

I was saved by the younger Mr. Reed. Just before I returned for the summer holidays that year, he strained his back lifting a gate to its hinges. He was ordered off all heavy work, an order he promptly ignored, like any decent working farmer the world over; and duly paid the consequences, a fortnight in bed, and at least four more in a chair. We had received too much kindness from the family over illegal food for my father to be able to refuse Mrs. Reed's suggestion that she needed my help that summer more than anyone else in the parish. I arrived home to find the matter cut and dried. I was hired out for thirty bob a five-and-a-half-day week, which was slave labor.

But the sixteen-year-old slave didn't care. Those previous Easter holidays he had met Nancy only once—and in the far from erotic setting of a Mothers' Union tea-party at the Vicarage; but it had been enough. He and she had been set to handing round the cups and saucers to the assembled logorrhoea of ladies. Her fair hair was done in something approximating the Betty Grable style, which he liked; and if she lacked the svelteness of a Deanna Durbin (his current ideal woman), the dark blue satin short-sleeved party dress she wore, puffed at the shoulders, flared skirt, showed that "rather fat" was unjust. A shade plump perhaps; but very clearly breasted and waisted; and he'd grown fast, he was an inch taller than her now. She was shy, probably for class reasons, and they hardly talked. He wondered if he dared ask her out into the garden, but so many witnesses . . . and he couldn't think of a good excuse. She had lavender-blue eyes, arched eyebrows, long lashes, a face that might have been too round-cheeked without the eyes, but somehow suited them as it was. She sat demurely by her mother after a while and he had had to be content with stealing glances. But that night . . .

He was head over heels in love with her after just one day's happy slavery at Thorncombe; awful, terrible, unable to look at her when she was beside him, unable to think of anything else when she wasn't; and the endless banal questions over supper at home. Yes, Old Mr. Reed had showed him how to scythe, he'd scythed half the orchard, all the nettles, it was terribly skilled really. The impossibility of telling them even that, the old man showing him how to set his hands, the rhythm, the slow-and-easy, not-too-much-lad, who labors longest labors best, the old man leaning on his walking-staff beneath the apple-branches, smiling and nodding. The art of whetting. How hard it all was, look at the blisters on his hands. They had brought a chair out for the old man to sit in and watch, by the bee-hives. He told that, but not of the girl who came with their ten o'clock bait, cake and tea, and gave him one smile. She wore a red scarf, she was covered in flecks of down, plucking chickens in the dairy; but those shy eyes, a subdued awareness of him, that one curve at the corner of the pressed lips. Then "dinner." Pasties and potato-cake (Mrs. Reed was half-Cornish). Then mucking the byre out with Louise, dung to the midden, spreading straw. Then this, then that, Aunt Millie smiling, his father approving.

To bed at nine, dead with sleep, just two minutes to recall the untellable worst, the end of the day. Collecting eggs, alone with *her*, holding the basket while she delved in the boxes, watching her profile, the stink of the hen-houses, the clucking, her soft voice to the hens, as if he wasn't there, but knew he was; less shy in that, if still not with her eyes. Suddenly feeling how small she was, how frail, how female. Sensing a sudden erection, using the basket to hide it, ducking more than he needed under the roof. Better outside, hunting down the hedge for the wild layers; the slanting sun, an angle of skin through her cotton blouse when she bent; then finally to the barn where an old Rhode Island Red called the Loony laid up in the straw, "if the bloomin' rats haven't got 'em." The hen runs in circles on the cobbled floor, in outrage and alarm. Nancy clambers down with two eggs, puts on a broader accent than her usual one.

"Oh, do 'ee be quiet, Loony!" And she bends forward, kissing at the agitated russet bird.

He says, "Nothing's loony that lives here."

She comes and takes the other side of the handle of the basket he is holding, as if to see how many eggs there finally are.

"It's just a farm. Working."

"Don't you like it?"

"Sometimes."

"Are you glad I've come to help?"

Her bent head. "Course we're glad."

"I meant you."

"If you're not stuck-up."

That shocks him. "Do you think I am?"

"Used to be. At Sunday School."

"I didn't mean to be." She says nothing. "I wanted to talk to you. At home. Last Easter."

She turns over a brown egg and rubs a speck of straw from its shell; then turns away into the wide barn door; gives him a quick shy look, and down.

"Do you remember Bill?" She gives a little nod backwards, to the north. "From out over. Bill Hannacott?"

He knows rather than remembers the Hannacotts; they are chapel, not church. They have a farm the other side of the main road.

"Not really . . . I know who you mean."

She crosses her arms, in a way her mother does, speaks to the ground.

"We're in the same class now."

What could be more delicately put? Yet at the time it seemed brutal, catastrophic, an atrocious let-down after the promise of that day. Imminent zenith to realized nadir, all in two seconds. He saw her with Bill Hannacott down and back every day in the bus to Newton; in class; giggling hand in hand. Stupid! As if Thorncombe were some secret island, non-existent without him, unknown to anyone but him. He felt his background again, intolerably; how it alienated from this simple world she lived in, how he was condemned always to do the rural equivalent of slumming. Perhaps it should have devalued her in his eyes, this fancy for some clodhopper from "out over"; but it didn't, it made her ten times more desirable.

"Got to count 'em up now," she said.

He followed her with the egg-basket to the dairy, where Mrs. Reed was—and insisted at once he go off, it was "after his time." He went for his coat in the orchard. But as he came back past the farm, Nancy ran from the side with a paper bag in her hands, up to him.

"Mum says to take to Miz Martin. 'Cos you worked so hard."

Six of the brown eggs lying on a handful of straw.

"Oh . . . thanks awfully."

"Now doan'ee drop 'em."

Again that mocking exaggeration of accent. He looks hurt.

And just for a moment she has a strange little doubtful look that somehow isn't about eggs; that is curious, and puzzled. Then she turns, waves her hand back to his "See you tomorrow?" as she runs to the dairy.

He sleeps on that look.

He doesn't get much else for . . . how long, I can't remember now, but it must have been two weeks or more, the beginning of harvest. He discovered that Nancy was the spoiled pet of the family, most of her work was helping her mother around the house, in the dairy, with the meals. Usually he was out with one or both of the twins. Mary was engaged to a young man from the other side of Totnes, exempted because of his farming; Louise was also "walking out." They were twenty-one, far too old for him, and in a way he found them easier to be with, though at first he felt they thought he was just a nuisance, they so often told him to do things and then moved to do it themselves at his slightest bewilderment or clumsiness. Neither of them talked much. They lived for the farm, for getting the work done, for proving that they could run quite as well as the sons their parents must originally have hoped for. It was the first time he had really done the countless jobs besides harvesting that a farm demands. He learned to use hook and hoe, how to hoy the cows in, how to wash and handle churns, how to muck out, feed the pigs, set gins for rats, there was a plague that summer; the killing hardness of some of it, the poetry of it too.

One late afternoon he went up on the tractor behind Louise with the hay-mower to cut the top ley clear of its nettles and thistles. He followed after her with a pitchfork, heaping the cut stems for later burning. But when it was done, she unhitched the mower and let him drive the tractor around the field, a waste of time and rationed fuel he knew delightedly was also an acceptance that he was useful after all, that he began to rate as one of the family. Louise had Nancy's blue eyes; a ruddy skin, a slow laconic smile. He liked her better than her twin sister, in spite of the identity of looks. He began to admire and like them both really; their asexual toughness and briskness and know-how was so much easier to cope with than Nancy's ambiguities.

But he liked best the milking. It embarrassed him, too. He had too much imagination, it was too near suckling and masturbation, too erotic. Yet like them, nice. They showed him how to do it, but he never really got the strange wristy knack of it, just the right pressure and timing. Mrs. Reed would be through three cows before he had finished one. The girls called her a show-off, muttered endlessly about the folly of not having installed machinery before the war and her continuing pigheadedness over it. She would smile and milk. No cow of hers would ever have rubber teat-holders instead of hands at its udders; and her dairy proved why. Daniel was usually put to lugging the pails to the churns and the separator, which gave him time to stand and watch the byre of female things at work; those smells and lights and shadows and murmuring voices among themselves and to the cows. The quick spurt of the first milk on the zinc. Like the woodlark.

There were times alone with Nancy; egg-collecting, once or twice she came to help him bring in the cows. They spent an hour one afternoon in the orchard, picking the first eating apples for Louise to drive into market the next morning, Daniel up the tree, Nancy below to take the full haversacks he handed down and transfer them to the boxes. One tipped over before she could reach up to grip it and she screamed and twisted aside and fell in the grass under the shower of Beauty of Bath. Astoundingly, they laughed. At ground-level they picked side by side and talked, shyly, politely about her school and his, the war. Her parents wanted her to be a school-teacher, but she didn't know. For the first time in his life he found himself talking almost like a socialist. How snobbish his school was, how he hated it really: she said nothing, but she seemed to understand. They did not talk about Bill, or other boys and girls, or love, or anything like that. He was still the vicar's son and she, the farmer's daughter.

His father came out sometimes on his rounds. Daniel hated that, to be reminded who he was, even if it brought flattery. He came back from one of the fields one day to find his father talking under the porch with Mrs. Reed and Nancy. "Now if only your school reports were as good as the encomium I've just had from Mrs. Reed, Daniel, I should be the happiest father in the country." Why did he have to use words like that? Nancy was biting her lips at me. And it wasn't fair. I always got rather good reports.

We all had the midday meal together in the kitchen, with Old Mr. Reed, Grandpa, at the head of the table. I think he liked me there, to have someone to reminisce to. He'd been a Regimental Sergeant-Major in the Devonshires in the First

World War, all his medals were under glass frame, on green velvet, in the living-room. I could see he bored the girls sometimes; or perhaps they were afraid he would bore me. But there was a great deal of love and tolerance in that room. It remains his room. I still eat in it, though it is no longer the kitchen; though none of the old furniture remains, something of the Reeds still does. Mrs. Reed always sat opposite the old man, in her husband's absence upstairs, at the other end of the long ash-wood table. Then the two twins side by side, and Nancy and I opposite them.

One day we were still at table drinking tea, there was always a pot of tea at the end of the meal, when my dreaded rival appeared in the door. I knew he was due to come, a huge beech had fallen in a gale the previous winter on the hill behind the farm, and branches had to be sawed into manageable lengths with the two-man crosscut before they could be dragged down to the circular saw in the yard. Bill had promised to come and help do it when he could get away from his father's farm. He was a big seventeen-year-old, I thought him terribly ungainly, a much coarser stock than the Reeds; not my idea at all of that already ignominious breed, the grammar-school boy. He bobbed to the old man, Mrs. Reed, the twins. "Hallo, Nancy." There was a brightness in his eyes as he looked at her. I was introduced, and had my hand wrung. He had a cup of tea before we started work. There was farm gossip, when they were going to "cut" out over, Mr. Reed upstairs. He said nothing directly to Nancy, just those little bright looks. He ignored me, too. I couldn't tell what she was thinking, whether she was proud of him or thought he was talking too much. I thought he was talking too much, and I bitterly envied him his ease, his knowingness, his being of their same earth.

An hour later I was doing much more than just envying him; I was hating every inch of his body. I had had the foolish idea it was going to be (at least in work terms) something of a jolly afternoon off. That was before he and I started sawing the branches off the main trunk, while the twins stood by with the tractor and chains to haul the cut balks down. Of course he was peasant-sly, Nancy was also there watching, he was bound by rural law quite apart from what he might have already sensed in the situation, to turn it into a contest of strength. He set the saw across the first bough, as if I must know as well as he did how to use it; which gave him the chance, after the first few to-and-fro's, laboriously to instruct me on how to stand and hold the thing. But once we got started he wouldn't stop. After a minute or two I could feel my arms ready to drop off with exhaustion and pain, and we weren't even halfway through. The return thrusts from my side got feebler and feebler. I had to stop.

"Too fast, is it, then?"

"Of course not. Just get my breath."

"Smoke?"

He thrust a packet of Woodbines at me.

"No thanks."

He lit one, then winked behind me to where Nancy was sitting; then spat on his palm and took the wretched saw-handle again. After a time he began sawing single-handed, and smoking, setting a much slower rhythm, but making it quite clear whose fault *that* was. He was so blatantly deter-mined to put me down that he gave me strength; and it mer-cifully wasn't all sawing, the stems had to be levered and rolled down to the cart-track where the tractor waited and chained up for dragging. He was strong as an ox, I had to give him that. For the first time I realized that the twins weren't. After a while, I began to take the sawing better, ex-hausting though it was; but he was relentless, perhaps there was a bit of the old chapel-church hatred in it as well, in showing me up as a weak-muscled tyro. Then right at the end of that afternoon of torment, I'd just rolled down one of the smaller branches by myself to the track . . . he was standing watching beside Nancy.

"Turn 'im arsy-varsy, Danny." He had kept calling me by the hated version of my name from about mid-afternoon, an-other gross crime. "I keep telling 'ee. 'E'll jag else."

Nancy turned sharply away. The tractor engine was run-ning, I couldn't hear what she said to him, but I saw him take a step after her and put his hand on her shoulder—and have that sharply removed too. It didn't mean much at the time, I just felt angrier: that she had had to pity me. He was still there when I went off home, and I knew he was asked to supper. Even the twins saw it had been a tough afternoon's work and thanked me specially for it. From Nancy I got hardly a look. She had disappeared when I said goodbye. I cycled home aching, humiliated and furious with the world.

The next day she had gone shopping with her mother to Torquay and I didn't see her at all. We were going to begin the harvest in three days, this was their last day off before that started. I even begrudged them that; gadding about while

I had to grease the reaper and file endlessly at the teeth of the mowing blades.

The weather held good, and we were up in the two big wheat-fields the following day scything the first swathe round the hedges for the reaper to get in. We took it in turns, the twins and I, tying up the sheaves by hand, then scything. Nancy brought our lunch up and helped for an hour with the binding, but it was very hot, and we hardly talked. Again she had disappeared when I looked into the dairy to say goodbye to Mrs. Reed.

The road home led steeply up for a while, through a natural cutting, thick with trees and the thornbushes that must have given the combe its name. It was always shady, rather secretive, gloomy. There were old limekilns to the left, cut into a small broken cliff. Above and beyond that was a common, dense with brambles and bracken at this time of year, where we sometimes used to picnic before the war. After the incline the lane levels out, another valley; then up and in half-a-mile, the village. I was too tired that day to cycle up the first hill. I was pushing up the steepest part, thinking of nothing, counting steps. Then something moved, where the old limekilns were hidden behind the August leaves. Nancy stood out in the little path that led down from them above the lane. She was wearing a pink-and-white frock, one I had seen before, schoolgirlish, sleeves that ended just above the elbow. It had a darn at the bottom she had done herself, badly. Mrs. Reed had joked about it one day, at midday dinner, and Nancy had naïvely raised the hem and I had seen above her knees for a moment. Now she looked at me, then down at the sycamore leaf she was shredding.

"What are you doing?"

"Nothing. Just a walk."

"Where you going?"

"Old quarry. Mebbe."

"I didn't know you could get that way."

"There's a path."

She went on shredding the leaf, as if she didn't care whether I went on or stayed talking.

"I didn't know."

"It's a secret."

She didn't smile, but she looked at me, and I knew it was a challenge, not an announcement. I turned my bicycle across the lane.

"Can I come with you?"

She shrugged. "If you want to."

"I'll just hide my bike."

She nodded, and I hastily pushed it into the undergrowth on the other side of the lane, then went back across and started to climb up to where she stood. She turned before I reached her and led the way up through the trees to where the rocks rose vertically for twenty feet from the earth; then along the face beside the rubble-choked mouths of the old kilns. She stopped where the cliff gave way and there was a steep scramble going up. She stood to one side and smoothed her dress.

"You go first."

So I went first. It was difficult at the top, one had to yank oneself up the last yard or two by holding a tree-root. I turned there and held out my hand. She took it and I pulled her up, wondering if I dared keep hold of it. But she moved away and led me on up through the more gently sloping trees. I caught a glimpse of the farm down below through the leaves, the sound of one of the sheepdogs barking, one of the twins' voices stilling it. There was no wind. The pink stripes and bands of small roses of her back, the fair hair. She wore old black shoes, school shoes, no socks. I knew I had entered the Garden of Eden.

"It's not my real secret place."

"Where's that?"

She pointed casually back, beyond the farm, as she walked. "Up over." Then, "When I was little."

I wanted to say more, to make her talk, but I couldn't think of anything that wasn't silly, and she walked quickly, keeping to the trees on the east slope of the valley crest, though I could see the common in the evening sunlight to our right. It was peculiar, not a stroll at all; more as if we were walking somewhere with a purpose. At last she turned up toward the common and soon we were pushing through the green bracken. She still led the way. Then suddenly we were on the brink of the old quarry, looking out across the valley to the distant village. It was nice, a surprise, the sudden openness and view. The rabbits running, the greensward they had won from the bracken. She pointed.

"There's the church."

I was not interested in the church.

She walked on a little, to where you could scramble over the lip of the quarry and climb down a grassy slope to its bottom. She began picking centaury and eyebright there, then knelt by a clump of the pink-headed starry flowers. Daniel sat beside her, then leaned on his elbow. He felt abominably gauche and tongue-tied, at a loss before her apparent composure; still sought for something to say, something that ...

"They're not much good, actually. They won't open indoors."

"My dad likes 'em."

"They're called centaury."

"Earthgirls." Her blue eyes met his a moment, then away. "That's what we say."

He didn't find that quaint (or inexact, she meant earthgalls); but embarrassing. His intellectual superiority, he was so anxious not to seem stuck up, he shouldn't have showed off about the real name ... umbrage hovered permanently, and as if to prove it, she stopped picking and sat back; then unlaced her shoes and kicked them off; curled her toes in the short grass.

He tried again. "I thought you didn't like me anymore."

"Who says I liked you in the first place?"

"After the other day."

"What other day was that, then?"

"You said something to him." He picked at the grass in front of him. Bloody girls, why were they so impossible? Why did they have bare feet? "When he was trying to boss me about."

"He shows off. Thinks he knows everything."

"Is that what you said to him?"

"Mebbe."

"He's more used to it than I am. That's all."

"All he's used to is having everything his own way."

"I thought you liked him."

She sniffed, said nothing; and kept staring at her feet, as if they interested her far more than he did. He felt out of his depth; first she said one thing, then another. She seemed waiting, as if someone else was going to join them there. Almost bored.

He said in a low voice, "I like you awfully."

Suddenly she smiled back at him, a little flash of mischief, of her old Sunday School self.

"I'll tell your father."

"Well I do." He felt his cheeks going red. She went back to her toes. "Don't you care at all that I like you?"

"Perhaps I do. Perhaps I don't."

"You never call me by my Christian name."

"Nor do you."

"Yes I did. Only yesterday."

"Not when we're alone."

"I never know what to say." He added, "In case you think I'm being stuck-up."

"It's just the way you talk sometimes." Then she said, "I know you can't help it."

There was a silence. The green evening air, the hum of insects on the still warm rock behind them. Without warning she turned on her stomach, her elbows bent, her chin propped; then she reached out a hand and picked off a tiny branch of thyme. Bit it. Then turned a little to face him. They were three feet apart. Those arched eyebrows, that enigmatic mischievous-simple mouth. Her eyes. They were the color of germander speedwell flowers: shy and bold, dared and doubted.

"I bet you don't really like me."

He looked down. "It's all I think about. Seeing you. Not seeing you. Like yesterday. I hated yesterday."

"We bought you a present."

"Why!"

She smiled at his almost offended shock. " 'Cos we all like you so much." She bit the sprig of thyme again. "It's a secret. You mustn't tell anyone I told you."

"Of course I won't."

"Cross your heart."

"Cross my heart."

She said, "It's a book." As if a book were some rare object, and its matter irrelevant. Now she rolled away on her back and stared up at the sky; then closed her eyes. He stared at her face, those cheeks, those closed lashes, those much more than childish breasts beneath the pink cotton, those bare feet. He plucked nervously at more grass.

"I'd write to you. When I have to go back to school. If you wanted me to."

"Je suis, tu es, il est. Amo, amas, amat."

Now she was being much too subtle for him. What on earth was that supposed to mean?

"Would you write back?"

"I might."

"I wish you would."

But she gave no further promise. She just lay there, her eyes closed, as if she had forgotten he was present. Perhaps she would let him kiss her now? But he wasn't sure, all this stepping forward, stepping back, noticing him, ignoring him. He felt irresistibly drawn to lean forward across the turf; and just as irresistibly tied down, like Gulliver, by the thousand strings of convention, his home, his ignorance, everything. And supposing she should laugh; she were just teasing him, leading him on to make a fool of himself . . .

Suddenly she sat up and reached for her shoes.

"I'm going home now."

She was offended. He was an idiot, *wet*, he had missed his chance, he had . . . he watched her lace her shoes, then gather up the little bunch of flowers she had picked and stand. He followed her up the slope to the lip of the quarry again, waited while she picked one or two late wild strawberries, then through the bracken and back into the wood. Without a word. He could have walked beside her, there was room, taken her hand at least or tried to take it, but he trailed behind. Then. No warning. She just stopped and turned, so abruptly that he almost bumped into her; put her hands and the flowers behind her back and simply stared at him, the old game of staring. Five seconds it lasted. Then she closed her eyes and raised her mouth to be kissed. He hesitated, he poised, he somehow found his hands gingerly on her upper arms; then the entire world, or sixteen years of it, melted.

Her lips tasted of thyme and caraway seeds, her body was his lost mother's, her giving forgave in a few seconds all he had thought he could never forgive. From gentle he suddenly grew rough, pulling her to him. He had a strange sensation: the stable wood around them abruptly changed into an explosion, a hurtling apart of each leaf, branch, bough, smell and sound that constituted it. It disappeared, in fact. There was only Nancy, Nancy, Nancy, Nancy; her mouth, her breasts, her arms round his back, clinging as well, until she pulled her head away suddenly and buried it against his shirt. How small she was, how much more understanding touch was than sight, how all faults of size, curve, visual appearance disappeared before touch and pressure. And victory! By several metaphorical decibels, the loudest cocklecockadoo of all his life.

They said each other's names, at last.

Then they kissed again. This time he felt the tip of her tongue and began to have an erection. He was terrified that she would feel it. Perhaps she did, because she said, "Don't be so rough" and pushed him away; stood a moment with her face down, then turned and knelt and picked up the flowers she had dropped. He knelt beside her, put an arm round her waist.

She said, "We mustn't. Not any more. Not now. I don't want to."

"You do like me?" She nodded. "Very much?" She nodded again.

"I thought you were just teasing." She shook her head. "You never seemed to want to work with me or anything."

"It was Mum." She said, "I'll die if she finds out."

"What did she say?"

"That I wasn't to make eyes at you. Flirt." Still kneeling she spoke to her lap. "That day you dropped the apples on me. She must have been watching. She told me off afterwards. We mustn't let anyone see."

"No."

"You promise?"

"Of course I promise."

"She said you'd tell at the Vicarage."

"That's *stupid*." His opinion of Mrs. Reed suffered an abrupt drop. "I'd never tell them. Never."

"I know."

"Please let me kiss you again."

She twisted her head round, but wouldn't let it last. After a moment she took his hand, laced her small fingers through his, stared down.

"What about Bill Hannacott?"

"I sent him packing. The other evening. Great fool."

"Was he . . . angry?"

"I don't care what he is."

He felt her fingers lace his a little harder. It was like a dream, too delicious to be true. She liked him, she preferred him, she sought his protection.

"Will you come every evening?"

She shook her head. "I can't. She'll guess." But she added, "Sunday afternoon's best. They all go to sleep then."

Ten minutes later, having dawdled, stopped, kissed again, gone entwined through the trees to the cliff over the old lime-kilns, scrambled down, one last kiss above the road, desperate, as if it were their last, a moment's blueness in her eyes, still a doubt, a searching, a tenderness he hasn't seen before: she leaves. He watches her run down the lane, then break into a walk, around the bend and out of sight, in the green-and-gold evening light, toward the farm. Then he slowly drags his bike out of the undergrowth, stunned, ravished, rent with joy. Already distilling it, though not yet in words; that first touch of her mouth, that melting away of all her wiles and tricks, the taste of her, the feel of her, the mystery of her.

And the lovely guilt, the need to lie, he took singing home.

A heavy dew, the good weather had held, the cutting would start, the world was all Ceres and simplicity, green early sunlight in the tunneled lanes, and Nancy. He felt, that first fine tomorrow of victory, like a bird freed from its cage, totally liberated; too liberated, as she tacitly warned him by not looking at him, not noticing him at all, when he appeared in the byre. They hadn't finished off the milking.

Only a snatched half-minute alone, in the dairy, before they all went up to the field. It was fraught with an unexpected shyness—his move, this time. But when he managed at last to reach gingerly for her hand, as if she might leap away with a scream at the first touch, she turned at once. He didn't mind when she snatched away almost as soon as their mouths had touched; it was enough—and her mother did come in a few seconds afterward, as if to confirm how careful they must be.

Stooking, stooking, all day long; an old man hired out of retirement from the village for the day was there, and his grandson, a little tacker of twelve, and they helped. Even Nancy joined in. No opportunity to touch, but chances to look, to whisper a few sentences from time to time, the secrecy of it, the being so close, the endless re-run of that evening before (although she warned him she would have to stay at home this one, all the usual daily jobs down at the farm had to wait until the corn was "on its legs"). But she wished she could, she wished she could, she'd thought about him as soon as she woke up. The deprivation seemed less cruel than he expected. It was the old harvest magic, that primeval breath of relief—there was still the ricking and threshing to be done, but it was like a voyage safely done, a landfall and solstice achieved, a promise kept. Nothing could really go wrong now.

Treacherous England—it rained out of nowhere that night and was still drizzling when Daniel arrived at the farm the next morning. It stopped before eleven, there was even some sun again in the afternoon, but no cutting was possible. He had one long, heady kiss in the barn, a minute long; a cautious pressure from her foot under the table at dinner; and the midafternoon promise that she might be by the kilns when he went home. She was. They found a place under the cliff where they couldn't be seen from the road. He backed against the rough stone and held her clasped; their mouths glued, totally uninventive, just one long kiss after another. He had another erection, it was very embarrassing, but she seemed not to notice, or if she did, to mind. He closed his eyes to shut out all daylight; to feel only; her breasts, her waist, her thighs pressing against his. Her jumper and shirt rode up a little at the back and by accident his hand touched bare skin. Apparently she did not mind that, either.

At last they broke off to whisper. She had kissed several boys. She liked kissing him much the best. Yes, he kissed much better than Bill Hannacott. She never liked kissing Bill Hannacott, she didn't know what she'd seen in him. Then he was cross-examined; when he had first begun to like her, why, how many other girls he had kissed in his time. He lied abominably, but there was no doubting his sincerity when he said that she took the palm. Then they talked of their secret, how frightened she was of her mother noticing, if his father found out, the awful Romeo and Julietishness of their fate; which, at least in difficulty, was not so far-fetched, after all. They were well outside the codes and comprehensions of both their homes, they were outlawed. They began to kiss again. That time his hand went straight to the naked back beneath the clothes.

She had to go. There was the Sunday afternoon, forty hours away, she didn't know, she wanted to, but if her mother . . . in the end a plan was agreed. They would be at Matins, if he saw her drop a handkerchief and stoop to pick it up, it meant she thought she could manage to get away after dinner. He must go round by another lane, behind the farm, "up over," walk along the top of the hill till he came to the beechwood, enter it where there was an old stone linhay, in ruins and covered in ivy; then wait nearby.

He went to church especially early that Sunday, to be sure he could watch the Reeds come in. They did, but she didn't drop the handkerchief. The service seemed the longest of his life, his father's sermon the most boring; the lovely living sun outside, the motes of dust in the stained shafts from the church windows. There was a prayer for the Allied troops who had recently landed in Sicily; but all that was a world away. At last the purgatory was over. The Reeds left their pew, they stood in the aisle. Daniel said his first genuine prayer of that morning. Nancy turned and went back down her seat and stooped. He could hardly eat Sunday luncheon, he dreaded so much some stupid demand, some suggestion, some chore to be done, from Aunt Millie or his father. But his father seemed sleepy, and when Aunt Millie asked him how he was going to spend the afternoon, he risked the casual suggestion that he might bike over to the Common and "do some botany." It was an interest his father approved, and sometimes he would come with him, if pastoral duties allowed; whence the risk. But the gamble paid. Aunt Millie thought gently he was working so hard, he should rest. That was easily brushed aside.

He was at the old linhay a quarter of an hour before the three o'clock appointed; and still there, a quarter of an hour afterward. He had gone down into the wood, and sat against a beech-stump watching down toward the farm, which was hidden by the dense canopy of leaves. Part of him knew why she might be delayed, another part was shocked that she should fail to keep this rendezvous on time; and another part again half-hoped she would not come.

Instinctively he knew many of the stories he had heard at school were boasts, wish-fulfillments; that middle-class girls were not like that at all. But Nancy was not quite a middle-class girl. She had kissed lots of other boys (it never occurred to him that Eve also can lie), she was much closer to the natural, the animal. She let him touch her bare back, she did not seem to mind that he could not control (as he was sure sophisticated boys could) his erections. Supposing . . . he knew the girl had to have a (what he then thought was spelled) pestlery, or the boy a French letter. It was not just that he feared being despised for not having one, but Bill Hannacott had had spots on his chin. And then a story had gone round his dormitory that summer of an American G. I. who had gone out with a girl from the nearest town and got stuck inside, they had had to be taken to hospital and separated surgically (it was all to do with muscle cramp or something). The virgin under the beech-trees had been much haunted by this tragic tale. But above all he had a very real and growing sense of impending sin. Kissing and meeting secretly like this was one thing. The other—he now knew better than divine lightning and the instant thunderbolt, but not much; and the longer he waited, the more trepidation he felt.

At twenty-five past three he walked back to the linhay at

the top edge of the wood. Nancy stood from behind it as he came near, in a short-sleeved yellow shirt, a dark green skirt and Wellingtons, her milking "clompers." She had a brown cardigan over her arm, and her cheeks were a high pink, perhaps because there was a redness about the mouth that was not natural—indeed, rather startlingly unnatural. Not that he felt like criticizing it. To his eyes she looked frighteningly aloof and adult, two years older at least.

They didn't kiss, they had a little argument, standing six feet apart. She'd only been five minutes late, she'd come along the top; if only he hadn't wandered off. In the end, when she lowered her head and turned away, as if she wished she hadn't come, he went behind her.

"I'm not really angry, Nancy. Now you've come."

After a moment, she reached out a hand, and he took it. They began to walk away from the farm, to the north. He smelt eau de cologne. Their fingers enlaced. After twenty yards she pushed her shoulder against his, and he put his arm around her, while she slipped hers around his waist. Then they stopped and kissed, and it was all right. The lipstick wasn't lipstick after all, but cochineal stolen from her mother's pantry.

She led him on, entwined, to her "real secret place," which was out of the wood and through a patch of high bracken and gorse at the top of the farm combe, legally one of its fields, though it was too steep for the plough, useless land. A large flat-topped limestone rock stood there, the "Pulpit," isolated in the sea of bracken. Its downhill side was slightly convex, there was a small platform of flatter earth in front of it. Daniel and she stood there, chest-deep in the fronds. Her elder sisters had brought her there when she was little, they used to clear a "room" in the ferns.

Now they did the same, squashing the stems sideways with their feet, treading the stiff ends flat, till there was a close green-walled room again, six by four. She dropped her cardigan and knelt. He sank facing her and they kissed properly, erect on their knees, clasped, in a blasphemous imitation of that morning's kneeling in church. Then Nancy spread out her cardigan and lay on it, sideways. He lay beside her and found her cochineal-stained mouth. After a while he moved his right knee on top of her leg. She sank backward, so that he had to move a little more; then she gave a twist of pain, and they had to sit up, lift the cardigan and press flat an obstinate stump of bracken. But she let him resume his previous position, half on top of her. She became passive, just lay there, let him kiss her cheeks and her eyes and under the chin; then active, began to teach him eyelash kisses, "cowpecks," lizard kisses, little flicks of her tongue against his cheek. And the sun, the heat, the bracken-flies, a buzzard mewing somewhere out of sight, the cool shadowy depths between the still upright bracken stems around them; all beautiful, except the swollen agony of his penis pressed against her thigh. It threatened to burst, he could feel its wetness, he didn't know what to do. Suddenly he twisted away and sat up and prayed for continence.

"What's wrong?"

He shook his head. She sat up beside him.

"Danny?"

He shook his head again. (For some mysterious reason, he didn't mind "Danny" from her.)

"Danny, tell me what's wrong?"

He leaned forward a little. "Nothing. Just leave me alone a minute." He said, "Please."

She turned back on her elbow, away from him. There was a fraught silence.

"I don't think you really love me at all."

"Yes I do."

"All you think of is . . ."

"What?"

"You know."

"I can't help it. I do try."

Another silence.

"Is it when you kiss me?" He nodded. "We'd better not kiss anymore then."

"It's just . . ."

More silence.

"Boys." He said nothing. "It's the same for us. Only we don't make such a fuss about it."

He couldn't find the words to say that it couldn't be the same for girls. At least they could hide what they felt.

"Please don't be angry."

"I just want to kiss. That's all."

"I know."

"I'm only sixteen."

She spoke as if she were two years younger, instead of two months older, than him.

"I honestly can't help it."

He felt better, safely detumescent, but now he couldn't

look at her. They waited, like strangers. Then she spoke in a low voice.

"At least you don't show off about it. I s'pose that's something."

The tone was resentful, but he recognized that it held some sort of forgiveness—and some consoling information. Other boys had the same problem, it seemed.

"Did he. . . ?"

"He was horrid." She suddenly added, with a tiny touch of venom, "Disgusting."

"Why?"

"I can't tell you."

"I won't tell anyone."

But she avoided his eyes, still leaning on her elbow and half turned away, and shook her head.

"Is that why you sent him packing?"

"Perhaps."

He also leaned on his elbow, his back to hers.

"I'd never do anything like that. I love you."

"You don't know what it was."

"I can guess."

"I don't want to talk about it." She said, "And anyway. He doesn't know any better. He doesn't go to boarding-school."

Terrible: he'd never understand girls. Not in a thousand years. The silence grew unendurable.

"Nancy?"

"Yes."

"I wish you wouldn't be angry with me."

For a few moments she said nothing, but then he felt her turn and pull his shoulder gently around. She stared a moment into his eyes, then leaned forward impulsively and quickly kissed his cheek; then leaned away again. But he reached a hand behind her back and pulled her to him. Once more they lay side by side. Sonata form; *da capo,* though she pressed less against him and he did not try to climb on top of her again. After a while they lay with their faces a few inches apart, staring into each other's eyes, the tiff surmounted; the mystery of love, of liking, gender, this strange new closeness outside family, past, other friends. He let his hand rest on her waist, and once again felt bare skin; cautiously let the hand edge round the bare skin to her back. She closed her eyes. He ran a finger down the spine furrow, over the vertebrae. She gave a little squirm, but her eyes stayed closed. He began to smooth upward under the shirt. The underside of his forearm on her skin, the curved smallness of her back. He touched a thin strap. She opened her eyes; spoke like a village girl.

"You'm worse than Bill."

But she was pressing a smile out of her mouth, her eyes had depths.

"Your skin's so smooth."

He ran his hand along the strap toward where her arm lay down her side. She let it creep underneath, then pressed down.

"Please."

"You said you'd be good."

"I am being good."

"No you're not."

"Please."

"It's wicked."

"Nancy."

"I don't want you to."

"Just let me feel."

"Why?"

"Because I want to."

"You'll go all funny again."

"No I won't. Please."

She stared at him a long moment more, then she said, "Close your eyes."

He felt her push his arm underneath her shirt as she sat up a little. There was a brief movement, then she was back at his side. He opened his eyes again, but now hers were closed. He explored her side beneath the shirt to the strap again, touched its loosened end, then down in front, the curve of flesh beneath the now lax cotton cup. Again it was like a dream; quite literally, like ten thousand past daydreams. His fingers touched the infinitely secret, the so often imagined, and so seemingly unattainable: a stiffened nipple. She lay absolutely still. He covered the small breast with his hand, felt its silky smoothness, softness, roundness, firmness.

"Please let me see it."

"You said just feel."

"If only I could see it."

He ran his hand backward and forward over the breast, then down to where the other, pressed against the ground, curved out as well.

"Please, Nancy. I won't do anything. I won't be rough."

"Do you love me?"

"You know I do."

"You promise. Just look."

"Honestly. I swear."

She hesitated a moment more, then all in one movement half sat, pulled up the shirt as if she was going to take it off, but stopped at the armpits, then lay back with her head turned away, her hands still holding the sides of the shirt up, the breasts bare: a gesture and offering so naïve, so innocent that it was quite sexless. But the breasts were charming, irresistible in their plumpness, their pinky-brown excited tips, their invitation. The stomach, its navel, the naked waist; a little rim of pinching white lisle that peeped above the green skirt. He put his hand out. The shirt jerked down.

"You promised!"

"I want to kiss them."

A long moment, then the shirt was allowed cautiously up again. He touched the nipples with tight-pressed lips. But almost at once she pulled the shirt right down and sat up.

"That's enough."

"Oh please. Nancy? I wasn't rough."

"It makes me shy."

She reached behind as well to do up the straps of the brassiére. But he sat up as well and drew her back against him, slipped his hands up beneath the shirt, appled the budding curves again. She made a small struggle, tried to pull his hands away, then acquiesced. After a moment her head came round, and they kissed. He was tumid, of course, the same old agony, but somehow it seemed endurable after that early near-disaster. He felt drowned in happiness, which was only partly sexual; to have so many fears so comprehensively killed, to know that back at school the days of stupid lies and false boasts were over . . . he had kissed a girl, and touched her tits. Daniel sensed dimly, at long last, what all the filth and crudity was about: and how inadequate it was, how it left out of account the emotion, the softness, the wanting to please, not wanting to hurt; how girls were not just jam-rags and protuberances, revolting blood and masturbated semen, taboo and fetish; but all you weren't, and much, much nicer, softer, more mysterious.

How long they would have sat like this, his fondling, more kisses, whispers . . . there was a distant cry, from far below, the farm. They froze.

Na-an. Na-an?

Mrs. Reed. Wailing for her.

Nancy clasped her hand to her mouth and leaned away; began to do herself up.

"Oh lawky, it's Mum."

They heard the voice cry again, half a mile away down beyond the beechwood; the voice of the righteous and deceived, accusing their wickedness. It was all blurred then, beastly; hasty agreement that he would stay out of sight for another quarter of an hour, you could see the Pulpit Rock from the meadow opposite the farm, Mrs. Reed might be there looking back, two heads would be catastrophe; what Nancy should say; what pretend; a frantic licking of her handkerchief and rubbing the last of the cochineal from her lips (and his), a frantic last kiss . . . then she was creeping away, her head bent low, through the bracken toward the edge of the beech-hanger.

So endeth the first lesson.

It was nearly, as he learned in hurried whispers the next morning, ended all. Her mother had given her "such a funny look" when she arrived home. Bill Hannacott had called, it seemed, and was now gone away again looking for her. She had no right "gallivanting off" on her own all afternoon without telling them where she was going. Nancy had had to sacrifice a pawn: telling her mother she had gone off on her own just because Bill might come over. Which had led to a cross-examination under that heading—but finally a more sympathetic one, since Mrs. Reed (it was revealed later that evening) had never liked this threatened liaison with chapel (though the Hannacotts had good land and farmed well). If Nancy didn't want him coming courting, very well; but tell the lad out so plain, and her mother first. It seemed on the face of it a killing of two birds with one stone, since Bill had returned in due course, not seen Nancy (who'd hidden upstairs in her bedroom) and had been firmly dealt with by Mrs. Reed. That left one weak flank, however.

"Didn't she ask why you didn't like him anymore?"

Nancy gave him a mock-prim little stare. "Said he was always trying to kiss me. Said I didn't like boys like that." Then she looked demurely down and bit her lips. They had to turn away from each other to choke their giggles. Deception was fun again.

All this during harvesting. The weather reverted to good, they had it all done, the cutting part of it, by late on the Saturday. But they had no meetings. Though Daniel could see nothing changed in Mrs. Reed, Nancy insisted that she was "on the sniff." They had to be extra careful—so extra careful that he did not see her one single evening on his way home. She had promised to be by the kilns on the Wednesday, and he had passed a miserable half-hour waiting for her. But she hadn't come. Mrs. Reed had felt tired and Nancy had had to help get the supper ready. She was so contrite the next day, so frightened that he would be angry, that he forgave her at once. But the frustration grew intolerably.

There was only one moment of consolation; on the Friday. Nancy had already gone down to the farm to get the tea ready—Grandpa and Mrs. Reed were up with them in the field—and give her bedridden father his tea also. She had to stay for the egg-collection van, so Daniel was sent down to fetch up the tea-cans and the cake. He found Nancy in the kitchen, just putting the big kettle on the range to boil. They had five minutes. She'd been up to see her father, he was asleep. The farmhouse was silent. It was like being grown-up, married. Did he want to see her bedroom?

He crept up behind her up the backstairs from the kitchen, then into the narrow room (the "library" now) at the north-east corner of the house. He felt shy at first, the two short rows of schoolgirl romances and textbooks ranged on a home-made shelf, the trinkets, china horses, a present from Widecombe, Uncle Tom Cobleigh and his friends in hideous polychrome, the old chest of drawers painted pink to match the small wardrobe, the neatly made bed, the pillow with an embroidered spray of forget-me-nots in one corner, the heavy cretonne curtains at the one small window. It was more child-like than feminine, yet in some way a new dimension of her, a revealing, a baring, some kind of parallel to that innocent showing of her breasts "up over." She took his hand and led him to the chest of drawers, opened one of the half-drawers at the top. Stockings and handkerchiefs; hidden among the latter she showed him a little pressed head of pink century, and suddenly they kissed. He began his please, please, again; and found mercy. She shyly unbuttoned her shirt. He saw the cotton brassiére and its shoulder-straps, then how it fell loose when she unhooked it, and put her hands behind her back. This time she watched his face, however, as he raised the cotton, feasted his eyes and hands, then bent awkwardly. That time he learned not to keep his lips pressed tight. She stroked his head and whispered; then squirmed.

"Oh Danny. We mustn't. You're tickling. We mustn't."

Again they were interrupted. There was the sound of an

engine from the front of the house: the egg van. He was pushed away, and there was more panic. He ran on tiptoe, hearing Mr. Reed's voice from his bedroom down the passage, for once not soft-spoken.

"Ma? Nan?"

And Nancy's voice calling behind him.

"It's only the eggs, Dad. I'll bring 'ee your tea in a min."

The egg-man went straight up to Mr. Reed for a cup and chat, which gave them the chance to bemoan their fate as she made the tea. They must meet Sunday; they must, they must.

For Daniel, by good (or bad) chance, it was easy. His father and Aunt Millie were invited to tea in a neighboring parish, a visit he was excused, since their hosts had no children. He made the same careful detour as the previous week, hid his bike and slipped quietly along the hedges behind the combe, then through the rusty old barbed wire and down through the bracken to the rock. The bruised ferns, the space they had made; it had waited all week. Some of the bracken had sprung partially upright again, and he trod it down afresh. He had exercised much thought over the problem of disobedient erection; had gone at last to an old Christmas decoration drawer in the Vicarage sitting-room, and rifled about under the collapsed paper concertina-chains and tinsel and folded "bells" until he found an old toy balloon—it must have been from prewar days, but Aunt Millie carefully deflated them each Twelfth Night if they had not burst, to use again. It was a little perished, and much too tight at the neck to be comfortable. But he carefully cut that away, and it seemed to hold and not hurt. As an extra precaution he changed from his usual underpants into his swimming-trunks. They kept him pressed down better. It wasn't, of course, a question of a real contraceptive; simply of not wetting his trousers if he had to give way.

Nancy came at last, ten minutes late, and nervous, she couldn't stay long. Louise and Mary had gone over to Totnes, she had to help her mother with the evening milking, she knew she suspected something . . . there was no cochineal this time, but a catalogue of fears and woes. She wore an old cream blouse under the same brown cardigan, navy slacks and rubber boots; she looked hot, a little tired. Daniel felt vaguely disappointed, he had come with an image of her that reality did not match at all. In the end she took off her boots and rubbed a sore spot beside one of her big toes. He sensed that she was in a mood, a temper of some kind; and that even though it wasn't really with him, he did not dissipate it. They sat side by side, obstinately waiting for each other to move first. It was miserable. And the weather. It was warm, but there was no sun. A tired, diffused light came from the lifeless canopy of clouds. There was no wind, either. The summer wanted autumn, and Daniel wanted summer till the end of time.

"Aren't you going to kiss me then?"

"If you want me to."

"Not if you don't want to."

He pulled out a bracken-haulm beside him.

"It's so rotten. All this being frightened they'll find out."

"Well I can't help it."

She kept rubbing the sore place. He said nothing. Then she drew up her knees, crossed her arms on them and, hunched up, hid her face as if he bored her. He was stupid, he didn't understand. She turned her buried face even farther away.

"Nancy?"

She shook her head.

"I do want to kiss you."

"No you don't. You think I'm just a silly country girl."

"That's stupid."

"You don't think I'm pretty at all." She sniffed. "Stupid old clothes."

"I don't mind. I like them. Honestly."

"You doan' know what 'tis like."

There had been a sudden little upward break in her voice. With a shock, a strange being cleft, he realized she was crying; and he was as suddenly touched, all his own sulkiness blown away like thistledown by that one note of despair in her voice. He gently pulled her around, saw the wet rims to her eyes, then pulled her less gently down beside him and held her, kissed the tears.

"I do love you, Nancy. I don't mind. About anything. I just love you."

He crushed her mouth, and they clung to each other in a fever of remorse and re-awakened passion.

She asked if he wanted to see her breasts again; he had his first taste of exploiting an advantage in the sexual war. She'd been "silly," he'd been generous, she owed it to him to be less shy. He was allowed to slip down and kiss them, to suckle them. She caressed his head. He took his first great initiative. He knelt back and peeled off his own shirt. She stared up at him a moment, then let him pull her up, and raised her arms as he peeled off her shirt and the tangled bra. The sweetness of those bare arms, that neck, the firm breasts pressing against his own, her surrender to it. He knew it was all getting out of hand, their tongues enlacing, searching, his loins bursting. He lay on top of her, crushing her down . . . until she twisted her mouth away.

"I can't breathe, Danny. You're hurting."

He rolled away, it was high time he rolled away, in any case. She sat up and rubbed her back, then suddenly turned toward him, knelt across him before he could stop her, on all fours, her hands beside his head, staring down at him, teasing . . . and something else, wicked, abandoned, much older. He reached upward to the hanging breasts, cupped them, then saw her eyes close as she sank down. Her loins pressing against his, the weight of her, the rough ground at his back, he knew it was awful, he couldn't stop it, he had a terrible fear the wretched red balloon had slipped off, but he couldn't stop it, he didn't want to, he had to cling to her . . .

It was paradise and a little bit painful, and he couldn't hide it, at the same time as he sensed obscurely that she too could not hide something: a sudden burying of her face in his neck and trembling below in a strange down-pressing way, once, twice, three times. By a piece of outrageous beginners' luck, they had achieved a simultaneous orgasm.

At least I suspect now that is what happened. We lay there so long afterward, we were so silent, we knew we had done something terribly wicked, something new to both of us, and we felt the primeval shame. Eventually we disentangled ourselves, we dressed, we couldn't look each other in the eyes, we hardly spoke. I was shocked, far more than when I lost my virginity in the full sense three years later. The famous descent of sadness, which is really just a re-awareness of one's surroundings, took me by surprise. This girl, this silent bracken, this overcast sky, this person with nothing but a tell-tale wetness in his swimming-trunks . . . they were totally strange. Everything had changed.

On the Monday, the next day, things seemed, after an initial moment of shyness, much better. Mrs. Reed had appeared to suspect nothing, the darker side of the previous day's madness disappeared. We managed only one kiss, but we found time to whisper that we loved each other, we couldn't wait till next Sunday . . . though we had to, of course. But on the Tuesday, a sinister incident, a premonition. I was pushing my bike up the hill home, when without warning a stone hit the lane six feet in front of me. I thought it must be Nancy, though she'd been sure that she couldn't slip away that evening. I stopped, staring up through the trees toward the kilns, expecting her to show herself. Instead, another stone came sailing out of the sycamores on the cliff above the kilns. This time it was too big to be a signal stone—and it came much too fast to have been thrown by a girl's arm. It was also aimed straight at me, it crashed on the road and then into the spokes of the front wheel. I was very frightened. I began to run up the hill, then I jumped on the bike and started to heave frantically up the last few yards of the gradient. Another stone landed and hit the road close behind me. I drove down on the pedals, standing on them, in a panic of fear.

There were no more stones, and I got away unscathed physically. But the damage was done elsewhere.

I told Nancy the next day, and we decided it must have been Bill Hannacott. She said he was a coward, everyone at school knew he was a coward, but he hadn't looked like one to me at our only meeting. I dreaded that journey home from then on. It was like running a gauntlet, a constant terror—less of stones than of his suddenly standing out in the road, a fight . . . and what it meant that he knew about me and Nancy. That frightened both of us: that he might have watched us that previous Sunday. Like all the village boys, he was used to slinking about without being seen. Then my imagination . . . it wasn't only stones and fist-fights I feared, but gunshots. I knew he had a gun, he shot pigeons and rabbits. I saw my gravestone beside my mother's. His choice of ambush also made our assignation place by the kilns impossible.

But as Wednesday and then Thursday passed, and I had still not been shot in the back or pummeled to dust, I felt a little more cheerful. On the Saturday afternoon Mrs. Reed, who had gone into the village, had still not returned when I was due to go home. Mary and Louise were out working, the house was empty except for Old Mr. Reed and his son and they were talking in the bedroom upstairs. Nancy and I crept into the barn, into a dark far corner where there was an old stall used for storing the hay they fed the cows during milking in the byre next door. We had our usual kissing and feeling, whispering about Bill and what his game was, how horrid he was, how had she ever seen anything in him . . . She had turned and I had pulled her back against me, my hands on her breasts, beneath her clothes, a pleasant posture we had only just discovered. Perhaps it was the darkness of that corner. Something had haunted me since that first Sunday: what Bill had done that had shocked her. I asked now. She wouldn't, she couldn't; but then she whispered. One evening. He wanted to take "it" out and have her "squeeze" it. I was shocked into silence; that he should actually say what I could only dream of—and to be told it, to have it shared.

"What did you tell him?"

"I didn't tell him anything. I slapped his silly gurt face." She said, "Bloomin' ol' cheek."

"Did you let him do this?" She shook her hair against my face. "I bet you did."

"You're the only one. 'Cos I trust you."

I held her breasts a little tighter.

"And I can't help it."

She wiggled her bottom and put on her village voice. "Doan'ee be naughty now."

"I'm not naughtier than you are."

"Oh yes you are."

"I'm not."

"You want me to do what Bill did."

"No I don't."

"You're all the same."

"I want to touch you all over."

"Well you can't. So there."

"I only said it."

"Saying's as wicked as doing."

"You let me do this."

"That's different."

I had one hand across her bare stomach, the other on her breasts.

"Only touch."

"Always saying 'only.' "

"Didn't you like it last Sunday?"

"Perhaps."

"That's what *you* always say."

"Shouldn't ask rude questions."

There was a silence.

"I wish we were grown-up."

"Would you marry me?"

"Would you marry me?"

"I might."

"I'd learn to farm properly."

"Pooh, I don't want to marry an old farmer. I've had enough of that." She kicked at the hay they were standing on. "Rotten old life."

"Say you'd marry me, Nancy."

"Why?"

"Because I want you to."

"Why do you want me to?"

"Because you're always teasing. I never know if you really . . ."

"I'm not really teasing."

"Then would you?"

He felt her hair shake up and down. Then she suddenly turned, and they kissed; a melting, a not teasing at all.

"Oh Danny, I love you. I love you so much." Then, "You don't think I'm wicked?"

"Why wicked?"

" 'Cos I tease you. 'Cos I . . ."

" 'Cause you what?"

"Like you touching me and . . ."

"And what?"

She spoke into his shoulder, hardly audible. "I'd do what Bill wanted. With you. If you really . . . if you'd love me more afterwards. If you'd promise you would."

"Would you let me touch you all over too?"

He felt her head nod, still buried against him.

"You promise?"

Again she nodded.

"Up over tomorrow?"

And once more she nodded her head against him.

They heard the sound of the tractor coming down with Mary and Louise. One swift kiss, one intense look from those shadowed blue-violet eyes, then she was running to the barn-door, out and down the side back to the house. He knew that they had been foolish, it was after his going-home time. His bike was leaning in full view by the gate outside, where he always left it. The twins came into the yard on the tractor. Normally he would have stopped and talked with them but now he waved, as if he was in a hurry, and went out to his bike. They might think it strange, but better that than have to lie about why he was still there.

So down the bumpy metaled road to the public lane, then over the bottom and the culvert that took the little stream, Thorncombe Leat. Up the hill past the kilns, too happy now, too excited to do more than give one passing thought to the possibility of Bill waiting there—and he wasn't. Halfway to the village he met Mrs. Reed in the old Riley and got off his bike to let her pass. He thought she would stop and give him his wages, that was always on Saturday, but she must have forgotten, she drove on with merely a wave, her eyes on the road. Probably she knew she was late for milking. She was all dressed up, she'd been visiting or Mothers'-Unioning.

No warning. Aunt Millie was her usual innocently inquisitive self about the day; easily dealt with. Father was preparing his sermon in his study; there was my favorite supper to come—eggs and bacon and baked potatoes. I went up to my room and lay on my bed and thought about Nancy and her breasts and her eyes and her still unknown body and being married to her and living at Thorncombe and . . . the gong sounded downstairs. And still no warning, even at supper: the same old fusty nothings of conversation. My father was rather silent and preoccupied, but that was a familiar thing on sermon-writing evenings.

The meal ended, and Father said grace; then ringed his napkin and stood.

"I have something for you in the study, Daniel. If you would spare me a moment."

I followed him across the hall into his study. He went straight to his desk, hesitated a moment, then picked up a small brown-paper parcel. He spoke to it, not me.

"Mrs. Reed came in this afternoon. She tells me her husband's recovery will be slower business than was at first thought. I understand the authorities have found a fully skilled farm-worker to help out over this winter. He starts on Monday. She will accordingly not require your assistance any more." He held out the parcel. "She asked me to give you this, Daniel. And your final wages." He turned away. "Let me see. Where did I . . . ah yes." He picked up an envelope and put it on the red-extended parcel.

I knew his eyes were on me and that I was going a deep and intolerable red. I guessed in a flash, of course; knew why Mrs. Reed had passed me in the lane without stopping. I somehow managed to take the book and envelope from him.

"Well. Aren't you going to open it?"

I tried to undo the knot in the string, but in the end he took it away from me and used a pen-knife he had on his desk; then he handed it back. I unwrapped the paper. It was a book, *The Young Christian's Guide to English History*.

There was an inscription on the fly-leaf in an old-fashioned, laborious hand.

> To Mr Daniel Martin
> With all our gratitude for his
> help in our hour of need and our
> sincere prayers for his future happyness.
> Mr and Mrs W. Reed

My father took it gently from my hands, and read the words.

"Most kind. You must write and thank them."

He handed the book back. "There. Now I must get on with my sermon."

I was back at the door before I summoned up enough courage, or sense of outrage, to speak.

"Can't I even go over and say goodbye?"

He had sat at his desk and made some pretense of settling to work, but now he looked up across the room at me.

"No, my boy. You may not." He stopped any further protest by going on—so calmly, neutrally, his eyes back on his papers. "I understand Nancy is going to her aunt near Tiverton tomorrow. For a holiday." I stared at him with a total incredulity, unable to move. He glanced up again and surveyed me for a moment. "I have great confidence in your intelligence, Daniel. As also in your sense of what is right and wrong. The matter is closed. I wish you good night."

It was monstrous, of course; the matter had been opened. I went straight to my room without saying good night to Aunt Millie, consumed with the most un-Christian hatred and impotent despair that can ever have seethed inside that house's walls. The cruelty, the stupidity, the vile meanness of adults! The shame, the humiliation! If only he had raged against me, if only he had given me a chance to rage back! The duplicity of Mrs. Reed, the cunning of her! The agony of not knowing, and *never* knowing, what was happening to Nancy at that moment, her tears, her . . . I would steal out, I would go to the farm in the night, stand below Nancy's window, we would run away together. I thought a thousand things; and knew I was trapped by convention, by respectability, by class, by Christianity, by the ubiquitous wartime creed of discipline and self-restraint as the ultimate goods. But the worst of all was knowing that I had asked for this terrible disaster. I believed in God again that night; he had my father's face and I cried with my loathing of his power.

I came to see later that it was really my father who was to be pitied . . . perhaps even admired, in his trusting me to condemn myself and find my own way out of the consequent Slough of Despond. I think Mrs. Reed must have put the matter diplomatically; not accused us of more than an illicit meeting, a stolen kiss or two. Whether she simply read Nancy's face, whether Bill Hannacott sneaked on us in some way to her, I was never to discover. But if the charges had been more serious, my father would not have felt free to burke the issue. I suppose he must have been aware what he was doing by giving me no comfort, so pointedly not asking me, then or ever, what I felt about Nancy; for all his faults he was not a sadist. I suspect he regarded all sexual feeling as childish misbehavior, something one grew out of as one "matured." To be fair, both he and Aunt Millie, whom he must have spoken to that same night (since she showed no surprise at this abrupt end to my laboring), did their best to ignore my melancholy and sullenness and chivvy me out of it.

I sneaked back once or twice to Thorncombe, spying on the valley and the farm from the surrounding woods; and saw not a sign of Nancy. Only Old Mr. Reed had been in church the day after the dreadful ukase. I had walked back to the Vicarage the moment the service was over. I thought the whole village must know (as they very probably soon did, Bill Hannacott and rural tongues being what they were). I longed for a letter from Nancy, but none came . . . or none that I was allowed to see. The one consolation of going back to school was that she might write to me there, as I had once suggested. But I was too scared to write to the farm myself in case my letter would be intercepted, and it was silly to suppose she should not feel the same. No letter came.

That following Christmas, perhaps to make certainty twice sure, my father took his first holiday of the war. He and Aunt Millie and I went up to their other sister and her family in Cumberland. She was married to a solicitor at Carlisle: two of their children were away fighting, there was another son just about to go; and then their youngest child, Barbara, who was six months older than myself. I hadn't seen her since 1939; she was very shy, but not unpretty; quite without the warmth and provocation of Nancy, yet I found her in-

creasingly attractive in the fortnight we spent with them. We
didn't kiss, except under the mistletoe, but we agreed it would
be nice to write to each other, to become pen-pals. I thought
of Nancy, and Thorncombe, less and less. I did not return
home that Christmas, but went straight back to boarding-
school.

I saw Nancy just once, in which, those next Easter holidays. If part of me felt sorry for her—not least because Aunt
Millie had written during the previous term to say that Old
Mr. Reed had died—another and meaner part now found her
provincial and farmery and plump beside my slim little
middle-class cousin from Carlisle. We had been writing long
letters and kept wishing we could see each other again. I had
learned my lesson and let them know at home I was "hearing" from Cousin Barbara. It was evidently approved; during
those holidays Aunt Millie asked if I would like her to suggest Barbara spend part of the summer with us. I said yes, at
once.

So she appeared at the Vicarage that following August. We
cycled about together, did some harvesting, played tennis. I
did not see Nancy once. Something seemed to have gone out
of the Reeds' religiosity with the old man's death. Mr. and
Mrs. Reed still appeared in church, but the girls were never
with them now. I still hated going past the farm and avoided
it as much as I could when I was out with Barbara. The face
I dreaded meeting in that lane was no longer Bill Hannacott's
. . . not that I ever got very far with Barbara. Her shyness
and niceness in the flesh proved far stronger than a certain
veiled emotion that had flavored (or I had read into) some
of her letters. Five years later she was to cause a great family
to-do by "turning" Catholic (not Anthony and Jane's sophisticated kind) and soon after becoming a nun. Her distaste for
the flesh was already apparent beneath a very timid desire for
young male friendship; I had no erection problems with her,
though we kissed once or twice at the end of her stay. I
needed to prove to myself that I had "overcome" Nancy. She
must have known "Mr. Martin's niece" was at the Vicarage,
poor girl.

That autumn I had news from home that did shock me
deeply. Thorncombe was up for sale. Mary was to marry,
young Mr. Reed had never fully recovered, he had the
chance of a smaller farm near another of Mrs. Reed's sisters,

outside Launceston, they were taking the cattle with them
. . . all the motives and details I didn't care about . . . but
Thorncombe without the Reeds! I couldn't imagine it, in
some way it seemed a worse denial of natural order than all
the far greater upheavals going on in the outer world. I think
I first began to get my guilt about them then; some sense I
have never quite lost of having been the precipitating cause
of all their disintegration, the old man's death, the leaving the
farm where they seemed to belong immutably, unimaginable
elsewhere . . . it wasn't only Nancy. I couldn't see Mrs. Reed
in another byre and dairy, Mary or Louise perched on the
tractor in any other fields, any other figure but Old Mr.
Reed's, bow-legged gaiters and gold watch, thornplant and
white moustache, about the garden and the yard. For the first
time in my life I realized how profoundly place is also
people. I could live a thousand years in this house where I
write now, and never own it as they did; beyond all artifice
of legal possession.

One last shot.
*Many years later,* as they used to say in the old sub-titles
. . . the early September of 1969, to be precise. I was down
at the farm for a fortnight, alone one afternoon, Ben and
Phoebe had gone into Newton Abbot shopping. I came out of
the front door and saw a man leaning over the gate down by
the lane. There was a car parked behind him. I shouted
down, he seemed lost. He opened the gate without answering
and started walking up, so I went to meet him halfway. I
could see he was a townee, he wore a lapeled cardigan with
a zip, and looked like one of the countless Midland and
North-county grockles that invade the West every summer.
A tall, thin man of about my own age, with hair plastered
back over a bald patch, and a gold tooth: he was grinning, a
shade embarrassed.

"Sorry to barge in an' all that." He had a faint Cockney
accent. He jerked his thumb back to the Cortina. "The wife
used to live here. Years ago. Too shy to ask if she can come
and have a dekko."

I hardly recognized her, she'd got so heavy-limbed and
stout, her tinted hair done back and up in a kind of bouffant
style, like a pub landlady, in a pathetic last attempt at attrac-
tiveness. She was in absurd crimson-red pants with a gilt-but-

toned navy blazer draped round her shoulders; just the eyes, they'd lost to the bloated cheeks below, but there was still a wash in them of that old azure-violet, the germander speed-well blue. She was hideously embarrassed. I realized at once that she must have known I owned the farm now, something had drawn her back to it, but she hadn't really wanted to see me. Her no-nonsense husband had forced the issue. He was self-assured, and very anxious to let me know he was quite as good a man as the next. A foreman at Dagenham, it seemed; "nice little place" in Basildon New Town, did I know it? He was clearly used to handling the shopfloor and a fat wage-packet. They'd been touring down in Cornwall, "giving the old Continent a rest" this year. Nancy still had a trace of a Devon accent, but she was so worried about intruding, so anxious to be nothing but correctly polite . . . it was painful.

Her father was long dead. Mary still farmed, up-country, in Somerset. She was become a grandmother now. Her mother lived with them there, same age as the century. Louise had never married. And she herself? Had they children? Three, the oldest had just got into university.

"Real bright kid," said her husband. "None of your hippie nonsense."

I showed them round the inside, and she came to life a little, though she found it all too beautiful, stock compliments, marvelous what I'd done; but something in her eyes was also seeing the past. I tried to coax her, make her remember where furniture had been, what rooms had been used for in the old days; then around the barns, the converted one Ben and Phoebe now lived in, where we had stood in the dark corner that last day. Very nice, she kept saying; hardly seems possible.

I gave them a drink back in the house, we talked casually about the general past, changes in the village, the rashes of bungalows; but not a single reference to the secret past. I wouldn't have minded if she'd just for one moment seemed sad, nostalgic; paid just one tiny tribute, even mocking, to that "tragedy" in our adolescent past. But she sipped her Dubonnet and played resolutely genteel second fiddle to her husband. I had only one minute alone with her, when he asked for "the gents'."

"Has life been good to you, Nancy?"

I hadn't used her Christian name till then.

"Oh well, can't complain." She pursed lips to her cigarette. "Harry's done very well. Considering."

"You haven't missed the old life?"

"Not the same now, is it? All chemicals and machinery. Not like the old days." She looked out of the window. "Good riddance, if you ask me. The way we had to work. Don't know how we stood it, really."

"I've never tasted cream like your mother's since."

"Given all that up now. Not worth it with Holsteins and Friesians." She said, "All seems so long ago somehow."

I smiled. "All of it?"

Just for a second her eyes drifted and cautiously met mine, then looked away with a prim little smile. "You don't smell those rotten old cows now. That's one thing I'll remember till the day I die."

"I just get a whiff sometimes. Like a ghost."

"I wouldn't fancy that."

I stood to refill her glass, but no, she really wouldn't, thanks very much. Then she wanted to know about the carpet. I told her about copal matting. Her husband came back.

I found it all vaguely amusing at the time; it hadn't really distressed me till now, when I set it down. It was my fault, I played my father's son, a kind of inversion of that scene when he so comprehensively outmaneuvered me in his study; if only I had broken through the wretched plastic shell of that meeting, through her frightened gentility and my equally odious urbanity. We think we grow old, we grow wise and more tolerant; we just grow more lazy. I could have asked what happened that terrible day: what did you feel, how long did you go on missing me? Even if I'd only evoked a remembered bitterness, recrimination, it would have been better than that total burial, that vile, stupid and inhuman pretense that our pasts are not also our presents; that what we did and felt was in some way evil and absurd . . . immature. Ban the green from your life, and what are you left with?

I walked down to their car with them. They must call in again if they were ever down this way, Phoebe would always give them a cup of tea if I wasn't there; walk around the fields again. I could see they thought I was merely "being polite," condescending perhaps, though I tried sincerely not to be; but I had been to Hollywood, I had actually met film-stars, I couldn't really mean it. I can't have, since they have never taken up the invitation.

We shook hands, I was thanked everso for sparing the time.

"I think you've done it all beautifully." She gave the house one last look back. "I really wouldn't have known it. Inside."

> *I found a stock-dove's nest,*
> *    and thow shalt have yt.*
> *The cheese-cake, in my chest,*
> *    for thee I save yt.*
> *I will give thee rush-rings,*
> *    key-knobs and cushings,*
> *Pence, purse, and other things,*
> *    bells, beads and bracelets,*
> *My shepe-hooke, and my dog,*
> *    my bottell, and my bag—*
> *    yet all not worth a rag:*
> *        Phillida flouts me.*

# Thorncombe

Phoebe had lit a fire in the living-room, supper was on. I showed Jane and Paul to their rooms, and then around the house. It seemed tiny after Compton, and unsure of itself; perhaps, though Phoebe had done her best, just insufficiently lived in.

I had begun by attempting a very simple and exorcising decor, all wood and white walls; but the place was much too old to tolerate the fashionable Finnish starkness I first tried to impose on it. I introduced more clutter, the odd print or painting that took my fancy, pieces of Victorian furniture picked up in local antique shops. One day I had disinterred the old canvas of my episcopal great-grandfather from the junk-cupboard in the London flat where Nell had long ago relegated it, and had it cleaned and re-lined. It now hung over the fireplace, disapprovingly grave, one of those portraits whose eyes seem to follow you everywhere. I had turned a dead ear to Caro's and most other people's horror of the thing. As a painting it was certainly not good enough to occupy the place of honor, and not quite bad enough to be amusing; which very probably represented its subject's true worth. But I had come to feel affectionate about the unremitting sternness of that gaze; and there were other family relics I had reinstated, one or two silhouettes and miniatures of forgotten ancestors, a favorite photograph of Aunt Millie and my father taken in 1938 . . . the house would no longer have pleased an art director, but it felt (at least until I had, as that evening, to see it through other eyes) more like a home.

Jane rang Dartington to see about bringing Paul back; while I found the old deed-map with the field boundaries for him. Then I produced the little presents I'd brought Ben and Phoebe from America, a bottle of Bourbon for Ben—knowing that with whiskey his respect for money overcame his love of alcohol—and some allegedly Navajo place-mats for

Phoebe, bought in transit in New York and (I suspect) manufactured there . . . but anything garish and suitably exotic pleased her. She had no visual taste whatever; even Ben complained about the collection of gewgaws she had amassed in their own quarters. No day-trip for her was complete without some ghastly new piece of tourist china.

We had supper—not one of her best, though Jane and Paul were polite about it. He was to be handed back at ten the next morning, but was desperate to get out and have a look at the fields before he left. So we agreed to that. He was markedly easier, perhaps because of the day, but also because Jane had evidently taken our little conversation about fussing to heart. She prompted him less, and he talked more. I told them about the old days, working at Thorncombe as a boy; about being the vicar's son, the antiquated social system; and watched Jane's eyes slide covertly toward Paul once or twice, as if to see what he really thought of this prodigal uncle returned to the fold.

She sent him off to bed at half past nine, and we took our coffees in front of the fire. Some successor of the Reeds had blocked up the wide old chimney with its bread-oven, but I had had the suburban tiles and the backing rubble out again. I sat to one side, in a rocking chair, Jane on the couch in front of the hearth, in the trousers and navy-blue polo-necked sweater she had worn all day. I had laughed when she asked if she should change. Now she delivered judgment.

"I think you've made a conquest."

"I'll give him the phone-number. It's really very close."

"I should be careful. You may find you've acquired a limpet."

"I'll warn him I must work. For a few weeks, anyway." I said, "And you must come and stay longer, Jane. Seriously. And let me meet your friend."

She stared into the fire and didn't say anything for a moment; then smiled wrily. "My ex-friend, Dan." She avoided my surprised eyes. "I'm afraid."

"But I thought . . . you said he'd written."

"Yes. He did. He's" . . . she sought for suitably old-fashioned, dismissive words . . . "he's formed a new attachment." She added lightly, "Not to worry. These things happen." Then at last she did permit herself a less clinical, or more feminine, moment. "Especially to Peter."

"I don't think much of his sense of timing."

"Apparently it's been going on for some months. And it did rather have to be now or never. He was very contrite. Self-accusing."

"I'm so sorry."

"It wasn't altogether a surprise. My only regret is that I didn't do that dear-Johning myself." She took a breath. "Fidelity was never his strong point. I think it's something to do with philosophy. You spend so much time in a rarefied stratosphere that you have to compensate when you descend from it. Be an ordinary mortal."

"Someone over there?"

"She teaches history at Harvard, it seems."

"You're being very brave about it."

She shook her head. "I've told Roz. Now you. So I don't even have to feel very humiliated. And there was the age thing. It was never really on."

I thought of her having nursed this news all through the week-end; and began to forgive her some of her calculated distances.

"Men are shits."

"At least honest ones. In this case."

"Even so."

She shrugged, and I left a sympathetic silence.

"Have you thought any more about the future?"

"Not really, Dan." She twitched at a horsehair that had poked through the fabric on the arm of the settee. "That's not quite true, I'm half thinking of selling the house and moving to London. A flat perhaps. Somewhere smaller."

"That sounds fine. And nearer Roz."

"If that's a good idea."

"What does she think?"

"She's all for it."

"Then why not?"

"I suppose doubting whether I could make a new life there for myself."

"You've abandoned the other idea?" She looked at me, rather revealingly unable to remember what the other idea had been. "Following in the footsteps of dear old Lenin's widow?"

"Not absolutely."

There was a reluctance, a brevity in her voice.

"Jane, if you don't want to talk about it, you know . . . I fully understand."

She smiled, still hesitated, then came to a decision; but

spoke to the fire. "You please mustn't take what I said that evening too literally, Dan. I do have very strong leftward feelings at the moment. But I'm not at all sure of the best way to use them. Roz is trying to push me into taking some sort of extramural PPE degree. Or a teacher-training course."

"But you're not called?"

"In a way, very much. As long as it wasn't at Oxford."

"A lot of women seem to do it nowadays."

"Yes, I know."

"A counter-argument?"

"No, of course not." She looked down, then glossed that. "Roz's motives get a tiny bit transparent at times. I hate feeling I'm both a problem mother and just one more blow for the cause."

"Except that it's a good cause? And you do have a problem."

She said nothing for a moment. "May I put my feet up?"

"Of course."

She kicked off her shoes and stretched her legs along the settee, then made a face across at me. "Varicose veins."

"Oh God."

"I've had them for years. Not even worth operating on. They just ache sometimes." She went on quickly, back to her psychological self, staring down at her lap. "I suppose it's a burden of frustration. Having got yourself into a state where nothing seems sensible enough. You know? Your heart aches for a huge step and you can't face any of the little ones. You lose your head, as I did that dreadful evening with you. Say things you don't really mean."

"But the heart wants to mean?"

She reached an arm on the couch-back, leaned her head against her hand, stared again at the fire. "I just feel our society has got so blind. So selfish. It's all I can ever see nowadays. And the only people who could change anything, change it intelligently, do absolutely nothing about it. Refuse to give up anything. Share anything. It seems almost beyond politics. A kind of universal blindness. Which means you turn to anyone who appears to begin to see. The Maoists, the Communists, anyone."

"But isn't the trouble—if you throw out all the bad freedoms, the good ones go with them?"

"Oh I know I'm in a dream-world. Especially on the historical evidence."

"The only place where I thought that wretched Fenwick

character had a point was on biological grounds. That we can't evolve without at least some freedom to go our own peculiar way."

She stretched the arm along the back of the couch; still hypnotized by, or finding sanctuary in, the fire.

"I heard a Marxist economist lecture a month or two ago. About the production costs of the British food industry. The ludicrous proportion of the whole that's taken up by advertising and packaging. Apparently it's even worse in America."

"No one would argue over that. A bad freedom."

"But no one *does* argue, Dan. Except the extreme left. That's the real horror."

"Perhaps you should stand for Parliament."

She smiled. "La Pasionaria of the detergent counter?"

"Seriously. Local government, anyway."

"I have thought about it." She added, "As schoolgirls dream of winning Wimbledon or dancing with Nureyev."

"Can you project. That's half the battle."

"Could project."

"It would come back."

Again she was silent a moment, searching for words. "It's the battle in myself that has to be won first. When I knew Anthony was going to die, I had a sense of release. So many things I was going to do. It's almost as if they've all died with him. I feel a terrible lack of energy. Not physically. All this useless, diffuse anger churning inside me, and knowing I just let it churn. Never do a thing about it. Just go on leading my same old life."

"You're not giving yourself any time."

"But I don't have that feeling anymore. Of release." She had folded her arms now, sat propped against the far inner corner of the couch, staring at her stockinged feet. "I have a rather symptomatic longing to renounce all my money. I can't in fact, obviously it's morally in trust for the children."

"Symptomatic of what?"

"I suppose of disgust with what I am. Wanting to have it all taken out of my hands." She grimaced to herself. "I know it's all ominously like what drove me into the Church."

I was tempted to go back to that, but knew, or guessed, that the past was not at issue.

"Perhaps what you need to renounce is some of the idealism."

My sympathy had to be acknowledged, but she gave the

impression that I had failed to realize the complexity of her case and her predicament.

"It's like waking up twenty-five years too late to what you are."

"We all have to face that."

She looked up and across the coffee things at me: those always rather Socratic dark brown eyes.

"But you do have an interesting career, Dan. It really is rather different for us. My kind of woman. At my age."

"But you also have more potential freedom now. I'm stuck with what I've learnt to be good at."

Again she smiled—at the kindness, not the validity of the argument; then shrugged.

"I suppose becoming a Labour Party activist would really be the most sensible thing. Our present man in Oxford is hopeless." There was another silence, then she looked at me again. "Do you ever regret having been an arts graduate?"

"And social drone?"

"Being left helpless in front of economists and people like that. Eternal amateurs."

"I once got up American corporation law in two days. Enough to kid the public, anyway."

She grinned. "That's very wicked."

"It's not a cheat. An audience likes to feel the details are right, but that's not what it's all about. It's a character's general plausibility as a human being. I'm sure the same's true of politics. Getting the details a bit wrong can even add to that. Look at Heath and Wilson. Or Johnson and Nixon. They've all been too concerned to be right to be plausible. There is a place for honest innocents."

"Hardly a category I belong to."

"I shouldn't be so sure."

Our eyes met a moment, as though she wasn't prepared to take that contradiction as lightly as I said it. But then she turned and put her legs to the ground again.

"I'd better just see if Paul's turned out his light."

She bent and slipped on her shoes, then went away upstairs. It was strange how she shifted, or had shifted as we talked—something still to uncover, to reveal, despite the apparent frankness; shifted in her age, from being it fully to someone younger . . . shifted in her voice, in the hints of the student revolutionary behind the dry self-dismissal of a woman in her forties; even in her body, a certain kind of studied formality, elegance, in some movements, a domestic simplicity in others; a kind of uneasy battle between the widowed mother of three and the eternal ghost of a much younger self. She was away for five minutes, and I got up to put some more logs on the fire; then stood in front of it and stared at the bishop, who contemplated with his usual air of disapproval. Perhaps he discerned the possibility that had sprung into my mind after her unvexed news from the Bermoothes; and left me torn between an instinct and a common sense; or to be more exact, between an instinctive idea—it had certainly come from nowhere conscious—and an inability to see how it could be expressed. The conflict was not resolved when Jane returned. She was pressing a grin out of her mouth.

"You have made a conquest. I've just been asked why *we* can't live in a place like this."

"Perhaps that's the answer. Cultivate your garden."

She sat down again, and once more put her feet up. Yes, all right, she'd have a whisky. There was another shift of mood; brisker, determined to leave her discontented self behind. She spoke to where I stood at the drinks cupboard at the end of the room.

"I do envy you. Being in touch with nature and all that."

"It is a relief from people."

"I looked out of Paul's window. The peace. All that darkness, things asleep."

I came back with the glasses.

"But unreal?"

"A little."

"Still quite cheap to buy."

She smiled, toasted me silently. "Get thee behind me."

"Anyway, I'm about to discover how unreal it is." I sat down in my rocker. "I'm going to give myself a year off after this current script."

"And live here?"

"If Ben and Phoebe don't drive me mad."

"How will you spend your time?"

I bent to replace a log-end that had fallen out of the hearth-stone. "God knows. Probably a sheer relief at not having to think cinema for a while." Now I hesitated. "I have a ghost of a notion I might try a novel."

She was surprised.

"Really?"

"Unreally. It's rather like your dream of standing for Westminster."

She sat again with an arm cocked on the back of the couch; the whisky in her lap, in a quite unconscious imitation of Mme. Récamier; for some reason, perhaps just at the change of subject, more alert, amused.

"Do you have a subject?"

"Just a ragbag of ideas that never got into my other work. The facts behind the glamorous movie scenes. That sort of thing. Hardly original. And potentially very tedious."

"Then it wouldn't be like anything else you've written."

I smiled down at my glass. "You're disappointing me, Jane. I was hoping you might argue me out of it."

"Why on earth should I do that?"

"I thought the novel counted as ego-perpetuating bourgeois decadence."

For a tiny moment she was inclined to take offense. Her eyes rested on mine, but then she looked down and murmured, "You're breaking our agreement."

"Rather more putting a serious question flippantly."

"Then I don't understand it."

"Whether it isn't a form of self-indulgence."

"I should have thought that depends on the end-product."

"Obviously . . . and when it's so uncertain?"

"Have you read Lukács?"

I shook my head. "Why?"

She bowed her head. "I just wondered."

"Tell me."

She shrugged.

"Only because he's rather wise on . . . well, all art, but particularly the novel. Its proper and improper uses."

"According to the canon?"

She looked up again. "He was a very great humanist, Dan."

"I must confess I haven't read him."

"Not very brave when the Stalinist screws were put on. Not a mad martyr à la Solzhenitsyn. Like most of us, really. Just wanting something better . . . inside the system." She looked down, as if ashamed to be so positive; then spoke more gently, like a guest. "I think you'd like him. He's very shrewd. Behind all the -isms."

"It's whether I could rival the supreme honesty of a novel I saw in California recently. It was called *The Life and Times of Jonathan Doe*."

"I haven't . . ."

"It consisted of a title page and two hundred blank sheets. All rather nicely bound."

That made her laugh, but she wouldn't accept such diffidence; having written so many scripts must help, if only with the dialogue.

"It's the bits between I fear. All the stuff the camera does for you. And finding an angle. A place to hide."

"Why must you hide?"

"I couldn't just write a novel about a scriptwriter. That would be absurd. A novelist who wasn't a scriptwriter might do it. But I'm a scriptwriter who isn't a novelist."

"Until you try."

"I'm slightly tempted to use someone like Jenny McNeil. Seeing it all through her eyes. If I could ever get inside a young female head."

"She sounds very intelligent."

"A lot too much to be a good actress."

"I should once have taken deep offense at that."

We smiled, looked down. My own smile was even then partly at my own duplicity, my knowing that Jenny's was not the only female head I must try to penetrate. Tensions, poles; the mysterious architectures of secret reality. I poked the logs together, then threw on some new ones.

"Not serious. Merely a touch of your own disease."

"I must say you seem remarkably free of the symptoms."

"I feel my life's been rather like the lanes round here . . . going the long way nowhere between high hedges. It isn't that I haven't enjoyed the hedges. But there comes a time when you want to look over them. Get your bearings, I suppose." She waited, the listener now. There was the sound of a car, one of the rare ones that used the lane at night. I remembered that other car that had passed in the Oxford night; and let the sound of this one die away. "A little peck at one's liver. The whole culture's, really."

"Prometheus in the Augean Stable?"

I smiled. "I know. And where the hell one would start. A Russian like Solzhenitsyn—he's got his dragon on every street-corner. It's where you find it in a society drifting slowly downstream into oblivion."

"Anthony would have said the terms of your statement answer it."

"The drifting? But that's not an external thing—like an inhumane political system. Just in the nature of history and its ends."

She mimicked the don's wife.

"History doesn't have ends. History is the actions of men in pursuit of their ends."

"Sartre?"

"Marx."

"I wonder if he could have imagined a nation with only its past to live for."

"Perhaps that's where the solution is."

"How?"

"Our moral tradition. Belief in personal conscience. Instead of being tied like an old boot behind American and EEC capitalism." It was my turn to wait; and once again I sensed a struggle in her between retiring and going on. It was not unlike trying to persuade a wild animal to feed from one's hand; the patience one needs sometimes, watching birds. She hopped, shyly. "I'm reading another very interesting Marxist at the moment. Gramsci."

"Yes, I saw you were." She glanced up. "It was in your living-room." I smiled. "And once again—only a name, I'm afraid."

"He tried to evolve a socialism for the Italian situation."

"And failed?"

"In terms of Mussolini and his own Communist Party, totally. But he's having his revenge now. In the modern CPI."

"And he's relevant?"

"Not in practical terms to the British situation. But I find some of his ideas sympathetic." She was staring into the fire again. "He's really another of the Marxist anti-Jacobins . . . a humanist, underneath the jargon. There's a thing he labeled ideological hegemony." She followed that with the faintest suggestion of a wince, but went on. "By which he meant a sort of all-pervasive organizing principle in bourgeois society—a belief-system that more and more takes the place of the overt police state . . . totalitarianism proper. It permeates all society, supports the established system through the mind—the unconscious. It works by what Marxists call mystification. Confuses all power relations, all major issues, the way people see events. Prevents them from judging them. Everything becomes reified, human beings become commodities, to be bought and sold. Mere objects, market research statistics—things to be manipulated by images and all the rest.

[ 417 ]

Which means that socialist intellectuals and activists have nothing to work on in the ordinary consciousness. They become inorganic, they're either driven into isolation on the political side-lines, or if they do get power, forced to follow the old Leninist heresy. Government by force and apparatus." She paused, then ended rather bathetically. "Unfortunately he's far better at defining that than explaining how one could create a counter-hegemony. The evil, not the cure."

All of which was said with a continuing shyness, tentativeness; it was less Gramsci than his exegetist that interested me—as always, far less the political than the biological view of life: not what she said, but why she was saying it; why I was allowed to hear what had been so firmly banned the previous evening at Compton. It seemed a compliment, yet I wondered; perhaps it merely implied, once again, that my political indifference and ignorance needed reprimand.

"I suppose I'm a victim of it in a way. Buying the American view of this country. From over there it does sometimes seem a hopelessly inturned and stagnant place."

"Because they say so?"

"Because of what they are themselves. Nine tenths of their energy may be misapplied, but it still represents a power to choose that we seem to have lost. All right, history may be the actions of men, but we've surely lost all emotional belief in the proposition."

"Gramsci would claim that's a function of the hegemony."

"I appreciate that, Jane. I have read Marcuse. It just seems deeper than . . . than media manipulation, all the rest. I think most people here do actually sense the Gramsci thing. That's part of the hopelessness. On the one hand we've decided history is a corrupt judge, has wrongly sentenced us, on the other hand we refuse to appeal. I'm not really arguing with you. I agree we've become almost totally the victims of social forces we can't control. But it seems to me something more biological in origin. I don't know. Blindness. Impotence. Old age. Not operable. In the nature of the process."

"And the young have to accept that?"

"I'm not sure they have a choice. Cultures are like species, they decline and fall. Perhaps the racial *Geist* is also mortal."

We were by then preferring not to look at each other; and there was a perceptible, if infinitesimal, tension. I knew I was being a man of little faith, a Job's comforter; but it was also for tactical reasons, to provoke her into showing how genuine her own pessimism was.

She said, "I refuse to believe our children have no choice at all about the kind of world they live in."

"But the choice does get more and more limited?"

"Perhaps physically. But not morally."

Anthony's ghost—or something else that had been concealed, an identity beneath all their disagreement—was suddenly very present between us. There was a lamp still on at the supper table at the far end of the room, but where we sat only the occasional flames and the red glow of the fire lit her face. She sat with her head slightly bowed, retreated into herself again . . . and I knew continued argument would drive her only farther away. Once again the dreaded theory of reserve, our Englishness, was upon us.

"It's not that I wouldn't like to believe as well."

"I realize."

But she didn't look at me. I stood up.

"Let me get some more whisky."

"No really I . . ." she glanced at her watch, one of those gestures that has to be followed by a move or else be fated to suggest politeness conquering boredom. "Do you keep country hours?"

"Not at all. But if you're tired."

"Just a few more minutes. This fire's so lovely."

I gestured with my glass. "You're sure?"

"Absolutely."

I went to get myself another Scotch, and looked surreptitiously back at her. She was staring into the fire again, absorbed in it. Her hair was without the silver comb she seemed to like to wear, or had worn, like some Tudor woman with a favorite jewel, as if it had some obscure talismanic value, on the later occasions I had seen her since the first; perhaps the lack of that, with the rather bulky sweater she was wearing, the apparent informality, was what redeemed the distances elsewhere. It certainly wasn't a sexual feeling, but much more one of mystery; to see her like this, both past and present. Though I knew that she felt something had been skated over, words had once again failed—that the infallible Pythia, for all her self-mockery, was still making secret oracular judgments, I somehow didn't wish her any other than she was: not predictable, not amenable, indeed in one way not too far from Nell's little gibe. A slippery eel. I had questions I should have liked to ask: why she had refused the previous evening to discuss what she had not shied from on this; what new thoughts she had on Anthony's death; how seriously she believed what she had said to Caro of me. But I knew I didn't yet know her well enough as she had become.

I sat down again. She asked what wood it was we burned and I told her: apple. With beech and cedar, one of the great trinity of logwoods. She shifted her head, as if she hadn't heard that before; then was silent. I watched her watching the fire, then looked down, and let her have her silence. This obstinate privacy must have grown slowly all through those years with Anthony, and been partly formed by the deserts in their marriage; but reached farther back . . . past the champagne bottle thrown in the river, the giving herself to me . . . to the small girl who had somewhere never forgiven the lack of love at a crucial stage in her life. It explained that married rejection of her outward persona as a student, of what we had then all thought of as her "natural" talents—her enthusiasm, acting, "style," independence. But they must always have been truly a mask, evolved to cover an earlier scar. The real secret behind her marriage had been that Anthony was also to be a convert, but to the needs of that insecure and thwarted child. The attempt must have been foredoomed, and perhaps largely a product of all that silly talk about steps in the dark; perhaps she had even half sensed it, and yet made withdrawal impossible by putting on the Catholic chain. The unconscious demand had totally trumped all conscious judgment.

I doubted if Anthony had ever truly realized the role he was meant to play. He had possessed intellectual gifts of fidelity, honesty and tolerance in many things; but no natural capacity for emotion, let alone passion. He had come himself from a happy and normal family background—how could he have shared her secret, even with a far better balance between thinking and feeling? Jane would have retreated again behind a new mask, much drier, cooler, smoother-armored, far less penetrable, until it formed a crust that could not be broken—which might explain her apparent calm over the loss of her friend at Harvard. He must have been, however different in outward personality, another form of Anthony, a liaison entered upon almost as a perverse proof of her side that the original problem remained insoluble.

I began to see a chain of dim points, the first faint outline of her constellation, the inner destiny I had never perceived in our past: the silences, the pretense that she had no conventional faces left (a claim her behavior denied all the time), the constant to-and-fro between the woman who argued every step and the woman who declared herself unreasonable; who asserted, then backed down; who had no hope for herself, but would not accept hopelessness in anyone else. Then there was that one revealing phrase about the heart aching for a huge step and the bizarre political step she had proposed as a substitute . . . and its constantly hinted motives, universal worry, universal concern, her revised lay version of the old Christian escape from practical responsibility. I had heard my father, not two miles from that room, preach too often about universal love and the brotherhood of the church ever to have had much time for rhetorical and abstract sympathy of that kind.

The comparison between Jane and my father is not fair, of course. She didn't preach, but had it dragged out of her; and was far more aware than he had ever been of the difference between creed and action, *doxa* and *praxis*. Yet just as I had been so deeply formed by antipathy, so had she. My father had talked love, but seldom been able to show it in the flesh; hers had simply not shown it at all. And her case had been worse on the distaff side. I could hardly accuse the mother I had never known of not loving me. But Jane's had shadowed all her life until recently: a woman who had essentially never quitted the shallow, well-heeled 1920s of her youth.

This says what took less time to think . . . or to feel, because it was more an empathetic insight than anything very consciously arrived at. It was a somewhat odd and paradoxical experience, in fact; a feeling that despite all the outward differences that had to be absorbed in meeting after so many years—the changed ways, views, appearance, the loss of sexuality, all the alienations of intervening circumstance—despite all of this, I perhaps saw her better now than ever before. Vanity played its part: one of those rare moments when one can concede more depth of understanding—as opposed to confirmation of prejudice—to growing older. I felt a kind of dry tenderness of time; its wheels, that we should become together again in that silence; hardly a present sisterliness in her, but at least a memory of it. Of course the ghost of that one carnal knowledge of her, though long become far more an emotional memory, did still faintly haunt the air, as the Reeds would for evermore haunt the house we sat in. But I knew something in Jane's presence satisfied some deep need in me of recurrent structure in both real and imagined events; indeed, married the real and imagined; justified both.

Our silence.

And withdrawing. I drained my glass, then spoke, guessing at where her mind had wandered.

"If I were a doctor, I think I'd recommend something very traditional and simple. Like a holiday."

"That's what my real doctor says. I suspect just to get me out of her hair a few weeks. Poor thing."

"She knows . . . ?"

"About Anthony and me? Yes. She's divorced herself. We've grown quite close friends over the years. She's made rather a speciality of unhappy North Oxford wives."

"Too close for you to take her advice?"

She shrugged. "I'm sure it's excellent. In itself." She made another face. "If it didn't seem so like chapter one in a woman's magazine story. Our lonely heroine looking for Mr. Right at the nearest ski-resort."

"Such cynicism."

"Cowardice, Dan. I don't think I could face that sort of experience at the moment."

I waited, watching her; hesitated, then joined her in staring at the fire.

"I have a wild idea, Jane. It's just come to me. Really off the top of my head. Would you be prepared to listen to it?"

"I thought I had the corner in wild ideas."

"Not quite." I stood. "Just let me get a little more Dutch courage. You won't . . . ?"

She shook her head, and I went away to the cupboard, and began talking.

"I have to go to Egypt for a few days soon. About the script. Cairo, then down to Aswan. They run rather a jolly one-week cruise down the Nile. From Luxor." I turned and smiled back at her. "Why don't you come?" She stared at me for a moment, as if I couldn't be serious. "Purely, in all senses of the word, as an old friend."

She let out a breath.

"Dan, I couldn't possibly. I didn't mean . . ."

I topped my whisky with water. "Why not?"

She put her legs to the ground, leaned forward, clasping her hands.

"Because . . . a thousand reasons."

"You haven't been there?"

"No."

"It's just sitting in the sun on a nice old boat. Doing the tourist bit if you want to. Resting, reading. I shall be busy writing and seeing people most of the time."

"It sounds heavenly. But I—"

"Only ten days." She had rapidly retreated into convention; wore that faintly rueful, faintly amused face of indulgent mothers faced with preposterous ideas from their offspring. I came back toward her. "I did the cruise with Andrea once. It's very relaxing, very peaceful. The climate's a dream at this time of year." I went in front of the fire. "Discount air-fares. Your dragoman for free. You'll never get such a bargain."

"I really couldn't, Dan. Honestly."

"But you've just said—"

"Not to be taken so literally."

"Give me one of these thousand reasons."

"The children." She shrugged. "Everything."

"May I go and ring Roz and see what she thinks?"

"I've more or less promised to go and see Anne in Florence."

"Nothing easier. Stop off at Rome on the way back."

This geographical common sense seemed for a moment to shake her; or at least to force her to search for better reasons.

"Everyone would think I'd gone mad."

I smiled. "Some of them think that already."

"I'd feel I was running away."

"That *is* mad. You've earned a break." She folded her arms on her knees, sat hunched forward, staring at my feet. "What you said to me in Oxford. About what one missed if one hid behind one's years."

"Dan, it's most terribly sweet of you to suggest it. But I . . ."

She gave up, as if the "terrible sweetness" was beyond further words—and my suggestion beyond serious discussion. I sat down again in my rocking-chair.

"It's not because of anything Anthony said. I simply think it would do you good. A new experience for you. And I'd love to have a companion."

She spoke gently, yet I sensed a relief that I had raised an obvious objection.

"I'm hardly the person you should be with."

"If Jenny was here, and she knew you, she'd be urging you to go. That's not a problem." But something in her face remained dubious. "You must know from Roz. Their generation don't go in for false propriety."

She made a sideways movement of her head. "I really do have so much to do."

"That can't wait a couple of weeks? The production office can do all the arranging. You'd only have to sign a visa form." She said nothing. "Look, Jane, I know what I owe you over Caro. If you'd think of it as a small token of gratitude. From both of us."

"There's nothing to feel grateful for. I did it because I'm very fond of her."

"I know that. And also what we both feel."

She lay back again in the couch and stared up at the bishop, then raised her hands to the sides of her neck, smoothed them forward, clasped her cheeks a moment: it was like that gesture she had made the night Anthony died, in her Oxford living-room . . . a loss for more than words.

"If I wasn't what I am, Dan. I just don't feel I have the right to . . . oh dear."

"To what?"

She took a breath. "In view of . . ."

"The past?"

"A little."

"Surely we're both old enough now to be able to smile at that."

"But you have work to do."

"You forget I'm a first-class dodger of all unwished-for encumbrance. I've had a lifetime of practice at it."

"Dan, I'm touched. But I really can't. I know I can't."

I stared down at my whisky.

"Now I'm offended."

"Please. That's the last thing I want."

"I'm still not forgiven?"

"Now *you're* being absurd."

"At least still to be feared—when bringing gifts?"

"Of course not. It's just . . ." She took another breath. After a moment she said, "I suppose it's a kind of pride. Wanting to get through on my own."

"The idea doesn't attract you at all?"

She hesitated, then said, "Of course. In the abstract."

"Then you're being quite unnecessarily puritanical."

Again she was slow to answer. "I'm so frightened of losing

what little ground I've made towards being a less self-centered being."

"Where on earth did poor old Rabelais go?"

"I'm afraid he long ago lost patience with me." She watched the fire a long moment, then murmured, "Like everyone else."

I disliked intensely the tinge in her voice, as if she knew she was being very unreasonable in casting herself again as Christ to my Satan, and half-apologized for it, like an unwilling martyr to her own pig-headedness. It smelled Jesuitical, of both her Oxford and her Catholic past; once again of seeing the ethics of situations rather more nicely than the common outside herd. But every war invents its new strategies, and I decided to make a withdrawal.

"Will you at least agree to sleep on it?" I said. "And at least forgive me for having sprung it on you like this."

"I'm the one who needs forgiving."

"Just think about it for a day or two."

She was cornered, of course, and could not quite refuse that; nor hide that she would have liked to.

"It's so kind of you, Dan, I . . ."

I stood up. "Not just kind. I have to go, anyway."

"You did say it was a wild idea."

"They're often the most sensible." I gave her a small smile down. "Especially when one's faced with circumventing an ideological hegemony."

She looked up from where she sat, as if set back by such impudence, but couldn't quite keep an acknowledgment of its partial justification out of her eyes. For a moment she stared down at the carpet; someone who could speak worlds, but knew her chance was past; then stood. I was carefully brisk . . . not to worry about the coffee-things. Phoebe would do that in the morning. I bid her good night at the foot of the stairs, killing any chance she might still have sought to do more eeling. She had everything she needed? Then sleep well.

I returned to put a guard in front of the fire, then went outside for a minute or two. It was very mild, one of those nights when there seems wind in the sky but not at ground level; a wrack, a delicate powdery drizzle out of the southwest, and the first hint of spring, a haunting green must in the air, something peculiar to Devon and the first two months of its year, the groves and orchards of milder climates, of the Canaries, stealing their tentacles through the gray winter. High overhead, a curlew cried, then another, answering, on their way down from Dartmoor to the flats of the Teign estuary; then a tawny owl, from somewhere among the beeches behind the house. The dense, traditional night.

Then he began to wonder what he had done.

# In the Orchard of the Blessed

If Dan had launched a strange ship on impulse, he had behaved much more habitually in another matter. The truth was that he was falling very rapidly in love with the idea of his novel. In his continuing reticence about it with Jane he had been playing English. In secret fact it was daily becoming—though the experience was not altogether unlike that of a tobogganer who discovers he is on a steeper slope than he realized, that is, Dan also felt a growing trepidation—less a possibility than a definite intention. He was still bare of a story or characters in any practical sense, but he began to see, dimly, a kind of general purpose or drift; in architectural terms, a site, if not yet the house, and even less the family, that would go on it. But then, as his vehicle gathered momentum, he also began to see what he suspected was a very ugly obstacle half-buried in the snow ahead.

He had already, without having admitted it to Jenny, borrowed her proposed name for his putative hero: the ghost of Altadena Drive, the pin-found "Simon Wolfe." He didn't like the name and knew he would never use it, but this instinctive rejection gave it a useful kind of otherness, an objectivity, when it came to distinguishing between his actual self and a hypothetical fictional projection of himself.

He remained by the front door, under the dated porch, for a minute or two; and then felt a whim to be more truly in the night. He turned and took an old coat off a hook, kicked off his shoes and put on a pair of rubber boots; then went down the path to the gate of the front garden. He looked back there a moment, and saw the one lit upper window, its translucent curtained warmth subtending a faint halo in the moisture-laden mist. Jane's bedroom; but he thought less of her than of the light, also diffused, she had unwittingly thrown on his problem. He went through the wicket, crossed the little drive from the lane up to the farm, then quietly unhooked an old gate and went into the small orchard he had once scythed as a boy, always one of his favorite places at Thorncombe. Some of the trees were too ancient to crop, and the bulk were inedible cider-apples. But he liked their twisted and lichened stems, their spring blossom, their age and always having been there. He began to walk slowly among the old trees. From the bottom there was a familiar low gurgle of water where the leat ran shallow over some stones. He did not hear it.

The obstacle was this: he was too fortunate, and this gave him, in his "Simon Wolfe" projection, a feeling of inauthenticity, almost of impotence. He had sensed it as he secretly criticized Fenwick at Compton—that he had no real right to criticize someone who so complacently forecast national disaster, since at a personal level he was guilty of the same crime, even though he did not predict the same disaster. And then again at Compton: all his talk of failure was only too like Nell's presenting the place as a white elephant, a constant agony to live in—and he had smiled at her for that.

In short, he felt himself, both artistically and really, in the age-old humanist trap: of being allowed (as by some unearned privilege) to enjoy life too much to make a convincing case for any real despair or dissatisfaction. How could there be anything "tragic" in a central character who had some fictional analogue of a Jenny, a Thorncombe, a still warm window just back there up the hill announcing a long-wanted reconciliation? With all his comparative freedom, money, time to think? His agreeable (despite his present grumbling) work? All artistic making, however imperfect, however tainted by commerce, was contenting compared to the work most of the rest of the world was condemned to. Even as Dan walked, he knew himself, partly in the very act of walking and knowing, and partly because of what had been happening during those last two weeks, dense with forebodings of a rich and happy year ahead. It was as ludicrous as that: forebodings of even greater happiness—as if he were condemned to comedy in an age without it . . . at least in its old, smiling, fundamentally optimistic form. He thought, for instance, revealing instance, how all through his writing life, both as a playwright and a scenarist, he had avoided the happy ending, as if it were somehow in bad taste. Even in the film being shot in California, which was essentially a comedy of misunderstandings, he had taken care to see hero and heroine went their separate ways at the end.

[ 428 ]

He was not wholly to blame, of course. No one, during all the script discussions about other matters, had ever suggested anything different for the close. They were all equally brainwashed, victims of the dominant and historically understandable heresy (or cultural hegemony) that Anthony had derided by beatifying Samuel Beckett. It had become offensive, in an intellectually privileged caste, to suggest publicly that anything might turn out well in this world. Even when things—largely because of the privilege—did in private actuality turn out well, one dared not say so artistically. It was like some new version of the Midas touch, with despair taking the place of gold. This despair might sometimes spring from a genuine metaphysical pessimism, or guilt, or empathy with the less fortunate. But far more often it came from a kind of statistical sensitivity (and so crossed a border into market research), since in a period of intense and universal increase in self-awareness, few could be happy with their lot.

The dooming, self-accusing artist thus became like an Irish keener, a paid exhibitor of token feeling, a mourner for the unmourning. Perhaps the more real comparison in the majority of cases was with some absolutist monarch coming to cautious terms with the dawn of enlightenment; or with contemporary management going in for good labor relations. Where such parallels collapsed was in the motivation. The artist was not in pursuit of unfair political or economic power, but simply of his freedom to create—and the question was really whether that freedom is compatible with such deference to a received idea of the age: that only a tragic, absurdist, black-comic view (with even the agnosticism of the "open" ending suspect) of human destiny could be counted as truly representative and "serious."

All this had descended on Dan like an unpleasant revelation. When he had first begun to think of self-accountancy—or escape—through a novel (actually for some time before that day at Tsankawi) he had genuinely attributed his depression to an unhappiness at what he had become. But the mere ability to recognize this already initiated a subtle osmosis; and now he had thought more practically—and though not consciously, with all his professional experience of extracting the essential from the prolix—he had realized his true dilemma was quite the reverse. He was, if he was honest, under the looking-glass of eternity, a good deal less unhappy at what he had failed to be than content to accept his lot. It was not that he discounted the failure; but simply that his *ens*, in the old alchemists' sense of the word, "the most efficaceous part of any mixed body," triumphed over his outward biography. He had perhaps learned to live much too comfortably with his failings—but he lived in a world of far more vicious ones, both personal and public; and he knew too that at least some of the failings were so deeply imbricated with whatever virtues he had that the first could not be removed without weakening the potentialities of the second.

That, profoundly, was what puzzled him about Jane. He detected in her a potency of self-disappointment, self-slander, self-distrust, that he might in the past have aped (as he had just aped a sympathetic pessimism), but had never really felt. One part of him, the side that loved the poetries and sciences of nature, could observe and fault her; explain her, as he had done during that silence, more or less psychiatrically; and still feel sympathy for her, of course, since the ability to empathize, to see, lay at the root of his *ens* happiness. But another side continued to feel diminished by her . . . as in the past, though for different reasons now.

It may have been something in femininity, in femaleness, but she was both her own, in a way he had never quite managed, and not her own, where he only too lazily and complacently was. That was why he had issued his strange invitation; made a necessity of going to Egypt when there was none; refused the chance to drop the idea in the discussion afterward. She was like an old enigma in his life, and she had to be solved; tamed and transcribed. Perhaps, though once again he did not think this consciously (but since characteristic structures and procedures in ordinary life so seep down and shape those of the unconscious), she had some kind of kinship with the Kitchener script: a problem to crack, to be converted to another medium, though in the emotions, not on the page.

Already he had toyed with two solutions in his other and increasingly related problem with his novel. One that he had considered, enough to make a note or two concerning it, was to give "Simon Wolfe" disadvantages he did not have: an even hollower career, an unhappier family background, no Jenny in his life. He had even descended, under the real experience of Anthony (and the influence of a film he had deeply admired when he saw it, Kurosawa's *Living*), to contemplating cancer in some less terminal form. Part of his present malaise, so simple was one aspect of the man, came from the realization of the fact that he did not, actually, himself, have cancer, and that to claim he had it, even through a fiction, but a fiction whose inner private symbolisms he must face, would be a lie. That is, such deference to the *Zeitgeist* would mean that he could not honestly set out for the land that inspired the proposed voyage: himself.

The other solution he envisaged was to present a character less self-absorbed, less concentrated on his own perceptions, less inclined to root all pleasure in them, even when they were hostile to and critical of the self; someone less conscious, in effect—and in every sense of that adverbial phrase; who saw himself as Dan suspected Jane now saw herself . . . largely misgrown and to be censored. But this, on reflection—those eternal mirrors that dogged his life—seemed what he had already always remorselessly extirpated from what he had written: the very reason the problem had arisen in the first place. Forbidding himself a real self reduced him to being a psychic investigator who began his inquiry by requesting a service of exorcism that, if it worked, would leave no ghost to inquire about.

The least thinking reader will have noted a third solution, but it had not occurred to the writer-to-be until this moment. Dan was at the bottom of his orchard by then, just above the stream. There was an obscure scuffle in the hedge to his right; some nocturnal animal, a hedgehog perhaps, or a badger. It was too dark to see. He waited a moment or two, distracted from his self-preoccupation, listening for a further sound. But none came. He felt, transitorily, though not for the first time, a paradoxical sort of determined imprisonment compared to the existence of the small wild beast he had disturbed; almost an envy of the pleasures of a life without self-consciousness.

Free will.

And then, in those most banal of circumstances, in the night, in his orchard, alone but not alone, he came to the most important decision of his life. It did not arrive—nor do most such decisions in reality—as light came on the road to Damascus, in one blinding certainty; but far more as a tentative hypothesis, a seed, a chink in a door; still to be doubted, neglected, forgotten through most of the future of these pages. However, Dan wishes, for reasons of his own, to define it as it was to grow; and to point out that though it may seem a supremely self-centered declaration, it is in fact a supremely socialist one. That it would not be recognized as such by a nearly entire majority of contemporary socialists is, or so he will come to think, a defect in contemporary socialism; not in his decision.

To hell with cultural fashion; to hell with elitist guilt; to hell with existentialist nausea; and above all, to hell with the imagined that does not say, not only in, but behind the images, the real.

# Rain

The drizzle had turned to rain when the alarm-clock woke Dan the next morning. He felt tempted to turn over and go to sleep again, but he could hear Phoebe downstairs and Paul had been promised that weather wouldn't stop their walk. So Dan tapped on his door, and spared his mother's. There was wind now, a gale threatening, as Phoebe, who never really believed anything unless it was first announced on the wireless, needlessly warned when Dan showed his face in the kitchen. Paul appeared, and they had a quick mug of coffee.

Five minutes later they were climbing up through the beechwood to the top. From there they were blown along to Pulpit Rock, where Dan had once lain with Nancy. It gave the best general view over the combe. The rain temporarily eased a little, but an endless gray mass of cloud, like an inverted sea, and low enough to hide Dartmoor, normally visible from this place, blew out of the south-west; the drenched countryside, the sodden dead bracken; the boy, in gumboots and an old riding-mac of Caro's, with his previous day's enthusiasm only too visibly dampened by the weather . . . Dan pointed out the faint remains of two Iron Age tumuli in one of the meadows below and the ancient plough-rigs in another. They tried to work out where the field-boundaries had changed, which might have been the oldest, but it was difficult without the deed-map in hand to compare. They wandered on for a while, over fields that were not Dan's, along the northern lip of the combe. The landscape seemed far more dead by day than it had by night: a few leaden wood-pigeons, a pair of crows torn ragged in the squally wind, mournful cattle.

Yet it was curious—or seemed curious to Dan, since he had come back from his midnight stroll in the orchard under the impression that he had decided nothing . . . but he unexpectedly enjoyed that walk. He had felt it in the hanger, his beechwood, though he despised the notion of possession of

the old trees. They were far more a noble congregation of ar-
boreal patriarchs, a little where the ancient upright soul of Old
Mr. Reed had gone. Half a dozen times during his ownership
of Thorncombe sharp-eyed tree-fellers had knocked on the
door and made an offer for the timber there, and Dan had
evolved a reply. They don't belong to me, he'd say; they
belong to themselves. Only one man understood; smiled,
nodded, argued no more—and had promptly been granted
what lesser sawing jobs had sometimes to be done about the
place.

That walk brought him home to ordinariness, to simpler
lives; finally home from the stale paradise of California's eternal smog-filtered sun to a much tenderer, if damper, matrix.
Such weather, drizzling and driving, interminable and salt-
laden, was far commoner when he was a boy, Paul's age. I
cannot remember Dan's ever having really disliked it, whatever his father's and Aunt Millie's complaints. It somehow
cocooned, enwombed, always set one dreaming of all the
places, both near and far, one couldn't go to; and long before
science, even in earliest childhood, one knew it was necessary—necessary not only in the sense that it bred the miraculous early springs, the celandines and violets and primroses of
every banked hedge, and the rich green-tunneled summers,
but necessary also in a far profounder sense. Life was more
enjoyable so, with each day's weather always a throw of the
dice, a hazard . . . and Dan had never really become accustomed to the boredom of unchanging skies, or fallen in with
the symptomatic modern fashion for equating holiday happiness with sunshine—the triumph of the Majorcas and
Acapulcos of this world over its true climatic poetry.

He wondered whether this would have meant anything to
Paul, as they trudged along the edge of a cabbage-field, the
rain driving harder again. He doubted it. For all his current
interest, Paul was a town boy, and with all the new town-
dominated media conforming his and his generation's mind
. . . even the ploughmen carried transistors in their tractor
cabins now. There was a village joke about one who got so
drowned in some pop tune that he forgot to lower his shares
after a headland turn and was seen driving all the way down
the return furrow with his tail cocked up "like an ol'
pheasant."

And anyway, who was Dan? He walked wet fields once a
year, between cities; and loved it only because he so largely
escaped it. Yet in a way this attachment to a climate, a land-

scape, was the only decent marriage he had ever made, and had perhaps been the deepest reason he had returned here in the first place—that is, the knowledge he would never make a satisfactory marriage anywhere else.

They got off to Dartington soon after breakfast. The rain had really set in, and Paul had grown silent again. They went by the main road, through Totnes; and then he and Dan were shaking hands, the latter doing his avuncular act, renewing invitations already made. Paul had the number at Thorncombe, if he ever wanted a day away from school, with a friend perhaps . . . Jane disappeared inside with the boy, she wanted to see the headmaster, and didn't come back for twenty minutes.

"Okay?"

"They seem to think he'll survive."

She had rung up about her train before they left Thorncombe. There was one she could catch at half past two, she was to spend a night in London with Roz before returning to Oxford, so there was time to spare and Dan drove the slow way, over the Dart bridge at Staverton and back through the maze of lanes eastward. They talked about Paul and the school for a while. Dan was determined not to be the first to broach Egypt again, but it must have been on her mind. She used the first lapse in their talking to return to it.

"Dan, about last night, I must have sounded terribly ungrateful."

"Not at all. Don't be silly."

"It did come as a shock."

"My fault."

"What I was trying to say is that I'm not really fit company for anyone at the moment."

He smiled, his eyes on the narrow lane ahead. "I should let other people judge that."

"You must have so much to do while you're there."

"Very little, physically. Bar looking at a few locations in Cairo and Aswan. On which I should value your advice, anyway."

"Please be serious."

He smiled again. "You can be as solitary as you like, Jane. As difficult as you like. As silent as you like. But I won't take it as a reason not to come."

She said nothing. He slowed down at a deserted blind crossroad, and looked at her face before he edged forward. "You won't be in the way. Will you at least accept that?" She bowed her head, but still did not answer, clearly embarrassed by his persistence. He left a moment or two, then spoke again. "What people might think?"

"I can't imagine Nell would see it as being in the best of taste."

"As her last instructions to me were to win you back to the bourgeoisie, I rather doubt that." She gave him a sharp look, but he concentrated drily on his driving. "And since when did either of us take her view of life seriously?"

"What did she actually say?"

"Beneath the sarcasms, that she loves you. Is genuinely worried for you." He waited, then went on. "I don't think she really minds what you are. She does mind that you seem unhappy." He added, "I'd be only too pleased to ring her when we get home and put the idea."

"I'd rather you didn't."

"Then why not?"

"It's not really Nell."

He drove a little way in silence.

"What Anthony said to me? I'm just being decent?"

"I suppose . . . yes, partly that."

"So you can't do something perfectly normal and sensible because he recommended it."

"Because I'm sure he didn't mean you should put yourself out so much."

He left a longer silence, trying to decide his next line of attack.

"I think he killed himself at least partly in an attempt to make the attitude you showed me before we knew he'd died impossible to maintain. I don't mean the attitude to me personally. But what it betrayed of your apparent attitude to everything else. I begin to think the real huge step you have to take is towards conceding some right in things as they are."

"Not in things. In myself."

"That still doesn't mean Anthony wasn't wise to the problem. He said things about you that night that you've repeated to me, almost word for word, since."

"He never understood that I can't forgive myself."

"I disagree. I think he did. And even if he didn't—now you can't come because you can't forgive yourself. That's masochism. Self-flagellation."

"Only because everyone else seems so determined to forgive me. As long as I look happy."

He gave her a glance. "You can't treat being concerned for you as some sort of temptation from Satan. It's absurd."

"Dan, I don't not know it." But she corrected that slightly. "I know you're being very kind . . ." there was a little breath. A spirit cornered; but unsurrendered.

"Is it something to do with that old business of feeling right?"

She was slow to answer; and didn't answer his question directly.

"I woke up this morning absolutely clear that I couldn't possibly go."

Dan had already noticed how, when she was cornered, she retreated into a thoughtless (as opposed to a merely guying) middle-class language that was normally foreign to her; those stock intensifiers, that "couldn't possibly"; it was also a stock English retreat, of course, from the kind of frankness every other nation in the world accepts in ordinary conversation between people who know each other well. Yet he wondered whether it wasn't in fact like the rain that lashed the windscreen in front of them, and out of nowhere remembered the quatrain, Henry VIII's favorite, from the early sixteenth century:

> O Western wind, when wilt thou blow,
>  that the small rain down can rain?
> Christ, that my love were in my arms
>  and I in my bed again!

Neither the first nor the third person that he also was wanted Jane in his arms again, at least in the sense that the old royal lecher would have understood it; but just as certain kinds of weather always drove him back into the imagination, so this shrouding use of psychological cloud and rain, of conventionality of speech and reaction and attitude, in denying the inner landscapes, suggested them, invited their future exploration; instituted an unknown quantity, a mystery, in even the simplest exchange. And just as he had dimly known as a small boy that cocooning winter weather like this was necessary, so, it occurred to him, now was the opacity in present behavior; that too always required its victims to believe in its intrinsic fertility, to gamble on an imago to come, clearer weather ahead.

In the real present he had reached and touched the sleeve of her coat.

"I'm only proposing a small step into the sunlight. For a change."

She smiled, a shade wistfully. "I must admit, on a day like this . . ."

"Will you at least talk it over with Roz tonight? If she pales in horror, I'll accept defeat."

She still faintly smiled, hesitated, then gave a nod of temporary acquiescence.

"Yes. All right."

He knew she really wanted to bolt her refusal beyond any re-opening; but was now caught the other way by convention, and forced to leave the option alive.

They came to the village by the far side from Thorncombe and he asked her—the rain had once more relented—if she'd like to have a look inside the church. He thought it might remind her that other childhoods had also had their purgatories. But Jane did not find them very obvious—she liked the church, its openness, ragstone pillars, exuberantly carved and painted roodscreen. Then they talked in the drizzle for a few yards down toward the two graves; and Dan showed her, over the Vicarage gate that led out of the churchyard, the house where he was born. She stood again a moment when they turned, reading his mother's headstone. It had tilted forward very slightly, and drips fell from one corner, as if in reproach for the tears her son had never, at least to his memory, shed.

"Why did you keep so quiet at Oxford about all this, Dan?"

"Trying to pretend it didn't exist?"

"I can only remember you laughing at it all."

"I did write that play."

"Yes of course. I forgot." She gave him a small smile, looked again at the grave. "I envy you. When I think of our own traipsing from one embassy to the next."

"It was when I began to see through it all. I had to hide such a lot." They turned and began walking back to the car. "I was far worse than Paul. At least he can show what he feels. I wasn't even allowed to do that."

"What made you come back here?"

They had talked briefly about that at supper the previous evening, but she must have sensed he was being less than frank. Dan looked down at the path, then slipped her a faintly mischievous look.

"A rather fat girl with heavenly blue eyes."

And suddenly she grinned, clasped her gloved hands in front of her, a flash of her old self.

"Oh Dan. How touching."

He murmured. "Truer than you think."

He told her about the Reeds and his tragicomic romance with Nancy, as they drove back down that same lane he had once bicycled every morning.

"And you never saw her again?"

He told her about the seeing again.

"Poor woman."

"I'd almost forgotten her. She wasn't really the reason. That first time I brought Caro here . . . I suppose it was the lost domain thing. I felt it this morning out walking with Paul. It seems absurd on a dreadful day like this—but a kind of innocence regained? I'm not sure it's very healthy. A bit too like the way millionaires buy the humble houses they were born in."

"I can think of worse things millionaires do."

Dan grinned at the dryness in her voice.

"Presumably they do it to remind themselves how far they've come. At least I've grown to suspect that I did it to learn how little I've left." He added, "Which is probably why I have more sympathy for Andrew than you."

"I've never laughed at that side of his love for Compton. It's what we so lacked in childhood. Belonging somewhere."

"At least Nell has it now."

"Yes. I envy that, too."

He glanced at her and she pressed her lips together in a rueful acknowledgment that not all sisterly differences were merely political. Then she asked Dan, a shade too quickly, as if they had been sinking too far below the surface of things, whether he'd seen Albicocci's film of *Le Grand Meaulnes*.

They ran over the last hill and came steeply down beside the limekilns with the farm in sight on its first slope opposite.

Her train was on time at Newton Abbot, a couple of hours later. Dan attempted to buy her ticket, but that was not allowed; so he saw her on board a second-class carriage and then stood on the platform smiling up at her in the corridor window.

"Thank you so much, Dan. And for being so patient."

"You think about ten days in Egypt. I just need a word, and hey presto."

He had not attempted to persuade her directly again, but

he had talked about Egypt, the Nile, during lunch; and elic-
ited a tiny fact. Several years before she and Anthony had
thought of doing a similar cruise; but it had come to nothing.
Now she looked down into his eyes, trying to find words. He
spoke before she could open her mouth.

"I shall most certainly hold it against you."

She smiled, still searching his eyes for some confirmation
of her own doubts; a final pretense of defenselessness now, as
if she had been unfairly teased.

She said, "I love your farm."

A whistle blew, and she thanked him once more. The train
began to move, and she raised a hand, a rather pale, self-contained, politely receding female face, which seemed at this
very last moment to have something puzzled and regretful
about it, as if she had come knowing who Dan was, but not
now so sure.

He watched the train go, long after she had withdrawn
from the window to regain her seat, already trying to think of
convincing excuses for why, when she finally refused to come
to Egypt, he should have decided the trip dispensable for
himself as well.

Phoebe had come in with them to Newton Abbot to do
some shopping, and he had half an hour to wait in the car-
park near the market where he had arranged to pick her up.
He sat smoking, not really seeing anything he looked at. A
part of him knew only too well that Jane was right to shy at
the idea. It was less the loss of time—the script was taking
shape, was back on schedule, he could do some work in
Egypt, and in any case Malevich had given him the extra
lease on contract—than Jenny. She was not as open-minded
about other women as he had suggested. Face to face, he
could have convinced her; even if she had met Jane, knew
all the circumstances; but over a telephone, and thousands of
miles away, was another matter. She wouldn't like the smell
of it, and he would have to be very clear why he was taking
pity on someone who for years had been a stranger, whom
indeed he'd never talked to Jenny of, except in the vaguest
terms; and even those that final night, Jenny had instantly
bridled against. He had said more about her in one or
two of the telephone calls since Anthony's suicide, but Jenny
had proved much more inquisitive about his reactions to Nell
. . . and concerning Caro.

So what could he say to her? There was the plea that he
wanted to show he was not too grand and internationally suc-

cessful to ignore an old friendship, to want to seal a family reconciliation. Gratitude for the help to Caro—that he had fortunately already mentioned. But this was about it. He could defuse the inevitable sexual suspicion but not admit the other truth, that this obscure ex-sister-in-law was someone whose spirit remained not quite like that of any other woman he had ever known; that there are some people one can't dismiss, place, reify . . . who set riddles one ignores at one's cost; who, like nature itself, are catalytic, inherently and unconsciously dissolvent of time and all the naturalist tries to put between himself and his total reality.

He thought back again to the morning, that drive in the rain, to what had been said, and not said. It was almost a heuristic quality. Even when she was being thoughtless, she made him think. It may have been connected with that opacity of temperament, it was certainly connected with her role in his past; but increasingly he knew it was of value to him, to both of him, Daniel Martin and "Simon Wolfe." His *métier* had forced him for so long to think in terms of visual symbolisms, of sets, locations, movements, gestures; of the seen actor and actress. This psychologically obscure creature belonged, or had grown to belong, to another art, another system, the one he was trying to enter.

Above all he had to distinguish his real self from his putative fictional one; and though his training in an adamantly third-person art and angle of vision might seem to facilitate such auto-surgery, he felt deeply unsure about it. There too he had an apprehension that Jane could help—that the "making him think" was essentially a making him look at himself through her eyes. And through her opacity . . . it struck him that she was also unique in not mirroring him clearly; did not reflect what he saw in the less thinking, less perverse and perhaps less distorted glass of more ordinary minds. It remained that somewhere he did not feel right to her, whatever outward returns of old familiarity had begun to show. She still, as she always had, disturbed images, changed voices, recast scenes; as Jenny did also, in her different way—more artificially, calculatedly, aggressively, and as a kind of intimate extension of her professional determination not to be type-cast.

In fact he felt all this more than he thought it; felt an interweaving of strands, both of and of far beyond that last twelve hours, an obscure amalgam of rain, landscapes, pasts, fertilities, femalenesses, all of which could perhaps have been derived from that one wet gravestone, his unknown mother's, he had stared at briefly that morning; and which would certainly have been so derived by the verdigrised old sage in bronze whom Dan had passed, with no more than an amused glance, in Dorchester that previous afternoon.

But I didn't derive it so myself, in the implacable first person of the moment, because a much more prosaic femaleness was suddenly standing at the passenger seat door and gently tapping on the glass. And Phoebe brought a more prosaic reality. It was so unlikely that Jane would accept, and I would thus be spared my white lying.

Yet having driven Phoebe and her shopping-baskets home, I went straight to telephone Roz at her office. I knew she worked at the Kensington House branch of the BBC. My luck was in. They tracked her down; and yes, she could talk. How was the week-end? I told her briefly about that, then got down to brass tacks.

"Roz, I've just put your mama on the train in a slightly shocked state. I've got to go to Egypt for a few days, about the script, and I've rather brashly suggested she come and does a week's cruise down the Nile. She told me about the end of the affair. I've been left feeling I shouldn't make such immoral propositions. In spite of having very carefully made it clear that I wasn't."

I had feared hesitation, another shocked reaction. It was refreshingly quick.

"But it sounds smashing. Why won't she . . . ?"

"I've asked her to talk it over with you, that's why I'm ringing. She seems to think she's too much of a social leper to be traveled with."

"Oh she is so *stupid*."

"And the expense."

"She's not even remotely hard up."

"Then what would people think."

"I know what that means. All her miserable Oxford lefty chums."

"And I suspect worried about Paul."

"It's high time Paul was less worried about. Anyway, I can cope with him."

"I don't want to force her, Roz. But I can't help feeling it would do her good. Perhaps she just needs a push."

"Don't worry. She'll jolly well get it. And I think it's terribly sporting of you. It's just what she needs."

"If you could let her bring it up. I don't want her to feel . . . you know."

"Of course."

"It's ten days, two weeks at most. She can stop off and see your sister in Florence on the way back."

She said nothing for a moment. "Fairy godfathers."

"Guilty ones."

"If she doesn't go, I shall offer myself as a substitute."

"I could certainly use a trained research assistant."

"Are you really sure you want an old drag like Jane? I'd be much more useful."

We pursued this treacherous teasing a sentence or two, then I went into more detail on the trip; and by the time she rang off, Jane was going . . . at gunpoint if necessary.

I knew there was a slight risk in invoking Roz's aid—that it might bring Jane to reveal things her daughter didn't know, and lend her refusal more emotional validity. She had also built up a life so firmly founded on original mistakes and wrong decisions that their removal must seem a threat; and I guessed that I remained (whatever comparative innocence I was granted to my face) the seeming cause of a far-reaching accident . . . like a mistake on a chart, forgiveable inasmuch as it arose from an ignorance on the cartographer's part, but still blamed for all that ensued. Such blames can assume formidable importance in the underlying structure of a mental life, and that was probably what most troubled Jane. To come must mean partly to pretend. Yet this could also prevent her from telling Roz the truth, and so make her arguments for not coming all the weaker.

Meanwhile, I took refuge in Kitchener; read back over what had been written to date; jettisoned one draft scene, and rewrote it; saw a chance to use a flashback inside a flashback, and possibly a flashback inside that as well; a Chinese-box gimmick, but with possibilities. Then I forced myself to analyze the problem of cramming Curzon and India, seven years, into twenty minutes of screen time. Eight hours later, near midnight, I hadn't solved the problem, but I did begin to know where to concentrate my energies. In India Curzon and Kitchener were like a pair of rhinoceroses, two ponderous and monomaniacal ambitions arrived, by reciprocal double-dealing, on a collision course. Dramatizing the actual clash of horns in India wasn't the difficulty; but conveying the furious establishment string-pulling the two men indulged in at home. However, by the time I took myself to bed, I thought I saw a way through that. I did now and then wonder what was happening in London at Roz's flat, and kept half an ear open for the ring of the telephone. But I didn't really expect it, knowing that my own combination of wiles and forthrightness had failed and that Jane was not a person to be bullied, even by her daughter.

Before I was to have that mystery solved, another was set. The telephone did ring, but at seven the next morning, the Tuesday. I was asleep, but Phoebe was up to answer it, and woke me. It was Jenny. Her second "contribution" had arrived in London three or four days before; and been discussed. Now she was in the Bel-Air cabin, just about to go to sleep. Like Roz, she wanted to know how the week-end had been, what it was like being back at Thorncombe, what time it was, the weather . . . all, as I very soon began to suspect, to hide something else. There was a silence.

"Is something wrong?"

"Yes."

She was silent again. "Jenny?"

"I'd have caught a plane home if you hadn't answered."

"What is it, for God's sake?"

"I don't know how to tell you."

"Something at the studio?"

"No, it's us. Not work."

"You must tell me what."

"I've written something."

I relaxed, even smiled to myself. "I thought it must be at least an orgy down at Malibu."

"Oh God. Why did you have to say that?"

"Come on. You write jolly well. I enjoy it. I don't mind all the home truths."

"It's not really about you this time. It's not true, Dan. You mustn't believe a word of it."

"What is it about then?"

"I posted it this morning. I spent the whole week-end writing it." Then she said, almost violently, "Promise you won't believe it."

Dan looked uncomfortably toward the kitchen door. It was not quite closed, and Phoebe's usual radio was not on.

"I believe everything you write."

There was yet another silence. "You don't know. And don't tease."

"Then I don't believe a word you write."

[ 444 ]

"I want you to burn it unopened." I said nothing. "It's my period. I went slightly mad. Trying to convince myself I don't need you."

"*Is* something wrong at work?"

"Please promise you'll burn it. Unopened."

And at last something about her voice, the constant pauses, changes of direction, struck me.

"Have you been smoking, Jenny?"

"I feel so miserable."

"It won't help."

"I know." She said, "It's all imagination. I made it up."

"Is Mildred down at the house?"

"I don't want Mildred. I want you."

"I thought we agreed——" I was going to say something about smoking, but she interrupted.

"Promise you'll burn it. I swear it's not true."

"Then it won't hurt."

"I've been such a mess today. I couldn't think of anything, I kept on forgetting lines. If only I hadn't posted it."

"You must calm down."

A longer silence. Then a forced, more formal voice.

"Is it nice? Your little gray home in the west?"

"I saw the first primroses this morning. Wished you were here."

"Damn you."

"Why do you say that?"

"Your famous imagination has failed you for once. You don't realize primroses seem like another planet."

"Only seem."

"Dan, I don't want to be in this fucking awful game any more."

She very rarely used such language.

"I wish you'd go down and see Mildred."

"I'm all right." She added, "Just ashamed."

"You shouldn't take things so seriously. Me, least of all."

"You've got your awful calm-the-star voice."

"It is what I'm trying to do."

The silence this time was so long that in the end I said her name again.

"I was just trying to think liberated. Great. You gotta believe."

"I need a translation of that."

"Why I have to tell myself so many lies."

"That's not confined to your sex."

"Are you sure you aren't on the moon?"

"Why do you say that?"

Another silence. But then suddenly her voice was near normal.

"Tell me something you're looking at where you are. Anything." I hesitated. "Please."

"I'm a couple of feet from an excruciatingly bad watercolor of my father's church and the village. By someone called Eliza Galt. Dated 1864. I think it's an adaptation of a religious print. It has 'The Lord watches over all' written in a sort of black rainbow across the sky."

"It sounds ghastly."

"Eliza ran short of space in her sky, so 'over all' looks like one word. God watches an overall. That's why I bought it."

"I thought you despised camp."

"Not when I feel affection for it."

"Is that meant to put me in my place?"

"Don't be so touchy."

"You keep sounding exactly how I was afraid you'd sound."

"I've been back here barely thirty-six hours and I've already thought a hundred times, is she going to like it?"

"What I wrote, it's because I don't really know you. I just think I know you."

"Are you sure it isn't that you don't always know yourself?"

"That as well." She said in a quieter voice, "Promise to burn it when it comes."

"Okay."

"I'm the one with the rather neat italic writing."

"I do just remember."

"Swear."

"Sworn."

"Cross your heart."

"You cross it. It's somewhere there beside you." Silence. "I want you to sleep now."

"What are you going to do with your day?"

"Work on the script. And think of you sleeping."

There was the last silence of the many that studded that conversation.

"Pick me a primrose. I love you."

The receiver had gone down before Dan could answer. He contemplated trying to get a line back to California, to ring the house and ask Mildred to go up and see if Jenny was all right; but then decided she was sane enough to do that for herself if she really needed a shoulder to weep on; and that it was better to book a call for when she woke up, later in his own afternoon in England. So he did that.

It had been doubly unfortunate. He had had Egypt, and Jane, on his conscience as soon as he heard Jenny's voice; but had waited to gauge her mood before confession, since it was not yet strictly necessary, though he had decided it was wiser to let her know what was in the wind, perhaps to pretend he was consulting her first. But of course she had made even that very dubious way of easing his conscience impossible. It was not quite the first time he had heard her so. Earlier on there had been a bad day at work, bitterness, tears . . . not unexpected, since he knew, perhaps better than she did, the extent to which actresses live on their nerves; and the mistake of thinking they were doing anything more than using pre-menstrual depression to toy with the part of the common Eve— and having toyed, to revert very rapidly to their usual abnormal role. But the call had unhappily emphasized the artificiality of their relationship. As always, Thorncombe had already made him retreat into the past, his lost domain, his other world, and it had not needed her voice to remind him of the new distance between them; almost the distance of the imagined from the real.

It was not fair to Jenny—not even fair to himself, since he had felt a protective desire for her as she spoke; and had not lied, merely exaggerated, over the number of times he had thought of her since her return to the farm. He cherished the idea of her there, at the same time as he knew it was, in any but a visiting way, the least conceivable of their futures: how bored she would be, if she gave up her career for this "nowhere"—and yet still, adolescently, dreamed situations in which, by some miraculous change of nature, she happily accepted such a life. He was also missing her physically: her casual grace, presence, voice and movement near him, as well as her naked body.

He had long considered himself disabused of the notion that much-photographed faces must axiomatically be accompanied by altogether more amusing, profound and human personalities than those of the rest of mankind; when off the screen, or stage, all the evidence, public and private, demonstrated the very reverse. But he wondered now if he was not still a little its victim; gulled by Jenny's intelligence into forgetting how desirable she was by more ordinary male standards—and would have remained, with far less interesting a private personality. He was like someone who had captured a princess, only to discover himself captured in return by her title and all that was attendant on it; silken skeins, of course, but fundamentally absurd. For some reason the long-distance call had seemed far more indulgent at Thorncombe than those in London. A folly had hovered over it, almost something from Restoration comedy, a mannered obliviousness to ordinary reality . . . the careless pounds and dollars spent on a complex technology to establish that they were simply in need of each other. It did not jibe at all with the feeling Dan had had on his morning walk with Paul; or with a tiny incident from later that previous day: the very small matter of Jane's electing to travel second-class, not first.

Shaved and dressed, Dan stood for a moment at his bedroom window, staring out down over the orchard; and wrily remembered Midas again. Sometimes having everything is closer to having nothing than the unsuccessful will ever imagine.

He went down for his breakfast. It was still cloudy, but the rain had stopped in the night and there was now no wind. He listened to Phoebe's chatter for half an hour, told her more about Jane, and Paul, and the other two daughters—a little to cover the fact that he was not going to tell her who his telephone conversation had been with. Phoebe approved, though whether that was out of genuine liking for Jane and her son or because she felt he was at last producing some sort of family besides Caro, he could not tell. Then he strolled out in the garden, where Ben was already working, to be shown what had been happening in his absence: a ritual the weather and his visitors had prevented before that.

He walked slowly down the paths behind the old man, listening to his commentaries, the spring broc's were coming on not too bad, leeks been fair enough, the "celery roots" (like Phoebe in the kitchen Ben found difficulty over some of Dan's more exotic demands, such as this bed of celeriac) seemed to like it . . . and there were the first of the new season's plantings, the shallots already sprouting green from the red earth, and the heads of the broad beans. Talk of seed potatoes, which Ben must order soon: a familiar debate between flavor and crop, which was always decided the same way. Ben grew his own King Edwards and the rest for size and sanity, and Dan was allowed a row or two of his Catriona and Fir-apples, if they could be got, for showing off to his fancy London friends.

From there they progressed to the iniquities of the American vegetable-growing scene, a woeful story Ben never tired of hearing; perhaps some atavistic nineteenth-century peasant's vision of the United States as the land of the blessed, where everything grew bigger and better, lingered in his mind, and it pleased Ben to have Dan demonstrate that he and his forefathers were wisest to have stayed put. They've declared the Cox and the Blenheim lost apples, says Dan; and Ben shakes his head in disbelief. He cannot really imagine a country where every man is not some sort of gardener, or at least understands the points of it (Dan is seldom actually seen spade in hand, I'm afraid).

They stand over another of Dan's new-fangled importations, a row of artichokes, their gray-green leaves already on the shoot. Neither Ben nor Phoebe will eat the heads, but the old man stoops and ruffles the leaves of the most advanced plant with an indulgent toleration for this foreigner. Like all gardeners he admires plants that show early, announce spring before winter is over; and Dan, too, has a pleasurable sense of seasons, of awakening. He thinks back again to Jenny, artifice, calls from California. Yes, the real inhabits here.

An hour later, he had returned to the unreal in his workroom, the telephone rang. It was Roz, she had just seen her mother off back to Oxford; and she thought her hash was settled. It had finally all boiled down to two contradictory things: to a matter of socialist principle, refusing to travel first class, and to Jane's feeling it was not quite *comme il faut*—what Nell might say. The latter objection Roz, in her usual manner, had solved by immediately ringing Compton. Nell (at least according to Roz) had laughed at Jane's scruples; wished someone would ask *her* to loll about in the sun, it was a super idea, just what Jane needed . . . though Jane herself, it seemed, had still not been quite convinced.

"She kept on talking about self-indulgence. I got really angry with her, she's become so silly about it. I told her she wasn't a socialist at all. Just a stuffy old spoilsport."

"What happened finally?"

"She did concede she was rather tempted. I think she'll come round. It's just she gets so mulish when everyone starts telling her what to do—was she like that when you first knew her?"

"Rather like her elder daughter, actually."

"Hey, that's not fair. I'm very suggestible." She said, "Anyway, she's going to ring you when she gets home."

And once again, he was thanked.

He then telephoned Malevich's London office, to make sure that things could be arranged as quickly and easily as the producer had claimed. They could, at any rate as regarded the visas and the traveling. The secretary he spoke to would see about the Nile cruise, and ring back; which she did, some twenty minutes later. There was a cruise starting from Luxor on Thursday week, and she had already reserved two single cabins. It was not fully booked, and they could be canceled.

Dan went back to work. The Indian scenes began to take shape, to feed one another. Then there was suddenly a page of dialogue that came to life, that would be good to act. He ate the sandwiches that Phoebe brought him, and gave himself a break afterward. He put on a Mozart record, the G minor symphony; and sat smoking, staring out of the window. It had begun to rain again. He went to the window and stared down at the rivulets of water on the drive up to the house, at the snowdrops that clustered around the two old rick-stones that bordered the path to the front door. The music behind him: he felt an abrupt wave of happiness, richness, fecundity, as if he was in advance of the actual season outside and transported two months on into full spring. The seed was swelling, the chink in the door widening a centimeter; though he still felt it was a selfishness, an unwarranted optimism. Perhaps it all came from the simplicities of his childhood. He needed complexity, multiple promise, endless forked roads; and simply, at this moment, felt he had them. Just as the green-gold music had, beneath the balance, the effortless development and onwardness, its shadows, so also was there a component of sadness in Dan's happiness: he was happy because he was a solitary at heart, and that must always cripple him as a human being.

It had come to Dan often, working on Kitchener—not only in reading the old man's life but in researching all those other lives interwoven with his—that their Britishness, their obsession with patriotism, duty, national destiny, the sacrifice of all personal temperament and inclination (though not personal ambition, of course) to an external system, a quasi-mythical purpose, was profoundly foreign to him, even though he was a myth-maker of sorts himself. Empire was the great disease . . . *aut Caesar, aut nullus*; and profoundly un-English. The whole nineteenth century was a disease, a delusion called Britain. The true England was freedom to be self, to drift like a spore, to stay unattached to anything, except transiently, but the drifting freedom. Very few were lucky enough, as Dan was, to be able to live that freedom in almost literal terms: live where they want and how they like . . . whence came the national evolution of the inner world and the stiff outer face that jealously guarded it. This Englishness was even, in retrospect, immanent in archetypal red-white-and-blue Britons like Kitchener. His face may have personified British patriotism and the Empire, but his inner soul was devious, convoluted, far more tyrannized by his own personal myth than the public one he appeared to be building.

Not to conform . . . whatever the cost, not to conform; and that, obscurely, biologically rather than politically, was what was wrong with Jane's Marxist solution.

The last movement had begun, though Dan had stopped listening to the music except unconsciously . . . or to anything else. He heard Phoebe's voice calling: the telephone again. He looked at his watch, thinking it might be the Californian call he had booked, but there was an hour to run before that was due; and when she saw him, Phoebe said it was Mrs. Mallory. Downstairs he hesitated, took a breath, then spoke.

"Hallo, Jane. Home safely?"

"Yes, Dan. Thank you." There was a tiny hesitation. "I gather Roz has spoken to you."

"She tells me it's three against one now."

"I feel the victim of a cabal."

"The beneficiary. Will you come?"

"Only if you're absolutely sure you can stand the thought of it."

"I wouldn't have suggested it otherwise."

"You are sure?"

"It's a lovely experience. I know you'll enjoy it."

"Then I'd love to come. If I may."

"Now I really feel forgiven." There was a moment, she said nothing, but he waited.

"That was granted many years ago, Dan."

"Symbolically, anyway."

He went briskly on then, and told her about the next cruise from Luxor, and that he would like to be in Cairo on that day week. She flinched a little at this, as if such long journeys

[ 451 ]

still needed a Victorian thoroughness of preparation. But he assured her all the bookings would be made, that the cruises were very informal, no fancy wardrobe was needed. If she could get up to London on the Monday, they could see about the visas then. He expected further flinching over the cost, but curiously she didn't ask about that . . . or perhaps had already checked on it with some local travel agency, and decided she would afford it.

"You must tell me who to pay."

"We can settle all that on Monday. They probably won't know, it's all done on account. So don't worry."

"I insist on paying my share."

"Of course. We're going Dutch. It's the movie business. You always pay later. Literally and metaphorically." He sensed, down the line, that she did not like that; she was not even being allowed to pay on the nail for her wickedness. But she did, finally, reveal something more innocent.

"I feel like a small child being offered a totally unexpected treat. Not quite able to believe it."

"There are all those boring old pharaohs. You may hate that."

"I must get a book and read it up."

Dan told her not to buy a guide, he still had the one he had used before in London. They talked a minute more about the arrangements. Then she thanked him again, and for the night's stay, and rang off.

He went into the living-room and poured himself a small whisky. The die was cast, and very soon he would have to speak to Jenny and take his own decision. He need not tell her yet. But Dan was an old hand at deceiving. The later you left it, the more difficult it became to justify. He stared at the bishop, and began to rehearse.

The booked call came through on time, sooner than he wanted. Jenny was already, though only just, up; and delighted, she hadn't expected it.

"I'm so sorry about last night. I won't do it again."

"Swill the bloody stuff down the drain."

"Yes I will. I promise."

"Where did you get it from?"

"Just someone at the studio."

He knew she was lying, he couldn't quite say why: simply that in other circumstances he would have pressed to know more about the "someone."

"How do you feel?"

"Okay. I'll get through. Now you've rung." She added, "Perhaps you'd better read what I sent. Just to discover what a bitch I am."

He felt the relief of a chess-player shown at least one clear move ahead.

"You're going to feel the same about me in a minute."

"Why?"

"I've got some news, Jenny. I was going to tell you last night, but it seemed hardly the moment. I'm going to Egypt for a few days next week. I'll be back before you return."

"Oh *Dan*. You mean thing."

"I desperately need some new ideas."

"But I thought you said—"

"I've had to change my mind. It reads like a history cram course at the moment. It's getting some atmosphere in."

"You can't delay it?"

"I wish I could."

"I don't trust you with all those slinky-eyed belly-dancers."

"I may be taking a chaperone. If that's any consolation."

"Your daughter?"

"The great family problem of the moment. Her aunt."

There was a tiny silence; then an incredulity.

"Your ex's sister?"

"Everyone's at their wits' end about what to do with her. She's got very withdrawn and depressed. I just suggested it out of the blue, God knows why. When she was here. My good deed for the day or something."

It had plainly set her back. Dan waited. Then her voice returned, guarded, sober, yet for some odd reason closer.

"I thought you were hardly on speaking terms."

"It's all peace and forgiveness at the moment."

"And she's said yes?"

"We're all trying to persuade her."

"And your ex approves?"

"Jenny, we're talking about a rather lost middle-aged woman. Who you'd like and feel sorry for if you knew her. It really is pure charity and . . . well there is something else."

"What?"

"Just Caroline. This ancient vendetta among us all has disturbed her a lot. I suppose I want to show what a decent fellow her father is at heart. In view of all my other sins."

"Meaning me."

"Among others."

"How's *her* madness going?"

"I gather it's being conducted in Paris this next week-end. No sign of sanity yet."

"If only I had a nice traditional gentleman friend like that." But she jumped on before he could answer. "Do you fancy her?"

"Passionately. That's why I'm telling you about it."

"Be serious."

"I've always liked her as a human being. In the days when I knew her well. But not otherwise."

"It's not pure charity then."

"You would like her. And feel sorry for her."

"That's what male rats have said ever since time began."

"Still true. In this case."

"At least I only betray you on paper. I don't think you're my Mr. Knightley at all."

"Never one of my ambitions."

"You're not even trying."

"Because you aren't an Emma."

"Soapy water."

"What's that mean?"

"What you wash hands of things with." He said nothing. "I think you're a bastard not at least warning me."

"I wanted to last night. It may not happen."

"If only I could see your face." Then she said, "Oh God, now my driver's knocking. Hang on."

A few moments later she returned.

"Dan?"

"Are you late?"

"No, but I must go. I'm not dressed. Will you ring tomorrow evening?"

"Yes of course."

"You're enough to put anyone on the hard stuff. You know that?"

"That's California talk. Not you."

"She'd just better be as scrupulous over personal relationships as you told me she was."

"She's already raised that problem. And I assured her you were much too intelligent not to trust me."

"Tell her that reads better without the 'not.' "

"She's also a very left-wing lady. With no time for capitalist layabouts like me."

"Except when you invite her to Egypt."

"I suspect only to try to convert me. If she does come." He said, "I so wish it was you."

"Me what?"

"Coming. And here now."

"I am. By post. I'm rather glad now."

"Tomorrow?"

"Only because I haven't anyone else to talk to."

"Of course."

"You needn't think I'm going to say goodbye. I'm only hanging on to cost you more money."

"I guessed."

"How old is she?"

"In her late forties. And with varicose veins, if you're interested."

"I'm not."

"Well then."

There was a silence, then her "small" voice; a curious flat tone she had used effectively in one or two of her already filmed scenes.

"I'm gone now."

"Jenny."

"Really gone."

Still she left a silence, but then the receiver went down. Dan was left staring at *The Lord watches overall*, though with a strong feeling that it was not quite all; certainly not over his skill at the half-truth. Yet strangely, the hurtness in Jenny's voice, an uncertainty of tone that was not characteristic of her, had touched him, and helped restore the balance he had lost after the earlier call. A fear, a loneliness, a simplicity, a humanity . . . something at any rate that remained when one had subtracted the indulgence and the artifice; he foresaw a day when she would meet Jane, and he would be forgiven.

He had remained standing by the telephone, but now, through the living-room doorway, he saw a low shaft of sunlight, entered by the westward windows, on the rush matting that covered the floor. A white wall beyond shone as in a Vermeer interior. Dan went and opened the front door and stood under the porch. The sky was clearing to the south and west, and the setting winter sun had got through for the first time since his return. Torn wisps of dark-gray vapor, silhouetted, floated against the limpid yellow upper air. Everything in the combe before him was stained a faint gold, the wet garden, the meadows, the glistening drops on the branches. To the south, over the English Channel, there lay a long soft bank of rain-cloud, curled at one end, like a fifteen-mile plume, and tinged an exquisite and evanescent dove-gray. All the clouds in that direction held delicate violet and amethystine washes in their billows and folds.

A hidden magpie chattered from the far side of the combe, and there was an angry cawing from a pair of crows. They flew overhead, purposefully, in hue and cry, and Dan walked down the wet paving of the path to where he could turn and look back over the roof of the farmhouse. It was a buzzard, circling high over the beechwood, the soft light from the opened west catching, as in some gentle, delicate searchlight, the brown-and-white underside of the bird's flexed wings. It mewed, majestic, golden, apotheosized, against a dark cloud above. Dan stood and watched till it was chased off, remembering Tsankawi. All his real but unwritten worlds; his past futures, his future pasts.

# A Third Contribution

Written in *anger*.

There was a change in the Prick when you left. He even pretended quite convincingly to be sorry for me when he heard the next day. He was having a party that evening, if I had nothing better to do—he made it clear there would be lots of people, it wasn't a pass. I didn't go, or want to. But he behaved better on set, even Bill noticed it. And between takes. He actually said another day it would be great to work together again. Perhaps he was making a bid then, but it was partly meant at face value.

I think I'd better call him by his proper name from now on. Steve, if you remember.

I've despised so much in him, but there's also something I've envied—the American thing again, I suppose. A kind of ease, a nonchalance, the way he won't be put down. Even the way he doesn't take his acting very seriously (behind all the talk). Life's fun, he's generally happy, he's got his girls and his Porsche and his tennis and his body. If I'm honest he relaxes me now as often as he irritates. That thing you never understood about us poor cattle, how we sometimes develop really rather good relationships somewhere between what we're acting and what we are outside the whole shmeer. Because no one else quite knows what being on camera's like.

This started happening before you left. I hid it, because I began to see I understood him better than you did (in spite of your foul double-dealing, of which more in a moment), and I know you don't like that in people. Their understanding better than you. Actually we've begun to get it righter and righter since you ratted. He's not trying so hard to be clever and trying much harder to be natural. The smidgin of edge I like between me and my acting man is still there. But it helps now, instead of getting in the way.

I guessed he must have found another girl: and there she was on set one day—this was about four days after you went.

And yes, I haven't mentioned her, either. Her father's some kind of legal big wheel, drips deals, land, corporations. Offices in San Francisco and New York. Her name is Katherine. Kate. She was sexy, cool, but polite. She'd been in England last summer, and we talked about that. Then Steve said they were going to the new Fellini, if I'd like to come with them . . . I tried to get a cue from her, I did quite want to see the film, but not if she minded. She didn't seem to. I thought perhaps he'd told her I was lonely or shy or something. I don't think it was planned. It may have been. It doesn't matter now.

We went to his place for drinks first. She knew Abe and Mildred slightly, it turned out her parents live in Bel-Air too. She majored in English and drama at UCLA, but no stage ambitions. She's known Steve "since ever." They were at high school together. We talked about the picture, Steve was nice about my work. Kate and I talked about drama teaching. We went and saw the Fellini, had a meal. I began to like her better. She seemed to have Steve and his emoting in perspective and we even sided against him in a bantering sort of way a couple of times. She seemed to do him good, too. Sobered him down, as if he knew she knew him too well to risk his cornier lines on politics and acting. They didn't touch, they might have been married, or brother and sister. The latter really.

The meal came to an end, I said something about finding a cab, I assumed they'd both be returning to his place. But no, he was driving her home to Bel-Air . . . and me as well. I still thought they were just being decent. They'd drop me and then go back to his place. But even that was wrong. Her house came first and he took us there. She asked us in for a drink, but I didn't have to speak. Steve turned it down for both of us—it was midnight, we had to sleep. He got out and kissed her briefly. She bent down at my window and repeated an invitation to come over, go shopping, a drive, any time I was free.

Two minutes later Steve and I were in front of Abe and Mildred's. I was suspicious by then, and very sure he wasn't even going to get the chance to refuse an invitation to have a last drink from me. As soon as the car stopped, I thanked him for the evening, and made to get out.

He said, Jenny, there's just one thing. Would you believe me if I said I truly enjoyed this evening?

I said that I'd enjoyed it too. I liked Kate.

I kind of got us off on the wrong foot that first date we had. Right?

I said it didn't matter. It might even have helped.

I knew I was being English. But it was all unnecessary. It didn't need spelling out, we'd been working better together for weeks. He was staring down at the wheel. He has angles, that moustache and the hair, a sort of sensitive Jesus look. It was put on, but something made me feel sorry for him. I leaned across and pecked the side of the hair, then got out.

I heard him get out as well, as I set off toward the house. I thought for a horrid moment that he was going to come after me. Ridiculous, when you're scared to give people even an inch.

I looked round, but he was standing there beside the car.

I watch you to the door, he said. Local custom.

Yes, I know Bel-Air is safe, that that also wasn't really necessary. Phony gallantry. But it made me feel a pig.

The next day, the first time we had to talk, he went back to how nice the evening had been. Kate liked me, he knew she liked me. That was apparently some kind of feather in my cap. I said again that I'd liked her, too.

I had a day off soon after that, while they did some of the odds-and-ends covers and sequences with Steve alone. Perhaps he let her know, anyway Kate rang and asked me over to lunch and suggested we go shopping. I've been good about clothes, I felt I'd earned a little binge. Her parents were out. We had a swim and a sunbathe and a salad. We talked about Steve. Though there were things she evidently accepted in him because they're a part of the standard young California male (things I couldn't take, though I didn't say so) she wasn't at all dewy-eyed. She said they knew each other too well, they couldn't ever really make it. "Like marriage, a serious commitment. You know what I mean?"

I didn't really. I supposed she meant they had been to bed, but now were just good friends. Perhaps it was a green light, and she really wanted to know if I was driving in that direction. But she didn't probe at all. She said she could guess how difficult he was to act with, he had no technique to fall back on if he couldn't "relate." I said he was fine when he did. It was all very diplomatic.

Their pool's enormous and the house something. So are some of the paintings on the walls. She showed me round, there was a touch of the bored young aristocrat about her,

[ 459 ]

very casual, not guying it as an English girl in that sort of parental shop would have done. Even rather modest about it, as if I probably lived in a castle *à la* San Simeon at home and wouldn't be impressed. I suppose it's wrong to talk as I did last time about Americans chasing a dream, when some of them have achieved it. Steve told me later that her Irish great-grandfather stood on Ellis Island with a small sack of nothing in his hand. Which makes it more of a fairy-tale. Her poise is quite something, also.

She took me off shopping, down to a smashing place in Santa Monica. Just my clothes. I enjoyed it much more than I expected, perhaps because the shop knew her and pandered to us. I pretend I despise clothes-buying, and I don't at all really. I began to like Kate. There were distances, she gushed too much over England and her tourist's view of it, but one sort of felt one could show her the real England and she'd understand. She has lovely greeny eyes, rather intense. A tan I can only dream about. She's a year younger than me. A little bit like an Israeli *sabra* girl. Her mother's Italian stock (strictly non-Mafia, she says). Rather small, apple cheeks and a boy-girl's body. Long hair, very dark, almost black. She's cool and warm, a nice mouth. All this for your benefit. You'd fancy her.

She asked about you, but very tactfully—whether you were coming back. I said you weren't. And we had a general kvetch about relationships with older men. Marriage, working, Lib. There'd been something with one of her UCLA teachers when she was a sophomore, she went into that in some detail and I was probably meant to respond in kind, but I didn't (all this was at a so-called English tea-room in Santa M.) and it ended in our agreeing there weren't any rules, the one thing one mustn't do is fake it . . . you *would* like her, Dan, even though she's a Californian-style poor little rich girl, ten planets away from Europe and its shabbiness and poverty and making do. She's rather refreshingly apolitical. Doesn't pretend, but feels as we do about studio shills and the boostering, things like that. The con game the success life is here. I realized it seemed years since I'd talked to another girl I liked, could feel with. She was so outgoing, articulate about it, being the only daughter (she has two brothers, one's at Yale and the other's a lawyer in daddy's New York office), what's wrong with the Coast . . . but all these are lines you can read between.

She drove me home about six. There was some dinner-party her parents were giving and she had to be at—I could have come, her parents were dying to meet me, but it would be a terrible drag. So another day. I hadn't been back in the Cabin ten minutes when the 'phone rang. It was Steve. Ashkenazy was playing downtown. He had two tickets, would I use one? It seemed so spur-of-the-moment on his part, he'd helped me meet Kate and I understood the situation there now (or thought I did) and that I wasn't two-timing her in any way. I'd bought a dress I wanted to baptize. And the evening to face. A restlessness. The L.A. thing. Shape up or ship out.

Most of all though, you vile rat, it was you. Something that had made me so angry two days earlier. The Topanga interior, Steve's come-uppance. That worked, Bill was pleased, he took me aside afterward to say how pleased he was. And I gave Steve his due, after all it's his scene, and he'd truly given all he knows, and I said something about him doing pretty well for a second choice. Bill gave me a look, I could see he'd forgotten all about that. I said, That's what you told me. He hit his head. He said, Dan didn't come clean? All right, perhaps I had to be cosseted and set up at the beginning. But I hated you for days. I couldn't even bring myself to talk about it on the 'phone. It's not an excuse that you'd have told me if I'd ever asked point-blank. If you were honest you had to tell me once it happened between us. I would have understood then. But suddenly it was like your practicing all you claim you hate in Hollywood: fool the stupid broad, never mind what lies you tell her as long as she gives a better performance. It threw everything in doubt, you must see that.

So Steve came and I asked him in for a drink before we set off. It was odd, he seemed both shy and curious. To see how I lived, but not to ask about it. The new dress was "sensational." Your blue flowers watched, but said nothing. He was wearing a suit and bolo tie, I like that. It was the first time I'd seen him dressed fairly formally.

I didn't hear much of the concert—we got there late, anyway, and they wouldn't let us in till there was a break. I was thinking things out, I won't pretend I wasn't. I knew it was there. That he probably wouldn't make a move, but expected me to. That I no longer flinched at the thought of it. That I felt rather like it. That I didn't want to be involved, and wouldn't have to be. That I felt frivolous and a little bit in heat. I'd known it beside the swimming-pool that morning with Kate. I'd like to have been there with a man, one of those any-man moods. Instead of dutifully admiring the Utrillos and the Klees. Of course for Steve I'd just be a score, something to boast about as soon as I turned my back. Just one more chick he'd been tailgating and could now overtake. But then the hypocrisy of it. We'd been to bed together in front of the camera, simulated it, he'd kissed me hard and it hadn't always been just for the camera. I'd felt his body a hundred times, and he mine. It didn't seem very much to see what it was like for real.

That left you. You had begun to seem—but I said it all last time. Bar that final revelation of what a crook you are. You *could* have flown back here, Dan. If you really wanted me . . . instead of just my memory. I don't want to sound too calculated, the thought of you *was* what kept me not making up my mind at once. If you'd walked into the concert-hall or Perino's (no expense spared) afterward, Steve wouldn't have had a chance. You understand I'm trying to say how I felt that evening (or imagining how I might have felt if there ever had been such an evening, if you want it that way—but will you, she wonders). Let's call it a test run for the final exorcism: to see if it matters, betraying someone you think you respect. To see if it helps.

And yes, right. I'd been thinking about Steve in bed before that evening.

You may not think it's necessary to say any more. But we've always been honest, in our fashion. No copyright. It's a present, alter and add to it as you like. Or tie it in black ribbons and forget.

It was quite funny, actually. I decided that at least he wasn't going to do the seducing. The inevitable suggestion came that we go to his place and play a few records. Strictly just that, he said. So we get in, and he puts an Indian raga on and fetches me the iced tea from his kitchen and says he'll be with me in a moment. I watch him go into his bathroom, then I take all my clothes off and lie on his fake leopard-skin couch. It's the first time I've ever seen him caught really off-balance. I just watch him, and he nods and nods. For once he really can't think what to say. He comes closer, his hands in his suit-coat pockets, looking absolutely gauche, there's no other word for it. I sit perched up like the Goya painting and toast him with the glass of iced tea.

I say, As we've both got a free day tomorrow. (It was Sunday, we had.)

He says, You're beautiful.

He looks at me for so long that I begin to think that perhaps he's impotent or gay or something. It was so strange. I actually made him shy. Threatened his machismo or something.

I say, Aren't you going to join me?

So I watch him undress. The little white band where he wears his swimming-slip. We kiss and it's nice, sexy at once. There's a light on in the far corner of the room, and the Indian music, and he smells nice and tastes nice. It's so nice to feel a lean, hard young body. He begins kissing me all over, and playing with me, exciting me. He's read all the books, very expert. A little too studied, but you can't have everything. He keeps telling me I'm beautiful. Like some sort of mantra—almost as if it's to himself, not me. I can't believe he's usually as gentle as this. I stroke his hair and let him do what he wants.

Then we stood up and he put his hands behind me and I locked my arms round his neck and we rocked a little. It wasn't really dancing. Just feeling. Naked flesh and his thing squashed between us. Then we fell back on the couch and I let go, played wild to please him. I thought it was rather decent of him—all the girls he must have had, yet still enjoying it so much. To have it without any sort of love. Just through the body. Knowing yesterday doesn't matter, tomorrow doesn't matter. Only not caring matters.

We smoked, listened to more music, talked a little. Then he came inside me again and we lay for hours, what seemed like hours, I don't think it was just the pot. He does it better than he acts. Then we had a shower together and went to bed. I slept at once, we didn't wake up till after ten.

I haven't finished (if you're still with me).

We were still in bed. He was still asleep, I could see sunlight between the blind slats and hear the traffic outside and I was thinking my body was glad about the sex and my mind was glad about the humiliation and there was something to do about America. Something in me that had stayed foreign to it and wasn't anymore. An American body had entered mine, and I needed it. I thought about you too, Dan. How I would have to tell you and make sure you knew you were partly to blame.

Anyway. Suddenly I heard a door in the apartment close.

It gave me a shock, I looked up from Steve's shoulder at the bedroom door, which was half-open. Then up at Steve's face. He'd woken, but his eyes were closed, he was smiling. He patted my back.

(I probably shan't get his language quite right. But then you did once say it was almost an honor to get his way with it wrong.)

Relax, nothing.

The cleaning-woman?

He grinned. Right.

I said, The door's open.

Then there was a voice close outside it.

Steve?

I nearly jumped out of my skin. But he was very quick. He held me tight down against him with his arm and with the other felt for the sheet we'd thrown aside and yanked it back across us.

In here, Katie.

It all happened so fast. She was in the door. Steve said, We finally made it.

She must have known, seen the dress and my tights and things over a chair in the other room. I looked from Steve to her and back to Steve again. He was still smiling. He turned and pecked my cheek.

Relax. She doesn't mind.

I wanted to say, But I do mind, thank you very much. I wanted to bury my head under the sheet. But she was coming across the room, in a little indigo singlet and white shorts. A kind of knowing grin. She knelt on the bed and leaned over and kissed Steve quickly on the cheek, then me on the top of my bowed head. He was still holding me so tight. I couldn't have got away without a struggle and it takes two embarrassments to make a scene. Then she sat back on the bed on the other side of Steve.

Two happy people?

Steve said, Great. Just great.

I knew it would be.

She's beautiful.

He kissed the side of my head again, and I managed a rueful smile at Kate.

I said, And embarrassed.

But it's so nice when you really make it. Nothing to be ashamed of.

Steve said, You're in California now, baby.

He reached up his free arm and touched his forefinger on one of Kate's nipples beneath the blue singlet.

Hey, girls get raped for wearing things like that.

That's the idea.

She got off the bed.

I came to play tennis. Remember?

Oh Jesus.

Okay. Coffee, anyone?

I said, I'll come and help in a minute.

But she held her hands out, stopping me.

You go together. Don't spoil it.

She went out to make the coffee. He relaxed his grip, and I sat up.

Does she always walk in like this?

She's kind of a kooky kid. You know. Like I'm her sister.

You mean brother.

That's straight. She's kooky.

I said I must go to the bathroom. He didn't stop me, there was a bathrobe behind the door and I went and put it on. But I wouldn't look at him, I suppose he must have realized.

He said, Jenny? She didn't mean to make you uptight. She really likes you.

And not you?

Hey. Come on.

I just wondered.

He came out of bed then and across to where I was. Put his hands on the door behind me, so I had to look at him. Leaned forward and kissed me, then spoke down at my feet.

Listen. You're very beautiful, you're very sweet. You're beautiful, I wouldn't want you any other way. Except . . .

He did his nodding, his I'm-so-serious-I-can't-find-the-words bit.

I said, Stop thinking it's a private thing?

Give a little. Learn the way we are. (He looked up, playing director now.) Those first scenes we played. You knew I was shit scared. Right? So we acted like two other people. When all the time it could have been simple. Like last night. We never took the time. Find out who we really are.

He must have seen the doubt in my eyes. He dabbed my nose.

Like she's my favorite sister. That's all. We're something different. We don't get jealous. Okay?

He parted the robe and put his hands on my breasts and

[ 465 ]

kissed me again. I think he'd have made love, but I wouldn't let him.

When I came out of the loo I found them both in the kitchen. Steve had pulled on a pair of old jeans. We had breakfast, I did finally relax, though I felt out of my depth, I couldn't rival their naturalness, get over the feeling that sex was something that ought to be hidden. I also felt it was stupid to feel shy at being "caught." When I hadn't been shy at all the night before, when it came to it. And Kate's total lack of embarrassment was like her poise in her Bel-Air palace. Yes, all right, there was something unhealthy by home standards. But something else unhealthy was being rejected. And after that first exchange when she came in, our having made it wasn't discussed. Just three friends, a jolly breakfast. Though I could tell by the way she moved around his kitchen that she knew it backward.

Steve still wanted to play tennis, but they'd missed their club reservation now. And I hadn't any clothes. So Steve drove me home and I went up to the Cabin and changed. He waited in his car outside. Mildred and Abe weren't around, I think they must have been out, so you haven't been publicly cuckolded yet. We went back to Kate's, she'd rung some friends, there were nine or ten of us in the end. Once again her parents were away—down at Palm Springs this time. Some of the others played tennis on their private court, we swam, lay around. Kate was best of the girls (at tennis), Steve a long way the best of the men. I suppose he was showing off. It was a new side of him. Apparently when he was in his last year at high school, he was nearly good enough to go pro. Very serious on court, he keeps hyping himself after a bad shot, like a Wimbledon star. That was the un-English thing—no one laughed at his muttering and thigh-slapping, the Jimmy Connors performance. I quite liked the other people, they were all our age, one or two married, there was a girl with a baby, a loose gang. A lot of joshing off-court. References back to things I didn't understand.

I enjoyed it. Watching them and talking to them and liking them. Being conscious of Steve all the time, though he was mercifully discreet. Perhaps being cocky about his tennis was a substitute, but he didn't broadcast anything. Americans: they're so knowable so fast. The transparency seems so good sometimes. The lack of the old hide-and-seek at home. I can see you hating this, Dan, the sun and the swimming and the luxury and the mindless ball-hitting and the total failure to see that any other kind of world or feeling exists, what you once called the silly mental whore in women, and I know a sense of loss is also a sense of reality, both in the present and the past, but it's the happiest private day I've had here. That part of it. Away from you.

Well. I still haven't finished.

The others drifted away, Steve went off for a bit with one of the other men to try out some newer-model Porsche than his own and Kate took me to her "suite" to shower—fantastic, it's really a whole separate flat, a living-room, a bedroom, a bathroom that would do for a rugby team (in size), even a little kitchen of her own. Actually we decided to have a drink first, we both felt tired, so we lay propped up on the 50,000 cushions on her huge double bed, chatting about the others who'd left, she told me all sorts of things about them (mostly woes), and then I began to tell her what I felt about California. It was that nice thing, you know, when national differences begin to disappear, you start finding common feelings, understandings, beyond all the language and life-style problems. Female feelings, I don't know if it happens like that with men. Well, yes, you and Abe perhaps—translate from there. We were still in robes, just sprawled out. Like two girls in a school dormitory, really. If it hadn't been for the decor and the drinking.

Then at last—it must have been nearly an hour later—Steve appeared in a white bath-wrap. He'd come back and had his shower in one of her absent brothers' rooms. *De trop* so far as I was concerned. And I think for Kate a little, too. But he went and got a drink from the living-room, and us another, then came back and clambered between us on the bed. It was absurd, a replay of that morning. But it didn't seem to matter very much anymore. It was dusk by then, that lovely fast dusk here. I could see palm-trees, black plumes against a rose sky, through the window, the house very quiet. All good comrades together. Kate and I went on talking across him for a while.

Then there was a break. Steve turned his ankles out and touched our bare feet with his own.

I should be so lucky. Not only beautiful. But clever.

Kate said, Lucky shmucky.

Not you. You're just a kook.

She hit him with her elbow. And what's Jenny?

Like trying to make it with an icepack.

She leaned forward and pulled a face at me.

This is what we call the American way of love.

He put an arm around each of our shoulders.

You mean there are other ways?

We're not in the mood for MCPs. Are we, Jenny?

I said, Certainly not.

He pretended to be surprised.

You mean you're really a normal pair of chicks?

She said, Oh boy. Thanks for the Polish apology.

Then we got on to Polish jokes. Wasp jokes. Black jokes. Kate said, They kill my father. He's collected a whole book of them.

Then she asked me about my father, and I told them about him. About real home. Boarding-school, working in rep. The light outside faded, everything in the room lost color, became shadowy. We'd all slumped down a bit, he still had his arms loosely round us. I wasn't sure he hadn't dozed off, his eyes were closed. For ten minutes or more it was all between Kate and myself. Then I suddenly noticed. His wrap had fallen nearly open, and he wasn't asleep at all.

He murmured, Hey, look what's happened.

Kate said, Why are you such a show-off, Steve?

But yes?

No.

Jenny baby?

No thanks.

There was an odd little silence. I couldn't look at Kate, but I waited to see what she'd do. Then Steve spoke.

Let's reshoot this whole scene. I dig you both like crazy. You dig each other. We all dig each other like crazy. Friendship is loving people, right? Touching people, kissing people, balling people. How does that sound to you two young cats?

I said, Oversimplified.

He took his arms away then, turned toward me. Ran his finger over my mouth.

So what are we scared of?

Nothing. Just the way I am.

Which is sweet and kind and beautiful.

And old-fashioned. About some things.

He moved down from my mouth and tried to tease the robe loose. I caught his hand, but he'd already found his way through. He whispered in my ear.

Like school. Soft and sweet. All together.

Steve, please, no.

He whispered again. Katie's kidding. She wants it.

I couldn't understand why she said nothing. No, began to understand why. Now he spoke to her without turning his face.

Katie baby?

Not if Jenny doesn't.

I don't know what it was, Dan. I was actually a little drunk, we'd been having some tequila concoction Kate had made up. It didn't taste strong—anyway, I'm not making excuses. It all happened so fast. I did feel tricked, outraged. More at Kate than at him. That change of sides without warning. Then frightened at seeming what I'd just said I was. Knowing I was a long way from home, but perhaps I needed it. Being hung for a sheep. All sorts of strange things.

Steve said, One happy brave, two happy squaws.

And then Kate again.

We think of it like togetherness therapy. You know?

I said, Who's we?

Anyone you . . . if the vibrations feel good. And you want.

I was holding his hand against my breast, not letting him move. Kate had been leaning on an elbow, but now she sat up and reached and took my other hand. It was so strange, but I knew she was being honest, in her fashion.

Jenny, it just happens. You feel yes, you don't, it's as simple as that. If you don't want to feel that way . . . you know. We understand. That's truly all it's about. Behind the crazy-people thing. Just a way of feeling close. Not only for Steve. For you and me as well.

Steve said, Right.

Kate said, But only if you feel the same.

Then she pressed my hand, as if to give me courage, and let go of it. I know, perhaps she was just being clever. I think if they'd tried to argue or coax any more . . . but they didn't. There were so many places earlier where I ought to have drawn the line. She lay back, I felt them waiting there beside me and in spite of what she'd said I still suspected it was partly a setup, but then also that I helped them do it. Enjoying the long gossip with Kate, not getting off the bed when Steve came. Part of me was walking away, Dan. But another, perhaps it was the tequila, knew it wanted to wait and see. I felt I'd become someone else, what I'd been only a day before wasn't me any more, or no longer had to be me.

I don't know, but I let his hand escape. Again he was very

gentle, undid the sash of my robe, I hadn't got anything on underneath, my swim-things had been wet. It really was happening to someone else by then. A few moments later I was aware that Kate had slipped off the bed and gone away. She came back again almost at once. She'd taken off her robe, and lit up. It was too dark to see much by then. She knelt beside Steve, helped him get out of his own wrap. Then me out of mine. We lay, smoking for a minute or two. The best, of course.

Nothing more was said. I tried to feel shocked, that I was taking some awful step into the pit of iniquity. Then for God's sake, it was hardly an orgy, even if Kate was a perverse little bitch who'd obviously played this game before. And if it gives pleasure and it doesn't hurt anyone . . . all right, begging questions. But somehow her taking part made it less— you know. If she hadn't. Just watched or something. And there *was* a togetherness of some kind. Not sexual, something in me was too nervous, I didn't know where it would go . . . it was just masturbating, in fact. Being petted. Naughty adolescents. It even became rather trite and tame, if you can understand that. It did have a sort of sexiness, finally. But it wasn't adult.

When it was over, he'd had to break the silence I didn't want broken, the usual moronic "great" and "beautiful," what a great pair of chicks we were, something strange happened. I knew she was like me, she didn't want to talk. Perhaps it got through to him. Anyway he sat up, kissed us both, then went to where he'd left his clothes. There were a few moments of silence, and I was wondering what next, what have I done. Then Kate moved in the darkness toward me, it was so peculiar, just like a small girl wanting to be held, she made me turn on my back, then lifted my right arm over her shoulders and sank beside me, her mouth against my shoulder, just one small kiss there. I was thinking, oh God. Ready to jump a mile. But she reached and found my free hand again and held it against my stomach, pressed it there, as if to tell me it wasn't what I thought—what you must be thinking. She did put a leg a little over mine to get closer, but I can't tell you how, I knew it was only a clinging. In the end I didn't mind feeling her warm naked body at all. It seemed sexless, like a child's. Her skin was very soft after a man's. It was funny, knowing what it is to be you (a man). To have something like that against you. It was also some sort of declaration. As if Steve had just been the catalyst. Not sex. Something about

[ 470 ]

the American heart. I don't know. So many mechanical and non-human toys to play with and only the flip little vocabulary to cope. Only another female body to explain to. The loneliness. Having it all, and underneath not knowing, remaining insecure. In Kate's case, not even able to escape her home, her family, her money. I'm trying to say it was mysterious, Dan. And innocent, you can't imagine. For a moment or two, so much closer than my real sisters have ever felt. Somehow more moving, disturbing, than anything with him.

And she didn't say a word. Nor did I.

Finally Steve came back dressed and stood in the doorway. Some light came through from the living-room and he could see how we lay and of course.

So that's the way it is.

Idyll broken.

What *is* kooky about her is the way she slips out of one mood into another—as if the last has been an act. Suddenly she was out of that lonely clinging child into her other self. Steve was told to take himself off. We showered, dressed, and she went on talking all through it as we had before he came in, there was even a whole bit about how one's (women's) feelings changed over clothes colors. Just as if nothing at all had happened, it had all been a dream. I can't tell you how odd it was. I think she is a little around the bend. At least two quite different people. I mean even Steve—she cooked us hamburgers afterward down in the main palace kitchen—even he admitted something had happened, the way he looked at us (though he too *said* nothing, they're so compartmented).

I felt so far from both of them down there, suddenly. Yet also close, I can't explain. And released, I think even amused. Steve rooting about in the icebox for some special beer he wanted, Kate talking about the art of the hamburger to me, just two girls in a kitchen. I'm sure it didn't mean very much to them. I suppose I felt let off lightly, too. There must be worse things three young people can do than just lie in the dark and play with each other's bodies. Perhaps next time there would be another man—lots of other men and girls. I didn't know, I was suddenly glad I had done it *and* that I was coming home soon. Even though you won't be there to meet me now.

Dan, writing this down has exhausted me almost as much as taking part in it would have done. I know it's a mass of contradictions. You'll probably know what it really means better

[ 471 ]

than I do. It's taken two long evenings and a whole day and I'm sorry about all the crossings-out and alterations. And bad taste. But not sorry you may not know whether I'm pretending it hasn't happened or pretending that it has.

I know this isn't what you want. But it's what you asked for. I just won't be *only* something in your script. In any of your scripts. Ever again.

# The Shadows of Women

That little document from a different world had come by the Saturday morning post. We had spoken twice more during the week. It was not altogether a shock, since by then I had dragged out of her, in the intervals between her interrogations concerning Jane, that it was "about imagining being unfaithful to you." The nonsense about burning the thing without opening it had been dropped. She called during her lunch-break at the studio; about nine that Saturday evening, for me. There was no beating about the bush.

"Has it come?"

"Yes, Jenny."

"Do you hate me?"

"Only for being able to put yourself down so well."

There was a silence. Then another question like an accusation.

"Did you believe it?"

"Not that it happened."

"But what?"

"Whether you wanted it to happen?"

A quieter voice. "Why didn't you believe it?"

"Because you wouldn't have written about it. And you haven't answered my question."

"Kate exists. We have got quite chummy."

"Good."

She didn't like that, but swallowed it. "It was based on an evening the three of us had together. Just a feeling in the air."

"Dangerous liaisons?"

"Something like that. Kate's been in that scene. Though she claims it's all over."

"I see."

"You are angry."

"You still haven't answered my question."

"Because if you don't know the answer—" but she broke

[ 473 ]

off, and changed tack. "All right. A tiny, tiny part of me. Which I despise."

"And it had to be him?"

"I don't know anyone else his age here."

"He's made another bid?"

"He lets me know it still holds."

"And you're tempted."

"I'm tempted to pay you back. Among other things for the reason I wrote. Which I notice you're carefully avoiding."

"All that was to help, Jenny."

"It hardly flatters your opinion of me as a human being. Or an actress. And don't for Christ's sake start quoting Falconetti at me."

I had once told her the story about Dreyer's cruel practical joke during the making of *The Passion of Joan of Arc*; how he had coaxed Falconetti into a real *oubliette* in some castle, to see what it was like to sit couched in eternal darkness, and then locked her in until she was hysterical enough to give him the martyred Joan no other actress has ever come within a mile of. I had told Jenny the tale was almost certainly apocryphal, but it had registered.

"We were overprotective. But the rushes were arguing for it."

"And of course the silly vain cow couldn't conceivably have lived with the knowledge."

"I am sorry, Jenny."

She was silent a moment, then changed from bitterness to reproach.

"You don't know how difficult it is. I can't slap his face. And I still quite like this girl Kate, even though I know she's . . . I suppose a little bent. Cracked. They're so innocent underneath. You know what they're like."

"Is it she who's put you back on pot?"

"I haven't smoked since that evening. If it's your business anymore."

"I'm concerned that you know what you're doing."

"I haven't much choice. A lousy old two-timer like you or a lump of bronzed nothing. Neon lights or welly-boots."

"At least you'll agree the last two aren't compatible."

"I spend most of my time thinking of ways they could be."

"At the cost of a fortune in long-distance calls."

"Which we can both afford."

"I'm not talking just about money."

She left a silence again. "Every time we speak you seem

further away. That's also why I wrote it." She added, "What might happen to me."

"It's precisely because you can imagine it that it won't."

"Optimist."

That was the first sign of her more normal side, and I used it to move us to less emotional matters.

"How's it gone this morning?"

"Okay. We're doing the second visit." That was a scene early in the story when the nanny Jenny was playing had a surreptitious evening visit from the boy, her bosses being out to dinner . . . a difficult one for her partner, but fairly straightforward for her.

"Bill's happy?"

"I think so. We cut a couple of lines. He did ask if I thought you'd mind. I'm sort of treated as your agent these days."

She told me which lines, and why.

"All right. But tell him it's a bad principle."

"Yes, sir."

"Have you had your lunch?"

"Now you've forgotten I don't eat on the job."

"That's another bad principle."

"I'll have a yog. Just for you. Have you got your T. E. Lawrence gear packed?"

"It's all in town. I'm going up tomorrow."

She was silent a moment.

"I get so lonely, Dan. Abe and Mildred are sweet, they do try, but it's not the same. I seem to have forgotten how to talk to anyone except you."

"And this girl?"

"She's only a substitute. Anyway. She does most of the talking." She added, "It wasn't true."

"I know."

"I'm writing one last thing. You'll be gone before it comes. About New Mexico."

"You are an extraordinary child."

"I should have written it first. And nothing else."

"I wish I could read it now."

She waited, then said, "I must go." There was the suggestion of a sniff down the line. "Be someone else you imagined once."

"Soon over now."

"You do forgive me?"

"Of course."

[ 475 ]

"And you will miss me?"

"Every minute."

"Hold me a moment."

Then, as before, in the last of the silences, defeats, film without vision, she put the receiver down. Dan did the same with his, but remained staring at the stone flags he stood on. It was true that he did not believe it had happened; but he had suspected that something more than she was alleging had happened. He had realized too that it was half written to bring him back, a princess's message to her errant, and erring, knight; before, of course, she knew he was otherwise engaged. He would not know the truth until he possessed her again; and the side of him he has rather suppressed here, the animal, never happy when too long deprived of a naked female body, though now it was less the act than the adjuncts, the mere diffuse sexualities of another close body—warmths in the night, dressings and undressings, domesticities (the illusions if not the realities of what she had called, or been taught to call, togetherness)—that he missed . . . this animal side of him stood there imagining the repossession; remembered how Jenny was sometimes, since her writing had not, as she perhaps intended, in any way displeased the erotic side of the same animal. At such times she was much more as she had made Kate at the end, in her adventure, than herself . . . clinging, young, not independent at all.

In the night of the future he kisses tears from invisible, surrendered eyes; and in the electric light of the present tells Phoebe the apple-pie was superb but he can't eat a mouthful more.

Dan arrived at the somehow doubly empty—Caro being in Paris, and having in any case moved out—flat, the next day, feeling vaguely depressed. It was not so much Jenny, since on a third reading he had decided to see what she had written, and whether it was true or imagined, as a sign of health, that is, of independence, weaning; but considerably more a belated wondering why he was once again forsaking Thorncombe. There had been a reproach in Phoebe's eyes when he had told her he was off so soon after arriving; and he had sensed that she did not really believe his assurance that he meant to be "home" through most of the rest of the year ahead. By an irony he had left the farm on the first truly clear and springlike day since he had returned, and with a distinct sense of foreboding, a potential grim smile from destiny. There would be a plane-crash, he would never see it again . . . when it was so near, need never have been left. Egypt seemed like an unnecessary last gamble—he even cold-shouldered a quite normal pleasure he found in the prospect of revisiting the place, of watching its effect on Jane. He knew better: he was at the old game of trimming, of shuffling off decision.

He had not spoken to Jane again except once, and then only about practical matters . . . the visas, how many traveler's checks she should take; and Roz insisted he should come to supper at her flat and bring Caro, the evening before they left. In reality he knew he was beginning to lose the impulse of his good deed, perhaps because he had during that intervening week been reduced to so much prevarication over Jane with Jenny, and had come half to credit what he said to her. His professional excuses had not been totally invented; the script did lack atmosphere, and would benefit—but he knew he would not have been conscientious enough to have bothered to go on his own. In any case he was too old a hand not to know that specific location recommendations in a script rarely survived to the final product.

At least he was going with general approval inside the family. He had spoken to Caro later the previous Tuesday, after he had told Jenny. She seemed more surprised than he had expected; almost as if she needed to know, before she approved, that her mother sanctioned such anomalous goings-on; but when Dan told her she had been consulted by proxy, and given her *imprimatur*, Caro warmed rapidly to the idea. They were to meet this day, the Sunday, after her week-end in Paris—she would come straight to the flat from Heathrow. That had left one other voice to face. He had not given himself time to hesitate; but no sooner said goodbye to his daughter than he dialed her mother's number.

"Hallo, Nell. It's Dan."

"How extraordinary. I was just going to ring you."

"Have I done the right thing?"

"Now I've got over the initial shock."

"She said something about feeling she needed a holiday. That's how it came up. Since I've got to go . . ."

"I think it's a marvelous idea. Actually I'm green with envy."

"It's only ten days."

"It'll be good for her. Seriously. I'm just amazed it did anything more than precipitate another fit of the Marxist vapors."

"It did a little. And more conventional ones. About how you'd react. Which is rather why I'm ringing."

"I'm equally amazed she remembers I have reactions. After Caro."

"She does feel bad about that, Nell."

"So she should. But never mind."

"As long as you don't think I'm outraging propriety."

"My dear man, I'm not that stuffy. Yet." As always, fatally, they were slipping into the language of the double edge; but she must have heard it as soon as he. "I'm all for it. Honestly. Andrew and I think you were terribly clever to suggest it." She added, "It's left us a bit breathless, but not because we're not grateful."

"I suspect the culture shock may do her good."

"Perhaps you can get her off with some lovely oil-sheik."

"I don't think I'll quite promise that."

"Did you find her any more forthcoming?"

"A little. I think she knows she's trying to solve the world's problems as a substitute for facing one or two of her own."

"I've been trying to suggest that for years." She hesitated, then said, "I am worried for her, Dan. I know she's holding so much in. In spite of the way I talk about her."

"I know."

"You have my blessing. For what it's worth. And sincere thanks. At long last." She said, "Also for bearing the current brunt of our wicked child."

They had talked about Caro and her problems then.

She continued a minor problem that Sunday night. Dan waited, drinking too much, for her to appear. She hadn't been sure which flight they would catch, so it was not really her fault; but it irritated him obscurely. In the end, after nine, he left a note and took himself off to an Italian restaurant around the corner from the flat. She appeared there just as he was finishing his meal, a little breathless, and contrite. She wasn't hungry, they had had an early dinner in Paris, but he ordered coffee for her. She looked tired, as always, but seemed cheerful enough, full of chatter about her week-end. Barney had gone for some interview with one of the French Common Market high-ups. It hadn't gone too well, but otherwise she did not mention him. Then she broke off about Paris. There was a certain amusement in her eyes, as if he had been belatedly converted to a cause, when she asked him if Aunt Jane was excited.

"I hope. She was taken aback at first."

"I should think so. Whatever next. A man with a reputation like yours."

"I find some of you young people very behind the times."

She slipped out her tongue. "And how's the other bit of young people in your life taken it?"

"With a becoming common sense."

"There was a photo of her in an old *Paris-Match* at the hotel. I meant to tear it out." She sniffled. "Not bad. At least she was dressed."

"Don't be catty. I want you to like her."

"I'll try."

"You do have a mistake in common."

She looked down at the pink check table-cloth. "Does she think so?"

"Rather less than I wish she would."

"We must get together."

"Hers is a special case, Caro. No comparison, really."

"Oh sure. I'm just ordinary."

Dan smiled. "Not worth answering. You're much luckier. Jenny's condemned either to independent men and long separations or dependent men who become mere Mr. McNeils."

"And she hasn't realized that yet?"

"Realizing and accepting are two different things."

Caro looked down again. "As I'm discovering. His wife's found out about us."

"Oh God."

"It's all right. Apparently she's resigned to it. She even told him I was an improvement on the last." She gave Dan a twisted little smile, and lit another cigarette from a packet of Gauloises. She had begun to smoke more than he liked.

"How did she find out?"

"I thought you might know, actually." She must have seen that Dan didn't understand what that meant. It sounded almost like an accusation. "There was a snippet in *Private Eye* last week."

For a brief moment Dan became his Victorian great-grandfather, a severe face on a wall. Fortunately she was avoiding his eyes, and he spoke gently.

"What did it say?"

"A year or two ago he wrote a piece in favor of marriages, lovers, being the same age. You know how he writes, it wasn't very serious. Just arguing a line for fun. They lifted a quote from that. Then something about" . . . she stopped, as if to get right lines she now knew by heart . . . " 'the piece is causing grave concern to his current twenty-year-old secretary'—they couldn't even get the age right—'who has cast modesty to the winds under the bizarre illusion that Boring Bernard is the only upright man in Fleet Street.' " She added, "They're so foully below the belt sometimes."

"Were you named?"

"No." She added, "We've tried to keep it secret. But they're always going for him. *Private Eye*."

The nasty thought crossed Dan's mind that Barney was not above leaking the information himself; but it was fairer to say that once he would not have been above leaking it. At any rate he had made part of his reputation as a student journalist, as Dan had had reason to know on more than the one occasion previously mentioned, precisely on such gossiping innuendo. Barney, in a Fleet Street now dominated by his own Oxbridge generation, could hardly cry outrage at something he had helped set in motion.

"Is he upset?"

"For me." She had another thin smile. "He says he wishes the days of the horsewhip weren't over."

"If he wants it to make the headlines."

"He's desperately sorry about it."

Dan ventured a tentative step further.

"He's not talking of . . ."

"Of what?"

"Leaving her for you?"

She stared down. "Daddy, I'd rather not discuss it."

As so often in the past, the "Daddy" was a tacit reproach; a reminder that he had long ago forfeited at least some of the prerogatives of that relationship. She had—Dan had been thinking till then how rapidly she was leaving her earlier self behind—suddenly reverted to the past. Her cheeks had gone a little pink and she would not look at him; but did not quite know where else to look. For a moment they were back to the days when he would probe too far, or too obviously, into her feelings about Nell and Compton—only to realize, too late, that he had trespassed across some invisible boundary in her mind.

"Then question withdrawn."

She said nothing for a few seconds. "It came up over the week-end. He was depressed about the interview. He keeps on talking about getting out of the rat-race. Writing a sort of autobiography. Dillon's History of a Very Small World—he jokes about it. And he can't really. He hasn't got the money."

Dan had to give a slightly sour inward smile at that "sort
o^ ... ^ndered whether he was being told to
reflect on his own good fortune.

She added, "I'm not starstruck or anything. I went wandering round the Latin Quarter on my own yesterday afternoon
while he was doing his interview. All those students and
people my own age. I did a bit wonder what I was losing."
Then, as if she were giving her father too much rope, she
said, "He is terribly sweet to me. Patient. Not like some
people."

But that definite dig went with a mocking slide of her eyes.

"That's because I know you're much brighter than you
sometimes pretend."

"You hope."

"Know."

She was wearing a dove-gray corduroy trouser suit with a
Liberty shirt, which suited the natural rather high color of
her complexion; and her long hair. It wasn't a very photographable face, as Dan had discovered in the course of family
snapshots . . . a conventional face, just as she was no more
than a conventionally not unpretty girl; always a much
younger girl lurked in it, as it had in her mother's at the
same age. And just as he had secretly liked the rare—increasingly rare, alas—childlike side in Nell in the old days, he
recognized a same feeling about their daughter. He had a
sudden wish that he was taking this slim little problematic
and obstinate creature beside him to Egypt; and said it.

She grinned. "I wish I was free to come."

"You're not too unhappy?"

She shook her head, very positively. "I think I feel happier
nowadays than I ever have in my whole life before." She
shrugged. "Which proves I'm not very bright." That amused
Dan, and she bridled a little. "When everything else is in such
a mess."

"You mean the world?"

"It's all we ever hear at work."

"Newspapers live on doom and disaster. Good for circula-
tion."

"The awful thing is I know I rather like it in a way. Nothing being certain. Living from day to day. Everything that
Compton isn't." She gave Dan a dry look. "I didn't tell you, I
got a real talking-to from Mummy and Andrew after you left
last Sunday. They were perfectly nice. Just incredibly square.

As if you were done for if you didn't have your whole life planned and secure for ever."

"The opposite theory also has its drawbacks."

"It's just sometimes. I read a piece we're running in the color supp. next week. About nurses. It made me feel how ridiculous it is that I should get paid more than they do. And have all the fun as well."

"Nursing's like acting. A vocation."

"It's still not fair."

"Do I smell your Aunt Jane?"

That in turn amused her. She said with a mock primness, "I begin to see what she's on about."

"Good."

"Well you haven't had to hear all the anti-propaganda I have."

"True."

Now he was queried.

"Did she talk a lot to you at Thorncombe?"

"Yes."

"What about?"

"You. Paul. Politics. Everything."

"I couldn't believe it when you first told me about Egypt."

"Why not?"

She shook her head. "I suppose I've always thought of you living in two totally separate worlds. That could never meet."

"We once met almost literally every day of our life, Caro. At your age. We've even been on holiday before. We all spent a summer in Rome once."

"It's just that you've never seemed very interested in her."

He hesitated, then covered hesitation with a smile. "I didn't only lose your mother when we divorced, Caro. Lack of interest doesn't always mean lack of memory. Rather the reverse, in fact . . . sometimes."

"Does she seem very changed to you?"

"Outwardly. Not deep down. I felt she's been living in a world where only bad things happen. So a good happening might make a change. That's all." He smiled again. "Amateur headshrinking, really. And to show I'm grateful for all the help she's given you."

"Did you tell her that?"

"In Oxford. The night Uncle Anthony died."

Caro was silent a moment, avoided his eyes.

"Daddy, why did he kill himself that night of all nights?"

She asked it as if she knew that she was now the one

crossing forbidden boundaries. Dan stared across the restaurant.

"He was a teacher all his life, Caro. I think it was a kind of lesson."

"Who to?"

"Perhaps to all of us. On taking responsibility for your past."

"What responsibility?"

"For having hated, lied, deceived. When we could all have tried to understand a little better."

"But why did he wait till you were there?"

"Perhaps because he knew I needed it more than most."

"But he hadn't seen you for years."

"Some things don't change about people."

Again she was silent.

"Did Aunt Jane need it as well?"

"Perhaps."

"You're being very cagy."

"Because I don't want to spoil what you quite rightly admire in her."

She considered that a moment. "Is it something about their marriage? I realize I always rather took it for granted. I was sort of presuming it was good one day with Roz. I felt I'd said something silly then."

"I think it had its problems. Mainly of temperament. Views on things."

"I'm so stupid. I never guessed."

"No one was meant to. I understand Jane turned to Roz a great deal in the last years. That's why she wouldn't have agreed."

"I always feel such an empty-headed little nit with her."

Dan signaled for the check to be brought.

"You can face this supper tomorrow?"

"Yes. Of course. I do like her really." By which, Dan suspected, she really meant "envy."

"I think you've got her rather wrong."

She seemed to accept that it might be so, but a dissatisfaction remained.

"That's why I've always been so fond of Aunt Jane. She's the only one of the university graduates I seem to be surrounded by who doesn't rub it in."

"The only one?"

"You're joking. You're the worst."

"I try very hard not to be."

"That's what makes it so obvious."

"I'll take lessons in Egypt." She gave him a bitten smile, then looked down, as if he were now the ingenuous one. "What does that Cheshire Cat smirk mean?"

She still kept it. "You need more than lessons."

"Then what?"

"That would be telling."

The waiter brought the bill, and Dan had to occupy himself with it. Caroline stood and looked for her coat, then waited for him by the door. He eyed her as he came up.

"Telling what?"

"What I know about you and you don't."

They moved outside. "Hopeless case?"

"Why you are."

"Don't I have a right to know?"

"Not yet." And she took his arm then, flagrantly changed the subject. "Hey, you haven't asked about my flat."

Two or three minutes later he was kissing her good night by her Mini; then waving her on her way. He went to bed himself as soon as he had returned home. But in spite of having, finally, enjoyed his hour with Caro, his earlier depression remained. He kept thinking of all the things that had to be done the next day. He had arranged to meet Jane briefly at the Egyptian Consulate the next morning to see about the visas, she was traveling up to Roz's from Oxford that evening. And then Caro—he began to write one of his instant scenarios: in which the worst came to the worst, Barney left his wife and persuaded her to live permanently with him. He even added a development (and if she really wanted, why not?) in which he stopped playing Sidney Carton and settled into some similar permanent arrangement with Jenny. He tried to imagine the friendship between the two girls he had said he hoped for . . . but the scenario died when it came to a plausible relationship between Barney and himself. Somehow he saw that too clearly through Jane's truth-seeking, and Nell's cynical, eyes.

He had to see his London agent that following afternoon. A month before, in Hollywood, he had turned down a script for after the one on Kitchener, and discountenanced any further approaches. But he knew at least two more nibbles concerning other properties were now waiting and had to be decided on. There, the folly over Egypt helped; it made resisting whatever blandishments his agent intended to try an easier matter. He would stick to his original plan: Kitchener, then retreat, Thorncombe, peace; a long green spring and summer. Egypt, and Jane, he must regard as an initiatory ordeal: a gratuitous one, but unavoidable now.

It was also, and more than partly, the old lone wolf, the hater of encumbrance in him; of the effort, the energy and time and diplomacy involved in walking the tightrope between all these contradictory female faces and forces in his present life. And perhaps an added attraction of the notion of a year's retreat to Thorncombe was its certain echo of that very ancient male dream embodied in Mount Athos and its monasteries. He had just spent long days on the Kitchener script, but aware that it was less out of true conviction than a subdued exasperation to get the thing over and done with. Ideas for his novel had kept on breaking from behind the page before him. He felt like someone who had done quite enough field research, who now longed to get back to the laboratory, to draw the conclusions.

Then he did something absurd. He got out of bed and found his notebook in his jacket pocket. There he jotted down not something profound about intimations of approaching changes of key in human minds, but the words: *Remind Ben—mangetout peas.*

He had remembered they were one of Jenny's greeds.

# Pyramids and Prisons

Dan developed, during the six-hour flight to Cairo, further doubts about the days ahead; or at least wondered if he had not underestimated the difference between an evening alone with someone and the kind of companionship now in prospect. Jane also seemed to be caught unaware, by reality: they were too trivially tritely solicitous toward each other to be natural. She had been far more at ease the day before, when they had met to get their visas—only briefly, for she had gone off, once the formalities were completed, to meet Roz and do some last shopping; and later, when they had met again at Roz's for the family supper. It had gone well, Roz had put herself out to be nice to Caro, who had responded and perhaps learned from the brisk way her cousin handled her mother . . . teased her over her still latent financial and other qualms. Indeed, she had been more at ease earlier that very morning, before the take-off. Roz had driven them to Heathrow, and kept the reality at bay.

Now they sat side by side, eating their lunches. She ate more of hers than he did. Dan had long ago preferred to go hungry rather than face most airline food; while there was a tiny air about Jane of being determined to have her money's worth, like any true tourist. What conversation they had later was mainly about what they were reading: in Jane's case, the old Blue Guide he had brought along. He was once more jumping through the biography of Kitchener he was using, to refresh his mind about one or two locations he must visit. He was already a little on the defensive there, explaining what it was about the old man that intrigued him. He felt Jane's show of interest was diplomatic rather than genuine; as usual, she was forming her own opinions behind what he said. They talked for a while about the technicalities of film production. He suspected that this too was a sop to his vanity, her proof to herself as much as to him that she was not going to be critical of his way of life, but dutifully, or gratefully, con-

cerned to know it better. They were much more like chance
embarrassed strangers than he had foreseen; perhaps on neither side able to forget the misleading impression given by
the ring on her wedding finger.

And perhaps because he had had, soon after take-off, a reminder that they were separated by more than private and
personal things, for all their sitting side by side. There had
been a first break in their conversation, and he had asked if
she had brought plenty to read; then passed her the Blue
Guide. As if she had forgotten, she stooped to the traveling
bag by her feet and came out with a paperback and handed it
to him with a small smile.

"You don't have to if you don't want to."

It was an anthology, *Lukács on Critical Realism,* issued by
some small left-wing publishing house Dan had never heard
of.

"That's sweet of you, Jane."

"Since he was mentioned."

"I'll read it where I can concentrate. On the boat."

She glanced down at the book as he fingered through it, almost with a dismissiveness, now it had been presented.

"There are bits."

"I'm sure. I shall look forward to it." He smiled. "Actually
I must read for Cairo a bit now."

She did seem to be genuinely eager for the experience of
Egypt. It had been most noticeable when they met outside the
consulate the previous morning. The first thing she had said,
with a smile, was that it wasn't too late for him to say no;
and then that she would still get a visa, because she was "so
hooked" that she couldn't not go now—even if it had to be
alone. There at least he detected in her readiness to be converted, the tentative resumption of an old and more extrovert
self.


The two hours' advance in local time meant that it was
near sunset when they landed at Cairo. Malevich's London
office had already arranged a program for Dan the next day,
and had asked for him to be met. but he was not too sanguine that they would be; and even less so when they cleared
immigration and customs and finally emerged into the
seething and galleried central hall of the terminal—so much
turmoil, so many faces of every shade of brown, the immediate plunge into the non-European world, and at first sight one
principally indifferent to chaos and dirt. The place had the

feel of a country at war, of an upset hive. Dan glanced at Jane beside him, as they were besieged by taxi-drivers and hotel touts. She smiled, but he could see this chorus of alien, demanding voices, the primeval mob, had set her back.

Then someone was sharply calling Dan's name, and they turned. A tall, bald man stood by a pillar. He was well-dressed, in a light mackintosh and dark suit; he had a moustache, a broad, flat face, faintly hooded eyes, a kind of aristocratic disdain for the less fortunate beings around them. But when he saw he had guessed right, he smiled, raised his hand, and came quickly forward.

"Mr. Martin? I am very pleased to meet you. I am Jimmy Assad."

Dan already knew of his existence. David Malevich had met him and meant to use him for the Egyptian side of the production.

They shook hands, and Dan introduced Jane, whose hand Assad rather formally bowed over; but the old-fashioned courtesy disappeared when it came to dismissing the touts and taxi-men who still clamored around them. He drove them away with one or two sharply guttural Arabic phrases, then smiled at his guests, as if to tell them European civility cut no ice here. He had a car and driver waiting. Dan had a suspicion that for once Jane did not regret leading a privileged life.

They set off for Cairo, and found out more about Assad. He was a Copt, it seemed, not a Muslim. He had been in the local film industry most of his life, but had also worked briefly in England, where he had picked up his inappropriate first name, just after the Second World War. He didn't speak the language very idiomatically, but fluently enough, and he seemed well informed as to what was going on in the rest of the movie world. They took to him: he showed at once a nice dryness both about himself and the faults of the United Arab Republic—like the airport, Cairo was overcrowded, it was because of the war situation, so many refugees from the banks of the Suez. Jane asked if a resumption of hostilities was likely.

"You will see. In the newspapers. Every day it is going to happen tomorrow." The eyelids drooped. "You think Mr. Churchill made great speeches of war? You have not heard Sadat. Here we call him Victory Tomorrow, Dirt Today." He slipped a look at Jane, twisted round from the front seat where he sat. "I say dirt for your sake, *madame*. Arabic is a frank language."

"*Merde?*"

"*Ah, très bien. Vous parlez français?*"

They established that they spoke French to each other's satisfaction; and Dan had to come rather hastily in. His own spoken French was very limited.

"Can one talk about the President like that in public?"

Assad raised his hand in regretful negation, but there was a glint in his hooded eyes.

"But we are very lucky here in Egypt. All our secret police wear a uniform." He glanced toward the driver, then one of the eyelids flickered, as if with a tick. "*Une stupidité stupéfiante.*"

One sensed at once with him membership of what is one of the most distinctive clubs in the world, and mercifully without frontiers: that of the political cynic. Dan decided he was probably a corrupt man, not above budget-fiddling, but an agreeable one.

It was dusk when they came into the city, with its unique mixture of the medieval and the modern: shabby boulevards, khaki and tired white façades, dust everywhere, the blend of European clothes and the flowing galabiyas, barefooted urchins, stalls, barrows, donkeys with vivid green bundles of fodder, the only fresh color to be seen, tied to their sides. Wafts of strange smells, dung, something acrid—according to Assad fumes from the Helwan industrial complex up-Nile ("We have to prove how Western we are, so naturally we start by giving ourselves the big pollution problem"); but other richer, more spicy scents came through the windows of the car on the mild subtropical air.

At last they came out beside the Nile, too late to see the Ghiza pyramids in the distance, but the great river was a pearly gray, serene in the fast-dying light; then they were drawing up outside the hotel. Assad came in to see their reservations were all right, and they had a drink in the lounge. He was supposed to take Dan to meet a ministry high-up the next morning, but it was apparently a mere formality, and could be skipped unless Dan insisted. He did not. Then they would spend the day driving round likely locations, the ones Malevich had already inspected and wanted the writer to look at. Dan had already suggested to Jane that she do the major tourist sites while this was going on. Assad offered his wife's services, but Jane declined them; so they went to the desk and fixed a set day-tour for her: the antiquities museum and the city in the morning, the Pyramids in the afternoon. The eyelid showed its tic again.

"Extremely boring, *madame,* but I think you must see them once."

Having assured himself that they really wanted an early night, and no entertaining, he withdrew. But the following night, he insisted, they should have dinner with his wife and himself and some friends.

They found they had adjoining rooms, overlooking the Nile, and that someone, perhaps Assad, had jumped to wrong conclusions. There was an interconnecting door. Dan did not try it to see if it was open. There was no key on his side, and he hoped it had been left on hers. Jane was going to have a bath, and he could hear the water running, occasional movements, as with tomorrow in mind he read through the Cairo scenes in the draft script copy he had brought with him. After a while he felt like opening the duty-free whisky he had bought at Heathrow and wondered whether Jane would like to join him; but he could bring himself neither to tap on the door between their rooms nor to use the telephone, which would somehow underline the awkwardness he felt. In the end he rang down and had Pellegrini and ice brought up; then, glass in hand, went to the window and stared down at the now dark river, with the lights of Gezira opposite tranquilly reflected in the water. There was far more traffic in this central part of Cairo than he recalled from his previous visit, an almost Californian stream of crawling headlights over a bridge to his right; and a continual blaring and hooting of horns. The whole city reminded him faintly of Los Angeles; perhaps it was the air and the temperature, the teem of it, the same stress, behind all the human and architectural differences. All cities grew one. Cairo was simply denser, older, more human. The medieval injustices and inequalities still existed, and everywhere; in the West they had simply been pushed out of sight. Here they remained open.

There were two taps behind him in the interconnecting door. He heard Jane call.

"Dan? I'm ready, if you want to go down."

"Fine, Jane. Does this thing open?"

"Yes. there's a key."

He heard her turn it, and she appeared. She had changed into the dark brown cottage dress she had worn for the funeral, and made up her eyes a little.

"I'm already beginning to feel I should have brought something dressier."

"Don't be absurd. That dress is charming. Really." She gave a little mock bow of her head. Dan smiled. "Sorry about the door. I suspect it's Assad trying to be sophisticated."

"I think it's rather charmingly old-fashioned. He reminds me of one of the Arabists at home. I always thought he was trying to be more Oxford than Oxford, but perhaps it's universal."

"How about a drink? Or shall we go to the bar?"

They elected for the bar. There were American voices, some French; and three men who Jane said were speaking Russian. Dan asked for first impressions. She thought time—layers of time, so many stages of history still co-existing here. The airport had shocked her; and the more crowded, working-class streets they had passed through. One forgot what real borderline poverty meant.

During dinner Dan suggested they could cry off Assad's invitation for the next evening if she'd rather; but no, she looked forward to it, unless Dan himself . . .

"Your treat, Jane. Your choice."

"I'd love to meet some real Egyptians. If they're being offered."

"I'm not sure they'll be very real. But let's find out."

"Not if you . . ." she smiled, she was insisting too much. "It's all so new to me. But I don't want you to be bored for my sake."

"The other guests will probably be people Assad wants us to hire for the film. And I'm not the one who has that sort of baksheesh to hand out. But don't worry. Let's go. We can always pull out early."

The hotel dinner then and there was rather pretentiously French, especially in its menu, though they decided they liked the unleavened pancake bread. But Jane did not appear to mind the gastronomic disappointments; all these things, the people around them, came fresher to her than to Dan, and not just because he had been, though not in this hotel, in Egypt before. He had the amused impression that she was now being her age, her Oxford and staid self, for his sake. Just as a slip can show momentarily beneath a skirt, he glimpsed a ghost of the girl he had known at Oxford. He could remember what she was like in those days before new experiences and new faces: a kind of impulsive intensity of interest, almost a concentration, that wasn't factitious (as it usually was in Nell, who had shared something of the same trait), but could be misleading, especially to men who didn't know her well . . . a directness, an absorption: this interests me, or you interest me, more than anything else at the moment.

They strolled through the traffic and beside the Nile for a few minutes after they had eaten. There were not many people on foot, just the passing cars; a little way along they leaned over a parapet and watched down to where three large feluccas were moored side by side. In one of them three men, perhaps watchmen, sat round a hurricane lamp; an older man in a white burnoose, with a black overcoat hiding his galabiya, and two crouched younger ones—one more small enclave from a much older world. Beyond, the lights of Gezira and Dokki glistened in the smooth water. Now and again one would break into lines as some minor ripple broke the reflection. He glanced at Jane staring down at the dim circle of light in the central felucca. She had put on a coat for the stroll, the rather Russian-looking one he had first seen her in when she had met him at the station three weeks previously. And she wore the silver comb again. He thought of second-class tickets; thrift, simplicity.

"What are you thinking?"

She smiled. "Nothing, Dan. Just looking."

"It's a marvelous river. Day and night. You'll see."

"It reminds me of the Loire, I don't know why."

"The feluccas are a dream in full sail. They're the Nile's *châteaux*, in a way." Those below had their masts lowered, to navigate the city bridges. "Not the boring old temples."

"I'm looking forward to them as well."

Once again he had that muffled, but unmistakable, feeling of being obliquely rebuffed: he was not to pre-judge her impressions or try to reform her scale of values. What she had really answered was, Yes, but I am waiting to judge for myself. They said nothing for a while, leaning on the parapet, and he thought of Jenny—how perhaps what attracted him in her was also this same always incipient contrariness, this refusal to accept his rules; although of course she was greener, less conditioned, far less sure of herself . . . which was equally attractive, in its way. He had spoken twice more to her since the Saturday of her third contribution's arrival; most latterly only early that same morning in London. Her call, agreed on, had awakened him at half past seven. It was really only to say goodbye, to tell him he was a rat, she hated him, but in the kind of voice that declared the opposite. She had rather noticeably said nothing about Jane. They had lost the spontaneity of the earlier calls; both knew it, and knew it could not be restored until they met again face to face. Instead, she had demanded, and he had granted: he would write, he'd try to telephone from Luxor or Aswan, he'd think of her all the time . . . women who always went head-on against, like a felucca going up-stream, or smoothly with the current; and women who always proceeded at a tangent from the male. Jane stood back and pulled her fur collar close.

"Cold?"

"It must be the river. It does seem colder here."

They wandered the few hundred yards back to the hotel. Was she sure she didn't want to go out on the town? Perhaps some belly-dancing? He hadn't proposed it seriously, but it precipitated yet one last conflict of politeness . . . perhaps he wanted to go somewhere? It even continued in the lift, when he thought they had firmly established that neither of them had a secret desire to do anything but go to bed. Was he absolutely sure . . . ?

"I should have gone to the bar and sulked if I felt thwarted."

She smiled, and he felt inclined to tell her to stop being so English. But they came to their floor—and to another potentially awkward moment, which he let her negotiate. In the corridor outside their rooms, she held out her hand.

"Good night, Dan. You have a very grateful acolyte."

"Early days yet."

She shook her head.

"I *was* thinking when we were looking at the feluccas. That it was worth coming just for that."

"We'll see much better."

She hesitated, then gave him another smile and shook her head, almost like a small girl not to be deprived of a choice of toy, however illogical some adult tried to suggest it was. Then she turned away and they went into their rooms.

Dan had very little time to think of Jane that next day. Assad had arrived to take him to his tour before they finished breakfast, and a few minutes later Jane left to get ready for hers. Dan was complimented as she walked away, a charming lady . . . and took the opportunity to explain the real situation before some Egyptian equivalent of male elbow-nudging appeared. The mention of Anthony's recent death took care of that. Assad made an Indian prayer-sign, as if he would have been even more courteous if he had known.

Dan discovered a good deal more about him in the course of the day. He seemed to have done everything in the industry; lighting, camera, production, directing, even on occasion acting small parts. He had lost count of the Arabic films he had helped make. The local industry was very fluid, most people in it had become jacks-of-all-trades, like Assad himself. He was very dismissive of the quality of the countless films he had been involved with; he would be ashamed to show them to Dan. There was not only no art cinema to speak of, there was not even a place for an intelligent commercial cinema. It was all rubbish for the masses, traditional themes and treatments were inescapable; plus the now obligatory political propaganda, with the Muslim priesthood forming a powerful kind of Hays Office on another front. Assad himself had given up hope of a serious Egyptian cinema, which was one reason he was excited by the prospect of *Kitchener*. He seemed to feel that it might with any luck rub his own national industry's nose "in the sand"— he meant in the dirt, but that was the phrase he used.

However, he was more optimistic with the other arts. There were some good writers—he mentioned one or two novelists, though Dan had to confess that he had never heard of them—and one very interesting new dramatist, whom he hoped Dan was to meet that night. He wrote satirical comedies and had lived a highly dangerous life under the Nasser regime, and a still precarious one under that of Sadat. They were talking about this over lunch, in a Lebanese restaurant Assad had taken him to—much more interesting food than at the hotel, and Dan rather wished Jane had been there to enjoy it. The playwright's name was Ahmed Sabry, he was a famous Cairo character, a great clown, it was a pity Dan could not see him in a cabaret-cum-music-hall act he occasionally did. Assad was obviously anxious that they shouldn't despise Sabry for not being very daring by British standards. He glanced round the crowded restaurant, then smiled at Dan with his lazily ironic eyes.

"Ahmed says nothing you would not hear at any table here. But to say it publicly—in this country, that is . . ." he opened his hands.

"It takes courage."

"Or a little madness."

On the practical side of things Dan very soon knew that

Malevich had picked a good man. Assad came out quickly with cost estimates for the most likely locations they saw; every so often he would stop, and make a director's frame-finder with his hands, to be sure Dan saw the visual possibilities. The kind of disruption problems that bedevil location work in other cities, the clearing of long shots, the traffic handling and all the rest, were not going to be allowed to hinder matters here. Dollars mattered more; the minister had decreed. Dan took a few photographs of various old khans and Mameluke town houses, though all this wasn't really his province, and he didn't intend to rewrite scenes just to fit likely locations. He did see one thing he was looking for, a corner of the great *souk* of Mouski that might do for a small incident (to show Kitchener's almost Goering-like mania for collecting antiques) he had yet to write. But that was about all.

Every so often they glimpsed the insubstantial papier mâché of the Pyramids outside the city, the ocher Mokattam hills, and Dan wondered how Jane was getting on. But he enjoyed the day, and ended it with a better feel for Cairo . . . tired, unwashed, seemingly full of aimless soldiers and burst sandbags, a sad little emblem of the nation's military pretensions—but a great city, for all that. He also culled from Assad a list of the Arabic phrases he needed to pepper some of his dialogue with.

Assad dropped him at the hotel just after six, and offered to come back to pick them up for the dinner at eight. But his flat was only half a mile away, and Dan insisted that they could do it by taxi. He knocked on Jane's door, but there was no answer; which was explained by a note that had been pushed under his own. She had had a "fascinating" day, she was having her hair washed. He had a shower and changed into a suit; then sat down to write some notes. A minute or two later he heard Jane enter her room, and called through to tell her he was back; and how about a drink before she changed? She came through at once, still in her clothes of that morning.

"Good day?"

"Incredible. It's been so interesting."

He poured her a whisky, and she sat in an armchair near the writing-table. She smiled.

"And I don't agree at all with you. They took us round one of the mastabas at Saqqara. I don't think I've ever seen anything more beautiful. So delicate. It's like the Renaissance three thousand years before it happened. All those lovely birds and animals."

"And the Sphinx?"

She tilted her head. "A shade *déclassé*, perhaps? But the museum—I could have spent hours there."

He asked her what else she'd seen: the *souk*, El Azhar with its Muslim "dons" ("I could just see Maurice Bowra and David Cecil . . .") sat by their columns with their classes squatted around them, what thirteenth-century Oxford must have been like; some Coptic church, Sultan Mohammed Ali's mausoleum . . . and what on earth were the huge brown birds that floated along the Nile?

"Kites. They were city birds in Europe once."

"The American woman beside me insisted they were vultures. I knew they couldn't be." She pulled a face. "Incidentally she gave me a copious list of all the medical horrors. I shall see bilharzia and even more ghastly diseases on every plate now. Absolute old ghoul."

He grinned. "Did you tell her so?"

"Of course not. My father would have been proud of me."

She had caught a little color during the day, from the sun.

"Were there many on the tour?"

"Americans? No, hardly any. Just two other couples. Far more Russians and French."

"I should have warned you about the beggars. They're like piranhas if they see you're a soft touch."

"They warned us on the coach. It was curious, it must have been my coat. They apparently thought I was Russian too. Hardly pestered me at all, compared to my blue-rinse friend. I didn't realize at first. I was quite hurt."

"They obviously knew a hard-hearted socialist when they saw one."

"I did give one rather beguiling little girl something. But she was so surprised she forgot to ask for more."

"Probably because you gave her far too much in the first place."

She smiled, then looked down at her glass. "I bought a booklet at the museum. About the fellaheen."

"People-shock?"

"Yes. I think it's what I'm going to remember most."

He wondered what she really thought—how theory and intellect met a situation where it was so obvious that no political system could provide an answer. Perhaps she was playing polite again, and letting her tourist self camouflage one that was secretly outraged. She asked then about his own day, and Dan was left no wiser. Soon after that she went to get ready for the dinner-party.

Though there were a pair of cronies of Assad's from the Egyptian film world, Dan's fears that he would be solicited for jobs proved wrong; and it turned out to be a surprisingly enjoyable evening. The flat wasn't very large, but it was furnished in a pleasant blend of the European and the Oriental. Assad's wife was a plump but still quite attractive Lebanese woman in her late thirties; apparently one of the best-known translators in the Arab world from the French. According to Jane she spoke the language flawlessly, though her English was much poorer than her husband's. They were introduced to the other guests. Besides the two film men and their wives, there was another couple, an Egyptian novelist—who also did filmscripts—and his Turkish wife, and two unattached males. One was a professor of history at the American University in Cairo. Assad smilingly said, "We have to tolerate him, because he knows more about Islam than any of us"—and he also knew all about the Kitchener period of Egyptian history, as Dan was to discover in the course of the evening. He turned out to be an untypical Texan—indeed Texan only in his drawl: an agreeably dry man, like his host; a collector of Islamic pottery; and militantly indifferent to the ancient culture. The other single man was the promised satirical playwright, Ahmed Sabry.

He was the only one there not conventionally dressed; a huge seal of a man with a laconic, rubbery face and melancholy, pouched eyes, that reminded Dan at once of a younger and sallower Walter Matthau. He wore an old jacket, a black polo-necked sweater; one guessed at once at a born anarchist, though he said very little before they ate. Assad apologized for giving Dan Lebanese food again, but it was excellent, countless small dishes and titbits, to which they helped themselves from a huge circular brass table. The informality suited such a hotch-potch of backgrounds and nationalities. They disposed themselves round the room in loose groups, in a mixture of the three great languages of the Levant: English, French and Arabic.

Dan saw Jane across the room, talking French with Mrs. Assad and one of the local movie-world couples. She had put on a black dress, very simple, Empire, rather low-cut, a cameo pendant on the bared skin, making her look like a latter-day Jane Austen. It had made him tease her when he first saw it at the hotel—it was apparently one of her last-minute buys, and he informed her that she wasn't doing too badly for someone who had brought nothing dressy. He was sitting himself with the novelist and Ahmed Sabry. Assad had rather boyishly shown Dan, before they ate, his "proudest possession"—a framed photograph of himself, slimmer and younger, though even then going bald, standing with Bernard Shaw. He had worked in England on one of Pascal's film productions of the plays, and the old man had come to watch the shooting one day. The photograph was signed by Shaw across the bottom.

Though Sabry's spoken English was erratic, and voluble to the point of incoherence, he turned out, once his initial mask of withdrawnness was dropped, to be a great admirer of Shaw, though with all that characteristic foreigner's ignorance of how the dead are now regarded in their own countries: an obviously intelligent man, and a heavy shade larger than life. They soon got onto politics; Nasser, Sadat, the economic problems of Egypt, the "grand folly" of the Aswan Dam, the dilemmas of Arabic socialism.

Dan began to wish Jane were there to hear all this; and he took a chance, when he and Sabry wandered over to get more food, to join them to Jane's group. Sabry sat beside her, and then realized she could speak French. He slipped into it himself, and seemed much more at home there. Then he said something that made Jane and Mrs. Assad laugh. He was sitting on a small wall sofa beside Jane. Assad came up and winked at Dan; a little circle began to form, then Sabry said something in Arabic, which again made those who understood laugh. Assad translated. Those who thought two and two made five must leave the room—a first crack, it was to be the first of many, against the naïvety of the political police.

Slowly Sabry began to perform, though with a lugubrious reluctance; then a stream of stories and one-liners, in a mixture of French and Arabic, began to pour out of him. He had the born comic's mastery of the deadpan face and there was now an increasing touch of Mort Sahl about him, as if the more his audience laughed, the more he gave up hope for the human condition. Some of the jokes in Arabic were apparently too broad for European ears, but he took to using Jane beside him as a combined interpreter and feed, making her translate the less scandalous gibes into English. Here are one or two that Dan recalls.

They find a stone statue of a pharaoh at Luxor. The inscriptions are indecipherable, the archaeologists at a loss as to who it is. The statue is brought to Cairo and cleaned, but still the experts are baffled. At last a secret policeman asks if he can see it. He is taken to the room, he goes in and locks the door. An hour later he comes out pulling his coat on and wiping the sweat from his forehead.

"It's okay," he says. "He confessed."

A well-known political suspect is recaptured after an escape, not his first. The chief of police racks his brains to think where to put him. A young inspector speaks up.

"I've got it, sir. One of those old prisons outside the city. I've never seen thicker walls."

"Which prisons?"

"You know, sir. The ones at Ghiza. Foreigners call them the Pyramids."

There was a joke for Assad. Sadat rings up the Coptic Patriarch.

"Your grace, we must stop using these words Muslim and Copt. We are all Egyptians. That is enough."

"Yes, Mr. President."

"And by the way, I've decided to appoint Ibrahim Shafir as your bishop in Alexandria."

"But he's a Muslim, Mr. President!"

"There you are—using that word again!"

Some of the jokes must have been as old as Egypt herself. Nasser is reviewing troops. He comes on a soldier with exactly his own face. He smiles.

"I know where you come from, my lad."

"Same village as yourself, Mr. President."

"Ah. So your mother was a servant in our house."

"No, Mr. President. My father."

Then there was a seditious and vitriolic group about the ignorance and ineffectiveness of the Egyptian army. One soldier came back from the Sinai front.

"Allah, how those Germans can fight!"

Or this: an army truck drives toward the Israeli lines. The officer beside the driver feverishly eats pistachio nuts and throws the shells out the window. The driver looks at him.

"Why are you doing that, sir?"

"So I can find my way back, you fool!"

Sabry was obviously in the Ustinov class as a raconteur.

Dan enjoyed this impromptu cabaret act, and guessed that they were privileged to hear it. He thought he detected, at least in the faces of one or two of the wives, a certain shock at the more violent digs against Nasser and Sadat; which seemed an added reason to admire this rancorous, mocking, sardonic tongue. He felt his own mind being opened, since just as Sabry's appearance and delivery recalled Matthau and Sahl, the bitter self-denigration of his jokes sharply echoed so much Jewish humor. Dan imagined his Hollywood friend Abe beside him, and thought of countless other acid-tongued scathers of pretension he knew or had known in his years in the Jewish-dominated world of the cinema. It seemed insane that two such identical senses of humor could think of each other only in terms of hatred and destruction. He suddenly saw the political establishments of the world as a conspiracy of the humorless against laughter, a tyranny of stupidity over intelligence; man as a product of history, not of his true inner, personal, nature. He might, if he had browsed further in the book he had picked up in Jane's drawing-room at Oxford, have seen that Gramsci had once said almost exactly the same thing, though he had derived his proof of it from the failure of mankind to make socialism universal. Dan saw it much more in existential terms, a universal failure of personal authenticity, faith in one's own inner feelings.

He wondered if Jane felt the same—probably not, she would regard it as elitist to dismiss the great bulk of mankind, both rulers and ruled, as stupid and brainwashed. But Dan, with his usual fatalism, from his favorite stance of outside observer, saw privilege as something evolutionary and pre-ordained. One was condemned without choice to enjoying such experiences, to having knowledge of the world, to valuing wit and use of language because one was genetically, and by hazard of birth and career, endowed with the faculties to appreciate them. He felt he understood the bitterness and blankness of the Keatonlike masks Sabry kept assuming; they were not merely a part of his act, but a knowledge that it was fundamentally futile, a selling to the already sold. The real clowns of the world, he seemed to be saying, were those in power—and who would remain in power.

Another of Sabry's jokes concerned Nasser's funeral cortège. A woman wails and wails until she is allowed to stand over the coffin and see the dead leader one last time. She stares down a long moment, then looks up with a beaming smile.

"So he really is!"

If not the funniest, it was perhaps the profoundest of Sabry's stories. He had preceded the punch-line with a beautifully exact mime of a stupid old woman's smile of joy; beautiful in its glistening idiocy, its happy blindness to reality. Actors very rarely impressed Dan, and perhaps comic actors least of all; but this one touched some deep affinity, an angry despair that he rarely admitted was also inside him.

Through all this he was also watching Jane, who had become a secondary center of attention for those who didn't speak French. At first she translated the jokes into English a shade hesitantly, mainly toward Dan; but then gradually something of her old theatrical sense of timing, of the right turn of phrase, began to come out. There was an animation about her, a sudden willingness to perform a little as well. When Sabry finally declared himself exhausted, he turned and kissed her hand—he would never again tell an unkind joke against an Englishwoman.

They split off once more into separate groups. Dan turned away and talked with the history professor. Jane remained sitting for some time with Sabry, talking more seriously. He used his hands a lot. Occasionally she nodded, as if in sympathy with what he was saying. After a while Assad and the novelist joined them, and then she was talking more. She was plainly making a sort of hit. It both pleased and in some odd way offended Dan, who was beginning to get rather bored and would normally have been thinking of leaving. But he didn't want to tear her away when she was enjoying herself; and did want to suppress his slight resentment that she seemed more at ease with these strangers around her than she was with him. The other wives had gathered in a corner, and some sort of women's klatsch, in a softer, more lisping Arabic than the men's, was in progress; perhaps unintentionally, they seemed to imply that they could not rival this foreign woman and her Western ways with men.

Another Dan was rather proud that she had this power to attract still. She must have been the oldest woman in the room, but the black dress with its open neckline suited her, lost her a few years; was rather striking beside the somewhat conventional evening dresses of the others. Assad's wife eventually came with more cinnamon tea to where Dan and the American were sitting, and smiled down at him. His "friend" was putting them to shame. It wasn't like this in the Lebanon; but always at parties in Egypt, she complained, the women, however emancipated they tried to be, ended in a conversational harem. The little Texan beside him tried to defend the custom, he had come to Cairo to escape women trying to out-talk every man in sight. But Dan was finally led into the harem, and became for a few minutes a center of attraction himself. They questioned him on the film; then on his previous trip to Egypt, when he confessed to that. It was provincial chat, and at last he could face no more of it. He managed to catch Jane's eyes across the room, and she raised her eyebrows in quick interrogation. He nodded and stood.

Once they were in the taxi, he looked at her.

"Survived?"

"I wouldn't have missed it for the world. I'm so glad we went."

"I think you made a hit with Sabry."

"Extraordinary man. He gave me all his life-story afterwards. He's completely self-educated. His father was just a peasant."

"I wonder what his plays are like."

"One sounds rather interesting. It seems to be a sort of Arab version of *The Entertainer*. He's never heard of Osborne." She let out a little sigh. "He's half-inveigled me into trying to write an English version. Apparently it was done in Paris last year."

"I should make sure someone will put it on first."

"He's going to send the French translation to me."

"Well. Perhaps you've found your *métier* at last." She said nothing, as if he were now being the spoil-sport. "Did you like Assad's wife?"

"Yes, I wished I'd talked longer with her."

"I must send her some flowers in the morning."

She leaned forward quickly, turned to him. "Oh you must let me send them, Dan. Please. I'd like to."

"You're in the wicked film world. Neither of us pays for flowers. The production does." She looked down. "In due course it will also pay for tonight. So don't feel conscience-stricken."

She hesitated, then leaned back, but the concession was reluctant.

He said, "All right. But we'll go Dutch on them."

"Thank you."

Her eyes had a momentary glint of an old knowledge of him behind their amusement, and he smiled away.

"I keep forgetting I'm with a philosopher's widow."

"I think there is a case for paying for one's own gratitude."

"Of course. And have patience. I've lived too long in a corrupt world."

"I begin to see its temptations."

"I was rather hoping you'd help me see through them."

She shook her head.

"Too fresh from the cloister for that."

He smiled again, and there was silence between them. He slid one very brief covert glance toward her corner, a mere flick of the eyes as she stared out of the side-window of the taxi; perhaps it was the dim light, or the transience of his look, but he retained a ghostlike image of a much younger profile. Something in it, or in their silence, his sense that she did not want to talk about the evening, was disturbing. He had of course accepted the presence of a residual attraction, one couldn't reject all memory. Some kind of analogy to what he had felt about Sabry crossed his mind as, like her, he stared at the passing streets and embankments: the tyranny of the stupid. It was not at all a moment of physical lust, a phenomenon he associated with the imperative mood (seduce this girl, get her clothes off, bed her). Such moments were always spiced with ignorance and risk; had a sense of adventure, devil-may-care, some affective equivalent in the mind of erection at the loins. He did not feel that; not a trace of an imperative; much more a sudden tenderness, a wish to be intimate in a way she was establishing that they could not be. It was absurd, in the way that the reciprocal hatred of Jew and Arab was absurd, that he couldn't even reach out and touch her hand, that they so scrupulously avoided even the most innocent physical contact.

If he did speculate a little beyond that, it was coldly, idly, purely—almost in both senses—as he so often hypothesized imaginary futures from trivial presents; and only very briefly. Jenny scolded in his mind; and Jane herself, or her moral values, in some way not unlike those of the far more famous Jane she had already reminded him of that evening, equally rebuked the very idea of such multiple betrayals. It was merely his imagination mutinying against the pre-ordained, as children will sometimes test their parents' indulgence . . . and secretly want to fail, to be duly disciplined; merely and haphazardly triggered by that drily meant remark about leaving the cloister, by a momentary impression, in the line of a cheek above a furred collar, of a loneliness in her, of someone too finely poised to be as secure as she seemed.

This time, back at the hotel, they did not even shake hands. The formality of the previous evening had been only to set the correct key. She had thanked him genuinely enough—it had been a fascinating day, a fascinating evening.

Alone, he had not undressed for a while. He poured himself a whisky he didn't really need. The small sounds from Jane's side of the door soon ceased. It was one o'clock, she had gone straight to bed.

Dan went to the window and stared down at the dark silence of the Nile: endless, indifferent, like time itself. He felt obscurely trapped, not master of his own destiny at all, at a nadir from his moments of happiness at Thorncombe. Strangely his mind slipped away from the nocturnal view to his father; to a wondering, not the first of his life, whether he hadn't . . . in depths beyond his conscious reach, and therefore perhaps qualifying for the passive tense—whether he hadn't been formed in his father's image and in a sense not too far removed from that father's God and *his* son; almost, that is, for a secret paternal purpose, though in Dan's case it would be more accurately called a paternal defect. He thought of the old man's flight into stasis, unchangingness, immemorial ritual and safe tradition.

Never mind that Dan had rebelled against such timidity in countless outward ways, he still strove, even in the shifting nows of his life, always for control, a safe place. The nature of his work, his frequent experience of beginning a new script before the last one was fully realized, was parallel in his private life, in the way he would so often think himself out of relationships with women long before they actually ended. That might seem to argue against a desire for stasis. But perhaps it was simply that the old man had found—by hazard and unthinkingly, since Christianity in this context was no more than the answer to fear—what his son was searching for. Dan's solution had been, like some kinds of animal, to find safety in movement; to be Jenny's suitcase in eternal transit; a windblown ball of tumbleweed. His father had chosen attachment to the established order, social and metaphysical; Dan had tried a little of the same with Thorncombe, but otherwise his religion had been non-attachment . . . what the woman now sleeping on the other side of the door had said to his daughter. Yet somehow this seemed a very superficial paradox between father and son. In both cases there was a same flaw of nature: a need not to question, to ban certain possibilities.

He did think of Jane again while he undressed, but more practically. One couldn't really do anything about the situation and its minor embarrassments: it was as irremovable as the wedding-ring on her finger. The scenario was already written, by their past, by their present, by Anthony's ghost, by their family relationships and responsibilities; and Dan was a great believer in keeping to the agreed lines in scripts. Behind all this, in any case, lurked the knowledge that he might amuse Jane, that she might be grateful to him, that she liked him and might even admire him a little; but she was not satisfied by him. Still, as he always had done, he failed where she could not relax her standards; and he could not resent that, since increasingly he doubted even his own.

Once in bed, to stop any more of this and send himself quickly to sleep, he picked up the Lukács paperback he had been given.

# Barbarians

Luxor, after a further jading experience of the airport at Cairo and an uncomfortably crowded flight on an Ilyushin, was a relief. The actual town, with its tired corniche, its two or three would-be grand but apparently deserted hotels overlooking the river. did not impress them. But the warmth was delicious; the brilliant azure sky, the mimosas and acacias and poinsettias in flower, the drifting feluccas, the shimmering water tinged a pinkish ocher by the reflections of the cliffs of the Theban necropolis to the east . . . it was one of those landscapes, and climates. that immediately justify their reputation. Even the provinciality of the little town, its air of run-down indolence, of trying to get itself into a Graham Greene novel, was appealing after the stress and noise of the capital.

The modern white "floating Hilton" that was to be their home for the next week. and which they found moored beside the corniche, seemed clean and efficiently run, if lacking in the picturesqueness of the old Nile steamer Dan had taken his previous cruise in. Their cabins were on the same side, but separated by three others. Dan had hoped they might get a table to themselves in the dining-room and tried, when they went to lunch, to bribe the head waiter into fixing it; but it couldn't be done. All he could offer during the cruise was a table with an American couple. There were two large parties of French and East European tourists; the Americans were the only other native anglophones aboard.

They turned out to be a rather shy young couple in their late twenties. Dan and Jane consoled themselves, when they were alone afterward, that they might have done worse. He suspected she might have been happier at one of the French tables, but he felt loth to leave the one little Anglo-Saxon island, in the babel of tongues surrounding them at lunch, available. Besides, the American pair seemed to have been abroad long enough—they had been in Cairo some four months—to have quelled that least attractive (to Dan) of national characteristics: the need to overwhelm you with personal information and then demand yours. The occasional conversation at lunch—it was properly a rectangular table for six, which allowed them some separation—was almost English in its generality.

The *lingua franca* of the East Europeans seemed to be German—they were mainly from the Democratic Republic, with a few Czechs and Poles thrown in . . . "kind of rivals of mine, I guess," added their table companion, who had been chatting with one of the ship's officers. Most of them were working in Egypt under various industrial and technical agreements; and so was the American. He was a computer expert, on a year's loan from his company to the Egyptian government, training programmers at a new branch of the Ministry of Finance just outside Cairo.

They were all taken after lunch on their first tour, a mile or so north in fiacres, to the Temple of Karnak. Dan had privately decided that he would cry off some of these sidetrips on the cruise, but felt he should show willing on this first day; he was curious, in any case, to see how Jane would react to the first full frontal assault of ancient megalomania. Somewhat to his relief the cruise guide took the four English-speakers aside when they were assembled outside the temple. He was embarrassed by the predominance of French-speaking passengers—the East Europeans had brought their own guide—he would have to use that language, perhaps they could follow him? Jane could, the American girl said she would try, while her husband and Dan held up their guidebooks. Neither of them, it turned out, was a conscientious tourist, and both preferred, amid such regimented sightseeing, to wander about on their own. The American was at least characteristic in his mania for photographing everything; and that left Dan free to let Jane translate the essence of what the long-winded little Egyptian guide said or to drift off.

He soon felt the same reactions as on his previous visit. The place was graceless, obsessed by the monumental, by exactly that same sort of grandiose and bloated vulgarity some more recent dictators had favored in their architecture. At this distance it was even rather ludicrous; the way each succeeding pharaoh seemed to have spent most of his life ripping out his predecessor's stone bellows and trumpetings for the attention of posterity . . . as mockable as the more contemporary delusions of grandeur Sabry had been attacking. The large complex had a certain theatricality, but he enjoyed the incidentals much more than the tour proper: the names of early nineteenth-century French, Italian and British travelers carved high up the huge phallic columns—high, because they had once, before the sand was cleared away, been at ground level; and he liked the inner lake, where the sacred barges had once been brought. That still had a charm. He spotted a magnificent bird there, an emerald-green and copper bee-eater, and took Jane to see it closer; then felt a secret irritation when he could see she was anxious about missing the guide's eternal lecture. He began to find her disconcertingly dutiful, almost Teutonic in the way she solemnly stood and listened to the outflow before each bas-relief and building. But he found he was doing her a partial injustice.

They were taken into a room to see a delicately incised wall-carving of the ritual pouring of the flood waters of the Nile, and he and she stayed on to see it better when the others followed the guide out. Two divinities, a male and a female, faced each other, holding up tilted flasks from which the water poured in two curved and crossing lines, forming an arch; except that it wasn't water, but chains of the ancient keys-of-life, cascades of little loop-topped crosses.

He murmured, "Three stars, that one."

"Yes, it's very moving."

They stood there, alone in the shadowy room now, in silence, staring at the Isis and Osiris, brother and sister, husband and wife; for the first time since their arrival he had a sharp recall of Andrea, of standing here with her nearly twenty years before, in exactly this place, this same time of year—even alone like this, and for the same reason, wanting to savor by themselves this clear small masterpiece embedded in the oppressive and elephantine architecture outside. In spite of the stylization, the scene had deep humanity, a green fuse. Jane turned and saw something in his face that he hadn't really meant to show; but which he acknowledged with a wry smile, as if he was being foolishly sentimental.

"Andrea. Standing here with her once." He nodded. "She loved that."

They stood a moment, still looking, and Jane said gently, "I always remember that marvelous passage in *Mrs. Dalloway*. About the only conceivable life after death being the memories people retain of you."

"I doubt if that would have satisfied dear old Queen Hatshepsut and her brood."

"I think one has to envy them in a way. Their innocence."

"I wonder. I have a suspicion they were running scared. All the bad vibes in places like this must come from somewhere."

"It is a bit much." They turned away to move outside and rejoin their party. "Except it's so remote. Like Stonehenge."

"I don't know if it is remote. When you think of the way we're ruining London. San Francisco. Andrea wanted to mount an exhibition here. Megalopolis through the ages." She smiled, and they came out into the sunlight. Dan glanced at her. "Money back?"

She laughed and shook her head. "But in a way I'm glad I'm seeing it all later in life."

"We saw through Rome. I think we'd have got it right. Even then."

"I've been thinking that as well. How Roman it all is."

"How Egyptian Rome was."

"Of course. I suppose every great civilization needs its Etruscans."

They were nearing the twenty or thirty passengers gathered around the guide.

"Or its French?"

She stared drily ahead at them.

"They take it all so seriously. Have you noticed the one like an old-style actor-manager?"

Dan had noticed him, there was an outrageously handsome and unmistakably queer young man with him; a gentleman in his late fifties, with a face eternally poised between aesthetic eagerness and a supercilious air of aristocracy—or at any rate considerable superiority over the heterosexual world around him.

"I'd rather marked him down for you, Jane."

She bit her lips.

"I hereby baptize him the Barge-borne Queen."

And Dan was left, because they had regained the group, with the image of her bitten lips and the clearest flash yet of her old self. She moved forward from him, in response to one of those mutely reproachful looks at laggard sheep that guides in full spate employ, and he watched the back of her head. He felt the dead around him: the ancient and their own dead, Anthony and Andrea; but richly, poetically, in the late afternoon sunlight. It occurred to him that he was perhaps not so removed from these ancient kings and queens as he liked to think. He too was haunted by remembering and being remembered, by death and his own death; intimations of mortality—but they came to him with a patina of contentment, one was dying perhaps, but one knew more, felt more, saw more; all she had meant by her "later in life."

On the way back to the boat they stopped for half an hour to look at the other great temple of Luxor, where the wretched Ramses II, Il Duce of the dynasties, had had himself celebrated at every angle and in every granite vista, *ad nauseam*. Then they were allowed an hour's free period. Assad had given him the name of the "only honest antique dealer" in Luxor, a Mr. Abdullam, and Jane and Dan strolled into the town to find his shop. There seemed to be antiquities shops of a sort at every turn, and they were continually pestered in the street. One man on a bicycle came beside them and thrust an object wrapped in newspaper at them, exactly like a spiv of the 1940s; it was a mummified foot, a hideous shape, like something in a Bacon painting, of twisted black and yellow and tawny parchment.

"Not today, thank you," said Dan politely.

The man insisted, with a wolfish impatience.

"Is true, is true."

"I'm sure."

"Lady!"

The grisly thing was thrust against Jane, who raised her hands and shook her head. He persisted for a few more yards, but then turned to waylay a French couple behind him. After a moment there was an angry Gallic shout.

"What did he say?"

"*Oh toi, tu m'emmerdes.* Thou art a pain in the neck."

"I think the Frogs are rather better at handling the natives than we are."

"That's because being French is a state of mind. I heard one of them at Karnak. She said in a somewhat surprised voice to her friend, *Il y a des abeilles.* There are bees. Then she said, I have also seen flies. Even insects don't truly exist until their presence has been announced in the only real language."

"I wish I spoke it."

"I don't think you're missing much. They sound a ripe old bunch of Gaullist *nouveaux riches*."

"Yes?"

"Actually I wish we spoke German. Apparently their guide's a professional Egyptologist."

"I know. He looks a learned old boy."

They came to the shop they were looking for and found, talk of the devil, that they had been forestalled; the German-speaking group had preceded them on the two sightseeings and as they entered the narrow room with its glass-cased walls, they saw the "learned old boy" sitting on a chair at the back talking with the hawk-nosed and even older owner. There were two small coffee-cups. As soon as he saw them, the dealer came to meet them. He spoke a broken English. They wished to buy antiquities? Dan said they wished just to look a little; then mentioned that the shop had been recommended by Assad. The old man bowed his head respectfully, though Dan suspected that the name, or his pronunciation of it, meant nothing. They wished scarabs, beads, figurines? He was a shade too eager.

"If we could just look." Dan gestured toward the back of the shop. "And please . . ."

But the man there raised a hand in polite refusal.

"I am a friend. Not a customer."

They smiled, surprised, his English accent was so good. He was a thin old man with a last forelock of ashen hair and an almost white close-trimmed Van Dyck, or perhaps it was an Ulbricht, beard. It was a face that had a faintly circumspect, yet alert, authority. He had a walking-stick beside him. Dan had seen him at Karnak, using it as a pointer. Mr. Abdullam began to pull out trays of scarabs and beads and they stood at the counter, slightly embarrassed by all this attention and the watchful eyes of the old dealer. Jane took to some rows of beads made of countless minute sea-green discs interspersed with tawny cornelians, and asked where they came from. They came from graves. Yes, but she meant from which site? That seemed to confuse the dealer, and he turned and said something in Arabic down toward his guest at the back, who now spoke again.

"The beads come from different places, *madame*. They are put on strings here by Mr. Abdullam. They are old, but they have no archaeological value."

Jane said, "I understand. Thank you."

Mr. Abdullam produced a key and unlocked a shallow drawer below his counter. That was full of better authenti-

[ 511 ]

cated strings, but the prices were much higher, and the oracle at the back of the shop was silent now—they had no idea whether they were cheap for what they were, or exorbitant. They went back to the made-up strings, whose prices seemed to vary between three and five pounds. Jane picked two for her own daughters, and then helped Dan pick one for Caro. But he noticed that two of its cornelians had suspiciously fresh-cut edges, and from some obscure feeling that one ought at least to go through the motions of haggling with an Arab merchant, mentioned his doubt. Again the authority at the back of the room was invoked. He held out a hand.

"May I see?"

Dan walked down with the necklace, and the old man produced a small pocket-glass and cursorily examined the cornelians.

"I think good." He pointed. "These rubbed ones are so because they are not fresh from the ground. They have been worn by village women."

"I see."

Jane had come beside him, and spoke more to Dan than to the old man, though he answered.

"I think that makes them nicer. Having been worn so long."

"I warmly agree, *madame*. Most certainly more human." The old man passed the beads back to her.

"I'm afraid we're very ignorant."

"Ah. Then let me show you something." He turned to the small brass table with the coffee-cups beside him and picked up an inch-long scarab in a curious stone, like beef marbled with fat. "This too has been worn as ornament by a village woman. You see how rubbed it is." He handed it to Jane, who turned it over in her fingers, and held it for Dan to see as well. "And how a hole has been drilled through for wearing as a bead . . . for so many generations that the string has made the end of the perforation funnel-shaped."

"Oh yes, I can see. How extraordinary."

"It is a very rare class of Eleventh Dynasty scarab. I know of less than ten others." He glanced down the room at the dealer. "I have just told Mr. Abdullam that in my opinion it is genuine." He opened his hands a little. "I have handled many thousands of scarabs, *madame*. I am not easily deceived."

"But . . . ?"

"Mr. Abdullam has just told me it was fabricated last year by an old man from a village near here. He watched it being made."

"Good heavens."

The old man looked up at them with a sage smile. "A good rule is the more humble the object, the more likely it is to be genuine." He took the scarab back and set it affectionately beside the coffee-cups.

Jane murmured, "It's very kind of you to show us."

He opened his hands: his pleasure.

"*Caveat emptor?* Yes? But you may trust our friend. His prices are fair."

They thanked him again; made their purchases, nodded and smiled to the old man with the beard, who gravely bowed back; were ushered out by Mr. Abdullam. But they had not gone more than a few steps back toward the boat before Jane suddenly stopped.

"Would you wait here a minute, Dan?" She said quickly, "Please. No questions."

He watched her walk back to the shop and go in again. She came out three minutes later with a small round parcel of white tissue, like a wrapped orange, and handed it straight to him.

"Oh Jane . . . for heaven's sake."

"I couldn't resist it. It was at the back of one of the cases. You didn't see it."

"That's thoroughly naughty."

"Do look at it."

He broke the Scotch tape holding the tissue together and unwrapped the object. It was a broken fragment of a hollow pottery head, blandly broadfaced, mere slits for eyes and mouth.

She said, "Who does it remind you of?"

He stared a moment, then suddenly grinned up. "Assad." He looked again. "How fantastic. It's the spitting image of him."

"It's the top of a Coptic water-jar. Our German friend assured me they're too common to be faked."

"How old is it?"

"He thinks about the third century A.D. Give or take a century."

Dan looked up at her, then caught her arm, leaned forward and kissed her cheek; which embarrassed her. She smiled and looked down as if he was making too much of it.

"As long as you didn't pay . . ."

"Absolutely not."

"It's delicious."

"Token."

"No. I really love it."

And he held it out again at arm's length; the similarity really was extraordinary—and touching, the enduringness of race, the genes.

They set off again for the boat, talking about the shop, the niceness of the old scholar. But Dan was remembering that contretemps in the taxi the night before: her lesson, acted on before they left Cairo, about the true meaning of tokens of gratitude; and remembered too that little delay in her decision to buy the head, which somehow pleased him almost as much as the gift itself; the conquest of caution, shyness, frugality, whatever it was, by impulse. He had expected too much, in Cairo; a wholly unreasonable and immediate gift of her natural self or at least of their old kind of camaraderie.

Dan was very slowly realizing something: that he was looking or seeking for her old self as if it were a reality she was deliberately hiding from him; which was not only, of course, to dismiss the much greater reality of all that had happened since, but betrayed a retardation in himself, a quasi-Freudian searching for the eternally lost, his vanished mother. There too, as with his father, he was much more deeply conditioned than he could easily admit. Something in him must always look for that, even in much younger women—one could invert the whole process and say he was looking for the Jenny in Jane still. All his close relationships with women, even his completely asexual ones (like that with Phoebe, which he had long recognized carried a very minor, comic, yet perceptible mother-son charge), were variations on the model; and broke down precisely because they could not support what his unconscious demanded of them. It was fundamentally absurd, a repetition compulsion, and his disappointments and vague resentments with Jane sprang very largely from it. He made a mental resolve: I must start treating this woman as she is.

They came on a more recently built arcade of shops, aimed at the tourist trade and full of gaudy tat, leading through to the corniche beside the Nile. They idled from window to window, looking at the prices. Jane wanted a basket to carry her things on the tours, so they went into one bazaar and poked around that; and emerged ten minutes later with a cheap rush bag. She lifted it to examine it as they came out under the arcade. A voice spoke from just behind them.

"That is not ancient."

It was the bearded old German on his own way back to the ship. He was rather formally dressed in a pale gray suit, a shirt and tie, a panama hat with a black band and curled-up rims, as if it really wanted to be a homburg—he had an air about him of being an old hand in this climate, and from before the era of "leisure" clothes. Perhaps it was the walking-stick or a white carnation he had in his buttonhole: a touch of the old cosmopolitan. They smiled at his small joke, and Dan thanked him again for having helped them, and in such excellent English; then, might they walk back with him?

They strolled on, with Jane between the two men. She said she was surprised to see so many antiquities on sale.

"It is a very difficult problem. At least here, it is in the open. You do what the Turks are trying . . ." he shrugged.

Dan asked what was going to happen to the scarab. The old man's blue-gray eyes showed a faint frosty twinkle. "No doubt it will one day make some American museum very happy. It will pass through several hands. By then the true story of its provenance will, how shall I say—have been lost?"

"I suppose, if it can deceive even an expert like yourself . . ."

He raised a hand. "It deceived me to look at. But I have had, oh, much experience. You learn never, but never, to believe your eyes. Even when you have dug up an object yourself. That is because many expeditions pay workers for good finds. So. Good finds are sometimes arranged." He pointed with his stick toward the Theban hills. "There is a village over there. Qurna. They are great masters at every kind of fake—and even at burying genuine things where they know you hope to find them. It is forgivable, from their point of view. Excavation means work, so why not?" He smiled at them. "Egyptology is not a pastime for innocents."

"You trust Mr. Abdullam?"

"Trust is a grand word, *madame*. I trust his knowledge. He knows a great deal. A spurious piece has to be very exceptional to deceive him. He knows all their tricks, how do you say, their trademarks." He tapped the side of his head. "He has many ears, as they say in Arabic."

"He's been at it a long time?"

"More than you may think. He was at the opening of Tutankhamun's grave in nineteen twenty-two. He was one of Howard Carter's workmen."

"Good God."

"A very interesting man." Then, as if all this must be boring them, he asked Jane where they lived in England.

"I live in Oxford."

That pleased the old German so much that he missed what she had meant to be the operative word in the sentence.

"Ah? So. I have worked at the Ashmolean Museum. I am very fond indeed of Oxford. One of the most charming cities in the world." He looked across at Dan. "And you, sir, perhaps you teach . . . ?"

That obliged Dan to explain the situation; that Jane had been very recently widowed . . . and that her late husband had indeed taught at Oxford. The old man expressed his regrets. Philosophy was a noble subject, as a young man he had thought of studying it himself. Though that "noble" made them both suspect he had a very old-fashioned notion of philosophy, this academic status by association apparently allowed him to feel that his until then guarded courtesy might become more open. As they strolled down the corniche he told them a little about himself.

He was not primarily an excavation archaeologist—his field was the economy of Ancient Egypt. He had had a heart attack five years before and had given up his active professorship at Leipzig, and now lived in Cairo with a kind of emeritus status, pursuing papyri related to his specialization—which was what had brought him many times in the past to England.

He didn't seem to feel it was necessary to apologize for his present role, and Jane and Dan decided afterward that they liked him for it. They supposed it brought him some extra money—perhaps, as the national of a socialist state, it was a condition of his emeritus appointment. He was seventy-two years old, and his name was Otto Kirnberger. Two years later Dan was to see his name again, in the *Times* obituary column; and to learn that this urbane and friendly old man was in fact a world authority on the pharaonic tribute and taxation systems, and a papyrologist of "unsurpassed breadth of knowledge."

Jane said, as they came to the ship, that they wished they could speak German, and follow his section of the tour, but he turned the intended compliment aside.

"I think you have the best of the bargain, *madame*. I am much the more pedantic."

They parted, and Dan and Jane went down to their cabins.

"What a civilized old man."

"Yes."

"I wonder what he makes of his charges."

"I expect slightly more civilized people, Dan."

He smiled, knowing by the dryness in her voice that she knew what he had really asked: what she herself intended to make of them. True to his new resolution, he decided himself not snubbed this time, but deservedly and neatly turned.

Dan waited for Jane in his cabin before dinner—the bar promised to be overcrowded and the price of its nips of Scotch was hair-raising. The cabins gave just room for two to sit. Theirs had wide picture windows, and were on the starboard side, looking across the Nile toward the setting sun. He examined the Coptic head again. He was genuinely pleased with it, although he was not a collector of objects. It sat on the folding table by the window, in the last sun, in some way both slightly smug and slightly worried—the latter because of some scratched lines above the slit eyes.

Jane knocked on his cabin door and he called her in, then rang for some ice while she installed herself by the window. When it came and they had their drinks in hand, he sat on the end of his bunk. They watched the sunset, a magnificent sky of pinks and yellows and oranges. It changed, and died, with a tropical rapidity, but there was a superb afterglow, reflected even more delicately in the shot silk of the water. A pair of feluccas passed downstream, exquisite black silhouettes, their huge lateen sails hanging down from the curved crossmasts; and the disturbed light was especially beautiful in their gently spreading wakes. Palm-groves on the far bank similarly stood a deep soft black against the luminous sky, and beyond them the cliffs of Thebes turned through pink to violet and then a deep gray. Bats began to weave past, the occasional one wheeling so close to the window that they could see the details of its body. There was a great softness, stillness, peace; in the cabin as well as outside. They fell almost silent while this peerless death of light took place.

She had put on a long skirt and a cream shirt, and one of the necklaces she had bought, "in case it had some ancient curse on it." Dan had set one of his suitcases opposite where she sat in the only chair, so that she could rest her "bad" leg. It ached a little, it wasn't the walking, but the standing about. A black shoe, like a ballet slipper, rather girlish, cocked up; she sat holding an elbow, the glass in her other hand, watching the sunset, occasionally sipping, until her profile too was a silhouette against it.

But their peace was broken. They heard the engines rumble, then throb quietly, and a minute later the ship began to move. The cruise commenced downstream, away from Aswan and back toward Cairo, so that they could visit Abydos; they would come back to Luxor for their day in the Valley of the Kings. Jane went and got her coat and they went up on deck to see the departure, along with most of the other passengers. The dark shadows of the Luxor and Karnak temples slid past. Their voyage had started.

Dan knew that the discreet distances of lunch could not last the whole cruise; and sure enough they had hardly sat down to dinner when the computer man announced that he was Mitchell Hooper, and this was his wife Marcia; to which Dan returned that "this," in his turn, was Jane Mallory, and . . . he had hoped his own name would mean nothing to them, but was destined to immediate disappointment. The girl gave him a quick look.

"The movie-writer?"

"I'm afraid so."

"I read about your being here. There was a piece in the Cairo English newspaper yesterday morning. Kitchener, right?"

"We hope. It's very early days yet."

Her husband eyed the girl, then grinned at the English couple. "This is going to make her trip. Oh boy."

"Mitch."

He ignored her reproachful voice, and went on grinning. "She's the movie-and-books freak. I'm just a scientist."

"We're on vacation. That's all. Like you."

"Sure. Great."

Dan's voice had been a little too anxious to kill any further questioning, and Jane stepped in with a subtler diversion. She looked at the girl.

"Could you manage to follow the guide?"

"Kind of . . . you know. So-so."

"If I can help."

"Thanks."

"Did you enjoy it?"

The girl raised her eyes. "Unbelievable." Then, "Didn't you think so?"

"I was very impressed." Jane smiled. "Not to say over-whelmed."

"Oh I know, I was just saying to Mitch before you came. It's all too much to take in."

"Yes, it is rather."

The waiter came with the first course, and they broke off the conversation. For the merest fraction of a second Jane's eyes met Dan's, though with a studious correctness of expression. Perfidious Albion had struck again; and the key of duplicity was set. They talked, or Jane and Dan listened, between courses. The American couple came from Joliet, near Chicago, but "Mitch" had worked for a couple of years in California. They liked Cairo, Egypt, the Egyptians. You just had to learn their methods. Like the man said, if you had no patience when you came, you learned it; and if you came with patience, you lost it. *Mallesh*, did they know that word? Apparently it meant "sorry, it can't be helped"; kismet. You had to learn to live with that. It was "the way their society was structured." They didn't want to go back to the States, they thought perhaps he'd try for another year here, or maybe Lebanon, they were really sold on Lebanon; or Europe someplace. They didn't know, they were playing it by ear.

Dan and Jane went up on deck after the meal. The desert air was sharp, especially in the slipstream of the ship's passage, but tolerable.

They leaned over a rail in the lee of the superstructure and watched the dark, silent shores slip by. Occasionally one glimpsed the white shadow of a house or a villa caught in the ship's lights; here and there a dim-glowing point, as of an oil-lamp; the stars, the quiet rush of the water. They discussed their table companions.

"I used to hate my mother, she used to be so cutting to them sometimes. But I don't know if it isn't more honest than playing games."

"You mustn't expect subtlety from the backwoods of Illinois."

"I'm not blaming them, Dan."

"Just us."

"In a way."

"If anything stands accused, I suspect it's the ridiculous notion that advanced technology produces richer human beings. When it's become only too clear that the contrary is true. I think those two half-know it. They're on the defensive about something."

"Yes. I felt that."

"Probably about wanting out. I suppose we're lucky. Being of a race where you're born out."

She stared at the bank three hundred yards away. "You forget what being English means. Until situations like this."

"I think I've become a tiny bit of a patriot in my old age. Perhaps it's having spent so much time over there."

She was amused. "Little Britain?"

He murmured. "If you hadn't given me that lovely present . . ."

"But we have just been Little British. At least they were being honest."

"According to an inadequate scale of values."

"But we hide ours as if we're ashamed of them."

He stared down at the water. "I'm a highly principled lady Marxist? I won't tolerate the glorification of the individual in any day or age? Do you think they'd buy that?"

He glanced, and saw the faintly impatient curve in her mouth.

"I thought we'd decided I was just a confused idealist."

"Equally beyond their ken." She said nothing. "They've paid hard-earned money to see this. The guide-books say it's great stuff. How can they think otherwise?"

"It is great stuff, Dan."

"Now you're being naughty."

"Why?"

"Because you know that's not what I'm talking about."

"I know they're not very imaginative as tourists. I'm just thinking of being at school there. They always seemed to be much more open, at least in terms of personal taste. Saying what they feel."

"I'm not accusing them of not saying what they feel."

"But not feeling enough?"

"Not even that. Not knowing enough. Not being allowed to know enough. That Gramsci thing you talked about." He added, "Always doing it by the book."

She was silent a moment. "Peter said something like that in one of his letters. How first you love the straightforwardness . . . then long for the curves."

"That's my experience. The transparency's fine. Until you begin to realize it's less based on an intrinsic honesty than on a lack of imagination. All that so-called frankness about sex. They don't know what they're missing."

"Some must."

"Of course. The lucky few."

"Isn't that the same everywhere?"

"Probably. But the basic opportunities to join the few are so much greater there. If they could only see it."

"I suppose. If you look at it like that."

"The absurdity is that they've managed to turn themselves into the most culturally deprived people in the advanced West. Outside the big cities. Therefore the most insular. How else could they have picked a pig like Nixon for President? And on that huge majority?"

"I do hate all that politics based on image."

He waited a moment, but she seemed content to listen, staring at the shore. He shrugged.

"How else could Madison Avenue function? They have no built-in standards. Which makes them wide open to every huckster, literal or political, who's around." Again he waited, then went on. "All the sales talk about total freedom being the greatest human good. Even though it's as clear as the stars up there that for the last hundred years total freedom has meant the freedom to exploit. The survival of the sharpest at making a quick buck . . ." he took a breath, then looked at her. "And this is absurd. You're making me carry coals to Newcastle."

Her head bowed, a ghost of a smile. She said nothing for a moment, and when she spoke, it seemed almost to herself, or to the night.

"I wish we could find out why they don't want to go back."

This time his new resolution did not help: he felt deflated. He had been talking too much to please her, and in terms of the widest generalization; while she thought only of two people somewhere on that same boat—whose views he knew she must see were simplistic, whose language she had listened to, as he had, as a professional pianist listens to an untalented amateur; yet would not admit it.

"I don't think that would be too hard."

She spoke as if to explain. "I was reading my booklet on the fellaheen before we had our drink."

"Yes?"

She hesitated. "How for five thousand years they've been given nothing, ignored, exploited. Never helped at all. Apparently not even been studied anthropologically until very recently."

"And?"

Again she hesitated. "What I really felt at Karnak today. Whether the way we lucky few live now is very different from those past lucky few. In terms of what's really going on outside."

There was something unusually tentative in her voice, as if she half expected his scorn.

"But someone has to pour the symbolic waters, Jane. For the poor devils outside as well."

"Except that at the moment there's an appalling and literal drought. I don't see much use anymore in symbolic waters."

"Civilization? Scholarship, art? Everything we both felt about the Herr Professor this afternoon. They all come from inside the walls. No?"

"I've heard that argument so often at Oxford. The supposed barbarian hordes as justification for every kind of selfish myopia."

"I don't defend that. But if you start regarding all complex feeling and taste as a crime, you surely also start forbidding all finer knowledge as well."

"If only it didn't cost so much."

"But is the guillotine the answer? They do need the Herr Professors. Even us, in a way. As we are, for all our faults."

Her eyes followed a winged white ghost, a disturbed egret.

"I just wish that so many of that 'us' didn't deny the primacy of the need. See privilege as an axiomatic birthright."

"We can't all be activists, Jane." She said nothing, and he went on. "I think certain intellectual climates also have to be preserved. Disciplines. Knowledges. Even pleasures. For when the revolution's over."

That seemed to silence her, finally, though he couldn't decide whether it was because he was being conceded a point or because she gave up trying to convince him. But then he stole a look at her profile, and sensed something else. It did have a kind of withdrawnness, a thinking to herself in the night; but not what he was looking for, the smallest sign that she wished they were not having this conversation. Something else in it had already puzzled him: her tentativenesses, hesitations, veerings, silences. He had supposed she must be used to much more sophisticated discussions, viewpoints, argument in such matters. Something of Anthony's mind and manner of discourse must have brushed off on her through all those years, the outward as well as the inward of the philosopher's widow. He had thought it perhaps a kindness to him, a dubious one, not very far removed from just that secret condescension she had accused them of showing to the young American couple.

But now, in their silence, it dawned on him that perhaps he was being kept less at a distance than he imagined, that precisely what he believed he was being denied was being granted: that is, she was revealing feelings, confusions, not intellect; longings, not propaganda. And he began to divine something else, that the more precise huge step she was unable to make was between a personal sympathy for her Marxist, or neo-Marxist, ideas and the public manifestation of them in practical, organized form. It was not difficult to trace her fears there back to her Catholic days; to see a parallel between the conflict of Marxism as a noble humanist theory and Marxism in totalitarian practice and the same conflict between personal Christianity and the dogmatic vulgarities and naïveties of the public Church of Rome. That must be the great stumbling-block in her: the fear of seeing personal feelings and judgment once more traduced. It was an important insight for Dan, for he was hiding something from her himself. Against expectation Lukács had not sent him rapidly to sleep that previous night in Cairo; and his split feelings there had been very similar to the ones he had just ascribed to her—he had felt personally drawn and publicly sceptical, approved a number of general premises, doubted their political consequences. In the here and now he guessed at an undeclared but fundamental similarity of situation. It was strange, almost like an invisible hand reached out to touch and reassure him.

She spoke out of the blue.

"Tell me about Andrea, Dan."

He smiled down at the water. "That's an odd change of subject."

"Not really. She's another American couple I've only played games with. Or listened to Nell playing games with."

"You're not cold?"

"Not if we walk up and down. This air smells so clean."

So they began to walk up and down the deck between the empty chairs, and he told her about Andrea: her faults, why he had liked her, why they separated, why he thought she had killed herself. Finally they went into the lounge and had a cup of tea, a shade self-mockingly, being staid old British; side by side on a wall-bench. But the conversation continued and shifted imperceptibly to what had gone wrong between him and Nell . . . at least in daily and psychological terms. They were both carefully objective, and he talked about himself as he talks here, in the third person; a rather blind and willful young man, still in full flight from his adolescence. He thought of telling her about his other and unforgivable infidelity with the British Open, but it was too near the knuckle, to the day of the woman in the reeds.

On the other side of the lounge the Barge-borne Queen seemed to have attracted a kind of court. Four or five of the other French passengers sat at a table with him. His young Ganymede, in an expensive-looking suit, with a black shirt open almost to the navel and a scarf tied winsomely round his neck, kept going to a jukebox in one corner. Dan and Jane fell at last into silence, watching this menagerie opposite.

"What are they talking about?"

"I can't really hear with that thing pounding away. I think it's about modern art. Painting."

"Dear old Frogs."

"One disputes. One is very logical. One shows off one's rhetoric. Above all one is much more civilized than that ludicrous Anglo-Saxon couple opposite." She nudged his arm. "What a pity you didn't bring a bowler hat."

"Are you sure you wouldn't rather be with them?"

"Absolutely. And I'm going to bed."

She gave him a little smiling look, and touched his hand; then stood.

"I'm not staying here alone. That boy looks dangerously bored to me."

But outside the lounge he let her go down to the cabins on her own. He felt unsleepy, and went out on deck again to smoke a last cigarette. But he turned back inside as soon as it was finished. The night, the stars, the onwardness, were somehow depressing now; monotonous, meaningless. He saw, through the glass doors of the lounge as he passed down to his cabin, that the French group had dispersed. Only the

Queen and his companion remained. They sat on opposite sides of the table. The older man seemed to be reproaching him for something; and the boy, who was facing the door, stared sullenly down at the table between them.

# Nile

The six days of their cruise were to flow almost indivisibly one into the other, as the placid yet perpetual river itself swam past its banks. The Nile and its landscapes they grew quickly to love—to love again, in Dan's case. Its waters seemed to reach not merely back into the heart of Africa, but into that of time itself. This was partly the effect of the ancient sites, and of the ancient ways of life of the fellaheen villages and fields they saw as they passed: the minarets and palm-groves, the women with their water-jars, the feluccas, the shadoofs and saqiyas—the great gaunt pole-dippers, the water-wheels ringed with earthenware pots and driven by a donkey or an ox; but its origin lay in something deeper, to do with transience and agelessness, which in turn reflected their own heightened sense of personal present and past . . . a thing they both agreed they felt.

The river moved and the river stayed, depending on whether one saw it with the eye or the mind; it was the Heraclitean same and not the same. It was the river of existence, and it reminded Dan of those magnificent opening verses in Ecclesiastes, of which most people remember only the phrase "Vanity of vanities," but which had always, perhaps revealingly, seemed to him—it had been a favorite lesson choice of his father's—unintentionally comforting. *The earth abideth for ever; and there is no new thing under the sun.* They both noted these biblical echoes, how often they had sudden memories of the misunderstood yet haunting imageries of childhood. They decided it was because the river, like the Bible, was a great poem, and rich in still relevant metaphors.

These usually had some visual objective correlative, of course; but just as there are passages in the Bible that must touch even the most convinced atheist, the Nile did seem to possess a metaphysical charm beside its more obvious physical ones. It cleansed and simplified, it set all life in perspective. The memory of its hundreds of generations, its countless races—all that had eternally vanished beneath its silt—sobered and dwarfed, cut the individual down to less than the tiniest granule of sand in the endless desert that haunted the skylines behind the cultivated valley. Yet so many of the great stream's moods and lights and vistas were ravishingly beautiful, especially at dawn and dusk; and seemed to justify the very life its ageless indifference, its mere geographical being, denied. Jane and Dan found themselves not entirely able, despite the poverty, the bilharzia, the thalassemia, and everything else, to pity this antediluvian peasant world.

A group of women bathing, like classical Greek statues under their wet outer garments, or watering, or washing clothes at the river-edge, would look up, laugh, retreat from the inrushing wake as the opulently white ship passed. At first, when this happened, they felt a guilt, as if they were part of some royal cavalcade cantering through a medieval hamlet, or looking out of the windows of some moving Versailles. Before the inevitable battery of cameras when they were close inshore some of these women would turn their backs, or with a Moslem dignity, both simple and grave—and sometimes faintly mischievous, since the younger girls would flagrantly peep, evoking harem and zenana, through their latticed fingers, veil their faces with crossed hands until the intruders had passed. And then there came what was almost an envy of the simplicities of life in this green and liquid, eternally fertile and blue-skied world; just as some denizen of an icier, grimmer planet might look on, and envy, Earth. Before certain such idyllic pastoral scenes, one's own overcomplex twentieth-century existence could seem like a passing cloudshadow; a folly, a mere result of climatic bad luck. Jane recalled Montesquieu—and they wondered whether all Western "progress" wasn't just a result of having to fill in a historical wet afternoon. One morning, when they were leaning over the rail in sunlight, she decided on an adjective for the river. It was wise; both in itself and to what it bore.

Then there were the other passengers, who also spoke parables of a kind. Dan and Jane derived a constant interest and amusement from observing them—and their own reactions to this polyglot microcosm on which they were temporarily marooned. If the Nile was human history, their ship was a pocket caricature of the human race, or at least the Western part of it. There was a certain mixing, after the first day, between the two main parties, the French and the East Europeans. During the cruising between sites, they shared a common mania for photographing and filming. When there were photogenic subjects on both banks, the crowded sun-deck became absurdly like a scene from a Tati film, as the tyranny of the lens and cries of excitement pulled the would-be Cartier-Bressons frantically from port rail to starboard, and back again.

Dan used his own Nikon very little, and only then for the kind of snapshots, of Jane, of the odd view, for her to show at home, that he might just as well have taken with an Instamatic. A lifelong avoider of other tourists, he had forgotten the extent to which every man is now his own image-maker. It was almost frightening, this obsession with capturing through one sense alone, and one that required (at least at the level of Jane and he watched every day) so little thought or concentration: a mindless clicking. It encouraged the clicker not to think; not to imagine; not to remember; above all, not to feel. Perhaps it was the ultimate privilege, on that ship already loaded with unfair advantage of a cultural and economic kind: merely to duplicate seeing, to advertise in some future that one had been there. He said all this to Jane, who mocked him for being a traitor to his own medium.

The next day she came up to him at the site they were touring, with a pretended downward glance of contrition.

"Dan, I know it's most terribly vulgar and philistine, but I wondered if you could just duplicate my seeing. That frieze over there."

He took the photo she wanted, but sniffed at her. "I'm still right."

She smiled. "I didn't say you weren't."

On deck during the cruising, all this photography, this comparing of cameras and impressions and backgrounds, gave an air of international comradeship. But the English pair found the East Europeans too guarded, on the defensive, the French too hedonistic and self-centered—duty obsessed the one group, pleasure the other. This wasn't without exception. It soon got about that Jane spoke French, and some of the East Europeans spoke passable English. Everyone showed off their knowledge of foreign languages.

There was a quiet Czech mining engineer, who had spent the war years in Scotland, and whom Dan and Jane got to like: and two young Frenchmen, a professional photographer and a journalist, who were doing an article on the cruise for some illustrated magazine. They both spoke fair English, and combined Gallic charm with a certain cynicism about life that Dan approved. There were very few young people on the cruise and these two rather took up with Dan and Jane, as if they were more amusing than their compatriots; or perhaps it was just to exhibit their anglophilia. They confirmed Jane's initial guess at Luxor—the young journalist, Alain, contemptuously slashed the back of his fingers down his jaw when the subject came up one day. He found his own national contingent *rasant*, distinctly tiresome and boring and offensively conservative. Like most well-educated young leftists, he retained an unhealthy respect for style. But he shared Dan and Jane's growing feeling that the fellaheen were as interesting as the ancient sites, and they forgave him. He and his colleague also shared their amusement over the preposterous Barge-borne Queen and his boyfriend. He was apparently a well-known art critic and man about fashionable Paris; he had known Jean Cocteau and never let anyone forget it. The boy, "Carissimo"—Jane and Dan found they were not the only ones who bestowed nicknames—was Italian.

The French in fact interested them most, perhaps because of their marked greater individualism, the transparency of their self-centeredness. It was hard to decide whether they were a nation left behind by, or in advance of the rest of, Europe. They could seem sometimes like antiquated peacocks beside the sober, solid East Europeans; individualists fighting a last lost guerrilla war against the necessary uniformity of the global future. At other times they seemed the epiphany of what the British themselves had been timidly trying to become over the last three decades—depuritanized, self-obsessed and self-indulgent . . . all that the word "British," with its connotations of national duty and the sanctity of the done thing, had once proscribed. Occasionally Dan imagined this contemporary human comedy under Kitchener's fierce blue stare. From that professional point of view he welcomed the experience, not least because he had already in his script "gone long"—in what he now suspected was a lucky hunch—on the Fashoda incident of 1898. Major Marchand, the intrepid French soldier-explorer who provoked it, had already taken his fancy, and he began to see him a little with their young journalist friend Alain's mobile and dry-tongued face; and how he could present the whole confrontation as a twentieth-century pulling of the nineteenth-century lion's tail. Britain and Kitchener had won the political issue, of course;

but Dan began to see ways of making it clear that the imperialist cause was even then lost.

He argued about it with Jane one evening: whether the acute new awareness of self—its demands, its privileges, its rights—that had invaded the Western psyche since the First World War was a good thing or a largely evil consequence of capitalist free enterprise . . . whether people had been media-gulled into self-awareness to increase the puppet-master's profits or whether it was an essentially liberalizing new force in human society. Predictably Jane took the first, and Dan the second view. He thought it meant finally more honesty in human affairs, though he secretly told himself he could hardly argue anything else, given his lifelong (and altogether rather French) respect for his own decisions and desires; while Jane saw so many carrots dangled before donkeys. She couldn't even see useful demolition being done, and he accused her of wanting a society as rigid as the old, if founded on different concepts of duty and national destiny. But it was a matter of her feelings about feeling: worship of self channeled all feeling inward, and that was suicidal in an age where the world clearly needed outwardness.

She wasn't sure that even Kitchener was not preferable; at least he had shown concern (she had borrowed Dan's biography), though in a wrong framework. She shared Dan's contempt for imperialism, of course; but even that sprang from rather different grounds. To her the British Empire had dissipated a potentially good moral energy, and because it had fundamentally been based on power instead of justice, it had ruined our reputation for good. We had lost all hope of becoming an arbiter among nations.

Dan said, with a touch of malice, that he could live with the idea of Britain not being the Switzerland of the twenty-first century.

She smiled, and held her tongue. But he knew she meant that she thought there were worse roles to play.

Their own roles amused them, too; their Englishness, the polite faces they put on, the occasional spanners they threw in the works of foreign stock notions. Like all minorities they were willy-nilly arbiters of a kind, and this brought them closer. But their new acquaintances, the fact that it was rarely possible to have a table to themselves in the crowded lounge upstairs, meant that they actually had less time alone together. By tacit agreement they continued to forsake the bar before dinner. Dan had drinks brought to his cabin when his own whisky ran out. He began to enjoy their half-hour alone then, when they could be themselves; and rather to dread the endless conversations after dinner. On his own he would have taken to retiring to his cabin as soon as the meal was over, but Jane seemed to enjoy the mixing more than he. She did not always say much, but he noticed how often she surreptitiously led conversations by a question, a polite disagreement. He accused her of it one night, when they went for a last stroll on deck, and she was faintly shocked, as if it might have been annoying him. It wasn't her fault, it was Oxford's: the Socratic method, seeing all the rest of the world as students . . . it was awful, she hadn't realized; and she was noticeably rather silent the next evening. Dan deliberately took her place, asking the same kind of questions, venturing the same disagreements. At one point, after the most flagrant of these interventions, their eyes met. Hers had a certain dryness, of the woman unfairly provoked, almost as if he were being impertinent. But she said nothing afterward.

Though it was discreet, expectable, both what he had predicted and what he had hoped, Dan was surprised by how quickly she entered the shipboard society around them; and understood better how Caro could have been deceived by an outward mode of behavior. It also made a final nonsense of Jane's claiming she had forgotten how to behave as other people wanted. He soon realized she had lost very little of her old expertise at suiting manner to circumstance. He knew it was not a conscious affectation—as the same diplomacy had once often seemed in her sister—so much as an interest in other human beings; but once or twice, before some vivacity with Alain, some show of interest with a more conventional of the French (where he knew little could really be felt), he returned her one of her own dry looks; though affectionately, less provoked than amused.

There were two quite pretty French wives, thirty-year-olds, both married to elder husbands, but among the more middle-aged of her sex in the two contingents Jane had little competition. Dan had soon been aware that he was envied her company, and not only for her emancipation and intelligence, but for his presumed access to her cabin. The mining engineer was also a recent widower, and Dan knew very well what so often drew the Czech toward them when they were all on deck together. In a different way it was the same with the two young Frenchmen; Alain especially very rapidly fell into that half-mocking, half-tender manner beloved of the males of his race. It was done quite flagrantly, even with a teasing air, sometimes, of friendly provocation toward Dan; asides in French, mock gallantries. Dan guessed, though he did not ask Jane, that she had explained the real situation there; and could not blame the dark-eyed and distinctly good-looking young man for assuming some license. It was not serious. He used the same manner toward one of the two younger Frenchwomen, when her husband's back was turned.

All this made Jane herself seem younger, or at least younger for her age than she had seemed in England; more and more Dan felt the older persona she had shown there was mainly reserved for him. She gave an impression, when they were alone, and at table, that elsewhere she was acting: this more sober and dutiful was her real, or realistic, self.

But that psychological distances were being dissolved did obliquely emerge in one or two conversations they had alone. Perhaps in return for his telling her about Andrea, she told him more one evening about her affair, and Peter: his faults and virtues. It was done lightly and dispassionately, and he had no sense of a buried distress; much more confirmation of what she had suggested when she first broke the news, of a qualified relief. Somewhere, it seemed, Peter, too, had never really passed the test. She also talked of Anthony and their marriage a little, again much more dispassionately now; but there he felt she was still hiding something. He did not press. Affection said silence: her choice.

Another evening, and copying her own dispassion, he took the opportunity to be franker about Jenny McNeil and his own dilemma. That is, he started meaning to be franker; but it soon grew, like an algebraic rendering-down, more a casual analysis of the general stresses of Jenny's kind of life, how they automatically forced one into a pseudo-protective role, than about his real feelings or the real relationship. If he was unkind in one way, talking of the *déjà vu* feeling he had at seeing Jenny have her secondary love-affair with California and its ways of life and language, he tried to be fair in others: her common sense, her honesty, her struggle to keep her private judgment uncorrupted.

It was a strangely complex conversation, since as before Jane rather stood up for her own sex's ability to know what it needed of such relationships. In being fair to Jenny and praising her intelligence, Dan felt he had cut the ground from under his own feet: he wasn't getting it sufficiently across that he knew he was being selfish, but not blindly selfish. He felt a hypocrisy, an artificiality (and also a treachery, since though he had posted a card to Jenny from Luxor, he had not even bothered to inquire about putting a telephone call through to America), in all he said. Then he was receiving a different kind of sympathy—in effect, it was a kind of condonation— from the one he was soliciting: to be told he was wrong . . . instead of, as it was, probably right. Indeed, paradoxically, the only real pleasure he took in that conversation was far less in its words than its silences and pauses.

For once again, as in the distant past, they had begun not to have to communicate by words. The situation helped, the constant occasions when they could not say, because of others, the Hoopers at table, what they really thought; when one had to use other signals. Even when they were alone, the silences became much less of a strain. One evening, when she came to his cabin for their pre-prandial drink, she sat writing postcards, almost as if she had forgotten he was there; and that secretly pleased him as much as if they had talked. Their companionship had become more real, at least in this; but by steps so small, barely perceptible, that Dan was not to realize them till he looked back and relived those days.

Something else was changing in him, in fact changing at the very moment she sat in his cabin writing her postcards, since as she wrote, he read the book—and by then not at all out of mere politeness—she had presented him with on the flight: the Lukács. By chance, as he was dipping through it that night in Cairo, reading pages at random, he came on a passage that immediately struck home, perhaps because it strongly echoed something Anthony had said to him on that unforgotten night. It ran as follows.

> Between these methods, between Franz Kafka and Thomas Mann, the contemporary bourgeois writer will have to choose. There is no necessity for a writer to break with his bourgeois pattern of life in making this choice between social sanity and morbidity, in choosing the great and progressive literary traditions of realism in preference to formalistic experimentation. (Of course, there are many writers who will choose socialism as a way of solving their personal dilemma. I only want to emphasize that this is not the only possible choice for the contemporary writer.) What counts is the personal decision. And today that is determined by the question: acceptance or rejection of *angst*? Ought *angst* to be taken as an absolute, or ought it to be overcome? Should it be considered one reaction among

others, or should it become the determinant of the *condition humaine?* These are not primarily, of course, literary questions; they relate to a man's behaviour and experience of life. The crucial question is whether a man escapes from the life of his time into a realm of abstraction—it is then that *angst* is engendered in human consciousness—or confronts modern life determined to fight its evils and support what is good in it. The first decision leads then to another: is man the helpless victim of transcendental and inexplicable forces, or is he a member of a human community in which he can play a part, however small, towards its modification or reform?

Dan immediately read that again, then marked it: and read farther. Again and again he felt politically unconvinced: decided he was on Brecht's side in the bitter 1930s quarrel between the two men; but then was dazzled by the famous essay on Walter Scott, if for no better reason than that he had, many years ago, written an abortive script for a proposed production of *Ivanhoe*—and recognized at once how valuable this masterly new angle on Scott's faults and virtues, on the cunning mediocrity of his gentleman heroes, might have then been to him.

In short, Daniel found himself falling under the great Hungarian critic's spell, or at least under the humanist, Erasmic side of it, that current that runs through Western history as the Nile itself through Africa. As usual it was principally because he saw something he could abstract by analogy, depoliticize, and apply to his own life—not altogether, as he later realized, unlike Lukács himself in his fierce refusal to take Thomas Mann at ("typical bourgeois arrivist, futile, useless, artificial books") Brecht's valuation. It was the emotional attempt to see life totally, in its essence and its phenomena; the force, the thought, the seriousness. It was medicine in a way, and the arrived bourgeois in Dan himself did not always like its taste. But he was unexpectedly impressed, and felt both his world-view and his own being as a writer enlarged and redefined.

More so than he admitted to Jane—he did not hide that he was interested, delighted for the introduction; but a little as with that about Jenny, he felt something artificial in the one or two rather neutral, guarded discussions they had about Lukác's views and theories. He knew he was not saying what he really felt, but rather more taking up circumstantial positions with or against Jane herself— or to be more exact, in an attempt to get her to admit the truth of his insight during that first evening's conversation on deck . . . the difference between theoretical, even emotional, agreement and where it always seemed to lead in practice.

One knew about the cost of suppressing inequality in Eastern Europe and elsewhere; and the East Europe in the flesh around them hardly argued for a more free, more joyous humanity, a triumphant counter-hegemony. There was a stiff and very middle-class formality about many of them, much more as if they felt secretly deprived rather than politically and philosophically liberated. Jane had to concede that—though she maintained it was a racial thing, the imposition of a Russian Communism unadapted to other national needs—but he detected the old irrational guilt in the background. We can't really judge, she seemed to be saying, we are too conditioned by our own culture. Nevertheless, he did become increasingly sure that underneath there was far less disagreement than there might seem; and yet in a way it was counter-productive to suggest it. She immediately suspected that, as if he was just being nice, merely sympathetic, hiding what he really thought. He gained another insight: she had an ignorance of him, of what he had become, and how he had become it, quite equal to his own of her.

But they also had their genuine agreements. These formed above all in their relationship with the young American couple and with the Herr Professor. In the first they gave, or tried to give; in the second they received.

They had been taken in a fleet of ramshackle taxis to visit Abydos, the day after their tour of Luxor and Karnak; and Jane and Dan had shared one with the Hoopers. The road went through endless fields of sugar-cane and beside a wide and stagnant irrigation canal. It was hot and dusty and the poverty of the villages—they had been warned this was a bad bilharzia area—and their inhabitants was distressing. Some of the little girls who ran out to greet the passing motorcade and to hold out their hands for piastres were vivacious and pretty in their gay-colored clothes, but the older women, in their funereal black, looked worn and emaciated. There were very few men. They saw children swimming or women filling their water-pots in the lethal waters of the canal; one had an impression of a stupid animal fatalism, even though Mitchell Hooper assured them starvation was not a problem. The great peasant bean staple, *foul*, was high in protein; and anyway, wages in the sugar-cane areas were comparatively good.

Dan sensed an obscure bewilderment in Jane at all of this, a kind of numbness, though it was only the practical demonstration of what her booklet on the fellaheen said. He guessed, or hoped, that it was less a shock at the helpless immensity of the Third World problem than a realization of the parochial irrelevance of so much politics at home.

Perhaps depressed by the approach, neither Jane nor Dan took to Abydos, in spite of the elegance—but even they had an effete, etiolated, Flaxman-like quality—of its wall-sculptures. Their longwinded cicerone, the claustrophobic feel in some of the smaller chapels, the absence of lighting—they and the two Americans discreetly detached themselves after a while and followed well behind the guide and the French passengers. However, there was another great bas-relief there, of Isis massaging up the penis of Osiris at her husband's annual resurrection from the dead. Dan remembered it well from his previous visit, a strangely eager tenderness in the goddess's face as she knelt over her hibernating consort, the echo of the Persephone legend . . . and remembered a private episode with Andrea. Because of her illness she had been off sex for some time, and the ancient erotic image, even though it had been successively bowdlerized by both Coptic Christians and Muslims, had brought a small resurrection to them as well later that day. Now he and his three companions stood before it without saying anything, each pair a little embarrassed by the other's presence. The atmosphere needed breaking.

Dan murmured, "Of course it's really D. H. Lawrence and Frieda."

The Americans laughed and Jane said, "That's wicked."

"Even down to the censorship."

"I'll agree there."

"Religion up to its usual tricks. Kill the body." But he realized, as soon as he had spoken, that he might have hurt, and glanced quickly at the other couple. "Sorry. No offense meant."

The girl answered. "Oh no, we . . . ." Then, "I adore D. H. Lawrence." Then she added rather shyly, as if they might not credit it without some academic evidence, that she had once done a term paper on him.

As they left the chapel, Jane asked where she had been at university and the two women began a conversation that continued spasmodically through the rest of the tour. Jane's side of it had, to Dan's ears as he wandered behind them, the air of a resolution being kept; of do-gooding. He had decided the girl was unexceptional and uninteresting, with only a degree of diffidence to mark her out from thousands of other young half-educated American women of her kind; and he found her husband—as usual he applied even harsher standards to the conversability of his own sex—rather ludicrously unimaginative. Though he photographed so much, Mitchell seemed to have no aesthetic instincts whatever. He was far more impressed by size, by how the hell those guys got this thing up—in the eternal manner of practical America.

Dan decided Mitchell was something of an Ancient Egyptian himself. There was such an obsession with multiplicity at Abydos and the other places they saw on the succeeding days; with numbers, with lists, with never using one when you could use several. Somewhere behind the Egyptian pantheon he detected a mathematical, possession-cataloguing super-god with a profound *horror vacui* or more exactly, *horror uni*. The Herr Professor was later to correct him on that, but Dan developed during those days a childish, and perhaps peculiarly English, image of civilizations being sorted into cricket teams. His opponents were here, in Rome, in modern America and Russia, in Kitchener's Britain; and his own team ran through the Minoans and Etruscans and the Renaissance to . . . well, not quite England as she is, but at least England as she sometimes still was; his England.

Perhaps his deepest dislike of this Egypt-captained "eleven" was that its art could not be romanticized. It was too adamantly based on conspicuous consumption and status; the pharaohs and their gods were the first smug bourgeois of the world—the birth of fire-brigade art, as Alain Maynard cuttingly put it. It reeked from the calculated precision, the formal, statuesque coolness of their paintings and sculptures. They had somehow banned personal sensibility, affection for life, all impulsive exuberance, all spontaneous exaggeration and abstraction. They had used art, instead of letting art use them; already Stalin and Zhdanov came.

But Dan was to feel kinder toward Mitchell Hooper a day or two later. Jane had learned at Abydos that the couple had no children; she came back from their long day at Thebes, when the ship returned to Luxor, with the news that the Americans had a small tragedy in their life. All the gynecological details had been vouchsafed: they could never have children . . . or at least Marcia knew that, though Mitchell still persisted in hoping that science would find a way. She wanted to adopt, but for him adoption had become an ultimate proof of failure and he would not accept it. Egypt had saved their marriage, the pressures to conform were so terrible in the States, Mitch's parents . . . their inner shyness, it seemed, was partly a lostness.

That was Jane's view, at any rate, and Dan did not dispute it. He tried to be nicer, the girl was a little bit awed by his "fame" and movie-world background; wanted precisely the sort of tattle and crumbs of gossip that he did not want to give in front of Jane . . . yet he took his cue from her, this simple curiosity was to be placated. Jane was rather rapidly cast as someone understanding—even at table the girl spoke much more to her, as if she knew she would meet more indulgence there. Once, at Edfu, Dan caught her looking secretly at Jane, who had by then told Marcia of the recent tragedy in her own life; a strange look, wistful, almost canine in its lack of envy. She told Dan one day, when he happened to come into lunch before Jane, that "Mrs. Mallory" reminded her of an English girl she'd known at Michigan. It was as if she saw Britain peopled with understanding and gently spoken women. She had never been there, and he did not disillusion her.

There was no real need by then to find out why the couple had left the United States, but Dan and Jane pieced together a picture: they were two young people whose values were changing, partly because of world events, partly because of their private misfortune. It was much more patent in the female of the species. Obviously the revelation of barrenness had hurt her more deeply. They were both Democrats, but there was a schism over Vietnam—all this came up at lunch one day. Marcia wanted out, they had no right being there; but her husband, with a sort of tattered chauvinism—he conceded they ought never have gone in—felt they should see it through. The two of them became quite heated. She had a small armory of statistics, the waste, the cost . . .

"I'm not arguing, Marcia. I know the figures. If it was just figures, no argument. We cut our losses, we quit."

The girl looked down. "Since when did you carry on with a program after you discovered a bug?"

"It's not the same thing, for Christ's sake. These are human beings. So we abort the whole project. Only just don't ask me to explain it to all the guys whose lives it's wrecked. I mean, what do you say? Sorry, you men, we kind of accidentally sent you to the wrong ball-game?"

"There's no need to get aggressive about it."

"Jesus. Aggressive." Poor hard-put-upon young man, he nodded his head several times, then managed a grin at Dan. "Sorry. We get mad over all this. Maybe we are short of experience of backing down."

The girl seemed unmollified and she glanced at Jane.

"What do people in England think?"

"I think we're rather split. As you are."

Dan said, "Jane was an active member of the Anti-Vietnam Campaign at Oxford."

"If being active is distributing a few leaflets."

Marcia said, "You're against?"

"I'm afraid so. Very much against."

The girl flicked her husband a look. "Mitch is against, really. He just won't admit it."

"He just won't admit he's certain. That's all." He looked across at Dan. "Europe, right? I appreciate, it's all one hell of a way away. But the way I see it it's like World War Two. How it was with you then, and the Nazis. I mean, if you don't fight them all the way, where the hell are they going to stop?"

Jane said, "I think Hitler did announce his intention of invading Britain. I don't believe the North Vietnamese intend to cross the Pacific."

Marcia said fiercely, "Exactly."

"Hold on. Forgive me, but isn't that a kind of simplistic assumption to make about Communism? What I've heard, someone else is behind Hanoi."

Marcia broke in before Jane could answer. "Okay, so we face that when it happens."

"Baby, it's happening. Jesus."

The argument went on several minutes more; and it seemed to Dan to be more and more a linguistic problem— perhaps in this case also a psychological one, a case of a threatened personal virility fearing a threatened national one—rather than a political issue; a lack of a register of discourse, of other horizons. He could see what really disturbed Mitchell, it was the question of freedom; even though he seemed to an outsider a largely conditioned young man, he had a terrifying belief in it as a universal panacea. Jane suggested the corruption of the South Vietnamese government hardly argued a free society; but he wouldn't wear that. There must be free elections. Perhaps that was a fortunate privilege of advanced democracies? But he symptomatically jumped on such monstrous elitism and pessimism. He didn't think "anyone" had the right to decide people were so damn' ignorant they couldn't be allowed to choose; and Dan was left once again wondering how the idea that pragmatism was the bedrock of American character had ever entered the world.

It seemed to Dan yet another Ancient Egyptian aspect of the United States. He had picked up a fact (been shown it with a smile by Jane) in the guide-book. For the Egyptians the land of death had been where the sun set, in the West; and their euphemism for the dead became "the Westerners." That once all-pervasive fear of death had turned into this all-pervasive fear of non-freedom; and it was as pathetic, or as futile, in the exaggerations of attitude and the blindnesses of reason that it induced, as all the pharaonic mania for assuring an afterlife. A million Asian peasants must die so that the illusion could be kept whole. The real and archetypal Red under the bed was determinism; and all the more terrifying for having its fifth column, its agents and subversives and brain-washers, in every act of life . . . and not least in the everyday language of life.

They left the table to get ready for their afternoon tour without any resolution of the argument. Marcia was silent by then, and she did not appear when twenty minutes later they assembled by the gangway to go ashore. Mitchell said she was tired, she hadn't slept too well the previous night. But during the tour he suddenly told Dan, when they were on their own for a minute or two and as if only another male could understand, about the childlessness problem; evidently he didn't realize that Jane had already been told. It made Marcia difficult at times, she kind of switched what she felt about that, and couldn't say, onto her feelings about the war. He guessed he shouldn't have argued.

Dan said, "That's tough." He smiled sympathetically. "Life can be a shit when it wants."

"You can say that again."

"You have tried . . . ?"

"The lot. I have a doctor friend. He keeps me up-to-date with all the latest research. If there's a break-through, we fly tomorrow."

And Dan was left with this sad little faith in technology as the key to the best of all possible worlds. That celebrated and pernicious myth seemed to underlie all his companion's attitudes. In the baseball imagery Mitchell was rather fond of, he had struck out; but he could not yet imagine not having another turn at bat—or that there was not even a pitcher involved, but simply the nature of things. For his kind of innocence, Virgil and Voltaire were still to come. He hardly photographed that day, but drifted glumly around, and Dan felt sorry for him.

However, Marcia appeared again at dinner. She seemed recovered, she had slept, evidently marital peace had been made; and as if to demonstrate it they talked about the Lebanon and Syria, a holiday they had had there soon after they came: Beirut, Damascus, Byblos, Palmyra . . . the latter especially, it was incredible, the strangest one hell of a place on earth. Jane had heard the same from someone once at Oxford. Wasn't there a Crusader castle? That was feeding Christians to hungry lions—they'd been there too. The Krak des Chevaliers, out of this world. Dan and Jane couldn't imagine . . . it was such a pity Mitch hadn't brought some fantastic shots he took. With which Dan secretly agreed; their enthusiasm grew more and more boring. A little traveling was a dangerous thing. Yet he listened and smiled and raised his eyebrows under the impression that he was obeying a humble Jane-inspired version of Nelson's famous signal at Trafalgar.

In fact, and although he had not, during that dull dinner, perhaps because of the too exactly pictured and specific set of Egyptian divinities closest on his mind, had the least realization of the honor he was being accorded, he was not just doing his expected duty—but meeting incarnate the darkest, strangest and most omnipotent god of them all.

# The River Between

A pleasure for Dan during the cruising—one Jane did not
share, though she showed an occasional interest—was the
bird life of the river. He had not this time made the mistake
of leaving his field-glasses at home. The Nile is both a major
migration route and a wintering place, and there were birds
everywhere: hundreds of wagtails on every shore, and often
on the ship itself; weaving clouds of swifts and beautiful
blood-red and indigo swallows; endless flocks of duck—pin-
tail, mallard, pochard, teal and others he could not identify;
the Egyptian wild geese whose remote ancestors he also saw
much closer at hand, painted on temple walls; herons and
egrets, hawks and falcons. All landscapes acquired, in his
eyes, a most characteristic emblematic bird; and here he decided it was the spur-winged plover, a cousin of the English
lapwings he sometimes saw on the Thorncombe meadows, but
a far more elegant little creature, Nefertite to a dowd. As in
New Mexico, and everywhere else in his life, all this nature
delighted and reassured him. The earth abided, and behind
surfaces and plumages there was no new thing under the sun.

In a way the birds were a primeval version of the fellaheen; they endured through simplicity, they formed an alternative world to the one on the ship, a sanctuary from the
neuroses, the over-sensitivities, the time-wastings, the illusions
and dilemmas of his own hyper-sophisticated species. They
also brought him back into conversation with the Herr Professor. It happened when they were sailing back from Abydos
to visit Dendera. Dan was at the rail at a place where the
Nile stretched very wide and sandbanks showed. There was a
voice beside him.

"You are watching the birds?"

Dan lowered his glasses.

"Yes. Though I'm a bit out of my depth here."

The old man pointed with his stick at a distant gathering.

[ 542 ]

"That is *Chenalopex aegyptiacus*. The Egyptian Goose."

"I've just been looking at them." He smiled at the professor. "You're an ornithologist as well?"

The old man raised his hand in a quick disclaimer. "I have had to learn their names as part of my work. They were sometimes paid in tribute."

"We saw a marvelous bird at Karnak. Green . . . a bee-eater?"

"Bee . . . ah, yes. *Bienenfresser*. Green like a parrot? That is *Merops superciliosus*." He shrugged, as if his knowing the Latin name was indeed pedantic. "That too was given in tribute. For its feathers. At least we think. The hieroglyph is in dispute." Then he said, "You know the Egyptians paid a great compliment to the bird? They allowed it to symbolize the most important word in every language. The soul. The spirit."

"I didn't realize."

Jane had until then been lying on a chaise-longue some yards away, reading the Kitchener biography. But now she came to join them. The old man raised his panama.

Dan said, "I shan't have my bird-watching laughed at again. Professor Kirnberger has finally justified it for me." And he passed on what he had just been told. She bowed her head in mock repentance, then addressed the old man.

"I come with a much more banal question, professor. I wondered what that plant is they grow along the river bank." She pointed back across the deck to the nearer side, where the river was bordered down to the water with little plots of vivid green.

"That is *barsim*. A kind of winter clover. For their animals."

"I suppose they've been growing the same crops for thousands of years."

"Not at all. It is the methods that have not changed."

A waiter came around with coffee, and they persuaded the old man to sit with them. He perched upright, with his hands cupped and folded over his walking-stick. Every so often he would acknowledge with a nod of the head some member of his flock who happened to pass. Jane had smiled at him when they sat down.

"Am I being very wicked in finding the fellaheen as interesting as the temples?"

He hesitated, in a way he had, as if he had to compose his

sentences carefully before he spoke. There was a little glint in his look.

"*Madame*, I suspect you know that your sex is never more charming than when it is being wicked." The sere skin beside his eyes crinkled. "So perhaps I should not tell you that you are not being wicked." He glanced out toward the bank. "We used to spend all our time digging for the past." He smiled back at them. "When the past was still living all about us. That is changing now. Our colleagues in anthropology are discovering many things."

And he began to tell them—they connived a little, already knowing some of it from Jane's booklet—about the fellaheen. The word came from *falaha*, to till. Their villages were both Coptic and Muslim, usually but not always separate. The curse of their history was the lack of a rural landed gentry. They had always been exploited by absentee landlords, who for millennia had relied on a ruthless caste of overseers. But all that was rapidly changing since the Nasser land reforms. Dan and Jane must not be misled by the apparent tranquility they saw: there were violent clan vendettas and rivalries, a great deal of thieving of livestock. They were forbidden guns, but they all had them; and they were also very fierce over female honor. Fellaheen versions of *Romeo and Juliet*, said the old man, were still enacted every day.

Jane asked if they sympathized with the socialist trend in Egyptian politics. The old man shook his head.

"It is beyond their conception. Cairo is as far away here as Berlin or London. They are very old, they have seen so many so-called superior civilizations pass—with all their cruelties, their lies, their promises. For them all that remains is their river, and their land. That is all they care about. For them socialism is no more than another foreign culture. Perhaps good, perhaps bad. Colonel Nasser gave them some of their land back. So good. But he also built the Aswan Dam, which means their soil is no longer refreshed by alluvium every year. That is very bad. What need have they of hydroelectricity? They wait and see—yes? From the beginning of time, and I think to the end of it." He looked out to the bank. "I admire them. For all their faults. They are brave people."

And finally he told them two words, without which one could never decipher the fellaheen character. One was *qadim*, which meant ancient, holding power from the past, therefore never to be relinquished. It was their key of life, their passport to survival. The other word was *kayf,* which meant sitting, thinking and doing nothing, existence as a waiting-room for a train that will never come. That was the image he used.

Jane said, "I find that very sad."

The old man shrugged. "It is a philosophy of necessity. They are always sad."

"But you have sympathy for it?"

"Let us say I have lived too long in this country not to understand." He looked down, with a minute, faintly birdlike tilt of his head, his hands still clasped over the handle of his stock. "It is for old men." Then he wrily sought their eyes. "And perhaps above all for old Egyptologists?"

Jane said, "Professor, I suspect you have far too good a sense of humor to be a fatalist."

That brought the old German short a little. He gave her a severe glance, as if he knew he was being teased, then looked down with another of his hesitations.

"I was taught humor at the source, *madame.* Many years ago I did something no true German, no very serious young scholar, should ever do. I fell in love with an Englishwoman. And what is worse, I married her." For a moment he enjoyed their surprise, their smiles. "She is long dead, alas. But in our most happy years together she did manage to persuade me that scholarship and solemnity are not always quite the same thing." Then he said, in a gentler voice, "A lesson it is a pleasure to be reminded of."

"When did she die?"

"Many years ago. Just after the war."

"She was an archaeologist?"

"No, *madame.* A doctor. I believe almost the first woman doctor in Cairo."

He mentioned her maiden name, which meant nothing to Jane and Dan; but her father had also been a doctor, had headed a Cairo hospital during the Protectorate. It was a name still remembered "with much honor" in that capital, the old man said; and despite the anglophobic side of Egyptian nationalism. There were two children, both sons. One now lived in East Germany, the younger in America: he too had become an archaeologist, though his field was the Mayan. The old man was a grandfather several times over.

He left them soon after that, and they speculated about the gaps in what he had said: his present political beliefs, how he had managed during the Nazi period. They felt he must have traveled beyond all that: behind his self-irony, his authority, his knowledge there lay a stillness, almost that of an Indian sage . . . but one didn't know if it came from *qadim* or *kayf*, from his profession and long expatriation or from his heart condition. Perhaps he was living now on borrowed time, waiting for the final stroke.

From then on they spoke quite often with him. They felt distinctly envious of the East Europeans when their party set off at the various sites. The French were beginning to get restless at the oratorical over-kill of their own Egyptian chaperone; and Dan and Jane were to have one small direct proof of what they were missing when by chance the two parties were close to each other, and given ten minutes' rest, at Queen Hatshepsut's temple at Thebes. The Herr Professor beckoned to them—and led them into the Punt Hall to show Dan some bird details in one of the paintings recording the queen's naval expedition to Somaliland; and he told them briefly about the queen and her history. It was the difference between mechanically repeated and lived knowledge.

They strolled back with the bearded old man down the incline to the waiting coaches, and gently probed him on this seemingly rather menial task he was performing. But he was quick to the defense of his flock. They were all experts in their own fields, they were doing invaluable work for Egypt, he was the fortunate one; and besides, he liked to have news of home, to meet people with other interests. He learned, always on such excursions, far more than he taught. And did not Oxford professors do such things, guide tours to Greece and Turkey? Dan and Jane agreed that they did, but couldn't quite convey to the old man that they felt he was doing something rather different, more truly democratic. Dan ventured one oblique question. He asked if there was a Marxist approach to Ancient Egypt. Their companion gave an inclination of the head.

"Most certainly. From that point of view Egypt is the most studied of ancient cultures. With Greece and Rome." It was a carefully neutral reply, but perhaps he guessed the real drift behind Dan's question. He gave him an oblique look. "You understand what *ka* means, Mr. Martin?"

"The soul?"

The old man raised a finger.

"Not quite soul. Etymologically it means the Greek *pneuma*—breath? It was personal. Each had his own *ka*. So

[ 546 ]

to say, it was a man's ideal image of his own life. It could survive death only in connection with the personal body, which is why the ancients were so anxious to preserve their corpses. You understand it best by contrast with *ba*. That was not attached to the body. It was individual, but after death it joined the *khu*—the divine spirit, yes?—which could not take bodily form. It is complicated. But we may say that *ka* and *ba* are ways of seeing man first as an individual . . . and then as one." He pointed to one side with his stick as they slowly walked. "As the artist does." He pointed to the other. "As the scientist. As a unique experience. As a processus." He looked ahead to where the two parties were boarding their coaches, then gave Jane and Dan a little smile. "Speaking for myself, I do not know which way is better. I think the ancients were wise. They knew neither was sufficient in itself. You understand?"

Dan smiled at the old man, then briefly across him at Jane, and then down at the ground.

"Yes. And agree."

"Good."

So they were left a degree wiser about the old man, and Dan had gained a new concept—that of *ka*, or personal immortality based on the body and its belongings and leavings, even if no more remained than Mrs. Dalloway's memories in other minds.

He and Jane talked about it before dinner that evening, overtly in connection with Kitchener, because Dan had immediately seized on an idea there . . . some scene between Kitchener and a Victorian Egyptologist, just such an explanation of what *ka* and *ba* meant, a light in the soldier's eyes; or if not as explicit as that, certainly a scene where the shrewd old self-promoter saw the valency of the concept in some ancient monument . . . the methods of conquering time; to each his pyramid. Although they did not argue about all this, Dan secretly thought that these two terms, *ka* and *ba*, applied also to their own relationship. He was the first, Jane the second; a would-be ambition, a would-be selflessness; and equally insufficient.

They persuaded the professor to sit with them again one morning, when coffee was brought round, though this time the Czech mining engineer was also there. Dan had revealed the real reason for his presence on the cruise, and the old man was interested. He had not come to Egypt until after the

British Protectorate was ended in 1922, but he had memories of those days. His English father-in-law had even met Kitchener several times as a young man, as well as Lord Cromer; and he still seemed to hold these two in a reflected reverence. Dan was able to do some instructing in his turn; and with his new scene in mind ended by suggesting that the more megalomaniac pharaohs must have set a bad example to the proconsul. The old German was amused, and turned to the Czech.

"These English set a very bad example for us other nations. They have no respect for their heroes." But he got no support. That was one of the things, the engineer declared, that he admired in the British. The old man nodded at Dan. "Very well. You may be rude to Lord Kitchener. But not to Ramses the Second."

Dan grinned. "Were they so different?"

He received a severe look.

"Such cynicism, Mr. Martin. This is most shocking."

"I rather hoped it was allowed since the Twentieth Congress."

They had already established that the Czech was not a Party member and far from being a totally uncritical admirer of five-year plans and state bureaucracy; and once again, with a wink, he took Dan's side.

"I think there is here too much cult of the personality."

"You must not use these modern terms, my friend. They are most incorrect." The old man wagged his finger at the Czech. "As I told you on our first visit, if you had been listening, even 'slave' is misleading."

Jane said, "Why's that, professor?"

"Because it requires a certain concept of freedom, of *not* being a slave. Of free will. There was no such thing in Ancient Egypt. In fifth-century Greece, yes . . . perhaps. But not here."

Dan risked one more provocation. "At least the early tomb robbers believed in free enterprise?"

But the old man would not treat it lightly anymore. "That is not what I am saying. Of course. There were bad men. Ambitious men. Dishonest men. But not groups of men who doubted the very principles of their society. How should they? They had no models. No comparisons to draw." He gently reprimanded Dan. "We must not think with modern minds, Mr. Martin. Then we understand nothing."

Dan complained next about the multiplicity, the obsession with lists; and was taken to task again for the gross heresy of ahistoricism.

"There are people from the very beginning of our modern age. Life is very precarious, all its processes are mysterious. Very slowly these men see that in small places it can be controlled. They make many mistakes. But they also see controlling is knowing, and that the greatest tool of knowing is the symbol that allows you to represent what is not present before your eyes. They are like children, perhaps they grow too proud of this little control. But how can one laugh at a child because he wants to learn?"

"But that's just what I feel is missing. The childlike—the simplicities of Minoan and Etruscan art."

"Forgive me, but you betray your ignorance. There was no art in cultures as ancient as the Egyptian and the Minoan. Conscious art did not exist for them. They wanted only to control. That is how they would want us to judge them—by how well they controlled. Not by how pretty they look to us modern men." He opened his hands. "And why did those other civilizations last so short a time?"

"Perhaps it's only that I find their . . . methods of control more sympathetic."

The professor shook his head. "No, Mr. Martin. More ignorant. More primitive, if you will. And I think you like them because you are overcivilized." He raised a hand before Dan could speak. "I know. Here it often seems so cold . . . formal, so royal. You wish there was more folk-art, art of the ordinary people. Just as I sometimes long for the Kaffeehaus music of my youth. But you must not blame the pharaohs. You must blame time. Time is the source of all human illusion."

"Which we're condemned to?"

"In our bodies. But I think we can try with the imagination. The other day you listened most sympathetically when I told you about the land-owners who once exploited our fellaheen friends. Yes?" Dan smiled, and nodded. "In history we are all absentee landlords. We think, those stupid people, if only they knew what I know. If only they had worked harder to please me, and my taste. Is that not true?" Dan smiled again, and had to concede that it was so. "And then—who made all these beautiful sculptures and paintings you are seeing every day?"

"But that's it. I think the wrong names got remembered."

The old man smiled.

"That is the voice of this epoch. Not the past."

Dan murmured, "The voice of my *ka*."

"That is natural. You are a writer. Ever since the Greek all artists have wished to be remembered by name—like the ancient pharaohs. Perhaps they are the only true pharaohs left in this world. I think you have had your revenge."

They began to talk of other things. But Dan had glimpsed another great spell cast by Egypt, all artistic creation seen in its light; perhaps it was even a growing spell, as belief in an after-life died away and people more and more turned to the arts for escape . . . something the very opposite of that fellaheen resignation, waiting for the train that would never come—a frantic entombing, mummifying, surrounding with personal achievement; a morbid need to pupate, to build a chrysalis before the grub was fully grown, and even though reason told one that there was no world in which an imago, the released *ka*, could ever emerge. And was Dan himself essentially different from the unknown mason carving a head of Ramses? He might claim he was examining, or even debunking, much more than he was glorifying. But all attention drawn was a kind of glorification; and when the strongest motive in the drawing attention was not really the object, Kitchener, but the act of pointing itself, one's own reputation, the element of parasitism was obvious. For a private self-mocking moment Dan wondered whether he should be the first screen-writer to demand not a larger credit, but none at all.

All this, though rather paradoxically, strengthened his decision to try a new medium, a new life, as soon as the Kitchener script was done; paradoxically, because he was gaining new ideas for it every day—it was at last beginning to brew, to grow rich. Perhaps the clue had lain in the Herr Professor's suggestion that artists were the only true pharaohs left; so let them be their own celebratory masons, and return to the self, abandon all the work on the other tombs and monuments. He sensed a great need to jettison, to simplify, almost like some painfully obese gourmet craving a stay at a health farm. Even this had a paradoxical element: at the same moment as he saw all art as a mere modern variation on superstitious tomb-making, absurdly elaborate and futile insurance against the unknown, the seeing brought a sense of freedom . . . or perhaps it was more a retreat into Englishness—conviction of the sheer silliness of taking anything in life (such as Lukács and theorists of total consciousness and authorial responsibility) very seriously. It was all also a game of chance, in which the part played by skill was far smaller than the world would admit. Not to see that was to be like the young American, for he also taught.

One was best: that passive third person.

The desert crept nearer as the days passed and they approached the Tropic of Cancer. Even the amateur photographers grew satiated, and increasingly the scenes on the banks, the passing feluccas, were allowed to go by uncaptured.

They visited Esna, a dirty town, with a temple in a huge pit in the center of it. Crowds of beggars besieged the tourists on their way to and from the site. A man with two reed panniers at his waist was especially insistent and one of the French gave the baksheesh he clamored for: a snake was produced, then from the smaller basket a huge scorpion, held by its depointed sting, its legs slowly crawling through the air. Suddenly the cameras appeared again in their dozens, a circle formed. One of the showman's friends began to block views, demanding more money. The picturesque was not to be had free. Without warning there was a fracas in embryo, as he pushed one camera aside and was shouted at and pushed sharply off balance himself in return. It was the Barge-borne Queen's Italian friend. He was calmed, but the Arab continued shouting insults.

In the background, outside a coffee-shop, a line of old men sat, two of them smoking narghilehs, watching all this with inscrutable eyes. Dan and Jane stood a little apart, with the French journalist Alain beside them. His photographer friend was busy, a neutral eye, snapping the snappers, with an obliviousness to anything but angle and rapidity of take. Alain said something in French to Jane, which she passed on to Dan: *Silly cunts are easily amused.* There was some kind of triple blasphemy involved; against nature, against humanity, against themselves . . . man the ape, all the babooneries, the wrong motives, of package travel.

Later that day they moored at Edfu to see the Ptolemaic temple of the winged sub-god Horus, with its magnificent granite falcons. Living kestrels still clipped and wove between the Assyrian-looking towers and in the evening light the place had a certain serenity. But there was something brooding also in the massive fortress walls of the temple, the ambience of a hermetic priest-cult barricaded in against outside reality; as remote, and perhaps as repellent, as the white sides of their ship to the peasants they passed each day.

A cabaret and dancing had been announced for that evening after dinner, and Dan and Jane arrived in the dining-room to find their own slight concession to this—Dan had put on a suit and Jane wore the same black dress she had baptized at the Assads' party—far outdistanced by the other passengers. They had treated it as a fancy-dress gala. There were some unlikely-looking peasant outfits among the East Europeans, a selection of would-be corsairs and toreros and the rest among the French. The only thoroughgoing costume, obviously brought in preparation for this evening, was that of the Barge-borne Queen's young fly-by-night. He was rigged out, bare-chested, and with some massive imitation jewelry, as Tutankhamun. The face was elaborately made up, and he looked alarmingly hermaphroditic. The Queen himself was got up in a puce coat with a large black cravat in the loose bow; they learned later that he was Baudelaire. The young man seemed hardly to eat, but flitted from table to table among the French party, showing off his bare torso and his finery, striking poses, oblivious to the ludicrousness of it all.

Even the Hoopers had fallen slightly prey to this madness. Marcia wore a long dress with a gilt cardboard crown over her republican hair. She wasn't quite sure who she was meant to be, the purser had lent her the crown. Mitch had similarly acquired—by right of nationality, he explained, not because he had any connection with Texas—a stetson. They were clearly worried by Dan and Jane's ordinariness—the purser had a whole cupboardful of hats and clothes, they were sure there were some left . . .

In a while the Hoopers took their headgear off, and the table showed a solid Anglo-Saxon front of refusal to conform to the nonsense around them. Dan had Jane's eyes at one moment.

"They must think we're the most awful snobs."

"Someone has to show disapproval of such rampant bourgeois narcissism. I wish I'd come as a KGB man."

She smiled, but her eyes lingered on his a moment more

before looking down. He was still not allowed, or only just allowed, to make jokes about such things.

He said, "You've caught the sun today."

"I can certainly feel my cheeks burning."

"Gives you a nice gipsy air."

"Home will soon take care of that."

He smiled back, but it struck an unwelcome practical note. She looked past him to the animated other tables. Even the East Europeans seemed to have relaxed a little. They waited then for the next course, in a silence, like a married couple; older than anyone else there. She had caught the sun, and in fact looked much younger. And the dress: already, on their way to their table, Dan had seen a discreet Gallic gesture of approval of that from Alain Maynard.

They were among the last to go to the upstairs lounge after the meal. All the tables seemed crowded. It had been festooned with decorations, and a makeshift folk-band had been assembled out of the crew. They saw their own soft-spoken Nubian waiter, in native clothes now, crouched over a pair of drums at the end of the room. There was another drummer, a man with a tambourine, a rebec-player; a microphone and amplifier, a pounding din. Dan and Jane stood watching a moment through the glass doors, and decided not. They turned away to the bar and bought two brandies, then carried them through to another small lounge that opened out on the sun-deck at the aft of the ship. They had expected it to be empty, but unexpectedly the Herr Professor was there.

They had noticed that he wasn't at dinner. He seemed to miss meals sometimes, or perhaps took them alone in his cabin. He sat now in a corner with a glass and a bottle of mineral water on the table beside him, reading a book. But he looked up as they came in and gave a dry bow of the head.

Dan said, "The noise is too much for us."

"You have my sympathies. My cabin is beneath the orchestra. Tonight I am homeless."

He explained that the company let him have a cabin away from the engines, as he was a very light sleeper; but on such gala nights he had to pay for his usual peace. Dan asked if he might buy him a brandy. The old man refused: he had a touch of indigestion. But please, they must sit with him, he was reading only to pass the time. The book had been lent him by one of his party. They could see it was in German, and he said it was a summary of the economic progress made in the DDR since the division of Germany. The old man contemplated the cover for a moment, then gave them one of his delicately ambiguous smiles.

"It is not light reading."

"Do you go home very often?"

He shook his head. "I have a sister. And my son and grandchildren. That is all now to take me back."

"You must find many changes."

"They were invited." He added, "Especially by my generation. I think we cannot complain."

Jane asked him what his son still in Germany did.

"He is a doctor. Like his mother and grandfather."

"You must be proud of him."

"Yes, he is a surgeon now. Of the eyes. I am told very good." But they sensed a tiny tinge of paternal regret in his voice: a fate accepted, but not quite welcomed.

Jane said gently, "You wish he didn't live so far away?"

The old man shrugged. "He has his work, his friends . . . and at least I have my memories." He gave Jane a small smile. "Which you awoke a little the other day, *madame*."

"Why was that?"

"You will think me very sentimental."

"Please."

He hesitated. "My wife's poor patients often had no money to pay her. They would bring her small presents instead. Sometimes they would be strings of beads of the kind you bought in Mr. Abdullam's shop. As an archaeologist, I would tell her they were worthless. But she would say . . . what you said that afternoon, *madame*. And something in the way you touched your beads. Your voice." He smiled drily at Dan. "I am sorry. Forgive me."

Dan indicated that there was nothing to forgive. Jane was staring down at her lap. There was a little silence. Then she looked up.

"I think I envy your wife, professor. For having been able to do so much more than feel."

"That is already more than most. Alas."

"She died here?"

"In Germany. At Leipzig. After the war."

"You spent that there?"

The old man shook his head, and spoke with a certain grimness. "In Palestine. In a British internment camp."

Then slowly, under their further questions, he must have sensed their curiosity, he began to talk in more detail of his past—quite objectively, as if he were a site, not himself; not unlike the way in which he had outlined Queen Hatshepsut's life to them at Thebes.

He had never been a fascist, but he took little credit for that. He had lived too much out of Germany in the 1930s. He had found the demagogy, the mass rallies, the appeals to *Volk*, unattractive, but no more than the vulgar trappings of a fundamentally necessary government. He could not remember "der Führer" and the rest of National Socialist jargon ever cropping up in conversation with most of his friends and associates without a certain irony. At the time it all came from another world, it was beneath serious discussion. One conveyed one's attitude by not talking about such things. Then there was his wife, and the entrée he had through her into English circles in Cairo. There too the subject was rarely discussed. The moment of truth had come when Hitler revealed his true colors in 1939. Many of his German colleagues in Egypt had returned home and he was ordered to do so himself.

"So. At last I was forced to think of a world beyond that of ancient Egypt and my wife and children. She helped very much. We decided our marriage was more important than our difference of nationality. That I would take my luck here. I had begun to suspect my country was wrong. I would not fight against it. But I would not fight for it."

During a year, in the phony war, he had been allowed to continue his archaeological work. Then he was interned, and had spent the remaining years in a camp in Palestine. He said the conditions had not been comfortable, but the company had been valuable. He had learned a great deal about something of which he had hitherto been "a little ignorant": other men.

"Of course I knew when the war ended that my country had deserved its defeat. The Jewish genocide. I was brought that news—the first discovery of the concentration camps—by my wife. I can still see the newspaper. The *Daily Telegraph*. The photographs. I wept, but I am afraid it was not for the dead Jews, it was for myself. My race. I could not look at my wife. She had supported me and my children so bravely through those unhappy years."

Jane said gently, "But she can't have blamed you?"

"No. Not at all. But our two sons . . . it was difficult for them, poor boys. I think perhaps they judged better. They knew their father had failed. As his fatherland had failed."

"By omission?"

"I thought of it by an example from my work, Mr. Martin. If I had transcribed only what I could read easily of a papyrus, and pretended what needed more patience, more examination, did not exist. I recalled so many things, so many signs I had preferred not to see or hear before the war. The part of the papyrus I had neglected to read—that was not difficult to see."

Then outside circumstances took a hand. His "unpatriotic" attitude at the outbreak of the war and the fact that so many contemporaries in his field had died or disappeared, or elected now to stay in the West, made his specialized knowledge a rare commodity. Out of the blue he was asked back to Leipzig to rebuild the faculty—"if you can call a faculty a large hut without students. A collection of packing-cases. An almost total loss of records."

"We had much discussion. My sons did not want to go. But their mother knew I would not be at peace if I did not go. We tried to explain to the boys why it was our duty to go."

"The political side didn't worry you?"

The old man smiled. "A little, yes. You must understand, we were not sophisticated people in that way. There was work for Constance—she had always worked by preference with children. I had my old university. My great feeling I must help now, even though it was too late."

So they had gone. His wife had died during their third year in the ravaged city—a great shock, an unexpected hemorrhage after a hysterectomy. But he thought her last gift had "in a most sad way" been to leave him a German alone in a Germany he now belonged to more out of a sense of duty than from any deeper attachment. He was forced to re-examine his beliefs. He had never joined the Communist Party, and his status as a scholar had put him in a privileged position as regarded "official pressures"; but he had come to accept that socialism was best for the country and the time in history. It had its inhumanities, "its blind places"; but so perhaps began all new and better societies.

Though he had passed very briefly over his wife's death, and left so much unsaid, they had a sense of a very real marriage; as, too, of an innocence in the old man and his dead wife; of two people alienated from both sides, split across the Iron Curtain, with only their mutual respect and love to sustain them, their professional work. He even said as much, how his two sons' practically demonstrated division of feeling reflected something of his own.

He told them then that his younger son, the one who was now an archaeologist in the United States, had originally escaped to the West. The old man smiled.

"He took after his mother. In character. I call him my English son."

There had been nothing dramatic in his escape. He had been on holiday in London with relations of his mother, and had simply not returned. He had just had his twenty-fifth birthday. The professor had tried to make him come back, but not very seriously.

"At his age it is sometimes more important to take decisions than to be sure they are right."

Dan said, "At all ages?"

"Perhaps."

Jane asked if the two brothers remained on good terms.

"Yes, *madame*." He added, "Now. Hans, my older son, the doctor, he would not accept such treachery to begin with. But he is wiser now. I believe they sometimes argue very much. When they meet. But like brothers."

"And you don't take sides?"

"I find my younger boy a little too American now. We do not see things the same way. But why should we? My generation were blind—especially we so-called students of history. We must pay for it. His is innocent. And as I say, he takes after his mother. Or her country." He smiled at them both. "The Sphinx of Europe."

Dan said, "More familiarly known as the Sick Man of Europe."

"If obstinacy is a sickness."

"Surely not very enigmatic?"

"There I must disagree. To us foreigners . . ."

"But your English . . ."

"Oh yes. I speak the language. I understand English ways. I even grew to like English cooking—steak-and-kidney pie . . ." and he lingered a moment, as if over the memory of some rare claret. "But your soul. That is another question." He raised one of his admonitory fingers. "And above all in this matter of freedom. A German cannot think of freedom without rules. That is much more than our love of goose-marching and military discipline—which is a Prussian matter, in any case. It is in our philosophers. In Kant, in Marx. In Bach. Goethe. For us, all freedom is no freedom. We may dispute over the rules, but not that they must be there.

Dan smiled. "But our freedom is largely an illusion. As we're beginning to realize."

The old man was silent a moment, then quizzed them.

"You know the story of the West German cousin who visited his East German relations? The talk came to politics. The West German told his relations that their lives were dictated by the state, by the Russians. They retorted that his half of Germany was no better—it was the most Americanized in Europe. Perhaps, he said, but at least we have freely chosen it, in the democratic Anglo-Saxon way. Ah, said his uncle, but so have we freely chosen, my boy. And what is more, in the democratic German way." The old man acknowledged their smiles, but went on. "I think the point is this—whom is the joke against? I have heard it told as a satire on East Germany. Yet I think it may be told also in its favor. It depends, you see, on how you define the contrary of freedom. For us, it is chaos. For you . . ."

"Authority?"

He nodded. "That is the true curtain between East and West. In my opinion. We sacrifice some of our freedom to have order—our leaders would claim social justice, equality, all the rest. While you sacrifice some of your order to have freedom. What you call natural justice, the individual rights of man." He suddenly smiled, as if they were becoming too serious. "May I tell you one more story? It is against the English, but it was told me many years ago by a compatriot of yours."

"Of course."

"An Englishman in French Africa goes swimming towards a place where there are crocodiles. A native on the bank who speaks English cries to him. 'Turn back! Danger! Turn back at once!' The Englishman hears, he looks round, the black man cries again. But the Englishman takes no notice at all. He goes on swimming. And he is killed. The French authorities hold an inquiry—no one can understand why the victim ignored the warning. But another Englishman stands up to explain. The warning had been given in incorrect language, it would not have been understood. Ah. Then would monsieur please tell the court the correct call, in case such an unhappy event occurred again? The Englishman thinks, considers very deeply, then he says, 'Would you mind awfully turning back, sir, please?' "

They smiled, a little less genuinely than before.

"It is cruel. But I have a suspicion that something in your country would still rather drown than be given good advice by a foreigner. That is the freedom I do not understand."

"We don't understand it very well ourselves."

The old man smiled. "Never mind. Who knows? Perhaps that Englishman wanted to be eaten by crocodiles."

Dan glanced at Jane, who had been silent for a while; but there was a gentleness in her eyes, an agreement, at least as regarded the old scholar. They looked down, then Dan spoke again.

"Do you have any hope for the conflict between East and West?"

"I used to feel guilt that I have spent so much time studying the past. I saw my papyri as screens I had put up to hide what I did not wish to understand. I now see everything is a kind of screen if one wishes it so. An excuse for not understanding." He paused, then went on. "I remember—this is before the war—a dispute between two villages on opposite banks of the Nile. North of Luxor, where I was then working. It was over rights of fishing. It became very bitter, blood was shed. One day I asked one of the headmen concerned—a peasant, illiterate, but a very wise old man—why he and the other village leader could not settle the matter by compromise. He reprimanded me for such foolish optimism. He told me there would never be peace among men, on either bank. Only in the river between."

"The one place we can't live."

The old man opened his hands.

And then he told them a last story: a personal one, what he called a ghost story without a ghost. It had happened soon after he first came to Egypt, in the late 1920s, before he had specialized in his subsequent field. He had been working one day in one of the recently excavated noble—as opposed to royal—tomb-chambers in the cliffs opposite Aswan; and became so absorbed in his work, recording a wall-painting, that he stayed on later than usual. Working by artificial light, he had not noticed that dusk had fallen outside. But then something, perhaps caused by his long hours of concentration, perhaps by an unconscious realization that all was now silent on the site, happened. He had a curious sense of a living presence that was not his own. It was for a moment frightening, indeed he shone his light round the tomb, but he was not in the least a believer in the supernatural . . . in "curses and such nonsense." His fear was a more straightforward physical one—that some thief had sneaked in. But there was a night-watchman who guarded the access to the site. He thought perhaps it was this man, he even called his name. There was no answer, and then he had stared again at the wall-painting, which happened to be in an exceptionally fresh state.

He had paused at that point in his story. They heard someone come into the lounge behind them, but neither Dan nor Jane turned; and whoever it was, went away again.

"I have had this experience again, but never so vividly as on that first occasion. It is of a most strange . . . like a broken link in time."

"A dislocation?"

"Yes. Thank you. That is a better word. For a little interval time does not seem to exist. One is neither the original painter nor one's own self, a modern archaeologist. If one is anything—I speak metaphorically, forgive me, I lack words to express it in any other way, one is the painting. One exists, but it is somehow not in time. In a greater reality, behind the illusion we call time. One was always there. There is no past or future. One's knowledge of history, chronology, seems like one of those screens I spoke of just now." He smiled at them. "This is not to do with mysticism. It is almost physical, something hidden in the nature of things. I once had a similar experience, also after many hours of work, with a difficult papyrus. I became the papyrus, I was beyond time. Yet it did not help me decipher it at all. So. It was not in that sense that I was the papyrus. Perhaps I was the river. For a few moments whatever in the river does not pass. That river between." He said nothing for a few seconds, then gave Jane and Dan a little look. "I am afraid that is what they will never understand. The river between."

Jane murmured, "Who is 'they,' professor?"

He gave her another look, as if she were teasing him again.

"I think you and Mr. Martin know, *madame*." He left a moment's pause, and there was a glint, both of latent irony and of conspiracy, in his old blue eyes. "There are many languages on this planet. Many frontiers. But in my experience only two nations."

In the silence, they heard the faint continued throbbing and pounding of the drums from the forward lounge; and knew he did not mean East and West, and even less his Germany, or their England.

# Kitchener's Island

The boat's constant progress, the transience of each land-scape—it might in many ways be a delightfully indolent way of traveling, but it had mysteriously heightened some obscure metaphysical pressure in Dan. It was all very well the Herr Professor talking about time being an illusion, but time seemed both ever-present and distorted on that southward journey. It gained a strange brevity: the cruise had hardly begun before it was nearly ended, almost as if there was a cheat about it, a temporal sleight of hand.

His malaise came from a blend of that and of an even vaguer awareness of shifts in the equilibrium of his life, beyond what he could consciously detect. But more and more he knew these shifts were in response to a sense of incompleteness that was also one of predestination. This lay behind, or deeper than, the effects of re-experiencing the Nile and the events and meetings of the cruise. He still clung to his inmost grain of conviction—that freedom, especially the freedom to know oneself, was the driving-force of human evolution; whatever else the sacrifice, it must not be of complexity of feeling, and its expression, since that was where, in social terms, the fundamental magic (or chink in the door) of mutation inside the nucleic-acid helix took place. All through that long last conversation with the Herr Professor he had secretly watched Jane's face, to see whether she was recognizing this implicit support being given to his case. But when the old man had left them, soon after the summary but touching reduction of the Tower of Babel to two tribes, he had not pressed it home. They had talked about him, not of what he had been saying; of whether he ventured upon such a line with his fellow-nationals on board. Dan had sensed that Jane, though approving of the old man's humanity, was not convinced. It was too like quietism. Western mankind was an unruly child, and could not be spared its left-wing rod.

The net result of all this was that Dan found himself wishing—though not overdoing a good thing was such a salient feature in his practical philosophy of pleasure—that the cruise were longer: another week, perhaps. It also suspended, postponed all decision. One waited and one watched; one did not have to act. Already he saw he had spent those days balanced between outward enjoyment and inward anxiety—or enjoyment in the now, anxiety about the future . . . a worry beyond normal worries, a fear of its arrival. It even worried him that he could not clearly ascribe this premonitory anxiety to anything. He did not need the passage he had marked from Lukács to feel that it was self-indulgent, unnecessary. In simple fact he felt a little bewitched by what these few days on the Nile seemed to have done to him: both calmed and unsettled.

But the Herr Professor had without knowing, without Dan himself seeing it, given the scales a small tip; then something happened that at last allowed him to perceive what he had been sailing upstream toward. It was not Aswan; but he only fully began to admit what it really was on their very last stop, the morning of the afternoon they were to arrive there.

This last halt was for a brief visit to the temple-complex at Kom Ombo. Set in a desert landscape on a low promontory over the Nile, it had a Greek quality; an isolation, a posedness, a sunbaked peace reflected in the blue water. It was much more as the other temple sites ought to have been: both beautiful in itself and beautifully framed. For some reason Dan had no memory of it from his previous visit.

The ship moored close by and they strolled across the sand. A band of mischievous Bedouin children ran and danced along the ridges of the dunes around them, and bronze-collared doves cooed in the acacias by the waterside. This time Dan and Jane did not even go through the motions of listening to their guide. The stone pavements and terraces over the river were too pleasant to stroll on. Then Dan was given an ornithological treat. He looked through his field glasses at a robin-like bird hopping in the shade by the river's edge. It was a very handsome little creature, a bluethroat, the first of the species he had ever seen. He stopped a minute or two to watch it, and Jane went idly on to sit at the corner of the terrace overlooking the river, facing upstream. Then she changed her mind and went out of sight, somewhere lower. When he got to the corner himself, he saw a collapsed wall made it easy to clamber down nearer the water. She was sitting on one end of the drum of a fallen column, in the thin shade of a sunt tree, her back to him, looking at the curving reach of the water to the south. He scrambled down to join her.

"Isn't this a delectable place, Jane?"

She nodded. But something in the way she nodded, and did not turn, both contradicted his light tone and warned him. He came beside her. She gave an embarrassed downward glance toward his feet, then looked back at the view. After a moment a hand came up and she touched her eyes.

"I'm sorry. It's nothing." She shook her head, to dismiss his solicitude. "Its all being over. And thinking of Anthony. How he would have liked it here."

He sat beside her on the drum of stone, then asked gently, "Why now?"

She had said nothing.

Then without warning her right hand had reached out and taken his, as if she were apologizing for turning female. She would have withdrawn it, but he caught it and made it lie still, under his own now, resting on the stone between them. They stayed like that for a few moments. He pressed the hand, felt a small movement of response; then saw her look down at the hands, as at things detached from the rest of their bodies. And suddenly he knew that something else was being said—in that way she looked down, as in that original gesture of reaching. He felt moved, yet strangely frozen. It was in those moments' silence, simplicity; in their very tentativeness. Part of him wanted to put an arm around her shoulders, but he knew that the instinct was in some way, echoing the curious swiftness of the cruise, too late when it was perceived; either done spontaneously, or not at all.

"My dear, he wouldn't want it."

"I know."

"And we could easily make this an annual thing."

She smiled, as he had meant her to, and quoted Eliot to the river.

" 'I read, much of the night, and go south in the winter.' "

"In a manner of speaking."

They heard voices behind them, some of the French at the corner of the terrace. She withdrew her hand, but they did not turn; sat in silence again, in the dappled shade. Three snow-white egrets flew across the river, but Dan saw them without thinking. It had been in that downward look at the joined hands. It had been a declension out of the theater of their behavior on the cruise into something undeclared not only between them, but also in each separately; and describable in the other sense of declension . . . a feminine look, not a neutrally companionable one. Almost reluctant, admitting nothing but its brief existence; yet there.

It had glossed that "its all being over," which had meant not just the cruise, the experience. He knew it had referred mainly to the past, and not to any specific past possibility, but all past possibility; what she knew he knew was lost for ever; but there was also some tinge in it, if only derived from the fact that it had been given in the now, of a present regret . . . for what had been rediscovered, for what, beneath all the change, had remained. Perhaps he had read too much into it. Yet what it really revealed was something in himself: the arm that had wanted to move, the knowledge that he hadn't honestly examined why he wanted the cruise to continue, that he shared this sadness at its ending; that he would miss this daily closeness, mind, intuition, shared age and experience, the restoration of the old empathy, far more than he was prepared to admit. It came so oddly without the usual clear knowledges of physical attraction; all those still stayed obstinately attached to the thought of Jenny, and not just out of fidelity. It was far more a matter of that sense of incompleteness—the extent to which it would increase when they went their different ways, a glimpse of a reality in the old Platonic myth, an echo of the old Rabelaisian one, *Fais ce que voudras* . . . it also frightened him.

He found his cigarettes. She took one and they smoked, both staring out at the river. The tears were quite ended now, as she proved when she broke the silence.

"I was also crying because I suddenly realized I was glad to be alive again, Dan. After what seems rather a long time."

"I prefer that."

"It was your stopping to watch that bird . . . we had an absurd row in Greece three years ago—our last proper holiday alone together. Because he'd held us up with his botanizing one afternoon, when all I wanted was a beach and somewhere to swim. He was so happy and I was so unreasonable."

"Are you sure he wasn't being unreasonable as well?"

"I sat under a tree reading. I only took it out on him later. He wasn't to know." She flicked ash from her cigarette. "Behind our screens."

"An accepted part of every civilized marriage?"

She smiled, but sadly, then took a breath.

"I think they must be right, the young. About the anti-quatedness of the institution."

"Their theory also has its price."

She left another silence.

"Have you ever missed it?"

"Sometimes." But that seemed not enough of an answer. He looked down. "Not often. If I'm honest." He added, "And once burnt, twice shy. Laziness. The other kind of relationship becomes a habit."

"And a freedom?"

"To be an aging Don Juan?"

She murmured. "That lovely innocent young man I knew at Oxford."

"Beyond salvation now." She glanced at him, but he avoided her eyes, knowing why she looked. "I'm only smiling because you know perfectly well he was never innocent. Lovely, perhaps."

She too looked down at the ground, then said slowly, almost as if to herself, "I always remember you as innocent."

"Unlike you?"

"I was so frightened of my real feelings."

Before he could answer there came, from behind them, a wail from the ship's horn. It was time to return.

"That's still a kind of innocence."

"It never seemed it. Even then."

"I think you're playing Cassandra backwards. My memory of you's quite opposite. That you always did show real feelings. When it mattered." He said, "Or much more than the rest of us ever managed."

"Emotions. They're not the same." But then she said, more lightly, "I'm trying to say thank you, Dan. That is a real feeling."

There was another peremptory wail from the ship. She stood and reached out a hand with a composed smile . . . long live convention, the foolishness was over. He pressed it as he stood, and they started back for the boat.

He remained disconcerted. There was something disturbing in the conversation, as in the look; that had not been in any of their previous conversations. She put on dark glasses, and they strolled slowly back through the ruins toward the entrance. A row of crocodile-headed divinities, Alain coming up to greet them, some joke . . . Jane smiled, and answered for them both; she seemed fully recovered from her brief bout of sentiment, as lightly guarded as always. Dan had a sense of missed chance, he should have put his arm around her shoulders, at least closed that space . . . this ludicrous emotional no-man's-land they had decreed between them, which perhaps their conversation had been directed, on her side, after the holding hands, to reconstitute. It had been like accidentally seeing a woman in her underwear through a bedroom door. Even though the undressing had been of a very different kind, he could not deny that, just as with the hands, it had held an erotic charge for him.

Later, when the ship was on its way again, and they sat on deck before lunch—their Czech friend and Alain were sitting with them—he found himself constantly contemplating Jane in secret . . . or at least if not literally so, then mentally. Alain was flirting with her again, in English, it was all innocent, she must come to Paris and let him take her to all the new *boîtes* and restaurants—and Dan let himself slip into the young Frenchman's imagined place. Perhaps that was at the root of it: a resentment on her side, though almost certainly unconscious, that Dan had so scrupulously not acknowledged what other males around them did: that she wore her age well, she retained an attraction. It had worried him slightly from the beginning, which was why he had been careful with conventional compliments about clothes, about how she looked.

On the other hand he was very clear that whatever else that gesture, that revealing, had meant, it had not been an invitation. And it was absurd because of Jenny; because of the memory of what Jane had told Caro, her view of him as someone in flight, eternally fickle; because of a thousand things.

So much bound them apart, and not least sheer ignorance of each other's secret feelings and emotions—as her very distinguishing between the two words had once more proved. Yet Dan fell, in his habitual hypothetical way, to imagining what, if he proposed when they transferred from the ship to the hotel in Aswan that they take a double room, her reaction might be. The only speculation involved was over how she would refuse: with anger, with disbelief, with irony, perhaps even with affection. What was certain was that she would refuse—or he knew nothing of women. He wondered if what nagged at him was merely her impossibility; that is, their joint impossibility. He remembered that she had an affair quite recently; and he could, just, imagine her having an affair, a night, with Alain, if he himself had not been there—a letting him into her bed if he insisted enough. But that would never do for them. And he knew, in some strange way, that even if she might, out of some part of herself so hidden that he had not even guessed at its existence, out of some brief conquest of feeling by emotion, not have refused, he would have felt betrayed.

The Hoopers, or their presence, made him say very little at lunch. He worried, like a dog with an old bone, at those brief tears, that one downward look: had it reproached him, or warned him? Jane gave no clue now, it was as if nothing had happened. Any reference, she managed to suggest, would have been to exaggerate the incident. But he wouldn't quite let her get away with that. She smiled at him as they waited for their dessert, her chin poised on her clasped hands.

"You're being very silent."

"That's how men cry."

"What's your woe?"

"I smell the return of reality."

"There's still your island. I thought that was why we were here." He tilted his head in reluctant acknowledgment: yes, one treat left. As if to cheer him up, she added, "And lovely memories."

He retreated behind a smile and a look aside; but then something, against his will, he was conscious that his smile had been too thin, made him seek her eyes again. In a way it was his equivalent of her look; certainly puzzled and questioning. Perhaps it seemed to her merely inquisitive, or contradicting the last words she had said. At any rate she gave a little interrogative shake of the head.

"No?"

He smiled more naturally. "I shall try to forget the food."

Their waiter came with the dessert, creamed rice sprinkled with cinnamon, and Jane began to eat at once, as if to tell him he was being unreasonable, spoiled indeed.

The landscape changed as they neared Aswan. The Nile ran through desert. Limitless sands, broken by harsh black basaltic outcrops, scorched by millennia of unrelenting sun, stood and waited, or so it seemed, for the great river to run dry. Tropical cabbage palms became the only trees along the banks, and desert ravens, recalling the Bible again, manna, as well as Dan's more personal memories, were the only birds. The sun burned down through a cool north wind.

Aswan itself came as a shock, brutally interrupting the increasingly barren solitude. The town had changed considerably since Dan's previous visit in the 1950s. Now it had the air of a boom city, with an imposing and traffic-filled waterfront, high-rise buildings, a monstrous new hotel complex on Elephantine Island. There were crowds of ferrying feluccas, motor-launches; and beyond, to the south, the blue sky was stained a pale yellow with the dust from the dam and its surrounding industries. The horizon there was festooned with wires and pylons, radar, all the ugly adjuncts of twentieth-century technology and war. Three MiGs tore low overhead as the boat came in to moor; and higher still the azure was lacerated with white con-trails.

Dan and Jane remembered what they had heard at Assad's party; what would happen if the Aswan Dam was breached, the terrible tidal wave that would destroy the whole length of the Nile Valley and half Cairo with it . . . and which made all bluster about total war with Israel a sour joke—the "final irrigation scheme," as Ahmed Sabry had sardonically named this sword of Damocles. Aswan was the return of reality with a vengeance, and Dan loathed it. He had an abrupt sense of a voyage ended; and the end of the dream of a different voyage, far longer.

Assad had wanted to put him in touch with the manager of a local studio, indeed offered to fly down himself, but Dan had declined. The studio facilities were not his business, there were obviously desert locations galore, and he merely wanted the feel of the place. He was even gladder now that he had been firm. They did not have to leave the ship until the next morning, when they would transfer for a couple of nights to the Old Cataract Hotel—dwarfed, he noted, by the ugly New Cataract beside it. On his own he would have moved ashore at once, but he knew that that would have offended Jane's sense of economy; so he compromised and suggested they skip the prescribed official tour that afternoon. They could go under their own steam . . . or sail, hiring their own felucca. He presented the idea as a professional necessity, he didn't want to rush things. Jane seemed content.

So they waited until the others had left, and then walked down the corniche to where a fleet of small feluccas waited; and to save argument let themselves be captured by the first boatman who approached them. He was a grave young man, in a white galabiya and black-banded headscarf, with a small boy at his side. His name was Omar, and he spoke a few very rudimentary words of English; beneath the dark skin he had strangely Anglo-Saxon features and rather pale eyes. There was a ghost of T. E. Lawrence about him. They tacked slowly into the wind as they headed north for the sandy cliffs on the uninhabited west bank, around the tip of Elephantine Island. The motion was pleasing, after the ship; its patience and gentleness. Kites glided overhead; then there were terns fishing, a falcon circling over the ocher cliffs, and a huge bird flapped off the buoy at the end of the island, an osprey. Dan began to feel happier as the busy town receded. He found their helmsman's taciturnity pleasing. Kitchener's Island came in sight, upstream of them, green and dense with vegetation, and he knew that there at least he would not be disappointed. Jane, too, was obviously enjoying this new scenery.

They landed and climbed up to see the rock tombs in the Kobbet el Hawa cliff, where the Herr Professor had had his strange first experience of timelessness. They had been too long occupied by nomads to show much more than pretty fragments and perversely, though he had complained so much at the royal sites, Dan now found himself missing their craftsmanship and finesse of detail. From outside the tombs they could look back over the midriver islands and survey the mushrooming town to the east, the industrial landscape stretching behind it and to the south. It was like a huge scorpion, pincered, menacing the little oasis of blue and green at their feet; reminded Dan a little of Los Angeles, seen from Mulholland Drive—or indeed, from Jenny's apartment. In some way this depressing sense of a spatial invasion transferred itself to his sense of personal time . . . how briefly they were there, how short the permitted entry into the oasis. The man who had guided them round the tombs pointed out various landmarks in the town, but Dan was lost in his own thoughts.

Then he had a very peculiar few moments of disorientation. Perhaps there really was some *genius loci,* though his experience was not of timelessness, but of somehow being outside his own body, as if he were a camera, merely recording, at a remove from present reality. For a brief but abyss-like space he was not at all sure where he was, what he was doing. This landscape, this voluble guide, the way the wind moved this woman's hair . . . it was like a mechanical trip in the normal current of consciousness, a black-out, an epilepsy, and he found it, during the few seconds it lasted, ominous, unpleasant; as if he, all around him, was an idea in someone else's mind, not his own.

He paid and tipped the guide, then followed Jane down the narrow path to where their felucca and its two attendants waited. He would have liked to try to describe to her what had just happened, but felt the old German had in some way pre-empted him; it would seem silly, like exclaiming over some experience of *déjà vu*, whose metaphysical strangeness could not be conveyed, and must always sound suspect to an outsider. The evanescence, the illusion of lost angle. He had had the same feeling once or twice before, when he was tired, on film-sets. Nothing existed except as a record of another pair of eyes, another mind; the perceived world was as thin as an eggshell, a fragile painted flat, a back-projection . . . and behind, nothing. Shadows, darkness, emptiness.

He watched Jane's back, as she descended the steep slope just before him. She was wearing bell-bottomed jeans, a pale terracotta-colored shirt beneath a kind of loose woolen cardigan-cum-coat, too long to be one, too short to be the other, that she had often worn on their forays from the ship. It was unashamedly *sui generis*, and managed to hit, more than anything else she wore, that blend in its owner between the ancient blue-stocking's indifference to clothes and a contradictory, but not altogether casual, respect for how personality is conveyed through choice of them. Then the rush-basket she was carrying—that touch of domesticity, of being on a shopping expedition as well: she was wearing the silver comb in her hair, but a dark strand had escaped.

And once again Dan had a moment, like that one on the Dorset down, of imagining that they had married, had been married since the beginning; he saw his wife, not Anthony's widow; a hand on her shoulder, a moment's stopping, a replacing that escaped strand, an indulgent little marital nothing. Then he felt frightened again. Perhaps his brief experience above, which part of him was already dismissing as a curious trick of the brain-cells, a second or two's lapse of those responsible for maintaining one's normal state of consciousness—was premonitory; just as he had, a few moments before it happened, slipped from an outer spatial to an inner temporal analogy over the invading town, perhaps there had been some warning of an imminent greater slip, into something pathological, a madness, a declared schizophrenia . . . the ground leveled out and he came beside her, damning death and introspection.

They set off again, against the current but with the breeze behind them, down the reach toward Kitchener's Island. The sun was beginning to decline and high on the sandy dunes that crowned the western cliffs there was a congregation of the kites, some twenty or thirty of them, perched on the sand, dark brown and hieratic. Omar brought them in past the first green walls of the trees of the island; strange flowers, leaves, boughs sweeping the water. There were no houses on this side of the river, the town was lost; and one might, as they came closer still beside the towering wall of sunlit vegetation, with the quiet water, have been on one of the summer Oxford rivers. Some hidden warbler bubbled an out-of-season song. It was delicious, after the arid desert of earlier that day: a profound and liquid, green and eternal peace. Once again Omar moored. They disembarked, and after a few steps up under a huge canopy of bougainvillea, found themselves in one of the island's walks.

Though some attempt had been made to maintain the island as the great botanical garden Kitchener had initiated—here and there massive leaden labels with exotic Latin names and distant countries of origin still hung suspended around trunks, and from time to time they saw gardeners at work—the place had a charmingly haphazard and unkempt quality. It had literally run to seed, and bred the pleasing air of a once stern scientific purpose succumbed to the mere existing of shady vistas, countless birds, coolness, simplicity . . . the simplicity of the finest Islamic architecture, of centuries of folk-knowledge exercised on sanctuaries against the sun. It was an Alhambra composed of vegetation, water, shadow; and perhaps nicest of all, it remained almost exactly as Dan had remembered it—one of the loveliest and most civilized few acres in his knowledge of this world, a tropical *bonne vaux*. He was careful not to prompt Jane, but she too fell for the place at once. They had strolled hardly a hundred yards before she touched his sleeve.

"I want a house here, Dan. Please."

He grinned. "That's what Andrea and I felt."

"It's like a Douanier Rousseau version of the Garden of Eden. And how clever of you to think of it for your film."

"I hope they'll use it. It'll make a nice point of return."

After a while they sat on a bench in one of the side-walks.

There were other strollers on the main paths, specks of distant color who idled through the sunshot shadow like figures not from a Rousseau, but in a Manet or a Renoir. They discussed what they would do those next two days, the other things to see, whether they should fly down to Abu Simbel or not . . . a number of their fellow-passengers were going to do so, the Hoopers had reported it was worthwhile, or so they'd been told, just for the vast landscapes of Lake Nasser—and the engineering side of it, of course, the "fantastic" raising of the temple from the ancient site. Jane had resisted the idea on the cruise, but now she gave way, one might never have the chance again; the day after next, they decided. Then a band of some dozen or so young Egyptians came by, a mixture of boys and girls, in European clothes. There were looks, things said, as they approached the two foreigners. And as they passed one of the boys cried, as if it were a joke, in English, "Good morning!"

Dan smiled and said, "Good evening."

"Ingleesh?"

"English."

"Very good. Ingleesh very good."

And suddenly the kids gathered round Jane and Dan, in a close little crescent, amused brown eyes, the girls biting their lips.

"You make holiday?"

"Yes. And you too?"

But the boy didn't understand the question. A girl beside him spoke; she was pretty, less broadfaced than most Arab women, with long dark hair and finely shaped eyes.

"We have free day today. No work."

"Speak Ingleesh very good," said the first boy.

She was shy, but she did speak better English. Her father was an engineer at the dam, a year ago a young sister had had to have some complicated heart operation, and she had spent three months in London with her mother and the sick sister. She was seventeen, she and her friends were from the leading high school in Aswan. She wished she could live in Cairo, they all wanted to live in Cairo, or Alexandria. It was too hot here, too "dirty." Jane asked if it ever rained.

"I live here two years, I never see rain."

There were giggles from her companions as she spoke, murmurs in Arabic, and every now and then her dark eyes would flash sideways reproachfully at whatever taunt she was receiving. She talked mainly to Jane, and the others began to drift away, until only the gazelle-eyed girl and two others were left. They learned English at school, but they had to learn Russian as well. They didn't like it, but it was the law. They liked English much better. She wished she could find an English pen-pal.

Jane smiled. "If you give me your name and address, I'll try to find one for you when I go home."

The girl bit her lips, as if set back by this direct response, and said something in Arabic to one of the other girls. Jane reached in her rush-basket and produced a pencil and a note-book. The girl hesitated, then urged silently on by one of her friends, sat beside Jane and laboriously printed out a name and address.

"Which would you like—a boy or a girl?"

"A boy?" Again she bit her lips. "You will not forget?"

"Of course not."

"You are very kind."

One of the boys called back impatiently from the opening in the main path.

"I must go. We have boat." But she stayed sitting a moment. "You have daughter?"

"Yes. Two daughters."

Impulsively, quite without warning, the girl took the long necklace of beads she was wearing and ducked her head out of it, pulled it free of her long hair, then put it on the bench beside Jane's basket.

Jane said, "Oh but . . ."

The girl was standing and made a bowing gesture, her hands folded one over the other between her breasts.

"Please. Nothing. So you will not forget." She bobbed again. "I must go now."

Jane picked the beads up. "But really I . . ."

The girl opened her hands as if to tell Jane it was fate, the deed was done, she mustn't remonstrate—then suddenly she had snatched one of her companion's hands and they were running away like girls half their age. There was a suppressed shriek of laughter, as if they had done something enormously daring. Their friends gathered around them on the main path to find out what it was all about. There was more laughter, but as they turned away the group waved back through the foliage toward Jane and Dan. She stood, they both waved back. Then she stared at the beads in her hands. They were brown, polished, some kind of seed. Her eyes, amused, still slightly aghast, sought Dan's.

"What an extraordinary thing to do."

"As long as they aren't coated in some deadly poison." She threw him a look for such an unkind thought, then, as if to contradict him still further, sat and slipped the beads over her head; then cast him another look. He grinned. "A nice kid."

"Wasn't she pretty?" She examined the beads again, then lifted them and sniffed. "Oh they've got some strange scent. Like patchouli." Dan bent forward and smelled the end she held out: a musty, sweet fragrance.

"Mm."

She sniffed at them again herself, then murmured, "It's so sad. All these young people so eager to make contact."

"I was just thinking—what could any Israeli boy in his senses want to do to a face like that? Except kiss it."

"I wish Paul was a year or two older."

"You could always try. She might enjoy the monthly ten pages on medieval English hedge-systems."

Jane grinned, still contemplating the beads, but said nothing; and he knew that this trivial gift, they were obviously bazaar beads, of no value, had moved her, penetrated that old openness to, recognition of, right feeling. He left a silence, then said in a lower voice, "Are you really happy to be alive again, Jane?"

"Yes."

"I've enjoyed these last few days so much more than I thought I would. Which sounds terribly backhanded. But it's true."

"Not fair. You've pinched my speech."

"Writer's privilege."

She still had a slight smile, still looked down; hesitated. "You were quite right. I did need something like this."

"And you'll leave the past behind now?"

"What I can of it."

"You've done your penance."

She made a sideways movement of the head. "By Ave Maria standards."

"Come on. What was that existentialist bit about using the past to build the present?"

"I think that really derived from the famous pre-Sartrean philosopher Samuel Smiles."

He persisted. "But at least the journey hasn't been quite wasted?"

"Of course not."

She half-smiled toward him, yet it was only a token acknowledgment; almost a withdrawal, a denial; at any rate, a not wanting to talk about it.

"I don't want to leave it behind here, Jane. That's all."

She didn't even answer that, but gave a small nod. She sat with her head bowed, quite unintentionally with something of the shyness of a schoolgirl, as if it had rubbed off on her from the beads she had put on; but now, as if she realized it, she straightened and looked up through the trees before them. What he had taken as embarrassment was perhaps simply thinking along other lines.

"That night . . . when he killed himself. What upset me so much was the feeling that he'd just turned me into an impediment. A sort of white elephant."

"That's ridiculous."

"I'm not defending what I felt, Dan. It wasn't a gender thing . . . whatever I said afterwards. Just that I felt I was relegated to being a burden on other people's consciences."

"Which is what they're for. If it was true."

"I think what this experience has done has made me see I never tried hard enough with Anthony in the last years. That's really why I cried this morning. But that in turn's because I feel better in myself. Less hysterical." She gave him another partial side-glance. "Whatever unfair demand was made of you in that last unofficial testament, consider it fulfilled."

"It wasn't unfair. That was what I was trying to say just now. I've also been realizing something here, Jane. How much I lost in you both over all those years. The debt goes both ways."

She smiled. "You should have been a diplomat."

"The last thing I meant to sound."

"I think my debt is much larger."

"Why?"

She replied very obliquely; answering his declaration of several sentences before.

"I think it's time I tried the reality of independence. Instead of leaning so much on kind friends and daughters."

"Perhaps they like being leaned on."

"Not fair to them. Or to myself."

"So you must leave it behind here? Otherwise you'll be back in prison?"

She said wrily, "I'm not putting this very well."

"Then try again."

"It's just that . . ."

"Just what?"

"Whether in the long run kindness is what I need. What should be prescribed."

"Is this a theory of your lady doctor friend's?"

"A little. She is quite strong on self-reliance in her female walking wounded. Rather aggressively so at times. But I think she has a point."

"And all males are to be feared, especially when bringing gifts?"

"I'm giving a wrong impression of her. She doesn't spread that creed at all. Much more that one should face up to the evidence of one's own past. That where there's a wrong man there's usually a wrong woman as well."

"Did you consult her about coming?"

"As a friend. Not as a doctor."

"What did she say?"

"That it was time I learnt to make my own decisions." She shook her head, as if that were not quite the truth. "And that I did need to get away from things."

There was a silence. Through the trees Dan saw the French party from the cruise, with the guide on the set tour, straggling down the main walk to their left; one or two of them looked across to where he and Jane sat. But Alain and the photographer seemed not to be with them; nor the Barge-borne Queen and Carissimo. Already the brief package disintegrated, the illusory togetherness dissolved. He spoke more lightly.

"Then I must learn to be unkind?"

She smiled. "Understanding. To someone who's much more grateful than she's managing to sound." He said nothing, and after a moment she put her hands in her coat-cardigan pockets and went on. "You've lived a so much richer life than I have."

"Are you sure you don't mean more corrupt?"

"No, not at all. Just . . . with different values."

"Which you mistrust?"

She hesitated. "Which I fear a little."

"Why?"

She showed a pressed, reluctant mouth, someone trapped in a chess-game, and did not answer for a few moments.

"You're very successful—sure of what you are. As you have every right to be. In a sense I'm only just facing up to something you did over twenty years ago. Leaving Oxford."

"What on earth makes you think knowing what you are is the same thing as being sure of it? Or even liking it?"

Again she was someone cornered; forced to think of a new move—though this time it turned out to be a very old one.

"It's probably something to do with male and female minds. You said at Thorncombe—I understand how you feel about your work. But I don't even have that. A direction ahead."

"You have a political one."

She took a breath. "My feelings there change every day. It seems like every hour, sometimes." She stared at the gravel on the other side of the path. "I think the curse of my life is having been born with a small gift for acting. Hating being able to pretend I'm someone else. Then using what I hate to be it." He had reached an arm along the bench, was turned toward her; quite deliberately, so that she would know he was scrutinizing her; and as deliberately said nothing, exactly as he might have written it in a film scenario—letting the place speak for him, really. Its peace, its presentness; almost its unspoken wondering why she was so deaf to it. In the end she said, "I don't quite know how we got into all this."

"For a very simple reason. I don't want you to think I shall breathe a huge sigh of relief as soon as we land at Rome." She looked down, as if she were unconvinced. He took his arm from the back of the bench and leaned forward with his elbows on his knees. "Jenny's very young, Jane. With her I have to live very much in the present. In today. The past becomes like an infidelity, something one has no right to remember or refer to . . . like a past mistress. You've given me a quite marvelous relief from all that." He left a pause. "That's my debt." He added, "And I won't have a perfect traveling companion going independent on me like this."

A moment, then she shifted slightly forward, gathered the handles of her basket; quick, too quick, to seize this opportunity to restore them to normality.

"Not quite perfect. Actually she must have a wee before she goes sailing again."

Dan allowed himself one small rueful smile; in check, just as he was about to claim victory; then gave in and stood up.

"There's a place at the end."

They walked down toward it, more briskly. It was cooler now. He held her basket while she went into the lavatory; and stared across a stretch of gravel at the silent river and the shadowed cliffs beyond. In some way the conversation had gone wrong from the start, it was like a scene one knew at the first re-reading was no good; simply chasing its own tail. He felt a distinct irritation, with himself as well as with Jane. He thought of Jenny, of a letter he had written her, in his cabin, nearly ready to post. He had already lied in it, claiming he had tried to telephone from Luxor, but had been unable to get a line.

Lies: not really saying what one felt.

Uncannily there came to him a faint echo of his experience outside the rock-tombs of an hour to two before. This time it was more with a sense of truancy: he had no right to be standing there, in this remote corner of an unknown country, he had forgotten what he was doing, the afternoon was somehow spellbound . . . he felt strangely purposeless, and he almost shook himself physically. It had also something to do with that little Egyptian girl, with her liquid almond eyes, the tight pullover she had been wearing. Watching her talk to Jane, he had approved her sexually, even jumped on to finding some tiny part for her in the film, in his early days Kitchener must have been offered such creatures . . . and he also knew, it had been building up, that the real scenario that was haunting him was not Kitchener's, but his own. He was approaching a fork, the kind of situation some modern novelists met by writing both roads. For days now he had been split, internally if not outwardly, between a known past and an unknown future. That was where his disturbing feeling of not being his own master, of being a character in someone else's play, came from. The past wrote him; and hatred of change, of burning boats.

Jane came beside him and took her basket back, and they returned to the felucca. This time they went south, heading for the Old Cataract, where Dan wanted to confirm their room bookings. The breeze had dropped and they drifted slowly through the islets, rocky and green, oddly Nordic, in the middle of the Nile. There was an obscure distant wail from the town, floating mournfully on the still evening air; the muezzin, relayed through loudspeakers. Omar asked Dan to take the tiller, then he and the boy knelt in the bows, facing Mecca, muttering, touching their foreheads to the deck. Jane and Dan sat in silence in the stern, embarrassed, like all intellectuals presented point-blank with simple faith. But when the helm was restored to the boatman, Jane murmured, "I may not have my house yet, but at least I've picked my chauffeur."

"Wouldn't it be nice. What would you do?"

"I'm sure I should find something."

"Good works."

"Of course."

"The Angel of Aswan."

She smiled. "With her out-of-tune harp."

After a moment he touched her hand.

"You're not cold?"

"I don't mind. The light's so beautiful."

They arrived where the river ran beneath the gardens of the famous old hotel. Omar would have waited still, but Dan paid him off, they would walk along the corniche back to the ship; tomorrow, perhaps . . . and then, well, why not, they made a definite appointment. He would take them again to Kitchener's Island. They climbed up through the gardens. The interior seemed mercifully not to have changed: the same pierced screens, huge fans, tatty old colonial furniture, stone floors, silence, barefooted Nubian servants in their red fezzes; so redolent of an obsolete middle class that it was museum-like. Dan settled Jane at a table, ordered drinks, then went through the arched rooms to find the reception desk. Their reservations were all right; then the girl telephoned about seats to Abu Simbel. They were lucky, there were two left for the day after tomorrow, and Dan took them. Finally he asked the girl to get him a Cairo number and went into a booth to take the call.

Jane had nearly finished her beer when he returned and sat.

"Sorry. I thought I'd better give Assad a ring. He sends his regards."

"I've been happy just sitting here. Absorbing the ambience."

"If only you had a nice print dress from the Thirties."

"And you in your linen suit and old school tie?"

"I think I'd have gone native, actually."

"That reminds me. I must buy one or two galabiyas before we leave."

"Me too. For Caro."

"I'm wondering if I ought to cable Anne to confirm Monday. If the post's as unreliable as everyone says."

He hesitated, staring at the brass table between them, then smiled up. "Could she stand a delay of three days?"

"Why?"

He looked down before her eyes. They were suddenly alert, faintly alarmed.

"We can fly back to Europe by Beirut. No extra charge. It only takes a few hours to get to this Syrian castle of yours and Palmyra. One can stay the night there. Then on to Rome."

Her shoulders slumped.

"Dan. This is wicked."

"Wonders of modern transport."

"But you know I feel bad enough already about—"

"You can pay me back in twenty-four monthly installments."

"That's not what I meant."

"You have to go by taxi. The Syrians won't let you in otherwise. They're very cheap. Assad says thirty pounds at most."

She folded her arms, sat up again.

"Is this why you rang him?"

"It may not come off. It's the Mecca pilgrimage season, and they apparently all go via the Lebanon. But he'll try and wangle us seats." He eyed her blandly, pressing a smile out of his mouth. "At this very moment Madame Assad is ringing her sister to find us a good driver."

She said nothing. Then, "I feel shanghaied."

"Wrong country. Valentinoed." She was not amused.

"I've got so much to do at—"

"You shouldn't have played up so to the Hoopers."

"I was only trying to be polite."

"Now you must suffer for it." She gave his smile a doubting look. He said, "Be brave. Palmyra's like the other place. Worth a mass. Even Assad says it's not to be missed. I'd like to see it too."

"Your script . . . ?"

"Three days' rest will do it no harm at all."

"Doesn't one need visas?"

"They give them at the frontier." He bit his lips, aware that her primness was fighting a losing battle against something tempted in her. "Scout's honor."

But he was not yet off the hook. He had her brown eyes again, suddenly very intellectual and authenticity-obsessed eyes, accustomed to cross-sectioning ethical problems with a microtome.

"Have you been planning this, Dan?"

Unaccountably, he found no further light answer, and looked down; then mumbled, like some small boy accused of cheating by a dragon of a headmistress, a truth he did not expect to be believed.

"No. And please."

# In the Silence of Other Voices

They had no time alone together, the rest of that evening, their last on board the ship. For a few minutes in his cabin while Jane changed, Dan read through his unfinished letter to Jenny. He had written to amuse her, playing down the pleasures, exaggerating the boredoms . . . to suggest there was nothing very much to envy. It was not even honest at that level; and in saying little about Jane—and even there presenting her as a latterday drawing-room socialist being taught reality—and virtually nothing about his own deeper feelings and perceptions, it was a tissue of lies by omission; a cheap throwing of dust, an odious placebo, an insult to all her own recent written honesties. He crumpled the pages up, opened the cabin window, then let the ball of paper fall into the Nile a few feet below. It drifted sluggishly away, disappeared. He found a postcard of Kitchener's Island he had bought at the Old Cataract and wrote the following.

*Set this with New Mexico, Jenny. I've fallen in love all over again with it. Water, silence, leaves, peace, out of time—too good for filming really. Though mercifully its real self can't be filmed. If this beautiful and noble river had one central place. It's all helped the script, more than I expected. And Jane.* He hesitated there, half a minute or more, then went on writing. *I was right to bring her. I think it has helped. We'll be here two days, then back by Beirut to visit a place called Palmyra two other passengers have sold us on. See you soon. D.*

He read what he had written. It was a worse lie; and (had he but known it) the first sentence, in view of that last "contribution" of hers, even then lying unopened, in wait, at Thorncombe, a worse insult; but now the omissions and ambiguities were so flagrant that he felt his conscience eased. He dropped the card in the ship's post-box on their way to dinner.

There was a general mingling afterward, as if the tacit barrier between the French and the East Europeans could be dispensed with now that everyone was separating. Expressions of international friendship were like infinitely post-dated checks, they would never be presented; and most of the bonhomie smelled distinctly spurious. But Jane and Dan felt a genuine sadness over saying goodbye to the Herr Professor, who received a little fêting from his flock and whom they failed to get on his own again; to the young Frenchman, Alain; and even to the Hoopers. They both feared a difficult future there, a marriage that must break one day. Dan had managed the grace, at dinner, to tell the couple that Jane and he were taking their advice and hoping to visit Palmyra on their way home. If the Englishman in him disliked having to concede that their opinion on such matters was worth something, a less snobbish self was amused, and touched, by the enthusiasm with which they greeted the news. Great, fantastic; they showered new descriptions, unnecessary advice, Syria itself was drab as all hell, a real police state, you had to watch with cameras . . . Jane did not say much, as if to warn Dan that she still did not totally approve this wild departure from plan, but he felt that at least she seconded the small fillip he gave to the American pair's lack of confidence.

The next morning they hired a droshky and were trotted with their bags to the hotel. There was a cable waiting from Assad. They had air reservations for Beirut, and a hotel, a car and a driver booked there. Whatever last reservations of the other kind Jane harbored were quelled, and she sent her cable to Anne about the postponed arrival in Rome. They went shopping, and bought their galabiyas. Then they drove to see the Temple of Philae; a long row out into the lake, followed by the slow gondola-like tour round the submerged columns, shadowy shafts in the translucent green water. An exquisite light shimmered and danced on the parts that rose into the air. They and the guide were rowed by two old men, with scrawny wrists and mummified bare feet. Every so often, on the long haul, the pair would break into a strange question-and-answer boating-chant, half sung, half spoken. Work on transporting the temple to its new site, the guide proudly told them, would begin within the next few months; very soon sunken Philae would be abusimbelized. They didn't argue with him, but voted it a vulgarity, the whole project, over lunch; which they took inside another vulgarity, the New Cataract Hotel. Its older branch no longer ran a restaurant.

The place was crowded, mainly with Russians working at

the dam, though they saw and nodded to some of their recent fellow-passengers from the cruise. But the Russians seemed to dominate the place: stolid-faced men and solid women, seemingly all middle-aged. The food was no better than on the boat, to Dan's taste; and the decor far worse, a ghastly hybrid between bad Egyptian and bad European interior decoration. It seemed particularly unforgivable with the model of the calm and elegant older hotel so close at hand; a small acme of twentieth-century stupidity, progress that wasn't, every decent architectural principle butchered on the altar of Mammon and Chauvin.

"Christ, one might as well be in Miami." They had just sat down at their table. "Even the people look the same."

Jane murmured, "Aesthete."

"Sorry." He cast sarcastic eyes down the long room. "I was forgetting how socially useful they all are."

She smiled, but said nothing; and some complex irritation in him, at the hideousness of the restaurant, at the memory of Philae, at Jane herself, very nearly made him force an argument on her. But then he remembered Philae again, the green water, the shadows, the way a ray of reflected sunlight from outside one of the cellae had momentarily caught her face, lighting it from below in a way that was natural in itself, yet artificial in ordinary terms: a strange softness, a gravity, she had been looking down through the water. It would have made a lovely photograph, but the moment was too transient; though that was also its beauty.

Many years before he had taken a brief interest in the Zen philosophies then popular in California, and discovered, with some surprise, that there were parallels with what he had always thought of as a product of his English country childhood, a mere way of looking at things induced by solitude and repression. Moments of intense vision had then always seemed an escape from the monotony of predictable weeks and years. He was too English, of course, to take Zen very seriously as a philosophy, but it had strengthened in him a feeling that some inner truth lay in the perception of the transient. He would have been embarrassed to define and justify it, but it lay somewhere in the importance of presentness in life; just as the value he attached to it was betrayed by his demanding or expecting more of the present than it was usually prepared to give. This was why, for instance, he had no deep political convictions, since they must depend on some form, however attentuated, of perfectibility, of belief in future; and why he could trace his actual feeling of irritation to the experience of Philae, a present about to disappear for ever, and to this crammed horror of a restaurant, a present one wished *would* disappear for ever; while Jane was a combination of both, a present about to disappear and, in her would-be socialist and independent self, a present that barred him from what little was left of the first kind.

All this thinking took place against a resumption of their conversation, about the shame of raising Philae, their afternoon plans, the food . . . but that one brief glimpse of her face in the haunting liquid and mobile underlight inside the temple had, so to speak, signaled the arrival at the fork, his growing feeling that some choice was very close, he must act; for something in the moment's message had also been, if still not quite sexual, distinctly sensual. Even as they talked about the afternoon, he knew he would really prefer to spend it, very close to her, saying all these things he could not bring himself to speak now; in a locked room, behind shutters. It was not love, not sex, but a need to exercise, perhaps even a little to exorcise, a deep and growing affection.

He mistrusted his mood; knew it was partly narcissistic, atavistic in terms of his past, his lifelong need for emotional relationships with the female, with mother-substitutes, or younger women carefully if unconsciously chosen to avoid that accusation, if such it was. He speculated again whether Jane was not indeed taking a small revenge by remaining so adamant over frontiers, so implicitly certain that no sexual current could pass between them because she did not possess that kind of attraction anymore. But he dismissed it. She was simply too proud, or too sensible, or too sure that she felt no equivalent being drawn toward Dan himself—the humiliation was his also, in other words. He kept thinking of Jenny, too. His childish old vice: wanting the impossible, so living it in his mind.

They found the silent Omar duly waiting when they went down to the landing below the Old Cataract; and once again threaded their way through the islets to the far bank. This time they landed below the Aga Khan's mausoleum, then walked a mile over the dunes to the ruined Coptic monastery of Saint Simeon: vandalized by six centuries of Bedouin nomads, but still a powerful ghost.

The place had the great peace of death, a solitude; an equal, if totally contrasting, beauty to that of Philae. They spoke of what was before them, like dutiful tourists, but Dan grew increasingly conscious of all that was not being said. It was far more like an embarrassment than an excitement; a growing embarrassment. It seemed to him almost silly, painfully adolescent—to have to think twice, as he did, about reaching out a hand to help her over rubble or on the erratic stairs to the upper terraces of the monastery; to answer nothings with even more careful nothings.

When they returned to the river, Omar took them back across to Kitchener's Island again. They wandered and Dan took some unnecessary photographs. Then they sat for a while, in a different place, a more formal garden over the river, among beds of gerberas and geraniums. It seemed to Dan that they had regressed since the previous day; he lacked even the energy to attempt what he had tried on the bench in the cross-walk. He had the impression that Jane was, if not bored, elsewhere; most certainly not thinking of him, or their relationship.

They went to their separate rooms as soon as they returned to the hotel, earlier than the evening before; he heard the muezzin after their return. She wanted a bath; and then she did not appear for drinks downstairs before dinner, and he had a miserable half-hour. In the end he telephoned up from the desk. She had fallen asleep. She appeared ten minutes later, her face clasped in her hands in mock dismay, as if he might never forgive her.

They found their table had gone, the huge room seemed even more crowded than at lunch. But there was a voice. It was Alain and the photographer, there were two seats at their table. Dan would have refused, but Jane seemed to welcome the idea. She was suddenly more animated, as if relieved to have someone else to talk to.

The talk was about Philae, where the two Frenchmen had also been that day: the pros and cons of raising it. There was no argument there, they were all against, and then, as if they must find something to disagree on, they somehow moved to general attitudes toward public art, what mattered most, utility or good taste. Dan, who lacked the courage to be as silent as he felt, put a version of his thoughts earlier that day: being was now and anything that destroyed or diminished the quality of life now—let expediency trump taste—must be inherently wrong. Jane thought that if the choice was between ugly building and no building, when there was a need, then . . . it went on and on, social art and socialist art, the onus on education, Gaullist elitism, *gloire* and *patrie* . . . a cloud of words. They began to distress Dan, and he said less and less. Alain sided with Jane, and he felt almost like snarling at times—the absurdity of this sophisticated conversation, use of language, being employed to argue a jettisoning of all other intellectual and artistic values, pell-mell, before the enormity of the socialist task: it seemed to him suicidal, a secret death-wish, precisely what Lukács had been essentially arguing against: the notion that the despised bath-water did not also contain babies. Yet he said nothing.

In fact the conversation split in two—Jane and Alain slipped into French, though still, as Dan could tell by the occasional word, discussing politics, while he and the photographer, who had done stills work in the past and knew the French industry quite well, started talking shop. He kept up a façade of interest, but one ear was listening to the other side of the table. He came away convinced that Jane had been using her table-companion to demonstrate to him the reality of that business of "different values."

At last they were walking back to the older hotel together. Alain and the photographer were going on to some night-club, but Dan and Jane had declined the invitation to join them. They had to get up early to catch the plane to Abu Simbel.

After a few steps in silence she said, "I'm sorry. You wanted to leave."

"It doesn't matter."

"You should have given me a discreet kick on the ankles, Dan."

"Because you were enjoying it?"

"Because I was slow realizing that you weren't."

"Never mind. It's that damned restaurant."

She left a pause.

"Are you sure you want to go to Abu Simbel tomorrow?"

"Don't you?"

"Yes, but . . . I mean, if you'd rather go off on your own. Your work." She added self-mockingly, "You worry me. I thought you'd be frantically scribbling notes all the time."

"Appearances aren't my job."

"I forgot. Just the soul."

"Plus dialogue."

They went into the Old Cataract. He thought of suggesting a nightcap, but decided his greatest need was to punish her . . . or perhaps, himself. He fetched their keys and they climbed the stairs. Their rooms were several doors apart. She reached out and took his hand as they came to hers, and pressed it a moment, staring at the tiled floor.

"Are you sure it wasn't me?"

"Of course not."

She gave him a look under her eyebrows, searching; belatedly aware how sullen he was, but even that belatedness irritated him; then pressed his hand once more and released it.

"Sleep well, Dan."

"And you."

He stood in his room a few seconds later; through the shutters there came the faint, obsessive sound of Arab music from some café loudspeaker on the waterfront to the north. He got undressed slowly, put on pajamas and a dressing-gown; then opened the shutters and stood smoking, wallowing a little in an attack of the traditional twentieth-century nausea: the otherness of the other. Everything was other: one's faults, one's situations, one's blindnesses, weaknesses, sullennesses, boredoms. They stood as unpossessed, as alien, as indifferent as the tired furniture in a tired room. He looked at his watch. It was just after eleven.

He went to get a yellow pad out of his suitcase, with the intention of sketching out the scene where Kitchener encountered his *ka* in the guise of an ancient monument. But then, seeing the Lukács book lying there, he took that out as well, and turned to a passage he had read on the boat and marked, since he had seen a relevance in it to Kitchener. It was in the disquisition on Walter Scott.

> The "hero" of a Scott novel is always a more or less mediocre, average English gentleman. He generally possesses a certain, though never outstanding, degree of practical intelligence, a certain moral fortitude and decency which even rises to a capacity for self-sacrifice, but which never grows into a sweeping human passion, is never the enraptured devotion to a great cause.

And having read that, Dan's eyes flicked to another passage, a little earlier in the essay, that he had also marked.

> Scott ranks among those honest Tories in the England of his time who exonerate nothing in the development of capitalism, who not only see clearly, but also deeply sympathize with the unending misery of the people which the collapse of old England brings in its wake; yet who, precisely because of their

[ 589 ]

conservatism, display no violent opposition to the features of the new development repudiated by them.

Mirrors: he knew why he had marked those passages and who was really being defined, and it was neither Scott nor Kitchener: but his own sense of defeat. He might have turned a page and seen how Lukács defended Scott and average heroes against the Romantic and demonic type of protagonist brought into popularity by Byron. But he had already read that, and seen in it nothing but literary criticism: not a partial defense of what he was, what England was. It was Kitchener's secret, perhaps; that driving ambition, that lack of decency (or manipulation of other people's decency) in pursuing it; that ability to do, to ride roughshod.

Daimon: choosing oneself. Dan stared across the room. He saw himself as being like someone with a deep feeling for an art, but no creative talent for it; what one felt occasionally before great composers and executants in music, great painters, what he had once or twice felt before great acting performances on screen, on the stage: the ability to assert the primacy of one's own genius . . . which was in turn a recognition of the extent of one's own inability and—in Dan's case—a contempt for his own safe, aided, compromising and communal art. His one hope had lain in the theater, and he had stifled that; in retrospect it now seemed almost at birth. He suddenly saw the proposed novel as a pipe dream, one more yearning for the impossible.

The terror of the task: that making of a world, alone, unguided, now mocked, like some distant mountain peak, mediocrity in his dressing-gown. He could never do it. Never mind that what he felt was felt by all novelists, all artists, at the beginning of creation—that indeed not feeling the terror was the worst possible augury for the enterprise; never mind that he held one very good guide-book in his hand . . . he could not do it. Above all he could not do it because his thoughts were metaphors; not really about artistic creativity, but the face he had said good night to in the corridor outside.

The cobbler and his last: taking sanctuary in his certain degree of practical intelligence, Dan put Lukács aside, sat down and began working on his scene. Half an hour later he was re-reading the three pages he had filled. He started striking out dialogue. Gradually it became clear that the gist could be conveyed in the way Kitchener rode up, in his gaze and face, the way he rode away; he needed to say nothing himself. It could all be done in the silence of other voices, was better so.

Dan wrote a second draft, only a page long now. He knew it was the kind of scene that would be the first to go if there was a time problem; and there would be a time problem. But he circled that one phrase as he re-read the new draft: *in the silence of other voices.*

Then he went to bed, able to sleep at last.

# Flights

They did not enjoy their day at Abu Simbel.

The civilian airport at Aswan had been taken over by the military, and they were driven many miles out into the desert, it seemed halfway back to Luxor, to find the temporary replacement. The flight south, over the moonscape and amoeba-shaped islands of Lake Nasser, the limitless rippling dunes of the Nubian desert, was spectacular enough; and at first sight, the resurrected temples also. But very soon they seemed factitious, a quite literally monumental waste of effort and money. Dan felt it most strongly inside the artificial hill raised to buttress—once more—the megalomania of Ramses II. Inside, it was a vast iron-plated cupola, a maze of steel ladders, generators, machinery . . . yet more misguided ingenuity, Ramses redoubled. It reminded him of a stage on a movie-lot; of the expensive artifices of his own profession.

They snatched a quick packed lunch by the water's edge, facing a horizon studded with brutal iron-gray kopjes; then were rattled back in an old bus to the desert air strip; after the flight, the tedious drive back to Aswan. It seemed a lost day to Dan, and he began to fear Syria, the possibility of the same boring and dusty journeys to nowhere for nothing.

However, he hid his feelings better than he had the evening before. Jane helped, at least by playing the perfect traveling companion in a more literal sense than Dan had meant—by making light of the day's minor setbacks and disappointments. Secretly this cautious, solicitious role granted almost as much as the argumentative one of the previous day. It was all very well knowing she was being nicer than she need as a sort of penance; but there was something intolerably distancing in all this discreet consideration for him. It seemed to him much nearer gentility than a true gentleness. But he could not complain.

They finally got back to the hotel about half past four, and had tea. When he asked her at the end of it whether she felt like a last visit to the island before dinner, he half-wanted her to refuse, to let him go on his own, so much had her presence beside him that day resembled an absence.

"Do you want to go alone?"

He very nearly betrayed himself. But then he remembered the tears at Kom Ombo, and what happened if one turned on Eurydice during her ascent from the underworld.

"No. But if you've had enough . . ."

She was smiling. "I was rather hoping you'd suggest it. I prefer that as a last memory."

There was a thin veil of high cirrus over the sky, but it was warm. The usual breeze seemed less, and a lethargy hung in both sail and landscape. When they came under the lee of Elephantine Island, the two boatmen—they had failed to find Omar again—began to row. But their destination seemed, in spite of their growing familiarity with it, even more delicious in its airy peace, its birds and water, after the dead landscapes they had driven through and flown over earlier in the day: a remarkable place, it had an almost human personality, vaguely feminine, at somehow touching variance with the character of the man whose name it bore. It also remained English in some mysterious way, behind the exotic palms and trees and flowers; green, a place to dream in. They had both been a little shocked at dinner the day before to detect indifference in Alain and his friend, as if to them the island was just one more *jardin public*. The two Frenchmen had been much more enthusiastic about a Bisharin village they had visited.

Now Jane and Dan strolled for a while, talking about French taste, its obsession with the formal, style as thought. Dan felt at last more relaxed, in sanctuary again. They sat to rest Jane's leg, it was aching, on the steps of a crumbled jetty at the southern end of the island, over the water, in the thin declining sun and listless air.

Jane leaned back, her hands clasped round a knee, looking at the water below them.

"I came to a decision last night, Dan."

It was unexpected, and he glanced at her. "Yes?"

She shrugged. "Nothing very momentous. But I think I'll definitely try for a teacher training course when I get home. If I can find a place."

She gave him a smile, as if she hoped this modest crossing of the Rubicon would please him. He remembered he had backed the idea when it had come up at Thorncombe. But now, for some reason, he read a rejection in it, yet another translating of "different values" into practice—and saw her behavior that day in a new light. Perhaps she had simply felt the contented peace of a resolution taken.

"What's made you decide?"

"I've been thinking about it quite a lot these days." She added, "And something you said last night. About the world people want becoming the enemy of the world that exists. Selling the present short, as you put it."

"I'm not quite sure how you teach that."

"Nor am I. But I think it might be good for me to try to find out."

She spoke with a kind of dull brightness, like that in the light around them.

"Now I feel I've corrupted a revolutionary socialist."

"It was high time she was suborned. Not from socialism. But into something more realistic."

He detected a patness in her voice, as if everything was clear now: a nice simple duty lay ahead, she need never bother him again. It was rather as if she had asked for a direction and was thanking him, with the careful politeness of urbans to rustics, for providing it before she drove on.

"I thought I was sowing on stony ground. Last night."

"You must make allowance for the fact that I'm only just beginning to realize that I've always been under Anthony's dominance intellectually. Even when I disagreed with him." She stared at the water swirling idly past the dilapidated foot of the steps on which they sat. "I've forgotten what it's like being with someone who keeps suggesting he's probably wrong." She said in a lighter voice, "Especially when he knows he's generally not." She leaned forward and picked up a long toothed leaf by her shoe, began smoothing it. "I have an awful feeling I hurt you that first afternoon here, Dan. By different values I didn't mean inferior ones."

"No. I understood."

But of course, he had not; and felt something both shift and melt in him, away from resentment; into self-reproach, for having doubted her sensitivity to the unsaid.

"I meant really to suggest doubt about my own. It's like changing into a remote key. Not quite knowing how one does the modulation."

"Now I think something else is being sold short."

She was smoothing the sides of the dead leaf, and he saw her smile; a shade wrily, she knew better, though she would not argue. Silence fell, as if they were doing no more than kill time, chat idly, waiting like the fellaheen for a train that would never come. He had a return of the sense of unreality, of being outside himself, that seemed to have infected him since their arrival at Aswan; only this time it was more or less conscious and strongly tinged with fatalism. He even asked himself—do I really want this resolved? Was it not merely some revenge of his childhood self, permanently unforgiving of its deprivations, on his adult philosophy of detachment? Perhaps that was why he had fled so long ago to the cinema, to its obsession with "moving somewhere," with peddling opium to the intellectually deprived.

Anyone intelligent who went in for the medium commercially must have a profound desire to limit his commitments, to whore after shifting gods; and this secret infatuation for a deeper relationship with far more than the ambiguous woman beside him went against every practical lesson he had learned from life. That with Jane it would, if carried to a conclusion, lead to a closing of all kinds of sexual and career and domestic options worried him a great deal less than the prospect of an irreducible obstinacy, a permanent psychological awkwardness she would bring. She was again wearing the ancient beads she had worn at Luxor; rubbed and unrubbed facets, angles no one life could ever abrade.

It was all a little ridiculous, anyway; part of a reciprocal myth. Just as Jane no doubt saw him as far more worldly-wise than he was, so he saw her—still like some freshman unable to credit the old quip that every don is half a donkey—as the product of a finer-honed moral world. He remembered the sitting beside another river so many years before . . . at least one had had the wit, the poetry, as well as the will, to take risks then.

"So what shall you teach—the river between?"

She gave him a look, amused; then put on—but this time it was clearly put on—a faintly prim voice again. "I shall teach set texts and French grammar. Racine and Balzac and the agreement of past participles."

"Pearls before young swine."

The smile lingered; then she admitted that she would really rather do primary-school teaching, but the course would be longer; and they discussed that for a while, the advantages of teaching children as against adolescents. It was a little to do with Paul, she felt he had not been well handled at his school in those years.

Dan realized, of course, that all this was being presented as an apology, as her way of saying that this new-found affinity between them was more important than intellectual disagreement; that she was grateful for the holiday, for the objectivity she had gained . . . and so on. But he had a sharp inner feeling that it was a decision almost as absurd as the ones she had aired at Oxford; simply swapping the role of world-changer for that of schoolmarm. She must have sensed his underlying disapproval, for after another silence came, she had gone back to holding her knees and staring across the river, she said, "I must do something, Dan. You can't imagine how strongly I feel I've wasted my life and—" but she broke off. "Not my life. But things I could have given life."

"We've all felt that, Jane." He added, "And done that."

"But not quite with my consistency." He said nothing, and after a moment she challenged his refusal to comment. "You still think this isn't the right answer?"

"My dear girl, it's up to you. If it feels . . . that famous instinct of yours."

"But?"

He murmured, "Château Lafite in a tin mug?"

"That's not fair to the tin mug. And an absurd over-rating of the wine in question."

He stared out over the river to the shadowed far shore.

"I don't know how people like us were meant to live this age, Jane. When it gives you only two alternatives . . . feel deprived or feel guilty. Play liberal or play blind. It seems to me that either way we're barred from living life as it was meant to be. I think if I ever had another child, I would pray that it was subnormal."

"That's a terrible thing to say."

"In a world where the future gets more horrible to contemplate every day?" She gave him a sceptical look. "Oh yes. I travel. I write. I meet film-stars. I'm a very lucky fellow." He added, "The last of the ancient regime."

His voice had been dry to the point of bitterness, and the delay in her answer underlined it.

"Then it is a privileged form of pessimism."

"Of accidie. Powerlessness."

"It's not very obvious, Dan. I think most innocent strangers would say you've acquired a rather formidable sense of balance."

"Alias the deadweight of inertia."

"Which still somehow manages to produce very literate scripts. Seen by millions of people."

"And forgotten by them. The next day."

"You're being naughty."

He smiled, half conceding the reproach. "It's not very difficult for people who never take risks to seem balanced."

"But even to seem requires some kind of effort? I should have thought a courage also."

"I don't think so. When it makes daily life easier. In an unbalanced world it can only be a kind of surrender."

She seemed to examine that; then moved ground.

"For so many years I've only known you through Caro's eyes."

"As a lousy father."

She said gently, "A difficult one."

"All those mirrors and masks in my room when I was a student. I think they just about summed it up."

"You should have tried the alternative. Surrounding yourself with book-lined walls. And minds."

They were both staring across the water at a trading felucca. It moved slowly down beneath the sandy cliffs opposite, floating on the current. He gave Jane's face a surreptitious glance. There was something both set and peaceful about it, keeping its own counsel; he did not know what she was thinking, yet he felt that unmistakable old empathy restored between them and knew she could not be totally unaware of it . . . that they sat on that remote, forever past, other river bank again. Forever barred, forever close. He remembered the phrase he had circled in his draft scene the previous night. Their truth lay in their silence, not the other voices of what they had just said to each other. He knew he wanted to speak, he was a man on a brink about to plunge: to make it explicit, she must feel it, she must know . . . yet something held him fatally back. Doubt of her, doubt of himself, fear of rejection, fear of response. Suddenly she tilted her head a little toward him, smiled.

"You're spoiling my good deed for the day."

He had been right to stay silent.

"What was that?"

"Cheering you up."

"I hate last days in places."

"But you'll be back when . . . ?"

"I doubt it. Anyway, I shall miss my perfect traveling companion."

She smiled again, as if such flattery were no more grounded on reality than his self-denigration; glanced at her wrist watch; and then once more, as he both clinically and resignedly noted, used this mention of perfection to prove a mundane opposite.

"I must have a bath and wash my hair before dinner. All that dust."

"Yes, so must I."

But he did not move, stared down at the water. She gave him a scrutiny, a moment, then she silently stretched out a hand and gave his wrist, beneath the sleeve of his coat, a squeeze of encouragement, sympathy, tacit appeal, he didn't know, except that this time it was not meant to say more than affection and friendship. Even if he had wanted to reach and hold the hand there, it left his sleeve too quickly, the gesture once made. Again it was oxymoronic: offended him by its tact, its timing, touched him in its seeming to know and remember more than it revealed. They stood, and remounted the steps, and she wondered how much colder it would be in the Lebanon. He knew she meant to say that it was not really their last day, but all he heard from then on was other voices. The compromises of his life seemed to lie on him almost physically, like warts. He no longer knew quite what was happening or what he was doing.

But alone in his room back at the hotel he decided, finally, that he must give up this adolescent toying and dithering. It must demonstrate that he didn't really know what he wanted. In a strange kind of way he knew much better what Jane felt; and that was certainly no encouragement. He had revealed too much already; if their old quickness at reading each other's moods and meanings had started the rot, its clear failure to bring them closer ended it. She must know where he had once or twice been leading, and had not followed. He had had his moment of decision on the steps over the water, and let it pass. He even saw himself describing it all, with appropriate meiosis, to Jenny; making her jealous; and making her laugh as well. After all, he too could make resolutions.

So when Jane came down and found him at the bar, he was much more the equable self of the earlier days of their cruise. And as if to confirm his admission of defeat, Jane herself seemed more at her ease. They had dinner, and carefully avoided anything that might lead back to self-analysis and soul-searching; then went back to have coffee in the Old Cataract, in a long lounge beside the terrace over the garden. There were normally few other guests there, but it began to fill almost as soon as they had sat down. They saw faces they had seen in the dining-room, Russian faces, coming as if to some meeting. Then a plump middle-aged lady, in an old-fashioned evening dress, heavy bare forearms ending in strangely delicate hands, went to the grand piano that stood at one end of the room. A man helped raise the lid. She began to play at once, without any formality, but the sudden quietening of voices, the way the people around them shifted chairs to face the piano, made Dan and Jane realize that they had inadvertently gatecrashed an impromptu concert. The lady began with a Chopin mazurka. Dan had no practical knowledge of music, but she was obviously either a very gifted amateur or a professional on holiday. There was discreet applause from the surrounding tables when the first piece ended, and he glanced at Jane for her opinion. She pressed her lips together: she was taken. More people, East Europeans and Russians, engineers and their wives, one or two of what must have been Egyptian colleagues, gathered at the end of the room. They had to stand, since all the chairs round the other tables were now occupied. The pianist played another mazurka. When she finished, to longer applause, the man who had helped with the lid stood and spoke in Russian—evidently what had been played, what was to come next.

Dan said, "I feel we're a little bit de trop."

"I know. It's just so nice to hear music again."

"Perhaps we could eavesdrop on the terrace?"

"Yes."

So they rose quickly and left, with a gesture from Dan to a standing couple near the door to take their vacated table.

"I think I'll go and get a coat."

"Fine. I'll find us a couple of brandies."

He went and did so, then took them out on the terrace and along the line of shutters to the one nearest the piano. There was a table there, and the window behind the shutter was open. The night, the faint smell of the river, stars, the filtered lamps from inside reflected in the exotic foliage below the balustraded terrace: Jane appeared, a dark figure, and walked down toward him, in and out of the latticed light. Inside, the lady was playing Chopin again.

"It's not too cold for you?"

"No. It does seem much warmer tonight."

She sat beside him.

"She's good?"

"That lovely Russian touch. I think she must have been listening to Richter."

They listened to her. After another Chopin piece, she played a Mozart sonata. There was applause, a little interval, a murmur of voices; then a hush, the man's voice in Russian. The woman inside began to play Bach. Dan looked at Jane inquiringly, and she smiled.

"The Goldberg. You're excused, if you want to be."

"No, I'd like to. I haven't heard it for years."

They sat in the endless sound, the precise baroque complexity, so calculated, so European; in the African darkness. Dan's mind drifted away after a while, into the night, the stars: saw the pair sitting down there, before a table, three feet apart, in what seemed to possess the lifelessness of sculpture, of waxworks, of unplayed instruments. And gradually there stole on him, both with the music and from outside it, a sense of release, a liberation from lies, including the one he had told himself before dinner. It was less that the music particularly moved him, he had never really enjoyed Bach, but it did carry a deep intimation of other languages, meaning-systems, besides that of words; and fused his belief that it was words, linguistic modes, that mainly stood between Jane and himself. Behind what they said lay on both sides an identity, a syncretism, a same key, a thousand things beyond verbalization. Strangely, out of nowhere, out of the distant night of his own past, perhaps out of facing across the Nile to the desert where Saint Simeon lay, came Langland's famous image, the tower on the toft, "Truthe is therinne"; of a truth on the long hill of their own two existences. It was not a wanting to possess, even uxoriously, but a wanting to know one could always reach out a hand and . . . that shadow of the other shared voyage, into the night. She was also some kind of emblem of a redemption from a life devoted to heterogamy and adultery, the modern errant ploughman's final reward; and Dan saw, or felt, abruptly, for the first time in his life, the true difference between Eros and Agape.

Yet it arrived in him less with emotion than with a sense of freedom; and not freedom from circumstance, but from what was false and temporizing in it . . . in terms of that old Kierkegaardian catch-image of their student days, the ability to step and to prize the step above the fear of the dark. Not stepping became the supreme folly and cowardice; even if one stepped into nothingness and fell, even if one stepped only to find one must step back.

There came a very slow variation, which seemed, or was made to seem by the pregnant manner in which it was played, to hesitate, to suspend, to hang on the brink of silence. It appeared to Dan isolated from the rest, symbolic of things he had buried or was not even aware of in his own being; in all being, perhaps. He stayed in it mentally, after it had finished; and to the end.

There was long applause from inside, one or two cries; then the murmur of Slavonic voices.

Dan said, "That variation near the end. I don't know why people think he lacks feeling."

"Yes. I've never heard it taken so slowly. But it seemed to work."

"The stars help."

"Aren't they beautiful."

And she looked up, as if she hadn't noticed them till then. He had a last moment of weakness, or irresolution. Perhaps if she had gone on to say something else . . . but she did not, as if she still heard the music, wanted to recollect it in silence a few moments more. He hesitated, unendurably, staring at the garden without seeing it, then took his step.

"Jane, four days from now we shall have gone our separate ways. Does that distress you at all?"

"You know it will. I've enjoyed—"

"I'm not talking about that."

Silence. She knew at once, of course; and said nothing.

He looked down at the table, at his empty brandy-glass. "I've become more and more aware these last two or three days that it's going to distress me very much. You must at least have suspected that."

There was a pause in Jane, not unlike one of those in the music they had just heard; a being suspended between logic and inspiration, conventional development and instinctive feeling. But the very fact that he already knew, in that telltale silence, what she would say, consoled him a little.

"I have the very greatest affection for you, Dan."

"But no sense of the wheel having come full circle?"

There was, again, a fatal slowness in her answering; a need to choose her words.

"I also have a very real sense of reconciliation." She added, "Far more than I've been able to express to you."

"That music. It made me feel the absurdity of this distance

between us. When there's all that frozen distance up there. I'm sorry, this is very trite, but . . ." She waited, as if she half agreed; or once again, did not know what to say. She may have suspected, but she was still taken by surprise. He said, "I had no idea this was going to happen. You please mustn't feel I've tricked you in some way."

Out of the corner of his eyes, he saw her shake her head. "I feel I've tricked you."

"How?"

"I have been on my best behavior this last week."

"I've allowed for that."

"You can't. Because you don't know what goes on underneath."

"And as regards me?"

She murmured, "Unlimited friendship."

"I want you nearer than that. Not only that." He half turned and smiled wrily in her direction. "You did do this to me once. It is my turn." After a moment he said, "This can't have come entirely as a surprise. You know what upset me yesterday evening."

"I knew you were upset."

"I know we disagree on many things. Intellectually . . . politically. It's when you use that to hide something else. Where we do agree." He hesitated. "I honestly thought that long-ago day in Oxford was dead, when I suggested this. But I can't forget it. It keeps on coming back now. It was what I was trying to say that first afternoon on Kitchener's Island. I know we did it for all the wrong conscious reasons at the time. But something in it wasn't wrong. I've only just fully realized that."

She said gently, "I so want not to hurt you, Dan."

"I'm wrong to think of it like this?"

"Wrong to suppose that what we were then is what we are now. What I am now."

"Which is?"

"I have so little to give."

"That exit's closed. And not for you to judge." Such finality reduced her to silence; and Dan himself as well for a few moments. It was not that her initial reaction was unanticipated, though he felt some of the disappointment of the eternally optimistic amateur gambler faced with the realities of probability; of the swimmer who knew the sea would be cold, but still finds it colder than the foreknowledge. Yet his old capacity for seeing alternative presents helped. She had not been shocked, not walked away, not laughed; but sat and waited.

"This business with Jenny McNeil?"

"That really isn't for me to judge."

"But am I talking in an empty room? You've felt nothing else?"

"Women feel all sorts of things. That they know can't survive the situation that gives rise to them." She added, "Or the ones they would give rise to."

"What Nell would think?"

"Among many other things."

"I think she'd understand. Even approve. Oddly enough." That too was met with silence. "Jane, a great deal of what you really feel is totally hidden from me. I may have misread things completely. But I keep on imagining what it would have been like if we'd spent our lives together instead of the last few days. And it seems like something so much better than actual history."

"I think the thing you're misreading is actual marriage. Especially to someone like me."

"And I think you're misreading something very real between us. We couldn't face it then, we're still failing now."

She hesitated, then spoke in a more placatory voice.

"Dan, I really have been keeping up a front these last few days—I don't mean that's a bad thing. As some parts are good for an actress . . . help her see outside herself. I do feel much more able to face all kinds of ordinary things. It's just what's still boiling away underneath."

"Such as?"

"Self-hatred. Guilt. Anger. Things without name."

"And I can't help?"

"You have helped. Very greatly."

"Then why can't I be allowed to continue helping?"

There was another suspension.

"Because I have no right to inflict all this on someone. I . . . I do have emotions. Of course I haven't forgotten that day, all those months, in Oxford."

"But it all happened to someone else."

"You were also someone else."

"For whom you now only feel friendship?"

"For whom I can't allow myself to feel more."

"That's an evasion."

A longer silence, like an indrawn breath; a being cornered.

"I also have normal female feelings, Dan. If that was . . ."

[ 603 ]

"The only obstacle?"

"If I was less . . . confused."

"I don't like the implication that I'd confuse you further."

"I didn't mean that."

"The last thing I'd want is to stop you living as you like. However, wherever. Being a teacher. An active Marxist. Anything. I'd just like us to try living together. For better or for worse."

"But you can't do that if you have no confidence at all that it would be better." She went on before he could object. "Quite apart from anything else, at my age of life . . ."

"You're not being honest. You know perfectly well half the men on the cruise . . ."

"Beside someone like your friend."

"That's not the comparison I'm making. And since when was it a time when women needed solitude?"

Beyond her he saw one of the barefoot Nubian servants come out for a moment on the terrace and look down toward them. Though the man made no offer of service, Dan waved his hand sideways, dismissing him. Jane glanced down to see what he signaled at; almost, he sensed, as if she were seeking help. He asked belatedly if she wanted another brandy.

"No thanks."

But she said nothing more. The servant went back indoors. High in the darkness over the river there was a thin trisyllabic call, piercing the stasis between them.

Dan said drily, "Special effects."

"What was it?"

"A sandpiper. Looking for somewhere warmer to live." He nearly added, Poor fool. Jane stared down at the table, very much as if she was too frightened to speak, to leave, to do anything. Her face was in shadow, but the edge of a bar of light from inside, through one of the shutters, caught the silver comb in her hair. He found a tone of resignation. "I suppose it's that third person who's always with us. Between us."

"Anthony?"

"Our familiar compound ghost."

"Which also joins us?"

"As crossbeams join girders. Making sure they never touch."

"But I am touched, Dan."

He stared out into the darkness. "It doesn't feel right?"

"It's felt right several times during these last few years that I should have taken an extra dose of sleeping tablets. There

[ 604 ]

was a period . . . just after Peter took himself off to Harvard . . . when I thought the only good reason not to do it was that it would have meant some kind of victory for Anthony. I'm not defending that. But it felt right."

"But if your instinct was wrong there . . ."

She sat with her hands in her coat pockets, hunched, head bowed.

"There've only been three men in my life—of whom you're one. The end product of all three relationships has been more pain than anything else. In our case, pain to you. In my last . . . adventure, pain to me. With Anthony—I suppose a drawn match. I can't not presume that the fault lies in me."

"And no pain for you, in our case?"

"Of course. At the time."

"And we never gave our relationship a chance." She said nothing. "I simply can't understand why your sense of guilt about it has to be kept alive in this absurd way. Why must self-hatred be more important than . . . what I feel we could still be?"

"It's not self-hatred . . . much more self-doubt. I can't control it. If it was just a matter of some freely takable decision . . ." but she broke off.

"Then?"

"I think even then it would seem like a daydream a much younger me is too selfish to give up. When the reality's a middle-aged woman who talks about teaching, simple little plans for doing good and keeping herself busy—and who secretly doubts her ability to go through with them almost as soon as she's spoken."

"Why can't these doubts be shared between us? Lived between us?"

He felt a growing frustration, as if all that really lay between them was a pane of glass; but unbreakable glass.

"It's nothing in you. You must believe me. I know you're a very gentle and understanding man . . ." Then she said, "If I need anyone, it's someone quite new, who probably wouldn't be sweet and gentle at all . . . someone who could carry me off and make me leave all my old world behind. Not set me right back in the heart of it."

"I've lived in exile too long to take nonsense like that. You can't leave old worlds behind. It's not on."

"I'm not trying to defend what I am."

"Then you're simply being perverse."

"I know I must sound that." She added, "Am that."

In his mind he circled, trying to find a breach; a door in the wall.

"You've tried to escape by joining outside things. And it hasn't worked. I've never even tried. And that hasn't worked, either. Which leaves us much closer than you imagine." He waited, then went on. "You can't talk about my so-called success as if that makes a difference between us. I know you meant it kindly this afternoon, but it's insulting, Jane. To all we both know we once believed in. And still try to believe in our fashion. When I decry it like that, all right, it is a privileged pessimism. But I know how the intelligent world judges what I am, and so do you." He paused, to see if she would speak, but she didn't. "You keep on talking as if you've changed completely. I can't tell you how little the part of you I always loved best hasn't. That night at Oxford after the suicide—it was suddenly still there again. It's been with us on the cruise. It's here now." He managed another smile at her. "I really wouldn't go on like this with anyone else in the world." He added, "Because I know no one else would understand." She was still staring down at the table. Again he waited, and again she refused to speak. "Does this mean nothing to you?"

"It means I feel more and more guilty."

"I didn't intend to provoke that."

Silence came again. There had been something in her answer, a hint of wistful reproach, a genuine plea for his forgiveness; for him to . . . something for which there was no accepted English verb . . . to long-suffer her.

"You've had so much freedom, Dan. You choose prison just as I'm trying to leave it."

"My dear girl, all my freedom's done has been to land me somewhere out there in the desert. You'll find out. It's not the way to Kitchener's Island."

"Where neither of us could ever really live. Alas."

"Then subtract all the romantic nonsense. But why should it have to be prison?"

"Because love is a prison."

He smiled in the darkness. "So if I felt less, the proposition would be more tenable?"

"I'm not nearly as independent as you imagine. That's why I feel I have to cling to what little I have."

He leaned back, folded his arms. "I sometimes wonder if you ever really left the Church."

"Why do you say that?"

"Self-denial and celibacy as the road to good works?"

"It was the other road that seemed the self-denial." She searched for, then found words. "If all I needed was somewhere to close my eyes and feel protected . . ."

"But the imagery's wrong, for God's sake. The last thing I want you to do is to close your eyes. You seem to forget the knight is just as much in distress as the damsel." He knew her silence disagreed, that perhaps here was where she remained most adamant. He leaned forward again. "Men like me can always find sex and new female minds to play with. What I need from you is that something inside you, between us, that makes half-living, half-loving like that impossible. It's not a function of intelligence, Jane. Jenny McNeil knows she's being used, she's as objective and open about it as . . . as any intelligent girl of her generation. Brutally honest about how she sees me. But then goes on letting herself be used. Which relegates me to the status of interesting experience. In terms of your new religion, she and I both reify each other. Become characters in a fiction. Forget how to see each other totally. So we invent roles, play games, to hide the gap. I meet you again, I suddenly see all this, what was wrong from the beginning, why you were the one woman who might have led me out of it." He paused a moment. "I didn't really expect you to say yes. But I've felt these last few days that we two are behaving like someone else's—or something else's—creatures. Behaving as all that was always wrong in our past expects. Not saying what we really think. Not really judging for our true selves. I just wanted to give us both the chance. That's simply all."

She sat as if frozen; and must by then have been physically chilled, as Dan could tell from his own body. He glanced at her, and something in the way she sat, her hands still inside her coat pockets, contrived to seem both obstinate and defenseless. He left a moment, then abruptly stood and went round the table and stood by her with his hands out.

"Come on. Before I freeze you to death both ways."

She took her hands slowly out of her pockets, let him draw her up, but then made them stand there a moment. He was not allowed to see her face.

"If I could only explain . . ."

"It doesn't matter."

"It's not in you. It is in me."

She pressed his hands, and they stood a moment longer. Then she withdrew her own and put them back in her pockets.

They turned and began to walk back toward the doors into the hotel. But just before they came to the light from them, she stopped; and for the first time since that conversation had begun, she looked him in the eyes.

"Dan, don't you think I ought to fly straight to Rome to-morrow?"

He smiled. "If you want me never to forgive you."

She searched his eyes, unsmiling, then looked down, unconvinced.

He said, "Anyway. It wouldn't be fair to the Assads. Now they've made all the arrangements."

"It's just . . ."

"And I thought someone said something about unlimited friendship."

She did at last, though reluctantly, bow her head in acceptance. He took a step toward her, put his hands on her shoulders, kissed the still bowed head.

"You go on up. I want a drink. Just one. Alone."

"I feel I should buy you the whole bar."

"Now you're being vain. Go on."

She went, but at the doors turned back a moment to look at him where he stood in the semi-darkness. It was a look of doubt, as if she still wanted to ask if he was sure she should not fly to Rome the next day; and paradoxically also a little that of someone unfairly dismissed, of a child being sent to bed. Then she passed through the doors. He turned away and stood by the balustrade at the edge of the terrace for a brief while, enough time for her to claim her room-key and disappear. He did not really want a drink, but simply to avoid the embarrassment of a good night in the corridor, with its solemn brass pots and aspidistras, outside their rooms. He felt oddly calm, almost assuaged, as if a burden had been lifted from his shoulders. It had been said, and something between them, if not his—or Eliot's—compound familiar ghost, had been removed.

A minute or two later he went up to his room, and forced himself to pack for the morning. Nothing had happened, it was all a dream, an imagined scene. Yet something in him also listened for a tap on his door, a standing there, a solution that would need no words; as it would happen in a script, where the brevity of available time trumped the sluggish recalcitrance of reality; yet also feared it now, knew it would be wrong, too easy.

He experienced a strange conflict of feelings—like some

equation too involved for his knowledge of emotional mathematics to solve. The pique of rejection, the trivial consolation that at least the barrier was apparently not physical, the irrelevance of that, the absurdity of her presenting refusal as some sort of kindness to him, the terrible fixity of her preconceived notions both of him and of herself, the growing physical desire he felt, the gauche suggestion about flying straight to Rome, how far apart they remained, how close they really were, Jenny, Caro . . . he gave up. Perhaps it was best as it was, left a secret between them, a canceled possibility.

In darkness, bed, that eternal nocturnal re-entry into the womb, he lay for a minute or two staring at the ceiling; then smiled wanly to himself, a kind of metaphysical smile, potential being making peace with actual being. One would survive, being English; knowing to the farthest roots of one's existence that it was all, finally, a comedy, even when one was the butt, and the great step in the dark only from *terra firma* to banana-skin.

# North

He woke up, much earlier than he wanted, at dawn. He lay there for a few minutes, in the silence of the hotel, the gray light through the shutters, trying to re-summon sleep. But he remembered at once what he had done the previous night, and now felt nothing but a condemned man's distress. The long day ahead, all the traveling, the leaving behind. He had a sad old memory of waking up on last mornings of holidays, at home, in the Vicarage; all that his wretched school uniform, carefully pressed the previous day by Aunt Millie and now hanging on a chair, waiting to be assumed, had represented.

In the end Dan got up and opened the shutters and the windows. The air was sharp, the sun had not yet quite risen: a great stillness, voiced only by the occasional raucous cry of inland gulls out toward Kitchener's Island. It was a time of day Dan always enjoyed in late spring and summer at Thorncombe; the last stars, the first green light, the untrammeled birdsong; the night-bathed coolness, refreshedness, the pristine dominance of nature before man sullied the world. He stood before its Egyptian equivalent: the smell of verdure, water, the Nile landscape. Somewhere down in the hotel garden, by the bank, a warbler "recorded" softly—its sub-song, not that of the breeding season. Of some unknown species, it chattered and fluted to itself, a smoky, princely, invisible babble, seemingly full of the contentment Dan himself did not feel; enviably able to remain. He craned out and looked down at the terrace where they had sat the previous night. He could even see the table to his right: the two chairs pushed back, the two brandy-glasses still waiting to be cleared.

A minute or two later the first sun struck the tops of the taller cliffs across the river, below the pure sky; the restless golden edge of day. An early car hooted from the other side of the hotel, facing the town. Then two men rowed past beneath where Dan stood, fishermen, nets piled in the bows of their small boat, and the suspension of time was lost. All moved again, into predestined pattern.

An hour later he knocked, nervously, on Jane's door. She called, and he went in. She was dressed, latching a suitcase on the bed, and she smiled at him in the doorway, a shade too normally, as if nothing had happened.

"My watch has stopped—are we late?"

"No. I was just going down for breakfast."

"I'll leave the rest. It won't take a moment."

She was wearing trousers, a dark green polo-necked pullover. She turned and reached for the suit jacket from a chair, but only to put it over an arm; then stopped, in an oddly histrionic way, as if to say she mustn't pretend that things had not changed; with her hands joined in front of her, the coat hanging between them; head down, a little pose of repentance.

"Am I forgiven?"

"No."

She looked at him, and he managed a smile. Her look across the bed lasted, as if she was not to be let off so lightly. She came round the bed, but stopped again short of him; seemed to wait for new words, but found only the simple ones she had used before.

"It's not you, Dan."

"Neither of us. Two other people."

She searched his face for a long moment, gave him a still faintly doubting smile back, then lifted her jacket to put it on. He took and held it up while she turned and slipped it on; but laid his hands a moment on her shoulders, so that she would stay turned away.

"You know how I feel now. I won't bring it up again. I promise. Let's at least hold on to what we've gained."

She stood motionless a moment, then raised a hand and pressed his where it lay on her left shoulder.

"I felt so dreadful last night. All I hate in my sex."

"I understood."

Her hand dropped away, but she did not move.

"If we were just . . ."

"I know. Born heavies." He pressed her shoulders, then took his hands away. "Palmyra? Then we're quits?"

There was an infinitesimal hesitation, then she bowed her head in acquiescence.

Four hours later they were coming down in the Ilyushin over Cairo. Dan's mood had changed disastrously. Though they had talked, even smiled over one or two things, exactly as before, it seemed to Dan an increasingly hollow behavior; behind their masks they were farther apart than ever. They had been much closer only twenty-four hours before; yesterday began to seem like Eden before the apple of knowledge. Confined to remarks about what was directly in front of their eyes, their conversation demonstrated that everything else was fraught, dangerous, forbidden. In spite of his promise, he had several times to suppress things he wanted to say. Pride helped. He began to imagine her secretly longing now for the wretched trip to be over; to be free of him; to be changing straight for the flight to Rome.

They landed just after noon. Assad was there to meet them. Their flight to Beirut was not till five and it had been agreed they should all have lunch together, do some last shopping in the Mouski. Assad's presence turned out to be more of a relief than Dan had foreseen, though it irritated him that it should be so. Jane and the Copt seemed happy to pick up the previously established relationship, the ghost of a flirtation; or at least Dan smelled that, in his hypersensitive mood. Assad's smiles and eyes, an even darker brown than Jane's, were mainly for her; and his questions. She was being no more than polite and Dan had no more right than he had cause to feel jealous. According to Alain, all well-to-do Egyptians, however far beyond traditional Muslim polygamy in cultural terms, still allowed themselves younger mistresses, and he guessed at something like that with the Copt—some comfortable socially sanctioned arrangement where he had the best of both worlds . . . his cultivated and intelligent Lebanese wife (he had brought from her an *ad hoc* guide, typed in French, to the delights of the Lebanon) and his secretaries and local starlets as well. He saw himself in Assad, in other words, and he knew what his real irritation was about: his suspicion that Jane saw Assad in him.

It was also something to do with that equating love with prison. He brooded most deeply over that; its injustice was before his eyes. She could enjoy this lunch, this chatter with Assad, only because he was at her side—was here only because of him. He called himself a male chauvinist, but the self-accusation came from liberal convention, not personal conviction. He remembered too what the Herr Professor had said about the German and English notions of liberty. Love might be a prison; but it was also a profound freedom.

They had a foul flight to Beirut. The plane was crammed

with Mecca pilgrims, there was constant turbulence, constant cloud outside, people vomiting, a mysterious silence from the pilot's cabin . . . even Dan, seasoned air traveler though he was, felt anxious. He hid it for Jane's sake. As usual, one saw the headlines, the future without one, the terminal incompletion; the bitter irony of dying at this point. He invented stories of far worse flights, as a substitute for holding her hand.

It had been raining heavily when they finally arrived in Beirut. The tarmac gleamed wet under the lights, and it was much colder, much closer to winter at home. It caught them both by surprise; as did the city itself, so much more European than oriental or African—the lights, the cliffs of lit hotels and flat-blocks, the traffic, with seemingly every other car a Mercedes; the wealth everywhere. They felt an abrupt nostalgia for the dirt and dust and poverty of Egypt; its shabby hotels, its inefficiency, its ancient humanity. Their new hotel was of the kind that makes all countries one, but in the wrongest way; distancing everything but the world of the expense account, the international executive. Dan telephoned Assad's sister-in-law; everything was arranged. Their car and licensed driver—one was not allowed into Syria except under such supervision—would be in front of the hotel at eight the next morning. They were asked out, but he turned it down, without consulting Jane—or even telling her, when they met again before dinner, that he had done so.

They walked afterward in the brilliant sea-front streets, shopgazing. By this time Dan felt appallingly depressed—less, or so it seemed to him, because of Jane than because of some feeling of having lost all the perspective he had gained at Aswan. Obstinately, in spite of what she had said, it attached itself to Kitchener's Island: a green place out of time, a womb, where all had seemed potential, something in the future as well as between Jane and himself melting . . . he had seen it too late, left it too late. Now they were back in the real contemporary world, consumer-obsessed, Gadarene, ephemeral . . . he could hardly bring himself to look in the shops they passed, felt the stiffness of his face; metaphysical humiliation, the world gone black and vulgar now, not comic at all.

He knew he was being burned in the oldest of fires, but still could not understand where it had come from—like some medieval disease, the bubonic plague, that modern science had supposedly controlled out of all practical consideration; an infantile happy-ever-afterward device from fairy tales, a ludicrous myth. It was almost as if that other great myth, destiny, was having its revenge on him for so many other affairs so coolly and calculatedly entered and enjoyed . . . he thought back to Jenny, the first weeks of that, how easy, balanced, amusing, agreeably exciting, all that seemed in retrospect. One stands beside a woman in front of a window of *couture* dresses and one wants to say, I need you beyond all my verbal capacity of defining need. Instead one plays pocket calculator, translating Lebanese prices into English pounds; hates her profoundly for this interest in gewgaws she patently exhibits only to fill a vacuum, a withdrawal . . . almost as if to show she is normal to the indifferent passers-by.

She must have known, of course; but said nothing. They returned to the hotel. Their rooms were side by side again, though they were spared the previous communicating door. Dan wanted, no, stated he was going to have a drink, and this time it was no subterfuge. If he didn't mind, she felt tired . . . whether it was diplomacy or not, he couldn't tell. She did look tired. There was just a moment, as she turned with her key, a circumstantial smile, when her eyes stayed on his: they showed both a probing and a solicitude, almost nurselike, but impotent, which he loathed.

He did not go straight to the bar, but stood at a kiosk in the lobby, staring at the English-language newspapers, as if the outer world and its affairs might cure him. But they only repelled. He wished he could have reduced the slick, plastic edifice around him, and all in it, to a pile of smoking rubble . . . a wish, had he but known, that history was to realize only a year or two after he made it.

He found the American-style bar and sat at one end of it with a double Scotch on the rocks before him. Two girls in black dresses, they looked German or Scandinavian, sat at the far end. Occasional glances in his direction said what they were. He stared through the shelved array of bottles on the glass wall in front of him at his own face: sullen, impassive, humorless, a locked suitcase with a destination label one couldn't read. He too felt tired, but not only physically; tired of himself, abominably alienated.

It was also an alienation from the distant dawn of that day, seven hundred miles and another world, an eternally lost world, to the south; and went with a corollary and overwhelming longing for the peace and solitude of Thorncombe.

Retreat, to lick wounds, to discover what had gone wrong, not only with Daniel Martin, but his generation, age, century; the unique selfishness of it, the futility, the ubiquitous addiction to wrong ends . . . not only a trip to nowhere, but an exorbitant fare for it. All the thoughtless effort, attachment to trivia, which was really a sloth—mindless energy as a substitute for true intelligence. Perhaps this always attacked writers worst. Other men could take refuge, as his father had in the dogma of his church, in the organization they were part of; share the guilt of the futility, the tedium of the treadmill, the horror of existence passed so, like caged animals.

The barren pursuit of false privilege: sitting, a shut-faced cosmopolitan, in an expensive bar, having only to turn, to mutter a word to the barman, to have the freedom of a body. The younger of the two girls had turned her back on him; and he could see it reflected in the mirror behind the bar. A tousle of Bardot-blond hair, the back bare to the coccyx, bralessness flaunted, the ease with which, one movement of the hands, her dress would fall. He felt momentarily tempted to that, out of his oldest and worst self: to plummet in one hour back to where he belonged. Which Jane also knew, and perhaps feared worst. He ordered another double Scotch.

Like a spoiled child deprived of a toy, barred by his past and his present from feeling anything but eternally spoiled . . . excluded, castrated by both capitalism and socialism, forbidden to belong. Our hero, spurned by one side for not feeling happier, despised by the other for not feeling more despair; in neither a tragedy nor a comedy, but a bourgeois melodrama—that short-lived theatrical fad, as he sourly remembered, dispatched into a deserved oblivion during the great crack-up of 1789.

Above all, he felt determined; and he knew he felt that in direct proportion to his obstinately growing recognition that in some way his freedom had lain in what might have been between Jane and himself . . . or if not freedom, some vital fresh chance; at the least, some true consolation. She had been like some radioactive particle slicing out of infinity and now away into it again: leaving nothing behind but a tiny damage to grow into an irreparable fault, the loss of the one good hope both heart and mind had needed. And twice in his life. The remembrance of a similar female particle that had sliced through his destiny came strangely to him out of the past: Nancy Reed. Perhaps that had been the essential predisposing event of his emotional life—less a particle than a first crystal, performing all future relationships in his life to its particular polyhedral shape . . . the illusory pursuit of a lost innocence, the seeking, or fascination, for situations that carried their own death in them from the beginning, that ensured an eventual determinism in the process . . . the appearance of it, whether it was really there or not.

Something in him did see, or was later to see, that the very perception of this was in itself a crystal, and of the kind that profoundly structures all narrative art; without which it collapses both internally and externally. But that night it seemed one more proof of how determined he was.

He drained his Scotch and stood abruptly. As he passed the two girls on his way out, the one facing him turned with an unlighted cigarette, with an obviousness that he met with a contemptuous cold gray stab of the eyes, like a sliver of steel; and stalked on. But if there had been witnesses upstairs, none would have realized that he had left the bar determined to have it out with Jane. When it came to it he walked past her door without a glance, not even the faintest hesitation, and went into his own carpeted, luxurious and inhuman cell; then locked its door.

# The End of the World

At least the monk without a faith, or indeed even a monastery, slept better, and the weather, when the desk woke him by telephone, seemed to favor their trip: a blue window and sunshine, the springlike air of the winter Mediterranean. Soon after eight they were heading north out of the city, and in unexpected comfort—a nearly new Chevrolet, an easy-mannered young driver. He had chestnut hair, not at all a Levantine face; he was a Maronite Christian, he explained in an English that kept stumbling, if not stopping, for lack of grammar and words. But it soon emerged that his real religion was the machine he was sitting in. He drove at a speed that made even Dan, not a particularly patient driver himself, catch his breath a few times. But the young man negotiated several at first sight rash attempts to overtake with a casual nonchalance. He clearly knew how to handle his chariot and after a while they grew hardened to his hatred of being made to wait by anything ahead. His garrulity, and curiosity about them, helped as well; and the new landscapes.

They were on the coast road to Tripoli in the north of the country. For many miles the littoral had been ruined by uncontrolled development, like the south of France, certain parts of California. But the sea was a deep, fierce blue, and inland, to their right, ran the long range of snow-covered mountains that spines the Lebanon. Past Byblos, the country grew wilder. The road ran under boulder-strewn hillsides; below, over the vivid water, lay dazzlingly white rectangular salt-pans.

After a while they had to travel more slowly, since the road narrowed and there were far fewer places to overtake: for minutes on end the red-haired driver would slowly tap his hand on the wheel. It was all the government's fault, they talked about tourism but they wouldn't build proper roads—he had a brother working for Volkswagen in Germany and had stayed on holiday with him, he knew what proper roads were.

Risking the young man's eyes in the driving-mirror, able to combine at least against this, Dan and Jane exchanged one or two covert glances: the sad innocence of backward countries. They were also warned about Syrian roads, that they were going into "a place where all is crazy, crazy people"—mainly crazy, it seemed, because they had no money under the Baathist regime. Labib liked driving customers there. "It make me so happy when I leave." And he grinned back at them, pleased at this wit. Dan gave Jane a dry little inquiring tilt of the head, and she smiled guardedly. Perhaps, she suggested politely, ordinary people were better looked after now? A dismissive hand waved back.

"Fool people. You will see. Not know what is money."

They gave up trying to convert this evident storm-trooper for laissez-faire capitalism. He switched on the radio and the car was filled with folk-sound. He fiddled for "American music," but they made him return to the original wavelength: a woman's voice, sinuous, alternately sobbing and languorous, against a plangent rhythm. She was famous, they were told.

"Every man in Middle East like for wife. Even Israel men."

They sounded him discreetly there, without need. He was happy to air his views. Though he was pro-Arab, he seemed to have a grudging admiration for the Israelis, and very little sympathy for the Palestine refugees. They were stupid people, lazy people; like the Syrians.

"I no have money, I no have work, so I much better man than you."

And again he waved his slack-wristed hand back over his shoulder at them, eyes on the road. It was a gesture they were to become very familiar with: the supreme asininity of the human species in allowing so many things to keep a man from making money. He was strange: both crass and open, and finally rather likable.

They bypassed Tripoli, then turned inland. Dour uplands began to rise ahead, and banks of cloud. They came to the frontier in the last sun. Dan handed over their passports and some money and Labib disappeared inside the customs office; ten minutes later he reappeared with two men in uniform, who came and stared at Dan and Jane. Some kind of argument was going on. There was a hostility, an indifference in the soldiers' eyes, that somehow chilled. The senior finally spat some word and turned away. It seemed, when Labib climbed back in and explained, it was nothing to do with them, but with some minor infraction of regulations he had committed on another trip a month before. He seethed with resentment over it for several miles, like some innocent landed in the middle of a Kafka novel. He claimed the soldiers simply wanted a bribe, as in the good old days; were afraid to ask for it, and took their frustration out on him.

Meanwhile, they were climbing under heavy cloud. The country got bleakly grim. They seemed in twenty miles to have jumped twenty degrees of latitude—into Scotland, or Scandinavia. One or two miserable villages squatted in desolate glens. A thin drizzle started, and the gray cloud pressed lower as they went on. The volatile Labib grew equally gloomy. He didn't think the cloud would lift. It was a bad time of year. He also had to drive with more care; there was very little traffic, but a fellow-driver had broken his suspension in a pothole only a week before.

They branched off, past the townlet of Tell Kalakh, for the Krak des Chevaliers. It loomed, a gaunt gray-blue, six miles away across a wintry plain; a formidable and forbidding catafalque of a castle that seemed tilted and sliding off its steep hill-top. They skirted the plain, through villages that recalled, in their poverty, if not their climate, Egypt . . . or medieval England, perhaps. There must have been a lot of rain recently, there was mud everywhere. Men in baggy black trousers, muffled in their checkered kufiyas, mere pairs of hostile eyes, watched them pass. There seemed no children, no hope; a world the rest of the world had forgotten, as far from the glitter of Beirut as the landscapes of the moon. Then the road wound endlessly up over bare, wind-scorched slopes, with runnels of water everywhere, toward the lowering Crusader stronghold. For the first time that day Dan felt happier. All this suited his mood. It seemed almost a welcome reality after the last twenty-four hours.

They arrived at the bottom gate of the immense fortress in an icy spatter of driving sleet. By the foot of the wall beside them there were cushions of unthawed snow. Luckily Assad's sister-in-law had warned Dan it would be cold, and they had brought what warm clothes they had. Jane pulled on a cardigan, Dan a sweater, then jackets and overcoats again. They followed Labib up through a long tunnel. The roof dripped water, the wind moaned, there was a dankness everywhere, one almost expected to see the Thane of Glamis stand out.

Instead, a resigned Arab in an ancient black overcoat came from a boarded-up recess at the foot of the inner wall. Their guide, he spoke only a tired, guttural French.

Labib disappeared, and they followed the man and his monotonous voice through a maze of underground stables, stores, magazines, kitchens, corridors; stared down over somber gray distances from occasional windows . . . and gradually, despite the cold and the wind and the desolation, felt their visit was worthwhile. It was the size of the place; its weight, its stupefying unnecessity, like that of the Pyramids; and, on the upper levels, the still sensible ghost of thirteenth-century elegance, the ruined stairways and delicately columned arches and terraced courtyards . . . its theatricality there appealed to both of them. On the highest battlements there were stupendous views. In one direction, back down toward the sea, they could even still see a countryside in sunshine. But to the north-west, where they were heading, there was nothing but endless cloud. They hardly listened any more to the guide; were far more conscious of a kind of quixotic English rightness in being at this monument to primitive power politics and human greed at this totally unsuitable time of year. Europe, out of gear since the beginning; one's permanent inner exile from its endless historical errors. It drew them close again, outside their own situation, since it was what had been lacking down the Nile: there, always the obscuring presence of their fellow-passengers.

They ended in a merciful warmth, in a room at the foot of one of the dilapidated wall-towers; a blazing stove, a serving-boy, Labib smoking; and a small brass pot of Turkish coffee, very sweet but strong; the best, they decided at the first sip, they had tasted. It was somehow Russian, very primitive and simple, a station waiting-room from Tolstoy. Labib and their guide talked in Arabic, the boy stared solemnly at them. But then Labib caught Dan's eye and tapped his watch. Dan glanced at his own, then grimaced at Jane as he prepared to stand.

"You could just about have been sitting down to a delicious Italian meal—you realize that?"

She did not answer, merely smiled. But a little later, when they were following Labib down a long flight of stone stairs to the lower levels and the tunnel out, she took his hand in her own gloved one and pressed it, without looking at him; kept it, until they got to the bottom of the flight; as if he must be good, like a bored child.

They drove back to the main road, then turned on for their next stop, the town of Homs. The route lay over long and treeless uplands, a barren and color-drained moor. Solitary lapwings stood by mournful pools. The road rose now into the base of the clouds. A thin mist settled, cutting visibility down to a mile at most, less in places. Labib shook his head. He had heard of weather like this, but not met it before. It was very evident that it was getting worse. A motionless human figure loomed beside the road, holding out a dead bird with an outstretched arm. Dan glimpsed a flat bill, a spiral of red and green on the head.

"What was it?"

"A teal."

He looked through the rear window. The man stared after them, the small duck still hanging from a disappointed outstretched hand.

Labib grinned round. "That is how they think business in Syria. I give you bird, you give me two packet cigarettes." The hand waved again. "Very stupid country."

After a few moments Dan murmured, "I handpicked him specially."

"I suspected you had."

He held her eyes. "Do you want to call it a day? I don't like the look of this."

"Faintheart."

He smiled ahead through the driving-window. "Only thinking of you."

"Adventure. I'm enjoying it."

But it began, as they came into Homs, to look more like the edge of a limbo nearest to a hell. It had started to rain. The town was awful in its feeling of ramshackle depression, of a society self-condemned to the utmost austerity. A drab grayness hung over everything: buildings, people, shops. They had expected a great contrast with the Lebanon; but this lacked even the individuality, the light, the laziness, the engaging humor of Egypt. Labib parked in the main square, carefully, opposite a restaurant window . . . where he could watch his car while they ate. Hubcaps, even wheels, would be gone in five minutes if he did not do so; or so he claimed.

The restaurant owner was a Beiruti, and the meal adequate, but the shabby decor of the place reminded Dan of the British Restaurant days of immediate postwar England. They sat with Labib in the window. He could see Jane was unsettled by the sight outside of two great puritanisms, the

Marxist and the Muslim, in joint practice; her eyes kept drifting out there, as if she were looking for some redeeming feature. There seemed to be many armed soldiers and army trucks about, which added a disagreeable air of enforced suppression to an already quite sufficient gloom. Dan observed her reaction with a kind of sour pleasure, wondering if she saw the parallel with the Krak des Chevaliers. This seemed to lack even the privileged graces for the few. He tried to discover more of political Syria from Labib, but the young man quickly shook his head and raised a finger.

"Not talk here."

It was like slipping back thirty years: Careless talk costs lives.

The Beiruti owner came up toward the end of the meal and chatted with Labib. He had heard there was fog on the road to Palmyra, still a hundred miles off across the desert. Traffic was getting through, but it was a slow business. They had a discussion. They couldn't possibly get there before dark now; their visa was strictly for one night, which would give them only tomorrow morning to see the ruins. But having said that, Labib declared himself for going on. He could get them there. They sensed that his professional mettle and his beloved Chevrolet were challenged. It was almost as if the threatened mist stood for everything he despised about the country. Dan wanted to go on for his own reasons; and Jane seemed still in her adventurous mood. Now they had come so far . . . or perhaps it was to demonstrate that she would not take the present appearance of Syria for its only reality.

They settled the bill and moved off again. For ten miles or so, the mist seemed no worse. But then, as soon as they branched off on the unmetaled desert road to Palmyra, it thickened down to less than a hundred yards. On either side, the sand stretched a little way; then the gray wall of vapor. Labib strained forward now, searching the road for potholes, down to fifteen miles an hour in places. At one point he swerved off the road without warning and stopped, his alert eyes having seen headlights ahead. An army truck thundered past, going a good deal faster than they had been. It was to happen several times more during that afternoon. Apparently the road was notorious for it, the army drivers didn't care a damn; and however innocent the driver of the car they hit, he would have the blame.

After some miles, they passed a congregation of domed clay huts, white and mausoleum-like; seemingly devoid of life. Then after that, mile after crawling mile. They all grew silent, the enclosed solitude and the monotony grew hypnotic. The strip of desert beside them seemed like an ocherous snow. One turned and looked at the tiniest distraction; a stone marker, the skeleton of a dead sheep, a scatter of low bushes. It became far stranger than anything they had bargained for: a fog in a desert.

Two cloaked figures, cowled and faintly monastic, hove into sight. Shepherds. Their flock grazed in a thin green rash of grass along the ruts beside the central camber of the road: the small ewes a soft orange-brown, the lambs piebald. One of the shepherds raised his hand gravely, almost forbiddingly, as if commanding them to stop, but Labib accelerated slightly and drove past. The road went arrow-straight, never deviating an inch. About four, when the light was already failing, the mist lifted slightly, and they could suddenly see a mile or more, only to realize they had been missing nothing—or a something that was in fact nothing: an endless expanse of sand, faint dunes, imperceptible escarpments, a huge emptiness like blank paper. They came over a small rise, however, to find something more interesting—two hundred yards away squatted a black Bedouin tent, fixed with long guy-ropes. Dan made Labib stop, and he and Jane got out for a few seconds while he took a photograph. It was bitterly cold, inhospitable, menacing. They retreated gratefully to the warm interior of the car.

Night had already begun to fall when they came to the Trans-Jordanian Pipeline pumping-station; a brief landscape of tortured pale-gray pipes, army sentries, a grimly shuttered hamlet; then they were out in the desert again, with the endless road in the headlights. The cloud at least had risen, and there was less mist. From time to time they saw orange specks in the desert, kerosene lamps in other Bedouin tents. Then a moment of drama—a chain of weird shapes in the headlights, strutting with a slow, awkward dignity across the road: a string of camels, each ungainly beast attached by a rope to the one ahead. They were very mysterious, not least because they seemed unattended. Labib eased forward, but just as they passed the place where the camels had crossed, there was a metallic bang behind the car. Dan thought it was a spring, a loose exhaust pipe, but Labib raised his right arm and made a throwing gesture.

"Stone."

"I didn't see anyone."

"He hide."

That, it emerged, was why he didn't slow down to exchange friendly greetings. The Bedouins were not friendly people. It was the army trucks. They killed too many of their sheep.

Dan slid a glance at Jane. "You may have your adventure yet."

"I already am. I feel as if I'm on another planet. Nothing seems real any more."

He reached in the darkness and took her hand; squeezed it as if to give it courage, and would have relinquished it, but the pressure was returned, and the two hands lay joined on the fabric of the seat between them; the last contact with lost reality.

Dan said, "Who would have dreamed this, all those years ago."

"I know. I was just thinking the same thing."

He felt a minute extra pressure on his hand; then a stronger one, and the hand pulled away, as if he might have misinterpreted her first response; this in turn was covered by her reaching down for her basket and fishing for cigarettes.

Labib spoke, pointing ahead in the sky. "Palmyra."

There was a distant luminescence. The country seemed more hilly. They climbed a slope and there ahead, below, lay a dim cluster of lights, the modern oasis. At last the road bent, as if it had decided to grow human again. A shuttered house, then a brief glimpse of a distant ruined arch as the headlights swept round. The car slowed, then swung at right angles off the road and bumped through an unreal petrified forest of broken walls, colonnades, fallen capitals. A few hundred yards on it drew up outside a long bungalow, bizarrely like the jerry-built 1920s clubhouse of some impoverished golf-course.

"Zenobia," said Labib.

It was Palmyra's only hotel, isolated in the huge graveyard of the dead city. They stood out in the windy darkness, the freezing air. The irregular stacks of a roofless temple stood obscurely silhouetted a hundred yards away against the light-stained clouds above the invisible modern village. There was a profound silence, macabre in the oldest, and appropriately Arabic, sense of the word. Then a door opened and a shaft of yellow light fell across the sand. Labib called curtly and the man in the doorway raised his hand.

If they had imagined relief from unreality at the Hotel Zenobia, they were not to get it. Its interior proved as strange as its site. They found themselves in a large room dominated by a huge stove, around which sat three men on wooden chairs. One, the oldest, had a squint, the other wore a long white, or once white, apron, the third was a younger man who had stood at the door. Dan and Jane were ignored. There was a conversation in Arabic, questions asked of Labib. The rear part of the room was arranged as a primitive dining-room. Some half a dozen set tables; embroidered saddle-bags, one or two carpets, on the wall. Behind the stove in the middle of the floor, against a wall, stood a high-backed old sofa, some relic of more bourgeois or more French days, covered in purple, red, indigo rugs and cushions, almost as if they were strewn there on sale; except that there was a newspaper and an indentation where someone had sat recently. The whole room was like a stage set eternally without a playwright. The cold and silence outside, the muggy warmth here, the way the men sat; evidently the hotel staff, but splendidly disinclined to show it by any welcoming courtesy or service.

Labib appeared to be giving a mile-by-mile account of the journey, but one of the men's questions must have concerned them, since the driver, as if remembering their presence, turned and asked if they wanted to see their rooms.

The oldest man, the one with the squint, stood and beckoned them to follow. They went through a door, into darkness and a much colder atmosphere. He twisted an old ceramic switch and a feeble bulb lit a long barrack-like corridor, a row of doors. He turned to Dan and questioningly raised one finger, then two. Dan raised two in return. The old man limped a few steps down the corridor, and opened a door. A bed, a chair, a wardrobe, two strips of worn carpet on a tiled floor, a paraffin drip-stove. The old man bent and lit it; a guttering flame. He gravely opened the wardrobe, and indicated more blankets. Dan set Jane's bag on the floor and followed the old fellow across the corridor; a similar bare room; the same process of lighting the stove. Dan turned to Jane, who had joined them.

"It's a bit larger. Would you rather have this?"

"I think it's even colder. Do you suppose there's a bathroom?"

Rather to their amazement, there was, farther down the corridor. The water ran cold, but the old man pointed to a plastic bucket, then to himself, made washing gestures—he would fetch warm water if they wanted. Labib appeared behind them. He had come to announce the menu. There was egg or lamb; noodles or rice. They chose lamb and rice.

Five minutes later Dan and Jane sat, obediently waiting, but at least warm, on the couch in the main room. The cook had disappeared, but the other two men now sat by the wall across from the stove, staring at the English couple in silence, as if they resented this irritating disturbance of their winter nights around the stove. Labib sat at one of the tables in the dining-room part, reading the newspaper. From behind a curtain at the back there came the sound of Arabic music on a wireless, the occasional scrape of a moved pan. But in the room a great silence, a formidable aura of waiting. Jane bent her head.

"I'm going to burst into giggles if you don't say something."

"I think that's the idea. They've had a bet on which of us will break up first."

"What an extraordinary place."

"End of the world."

"It reminds me of one of those time-warp plays."

He gave her a quick smile. "That's exactly what I felt. When we came in. Whether we've actually really got here."

"We're lying on the road out there somewhere."

"Labib's going to read about it in that newspaper. Any moment now."

She looked across at where he sat. The driver did, by chance, turn a page; and for a not quite pretending bated moment, they both watched. But then he merely felt in his pocket for a packet of cigarettes. Jane smiled down.

"What do you suppose happens if we ask for a drink?"

"At least ten years in the salt-mines, I should think."

But he went over to Labib. There was only beer; that was the law. Labib spoke back to the two by the wall. The younger man disappeared into the kitchen and came back with glasses and two label-less bottles. It was local beer, very thin, but drinkable. The silence welled back, the two men continued to stare across the room. Outside, on the road from Homs, they heard a truck. But it passed on. Somewhere out in the ruins a pariah began to bark, short intermittent yaps. Labib put down his paper and stared across the empty dining-room into space; then pulled out a notebook, and began to do some sort of calculation—or so Dan guessed, since the pencil was more poised than writing. He seemed bored, not behind his wheel; a centaur who had lost his body. Dan looked at Jane.

"Wish we hadn't come?"

"Don't be absurd."

"All that drag back tomorrow."

"I wouldn't have missed this for anything. Now it's happened."

"I feel the same." He murmured, "A loaf of bread. And thou."

She was dry in return.

"I don't think I could sing in this wilderness."

"I'd forgotten that part of it." She stared down at the glass she held perched on her crossed legs. He said, "Not breaking my promise. Just that I'd have hated every moment of today without you."

She said nothing, as if it could be treated as a remark that needed no answer. But the other silence, in the room, forced her to speak.

"It's all the other days, Dan."

He waited a moment or two, returning the stare of the man with the squint; seemed almost to address him, though their voices had dropped so that Labib couldn't hear.

"In which we travel alone."

"At places like this . . ."

He glanced at her out of the corner of his eyes. "But elsewhere, sentimental aberration?"

She still looked down at her glass. "What one feels one must."

Again he waited.

"I wish it was several hundred years ago."

"Why?"

"When it was literally a nunnery, one knew what one was fighting against."

"I'm sorry it seems like that."

"But it is a little?"

"In the sense that I feel I have no other choice."

"Then lack of courage of a kind?"

"I suppose."

But she said it like someone who had weighed the two sides, and accepted a lesser accusation to spare herself a greater. Dan stared across at Labib, who yawned and put his notebook away; then stood and disappeared into the kitchen at the back. They heard him say something to the cook.

"And you don't think I have enough for both of us?"

"One can't transmit courage like that, Dan. It's either inside you or . . ."

She shrugged, and her voice died away, as she clearly wished the subject would. Once again he stared at the two mute spectators opposite. Yet he clung to something. After all, she was there. She could have insisted that she did fly straight to Rome; or refused to re-open discussion now at all. There was a tiny hint in the way she sat of the disobedient schoolgirl, the waiting for further reprimand. Dan spoke quietly.

"We've just been through what must be one of the loneliest landscapes in the world. You called it unreal. For me it had tremendous reality. Symbolically, anyway." He glanced surreptitiously toward her still bent head. "Do you want me to shut up?"

She shook her head. He stared down at his own glass.

"I feel I've become a man driving through nothingness. Behind the screens the Herr Professor was talking about. This girl in California is just a carpet hung up to keep out the wind. I can't go on using her like that. Apart from anything else, she knows it." His voice was very quiet, as if they were discussing someone else. "I'm making it sound as if I want you to save me from her. It's not that at all."

"Nothingness is a very comparative thing, isn't it?"

"Meaning I'm not allowed to feel it? Economic privilege deprives you of all other human rights?"

"Of course not. Just that . . . nothingness is part of the vocabulary of despair."

"I shouldn't talk like Beckett?"

"Only to the extent that you are privileged in other ways."

He examined her downcast eyes, her obstinacy; and wondered why he now felt tender toward even this in her.

"That's even worse. The more you feel, the happier you have to sound?"

She made a little sideways movement of the head.

"I was thinking of that man by the road. Holding out the duck."

He knew what she meant: the real nothingness of some lives . . . of many lives. The younger man opposite stood and went into the kitchen; the murmur of voices there. The old man with the squint dropped his head, as if he had dozed off.

"I know everyone like us is profoundly lucky in a biological sense. Education, culture, money . . . all the rest. The logic I don't follow is that allowing a guilt about that to dictate every decision will help at all. I'm not saying that we haven't largely abused the gifts we were given. But when you even deny them intrinsic or potential validity—"

"I don't deny them that."

"Perhaps not in some abstract sense. But you do effectively. I'm not even allowed to have a real sense that I've abused them." He looked briefly at her face, then away. "We haven't tried enough, Jane. We've ratted. With less excuse than any other kind of human beings in the world. Anthony should have been a priest. You should have been my wife. I should have tried to be a serious playwright." Still she did not speak, and he lightened his voice a little. "I'm not sure you're not the most guilty of us all. You did half-glimpse it at Oxford. That we were living in a dream-world."

"And promptly entered an even worse one."

"I'm arguing for your instincts. Not your actions. And trying to suggest that once more you're making a wrong decision on right feeling."

"Dan, I'm simply trying not to hurt someone I'm very fond of."

"You may be trying. But you're not succeeding."

She hesitated, her voice dropped. "Because of what you say. My formidable past record of wrong choices."

"Did you mean what you said on Kitchener's Island? About my having helped you over what you'll do when we get back?"

"You know I meant it."

"I can't understand why you'll listen to me there. Yet not over this."

"Because I do value your opinions of life in general."

"But not of you. Or us."

"You're romanticizing what I am. Or not understanding what I've become."

"No man or woman ever fully understand what they've each become. If that condition has to be fulfilled, the two sexes ought to be living on different planets. It's an untenable thesis."

"But the pain it might cause isn't, is it?"

"Only if you grant it more probability than happiness."

Her head was bowed. "It isn't a deficiency in you. You must believe that."

"I think you're lying. Perhaps out of decency. But still lying."

"Why?"

"Caro told me something you'd said about me recently. About my being someone in permanent flight from his past. From all enduring relationship."

She took a tiny breath. "She shouldn't have told you that."

"Perhaps. But she did."

"It was meant to make things easier for her. Not to blame you."

"I'm sure. And I'm not disputing the diagnosis."

"I didn't suggest you were in flight from her."

He tilted his beer. "But you are afraid I might soon, once more, be in flight from you?"

"I do wish she hadn't told you that."

He looked at her. Something in her face was shrouded and embarrassed, at a loss as to how she should explain it away; asked to be let off this unpleasant hook he had kept stored for use.

"But since she has?"

"My fear is much more that I should make it only too justifiable."

"That's a kind of morbid false modesty. Assuming disaster before it's happened."

"I'm sorry. The fear is very real."

"I wish we could kill this notion of yours that secretly I mean to corrupt you in some way. I accept absolutely what you are. What you want to be." He took a breath. "And not only because I want to. I couldn't make you in my image. Not in a thousand years."

She shook her head, as if in despair at all these cross-purposes. "If it was just a matter of tolerance between us . . ."

"That is something."

"Which I fully recognize."

Once more they came to a baffled halt.

"It's not only the past, Jane. I have had to get to know you again. What you've become. I feel very close to that." He waited, then forced an answer. "Don't you recognize this at all? Some kind of elective affinity?"

"Yes. Sometimes."

"What I was feeling in Egypt was that for the first time in years I was undergoing a flight towards something. I haven't illusions about us. I know we've a formidable list of misunderstandings to sort out. If you could just accept that on my side I'm prepared to contribute endless patience. Sympathy. Love, whatever you want to call it. I want to write, but I can write anywhere. I just want to be beside you. With you. Wherever you are. Even if it never improves very much on this. I'd still rather have that than nothing. Than not at least having tried." He left a silence, but she seemed imprisoned now in a far deeper one. He spoke less urgently. "I can really see only two possibilities. One is that the old physical rapport between us no longer means anything to you. In which case—of course, I'll shut up. One can't dispute things like that."

"And the other?"

"Means you are just as much in flight as you claim I am. In a different direction, but no more honestly."

"Where?"

"To the idea that what's wrong inside you can be solved by sacrificing everything to social conscience . . . helping the underprivileged. All of that. At least I'd claim for my solution that it's much nearer home. I've betrayed the only two things for which I ever had any talent. Handling words, and loving one single other human being wholly." He added, "And that last one, you share." Strangely, it must seem very strangely in view of what he next said, there came to him the memory of that remote, endlessly stopping *andante* variation in the Goldberg; silences, and what lay behind them. "You murdered something in all three of us, Jane. Largely without knowing it, and perhaps murder is an unkind word. But you made certain choices, developments, impossible. We're sitting surrounded by what you did to us. Out there."

That last harshness visibly set her back again; killed whatever hopes she may have harbored of keeping the conversation within bounds. He went on.

"I can't forgive that analogy of the prison you used. I'd much rather you said you didn't trust me. At least that would be honest."

She leaned back a little, again shook her head. "I don't have to look outside myself for lack of trust."

"I think the difference between us is that there's a part of you I don't understand. That I'm even happy in a way not to understand. While for you I'm something in a cage. Only too easy to label."

"You know how to live with yourself, Dan. I don't."

"For which I get a black mark."

"That's not fair."

He looked down with a wry smile. "It doesn't have to be. My condition is traditionally excused." But even that plea for a shade less seriousness went unheard. He sensed that something in her was receding, not only from him, but in time, to well before his knowing of her; to an eternal unforgivingness, refusal to listen. He spoke more gently. "Perhaps that's the real difference. Only one of us is in love with love."

"In a fit state for it."

"It's not communion, for heaven's sake. States of grace aren't required. Or absolution." She said nothing. "We're two very imperfect beings, Jane. An egoist and an idealist. Not the Platonic dream at all. But that doesn't mean we couldn't give a great deal to each other." Still she would not speak. "Then we're back to animal facts."

He knew there was something panic-stricken in her, despite the stillness of her pose and expression; doubling and doubling, trying to escape.

"You make it so difficult for me."

"Then let me make it easier. I'd much rather it was something physical than what you're seeming to suggest."

He felt she was weighing the possibility of that as a loophole; which told him that it could not really be so. At last she looked up, across the room.

"I didn't go to sleep for hours in Aswan. If I felt nothing in that way, I wouldn't have talked about prison."

"Then what in God's name is it?"

"I suppose God himself. In a peculiar sort of way."

"What does that mean?"

"Whatever made me glad, the next morning, that nothing had happened." She added, "I knew I should have been lying to you. It wouldn't have been for the right reason."

"Then out of what?"

She paused, still unwilling to go on; but knew she must now.

"You've had lots of sexual experience, I don't suppose you can imagine what it's like for someone who hasn't had very much. How you . . . store the memory of what little you have had. This was one reason I hesitated so much over coming. Knowing . . ." but she broke off.

"Knowing what, Jane?"

"That old feelings might return." Now she went on quickly, before he could speak. "It's partly Anthony, Dan. I'm not really over that yet. I don't mean the death. The living with him. All the failures there."

"But I suspect he half-hoped this would happen."

"For reasons I can't accept. Even if his ridiculous scheme of metaphysics was true, he has to do his own penance."

"But you're behaving exactly as if it is. As if he's watching us, and you have to spite him."

"I have to take no notice of what he wanted." She appealed to him; or at least her head turned a little. "And of what something female in me also wants." She looked down again. "When you took my hand in the car just now, I wanted to cry. I know it must seem absurd. So much of me would rather be . . . not like this." She fingered the rim of her glass, letting the silence grow. Outside, the pariah was barking again. But then she continued. "It's as if the one part of you you don't want to be the acted part, the part that wants to give, to say yes, for some terrible reason still insists on denying the rest. What you expect from me is like something I'm told exists, I know exists, but in a country where I can't go. I lay awake that night in Aswan trying to be someone different. Telling myself this man has always attracted me, so why not. As an adventure. As . . . as it happened before. But I knew I couldn't." She waited, but now he was silent. "It's partly because I can't think of you objectively like that . . . as 'this man.' " She hesitated again. "I was given a little test on the boat. I was propositioned one evening by Alain—in a nice, discreet, traditional French way. As one makes an opening bid at bridge. But I looked across the room at you. If you could only understand the reason it would have been like betraying you then is the same reason behind now."

"And supposing I'd come, at Aswan?"

"I shouldn't have had time to think about it. But now I have."

He contemplated his glass.

"You can always tell a really bad film-script when the story depends on missed opportunities."

"But ours has. You said just now I killed a choice in all of us. I can't risk doing that again."

"Then we've learnt nothing all these years. Except how to make deserts even more barren still."

"I really shall cry, if you talk like this."

"I might well join you."

But he reached his hand, as if to stop such nonsense, and took hers. After a moment she returned its pressure. The joined hands lay on the rug between them.

"The one mystery to me is how I can have fallen twice in my life for such an impossible bitch of a woman."

"At least we can agree on that."

He banged her hand gently against the rug, but then let silence come. Both his tenderness and his irritation deepened: the tenderness because he knew what lay behind her refusal was also what he loved in her, the not being like any other woman in his life, despite the fact that this uniqueness came so strongly tinged with Anthony's old argument from absurdity—though it was less *credo* now than *nego quia absurdum;* and the irritation not only because she had admitted both nature and reason were on his side, but also because it offended some archetypal sense in him of right dramatic development . . . they had come to the end of the world, and not, at last, to be able to meet there denied that remote but all-powerful place in the unconscious from where his deepest notions of personal destiny came. He could have tried for years to imagine a better place and failed to create what one day's hazard had brought; so apt, so stripping of the outer world, so crying the truth of the human condition. He stared across at the particle of the human condition opposite, his head now sunk sideways, deep on a lapel of the old European jacket he wore over his galabiya: Tiresias, Muslim style.

Stalemate. But he would not relinquish her hand. He felt a more general irritation, against their history, their type in time. They took themselves, or their would-be moral selves, so seriously. It had indeed all been summed up by the mirrors in his student room: the overweening narcissism of all their generation . . . all the liberal scruples, the concern with living right and doing right, were not based on external principles, but self-obsession. Perhaps the ultimate vulgarity lay there: in trying to conform to one's age's notion of spiritual nobility—as if, though one laughed at the notion of an afterlife, one was not just an animal with one brief existence on a dying planet, but still had an immortal soul and a Judgment Day to face. And when what one wanted was so innocent, private, small: he felt tempted to put this to Jane. But then, perhaps knowing it was a lost cause, skipped the argument for the conclusion. He turned his head and looked at her.

"Jane, why don't we behave like two normal human beings and make it one room tonight?"

"Because it wouldn't solve anything."

He murmured with a mock tartness, "Speak for yourself." But she was beyond response, even the faintest smile. He pressed the hand, and spoke in an even lower voice. "You know it's not that. I'd just like to hold you. Be close to you."

She stared at the floor—almost through it, at something far beyond. He squeezed her hand again, but it was lifeless. He could detect no softening of the bleak perversity in her face, though it did have a sadness; a kind of ultimate being cornered, yet still an inability to surrender.

How that silence might have been broken he was not to know, because Labib—and by then it began to seem mercifully—reappeared and came to them. If they would sit; their meal was ready. They stood, and though they chose a table on the other side of the room from his, they felt more exposed, within earshot. The younger man served. A lamb stew on a small mountain of pilaf, very simple yet not unappetizing . . . a flavor of cumin, other exotic herbs, and the rice was good. Dan had another beer. They sat facing Labib, who ate the same meal twelve feet away. He seemed pleased to show off his English. The old man with the squint had awakened, between servings the waiter sat by him again; and the cook came and sat by the stove. For once Labib was prepared to concede something not absolutely bad about Syria—he had known the cook before, when he worked in a hotel in Damascus. They should go to Damascus, the *souk* was very good, very cheap, many folk-dresses, jewelry . . . Jane answered far more than Dan, playing the polite diplomat again, her father's daughter, across the space between their tables. It was as if nothing had been said; but they avoided each other's eyes.

Two dishes of yoghurt followed, and a bowl of oranges; then Turkish coffee. They discussed tomorrow with the driver. He wanted to be on his way back by midday. There was the museum to see, the baths, the tombs, the dead city itself . . . too much, they must rise with the dawn, at seven, if they wanted to see it all. He had heard a weather report on the wireless. The mist was not expected, but there would be cloud, perhaps rain. Tomorrow seemed already fraught with the press of time, with duty and gloom, by the time he had finished. Then he mentioned that there was an old French guide they could read if they wanted. He made the old man find it.

They retreated with the dog-eared pamphlet to their sofa behind the stove. His table cleared, Labib stayed where he was and began some kind of backgammon game with the cook. They played not with dice, but cards. The other two men moved and watched, made quiet comments; the occasional small clack of moved counters. Meanwhile Jane translated the guide for Dan's benefit, as if glad of this excuse to take sanctuary in something third, pedantic, stale; as if this small service might forgive her her sins. He listened to her voice, not what she was saying. If one part of him felt inclined to snatch the guide out of her hands and throw it across the room, yet another was in some way tranced by the strangeness, the suspense, the being there. He glanced at his watch. It was still not nine. It seemed they had been there for days, not in fact, less than three hours. She came to the end of her reading. There were exclamations from the four men, grins—some coup, some stroke of luck, for the cook against Labib; a new game was begun.

"Shall we take a sniff outside?"

"If you like. It is rather overpowering, this heat."

They stood, and Jane went through to their bedrooms while Dan explained to Labib what they intended.

The driver pointed. "Not that way. In ruin. Bad dogs." And he bit fingers against a thumb, to show what he meant.

"That way?" Dan pointed toward the road. That way, it seemed, was all right. Labib spoke to the younger man, who went and fetched a torch.

Dan found Jane with her Russian coat on, tying a headscarf, in the doorway of her room. There was a reek of paraffin.

"Oh Christ." He went past her, into the stench. "You can't sleep in this."

"It'll be all right. I'll open the window."

"And freeze to death."

"Not with all those blankets."

Outside, they found the wind had dropped, although a bitter dankness hung in the air. In spite of Labib's reported forecast, the mist had descended. Serpentine swathes of it wafted in the torch-beam, impelled by some ghostly breath. They moved past the black shape of the Chevrolet and down back toward the road, speculating about the mysterious dogs . . . perhaps he had meant jackals, neither of them was quite sure if they were found here. Dan had intended to argue again, but changed his mind; for her, now, to speak. But it was soon clear that she did not want to return to that. Nor would she allow silence. She played the perfect traveling companion again: set the immediate between them.

To the north the sky remained faintly lighter, but around

them brooded darkness and the scattered, veiled debris of a lost civilization: crumbled walls, a colonnade, a bank littered with shards. It was the weather, they decided; it took all the serene aura out of classical antiquity, reduced it to its constituent parts, its lostness, goneness, true death . . . and the contrast of the reality with the promise of the name: Palmyra, with all its connotations of shaded pools, gleaming marble, sunlit gardens, the place where sybaritic Rome married the languorous Orient. It was much more like Dartmoor, Scotland; the Connecticut where Jane and Nell had spent their schoolgirl wartime years.

They came to the harder surface of the road from Homs and walked a little way down that, but the vapor-laden cold was terrible. Somewhere in the mist to their right a sharp-eared dog, invisible but seemingly quite close, perhaps the same one they had heard earlier, began to bark with intense suspicion. They turned, defeated, menaced by the canine voice. It followed them sporadically, a soul caught between anger and despair, all the way back to the Hotel Zenobia.

The men looked up grinning from their game, as if amused to see these foreigners so soon thwarted and brought to sanity. Jane stood warming herself at the stove, while Dan exchanged a few words about the dogs. They were domestic ones gone feral, it seemed, breeding in holes in the ground, in the ruins. Their waiter at supper raised hands, aping a rifle and pressing a trigger; something, perhaps merely humor, yet which appeared vaguely sinister, glistening in his eyes. He said something in Arabic in a low voice, and the other men smiled.

"What did he say, Labib?"

"He say, like Israel men. When he shoot dogs."

Dan gave the upturned faces a circumstantial smile. "They'll wake us?"

"Sure. Seven o'clock."

He turned back to Jane. "Unless you want to sit and read?"

"No." She turned from the stove.

"Let's swap rooms."

"No really . . ."

"You can't sleep in that stink."

"Then why should you?"

She said good night to the men, and he added his own raised hand, then they went through into the corridor. She stopped at the closed door of her room, head half down: as if she knew nothing she might say would be adequate.

"At least let me turn the damn thing out for you."

She hesitated, then nodded and opened the door. The smell hit them at once. He drew a breath, then squatted beside the ancient stove and turned a tap on a fuel-pipe. It was wet with leaked paraffin. Another clogged wheel: the flame shone white a moment, then began to phut and smoke. He grimaced back up at her.

"Do let me get them to open another room."

She was staring down at the floor, her hands in her pockets. He stood and went in front of her.

"Jane?"

Very slowly her gloved hands came out of her pockets, then timidly reached for his. Her head, the green scarf she still wore, remained bowed as if ready to butt him again. He took the hands. Her voice was so low that he could hardly hear it.

"It wouldn't change what I said."

"But in spite of that?"

"I feel so cold, Dan."

He smiled, the statement was almost insulting, as if this fraught giving-way was a matter of temperature and quite beyond his powers of remedy.

"Any warmth. In a wasteland."

She stayed, as if already frozen; but then the gloved fingers clenched against his.

"I'll come in a minute."

He leaned and kissed the top of the scarf, squeezed the leather fingers back in return; then left and went to the bathroom. Her door was shut when he returned down the corridor. His own room also smelled of paraffin, but not nearly so acridly as hers; and it was warm now. He stooped to turn the stove out, then changed his mind, undressed, switched off the light, got into the cold bed. The sheets felt rough, unironed, distinctly damp. A phosphorescence shone on the ceiling from the blue flame of the stove. He heard Jane go along to the bathroom, then back to her room. Her door closed, and there was silence. He thought of Jenny, betrayal; bridges, brinks, wastelands. The silence went on too long. It was five minutes now since she had gone back to her room across the corridor, far more than she could have needed to undress, and spoke a terrible reluctance. He began to dread some change of mind. He saw her sitting on the side of her bed, with all her clothes on, unable to move.

He decided to give it a minute more; began to count; but then her door opened and closed very quietly. She came in. He leaned up on an elbow, and at first sight thought, since she still wore her outdoor coat, that she had come to say she could not; then realized, as she turned to close the door, that it was being worn as a dressing-gown. She came quickly to the bed and in one swift movement discarded the coat and threw it over his own clothes on the one chair. A moment later she had slipped under the bedclothes he held extended. Her face sank against his neck as he immediately strained her close against him; and suddenly, in that first naked contact, although he also knew, something in that buried head, that he was being allowed this body, not given it, there was no time, no lost years, marriage, motherhood, but the original girl's body. He had an acute and poignant memory, re-experience, of what it had been like, once, before so many other undressings and goings to bed had numbed it, to drop like this out of the intellectual, the public, into the physical and private . . . the strange simplicity of it, the delicious shock, the wonder that human beings bothered with any other kind of knowledge or relationship.

They lay embraced like that for half a minute or more, then he kissed her. She responded, yet he felt, if not a physical shyness, a reserve still. He released her a little and they lay like two children, noses almost touching.

"What took you so long?"

"When I was a Catholic, we used to call it praying."

But there was a smile in her eyes and mouth, and he smelled perfume as well, a more secular vanity.

"For both of us?"

"Mainly for you."

He smoothed down the side of her body beneath the bedclothes. "You're still so nice like this. You haven't changed."

"No memory."

"Every memory." He found a hand, laced fingers through it. "Haven't you?"

"Not physically."

"Emotionally?"

She stared for a long moment into his eyes.

"Do you remember that night at Tarquinia? When we had our night-bathe and all had to sleep in the same room?"

"Very vividly."

She looked down.

"I remembered it then."

"Tell me."

"I knew I was still in love with you." Her eyes stayed down. "I tried to tell Anthony when we got home. But I couldn't. Then to confess it. But I couldn't do that, either. I couldn't decide which was the worse sin. Still feeling it, or thinking it a sin to feel it."

She looked up into his eyes again then, with a strange mixture of gravity and timidity, almost as if Dan were the Anthony, or her unsought priest, of that time; and he knew that for some incomprehensible reason this was not a secret that brought them together, but remained a barrier; as if what was once suspect and illicit must always remain so.

The wretched dog began barking again somewhere outside, and he thought once more of T. S. Eliot: *oh keep the Dog far hence* . . . but couldn't stop to remember how it went on, conscious only of this oddly virginal, willing-unwilling body he felt and held; held against so many recent contradicting public images of her—the don's wife, the poised, discreet, the middle-aged Englishwoman . . . and now so disconcertingly reduced to a nakedness in more ways than the literal.

"The sheets are damp."

"It doesn't matter."

"Do you want me just to hold you?"

The head shook, and she closed her eyes. Her feet did feel cold, but not the rest of her body. She let herself be pulled to him, her head once more buried against his neck. In spite of her passivity he sensed an inner turmoil, a teeming race in the darkness of her mind. Half a minute passed, but then, in response to a movement he did not try to control, her hand slipped from his waist to the small of his back, and a moment later her head shifted, lifted, for him to kiss her; and she was no longer virginal. She yielded, at least to Eros; to being kissed, caressed, aroused, re-discovered. Somewhere beneath them a tired bedspring creaked, when he came on top. She let her arms fall sideways, but a leg bent, tenting the bedclothes, then splayed a little as Dan crushed her; as if there was indeed a physical longing for this, but her arms and hands could not sanction it.

It seemed to him, as they let sexual feeling dominate the next few minutes, that someone else was aroused, had taken over her body. It was not that she remained passive; the arms did rise and the hands caressed in return; but that in some paradoxical way made it seem a ritual, a concession to physical convention. For once in his life he would have liked his partner to talk, to know what she felt. He had pushed back the bedclothes and his own eyes, now accustomed to the dark, kept searching her face for answers; and even when they were joined, failed to get them. Her body excited him more than he expected—in the dim light from the fire it still looked, was young: slender-armed, small-breasted . . . and that side of it came almost as a last secret she had kept, an added unfairness.

Yet it did not take place as he had dreamed, did not reach that non-physical climax he wanted, fused melting of all further doubt. She had been wiser in not expecting it; though he still felt obscurely cheated by her not trying to create what she had not expected. But nor, finally, was she merely indulging him, comforting him. For a brief while she was the female animal; possessive, wanting possession to endure. It came to him, immediately afterward, when he was still lying half across her, that the failure could have been put in terms of grammatical person. It had happened in the third, when he had craved the first and second.

It left, too, a sad, sour little presentiment of age, of the death of the illusion that they could find each other as simply as this. It was too small, too short, too childlike a thing. Perhaps that was why he had always preferred, in more recent years, younger women: Jennies too green not to stay one with the myths of their bodies.

He moved beside Jane, lay on an elbow, an arm across her. She had opened her eyes and stared at the ceiling. That they were dry, still immersed in an inner self, seemed a final small confirmation of what he had just thought. It was beyond his power to change what she had said. It seemed almost as if she had let him "make love" only to demonstrate that a real love could never be made between them. In the end he whispered.

"What are you thinking?"

She smiled, then turned her face to him in the dim bluish light.

"How I wish tomorrow would never come."

There was at least a tenderness in her look, a confession of a kind.

"Which means you're glad now has?"

"You were so nice." She reached and found his hand.

"You feel a little warmer?" She nodded, still smiling. "Why did you change your mind?"

"Because I wanted you to know it wasn't this."

He raised their joined hands, kissed her. "I'm not going to accept just one proof. Now I've discovered what a sexy thing you are."

Her dark eyes stared gently into his. There was something in them that was both maternal and unchanged. She was still the girl who had never understood him, or herself; eternally tempted by him, eternally uncertain, almost as if their sexes were reversed, and he Eve, she recalcitrant Adam; but aware now of the pain she caused. He knew finally, he couldn't quite say how, but it was in the eyes, that nothing had changed. She was not convinced; or convinced only—that was what she had really been thinking—that this could not remove some profound incompatability between them. Her eyes closed.

"Tired?"

"Mm."

"I'll turn the stove out."

He bent over and kissed her mouth. Her arm came around him and held him close a moment, as if to ask forgiveness for what he had just read in her eyes. Then he got out of bed and extinguished the stove; undid the shutters and set one of the windows an inch or two open. Meanwhile Jane had pulled the bedclothes back. He came beside her again. They kissed briefly once more, then she turned her back. He slipped an arm under her neck to where the hand could bend down and rest on her breasts; then reached the other hand over her waist, to her stomach, and pulled her close. Her own hands came and lay on his, as if to keep them there. He began to feel, as they gathered warmth, knew each other awake in the darkness, that this innocent, silent nakedness was a nearer, deeper thing than the love-making; they were more coupled, thus, than when he had literally possessed her. The scent, light touch of her hair, enfolded body, those hands on his . . . it was an enigma to him that she still could not see her fears were groundless, her scruples nonsensical, her obsession with solitary independence totally foreign to her real nature; that something far more profound than hazard, than the coincidences of destiny, willed this.

Perhaps twenty minutes later he realized she had gone to sleep. He quietly removed his now stiff arm, then turned way. It must have awakened her a little. After a moment he felt her turn as well and lay a hand, instinctively, like a sleeping wife, across his hip; as if, in some dream, he was the one who escaped.

# The Bitch

Dan was deeply asleep when the knocks came on the door. He called, or groaned, from where he lay. There was an obscure mutter, footsteps went away. A cold first light came through the shutters. For a few moments, still half asleep, he had completely forgotten where he was; he lay trying to conform the room to his bedroom at Thorncombe, in a familiar maze between sequence-despising dream and coherent reality. Then he was aware that he was not wearing pajamas. He remembered. Yet for a few moments more he continued lying as he was, knowing he had only to turn, to reach back a hand. Something in whatever he had dreamed seemed to have washed his mind free of anxiety; in that shared stillness, silence, dawn, he would always regain her. He reached back a hand. But it met bedclothes, not the smooth, warm, female skin it expected. He turned sharply on an elbow, fully awake now.

There was no one there: an indentation in a pillow, the blankets carefully pulled up. Her coat had also gone from the chair. He thought perhaps she had slipped out to the bathroom, but then felt where she had lain; without warmth, she couldn't have left only a minute or two before. He stared down at where she had been, then across at the closed door. The air was cold on his shoulders, but even colder in his heart. He tried to suppose it might be some curious respect for the conventions, but already sought other reasons. Love, let alone tact or affection, could not have left him to wake up like that. Something else had to be shown, and brutally. It was almost as if she wanted to trick him into thinking he had imagined that previous night. But he could still smell traces of her perfume.

He got out of bed and pulled on the raincoat he had brought. Outside the door stood a bucket of water, steaming slightly in the cold. There was none outside Jane's room. He went across, knocked, then opened the door. Her bag stood packed beside the bed, her coat lay across the foot of it, but otherwise the room was empty. He went back to his own and threw the shutters open. And that too was a shock. The mist had risen, as promised, though the tops of the hills around the plain before him were only just clear of a gray ceiling of cloud. But he hardly noticed that.

The plain itself, which ran for two miles or more, was so extraordinary: an endless vista of ruins and isolated heaps of rubble, like a city stricken in some ancient nuclear holocaust and half buried again in sand. Forbidding square towers stood on a skyline to the west, above the plain. The scattered ruins were a heavy gray, tinged with russet and ocher. There was not a house, a tree, a figure in sight. One could not believe that the night had hidden so much, such a unique landscape, so chilling, so hopeless, so static, so vast; so without forewarning, so far, in its desolate immensity, beyond Herculaneum or Pompeii or any other ancient site Dan had ever seen. Indeed for a moment or two his reaction was purely professional: an amazement that this unforgettable scene had never been used by any film-maker, did not form a part of every educated person's common visual memory. He looked for Jane closer to the hotel, but could not see her. The entire landscape was lifeless.

He went to the bathroom and washed and shaved; then returned to his room and dressed. Her disappearing seemed more and more unforgivable, inhumane; as if they could not even share the first sight of the dead city outside. He went through into the room with the stove. She was sitting at the table where they had had their supper the evening before, a brass coffee-pot beside her. There was no one else there. She smiled across at where he stood for a moment, and held his eyes as he crossed to the table. He stood again a second there, searching her expression. Reading his own, it assumed apology.

"I woke early. I couldn't sleep."

"How long have you been up?"

"An hour."

He sat down, waited for some gesture, a reached hand. But she lifted the pot and poured him coffee, as if a banal domesticity could hide reality. It was so unexpected that it made him, quite against his will, fall in with it.

"I wish you'd woken me."

She smiled. "You were fast asleep."

The smile was additionally absurd; it was even, and intolerably, a little that of the mistress of a situation, of a wife, of someone who had slept beside him for years. She passed him the bowl of sugar, but he caught her hand before she would withdraw it.

"Jane?"

And as she had at Kom Ombo, she stared down at their two joined hands. She did not return his pressure, but it was done conventionally; as a plea, not as a recognition. Her eyes rose to meet his, confirming it. They admitted the existence of the night; but beyond that, they seemed to him to concede nothing. He spoke again.

"What's happened?"

"Nothing."

He tightened his grip, but now her hand remained inert, without response.

"Nothing?"

She looked down at the hands again, squeezed his, then released her own.

"Yes, of course something."

He took a breath, knowing the mood of his waking lay shattered; then stared at his coffee.

"Why did you have to get up?"

"A need to rehearse?"

"For what?"

"Rome and reality?" She sought his eyes again. "After the tenderest of dreams, Dan."

He felt outraged, and not least because she could now look him in the eyes as nakedly as she had met his body in the night; outraged like a man before a machine that will not function, although he has followed to the letter all the instructions for starting it. He thought of all his arguing and pleadings, both verbal and physical, and had an abrupt and hideously objective foreboding that he was dealing not with the psychological, but something pathological, conditioned beyond remedy. Already, perhaps even before the act, she had made up her mind to this: to give in order to prove that she could not. He knew he was on the very brink of a violent rage; perhaps even tears; but also that further pleading was useless. Perhaps she had done what she had done to make it so; and was certainly acting as she was now to prove it was so. We are civilized adults; but Dan felt a million miles from civilized adulthood. He stared at the table-cloth.

"Why did you tell me last night about Tarquinia?"

"To try to regain what I once did feel for you. When I had

a whole being." In his silence she said gently, "Have you seen outside?"

"Yes."

"That part of me can't. For your sake."

He left a pent silence; then burst out.

"Christ, and you talk about the language of despair." She looked down, and he went bitterly on. "That's what that bloody ring on your finger stands for. Eternal marriage to yourself. Undying love for your own mistakes."

The old man appeared from the kitchen with a bucket of fuel for the stove, with the cook behind him. The latter gestured to see if they wanted more coffee, but Dan curtly shook his head; then picked up his cup and drained it: the bitter chalice. The two men went to the stove, and the old man riddled it, with the cook watching. They spoke in Arabic, evidently something about the stove. Dan and Jane, her head bent, sat in silence, waiting for the others to go. But when the fire had been attended to, they drew up wooden chairs and sat by it.

She said in a small voice, "Do you want more coffee?"

"No. It tastes foul."

She swallowed that rebuff, used the same voice. "Then may we go for a walk?"

Dan hesitated. "I suppose."

"I'll go and get my coat."

He waited till she had gone through to her room before he moved himself; and once inside his own, waited till he heard her return to the main room before he followed. He managed to explain to the two Arabs, by pointing at his watch, that they should tell Labib he and Jane would be back in an hour's time. He had not appeared. Then they went out.

In the distance they now saw the date-palms of the modern oasis, and some flat roofs, but it seemed as if the modern town had retreated, lay in hiding, from the old. Its lifelessness was appalling, beyond all powers of humor or belittling. Now and then some species of lark would rise silently and fly out of their path across the sand; but there was nothing else. The wind had returned, the same bitter, penetrating cold, and they had to walk quickly to keep warm. Dan's face was set, shut, he would not look at her. When they had come out of the hotel she had pointed to the most conspicuous ruins.

"I think that's the Temple of Baal."

"Okay."

He knew as they walked that she wanted to speak, and he

was ready to bite off the first sound of her voice; or to continue the anathema. But perhaps she knew there was nothing more to say; she had asked for this, and she must bear it.

In any case, even at the best times, their wordless march would not have been inappropriate. The vast plain, the endless ruins, were their own inexorable commentary, as well as one on what lay between two the marchers. When they came closer to the square-walled temple enclosure, a flock of black birds rose; by a sour irony they were Dan's totem-bird, a whole colony of them; and for once he saw them as the rest of mankind and Edgar Allan Poe have always seen them, not as symbols of freedom and survival, but as the harbingers of ill-omen and death. They did give Jane an excuse to speak.

"What are they?"

"Ravens."

His tone forbade any further questions. They came to the temple and went inside. It had a massiveness more reminiscent of Egypt than Rome, a lingering smell of brutish heresy. Dan made it clear that it displeased and bored him, almost as soon as they entered. He watched the ravens circling overhead, croaking, then making a strange sound like dry bones clicking, a stick run down a lattice, while Jane wandered off for a minute on her own. He stood by the entrance gate, out of the wind, until she returned.

"Enough?"

She nodded, and he turned, like someone who had been unreasonably made to wait. They walked back through the center of the ancient city, under a triumphal arch, down a colonnade, past the melancholy tetrapylae in Aswan granite; and came on a theater, finely preserved, but somehow, like the whole site, cold and dead; then the ancient forum; and on, out over the plain past endless stumps of walls and mounds of collapsed building, toward Diocletian's Camp. They had, in the theater and the forum, exchanged one or two brief remarks, tourists' remarks, painfully artificial; but now again they fell silent.

They looked, yet—and both knew it—did not see what they were looking at. It was as if they had traveled one fatal day too long, and all their previous realities and pretenses had crumbled like the city. They were reduced to what, in their two sexes, had never forgiven and never understood the other. Now they walked without purpose, as if on some insane constitutional, its only recommendation that they did not have to put on faces for other people. Jane began to look peaked and haggard, her face as set as his. He felt all his hope for her, and of her, dwindle. It was crushed by her intransigence, drained away through some deep crack in her psyche. They had no free will, they were back, but in a far worse way than before, in this bitter, forsaken place, to not touching, not saying, not looking.

Palmyra itself stood between them: remorselessly dividing them because they saw it in totally antipathetic ways. For him, it was what he had made of his life; for Jane, what life had made of her. More exactly, it was what he claimed of his life in his more depressed and self-dramatizing moments; but what she derived from it, as from a faith, was something much deeper, though he saw it as a mulish irrationality, almost a snobbism, only too similar to certain kinds of intellectual Catholicism.

In her secret eyes he was eternally superficial, not an initiate, not able to see deep enough. He might use the landscapes of the last twenty-four hours as illustrations, parables, but somehow they remained external to him, while they were inside her . . . all that barely comprehensible talk of not being able to love, as if it were some impossible foreign language, like Arabic itself. Somewhere, deep down, she must, now, want it so.

Aided and abetted by his wounded vanity, he churned over the fallacy in her seeing, in all closet-intellectual seeing. It had no lateral or horizontal scope, it was all verticality, obsessive narrow penetration to supposed inner cores and mysteries—souls and absolutes, not skins and common sense; without self-humor, compromise, toleration, making-do, as if such qualities could not be a part of the whole, of truth, because they were so frequent, universal and necessary . . . and had to be demoted to the status of the mere misleading epiphenomena, like moments of animal closeness in the night, of a more elite reality. He blamed the mental influence of Anthony and all he had stood for: Oxbridgery . . . felt a growing seethe of anger with her, with this oversophisticated, hypersensitive system of valuation that immured her. Nunnery was right. The air of enclosure, masochism, of self-absorption disguised as self-immolation, louche and mystical marriages to Christ-figures . . . he loathed it all profoundly.

They stood at the opposite poles of humanity, eternally irreconcilable.

They had walked for several hundred yards in silence and were nearing the Camp at the end of the plain. He felt petrified in sullenness. She was behaving like an inverted Phaedra, a tragedy queen. He had also a blackly sardonic intuition that all his recent life had been leading here: to this potential climax and focus . . . and now all it produced was bathos. An act of charity, a sop to this male esteem, a solitary fuck; just as his career had given him "success" in a world that also became lost ruins in a lost desert almost as soon as it was achieved. And even that other, original, destiny had been inflicted on him by her. He cursed the day, that evening at Thorncombe, when he had first suggested her coming; invited the old pattern, the old doomed seeking of the doomed situation.

Then something he could not have imagined, or would not have imagined, happened.

Now very near the Camp, they passed a collapsed temple some forty yards to their right. It was no more than a gigantic pile of rubble. Huge squared stones, drums of fluted columns, fragments of carved cornice and capital, stone foliage and volutes, lay massed as they must have fallen in some earth tremor centuries before. But across the sand there seeped a sound from it: a whimpering, an unhappiness from the very beginning of existence. Involuntarily they stopped, puzzled, then Dan—almost with impatience, as if even distraction was an insult to his mood—walked to where the first stones had spilled across the desert. Then he saw the source of the sound.

Two dun-colored puppies stood at the mouth of a dark crevice in a conglomeration of cornices and column-drums littered against part of the temple platform. They were very young, evidently only just able to walk; too young to fear, since they stared at Dan from their hole without retreating as he went a step or two closer, though they fell silent. He looked back at Jane. She had stopped a few feet behind him, to one side. She too stared at the puppies, her hands in her pockets, as if she did not like being so close.

He said, "The last inhabitants."

Jane nodded to the left of the mound of debris, then said in a flat voice, "Their mother's over there."

He looked. A mangy bitch had appeared some sixty yards away, watching silently back at them; gray-black, of indeterminate breed. She loped a few paces across the sand; then stood and watched again. She was miserably thin, the ribs stood out over the swollen dugs—the size of a small greyhound, an air of being both cowed and vicious.

Watching the puppies again, Dan said, "Better not come nearer."

Jane did not answer.

He glanced back. She had turned away, as if out of boredom, and was walking slowly back across the sand toward the track they had left. He followed, came beside her.

"Poor little sods."

There was a movement of her head, a cursory ghost of a smile, as if, in spite of appearances, to acknowledge this tiny incident. But her head stayed down, her hands in her pockets; she walked now like someone about to stop at every step. He touched her arm.

"Jane?"

But she shook her head: it was nothing. They walked a few steps more. This time he took her arm more firmly and stopped her.

"Jane."

Again she shook her head, almost as if to drive him away. But he saw her bent face, and put an arm across her shoulders. For a moment they stood like that. Then, slowly, she turned against him, her face to his shoulder. It was so contrary to his mood that it took him foolishly by surprise. His other hand moved almost gingerly to pat her back. He looked across the sand to where the bitch stood. The animal at last allowed itself a more normal canine behavior. The muzzle lifted, scenting. He bent his head.

"Tell me what's wrong."

But her only answer was a pent-up expulsion of breath. Still she stood with her hands in her pockets, unwilling, unable to give; able only to cry. He embraced her more tightly, kissed the top of her head, but did not try to calm the sobs. She held herself so stiffly, and they seemed to force their way out of her, as out of a child. He divined, he did not know how, that gods take strange shapes; find strange times and stranger climates for their truths; and knew that all he had felt and thought for that last three quarters of an hour was also sand.

Beneath all her faults, her wrong dogmas, her self-obsessions, her evasions, there lay, as there had always lain—in some analogue of that vague entity the Marxists call totality, full consciousness of both essence and phenomenon—a profound, and profoundly unintellectual, sense of natural orientation . . . that mysterious sense he had always thought of as right feeling. But he had also always thought of it as something static and unchanging—and conscious, even if hidden; when of course it had always really been living, mobile, shifting and quivering, even veering wildly, like a magnetic needle . . . so easily distorted, shaken out of true by mind, emotion, circumstance, environment. It had never meant that she could see deeper. In a way it must be a thing that limited and confused rational vision, that would provoke countless errors of actual choice. Followed, it would always run her against nature, the easy courses of society; disobeyed, it would create anxiety, schizophrenia. It was simply that she *felt* deeper; and eternally lost conscious course because the unconscious knowledge of the true one always lay inexorably underneath. Mankind may think there are two poles; but there is, morally as magnetically, only one in the geography of the mind's total being; and even though it is set in an arctic where no incarnate mind can exist.

The wind shook a patch of sere foot-high thistles that stood between them and the dog; and as if it brought a stronger scent, the animal loped obliquely back another twenty yards —then once more stood and watched: the two bipeds as one, frozen, a hundred yards away. At last Jane managed to speak.

"Oh Dan."

He kissed the head again. "It will come. It will come."

Her face still buried, she was silent for a long moment. There was another sob, almost of disgust.

"You must hate me so."

"That's also a symptom."

"I don't know how you can stand me."

"Because you're such a clown."

"Alias ghastly neurotic female."

"I don't know how you can't read this place. What it really means."

"It feels so without hope. Those puppies."

He held her closer to him. "Then why do you reject all warmth?" She shook her head against him: she didn't know. "It's our stupid, one-dimensional age, Jane. We've let daylight usurp everything . . . all our instincts, all we don't know in ourselves. When we're still just as much animals as that poor creature over there." He raised a hand and pressed the back of her head. "It felt so right last night. Afterwards. Just holding you. Your being there."

She moved a little, and one of her hands went up to her face. There was a last small shudder of breath.

He said, "Didn't you feel that?"

"Of course I did."

"Then why did you run away?"

"Because I felt I'd done something dreadful. I didn't know where I was, who we were. How it could have happened." She sighed. "It suddenly seemed exactly as it was before. A sort of madness. A blindness to all the realities."

"Except the one you've just felt."

She stood away slightly, though her bent head rested against him and he still held her; as if somewhere he was still rejected . . . or not him now, but any consolation. She took a breath, but this time it was more banal, of apology.

"I don't seem to have brought a handkerchief."

So Dan released her, and made the oldest male gesture in the world. She would not look at him, but after a moment she turned and glanced over her shoulder back toward the dog.

"Why did she leave her puppies like that?"

"Why do you always jump to the wrong conclusions?" He took her shoulders and made her turn fully, then held her back against him, spoke in her ear. "It's not a lack of love, Jane. It's a well-known trick. What biologists call distraction behavior. Birds do it as well. She's offering a trade. To be hunted and shot, if we'll spare her young. That's why she's standing just out of gunshot. To lure us away."

She stared, curiously and touchingly like a small girl facing up to adult reason and life without tears.

"I thought she was just frightened."

"If she was just frightened, she'd be like you. Streaking for the horizon."

They watched, the bitch watched back across the sand.

She said slowly, "I should never have left the Church."

"You should never have gone into it in the first place."

"It's designed for people like me."

"Who won't believe in love?"

"Who fear it so much."

The bitch circled again, then disappeared behind the mound of stone.

"Will she go back?"

"Of course. As soon as we've gone."

She took another deep breath, as if unable to face such simple optimism; looked down at the ground for a moment. Then one of her hands came up and touched one of his where it still lay on her shoulder.

"Dan, I want to be left alone here for a minute. Would you start walking back? I'll catch up."

He was disconcerted, as much by a shyness in her voice as by the unexpectedness of the request.

"Why?"

"I want to do something. Alone. It won't take a moment."

"You mustn't go near the puppies. She might—"

"I know."

He tried to read the profile of her face from behind, but it revealed nothing. He pressed her shoulders, then began to walk away, slowly, toward the distant low speck of the hotel. He felt curious, and curiously embarrassed; but after thirty or forty yards he could not resist a glance back. To his astonishment she was sitting on the sand: her back to him, propped on an arm, her legs curled to one side, looking down at something in front of her. He stopped, infinitely puzzled—assumed some sort of prayer, a being too shy to kneel formally when he might turn like this and see her.

He would never forget that extraordinarily, almost surrealist sight: the bitter wind ruffling the fur collar of her coat and an end of her headscarf, the desolation, the hills behind with their grim watchtowers, the silent back, her sitting as if before an invisible picnic lunch; in the strangest echo, like Jenny, that day on the other side of the world at Tsankawi, pursuing Pueblo Indian shards. But that at least had been a rational pose, and one with movement. Jane seemed transfixed. It was like a supremely bizarre cinema still, of the kind that evoke far more than the film they transiently appeared in.

He went on another slow dozen steps or so; then looked back again. She was already on her feet and walking toward him. He waited, trying to tell from her face what she had been doing. But it was without expression until she was close, when she made a little grimace; stopped.

"Do my eyes look awful?"

He shrugged and smiled. "The wind."

She extended her hand before she reached him, to make him walk on. He waited for some explanation, both in the particular and in the general: what she had been doing there, what resolution, in both the decisive and the musical sense, they were brought to. But all he was granted was the hand. They walked fifteen or twenty steps in silence, then she pressed his.

"Tell me about distraction behavior."

"That's a perfect example of it."

His hand was pressed again.

"Talk about anything, Dan. But not me."

Half an hour later, when they were sitting and having a second coffee in the hotel, he was no wiser as to what was going on inside her. On the way back they had talked, in the end, about the site: the things they had not said before. Tourists again, old friends, at Oxford together—or so it had seemed to him, still bewildered by that enigmatic image of her sitting figure, by the emotion that had preceded it, by the speed of the recovery. It was almost as if she had made a resolution of a much more ordinary sort as she sat: not to bother him again with her "ghastly female" neuroses. Yet there was no attempt to restore the dreadful distances of earlier that morning; if anything, they seemed to have returned to the Nile, to mere close companionship. Labib, the other men, were in the room, so one was forced to play a role; but she seemed retreated beyond the need of that. He felt that needle still shivering, and was wise enough not to demand where it now settled.

It was to continue, as Labib drove them around. First into the shabby little oasis, where the museum was; he returned to the car, once he had put them in the hands of the guide who was to accompany them for the rest of the morning. A wizened old man, cramped in a threadbare suit, but who spoke a fluent, old-fashioned French. He knew his stuff, even had a certain dryness about it, which they shared, faced with the endless stone heads the ancient citizens of Palmyra had liked on their tombs: wall upon wall of them, in serried rows, ludicrously smug and Victorian; so many dignified Roman dowagers got up in their best jewelry, so many earnest gentlemen aping Cato and Mr. Gladstone. Dan watched yet another return in Jane of her Egyptian self; even an amused response to one or two comments from the guide.

*Un beau visage d'entrepôt, n'est-ce pas, madame?*

A nice eternal middleman's face.

Next they were taken to a clay hut beside the ancient site; and suddenly found themselves, another bizarre moment, in what seemed more like a football changing-room than anything else; a stinking steam, pegs of clothes, men in towels, laughter. They descended dank steps to an extraordinary basin of pale green soup, one of the warm subterranean sulfur baths that had attracted the Romans in the beginning.

Another dozen men, in white drawers, coffee-colored torsos, stood in the steaming water. Some smiled at the two foreigners, one or two turned their backs. Modern Syria, it seemed, still retained its sybarites, even if only underground.

Dan was to keep only the vaguest memories of those two or three hours. He would happily have forgone the tour, in fact. It was Jane who now seemed to want it—to be her housewifely self again, not to be short-changed of what had been paid for. In some atavistic way he did not really want to be put out of his uncertainty; perhaps still the victim of his love of loss, he secretly enjoyed prolonging it a few hours more. He avoided her eyes, rather than she, his. Twice, when they were in the car, her hand felt for his, but as it had at the Krak des Chevaliers, to comfort, to give patience. It was almost as if he were being obscurely teased, made to wait till they returned to Beirut for a full explanation. Now it was the tears that had never taken place, as earlier it had been the night.

Finally they were driven to a valley in the hills to the east, above the plain, the cemetery of the old town. They visited a tower-tomb, a kind of four-story columbarium, though stacked with stone sarcophagi, not urns. Even here, the guide told them, the Roman eye for business had triumphed—spaces in the best tombs had been excellent speculative ventures and had been bought and sold like contemporary flat-leases. A warren-like catacomb he also took them to had fetched especially high prices, since it was agreeably central-heated; somewhere close underneath ran the sulfur springs. Jane translated to the old man what Dan said of Forest Lawn in California. The old man's tortoise eyes crinkled. *Plus ça change* . . . they could not tell him anything new about human folly.

Soon after noon—they had deposited the old guide back at the museum—they were climbing out of the Palmyra plain on their long way back to the Lebanon; and listening to Labib expatiate once again on the Syrians' stupidity in not making more of the place . . . better roads, better hotels, a casino, an airstrip. When he fell silent, they risked a covert glance of knowing better. Dan, resigned now to being left in ignorance, moved his hand and took Jane's. After a few moments he gently rubbed a thumb across her knuckles. He had had all of their second breakfast to realize, and other occasions when she had taken off her gloves, but even usually observant men are peculiarly blind at times. He looked sharply down at the hand. The impression was still pinkly on the skin of the wedding-ring finger, but the band of gold was no longer there.

He gave Jane an almost reproachful look. She contemplated her own ringless finger; while he saw her sitting in the desert, staring down at the hidden ground. There was something in her face, both self-deprecating and shy, as if she wasn't quite sure it was her own hand. But when she looked up and met his eyes, though it was only very briefly, he knew he received his answer and his resolution. She looked away out of her window, and he through the windscreen, but their grip tightened. Nearly half a minute passed before she spoke, still staring out of the window.

"Do you think she will be shot?"

He pressed her hand again.

"Not now."

# Future Past

Dan watched Jenny standing at the bar, longer than she
needed to buy the drinks. The place had only just opened and
it was, as she had promised, nearly empty; her local, her
ground, this northern part of London had always been foreign to him. The wall behind the bar was covered with signed
photographs of television and show-business personalities:
good wishes, facetious messages; illegible scrawls, illegible talents. Jenny had told him once in Los Angeles that the pub
was an informal theatrical agency . . . where you congre-
gated on Sunday mornings, if you lived in the area and
hadn't quite made it; or even if, like her, you had made it,
but retained a belief that you were nicer if you sometimes
pretended you hadn't. Dan had not liked the sound of it then,
and did not like the reality of it now; but he knew she had
partly chosen it for that very reason.

The man she talked to, the landlord, evidently knew all
about her, and was being brought up to date. She turned
from him with a smile, some last remark over her shoulder,
and came back to the table with the drinks. A solitary young
man at the far end of the bar watched her cross to where
Dan sat. She was wearing Californian clothes still; a jeans
suit, flat shoes; a crocheted skull-cap of lilac, blue and white
wool; no make-up. It made her look less conscious, more
simple, more of an open-air girl, than she really was.

She put the glasses down: his whisky, her half-pint of
draught Guinness, then sat on the padded bench beside him.

"It's only Glenlivet. He doesn't stock Dettol."

He smiled. "Dettol" was her nickname for Laphroaig, which she knew he liked, though he had asked simply for Scotch.

"You seem very at home here."

"Sorry."

Dan smiled again; and tried again.

"I hear the studio are high." She gave a little shrug. "Bill rang the other day."

"Me too."

"You've signed and sealed for the new one?"

"Not quite. David's waiting for the good news to get round. So he can screw a bit more from them." David was her agent.

"But you will?"

She said nothing; then, "Dan, please don't be like this."

"Like what?"

"Like 'like what.' " She said, "I'm not your daughter." She added quickly, "Which reminds me." She bent to a basket beside her, and passed a small cardboard box without looking at him. "I thought you might like to give her this. You needn't say it's from me."

He took the lid off, and opened a fold of jeweler's lint. Inside that lay a silver chain, with one of the Tsankawi shards, framed in a rim of silver, hanging from it as a pendant.

"That's very sweet of you, Jenny."

She gave the pendant, or his examination of it, a brief sideways look.

"Perhaps it will bring her bad luck as well."

"I'm not going to rise to that." He turned, leaned, kissed the side of her head, then looked at the pendant again. "And of course I'll tell her it's from you."

She said, gauchely, "I went a bit mad. I had too many made."

"It's charming." He hesitated. "I bought you something in Egypt. But I didn't have the face to bring it."

"What was it?"

"Some old tomb-beads. You probably wouldn't have liked them."

She shrugged. "It doesn't matter. I'm going anti-jewelry anyway."

He folded the lint back over the pendant. "Caro will love this."

She sipped her Guinness.

"Is she still . . . ?"

"He's talking of getting a divorce now."

"And she?"

"I'm down to crossed fingers."

"Is she pleased for you?"

"She's always been very fond of her." He went on, a shade too quickly and lightly. "It allowed her to kill two parents with one stone. The first thing she said was, I always knew you'd picked the wrong sister."

Jenny did not smile. The interrogation proceeded. It was very tentative, and she did not look at him.

"And your ex?"

"She seems to have decided she can still speak to us. Since we were always two totally impossible people. As she delicately put it."

"What were you doing in Italy?"

"We stopped off a day or two to see Jane's younger daughter. She's doing a language course in Florence."

"And wrote me my letter of dismissal."

"Of reasons why, Jenny."

"I knew. That postcard you sent from Aswan." She picked up her tankard of Guinness, but did not drink. "I just wish you'd told me what was happening before you left."

"I honestly didn't know. You must believe that."

"You must have had some idea."

"Only that I was sorry for her. What I tried to explain in the letter."

There came a longer silence. Jenny drank some of her Guinness, then stared across the room at the bar. Dan hated it, he had come determined not to allow this. But from the first moment, the first sight of her, she was already waiting for him, her aloneness in the empty pub, an outdoor coat and the basket beside her, the taut small smile, relief that he had appeared, resentment; a token kiss on the cheek, a banal exchange over her insistence (they were back in London now) that she should buy the drinks . . . any chance of being natural had vanished immediately in the artificial naturalness they had both assumed. She spoke, still staring across at the bar.

"Every day I wonder what you're doing. Even though I know what a devious, lying bastard you are."

"You promised we—"

"I'm just telling you."

He left a pause.

"I sometimes wonder what I'm doing as well. If that's any consolation." He was aware of her glance at his face, but did not return it. "It gets tough when you're both older. All those bits of armor you've acquired and forgotten how to take off. The bastard knows what he's lost in you."

"I don't want your candy, Dan."

"I wish it was."

She put down her tankard, sat back, folded her arms.

"I'm going home tomorrow. Up to Cheshire."

"They know?"

"I've pretended you've been the perfect gentleman. God knows why." But she made an immediate grimace down at the table. "You're making me say all the lines I meant to cut." Then, "I only met here so that I'd be too ashamed to cry."

"You knew what I felt. Before I left."

She unfolded her arms, put her hands on her lap, smoothed a hem of her jacket sleeve.

"But you never knew what I felt. Deep down." She said in a lower voice, "Would it have made any difference if I'd written about Tsankawi first?"

He said nothing. He had come also determined to raise that as soon as possible, had even been given a perfect cue, with the pendant; and felt himself a coward, since he had guessed that his silence over it lay behind the brief telephone conversation that had preceded their meeting. She was back, she just wanted to see him once more; she wouldn't be emotional; only an hour; somewhere neutral and public. Now she looked at him.

"You did get it?"

"Yes, Jenny. And bullseye. Where it was aimed." She stared down, and he said gently, "The timing was appalling. I'm so sorry about that."

"And if it had been better?"

"I think one day you'd have been far unhappier than you are now."

She still looked down at her lap. "At least we'd have tried."

"My dear, you can't short-cut experience. How you handle all this. Discovering it with someone your own age. Who's also learning."

"I went through all that with Timothy."

"No. You only think you did."

She mulled over that for a moment; whether to argue directly or not.

"If only you could have understood that stupid pretense of being honest about you wasn't really about why I couldn't love you. But about why I did." She said, "That's the part of your letter that was so wrong. That hurt most."

"It wasn't stupid. It was brave. And very perceptive."

"For an actress."

"For anyone of your age. He's going to be very hard to find, Jenny. But you do know what you're looking for."

"I'm all right, then."

"You know I didn't mean that."

Her face was growing more and more ungiving.

"I wish you'd let me have them back."

"To destroy?"

"That third one makes me flush every time I think of it."

"Because it was honest?"

"Like masturbating on camera."

"Now you're being ancestral."

"I know you still think it all happened."

"I never thought that. I also know it doesn't matter whether it did or not."

She took a breath, then looked up. "The only thing I did in real life was not to go out with them together again. I think they decided I was rather dull, anyway. British." She sipped more of her black beer, then her mind made one of its jumps. "Can you remember your first return here?"

"That shock doesn't stale with age."

"Missing all sorts of things over there you thought you despised. Rediscovering so many things here you'd always taken for granted. When I picked up the first milk-bottle outside my flat, I nearly kissed it." Then, almost without a break, she said, "I'll never forgive you if you ever show them to anyone."

He smiled. "I might borrow the general idea. As you said I could."

"I know your game. We're all so much easier to live with when we're just notions in your past. I think you're the original male chauvinist pig."

"All writers are. Even women ones."

She seemed to want to challenge that; but once more expended her disagreement on the far side of the room.

"And where's that at?"

"Where I suspect it always will be. In contemplation."

"The script?"

"Being typed out."

"Pleased?"

"I enjoyed writing the final fade."

"As elsewhere."

"Not true."

"I suppose it's what it does to all of us. Two months on this. Then two months on that." She gave Dan a look. "I don't think you'll ever have the patience for a novel." He knew what she really meant by "novel"; but not how to answer without hurting her. "I bet you'll be back on scripts within six months."

"Not even a year?"

She shook her head, but in a way that made him, for the first time, look properly at her; then reach for her hand beneath the table.

"This is why I didn't want us to meet."

She sat forward and put an elbow on the table, the other hand against her cheek, stared down at her Guinness. The pub was slowly filling, there were now eight or nine people at the bar.

"I'm not going to cry. It's so humiliating." She took her hand away from his, and sat back. "I can't even face ringing up friends. Going home tomorrow. It's having to talk about it. Pretending it doesn't mean anything." She looked down. "If only you'd left me with some nice ordinary disease. Like syphilis."

"As opposed to?"

"A man tried to pick me up on the plane coming back. It was jampacked. He was sitting beside me."

"And?"

"He was rather nice. Very interested in the arts. The theater. A merchant banker, just been divorced. He told me all about it. He was an upper-class idiot. I'm supposed to be having dinner with him."

"Young?"

"Early thirties."

"You liked him?"

"He was rather sweet. Fun. He'd been on business in New York, he told me about some high-class call-girl they'd tried to fix him up with one evening. How they'd spent it just talking. They didn't go to bed. She told him it happens all the time."

"Why are you telling me?"

"Because I shan't have dinner with him."

"Why didn't he go to bed?"

"He thought it might be some kind of blackmail hustle. And don't change the subject."

"Tell me the symptoms then."

A group of young people came in, three young men, two girls; one of the latter opened her eyes and mouth as she saw Jenny, who raised a hand. The girl made a dialing gesture, and Jenny nodded; then she told Dan they had been in rep. together, at Birmingham. She watched the group go to a table at the other end of the room; and went on, still watching them.

"All the time I was on the plane I wished you were beside me. To tell me what to do. Find out what I felt."

"Then I was beside you."

"That's like so many of your lines. How things ought to be. Not how they are." She asked something naïve then; but of a naïvety Dan had always liked in her. "Does she realize this about you?"

He saw one or two covert glances toward them from the group of young people who had just come in—toward Jenny, of course; success; and wondered whether they wondered why she spoke so seriously, her face down at the table.

"You know me in cross-section, Jenny. She knows me historically. It comes to the same thing."

"Does she mind your coming to see me?"

"Not at all. She was quite a good student actress herself at Oxford. You've more in common than you might imagine."

"Except you."

It was said so humorlessly that Dan had to smile . . . and to think what they did not have in common: how much easier, if he were inventing it, Jenny's dialogue would have been. He was hiding so many very recent memories of Jane, and hiding now a certainty that destroyed the small hope he knew still lay buried in the girl beside him—though he knew also that it had not prompted their meeting, but had arisen, against her will, certainly against her original intention, as soon as it took place. It defined her nature far more than it flattered his vanity.

"I suppose you've told her all about me."

"All about why I never deserved you."

"I wish you'd write a script about a woman who kills a man out of rage at the phoniness of his decency. I could do that now."

"The actress in you."

"I didn't think you believed there was anything else."

"I wouldn't be here now if I believed that."

"It's almost as if you want me to become a hard-faced little ambitious bitch."

He left a silence, then spoke.

"Why do you think the friends of your friend over there keep sliding looks at us? The boys?" She said nothing. "They fancy you for your looks, Jenny. But even more for what you're becoming. You're condemned to be a sort of goddess. Still, even today. An untouchable vestal virgin. What every girl wants to be, what every man wants to have. It doesn't matter that they know you're not a virgin. Very soon you'll be sacrosanct in the popular imagination. You know the alternatives. You turn your back on that, refuse to play ikon. Or you accept its cost."

"I make a last phone-call and he's too important now to answer."

"Wrong culture. You'll never be Monroe. And fate settled that score." Again she said nothing. "You can't have both, I've been there too long. I know."

"I won't give up what I am."

"Then you can only choose which kind of new-style vestal virgin you'll be. Remembering you're in the sickest art of them all. Where even the best have been buggered almost before they've got their foot through the door. Where cretins have always ruled, and always will. Where the stock model for every relationship is that between a ponce and a whore. You know all this. And why."

"I think you have been there too long."

"I'm only making a plea for you not to give up what you are. But it doesn't come for free."

"I used to make nice bright clean decisions about things. All you've done is hopelessly confuse me."

"That's growing up. Not me."

"I was growing up perfectly well before we met."

"I'm not going to be cast as the Lovelace in your life."

"Who was he?"

"The seducer in *Clarissa*. Richardson."

Silence fell on them, of the worst kind; of the blind alley, the nothing more to say. There was something far more sullen and unconceding in her than Dan had foreseen, as if the return to her home environment had discharged an emotional static she had always carried in California; and left her, behind her looks, clothes, career and all the things other eyes in that room might see in her, small and flat and resentfully forlorn. He also knew what the end of roles sometimes did to actresses, and that her mood was partly dependent on circumstances beyond his responsibility. Yet he felt miserable, knowing he could not comfort her in the only way that might have worked. She broke the silence, in a fittingly mundane and dispirited voice.

"Do you want something to eat?"

"If you like—a sandwich?"

"I'll have smoked salmon if they've got it. It'll get so crowded soon."

"Another Guinness?"

She shook her head. "Just a coffee."

Dan went and waited at the bar for the sandwiches to be served. He saw Jenny go to the ladies', past her friend at the other end of the long room; she bent and said something very briefly to her as she passed, ignoring the young men. He tried to read the signatures under the celebrity photographs; most of them seemed to be of faces he had never seen before. When Jenny came back—he was already sitting again—she plumped down with a little air of new-gained resolve.

"I only wanted to see you once more. To let off steam." She squeezed lemon over her smoked salmon sandwiches. "If we ever meet again, you'll just be that peculiar mixed-up writer man I once had an affair with."

"I shall keep you much closer than that."

She started eating.

"Was Egypt interesting?"

He should have called that shameless shift of tone and subject; instead, he followed it. The pub began to be crowded. Dan knew she wasn't really listening; perhaps listening to his voice, but not his words; to their past, not their present. She was showing him now how he would be got over, *it* would be got over. Our time's slick comedown from Forster's *Only connect* . . . only reify. Then two girls came and sat in the chairs on the other side of their table. Dan and Jenny were silent for half a minute, unwillingly listening to their chatter. Then she said abruptly, "Shall we go?"

She pulled on her outdoor coat, suede patchwork, an extravagance she had dithered over for days in Los Angeles; picked up her basket. Dan followed her out to the pavement and the open air. Passers-by, traffic crawling up toward Hampstead. It was a fine day, presaging spring, a clear sunlight on everything. She held her wicker basket with both hands in front of her, and faced him, a brittle smile.

"Well. It was kind of you to spare me an hour. Mr. Martin."

He stared at her for a long moment, and she looked down.

"There's another opposite to how things ought to be, Jenny. How they ought not to be."

She gave a minute shrug, but still stared down.

"I haven't your gift for tasteful dialogue."

It was strange, Dan suddenly recalled talking with her on the beach at Malibu one day, the day she had written about: the same kind of aggressive shyness, even though it had been much more buried then . . . as if it was used, almost deliberately, to precipitate something better. There was something else, a much remoter ghost at his shoulder, his father's; all those years of seeing pastoral care in action, and never understanding it, despising it for all the inanities it generated, boring old parties one had to be polite to, endless chitchat over nothing . . . but a greater humanity than this. And a much closer ghost, ghost only in not actually being there, also watched him watching himself—stood beside him and told him that however much the needle veered, it was never as far from true course as this.

"Is there somewhere in the open we could walk for a bit?"

"The Heath. We could take a cab."

"Okay. Let's do that."

They stood in silence at the curb for a minute; then a taxi stopped at his outstretched arm. Jenny told the driver where they wanted, but once inside they sat in silence again. He took her hand, but she stared out of her window. Another battle with tears was taking place; Dan gripped a little harder. She did not in fact cry.

Five minutes later he paid off the taxi at the Whitestone Pond. Over the trees below, distant London lay spread, anesthetized, soft blues and grays and pinks, deceptively of its past still, Constable's London. They left the road and walked off down a gravel path; mothers and children, students, old men. A squirrel, wood-pigeons. She listened in silence, just an occasional question. He was aware, now that it came to it, the first time in words, not only of the difficulty of putting flesh on such remote bones, but even of articulating them: a world of value-systems, prejudices, repressions, false notions of faith and freedom, that he sensed she could hardly comprehend. He tried to tell her all his letter had lacked the honesty to tell: the real enemy she had always been pitted against. The day of the woman in the reeds, and all that lay behind it. And a little of Aswan and Palmyra, too. All rather drily, matter-of-factly, as he might have outlined an idea for an original to a sceptical but shrewd producer like David Malevich—slighting it rather than selling it, casting Jane and himself as middle-aged fools . . . strictly for that trade, not the younger generation.

Jenny was silent when he finished. They had stopped and sat on a seat for a while; were now walking on again, out of the trees and down a slope toward the one that led up to Kenwood House.

"Why didn't you tell me all this before, Dan?"

"Because I've never told anyone, Jenny."

She went a few steps without speaking.

"You're really in love with her?"

"In need."

"Has she changed very much?"

"Physically. Not otherwise."

"Soul-mates."

"Hardly. We disagree about too much."

"That doesn't fool me."

"I'm not trying to. We do agree where it matters."

Again they strolled steps in silence.

"I can see there were always casting problems. With us pale shadows who offered for the part."

"I'd long ago put it beyond the realm of the playable."

She slid him a look.

"I wish I'd known. I'd have put on my long nightie and danced through the palm-trees on Sunset." She struck a little pose and put on an *ingénue*'s face. " 'You can't arrest me, officer. I'm a figment in someone's imagination.' " She saw him grin, then suddenly came closer and slipped her hand through his arm. "I wish you'd get us all together. Then we could swap notes."

"I have got you all together."

"Like Bluebeard."

"Nonsense."

She jerked his arm.

"Only what you think we are."

"I won't have the great secret of my life treated as a subject for unseemly levity."

"Diddums. Did the naughty girl laugh at him?" He smiled.

Her hand slipped down and found his. After a moment she said, "I only wanted to feel close to you once more."

"It's not that I feel any closer to her, Jenny."

"But what?"

"Perhaps we're a little sorrier for each other. And with better reason."

She looked down at the grass.

"Is she in London now?"

"In Oxford. She's going to put her house on the market. She's there about that."

"And you'll play Darby and Joan in glorious Devon?"

"I've given up trying to sell that to the women in my life. We'll probably try to get a house here."

"And sell your farm?"

"Just use it as before. Perhaps a bit more often." He said, "Jane wants to go into local politics." He smiled rather sheepishly at her. "You're walking with a fully paid-up member of the Labour Party, by the way. As of last week."

"Seriously?"

"It doesn't feel it. But we'll see."

He had not provoked the smile he intended, one of amused contempt; but one of amused curiosity.

"Is she really very left-wing?"

"We're like two characters in a difficult play, Jenny. We know we both feel we want to do the parts. But we don't know how we'll get into them yet." He added, "Especially as neither of us has very much confidence in the director . . . or directors."

"That must be a very new experience for you."

He smiled at her dryness. "Where writers count for even less. That's the real problem."

He knew she was half-tempted to press him further; but then she decided not to relinquish the role she was now playing. For he also knew she was acting, though bravely; because she must.

"I think you'd make a jolly good politician. With your skill at conning and lying."

"I may surprise you yet."

She stole a look up at his face. "And really goodbye, screen?"

"I don't know. If a novel defeats me, I think I might risk my neck in the theater again."

"I wish you would. With a nice fat part for me." Then she

said, "I so wish I was going back into that. Now. Next week."

"Then do it when the next film's over. David's a good agent, but he'll run your life for you. If you let him."

She gave a small nod. More steps without speaking. Then she took his arm again.

"You will let us meet occasionally? Let me have a whiff of your rotten old mind. Even if it's only so you can tell me what a lousy vestal virgin I'm becoming."

"Of course."

"We'll walk here and then I won't see you for another year."

He made one of her own jumps.

"As long as he sees through Jenny McNeil."

"I shall bring him to be vetted."

"He won't stand for that. If he's any good."

"Then I'll use it as a test. If he knocks me to the floor at the very idea, I'll know he's all right."

"I should try this merchant banker." She shook her head. "Why not?"

"I'm off nice straightforward men."

They walked slowly up the slope to the cream façade of the house; wordless again, but she still kept her arm lightly linked through his. A few old people sat on benches in the winter sun and there was a dim roar of traffic from around the Heath. As they came to the steps up to the graveled terrace before the house, she reached down and squeezed his hand, but mischievously.

"I didn't tell you how sweet Abe and Mildred were. When you junked me."

"Yes?"

"He offered to divorce Mildred and marry me himself."

"In front of her, I hope."

"Of course. And you're never to have the Cabin again."

"But you are?"

"Any time I want."

He pressed her hand. "I'm glad."

After he had posted the letter in Italy, he had rung Mildred to warn her it was coming; and again, back in London, when he knew it should have arrived—and had. Mildred had said drily that she was doing his "dirty work" for him, but he knew whose side she was really on. He said nothing now. They came to the terrace and walked to where a tunnel-arbor led beside the eighteenth-century house. Then Jenny suddenly pulled him to a halt, as if they had reached a mark on set.

"I'm going to say goodbye now, Dan."

She turned in front of him, mimicking a niece at the end of a treat. A smile, a look into his eyes. "Thank you for having me. In all senses. And I think the rewrite of this scene's been so much better than the first draft."

"But how are you—"

"If you walk through here and up the drive, you'll be in Hampstead Lane. You can get a taxi there." She smiled again. "I'd rather walk home alone."

They stood frozen a moment, then she moved. Her mouth hardly touched his, for the briefest second he was allowed to hold her against him; then she was walking away. He stood watching her, feeling obscurely tricked, even in some way hurt that it had been her decision—which told him that it had been one that still, somewhere deep inside himself, he had not absolutely taken. At the top of the steps down, fifty yards away, she glanced back at him, and extended a discreet arm with the hand cocked up slightly, as if they were just saying goodbye for a few hours and she was late for some next appointment. Her face had turned away before she could have seen his own hand raised in return. He watched her walk quickly down, the woolen cap, fair hair, patchwork coat, brown wicker basket, over the long slope of grass to the footbridge that led across a brook and up over another slope to the woods. She did not look back again. He moved a few yards and sat on an empty bench, and watched her still, a speck with a basket, until she had walked out of his life; then lit a cigarette and stared unseeingly at the tame, tranquil landscape in front of him.

He felt bereft beyond his calculation of it; almost cheated by the understanding of himself he had arrived at over the last two months, and which he had tried to convey to her; trapped in his own trap, turned someone he wasn't. It was as if, having sucked the poison of her mood in the pub, he was left poisoned by it himself. In the end he stood and went through the hornbeam tunnel beside the house—but there, instead of walking up the drive to the road outside, on some impulse given realization by seeing two other people enter, vaguely remembering it was a public gallery, he went in himself. He walked around the place, not really looking at anything, until, by chance in the last room he came to, he stood before the famous late Rembrandt self-portrait.

The sad, proud old man stared eternally out of his canvas, out of the entire knowledge of his own genius and of the inadequacy of genius before human reality. Dan stared back. The painting seemed uncomfortable in its eighteenth-century drawing-room, telling a truth such decors had been evolved to exclude. The supreme nobility of such art, the plebeian simplicity of such sadness; an immortal, a morose old Dutchman; the deepest inner loneliness, the being on trivial public show; a date beneath a frame, a presentness beyond all time, fashion, language; a puffed face, a pair of rheumy eyes, and a profound and unassuageable vision.

Dan felt dwarfed, in his century, his personal being, his own art. The great picture seemed to denounce, almost to repel. Yet it lived, it was timeless, it spoke very directly, said all he had never managed to say and would never manage to say—even though, with the abruptness of that dash, he had hardly thought this before he saw himself saying the thought to the woman who would be waiting for him on the platform at Oxford that evening; telling her also what had gone before, a girl and a past walking into winter trees, knowing she would understand. He had lied a little to Jenny, to make it easier for her. But that was his secret now, his shared private mystery; which left him with the imagining of the real and the realizing of the imagined. Standing there before the Rembrandt, he experienced a kind of vertigo: the distances he had to return. It seemed frightening to him, this last of the coincidences that had dogged his recent life; to have encountered, so punctually after a farewell to many more things than one face, one choice, one future, this formidable sentinel guarding the way back.

He could see only one consolation in those remorseless and aloof Dutch eyes. It is not finally a matter of skill, of knowledge, of intellect; of good luck or bad; but of choosing and learning to feel. Dan began at last to detect it behind the surface of the painting; behind the sternness lay the declaration of the one true marriage in the mind mankind is allowed, the ultimate of humanism. No true compassion without will, no true will without compassion.

Some young schoolchildren came in, a babble of voices. The peace was broken, and Dan moved away. But as he left the room, he turned a moment by the door and looked back at the old man in his corner. The children were restlessly gathered before the painting, while a harassed woman teacher tried to tell them something about it. But Rembrandt's eyes still seemed to follow Dan over the young heads implacably; as many years before, when he was their age, his father had once unwittingly terrified him by insisting that Christ's eyes followed . . . wherever you went, whatever you did, they watched.

That evening, in Oxford, leaning beside Jane in her kitchen while she cooked supper for them, Dan told her with a suitable irony that at least he had found a last sentence for the novel he was never going to write. She laughed at such flagrant Irishry; which is perhaps why, in the end, and in the knowledge that Dan's novel can never be read, lies eternally in the future, his ill-concealed ghost has made that impossible last his own impossible first.

*For a biographical note about John Fowles*
*please turn the page.*

# About the Author

Born in Essex, England, in 1926, John Fowles was educated at Bedford School and at Oxford University. Following his studies in French at Oxford, Mr. Fowles taught in France and other places abroad before becoming a full-time writer. His first novel, *The Collector* (1963), was an immediate bestseller—a popular as well as a critical success. *The Magus* (1966), followed by the acclaimed bestseller *The French Lieutenant's Woman* (1969), confirmed Fowles' stature as internationally recognized writer of major importance. This novel was followed by *The Ebony Tower* (1974), five stories on love in its many guises, which was also critically acclaimed. His collection of aphorisms, *The Aristos: A Self-Portrait in Ideas* (1970), demonstrated the author's versatility in a literary form quite different from the novel.

Mr. Fowles lives in Lyme Regis, Dorset.

# GOOD READING from TOTEM

## Fiction

☐ **I HEARD THE OWL CALL MY NAME**     **$1.25**
MARGARET CRAVEN — A young priest, living among the Indians of British Columbia comes to terms with life and death.

☐ **COLLISION** — SPENCER DUNMORE     **$1.95**
Two giant jets crammed with passengers on a collision course over Toronto airport — a superbly dramatic novel.

☐ **BOMB RUN** — SPENCER DUNMORE     **$1.75**
Follow the fortunes of an RAF bomber crew as they set out on their last mission.

☐ **FINAL APPROACH** — SPENCER DUNMORE     **$1.95**
The whole history of aviation is bound up in this novel of one man and an airfield. By the author of *Collision.*

☐ **THE INTRUDERS** — HUGH GARNER     **$2.25**
Out of the conflicts between people at the bottom and at the top of society comes this rich and vivid novel.

☐ **FILE ON HELEN MORGAN**     **$2.25**
JOHN FREDERIC GIBSON — The author of *A Small and Charming World* writes about a young Indian woman in British Columbia today.

☐ **FLIGHT INTO DANGER** — ARTHUR HAILEY     **$1.50**
The modern Canadian classic — a remarkable novel of suspense in the air — told with breath-stealing attention.

☐ **CLIMATE OF CONSPIRACY** — PALMA HARCOURT     **$1.95**
Murder, sabotage and political intrigue in Ottawa. Tight, swift moving, plausible.

☐ **VIKING PROCESS** — NORMAN HARTLEY     **$1.95**
A terrorist organization holds the U.S. and Britain to ransom.

☐ **KING OF WHITE LADY** — R. LANCE HILL     **$1.95**
David Lee Henry is close to the top in the cocaine game. He wants out — will "they" let him?

☐ **NAILS** — R. LANCE HILL     **$1.95**
The Vancouver underworld is the setting for this tough, powerful novel about one man's pursuit of total freedom.

*Please turn the page*

# GOOD READING from TOTEM

## Fiction

☐ **THE BATTLE FOR SALTBUCKET BEACH**     **$2.25**
IAN McNEIL — Cape Breton Islanders pull the beach out from under the feet of Ottawa politicians and Bay Street big business.

☐ **EXODUS U.K.** — RICHARD ROHMER     **$1.95**
Another best selling novel by the author of *Ultimatum* and *Exxoneration*.

☐ **A LOVER NEEDS A GUITAR**     **$1.95**
DAVID E. LEWIS — The funniest, most down-to-earth portrait of life in a small Nova Scotia town.

☐ **MEDICINE MAN** — IVAN SHAFFER     **$1.95**
A blockbuster of a novel revealing the operations of international drug companies.

☐ **BUSINESS IS BUSINESS?** — IVAN SHAFFER     **$1.95**
In just thirty days Richard Rash makes it from bankruptcy to supersuccess.

☐ **SMALL CEREMONIES** — CAROL SHIELDS     **$1.95**
A novel for the seventies. Meet Judith Gill, successful writer — and suburban housewife. Somehow her two worlds are out of sync. "Superb bitchiness" — *Financial Post*

☐ **ON THE CIRCUIT** — JOSEPH F. SUESSMUTH     **$2.25**
All the glamour and danger of Grand Prix racing are captured in this novel by an author who has raced himself.

☐ **IN PRAISE OF OLDER WOMEN**     **$1.95**
STEPHEN VIZINCZEY — The amorous recollections of Andras Vajda. The Canadian novel that has sold over 2,000,000 copies worldwide.

☐ **ASH** — DAVID WALKER     **$1.95**
Ex fighter pilot, ex bush pilot, ex smuggler, Ash is a loner, with his own code of loyalty that brings him close to disaster.

☐ **BLACK DOUGAL** — DAVID WALKER     **$1.95**
Sir Dougal Trocher is a genuine Scottish Laird — and a jewel thief. Fast moving, high life entertainment.

# GOOD READING from TOTEM

## More Fiction

☐ **WINGED WARFARE** — LT. COL WILLIAM BISHOP  $1.95
The greatest Canadian fighter pilot tells his own story.

☐ **SHORT HAPPY WALKS OF MAX MacPHERSON**  $1.95
HARRY BRUCE — An affectionate look at the Toronto of
the Forties and Sixties.

☐ **BIRD OF PROMISE** — GREGORY CLARK  $1.95
A collection of entertaining short pieces by Canada's most
widely read author and grand man of humour.

☐ **OUTDOORS WITH GREG CLARK** — GREGORY CLARK  $1.95
The one and only Greg Clark, naturalist, humourist, story-
teller, invites you to come outdoors with him.

☐ **GRANDMA PREFERRED STEAK** — GREGORY CLARK  $1.95
Anecdotes and articles on all sorts of subjects, written with
warmth, wisdom and a sense of fun.

☐ **THE ANTE ROOM** — LOVAT DICKSON  $2.95
Volume One of the author's autobiography. A young man
footloose in Canada in the twenties.

☐ **THE HOUSE OF WORDS** — LOVAT DICKSON  $2.95
Volume Two of the author's autobiography. A fascinating
picture of literary London in the Thirties.

☐ **AND NOW ... HERE'S MAX** — MAX FERGUSON  $1.95
Enjoy the whole cockeyed world of radio and tv in this
different kind of autobiography by the man known to millions
as Old Rawhide.

☐ **MONEY PIT** — RUPERT FURNEAUX  $2.25
The mystery of Oak Island. Is the world's greatest hoard of
pirate gold in Nova Scotia?

☐ **A SMALL AND CHARMING WORLD**  $1.95
JOHN FREDERIC GIBSON — Share the bitter-sweet life of
the Canadian Indian in this eloquent book.

☐ **THERE'S A SEAL IN MY SLEEPING BAG**  $2.25
LYN HANCOCK — Funnier than fiction ... adventures of the
wife of a Canadian wildlife biologist.

*Please turn the page*

# GOOD READING from TOTEM

## Non Fiction